Seeker's Bane

by

P. C. Hodgell

SEEKER'S BANE

This is a work of fiction. All the characters and events portrayed in this book are fictional, and any resemblance to real people or incidents is purely coincidental.

Copyright © 2009 by P.C. Hodgell. *Seeker's Mask* copyright © 1994 by P.C. Hodgell. *To Ride a Rathorn* copyright © 2006 by P.C. Hodgell

A Baen Book

Baen Publishing Enterprises
P.O. Box 1403
Riverdale, NY 10471
www.baen.com

ISBN: 0-978-4391-3380-4   4355 3501
                                  9/10

Cover art by Clyde Caldwell

Maps by P.C. Hodgell

First Baen paperback printing, September 2010

Distributed by Simon & Schuster
1230 Avenue of the Americas
New York, NY 10020

Library of Congress Cataloging-in-Publication Data:
2009011731

Printed in the United States of America

10 9 8 7 6 5 4 3 2 1

IT'S RAINING FROGS

Cold drops stung Jame's face, while Kindrie hunched thin shoulders under his borrowed shirt. Only Jorin seemed unperturbed. He was taking this wretched weather unexpectedly well, Jame thought.

Strange. He didn't even look damp now.

When he returned, she found that his coat was quite dry. So was the road ahead. The rain, it seemed, was exclusively for her benefit.

It came down harder, laced with hail. No. With tiny, green frogs.

"Do you mind?" she demanded, extracting a wriggling froglet from deep inside her shirt.

"Geep, *geep, GEEP!*" cried a growing chorus.

"Will you *stop* that?" she shouted up at the roiling clouds.

The shower of frogs stopped. A moment later, rain began again—in a circle around them.

"This place has the damnedest weather," Jame muttered.

Kindrie stared after her. She *was* mad—and so was he, to be following her.

Why was he still in this lunatic's company? The last thing he remembered was challenging the Knorth about her Shanir blood. Then had followed the long nightmare of walking, stumbling . . . how far? His feet throbbed and he felt a sickening fatigue alien to his healer's nature. Where in all the names of God were they?

The naked slopes across the river were ominously familiar. So were the roofs of a manor he'd never glimpsed ahead over trees on the other bank.

"That's Tentir," Jame said in a stifled voice. "Which means the man inside is Gerraint Highlord—Wilden!"

He turned and fled.

Baen Books
by
P.C. Hodgell

The God Stalker Chronicles

Seeker's Bane

Bound in Blood

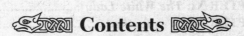

Contents

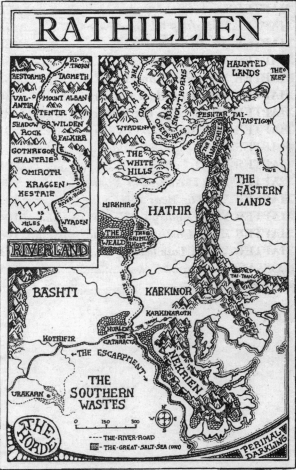

RATHILLIEN

RIVERLAND (inset map)

- HI-THORN
- RESTORMIR
- TAGMETH
- VAL-ANTIR
- MOUNT ALBAN
- TENTIR
- SHADOW ROCK
- WILDEN
- FALKIRR
- GOTHREGOR
- CHANTRIE
- OMIROTH
- KRAGGEN
- KESTRIE
- WYADEN
- MILES
- RIVER·ROAD

THE RIVERLAND

HAUNTED LANDS

THE KEEP

SNOW THORNS

THE GREAT GREY HILLS

WYADEN

PESHTAR

TAI-TASTIGON

EVER-QUICK

THE ANARCHIES

RIVER TONE

THE WHITE HILLS

THE EASTERN LANDS

MIRKMIR

HATHIR

THE WEALD

THE GRIMLY HOLT

TAI-THAN

BASHTI

KARKINOR

KARKINAROTH

THE RIVER

HURLEN

THE CATARACTS

KOTHIFIR

NEKRIEN

← THE ESCARPMENT →

THE SOUTHERN WASTES

URAKARN

THE HORDE

0   150   300

- - - - THE·RIVER·ROAD
▦ THE·GREAT·SALT·SEA (DRY)

PERIMAL DARKLING

P.C. HODGELL

SEEKER'S MASK

Dedication:

For Teddington Weir, who was and always will be Jonn,
and for Romney Marsh,
and for Melinda

PART

I

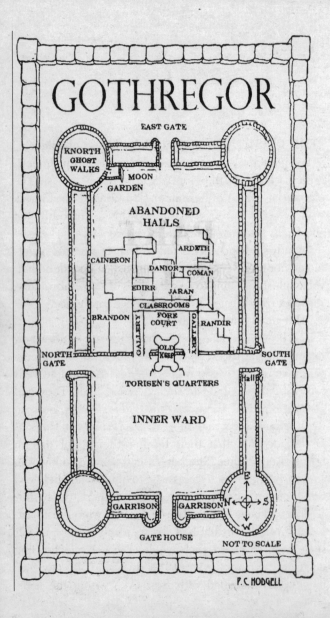

"THE FIRST DUTY of a Highborn lady is obedience."

So spoke the young instructress as she swept imperiously back and forth before her even younger class. The extreme tightness of her under-skirt obliged her to walk with tiny, rapid steps, but she did this so smoothly that she might have been mounted on wheels.

"A lady's second duty is self-restraint," she said, pivoting on her toes. Her full outer skirt belled out round her, velvet pleats opening to reveal panels of rich embroidery, restraint transformed by long practice into grace.

"Her third duty is endurance."

The little girls obediently echoed the words after her, fingers busy with the knot stitch which they were currently learning, eyes downcast behind the simple veils that were appropriate to their age and rank. They had already repeated these maxims endless times, both in their home keeps and here in the Women's Halls at Gothregor—not that their teacher thought of that in terms of endurance. She herself had learned to love the simple dictums which gave shape to her life, and believed that the more often her students heard them, the better.

That had been especially true over the winter just past. Never in her short life had she seen such snows, or felt such cold, or heard such winds as had come howling down the narrow throat of the Riverland. By day, her fingers had blanched with frost even within the halls,

1

while outside birds had plummeted frozen from the sky. At night, she had lain awake in the arms of her sister-friend, hearing the stones groan around them and the distant boom of ironwood trees shattering in the cold. Even on Spring's Eve, they had to dig into snow banks for the crocus with which to make their vows, guided by the flowers' violet glow beneath the ice crust.

Under these circumstances, the inmates of the halls hadn't been home since the previous autumn. True, the younger ones didn't expect to leave Gothregor before summer, but it made a difference, knowing they couldn't go home even if they wanted to. Still, thought the instructress, they had better get used to being homesick. Soon they would have to go wherever their lord sent them, to honor whatever contract he chose to make in their behalf. By then, of course, many of them would belong to the community of sister-kinship which would be their only true "home" as adults. At present, though, they were still the children of different, distant homes, in need of all the self-control which the Women's World could teach them.

Their young teacher had also felt that need, despite the warm arms of her Edirr sister. For her, the snow, the cold, and the wind of the past winter had been nothing compared to its strangeness. With most of the Kencyr Host wintering in Kothifir, the Riverland had been so *empty*. Now that the snow had finally melted, one heard first hand accounts of things only rumored before: of weirding mist and Merikit raiders, of strange noises in the earth and air, and of arboreal drift. Why, one hunter even claimed to have heard the demented howls of the Burning Ones, avengers of the slain, far south of their usual haunts—but that was nonsense. Everyone *knew* that they and their master, the Burnt Man, were mere Merikit superstitions.

Still, things *must* improve soon, now that Kencyr were beginning to return. The Jaran Heir Kirien had passed by some weeks ago accompanied by the haunt singer Ashe, bound for the Scrollsmen's College at Mount Alban. More important, only three days ago the first of the lords had returned. That it had been Caldane, Lord Caineron of Restormir, seemed an especially good omen, since she herself was a Coman with two Caineron grandmothers. The Highlord's garrison, on the other hand, had manned the walls as if expecting an attack.

Abruptly, another memory came to her, unbidden, unwelcome. Rumor said that just after the great battle at the Cataracts, Caineron had been stricken with some mysterious illness, which his randon commander had described as "not quite feeling in touch with things" —whatever *that* meant. The health of great lords affected everyone bound to them, even distantly, as she herself was. One more thing tottering in her world, one more thing insecure . . . .

So she glided back and forth before her class, repeating the great truths, demonstrating by her grace that the world still made sense, here in the heart of the Women's World where nothing ever changed.

Below, hooves rang on cobble stones. The windows looked down on the Forecourt, so called because it occupied the foremost open space in the Women's Halls, which themselves occupied the back half of Gothregor. At the center of the entire fortress was the old Knorth keep, whose own rear half projected into the Forecourt. A horse was clattering in through the gate which separated the court from the fortress's inner ward. But men weren't allowed here, the instructress thought, outraged. These were the *Women's* Halls, where even the Kendar guards were female.

Then she saw that the rider, although properly masked, was wearing a divided skirt and, yes, boots. Lady Brenwyr of Brandan had returned to Gothregor.

At the best of times, most people found this Highborn unnerving. The Iron Matriarch, they called her behind her back for her rigid discipline. These past few months, however, that control had seemed to slip. Everyone had been aware of her restless comings and goings, as if even in the depths of winter she had been unable either to stay in or away from the Women's Halls for any length of time.

The instructress had heard scandalized whispers about the Iron Matriarch's traveling garb, but had never before seen it for herself. It was indecent, she thought, and yet . . . and yet . . . .

She firmly believed that whatever her elders did was above criticism. The conflict between that dictum and her feelings confused and frightened her. Things should be one way or the other.

Brenwyr dismounted and disappeared into the north wing quarters of the Brandan.

"Forget what you can't help," the Women's World taught.

The instructress turned from the window, wiping what she had just seen from her mind.

"The fourth duty of a lady," she said firmly to the class, "is to be silent."

Traditionally, the response to this was mouthed rather than spoken. This time, however, a low but quite distinct voice in the rear of the classroom said:

"*Damn.*"

"Who was that?" demanded the instructress sharply, but she already knew. "*Now* what have you done? Come here and let me see."

The dark figure in the back row rose and glided forward into the shafts of late afternoon sunlight which fell through the windows like the memory of antique gold. Once her gown must have glowed in such light. Now the little girls snickered as she passed, pointing out to each other the tarnished silver trim, the threadbare royal blue facings, and the rich plum velvet, dulled by age to the color of a bruise.

Once they had laughed less cautiously. The instructress remembered their taunt: "Seeker, seeker . . . ." because of the eyeless mask with which the Matriarchs had tried to curb the newcomer's roaming. But then that blind face had turned toward the class and they had frozen, like . . . like the instinctive cower of small animals before a hooded hawk.

That was *not* a suitable image, the young teacher told herself sternly.

Anyway, now the oncoming figure wore a standard half-mask and ignored the children as she passed them.

But their giggles were still nervous, and so was their teacher.

For one thing, she wasn't used to pupils older than herself, if only by a few years. Worse, this elder girl was a Knorth, the Highlord's own sister. There had been no Knorth women at Gothregor for more than thirty years, since Bashtiri assassins had given the entire family a hard shove toward extinction. To have one here now, with her incredibly old, fabulously pure bloodlines, was like trying to deal with a creature of legend.

But the Matriarchs hadn't allowed her that status. Rather, they had subordinated her to her brother's limited term consort, Kallystine, and to any teacher whose classes she was ordered to attend. This was one of them. And, really, this Knorth was so very ignorant. Why, not only had she no knowledge of needlecraft—or of any other skill which any self-respecting lady should long since have known—but she wasn't an initiate into even the lowest ring of secrecy. Therefore, the instructress spoke sharply to her, but with a strong impulse to back away as the Knorth advanced, black gloved hands extended.

Then she saw why those hands were so oddly held: the Knorth had accidentally sewn them together.

The young teacher sighed, obscurely reassured.

"Oh, Lady Jameth. Not again. If those gloves make you so clumsy, why don't you take them off?"

"I prefer not to."

The voice was level, without emphasis, but with something so unyielding in it that the instructress felt piqued. After all, this was her class, and all the pupils here were under her authority.

"Don't be silly," she said sharply. "I insist."

"So do I."

The gloved hands clenched and parted, snapping the threads, diving out of sight behind the other's back.

Like two wild things escaping, the instructress thought.

For a moment, absurdly, she had been very frightened indeed, and that in turn made her angry.

"You *must* obey me!" she insisted, reaffirming the shape of her world. "The first duty of a Highborn lady . . . ."

". . . is obedience," finished that expressionless voice. "But why?"

"You mustn't ask that!"

"Why not?"

"Because . . . because it's forbidden!"

"That's circular reasoning. Why is it forbidden?"

This couldn't be happening. No one asked such things, especially in front of children. "All knowledge is the gift of our elders. They tell us what we need to know, when we need to know it. To demand an answer is . . . is sacrilegious."

"Not that, surely," said the Knorth. Her voice had lost its flatness, as if for the first time in weeks she was beginning to enjoy herself. "When the Three-Faced God drew the three people of the Kencyrath together to fight Perimal Darkling down the Chain of Creation, he (or she, or it) didn't give us any choice in the matter. I don't think that, ultimately, we could commit sacrilege against him if we tried. Anyway, he apparently abandoned us after our first defeat thirty millennia ago, so that we've been on our own, in retreat from threshold world to world, ever since. But we still have our honor, whatever god or man does to us."

"And a lady's honor is obedience!" cried the instructress, beginning to wax hysterical. Surely *that* must clinch the argument.

"But if she faces Honor's Paradox, ordered to do something dishonorable?"

"T-that's unthinkable!"

"But it happened."

And, suddenly, she began to chant, the old dark story rolled over the room like an eclipse, the daylight dying:

"Gerridon Highlord, Master of Knorth, a proud man was he. The Three People held he in his hands—

Arrin-ken, Highborn, and Kendar. Wealth and power had he and knowledge deeper than the Sea of Stars. But he feared death. 'Dread Lord,' he said to the Shadow that Crawls, even to Perimal Darkling, ancient of enemies, 'my god regards me not. If I serve thee, wilt thou preserve me, even to the end of time?' Night bowed over him. Words they spoke. Then went my lord Gerridon to his sister and consort, Jamethiel Dream-Weaver, and said, 'Dance out the souls of the faithful, that darkness may enter in.' And she danced . . . ."

"Stop it!" cried the instructress, hands over her ears.

But she knew all too well how that terrible story ended, as someday these children would too if their elders condescended to tell them. Two-thirds of the Kencyrath had fallen, soul-raped, and the shattered remnant had fled to the next threshold world, Rathillien. Three thousand years ago, that had been, but no lapse of time could dim the horror of that night or its repercussions in the Women's World, which paid daily for the Dream-Weaver's fall.

At least, so her elders had told her when, as a child, she had been so ill-bred as to question the restrictions which were to shape her life. That was when she had first heard Jamethiel's lament with its bitter coda: "*Alas for the greed of a man and the deceit of a woman, that we should come to this!*"

It had never occurred to her before that the Dream-Weaver had fallen through obedience to her lord.

But a lady's honor *was* obedience.

Stop it, stop it. Things *must* be one way or the other.

"W-we don't discuss such questions here," she stammered, struggling to wipe them out of her mind. "We practice obedience, self-restraint, endurance, silence . . . ."

"And knot stitches." The Knorth sighed. "Some of us do, anyway. Just the same," she added, regarding the sampler which the younger girl held, "a raised stitch like that might be useful as part of a code . . . ."

The instructress felt herself go cold. "Shut up, *shut up*, SHUT UP!"

And her hand lashed out, as if of its own volition, to deal that masked face the hardest slap it could.

The Knorth went rigid. Her own gloved hands were still behind her.

The nearest child, staring at them in awe, said, "Oh look, oh look!"

The teacher had fallen back a step as if shoved away by the other's sudden blaze of anger, remembering too late all she had heard about the deadly Knorth temper. She instinctively clutched the sampler to her chest as if sheltering behind it and flinched back as one of those gloved hands lashed out at her in a black and white blur.

Then the Knorth whirled about and left the room, moving with a hasty stride reduced by the tightness of her underskirt to a series of rapid jerks.

The instructress let out her breath unsteadily. She felt as if some appalling violence had just flashed past her, incredibly doing no harm.

Then the sampler fell to shreds in her grasp.

"Did you see her hands?" the little girl was babbling. "Did you see . . . ?"

"Be quiet!" snapped her teacher. "The fourth duty of a lady is . . . ."

But down the hall, another voice broke the rule of silence to exclaim, "Lady Jameth, be careful on that stair!"

That triggered a chorus of warnings, as the Knorth was hailed from the doorway of every classroom she passed: "Slow down!"

"Walk like a lady!"

"Watch your step!"

"Jameth!"

The instructress reached her own door in time to see the singing mistress, nearest the steps, pop out of her room to wail, "Remember what happened the last t . . . ."

Too late.

They all saw the Knorth hop down the first two steps—which was indeed the proper way for a lady to descend—but she was still going too fast. The next moment, she pitched forward out of sight. Her sharp cry echoed up the spiral stair as she tumbled down it.

A collective sigh rose from the instructresses in the upper hall: "Oh no. Not again."

II

ADIRAINA, the Ardeth Matriarch, sat by a window in an upper chamber of her family's compound, stitching a letter to a five times great granddaughter—one of a growing number. They did tend to accumulate, she reflected wryly, when one was over a hundred and twenty years old.

So did memories.

The spring breeze off the Snowthorns bought back an evening a lifetime ago, the child that she had been leaning on this windowsill, looking eastward over the jagged rooftops of the Women's Halls to the lights that sparkled in the Knorth family quarters, hoping for a glimpse of her new sister-friend.

Oh, Kinzi . . . .

How short that springtime together had been and how long the years apart afterward as each had served her lord wherever he sent her, in whatever distant house or bed. Highborn men laughed at the token cloths which their women seemed eternally to exchange. Adiraina touched the worn shawl draped across her shoulders. It had arrived on Spring's Eve almost a century ago, after a winter's enforced silence: Kinzi's vow gift, the stitched record of her winter days. Adiraina's fingertips remembered every detail, however many knots unraveled with age.

But at last the long separation had been over when they both returned to these halls, each now the matriarch of her own house.

Memories: another evening long after the first, standing by this window, the day's work done. Family business kept Kinzi to her quarters, but if Ganth returned soon from his hunt perhaps she could slip out.

Like children again, Adiraina had been thinking, *stealing sweet moments. What a good life we've had . . . .*

She tried to fix on that moment, the last of happiness, but memory swept her inexorably on: Cries in the darkness, and then screams as Bashtiri shadow assassins slashed their way through the unprotected tower. The blaze of Kinzi's helpless rage like a fireball in her lover's mind, suddenly extinguished. Dead, dead, Aerulan, Telarien, Kinzi—all the Knorth women but one, and that a child who must be kept hidden the rest of her unhappy life . . . .

It would be dark there now, in those apartments built for the Highlord's family in Gothregor's massive outer wall—dark and cold and silent. The Ghost Walks, people called them, and kept their distance. At least she was spared that dismal sight: the eyes on her gray, velvet half-mask were mere embroideries in silver thread. She had been blind since adolescence.

A pity, Adiraina thought, that she couldn't also claim to be deaf.

Behind her the Danior and Coman Matriarchs, Dianthe and Karidia, were arguing again; or rather, as usual, the latter was trying to pick a fight. As always, Karidia was advancing the interests of the Caineron, on the theory that since Caldane was the most powerful Highborn in the Kencyrath, he should be given more power still with first claim on the newly discovered Knorth, Jameth. "Dear Catti" would insist, if only she were here.

Adiraina smiled. "Dear Catti" was Cattila, the Caineron Matriarch and Caldane's great-grandmother, who had once called him the stupidest thing on two legs in the Riverland.

"Speaking of dear Caldane," she said, "has anyone heard exactly what has ailed him this past winter? 'Not quite feeling in touch with things' is not, I'm sure you'll agree, a particularly enlightening diagnosis."

She sensed rather than saw them all glance at Cattila's Ear, who sat in the shadows knitting their conversation into a scarf which she would subsequently dispatch to her mistress. Being an Ear, she of course said nothing.

"At least Lord Caineron sleeps at night," snapped Karidia. "That's more than can always be said of our fine, young Highlord or, recently, of his sister. Anyway," she continued, perhaps still thinking of lost sleep, "there's already an alliance between the Houses of Knorth and Caineron in that Torisen has taken one of Caldane's daughters as a limited term consort."

"Yes, dear," said Yolindra, the Edirr Matriarch, from a cushioned seat by the western window where, like a cat, she took her ease in the day's last warmth. "But I wouldn't count on that if I were you. When the Highlord stopped here last fall on his way to the Cataracts, he didn't so much as send her word, much less visit her. And he's had no trouble staying away all this past winter. It sounds to me as if he's begun to slip through darling Kallystine's grip."

"Nonsense!" snapped Karidia.

"About time, I'd say," Dianthe said briskly. "I've always had the highest regard for that young man's survival instinct."

With that, she swept off to take a turn around the room, with Karidia trotting to keep up, still arguing as fiercely as increasing shortness of breath allowed.

Dear Karidia, thought Adiraina. She did have such an unfortunate tendency to yap.

These squabbles would be amusing, if the stakes weren't so high. Ever since the Three-Faced God had created the Kencyrath over thirty millennia ago, its highlord had been Knorth. Everyone had thought that Torisen was the last of his lineage, had almost been glad of it, after the grief which his father Ganth Gray Lord had caused; but suddenly this girl, his sister, had appeared out of nowhere. It seemed inevitable that either her son or his would be the next highlord, the first in history with the blood of another house also in his veins. So far, Torisen had proven the impeccable instincts with which Dianthe credited him by refusing to give anyone a legitimate Knorth heir. It was unlikely, though, that the lords would permit him to be so evasive with his sister. If ambitious Lord Caineron did secure the girl's first contract with the option for a child, young Torisen Black Lord was not apt to get much older. That he would be better off dead than his sister would be alive under Caineron's roof, Adiraina knew perfectly well, but she gave it little consideration: in the Women's World, after all, one obeyed and endured.

Karidia trotted by, still trying to keep up with the much taller Danior Matriarch. "It isn't as if the girl is such a prize in herself," she was panting. "I *mean* so ignorant so clumsy . . . ."

This last made the Jaran Matriarch Trishien look up from her reading. Sunlight caught the lenses worked into her mask, fiery eyes in a cool face. "I'd like to see *you* fall downstairs even once without breaking your neck, much less make a habit of it."

"So she has . . . a brilliant future . . . as a tumbler," snapped Karidia, coming to a breathless stop before Adiraina. "Is it *really* possible . . . that this girl . . . is a pure-blooded Knorth? I *mean*, all the Knorth ladies died here over thirty years ago . . . except for the child Tieri . . . and we all know what became of *her*."

Adiraina's hand closed convulsively on the letter which she had been stitching. "It wasn't Tieri's fault that her lord brother went directly from the White Hills into exile, without her. Aerulan had saved her from the assassins by hiding her in the empty halls. I tried to do the same when I concealed her in the Ghost Walks for twelve long years and told no one, not even this council, not until she died in the moon garden, bearing an illegitimate child to an unknown father, to her utter disgrace. She was sister-kin to me, the daughter of Telarien, the grand-daughter of my dear, dead Kinzi. But here it ends. We will not speak of her or her bastard again."

There was a moment's embarrassed silence, even the truculent Karidia looking abashed. By the opposite window, Cattila's Ear had dropped a stitch. Adiraina released her cloth letter and removed the needle from her thumb.

"As for this girl's mother," she said, with an abrupt return to her usual calm manner, "all I know is that she was pure Knorth and a potent Shanir, as members of that house so often were. Remember, my own gift is to sense bloodlines by touch—back a hundred generations, if necessary."

"So you keep reminding us," Karidia grumbled. "Worth your eyes, was it? All right, all right: we *don't* know if developing the blood-sight caused your blindness: they just happened at the same time. A fat lot of good either does us now, anyway. Without the mother's name, we wouldn't know how to bring the daughter into sister-kinship even if we wanted to. And the darkling taint? You're sure that's in this uncouth brat too?"

"Regrettably, yes."

"So, we have here a purebred Shanir Knorth who probably knows who her mother was, but won't tell us. She also refuses to say where she's been for the past nineteen-odd years. Given the taint, it could have been in Perimal Darkling itself. And you once even said that she and the Highlord could be twins except, of course, that he's at least ten years older than she is. I ask you! What are we supposed to do with a mystery like that?"

"We crack it," said the Ardeth Matriarch tartly, "or we crack her. What else do you think we've been trying to do, this past winter? We *have* to know what we're dealing with."

"Make her drop the mask?" said Yolindra. "How indelicate!"

"Yes," said Trishien dryly, "especially since we forced her to wear it in the first place."

"I see now why you turned her over to Kallystine," said Dianthe, as she swept past yet again. "If you want to learn the worst about anyone, dear Kally will bring it out."

"I resent that!" yelped Karidia, and took off in pursuit.

Yolindra's chime of laughter broke as the sound of hoofbeats below made her glance down into the Forecourt. "Brenwyr," she said.

The others glanced at each other, momentarily united by the unease which the Iron Matriarch seemed to create these days.

"And she's wearing that horrid skirt again."

Trishien grinned. "Jealous, Yo? But I forgot: unlike some of us, you enjoy being hobbled. Never mind. I'm sure she'll change before coming up here rather than offend you or scare the children. At least, she's insisted that our young Knorth be properly clothed, which is just as well considering that her brother didn't make any provisions for her at all."

"Only you would call those old rags proper clothing," the Edirr Matriarch retorted with a sniff. "Still, I suppose they are better than that awful pink dress she arrived in."

Dianthe had come to stand beside Adiraina, scarcely breathing hard at all despite her brisk walk. *Ah, to be ninety again*, thought the blind matriarch. She felt her friend's hand on her shoulder. The fingers spoke to her with quick, deft changes of pressure.

Seriously, what does the Highlord think of his sister in Kallystine's tender care? It can't be what he intended when he sent her here.

Adiraina put her thin hand over Dianthe's. *It wasn't. He thought his steward Rowan would take charge of her.*

A Highborn girl alone in a Kendar garrison? Ridiculous!

So I said, and snatched her out of the steward's hands. Rowan must have told him that, but she doesn't know about dear Kallystine, anymore than he seems to have known that he should provide his sister with suitable clothes, quarters, and guards. So we have her quite to ourselves.

"Hmmmm." Dianthe's fingers drummed briefly. *At least until the Highlord comes home. 'Point of law,' as Trishien would say: custom may put her in our hands, but she's still Knorth. Be careful, old friend. About those clothes, though. Why did Brenwyr insist that she wear them? You do realize whose they were, don't you?*

Adiraina sighed. *Yes, I do. Having a Knorth in the halls again seems to have . . . set all the old ghosts walking, as it were. For me, Kinzi Kin-singer; for Brenwyr, in a more literal sense, young Aerulan.*

But this girl is so very different, Dianthe's fingers protested. *She's Knorth too, of course, and young, but so gawky, so maladroit . . . .*

You've forgotten what young Knorth are like.

Dianthe considered this rather blankly. "You're right," she said. "It's been so long." *If this girl follows the way of her house, she'll grow to be a beauty.* The fingers paused a moment. *I wonder if Kallystine realizes that . . . .* "What is it?"

Adiraina had suddenly stiffened. "Someone in the Halls has just experienced a berserker episode."

"I warned you!" Karidia burst out. "This comes of using Shanir powers and breeding for them. Oh yes, Ardeth, you and Kinzi did, admit it or not. Manipulating bloodlines, creating monsters . . . . And now that precious Iron Matriarch of yours has blown up in someone's face!"

"It wasn't Brenwyr," said Adiraina, shaken. "I don't know who it was."

The matriarchs looked at each other. Berserker Highborn were Shanir with a strong affinity to the Third Face of God, That-Which-Destroys. Adolescent girls sometimes passed through a mock-berserker phase, but the genuine thing was not taken lightly by anyone remotely interested in a quiet life.

"Well, someone's got to find out," said Karidia, and went.

The others were still discussing possibilities when she returned, hauling with her the young sewing teacher.

"It was that wretched Knorth," she announced, almost with satisfaction. "Tell them, girl."

The instructress told her story, stammering to find herself with such an august audience.

"I never said a-anything about using knot stitches as a code!" she wailed, clutching her shredded sampler. "That's a third circle secret. She shouldn't have known about it herself, much less mentioned it in front of the children. *And* she sang them Jamethiel's lament, a-all about obedience and Honor's Paradox . . . ."

"The trouble with that young lady," remarked Trishien after the instructress had burst into tears and been dismissed, "is that she isn't used to people who can think."

"Of course not!" snapped Karidia. "At that age, it's indecent! Honor's Paradox, indeed. As if anyone in that classroom was ready to learn about that, or perhaps ever will be. *And* the knot stitch code. That wretched girl has nosed out another of our mysteries, without being sworn to keep quiet about it."

"You can't have it both ways," said Trishien reasonably. "We haven't trusted her with the secrets of the Women's World, so she learns what she can and owes nothing to us. Excuse me." Her hand had written something in a spiky script. She read the short message and signed an acknowledgment in her own rounded letters. "A weather note from Kirien: Mount Alban reports increased weirding. The College thinks a storm is on the way. What a pity," she added, musing, "that this Jameth was born a Knorth. The Jaran would know what to do with a mind like that."

The Coman Matriarch flushed. "H-how *dare* you think of a purebred Knorth in those terms! You stick to corrupting your own women, you . . . you scrolls-worm! And as for your precious Kirien . . . ."

"*Karidia!*"

The collective voice and will of the other matriarchs brought her to a dead halt, a bit dazed, as if she had run full-tilt into a wall.

"Remember where and what you are," said Adiraina sternly. "Behave."

"None of us have been quite normal, I think, since that girl arrived," remarked Dianthe. "Haven't you noticed? She makes people forget themselves. I wish, though, that the sewing teacher hadn't slapped her. Have we really made the Highlord's sister so vulnerable?"

Karidia snorted, rallying. "Before you start thinking of that girl as helpless, you'd better look at this."

She held out the sampler which she had appropriated from her young kinswoman. They all regarded it at first with bewilderment, then with growing apprehension as Adiraina took it, spread it out on her lap, and examined the slashes by touch. Each of her fingers fitted into one.

"Oh dear," she said. "Oh *dear*."

III

JAME'S FIRST THOUGHT, as she pitched forward down the spiral stair, was an echo of the instructress's: "Oh no. Not again."

Then she gave a shout to warn anyone who might be on the steps below her, curled up, and rolled. The trick was to keep all extremities tucked well in and let the heavy velvet of her gown act as padding as she caromed down the stair's stony throat. It worked, as it had all too often over that long winter, until her hem caught on a broken tread. Suddenly checked, she crashed down full length at the foot of the steps and lay there for a moment, thoroughly shaken. Then, in a language which, hopefully, no one else at Gothregor understood, she began to swear.

"*What* was that?" voices exclaimed above. "Lady Jameth, are you all right?"

They were probably wondering if she had finally managed to break her neck. Here came one of them now, hopping down the steps to find out.

Jame struggled to rise, in furious contention with the tight under and voluminous overskirt. Dammit, she was *not* going to be found tied up in knots, like some poorly wrapped package. Her foot tangled in the damaged hem, ripping it more, as she floundered upright.

The lady on the stair bent to peer around its newel. No broken body huddled on the floor below. She descended to the arcade which extended around the Forecourt, under the classrooms. No one there either. Crossing the gallery, she examined the sweep of the court. Nothing.

"Vanished again," she called to her friends above.

When she had hopped laboriously back up the stairs, Jame emerged from a niche under them, shaking dust from her skirts. The sound of renewed lessons rolled down to her, the sewing teacher's voice shrilling above the others in praise of obedience, self-restraint, endurance, and silence, as if by sheer volume she could obliterate the past few minutes. Jame wondered what precious, petty secret she had stumbled across this time, to have made that little idiot panic so badly. Well, not an idiot, exactly—only willfully ignorant, like so many others in these halls.

Come to that, her own response hadn't been particularly brilliant.

She regarded her black gloved hands with disgust. The nails looked almost demure in repose beneath their ripped out fingertips—a secret of her own which she bitterly regretted having at last betrayed. The first time those retractile ivory claws had made their appearance, in her seventh year, they had gotten her thrown out of her Haunted Lands home. A fine joke it would be if the same thing happened here, and perhaps no more than she deserved.

In the meantime, though, what next? Back to her room in the Caineron compound to repair her damaged clothes? Although no needlewoman, she usually wasn't as inept as she had been in the sewing class. Indeed, certain individuals in the past had found her very nimble fingered, although not at skills which the ladies here would appreciate. She wouldn't have made such a mess this afternoon if she hadn't been worried about Jorin.

The Royal Gold ounce cub had been taken away from her on her arrival at Gothregor, after Kallystine had made a fuss. Jame had missed him terribly, especially on cold nights when she was used to having him crawl into bed with her, a warm, purring lump who usually by morning had appropriated both blankets and pillow. Even so, they hadn't been entirely separated. Blind from birth, Jorin used Jame's eyes to see; likewise, she was slowly learning how to share his other four senses. As a result, when he went for his daily run in the outer ward she, in a way, accompanied him. He should be out enjoying himself now. Perhaps the link between them was simply weak today, but what if the ounce was ill or hurt? She had been trying to contact him when she had inadvertently sewn her fingers together.

Worry again directed her: Jame found herself turning left onto the northern leg of the gallery, toward the inner ward and the subterranean stables where Jorin had spent the winter.

This section of the arcade and the apartments opening off of it belonged to the Brandan. A randon cadet and her captain stood by the main entrance, both wearing the dress grays and scarlet shoulder embroidery of their house. Although each compound was considered sovereign territory with its own small garrison, bemused guards had allowed Jame to explore all of them but one. She slowed, remembering her rebuff on the Randir threshold by its smiling, cold-eyed captain, whose name she had never been able to learn.

The Brandan captain looked up. Close-cut sandy hair, one brow broken by an old scar, flattened nose . . . a stranger.

Ah. This must be the Brandan's day to rotate the guard, new cadets coming down with their officer from the randon college at Tentir, the old either returning there or going on to the Southern Host. Would these two let her pass? The cadet looked uncertain, but the captain crossed low-held wrists in the salute of Kendar to Highborn, curiosity in her good-natured, bright blue eyes.

Jame passed with a nod, feeling suddenly shy. Who was she to receive tribute from a randon officer? Ganth Gray Lord's daughter, yes, but she hadn't known that until a few months ago. The last Knorth lady, clothed in rotting velvet . . . . Behind the mask, what was she becoming? Who had she ever, really, been?

Abruptly, she felt the touch of Jorin's senses. The surface under his paws was hard—stone, not packed earth—and he was running. The air smelled of stone too. At the end of the long gallery, a Kendar maid leaped aside with a shriek, her arm-load of clean linen flying. Through the blizzard of white sheets hurtled a silver-gilt form. Blind Jorin had apparently gotten this far by ricochetting off walls and was headed for another one when Jame saw him. Instantly, he straightened out, came pelting down the hall, and leaped into her arms. Struck in the chest by forty pounds of rapidly moving ounce, Jame went over backward. The Brandan captain loomed above her. Someone was shouting that the cat had attacked her.

"He did not!" she gasped, clutching Jorin.

"I can see that, lady," said the captain, amused, as the ounce hid his sleek head under Jame's arm. "Damned funny behavior for a full-grown hunting ounce, though."

"He is not full-grown . . . well, not quite . . . and he doesn't know he's an ounce. A tabby cat named Boo raised him."

"Ah. Well, that explains everything."

Someone shoved the captain aside. Jame saw riding boots, a brown, divided skirt, a heavy coat with inserts of braided leather, a masked face. Although she had never met this lady before, there was only one person whom she could be: Brenwyr, the Iron Matriarch.

What Brenwyr saw was Jame's torn clothes. Brown eyes widened, then flared red. The impact of her sudden fury seemed to pick Jame up off the floor and nail her against the arcade's inner wall. She slid sideways in a water flowing evasion, snatched up both of her skirts and ran, Jorin pelting after her.

Afterward, she supposed that they must have bolted right through the Caineron compound and into the derelict halls beyond, where the women of numerous minor houses had once lived. What brought her up at last, hard, was a wall which she had apparently also tried to run straight through. At least the collision had been muted by the tapestry. It hung before her now, frayed and faded but still wonderfully wrought: a moon garden full of pale blooms, seen through an open door.

Sanctuary . . . she thought, still half-dazed; then, as Jorin climbed into her arms chirping anxiously, *What in Perimal's name happened*?

But she already knew. When Ganth had realized with the appearance of her claws that she was Shanir, he had driven her out with just such a blast of mad rage. That time, she hadn't stopped running until she was across the Barrier into Perimal Darkling.

Trinity. That was another secret which she hoped these women never learned. Yet she had sung that song to those children, as if to remind both them and herself that there was more to their world than needlework. To that little sewing teacher, though, it had been only a tale of ancient days. Few knew or guessed that Gerridon, Master of Knorth, had indeed gained a semblance of that immortality for which he had betrayed his people, through the souls which the Dream-Weaver had reaped for him and the slower passage of time in Perimal Darkling. There in his monstrous house he still dwelt, deeper in shadow with each captured soul which he devoured, yet desperate for more as their number dwindled and darkness crept closer to claiming him as its own.

And there Jame had also lived, from the time of her flight from the Haunted Lands keep until two years ago.

That was hard to believe now.

Half her life had passed in those dark halls, yet most of it was a blur, like the fading images of a bad dream. Had she been made to forget, or willed it to protect herself? Sometimes she wondered: Had it even, really, happened?

When she had finally stumbled back to her old home two years ago, she had remembered nothing of the decade since her expulsion. Since then, fragmentary memories had begun to return, like snatches of an old, dark song: practicing the combat *kantirs* of the Senethar on the green-veined floor of the Master's great hall under the eyes of massed Knorth death banners; learning how to read the master runes in a pale book, in a library whose volumes slithered, whispering, on the shelves; dancing the Great Dance as her namesake had before her under the instruction of golden-eyed shadows; realizing at last with horror that she was being trained to take the Dream-Weaver's place.

Only afterward had she learned that this last was no coincidence.

Gerridon needed someone to reap souls for him, to keep him both immortal and human despite the shadows' hunger. Whatever the Women's World thought, his sister-consort had only been his tool, not understanding the evil which he had asked her to commit until too late. Her fall had not been complete, and in the end she had redeemed herself. Still, she had paid a terrible price. So massive an abuse of power had opened a rift in her nature to the chaos beyond, so that toward the end all souls which she touched were caught in the vortex and sucked down, irretrievably. Before that final stage, however, Gerridon had sent her to the exiled Ganth Gray Lord specifically to breed her own successor. Jame was the child whom he had wanted, or so her Senethari Tirandys had told her. No one had counted on twins. Likewise, Gerridon hadn't expected Tirandys to teach the new Jamethiel honor as well as the Senethar. When the night of her investment came, she had slashed the hand held out to her between the red ribbons of a bridal couch, taken the Book Bound in Pale Leather, and fled back across the barrier into Rathillien.

Thus, she had come again to the Haunted Lands keep, stripped of her memory, searching for the twin brother who had stood by while their father had driven her out but whom she still loved, almost as the other half of her soul. But everyone there was dead, slain by the Master in his search for her—everyone except Tori.

Her efforts to find him had taken the next two years, including a sojourn as an apprentice thief in the wonderful, god-ridden city of Tai-tastigon.

Now here she was at last, in their ancestral home, with a twin brother who turned out to be not only Highlord but (thanks to the slower passage of time in the Master's house) a decade her senior. Or rather, here she was without him. Judging from his continued absence, he wished that she had stayed lost. So did Jame, in a way, but she was Kencyr. She belonged with her people. It had crossed her mind not half an hour before that she might be on the verge of a second expulsion. If she was driven out again, this time from the heart of the Kencyrath, where was there left to go?

The image rose in her memory of a snowfield high in the Ebonbane, splitting open, thundering down into the maw of the chasm hidden beneath.

Why had she suddenly remembered that?

Ah. Over the tapestry was a wooden frieze depicting big cats at play—Arrin-ken, actually, third of the three people that made up the Kencyrath, once its judges. On the night of the Fall, many of them had been blinded with burning coals and then slain in the Master's hall, where their flayed skins still lay as trophies on his cold hearth. The rest had fled to Rathillien. A thousand years ago, though, they had withdrawn into the wilds. The carver, therefore, had never seen one. Jame had. In the Ebonbane, on the chasm's edge, Immalai the Silent had laid bare all the shadows which years in the Master's House had bred in her:

Child, you have perverted the Great Dance as your namesake did before you. You have also usurped a

*priest's authority and misused a master rune. We con-
clude that you are indeed a darkling, in training if not
in blood, reckless to the point of madness . . . .*

Under his silent voice in her mind had spoken all the
Arrin-ken in their distant retreats, a woven chorus of
power, judging her.

But in the end she had passed judgment on herself.
She had indeed done all those things and perhaps more
besides, which she had now forgotten. She could have
blamed the darkness bred into her or the training forced
on her, neither her fault. She could even have blamed
her Shanir blood, which had made the rest possible.
Instead, she had chosen to take responsibility for her
own actions, to jump into the abyss and die, if that was
required.

It wasn't. Immalai had overridden the others, sus-
pending judgment.

An unfallen darkling; innocent, but not ignorant . . . .

It was something, Jame supposed, to embody a paradox which could make even an Arrin-ken pause. Despite
all the dark things she had been taught, despite some of
the truly stupid things she had done, she hadn't yet fallen
from honor. So, be damned if she was going to let anyone
drive her over the edge of anything, if she wasn't prepared to go.

Nor was she ready to surrender Jorin. Jame looked
back the way she had come, out of doors hanging askew
down a long corridor half-sunk into dusty twilight. The
guards might try to follow her. She didn't think much of
their chances, though, in this wilderness of empty halls
which, thanks to a winter of ceaseless exploration, she
probably knew better than any of them did. No, no one
would take Jorin away from her tonight, unless she

tripped over a search party. Best, though, to keep moving.

She pushed aside the tapestry. Behind it was a door, and through that, under the grim shadow of the Ghost Walks, the moon garden itself.

Tall, windowless walls surrounded it. Pale comfrey sheltered against its northern end, three feet high with drooping, bell-shaped flowers on racemes as curved as a scorpion's tail. Then there were yarrow with their lacy, silver-gray foliage, white self-heal, wild heart's-ease already hanging their heads against the coming night, and a dozen other flowering herbs, all pure white. A small brook cut across the southern end of the garden, emerging from a tunnel under the outer wall and plunging under ground near the inner to join the fortress's subterranean water system. Beyond it, against the south wall, the delicate fiddlehead scrolls of young ferns arched up through the last, sheltered crust of snow. All the white flowers glowed slightly in the dusk (except the yarrow, still in tight bud), and white moths danced over them, wings luminous with pollen.

Jorin plunged into the deep grass with an excited bleat.

Jame followed more slowly. She was tempted to spend the night as she sometimes had in the past, escaping Kallystine, but didn't want to bring her bad dreams here. The garden had a dreaming quality of its own, haunted not so much by a ghost as by the half-forgotten memory of one. Against the south wall hung a tattered death banner. A gentle, barely discernible face gazed out of it, the texture of the wall behind showing through its weather-worn threads. It was a Knorth face, Jame thought, but she didn't know whose, much less why it had been exiled here while the rest of the family banners hung in state in the old keep. No, she would leave the garden and its lady in peace tonight. Bending, she picked a spray of white primrose. A light shake caused its buds to spring open and the pollen within to luminesce. Surrounded by a nimbus of eager moths and followed by a reluctant ounce, she entered the Ghost Walks.

Once the Knorth had occupied these mural apartments from the northern gate to the eastern, but they had been a dwindling house long before the massacre. On that spring night, the northeast drum tower had been large enough to house them all. A door in the herb garden's corner opened immediately into the kitchen. The family's guard had occupied the ground level, where they had slept through the slaughter taking place over their heads—inexplicably, some had thought afterward, but Jame suspected the expert use of poppy dust.

She was less certain about the Shadow Guild's claim to invisibility. Its members were said to wear clothes made from the fibers of the transparent *mere* plant, earned garment by garment as apprentices. Journeymen went on to a knife tempered in *mere* sap. Masters of the Guild acquired *mere* tattoos, bit by bit covering every inch of their bodies including eyeballs and as far into every orifice as the dye needles would reach. The Grand Master was said to be totally invisible, able to walk through walls, and quite insane from *mere* poisoning—if one believed that such an unlikely thing as *mere* existed.

A stair spiralled upward along the curve of the tower. The second floor, divided into apartments circling a hall, had been occupied by the family itself. Jame went through the silent rooms, the primrose wand dimly lighting her way. In the central hall she paused, looking about at the moldering rugs, the dusty furniture, the cold firepit. From the dark corners came a furtive rustling, instantly stilled. Jorin's nose twitched at the sharp smell of mouse.

"They were all here, you know," she said softly to him. "Mothers, daughters, aunts, nieces, cousins—the last dozen or so purebred Knorth women left on Rathillien, even those who had contracted out to other houses. It was their first family gathering after the thaws. They were up late, waiting for their men to come home. Ganth had gone off to hunt a rathorn, you see."

The ounce gave an uneasy, questioning chirp, as if he really did see. Perhaps he had plucked the image out of her mind of those eerie, armored beasts.

"That's right. Like the mare I killed in the Anarchies. Like that white, death's-head foal of hers who's probably still after my blood—small blame to him, even if it was a mercy killing."

All winter Jame had been hunting too, not for a slayer but for the slain. The dead could sometimes touch the living. Hadn't her brother carried the bones of a child all the way from Kithorn to the Cataracts and been helped more than once by her ghost? Hadn't she herself played tag–you're–dead in Penari's Maze with its very bad tempered, very deceased architect?

These walks were also said to have their ghost: a Knorth girl named Tieri, killed in the massacre, whose body had never been found. The unburnt dead always return, it was said. For years, lights and sounds had been reported in these dusty halls but never investigated, on orders of the Ardeth Matriarch, who had virtually ruled the Women's Halls during the Knorth's long exile. Finally, the disturbances had stopped. Jame's own prowl-ings had been in part a bone-hunt, as boys used to steal off to haunted Kithorn to retrieve relics of its slaughtered garrison for the pyre. They saw this as a test of nerve, as well as a service to the dead. Jame simply wanted to touch the family she had never known. Here in the Walks, though, there was no point of contact—not even with those faded blood-stains on the floor where, perhaps, her great-grandmother Kinzi, the last Knorth Matriarch, had died.

Nonetheless, when Jame regained the stairs, she again climbed.

The entire third floor had been reserved for the Gray Lord's use. It all looked gray enough now with dust and dusk, a desolation of public rooms serving as antechambers to the Highlord's apartment. Standing on the threshold of his bed chamber, Jame reflected that it had really been the Highlord's reaction which had sealed the tragedy.

Ganth had assumed that the Seven Kings of Bashti had commissioned the assassins. That still made a certain amount of sense. Collectively, the Bashtiri of the Central Lands hired more Kencyr troops than anyone except Krothen of Kothifir, and were always complaining that the Kencyr code of honor unduly restricted the orders which their mercenaries would obey. They might have reasoned that if they could eliminate the family which held the Kencyrath to its old, honorable ways, they could make contracts more to their taste with the surviving houses.

But there sense and sanity alike had ended for the Gray Lord. He had marched down into the White Hills where all seven kings were engaged in one of their usually bloodless squabbles and had attacked without parley, although his Host was not only greatly outnumbered but faced with the kings' Kencyr mercenaries as well. The end, after three bloody days, had been a stalemate and exile for the handful of surviving Knorth.

The Bashtiri kings still swore that they hadn't sent the killers.

It all seemed impossibly remote to Jame, like a tale told of ancient days. Yet the people she had known at the keep in the Haunted Lands had lived through this, even if Ganth had forbidden them to tell his children about it. If they had, though, would that have made it seem more real? Perhaps the impersonal past never did. Perhaps that was why nothing in the Ghost Walks touched her.

At least, so Jame thought as she turned to leave. A gust of wind blew through the broken windows behind her. It came again, harder, to rustle dry leaves across the floor, to lift and plait the tattered ribbons of arrases against the wall. The age-blurred hunting scenes shifted, and shifted again in the dimming light, dream images tumbling through the indistinct forms of leaf and bough, hunter and hunted. Gray, gray . . . not a forest at all but a city street, deep shadowed, down which dead leaves blew. One of the shadows moved. It was crawling toward her, flat on the ground, like a spreading stain. The leaves rattled over it. Its fingers slid, elongated, over the cobblestones, and seemed to clutch them to pull itself forward. Then it raised its head.

"Are you thinking of me, butcher of children?" Jame heard her own voice demand harshly, and knew that she was backing away. "Why can't you leave me alone?"

Something caught her behind the knees. Her hands leaped out to grab the window frame, to prevent her from tumbling backward out of the tower. Across the room, another gust of wind combed out the shreds of tapestry.

Jame sat down with a thump on the low window sill. Sweet Trinity. If her nightmares were going to pursue her into waking life, she was in deep trouble. Anyway, that particular ghost didn't even belong here. Bane was one of *her* dead, not Gothregor's—assuming that the Tastigon mob had finally managed to kill him.

Another attempt at mercy, another bloody mess . . . .

Most people would say that a man who mutilated children for sport didn't deserve even that much. But they didn't understand. Neither did Jame, entirely. He had threatened, tempted, and ultimately saved her when the mob had come to take him to the Mercy Seat to be flayed alive for the one murder in a score which he hadn't committed. Even then, he couldn't die without his soul, which he had given for safekeeping to the Kencyr priest Ishtier. Ishtier in turn had treacherously used it to create the Lower Town Monster, which fed on children through their soul-cast shadows. With Bane on the Mercy Seat, under the knife, Jame had tried to destroy the demon Monster to free his soul so that he could die. By then, though, the mob had been after her too, and she'd had to flee Tai-tastigon without knowing if she had succeeded. The alternative hardly made for pleasant dreams. It helped somewhat that Ishtier had paid for his betrayal with madness, but not much. In his warped way, Bane had been a friend—and blood-kin. Jame was sure of that, with or without proof. As much Ganth's son by a Kendar mistress as she was his daughter by . . . .

No. Don't even think it.

She had been careless before. There were women here, she suspected, who could pluck the very thoughts out of one's head. Ancestors only knew what would happen if they learned who her mother was. Luckily, they had decided that her own full name must be Jameth, the alternative never having occurred to any of them. She hid behind their mistake as she did behind the mask which they had forced her to wear. But hiding had only brought a stalemate. Now circumstances had forced her a little into the light, and she couldn't decide whether to advance or retreat again.

Jame sighed. So much at Gothregor confused her. She wished she could talk to Marc about it, but the big Kendar was still with the Host at Kothifir, enjoying his first rest in ninety-odd years. Not that he could advise her about the intricacies of the Women's World, of course, but problems tended to unravel before his tranquil common sense.

What are you hiding from, lass? he would probably ask now. *Wear that mask long enough and you'll forget what your own face looks like.*

Small loss that would be.

Even so, which will you choose—the face or the mask?

The Women's World prized the freedom which masks gave them to conceal their feelings from men, to live their lives hidden as they did within these halls in the mysteries of sister-kinship; but they hadn't chosen to share that life with Jame.

She remembered the children's taunt: "Seeker, seeker . . . " that damned game so much like blindman's buff, played with the eyeless mask. The blind seeker must catch someone, correctly guess her name, and then assume it while the mask passed to a new face and a new seeker groped for her lost identity among her jeering peers.

I'm groping now, thought Jame with a sigh.

The face or the mask . . . oh bother. Marc's "simple" questions never had simple answers.

There was a face at Gothregor, though, which the Women's World apparently hoped to recreate beneath the mask which they had made her wear.

Well, why not? This seemed to be a night for ghost-stalking.

"C'mon, kitten," she said to the ounce. "Let's go visit Aerulan."

 IV

LIGHT AND SHADOW interwove in the room where the Lady Kallystine sat at her evening adornment. Candles burned everywhere, their flames reflected in endless succession by mirrors lining the walls. All the fiery sparks danced restlessly: no amount of silken hangings, drawn however close, could shut out the fitful breath of the south wind called the Tishooo, which had risen within the past half hour. In the farther reaches of the large chamber, black-clad Kendar maids moved silently, ceaselessly, among the banks of candles, relighting those which the wind had extinguished. They had no need to approach their lady's dressing table, however: the candles there had a trick, after a moment's hesitation, of rekindling themselves.

By their light, Kallystine admired her reflection. Here in her own chambers, she wore no mask but a delicate lace-work of leaf gold, dusted as lightly on her face as the iridescence on a jewel-jaw's wing. Carmine brought a warm glow to high cheek bones and full lips. Powdered sapphire traced the veins of throat and snowy breast. Her personal maid, a young Kendar-Highborn half-breed, was brushing her long, black hair with slow strokes. Kallystine basked in the sensation, watching herself in the mirror through half-closed eyes. She was twenty-five years old, at the height of her power, and used to getting everything she wanted. What she wanted most at the moment, however, seemed perversely to have abstracted itself.

"Would it be too much to inquire," she asked the room at large, in her most languid voice, "if the Lady Jameth has yet been found? Can it really be that every spare guard is searching?"

"No, my lady; yes, my lady."

No expression colored the handmaid's voice or face. A winter in M'lady's service had taught her to keep her thoughts to herself. Kallystine noted the tone. She picked up a long, handsome braid of hair from the table, ran it through her fingers once or twice, then carelessly tossed it to the maid.

"Here. I shan't need this after all," she said, and smiled to see the girl receive back her own hair as woodenly as she had hacked it off earlier, so that her mistress could experiment with it as a fall. It was a Highborn's duty continually to remind others who held the power. Her father, Lord Caineron, had taught her that.

He had also commanded that she reduce the Knorth Jameth to a similar state of submission. "Break her into pieces," his last correspondence had abruptly concluded, "then grind them into powder."

Kallystine wondered what the creature had done, to make her father so angry. As always, she had tried to carry out his orders, with little success. Oh, the girl obeyed her, but with such cool reserve that Kallystine hadn't been able so much as to scratch her composure. Worse, despite the matriarchs' apparent indifference, she had found herself hesitant to use her usual, more direct methods: after all, the wretched girl *was* a Highborn Knorth, and a strangely intimidating one at that. Oh, it had been maddening.

Ah, but now, finally, she had something to work with. "Describe to me again that deplorable episode in the classroom," she said, selecting a candied tadpole from an alabaster bowl.

The handmaid again described in a perfectly flat voice all that the Caineron spies had been able to learn. However, no amount of coaxing or threats had induced the little girl who had been closest to say what she had seen, the moment before the instructress's sampler had fallen to shreds. She was an Ardeth, and the Ardeth Matriarch had sworn her to silence.

That blind bitch, thought Kallystine, biting off the tadpole's head. Why should she queen it here at Gothregor, over the Highlord's own consort? As for the cool way Adiraina had dismissed her plan to occupy the old Knorth quarters—

"Oh, no, my dear. That would hardly be appropriate."

Impossible, explaining to her father why she hadn't carried out that particular order regardless. Hard enough to understand it herself, or the Women's World at all, kept as she was at its lowest level—more of Adiraina's work, surely, as though she couldn't be trusted with their stupid little secrets!

(Not that Father wouldn't probably find them fascinating. If he *should* ask, well, the first rule of the Women's World was obedience, wasn't it?)

Secrets . . . .

The Knorth's hands and those perpetual gloves, hiding (oh, delicious thought) what monstrous deformity?

Kallystine's attention focussed sharply on her reflection. Was that a wrinkle? No, of course not. Just the same, her skin had been more radiant two years ago, when she had first become Torisen's limited term consort. She knew that he had consented only to stave off her father, but she had still managed to dazzle him. It had seemed inevitable that he would agree to a half-Caineron heir. Now, however, that contract had almost expired. She still didn't doubt her charms, but in order for them to work he had to be *here*. Somehow, it was that wretched Jameth's fault that he wasn't. But the man had to come home soon, and she must prepare for that day.

Kallystine's mirror reflected most of the room behind her, including a basin set on a tripod. She regarded it with discontent. The matriarchs (those meddling cows!) had forbidden her to experiment directly on the Highlord, but Great-aunt Rawneth had suggested an alternative. If only it worked, she could at least greet Torisen on his return with the same fresh complexion that had captivated him against his will two years ago. The potion lacked only the proper activating agent, which Great-aunt said she must discover for herself. The Kendar had proved useless. As for her half-breed servant . . . .

"Show me your hand."

Stony-faced, the maid obeyed. Her right hand was oddly withered, with blue, protruding veins, discolored spots, and swollen joints, the result of repeated immersions. What a pity that its lost youth had not proved transferable to the next person who had used the basin. Science was *such* a imprecise art.

Kallystine repeated these observations out-loud, adding over her shoulder, "Make a note of that."

In the dark corner by the bed, knitting needles began to click.

Ah, thought Kallystine suddenly, but what if she were to use a pure-blooded Highborn—the purest in Gothregor, by all accounts? That would be poetic revenge indeed, to make the one pay who was responsible for this long winter of lost opportunities; and afterward, given those omnipresent black gloves, who would ever know?

The Tishooo caught its breath. Hangings swayed backward out the first story windows, then in again as the wind exhaled—"Whoo!"—extinguishing a quarter of the candles. Maids hastily relit them. The room seemed surrounded by walls of moving air, as cut off by the growing storm as by the Caineron guards. Tonight, this was like a corner of Restormir, sovereign, inviolate, where a child of the house might amuse herself as she chose. So thought Kallystine, smiling at her reflection with half-closed eyes as she savored the other two pieces of information that she had gained tonight: a story and a fact which to her was the most exciting news of all: someone had actually slapped the Knorth Jameth, and gotten away with it.

Muted voices sounded by the door.

". . . tripped right over one of our search parties," a guard was saying. "No, we didn't see the ounce."

What a pity, thought Kallystine. She'd had such amusing plans for that cat. Still, one shouldn't be greedy.

"Lady Jameth," she said sweetly, turning. "How kind of you to pay this visit."

The Knorth stood motionless, a slender, dark form surrounded by candles. Her skirt spread out around her, its lower edge merging with the room's shadows, its folds concealing her gloved hands.

"Leave us," said Kallystine to her servants.

They went, all but the indistinct figure by the bed and the handmaid, who slipped aside at the door and remained in the room, concealed by a hanging, the severed braid in her withered right hand, the frozen expression still on her face.

Kallystine had risen and was slowly, languidly, circling the Knorth. Her train, iridescent as a peacock's tail, wound around the other's plum dark skirt. The jewels in her hair mocked the other's archaic simplicity.

"So," she said, regarding the Knorth's dusty hem. "You've been for a stroll in the abandoned halls . . . perhaps even in the Ghost Walks? Gone to visit the scene of past familial glories, hmmmm? What a pity the future will hold so few of them, but then there are so few of you Knorth left, aren't there?"

The answer to this apparently being self-evident, the Knorth didn't reply. Like the handmaid, she had learned to say as little to M'lady as possible.

"Well, perhaps there's one more of you than you think," Kallystine snapped, annoyed enough to play her main card before she had intended.

The other's poise broke. "What do you mean? Who else could there be?"

"Ah, someone in the shadows," said Kallystine, still circling, beginning again to enjoy herself. "Have you ever heard of a girl named Tieri?"

"The ghost in the Walks?"

"That childish story. Properly fooled we all were by it, too. Well, it seems that Aerulan hid the brat in the empty halls, where the Ardeth Matriarch later found her. A ghost she may be now, but she lived for twelve years after the massacre. The last Knorth lady, an Ardeth prisoner in her own halls—much good it did that blind hag in the end. Tieri died, you see. In the moon garden. Giving birth to a bastard."

"Poor Tieri."

"Rather pity yourself. She was your father's youngest full sister, your aunt."

"So the child was my first cousin . . . or is it still alive?"

"Who *cares*? The point is that there is, or was, a Knorth Bastard. Three of you left, my dear, and one a . . . a *thing*, that calls into serious question whether you yourself will breed true. I needn't tell you how damaging even the whisper of this could be to your prospects. But the secret needn't go outside this room, if we stay friends." Unexpectedly, her voice grew husky. She reached to touch the other's hair. "Such very, very good friends. . . ."

The Knorth pivoted away. Her hair slid like black water over Kallystine's white hand. Her heavy skirt, swinging, clipped the tripod, splashing some of the basin's contents on the floor. Oblivious, they stared at each other. The wind died between them. In the corner, for a moment, the knitting needles were still.

Kallystine sighed and withdrew her hand. "Then again," she murmured, "perhaps the other way is better. We needn't disagree, my dear, not if you serve me well. As a gesture of our . . . understanding, perhaps you will help me with a pet project." She faced the Knorth across the basin, smiling again with a sleepy, almost benign malice. "Such a small thing, my dear. Just stir this mixture for me. With your bare hand."

The girl stared at her. "Why on earth should I?"

A noise drew their attention downward. The ounce Jorin had emerged from under his mistress's full outer skirt to sniff at the puddle on the floor. Now he was scratching around it.

"Ah," said Kallystine. "I wonder. Is it true that ounces have special glands which produce the most exquisite perfume? Shall we find out?"

"Ah . . . oooo!" said the wind, and sucked the drapes out the embrasures into the night. The candle flames leaped and died. In the sudden, rushing darkness which followed, a strong hand grabbed Kallystine by the hair and thrust her downward into icy liquid. She reared back, sputtering, clawing at her eyes. Her face felt strange.

Then the candles on the dressing table flickered back to life and she saw herself in the mirror.

M'lady Kallystine began to scream.

V

ADIRAINA STILL SAT BY THE WINDOW, alone now in the falling night. The breeze off the Snowthorns had turned to a rising wind that lapped around her until she felt as if she hovered in it, perilously balanced.

It had taken her a long time to regain even so much poise as this. The old should be used to death's imminence, but tonight had brought back the memory of too many struck down too soon: strong Kinzi, sweet-faced Aerulan, Tieri . . . .

She had almost put that sad child out of her mind, until now. Growing up alone in the Ghost Walks where so many had died, herself the only ghost . . . . Had that long concealment really been necessary? What if she, Adiraina, had actually been punishing the girl for having survived when Kinzi had not?

No, *no*, NO.

"*I didn't have a choice,*" she had protested to Dianthe, when at last the secret had to be told. "*You remember what those times were like. Ganth's madness had thrown us all into chaos, defenseless. The assassins might have returned if they had known that any Knorth women had survived.*"

"*I can understand not telling the lords,*" Diante had agreed, "*then or later. Tieri was the last of her house, a prize—except that without her lord to give assent, any child of hers would have been a bastard. The Kencyrath was in trouble enough without that. But couldn't you at least have told us?*"

Not without knowing who had sent the assassins in the first place; and with Tieri dead, Adiraina hadn't wanted to know at all, when the answer might destroy what was left of her world. What did it matter if the blood price for the slain went unpaid when no Knorth were left to collect?

But now the Knorth had returned, brother and sister, Ganth's children.

And if someone still wanted all the women of that house dead?

They can't, she told herself. *Not after all these years.* Anyway, too many secrets have been kept too long. She daren't betray them now. Long awaited footsteps sounded on the stair. Silk rustled. So, Brenwyr had changed out of "that horrid skirt" but not, from the length of her stride, into the traditional tight under-gown.

"Greetings, Brandan," Adiraina said formally.

"Greetings, Ardeth."

A hand touched her shoulder. *Grandmother-kin,* said the fingers, with that special emphasis that indicated an embrace. "Sorry I'm so late," the Iron Matriarch added out loud. "I meant to attend the council meeting this afternoon but, well, something happened."

"So I heard. You finally met the Knorth. I have said all along that you should, but not quite like that. Do you feel better now, dear?"

"Of course," said Brenwyr, irritably. "Why shouldn't I?"

"You know perfectly well. You flared, my dear. A perfect example of a mature, berserker episode, the sort that always gives you such terrible headaches afterward. That's your touch of Knorth blood again, I'm afraid, the quarter that dear Kinzi gave you. Oddly enough, just before you someone else flared whom I never suspected before of berserker tendencies but should have, given her bloodlines: Jameth."

"Aerulan never flared."

"Dear Aerulan had none of the family curses. All in all, she was the most atypical Knorth I've ever met. But this isn't Aerulan."

"God's claws, don't you think I know that?"

"I have occasionally wondered. My dear, are you quite sure you know what you are doing?"

"No!" Her boots rang on the ironwood floor as she began to pace restlessly back and forth. "Sometimes I think I'm going out of my mind altogether—a proper Knorth response, eh? After I killed . . . ."

"My dear!"

"All right, grandmother-kin. After my mother died, all the self-control I have, I learned from you. I know what it cost you, too."

Adiraina dismissed this with a graceful gesture, even as the memory of Brenwyr's most recent flare sent a stab of pain through her head. Linked by her own Shanir traits to That-Which-Preserves, she knew that she had been lucky to survive her fosterling's childhood, much less her agonizing adolescence.

Brenwyr must have been watching her closely. "It seems that I can't help but hurt what I love best. Ancestors know, I loved Aerulan—but she's been ashes on the wind for thirty-four years! I was barely more than a child then. Since, I've honored a dozen contracts, borne four sons, managed my lord brother's keep, and become a matriarch on the council. You know the name they call me behind my back. Where has that iron discipline been this past winter? All I can think about is Aerulan, about ransoming her banner out of that cold hall, away from the moldering dead. Now. Before anything else can happen."

"Has Lord Brandan spoken to Torisen again about that?"

"He says he won't, that the Highlord doesn't understand, that the issue is too delicate to force. I ask you!"

"He might be right. I've often thought that Torisen Black Lord doesn't know our customs as well as he should, or is likely to with no Knorth Matriarch to instruct him. It occurs to me, though, that eventually there may be one here again."

"This girl Jameth? That's absurd!"

"No. I would say that it's inevitable. Who else is there? It's a disturbing thought, though, considering the example which she has already set for our younger sisters. Do you know what that child said when I told her to keep quiet about what she had seen in the classroom? 'Why?' Oh, she'll obey, but still . . . !"

"Are questions really so dangerous?"

"Now, my dear. You *know* they are."

"Why? All right, all right: it doesn't matter. After the massacre, though, didn't the Randir Matriarch swear that there would never be a Knorth Matriarch here again?"

Adiraina shifted uneasily. "What a foolish thing for dear Rawneth to have said. I'm sure she's long since thought better of it. It doesn't matter anyway, as long as no Randir Highborn are in residence here and Jameth has been forbidden to enter their compound . . . but perhaps I shouldn't depend on that: the Knorth are so unpredictable, so hard to manage! Why, even Torisen, quiet as he is, has given Cousin Adric some uneasy moments."

Despite herself, Brenwyr smiled. "*Does* Lord Ardeth try to manage the Highlord?"

"Of course. And yet, and yet . . . sometimes, late at night, I wonder. This impulse, this almost compulsion to control these two young people . . . . Do we find them so threatening because they remind us of what the Kencyrath once was like, and perhaps must be again if we are ever to fulfill the purpose for which we were created?"

"To defeat Perimal Darkling? Do you really think we ever will?"

"Ancestors only know," said Adiraina, and paused.

Before the Fall, her ancestors *had* thought they knew. Of course the shadows would be defeated, as soon as the three aspects of their god deigned to manifest themselves in the three Shanir known collectively as the Tyr-ridan. Earlier matriarchs had tried to speed that day by mating together potent Shanir. Whether they should have done so, especially within the bounds of blood-kinship, was still hotly debated. One such match had produced those dire twins, Gerridon and Jamethiel Dream-weaver, who in turn had been bred together with no issue except, perhaps, the Fall itself. Nonetheless, some matriarchs believed that in general their predecessors had in general the right idea.

Adiraina winced, remembering Karidia's taunt: "...*manipulating bloodlines, creating monsters* ...." True, she *had* suggested the blood-cross which had produced Brenwyr, but really ...!

"This much I do believe," she said: "unless our god has forsaken us utterly, someday the Tyr-ridan *will* come, and then we all will face the ultimate test."

The wind veered, bringing with it a distant, enraged shriek and the sound of shattering glass.

"Someone must have annoyed Kallystine again," Brenwyr remarked sourly.

"I do believe that you are right, although I've never heard her break one of her precious mirrors before. Amazing, the way sound carries tonight. Earlier, I thought I heard the Knorth. 'Butcher of children,' she was crying, if that can be right. 'Butcher of children!' It sounded almost like an evocation."

Brenwyr had come to stand beside her. "The Tishooo plays strange tricks. I thought I heard Aerulan calling my name, over and over, the night she died. Speaking of evocations, do you know where I met the Knorth this afternoon? In the arcade, just where Aerulan fell. There she was, in a heap on the floor with a cat in her arms and a torn skirt ... Aerulan's skirt ...."

Adiraina groped for the younger woman's hand and clutched it. "You mustn't ill-wish that girl," she said urgently. "You *know* how dangerous that can be! My dear, my dear, remember your discipline: forget what you can't help. We both must. It was all over so long ago."

"Thirty-four years ago tonight." The bitter twist in her smile was as audible as broken bones grating. "Why, grandmother-kin, don't tell me *you* forgot. This is the anniversary of Aerulan's death."

VI

THE MOMENT THE CANDLES BLEW OUT, Jame whisked herself through a window into the night, as handily as anyone could whose legs were practically bound together by a tight under-skirt. Jorin scrambled after her. They paused outside, listening to the commotion behind them.

"Now, that's a very excitable lady," said Jame to the ounce, "and not a very bright one. She thinks that you're a civet. Perfumes. Huh."

The screams resolved themselves into words. "You'll pay for this!" Kallystine was shrieking. "I'll see that you pay, you stinking Knorth!"

"Trinity," said Jame, as glass shattered in the room which she had just left, and again and again. "*All* her mirrors? Why? Let's just keep out of her way for awhile, eh, kitten?"

They went like shadows through the interconnected courtyards which separated the main hall blocks, a dark, gliding figure and a Royal Gold ounce cub silver-gilt with traces of its winter coat. Over black mountains to the west, the sky had shaded to a deep indigo spangled with stars. The wind whooped around them, swirling Jame's skirt until she was obliged to hold it down with both hands. It was turning into a boisterous night, full of vast uproar. As a rule, the Tishooo only visited the Riverland when the priests weren't paying adequate attention to the weather. Its name in Nekrien meant "The Old Man"—an odd title given its prankish nature. When it wasn't chasing its own tail or snatching up loose slates or plunging down chimneys, it was said to carry off unwanted babies and to turn shadows inside out.

Here was the Forecourt and across it, the old Knorth keep. Actually, the keep's lowest level long preceded the Kencyrath's tenure in this valley, or even that of the Hathiri. The ruins of ancient Merikit hill forts lined the Silver, many of them, as here, worked into the foundations of later buildings.

Inside, all was pitch black, heavy with the smell of cold stone and old cloth. Jame closed the door, groped for a box of candles on a shelf and lit one—cautiously, as she'd had chancy luck with fire ever since using its master rune the previous autumn accidentally setting fire to a blizzard. The flickering light revealed a large, low-beamed hall. Faces started out of the shadows against the walls, stirring restlessly in the wind that soughed under the door—death banners, row after row of them, woven of threads from the clothes in which each had died. These were her ancestors, such as had escaped the Fall into this new world, such as hadn't suffered exile with Ganth. All had the distinctive Knorth features—silver-gray eyes under arched brows; high, sharp cheekbones; obstinate chins—to which were often added the

hard lines of arrogance and cruelty, it being the privilege
of the Kendar weavers to portray the dead as they saw fit,
yes, even to that wild, sidelong stare or those fingertips
gnawed to white bone.

Who *were* all these people, anyway? Jame knew some
names from old songs but not to which banners they
belonged. *Her* people, lost in time, receding. When their
names, at last, were forgotten by all, would their faces
crumble away as already the oldest here had done?

. . . past familial glories, a dying house . . . .

But some were more recently dead than others. On
the far west wall, flanking the door to the inner ward,
hung the banners of those slain that terrible night in the
Ghost Walks. Above a strong-jawed, older woman who
might be Kinzi was the tapestry which Jame had come
to see, the only one there close to her own age. She
raised her candle in salute.

"Hello, Aerulan."

On first seeing that bright face with its whimsical
smile, no one thought, "This is a death banner," but
rather "This is someone I would like to meet." It came
as a shock a moment later to realize what that thin red
line across Aerulan's neck represented. She was so
plainly someone meant to love and be loved, not to bleed
to death with a slit throat in the arms of the girl who
would later become the Brandan Matriarch. Now it
seemed that she had died leading the assassins away from
where the child Tieri had lain hidden. That should have
made her even more real to Jame. It didn't. Oh, this was
hopeless, trying all winter to reach across a gap years
deep, full of pyrrhic ash. The burnt dead *were* dead, and
that was that.

She was about to turn away, sighing, when something
about the banner caught her attention. As a rule, one

only noticed Aerulan's face. Now, however, something about the dead girl's clothes, the cut of her tight-laced bodice . . . . Jame felt a jolt of recognition. It wasn't, of course, the same dress which she now wore—Aerulan's russet gown had been teased apart thread by blood-stained thread to make the weft of this tapestry—but the style was as distinctive as its owner's teasing smile:

Do you know me yet?

Jame's sudden grin mirrored that on the face above her, more closely than she knew. "Walking all winter in your shoes, standing here now in your damned swaddling shift, I'd better, hadn't I? Well met at last, cousin."

The door to the Forecourt opened. A blast of wind extinguished Jame's candle.

"I tell you, I saw a light under the sill," said a dark figure in the doorway, to someone behind her. "Where d'you say that box of candles was?"

Jame shrank backward in the rustling darkness, silently cursing. Betrayed by fire again. They would hear her if she opened the door to the inner ward, assuming it wasn't locked. She edged northward along the wall to the spiral stair in the corner, hitched up her skirts, and scrambled upward with Jorin bounding on ahead. Candle light danced over the steps at her heels. On the second floor landing, she paused to listen and learn that the people below were indeed Caineron guards, seeking the Knorth runaway.

They were climbing the stair.

Quick, quick—up to the lofty third-story chamber where the High Council met in the jeweled light of stained glass windows, up again into the northwest tower which Jame had never visited before, it having been so hideously cold here in winter. At the top of the stairs was an unlocked door. She slipped inside and closed it softly behind her. Her ear against its inner panels, she heard heavy feet mount the steps. The door started to open.

"Wait!" a guard called from the council chamber below. "That's Gothregor up there. Leave it be, for honor's sake, and help me search down here."

The door closed. Feet descended.

"Whew," Jame said, very softly, to Jorin. Then she turned.

The room was almost as dark as the hall below, except for what light seeped around its shutters as the wind rattled them impatiently. Jame groped over to the western window. When she unlatched it, the shutters flew open in her face and the Tishooo rushed in, exulting: *So there you are!*

Seventy feet below lay the grassy expanse of the inner ward, surrounded by the fortress's massive outer wall. Lights shone in the mural rooms opposite where her brother's Kendar were making themselves snug against the night. From this height, she could see over the battlements to the pale glimmer of Chantrie's ruins on the river's far bank. Jame wished that she had known about this vantage point when Lord Caineron had passed. As it was, she had spent the day keeping well out of sight, trusting Caldane no more than the Knorth garrison had. After all, the lord of Restormir had strong reasons, personal as well as dynastic, for wanting to get his hands on her again.

Thinking about Caineron reminded her of Graykin, his bastard son and erstwhile spy. At the Cataracts, though, she had accidentally bound Gray—something which only established Highborn males were supposed to do. There would be serious trouble if word got out about that, but nothing compared to the furor if anyone learned that she had also entrusted this Southron half-breed with the Book Bound in Pale Leather.

The Book, the Ivory Knife, and the Serpent-skin Cloak—those three objects of great if ambiguous power kept by the Master in Perimal Darkling after the Fall. No one knew what roles they might play in the final conflict, only that each was necessary. Now at last two of them had come to Rathillien. The Knife lay hidden in Jame's room here at Gothregor, sullenly eating a hole in her mattress with its malign presence. As for the pale Book with its collection of master runes, what a poor guardian she had proved of that. In Tai-tastigon, both the Sirdan Theocandi and the priest Ishtier had coveted the deadly tome and been destroyed by their brief possession of it. At the Cataracts, with Caldane on her heels, she'd had to entrust it to Graykin.

No word had come of it or him since.

In her experience, that damned Book could usually look after itself, using whomever it pleased to do whatever it wanted.

As for Graykin, though, sooner or later Caineron would realize that his son had changed sides. Perhaps he had already. Perhaps that was why Jame had felt so uneasy these last three days since Caldane's passing and why now, when thinking about Gray, she found herself leaning out the window to look northward, toward the Caineron stronghold, Restormir. Her bond with the Southron was only of the mind, not the blood, but still it twitched at her attention like a string tied to a broken tooth.

What was she doing at Gothregor anyway? Playing dolly dress-up, demonstrating incompetence at things she had no wish to learn, wasting time when she had urgent business elsewhere . . . . Damn Graykin anyway, and damn her too. Trapped behind a seeker's mask, searching for a name that would let her survive among her own people, how could she even defend herself, much less someone dependent on her?

Jame shivered. So this was what helplessness felt like: a cold draft up the spine, a premonition: *Find a way to fight back, soon, or be destroyed. Something is coming.*

"What?" she asked the breathing night.

No answer . . . no defense?

Other ladies would look for that from their kinsmen and guards. She was cut off from her brother's Kendar and her family was dead except for Tori—or was it?

Could she really have other surviving kin within the degree of blood—a first cousin, in fact, if a bastard?

Illegitimacy shouldn't exist among the Highborn, whose ladies usually controlled conception at will and grimly honored the terms of any contract to which their lord bound them. She remembered Lyra, Caineron's young daughter, contracted to Prince Odalian of Karkinor and longing for the child she would never dare have without her father's consent. To misbreed as Tieri had was black disgrace, dishonoring both mother and child. Now Kallystine claimed that it also called into doubt the constancy of all Tieri's female blood-kin.

No one had mentioned this last, personal application to Jame before or, she suspected, to Torisen. Either the lords didn't care, or knowledge of Tieri's disgrace was very restricted, perhaps to the matriarchs. Odd. Odder still that they would tell Kallystine, whom no one trusted. Perhaps they hadn't, directly. Everyone knew that when the council had met today, Cattila's Ear had listened in.

Jame knew through Jorin's senses that there had been three people in Kallystine's room when they had left it: M'lady herself, her maid, and a stranger with an almost familiar, earthy smell, like the inside of a potting shed. Perhaps that had been the mysterious Ear, who some claimed was not even a Kencyr, admitted only at Cattila's insistence. Whatever she was, though, perhaps she had been carrying tales.

One way or another, a great secret had fallen into enemy hands.

How damaging was it, though, really? Brought up by Kendar, Jame didn't share M'lady's revulsion at illegitimacy. If Tieri's misfortune got her off the breeding books, she didn't care if people expected her to litter kittens. Unfortunately, as long as the issue was legitimate, most lords probably wouldn't care.

Regarding the Highlord, though, when—if—Tori found out about the Knorth Bastard, how would he react? Kendar had raised him too. He was still said to feel more at home among the randon at Kothifir than here in his father's stronghold. Strange to think of the Highlord of the Kencyrath as an outsider. In some ways, she and he were still much alike. Old songs claimed that living or dead, twins occupied corners in each other's soul. Jame could almost believe that, asleep if not awake: all winter she'd had the recurrent dream of seeking her brother up and down Rathillien, as once she had sought him through the bleak rooms of the Haunted Lands keep. On Spring Eve, she had even dreamt that she had tracked him down at last, only to have her dream twist into the nightmares that had haunted her sleep ever since.

Jame hugged herself, shivering. *Think of something else.*

She turned away from the window to survey the room. Starlight revealed it to be circular, containing two chairs, a worktable, and a fireplace down whose throat the wind whistled off-key. On the mantle was a branched candlestick with wax guttered to the sockets. Behind that stood a pitted, bronze mirror, placed to throw back candlelight and, incidentally, a distorted image of the room. In it, she seemed to be wearing a black coat much like Tori's and almost his thin, handsome face, but so haggard . . . .

. . . looking like the unburnt dead . . . .

The faint, uncanny echo of her thoughts made her start; however, she was still alone in this cold, tower room.

Rumor said that Tori sometimes stayed awake for weeks on end. Well, if he was losing sleep because of her, it served him right. He should never have stranded her here. She stuck out her tongue at the reflection.

The surrounding walls were lined with shelves full of parchment scrolls. A second door opened off the south wall. Outside was a narrow platform and a catwalk swaying through dizzy space to the southwest tower of the keep which housed sleeping quarters. Now, where had she learned that? Then Jame remembered, and knew why the guard had called these upper reaches "Gothregor": It was customary to identify a lord, his possessions, and his chambers by the name of his fortress.

This was Tori's study.

The ladies of the halls speculated endlessly over the Highlord's refusal to reoccupy the Ghost Walks. Most saw it as a slap at M'lady Kallystine's ambitions, or an evasion of her company. However, faced with this austere bivouac at the very top of her brother's ancestral

keep, Jame wondered if in truth he loathed everything
that had been his father's. What had his life with Ganth
Gray Lord been like after her expulsion and before his
own departure, under mysterious circumstances, at the
age of fifteen? Twin or not, Tori was no longer the child
she remembered. Nameless boy under Lord Ardeth's
protection, young commander of the Southern Host,
Highlord of the Kencyrath, he had lived a lifetime since
their childhood together, and a life uncommonly private
for someone born to power. Look at this chamber. There
was hardly room here for his servant Burr, much less for
the retinue which his position would seem to demand.
Knorth poverty only explained part of it. The Caineron
guards had been right to respect such determined privacy. So should she.

But at the door she heard M'lady's guards still below.

Damn. She would have to wait them out. The thought
of inactivity, however brief, reminded her that, like her
brother, she hadn't slept in several nights. His chair, set
before the cold fireplace, looked dangerously comfortable. She sat down on the floor, her back to a bookcase.
Jorin flopped across her knees.

I need a bigger lap or a smaller cat, she thought,
bemused, and, despite herself, fell asleep.

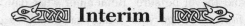 **Interim I**

Kothifir Encampment:
54th of Spring

"WHAT DO YOU MEAN," demanded Lord Ardeth: "'Something is coming'?"

Torisen Black Lord stopped short in his restless pacing, startled and annoyed to find that he had spoken outloud. What *had* he meant? The words had simply risen in his mind, out of a formless but growing apprehension. Dammit, lack of sleep was no excuse to lose control.

Turning, he tripped over a footstool.

Damn.

During his tenure as commander of the Southern Host, these lodgings had been sparsely furnished, each piece elegant and useful, with room in between to pace. Pereden, his successor, had redecorated according to his own tastes: gaudy, pretentious, cluttered. Dead as he was, that wretched boy would break Torisen's neck yet—turnabout fair play, perhaps.

The leavings of that other, worthless life seemed suddenly to press in on him. He had to get away, out into the desert dark, to prowl alone through the remaining hours of this interminable night . . . .

Ardeth stood in his way. "My boy, you mustn't."

"Thal's balls, Blackie," Harn Grip-hard growled from the table, crumbling the report which he had been pretending to read. "Your enemies already think you're half crazy. Wander around tonight looking like the unburnt dead and they'll be sure. Remember what day this is: thirty-four years ago your father ran mad as a gelded rathorn and most of us ran after him, all the way to death in the White Hills. No one in the Hosts, north or south, has forgotten that. No one ever will."

"Oh, really!" Ardeth protested—against the expression, not the facts. "Still, your behavior since the Cataracts *has* cost you much of the credit you gained there. This continued refusal to sleep, merely for fear of dreams . . . ."

"Who told you that? Was it Burr, spying on me again? No."

Torisen ran thin, scarred hands through his dark hair, gripping it briefly to remind himself with pain. Burr had been Ardeth's agent years ago, openly, when he himself had been a nameless boy in the old lord's service. Now Burr served him. After the events leading up to the Cataracts, everyone must know that he often avoided sleep, if not why. His three oldest friends, here in this room, knew full well that the pattern went back years.

"All right," said Ardeth soothingly. "We'll discuss that another time. But as for your refusal to make certain necessary decisions . . . listen to me: you *must* form an alliance with some house strong enough to protect your interests. If you're too fastidious to bargain with your own bloodlines, use your sister's. The girl *has* to be contracted out for the best advantage you can obtain. Oh, if only my son Pereden were alive to offer for her . . . !

"My boy, what's the matter?"

Torisen had turned sharply away.

He was remembering what it had felt like, in his tent by the Cataracts, to break Pereden's neck. Then he'd had to go into the Wastes with Ardeth to hunt for the bones of his "hero" son, knowing all the time that Harn had reduced them to ashes on a common pyre at Hurlen. Damn Pereden anyway, that vain, spoiled boy who had led the Southern Host against the vastly larger Waster Horde, against orders, in a stupid attempt to prove himself a better commander than Torisen had been. Captured, he had changed sides, seduced by the promise that the Horde would make him Highlord. And all because he thought that Torisen had stolen Ardeth's love.

Fathers and sons. How did any of them manage not to murder each other?

Pereden would have used the shame of his treachery to destroy Ardeth, if Torisen hadn't killed him first.

Right. Try explaining that to a grief-stricken father.

Torisen stepped out onto the balcony and leaned on the rail. The Host's permanent encampment formed a city at the foot of the escarpment, with Kothifir on the cliff-top above. To the south, over the garrison's roofs, he could see the Wastes, a line drawn flat on the horizon, black beneath, star-fretted above—*his* land, which Ganth had never even seen.

Still, the Gray Lord's shadow fell over him. Maybe he would never escape it as long as he claimed the Highlord's power as he had his father's ring and battle-sword, now hanging from a belt-loop at his side. Songs said that Kin-Slayer made its rightful owner all but invincible. For Torisen, however, it had remained sullenly inert, as if it knew how Ganth had died, cursing his runaway son, disowning him. Ironic, if the only thing he *had* inherited from Ganth was his insanity. He could feel the tug of it now. Somewhere, something was about to happen.

No. Think of something else.

He turned restlessly back into the room, trying not to chafe under the anxious regard of his friends. An aimless step brought him up short before another of Pereden's prize possessions: a full-length mirror in an ornate golden frame. He stared blankly at the shadow which fell mask-like across the reflection of his face, feeling empty with fatigue. Hounded day after day by the lords, haunted night after night by dreams . . . .

The face in the mirror stuck its tongue out at him.

Torisen recoiled, then controlled himself, furious. She was four hundred leagues away, wasn't she? He had seen to that.

But all winter, the moment his eyes had closed, he had felt her hunting him as relentlessly as she had as a child, playing hide and seek. She had almost caught him too, on Spring's Eve.

It was a dream, he reminded himself, scowling defiantly into the mirror. *Only a damn dream—wasn't it?*

It had, at least, been seven weeks ago, too long even for him to stay awake. Since then, when the need for sleep had overwhelmed him, he had hidden from her in the one place to which he thought she would never willingly return. In his dreams, reduced again to childhood, he had huddled miserably in the dark, cold hall of the Haunted Lands keep, hearing the tentative rustle in the shadows of dead Kendar returning to what, for a haunt, passed for life, hearing those other slow, dragging footsteps descending the stair from the battlements where his father had died but refused to stay dead, the mad mutter in the stairwell growing closer, more distinct night after night . . . .

He hadn't bolted the stair door. Did he dare rise to do it? Jame would, if she were here. No one stood up to

Ganth but her. She was so strong. He could stand anything, if only that door were bolted, but he wouldn't run out to find her. He *wouldn't*. He would stay here, with Ganth's madness fumbling at the door, mumbling through the cracks:

"It's all her fault, boy. She is strong. She has power. You've got to destroy her, boy, before she destroys you . . . .

"Drink, lord," said Burr.

Torisen looked down at the cup of mulled wine which his servant and old friend had thrust into his hands. His cold fingers curled around it, the lace-work of white scars grateful for its warmth. Had he spoken out-loud again? A fortnight awake, dreams bleeding into reality—he had starved himself of sleep often enough to know the signs. Dammit, why couldn't he master them?

Control. Must keep control . . . .

He raised the cup to drink, then in the mirror saw Ardeth's eyes on him. The wine smelled peculiar. A shudder went through him, followed by rage.

"Traitors!" he heard himself say in a harsh voice not his own. "You eat my bread and yet you conspire to betray me. You, and you, and you . . . ."

Burr's plain face had gone stiff. Without a word, he took back the cup and drank deeply from it, his mud-brown eyes locked on the Highlord's silver-gray. He blinked. Ardeth took the half empty cup from him before he could drop it. Harn threw a burly arm around his sagging frame to swing him around to a seat by the table, growling over his shoulder:

"Blackie, you damn fool."

Torisen Black Lord stared, beginning to tremble. "I . . . it wasn't . . . ."

The rage had gone as abruptly as it had seized him—but he wasn't a berserker, to flare like that, or to speak those words with that voice. All, all had been Ganth's, born of that obsession with betrayal which had driven some of his loyal followers to suicide and the rest to contrive his son's escape from the Haunted Land's keep. Those Kendar had ransomed Torisen out of darkness with their lives and honor.

Listen: hear them now in the shadows of the hall, bereft of honor and life, rustling, rustling . . . .

"No. I refuse to dream this."

He turned his back and stepped out again onto the balcony, to grip the rail, to master his shaking hands. Even now, she was seeking him, but he wouldn't hide again in the dream of that terrible hall, where madness fumbled at an unlocked door. He would stay awake—for the rest of his life if necessary.

Wait it out, just wait it out . . . .

PART

II

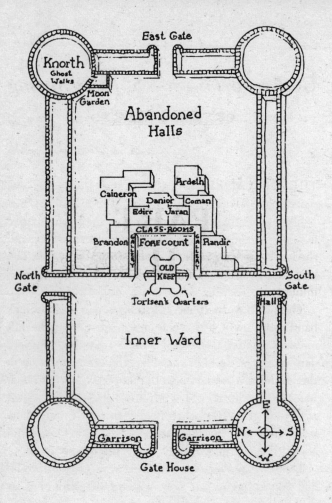

East Gate

Knorth
Ghost
Walks

Moon
Garden

Abandoned
Halls

Caineron

Ardeth

Danior
Coman

Edirr
Jaran

CLASS·ROOMS

Brandon

FORECOURT

Randir

OLD
KEEP

North
Gate

South
Gate

Torisen's Quarters

Inner Ward

Garrison

Garrison

Hall

Gate House

Gothregor: 54th – 55th of Spring

THE DREAM BEGAN as it always did: Jame was searching for Tori.

She was angry with him for letting their father drive her out, but she still had to find him because . . . because she had something for him. Ganth's ring and sword. The ring was on her finger; the sword, ill-omened Kin-Slayer, in her hand.

The sword worried her. It had broken in their father's hand, but now it was whole again, except for the hilt emblem. Under the cracked crest something moved, dark and wet: fleshless lips that muttered endlessly in their father's voice; sharp teeth that gnawed at her hand. She couldn't let go, though, until Tori took the sword out of her grasp. But when he did, he didn't notice how it had hurt her. He didn't care. So she didn't warn him about the mad, mumbling voice or the hungry teeth.

Then she was searching for Tori again because . . . he had sent her away, and now he was hiding from her, as if this were some silly game.

On Spring Eve she at last found him, standing at the edge of the Southern Wastes, his back to her. He was holding Kin-Slayer and listening to the voice. Unnoticed, blood ran down the sword's blade from his hand, where the teeth did their silent, malicious work.

She called his name: "Brother."

"I refuse to dream this!" he snapped, and walked rapidly away.

"Come back!" she cried after him. "You can't run away from me forever!"

But he had already disappeared into the blowing sand.

No, not sand but dry leaves, hitting her face with furtive, brittle taps. Before her lay a gray city street, lined with decaying houses. Something dark crawled over the broken cobblestones toward her, its shadowy fingers delicately probing the rubble as it came. Behind shut doors, children were whimpering in terror. The Lower Town Monster, not destroyed after all, whispered a voice on the wind. Her voice, from another place, another dream.

The gibbous moon emerged, white and cold. Not sand or leaves, but snow, hiding the summits of Mounts Timor and Tinnibin as they loomed above her. She was in the Blue Pass of the Ebonbane, facing east toward Tai-tastigon. Something was crawling toward her like a shadow cast on the snow. Then it raised its head, and she recognized Bane's features.

The wrong brother had answered her.

Turn. Flee. If only she could escape back into the waking world, leave him here where he belonged, nightmare creature that he had become . . . .

"You can't run from me forever," whispered the darkness behind her, mockingly. *"Blood binds . . . ."*

The moon waxed, waned, then waxed again, the snow melting under its pale light. The shadow-thing that pursued her sank into the green of spring, but still it came on, sometimes crawling, sometimes wrapped around some wild creature which it caught and rode until the soul was eaten out of it. One stag lasted a week before falling to pieces before the horrified Grindarks who were hunting it. On it came, down the trade road beside the Ever-Quick, through the Oseen Hills, over the toes of the Snowthorns, into the Riverland, and finally to the gates of Gothregor itself, to break its long fast and then to hunt . . .

Jame woke with a gasp. Slowly, the tower room redefined itself around her, Jorin's grunt of protest at the sudden tightening of her arms changing back to a drowsy purr. Calm down, calm . . .

Those damned dreams again. Bad enough that they repeated themselves every time exhaustion forced her to sleep. Worse, that each repetition ended with a new installment, as if the pursuit really was drawing nearer. But, after all, they were only dreams.

All right: she *did* resent the way that Tori had treated her. It hadn't been easy to restore Ganth's sword and ring to him. Some of the things she had done, some of the places she had been, would have startled him considerably, if he had bothered to ask. He never had. Of course, Marc could tell him, but Tori disliked spies so much that she didn't think he would seek information behind her back. Fine, then: let him stay ignorant . . . but she really should have told him that Kin-Slayer had been reforged in Perimal Darkling.

As for Bane, the Lower Town Monster might have been constructed around his soul but it had never (to the best of her knowledge) had his guiding intelligence. *Blood binds*? That made no sense either. Tori was the blood-binder, not she, not that with his terror of the Shanir he would ever admit such a thing even to himself.

Blood—its taste when Bane's farewell kiss had nearly bitten through her lower lip, the hidden scar which her tongue could still trace . . . .

That had been real enough.

As for the rest, it would be different if she were a far-seer. Never mind that her thoughts had actually crossed Bane's at least twice in Tai-tastigon, or that her mental distance from Tori had seemed to diminish greatly since they had both been exposed to wyrm's venom the previous winter. That wasn't farseeing. She had never far-seen anything in her life, dammit, and she wasn't going to start now.

But still the last image of this latest dream lingered: in the Brandan night nursery, a shadowy form creeping up the side of a child's cot . . . to break a long fast? Bane always liked little boys.

Ah, it was no use. Dream or not, Caineron patrols or not, she had to see for herself that her brother's house was safe.

Down in the Forecourt again, Jame cut across toward the Brandan compound with Jorin trotting at her heels. A bright, gibbous moon had just cleared the mountains to the east. Near midnight, then. Her shadow fluttered on the grass in the boisterous wind, as though at any moment it might shred and blow away. Shadows *had* become detached before, along with the souls which cast them. That, after all, was what the Lower Town Monster had been, while Bane had walked shadowless in the noonday sun. Then too, the Sirdan Theocandi had sent his soul abroad at night as the assassin Shadow Thief.

But neither he nor Bane had had to contend with the Tishooo, which was romping along with Jame, snatching at her hem like a playful dog.

"Stop that!" she cried.

"Whooo . . . ?" said the wind, and swept up under her full, outer skirt, inverting it.

Jame found herself cocooned in heavy velvet, blinded, entangled. As she struggled to free herself, she heard a whistle—shrill, excited, and very, very close. Jorin was growling. Then someone yelped, as though in surprise or pain. The taste of blood again—in the cat's mouth, not her own. Jame clawed the gown away from her face.

No Jorin, nothing but an empty courtyard full of wind.

Where . . . there, ancestors be praised: a glimmer of silver fur in the shadows, a very upset ounce slinking toward her across the grass. Catching him, she pried something out of his jaws. It felt like coarse cloth. However, except for a corner stained with blood, she couldn't see either it or her own hand, which the rest of it covered.

Sweet Trinity. Could this be *mere*?

Jame stood holding the scrap of invisible cloth against the wind's tug, feeling suddenly chilled.

"Kitten, let's get under cover. Fast."

Strangely, no guard was on duty at the entrance to the Brandan quarters. Jame crossed the arcade where, earlier, she had encountered the Iron Matriarch, and entered the compound proper. Still no guards or anyone else, although she could hear whistling in the distance.

The nursery was on the second floor, at the heart of the compound. The door stood half open, warm firelight spilling out of it. Jame slipped inside. It was a large, L-shaped room with many cots in it, all empty, as far as she could see. Nonetheless, fires were lit on the several hearths. *Someone* must be here. Jame stole silently between the rows of small beds toward where the room bent to the right. The hearth-fires danced uneasily as she passed.

The fire at the far end of the ell, however, had burnt down to tinkling embers. At one side of it sat a comfortable chair, empty. At the other was a cot, in which something moved sleepily. Bending over it, barely visible in the gloom, was a shadowy form. Jame could see the wall through it. It raised its head and looked at her out of eyes like the wells of night. The tenebrous planes of its face shifted. It was smiling at her. Jame went back a step, nearly stepping on Jorin as he scuttled under a bed. Then she saw that those shadowy fingers were resting in the creases of the child's blanket, inches from its sleeping face.

She heard herself say, hoarsely, "Don't you *dare!*"

Footsteps sounded on the nursery tiles behind her. She turned just as the Brandan captain rounded the corner and stopped short, clearly startled to see her. For an instant, Jame was also disconcerted: she thought she had seen something flicker aside between her and the sandy-haired Kendar, but nothing was there now except a stray shadow on the floor.

The captain advanced, scarred brow knitted in a frown. "Lady, what are you doing here at this time of night? Did you know that every Caineron in the halls is searching for you?"

Obviously, she hadn't yet seen the thing by the cot. She also didn't notice the shadow on the floor until her own, cast ahead of her by the room's outer fires, fell across it. Then she gave a sudden gasp and crashed to her knees. Her own shadow seemed to be floundering in that other darkness. As the two locked in unequal combat, she pitched forward and lay writhing on the floor.

"Get out!" she cried to Jame through clenched teeth. "Run!"

What in Perimal's name . . . ? Was this somehow Bane's doing?

But even as Jame turned to look back at the cot, where the child had woken and was beginning to cry, an all too solid arm slid around her neck from behind. It jerked her off balance. A flash of steel . . . . She barely got her own right arm up in time, the edge of her hand against the other's wrist, holding back sharp death for an endless moment.

Abruptly, she was released and flung sideways, almost on top of the stricken Kendar. Shadow hands were sliding over the woman's throat and face, fumbling at her eyes, while she tried futilely to tear them off. In another moment she would blind herself. Jame grabbed her wrists.

Above them, a shrill whistle began as if in triumph, but ended with a breathy explosion. Still gripping the Kendar, Jame twisted about to peer up over her shoulder. Something indistinct loomed over them— man-shaped, she thought, but somehow she couldn't focus on it. All that showed clearly were wild eyes without a face, a knife poised in midair, and below it a skinny, bare wrist, marked by Jorin's teeth.

For a moment, she thought that the assassin wanted them to "see" their killer, or rather to rub in that they couldn't. Then she realized that, just as he had caught her seconds before, so now he himself was caught. A shadowy something stood behind him, its indistinct arm around his neck, its ghost of a hand grasping his knife hand at the wrist.

M'lady, whispered darkness. *Have you noticed? Every time we meet, someone bleeds.*

The shadow hand tightened on the other's wrist. It drew the knife across some six inches below the terrified eyes, cutting slowly, cutting deep. The assassin jerked. Blood spurted, painting his neck, his chest. His breathing changed to a desperate wheeze as his trachea was severed, but without his soul he couldn't die. Jame flinched aside as his shadow fell away from the Brandan captain and scrabbled past her. The moment it reattached itself, the stricken assassin, crumpled, twitched, and lay still, defined against the floor by the spreading pool of his own blood.

The shadowy thing that was Bane rose from the corpse like black smoke off a pyre. It bent its head against the ceiling and spread wide its sooty arms. Out of that towering charnel cloud, the glimmer that might be eyes stooped over Jame . . . no, bowed ironically, then melted into the upper shadows, leaving behind only the ghost of a mocking whisper: *Later* . . . .

Jame gave a long, shuddering sigh. Later? Trust Bane never to do anything direct.

She released the Kendar's wrists. The woman huddled on the floor with her face hidden in the crook of her arm, clammy-skinned and shaking, but with her shadow still intact. No soul damage there. Perhaps the assassin's shadow-casting technique was limited to incapacitating his prey. Although it was screaming with fright, the child also appeared unhurt when Jame rose hastily to check it. As she scooped bedding off a nearby cot, Jorin crept out from under it.

"Some help you are," she told him.

After piling the blankets on the randon to combat shock, she gingerly turned over the sprawling figure. It no longer cast a shadow. So, Bane had broken his fast after all. Really, this *mere* cloth was amazing: only where it was soaked with blood could she see it clearly. She stripped off the other's sodden hood and stared down at the waxy face of a boy not more than fourteen years old.

"He's an apprentice in the Bashtiri Shadow Guild," said the captain behind her. She had sat up, clutching the blankets around her. Her teeth rattled together as if with the cold and her square, scratched face was haggard, but she came of hardy Kendar stock and had trained in a tough discipline.

"What's he doing here?"

"At a guess, trying to earn his journeyman's *mere*-tempered knife by fulfilling the contract which someone took out on the Knorth women, thirty-four years ago. I had kin on duty here that night. Bloody hell. Why didn't someone anticipate this?" She tried to stand up and failed, cursing. "Everything is upside down tonight. None of my cadets are where they should be. There's always some confusion, settling in a new garrison, but this . . . ! I should have realized that it wasn't just the other house guards ragging us."

Jame rose, the hood a flicker in her hand. "Well, he's dead now."

"He probably didn't come alone. There are usually thirteen shadows in a casting. Lady, I'm not sure we can protect you. Run. Hide. Trinity knows, you're good enough at that. The Caineron have been taking your name in vain from one end of the halls to the other, all evening."

The click of footsteps made them both start, but it was only the child's attendant, a Kendar maid, come back from whatever errand had drawn her away. She was outraged to find her charge shrieking itself apoplectic in the presence of two apparently indifferent adults, but then she saw the far end of the room awash in blood and showed signs of waxing hysterical herself.

"Don't!" said Jame, Highborn to Kendar.

The girl stopped with her mouth open. It stayed that way while she listened to the message which Jame wanted her to convey to the Brandan guardroom, in hopes that at least the watch officer would be on duty. She left still looking as if someone had hit her between the eyes with a board.

"You need help," Jame said defensively, meeting the captain's eye, "and someone's got to be told that there are foxes loose in the hen-house again. C'mon on, kitten."

"Lady, where are you going?"

Jame paused at the door, tucking the hood into her belt. Where indeed? To run, to hide? No. There was blood on the floor of her brother's house and blood in her veins, swift and hot after the winter's chill as she had never thought to feel it again.

"To warn the other house guards; then, perhaps, to hunt foxes."

II

BRENWYR STALKED through the midnight halls in one of her blackest moods. Talking to Adiraina usually calmed her, but not tonight, on the anniversary of Aerulan's death. It didn't help that during this short walk back to the Brandan quarters she had been stopped three times by Caineron patrols, on the last occasion nearly clouting the Caineron captain for daring to question her own presence, abroad so late. That entire house seemed to have run mad tonight, from Lady Kallystine on down—and no, dammit, she would *not* give them permission to search the Brandan compound.

As Adiraina had guessed, Brenwyr still had a splintering headache. Thirty-four years ago tonight, she had suffered an even worse one, brought on by a row that afternoon with Aerulan. No. The argument had been entirely one-sided, caused by her stupid jealousy over Aerulan's kindness to her cousin Tieri—a mere child, for God's sake! Aerulan had only laughed, and Brenwyr had stormed off. That night, the Tishooo had brought her Aerulan's voice, calling, calling, but she had heard it through such a haze of pain that she hadn't believed it was real, until too late.

It's my fault she died, the Iron Matriarch thought savagely, for perhaps the millionth time. *I ill-wished her, that afternoon—in a filthy temper, not meaning it, but it stuck, and it killed her.*

Not even Adiraina knew about that.

Sometimes, Brenwyr almost consoled herself remembering how the assassin had shrunk back as he felt her curse strike home: "*Shadow, by a shadow be exposed*"—whatever that had meant. More to him, obviously, than to her, as was often the case. No, that yellow-eyed bastard wouldn't soon forget the Brandan Maledight. But blood prices weren't paid by words, however blighting, nor the dead brought back by remorse. Because of her, Aerulan was both dead and unavenged.

Thus raging at herself, she entered the Brandan compound . . . and there, coming down the arcade toward her through slanting bars of moonlight, was Aerulan.

Someone whistled—a thin, high, excited note—and then something seized the slim figure from behind.

It was all going to happen again, thought Brenwyr, frozen in sick horror, and she for her sins must witness it, over and over and over . . . .

But this time Aerulan had a moment's warning from the ounce trotting at her side. She grabbed the invisible something which had her around the throat and bent sharply forward. An indistinct form shot over her head. Bright steel clattered on the flagstones at Brenwyr's feet. Hobbled by her tight underskirt, the girl toppled forward to land on something that fought back. The two, visible and otherwise, were rolling about the arcade, pounced indiscriminately by the cat, when Brenwyr finally realized what she was seeing. She snatched up the assassin's knife and ran forward.

The Knorth saw her coming. "No!" she cried.

Brenwyr hesitated, then struck almost at random with the hilt. "What in Perimal's name do you mean, 'No'?" she demanded as the Knorth shoved her stunned attacker aside.

"If he's dead, he can't answer questions. Besides, look." She pulled off the *mere* hood. Underneath was the face of a surprisingly young, blond boy. "I'd like to know who's sending children to cut my throat, and why."

"Children, eh?" Brenwyr tried desperately to wrench her mind away from the past, to focus on this stranger in Aerulan's clothes whom she had spent the winter refusing to meet. "And just how old are you, girl?"

The other snorted, a most un-Aerulan-like sound. "Older than this fellow, anyway, and better trained, for all that thrashing around just now. Still, he would have had me cold if he hadn't expected an easy kill. This damned dress!"

She hiked up her outer skirt, ripped open the undergown's side seam, and began to tear long strips off of it as the wind tried playfully to twitch them out of her grasp.

Over three decades preserving those clothes, carrying them to each new house where a contract sent her, clinging to them for comfort in each strange bed, to the last moment, until a stranger's footstep stopped at her door . . . .

Rip, rip, rip . . . .

Berserker heat flared in Brenwyr's blood, kindling red in her eyes, until the other's voice hit her like cold water in the face:

"Lady, for pity's sake, *not now.*"

Impostor, usurper, destroyer . . . .

No. *She* had made the Knorth wear these clothes. *She* had pretended that Aerulan again walked these halls, always just out of sight so as not to imperil the illusion. Delusion. Obsession.

"*Name a thing,*" Adiraina had told her, "*and you gain power over it.*"

What a fool the Iron Matriarch had been to believe that. But now, in this moment of hard won freedom, Brenwyr heard her own hoarse voice say, "Do what you must."

"Good!" said the Knorth, and bound the unconscious boy with Aerulan's dismemberments. Where he lay, in the shadow of the arcade's waist-high wall, the white fabric showed up against the *mere* as though it were wrapped around empty space. "Two down," she said, rising, "eleven to g . . . oh!"

A burly figure had suddenly appeared outside the arcade, thrown an arm around her waist, and scooped her out into the Forecourt.

"Greetings again, Matriarch," said the Caineron captain affably. "I thought I heard familiar voices. It seems that we won't have to impose on your hospitality after all. Lady Jameth, M'lady Kallystine would like a word with you."

The Knorth started to protest.

"Shhh," said the captain and put her hand over the girl's mouth. "Remember the fourth duty of silence. Malie, take that cat back to the stable. Good night, Matriarch."

She strode back across the courtyard with the Knorth, still uttering muffled protests, tucked under her arm. A cadet snatched the ounce as he tried to follow and bore him off in the opposite direction, too well-bred to bite or scratch but with all four legs stuck up in the most awkward angles he could manage.

This joint abduction took place too quickly for Brenwyr to protest; but then again, she thought, watching them go, why should she? The Knorth was a Caineron responsibility. Let them guard her. Brenwyr's duty lay here, with this trespasser in the Brandan domain.

"Two down, eleven to go," the Knorth had started to say. Thirteen what?

But her mind slid off the thought. The wind blew, the moon shone—and she stood at the very spot where Aerulan had fallen, with an assassin of the Bashtiri Shadow Guild at her feet. When this fellow opened his eyes, perhaps they would be yellow, like those of Aerulan's killer. Perhaps . . . perhaps she would wait and see . . .

III

IT WAS HER OWN FAULT, Jame thought, as she sat a virtual prisoner in the Caineron's second floor guardroom.

Of course, since Ganth's fall the Caineron had tended to treat all surviving Knorth as only temporary inconveniences. That Caldane hadn't seized power yet said more about Torisen's unexpected qualities as a leader than about any slackening of Caineron ambition. Jame realized now, though, that she hadn't helped by letting Kallystine treat her all winter as a servant. No wonder these Kendar showed her so little respect.

Worse, they had brushed aside her talk of assassins as pure hysteria. What else could one expect from the crazy Knorth? Not even the *mere* hood of the dead boy had impressed them, looking as it did only like a blood-soaked scrap of cloth. The Caineron captain had dismissed it with a glance: "That time of month, is it?"—as if some suspicion of hers had been confirmed.

Jame had seen no point, after that, in mentioning Bane.

At least the Brandan Matriarch knew about the assassin in the arcade. Even if she didn't realize that his brethren were abroad tonight, surely she would have her guard deal with the one they had captured. How frustrating that Jame hadn't been able to tell Brenwyr about her captain, incapacitated in the night nursery. Of course, the Kendar maid knew. Perhaps even now the alarm was spreading . . . but so far she heard no sound of it.

Meanwhile, the Caineron ten-commands sent out to search for the Knorth runaway began to check back in.

The first report came from the Brandan compound. The Caineron still hadn't been permitted to enter there, but a Brandan guard on the northern perimeter spoke of cadets lured away from their posts, locked on the wrong side of doors, tripped by wires, and in general victimized by tricks ranging from the silly to the malicious. Several Kendar had been slightly injured and a maid had been knocked unconscious by a tumble downstairs. It was all a damn mess, the guard had said in disgust, like an exercise in disruption or an assault by bogles.

"At least we've put a stop to that," the Caineron captain remarked, and shot a glance at Jame.

But it didn't stop.

"Lights, moving in the Ghost Walks," reported a ten-commander. "Wills-o'-the-wisp, like the old days when the Ardeth kept us out. This time, we investigated. Nothing. Ruin and shadows."

Shadows also figured in the next reports, coming mostly from the Edirr compound but spreading southward into the Danior. They seemed to be creeping everywhere, terrorizing whomever they met but as yet doing little harm. The only things which kept them out were bright lights or the wind, which had begun a restless prowl of its own inside the halls.

They're looking for me, Jame thought.

If she hadn't been in odd places all night, dodging Kallystine, the assassins would have run her down long ago. Now they were trying to flush her out. If she really was the only one at risk tonight, perhaps she had better stay in this brightly lit room, away from shadows of all sorts. Let Bane hunt the hunters, if he chose. Thanks to the Caineron, she was out of the game, safe.

But still her gloved fingertips drummed on the chair's arm, quieted themselves, and drummed again.

The captain was also beginning to lose patience. Word had come earlier that, in a final act of defiance, M'lady's servant had hanged herself with her own braid. Oddly enough, though, Kallystine seemed to blame the Knorth Jameth for all the evening's misadventures. On first hearing of Jame's capture, she had furiously demanded that the truant be delivered to her quarters, along with any instruments of torture which her guards might have on hand. The captain had blandly suggested that M'lady meet her errant charge here, on more neutral ground. This, however, Kallystine had so far refused to do. It wasn't clear to Jame who would win in such a tug-o'-war, randon Kendar or lord's daughter, training or raw power. She felt like a bone between two dogs.

Meanwhile, the captain's latest, carefully worded message had as yet gone unanswered. "What," she grumbled, "no more threats to tell daddy? Our runner must've fallen into a hole somewhere. Cadet, go see."

But it was no hole down which the messenger had tumbled.

"I found her at the foot of the privy stair, and another of those damned trip-wires at the top," the second runner reported, white-faced. "She's dead."

The captain turned on Jame with an oath, but the runner caught her sleeve, fingers leaving bloody prints.

"Ran, it wasn't the fall. Someone cut her throat."

Just then, the Tishooo found the guardroom. It flowed in past the captain and cadet, making the candle flames dance, stirring the arrases. These latter surrounded the room, enlivening it with their bright depictions of randon life, stitched in their off-duty hours by generations of Caineron guards. The hangings served the practical purpose of stopping drafts and, like most Kendar work, were peculiarly effective. Thus the Tishooo found itself trapped behind them. Jame marked its approach by the rippling of the tapestries until it slid out between two of them to tweak at her skirt.

Come out and play, it might have been saying. *Come out and play.*

The room had filled with sharp orders and activity, the prisoner forgotten. Jame slipped between the tapestries, edged her way behind them to the door, and darted out into the hall, still unobserved.

If she was the prime target, why this other slaying? From what she had heard, the Shadow Guild considered it unprofessional to kill without a fee. However, given the age of these would-be assassins, perhaps this was more than the settlement of an old contract: perhaps this was a blooding mission. If so, each of the thirteen might intend to claim a kill tonight in a kind of limited open season on Gothregor. Still, wouldn't they want to be sure of her before announcing their presence too openly? Logically, yes; but despite all their advantages, these were boys, off the leash for perhaps the first time, running wild. While she had sat safe in the Caineron guardroom, one of them had lost patience and bagged a cadet, not realizing how quickly the body would be found.

Damn. She had to do something about this after all.

What she did first was to descend to the ground-floor cubbyhole which Kallystine had assigned to her. If these brats liked sharp toys, she had one too . . . except that someone had beaten her to it. The tiny room had been torn apart. The Ivory Knife was gone.

DAMN.

Objects of power certainly fell into and out of her hands with unnerving frequency. Worse, if the Shadow

Guild *was* behind this ransacking (and how unlike it to stoop to theft), it meant that someone had told the assassins exactly which out-of-the-way broom closet was hers.

Betrayal.

She remembered Ganth raving about it in the Haunted Lands keep on those nights when no one slept. The stupid Caineron, the scheming Ardeth, the ambitious Randir, the whole bloody web of friends and foes who had entangled his house in such ruin. Now, thirty-four years later, who out of that snarled past wanted his daughter dead?

She could stay here, where the hunters had already searched, or flee into the empty halls as Tieri had . . . .

Run. Hide . . . .

No. Since when had she let good sense dictate to her or hesitated to act, however stupidly?

"I'm losing myself," she said out-loud to the stranger who stood, fragmented, in a broken mirror. "I'm half lost already."

Then stop hiding, lass, she could almost hear her friend Marc say. *Take off the mask.*

Well, yes: Although the matriarchs had forced it on her, she had used it quite literally as a way not to face life in the Women's Halls. Behind it, she had pretended to be someone else, a nameless seeker lost in a game whose rules no one would explain. But she *had* been told, repeatedly, that the girl behind the mask was ignorant, clumsy, and altogether hopeless. If that was true, the assassins' work was as good as done.

Why should she make things easy for them?

Jame dropped the mask. The face in the shattered mirror looked back at her, one brow raised and the other askew. Wise Marc. So there she was after all, cockeyed as ever. Time to gird up what was left of Aerulan's skirt, braid her hair, and get on with it—quickly, before good sense returned.

Out again in the hall, she paused to listen. The Caineron quarter was beginning to seethe. The guards' harried effort to find her would be nothing compared to the cold ferocity with which they would seek their comrade's blood-price. They were a self-absorbed house, though, intent on private vengeance; so far, no general alarm had been raised. Good enough, for her present purposes.

She drew a deep breath and let it out in a loud, long whistle. The single note hung in the air like an exclamation mark, as it had in the Forecourt and again in the arcade.

Here she is! Jame was almost sure it signaled. *Here, here, here*!

No answer. Had the killer already left the compound?

No. There came the reply, from some distance to the east, a warbling, inquisitive note which might have been dismissed as a trick of the wind.

Where? it trilled. *Where?*

Here! Jame whistled again, peering down the corridor toward where moonlight flooded into it through a set of arched windows.

The question came again, closer and more complex, as if demanding further information.

A shadow started across the moon-washed flagstones, then hesitated. Jame could almost see the boyish, *mere*-clad figure who cast it. Because her night vision was almost certainly better than his, she stepped into the light to give him a good look. With a muffled exclamation, the shadow darted toward her. She turned and ran, quick footsteps close behind her.

Among these intruders' disadvantages was not only their night vision but also their age: what boy could resist a really good game of hare-and-hounds? Now, to whistle up the rest of the pack and then . . . and then . . . . Well, she would think of something.

The assassins had apparently looked for her first in her own room, then fanned out to search the Ghost Walks, the Brandan compound, and the Caineron. Now most of them seemed to be moving southward. Consequently, Jame raced in that direction, through the dark corridors of the Edirr and Danior, hearing first the excited whistle of her pursuer, then answering signals ahead. Each trill seemed to convey complex information —more than she could decipher on short notice. Instead, she concentrated on pinpointing the position of each whistler, down what hall, around what corner, up what stair. In her mind's eye, she saw a complete floor-plan of the halls, in far more detail than anyone could who hadn't once been obliged to memorize an entire city. She used her training now to slip past the assassins ahead as they tried to intercept her, once cutting it so close that she heard two of them collide on her heels.

From the locked doors which she passed, Jame concluded that the inmates of the halls had finally realized that something was afoot. So much the better, if it kept them out of her way. Unfortunately, the closed doors also impeded the Tishooo, which was soon left behind. A pity, since she had hoped it would make shadow-casting too risky, as it apparently had in the arcade.

At least seven of the pack were on her heels by the time she was half way through the Danior compound. She was wondering, rather breathlessly, where the rest were and what to do with the ones she had when ahead voices warned her that she was about to run into a guard patrol.

One cadet dead tonight was more than enough.

She swerved aside and plunged down a stair into the sublevels, whistling to draw her deadly tail after her. Below, she went on as quickly as she could through the unlighted passageways, forced now to rely entirely on memory to avoid running into walls.

At the end of this long corridor should be the entrance to the subterranean levels of the Jaran compound. Jame was so sure of this that she ran into the closed door at a brisk trot, nose first. It took her a dazed moment to remember that there was indeed a door between the Danior and Jaran compounds, but she had never before found it shut, much less locked. Extending a nail through the tip of a ruined glove, she began to pick the lock.

The door swung open. On the threshold, in torch light, stood a tall woman with eyes full of reflected fire: Trishien, the Jaran Matriarch.

"Er . . . " said Jame, hastily putting her hands behind her back. "Hello."

"Good evening," said the scholar matriarch, as calmly as if every day she opened her cellar door to a Highlord's sister dressed in rags. "Is there, perhaps, a problem?"

"A bit of one, yes. Shadow Guild assassins are after me."

"Ah. You had better come inside, then. With the relocking of this door, the Jaran and Ardeth compounds will be fully secured." She smiled faintly at Jame's surprise. "Like me, many Jaran ladies are scrollswomen, and so are many retired randon. Our guards listen to us, and we listen to the Ardeth Shanir when they have nightmares."

The offer of sanctuary was tempting. A shadow might slip under a door, but if the assassin who cast it couldn't follow, surely it could do little harm. Never mind that the *mere*-tattooed masters of the Guild could reputedly walk through solid walls. These were only apprentices. Nonetheless, if she was right, there were at least ten more bloodings to prevent.

"Somehow, Matriarch, I've got to draw them off. All of them, including the three or four more who must be in the Coman or Randir quarters, if they aren't here. There isn't time to backtrack, either. I've got to cut through your compound."

"I . . . see. Child, are you quite sure you know what you're doing?"

"Very seldom," said Jame with a sigh. "Tonight, maybe. Lady, please. I-I can't explain it, but somehow this sort of thing is my job, my . . . responsibility."

"I see," said the Jaran Matriarch again, after a pause. "In that case, it would be more dangerous to get in your way tonight than in theirs. This corridor leads straight under the compound. We will clear it."

She departed with her escort, taking the torches with her. Jame waited in the dark, wondering how far a shadow might be cast in absolute darkness, if at all. Side doors closed, farther and farther away: the Jaran, sealing off the passage. For a moment, she wished very much that Trishien hadn't taken her at her word. Maybe it *was* mad to claim such a task. If there had been anyone else to deal with the situation . . . but no: somehow, there never was.

A glimmer appeared at the other end of the hall down which she had come—one, two, three . . . seven wills-o'-the-wisp, as the Caineron guard had described them. As the ghost lights bobbed closer, Jame felt her spirits bob up with them. Insane or not, this was still much, much better than practicing knot-stitches.

"Calli-calli-catch-me-if-you-can!" she shouted down the hall, spun, and darted away.

Swift feet followed.

 **IV**

"PUT MORE WOOD on the fire," Karidia ordered.

"Lady, t-there isn't any more," stammered a voice behind her.

The Coman Matriarch whipped about, skirt belling, to glare at the group huddled around the fire-pit in the middle of the great hall. Forty-eight frightened eyes stared back at her—the entire Highborn population of the Coman compound, most under the age of thirteen.

"You," she snapped at one of the few adults. "Go fetch a chair to break up."

"Y-yes, Matriarch," quavered the woman, but didn't move.

All the room's furniture was pushed up against its walls, well beyond the faltering ring of fire light. The first duty might be obedience, but no maxim had the strength to drive anyone here back into the dark tonight.

Karidia snorted, but didn't insist. She wasn't about to admit that nothing would get her to cross that stretch of shadowy floor either.

Even less would she acknowledge any flaw in her handling of the night's events. When word had come that the Ardeth Shanir foresaw imminent danger, Karidia had refused to listen. *She* knew how the Ardeth Matriarch schemed to make those precious freaks of hers seem important. Hadn't Adiraina even claimed that all matriarchs and lords must *be* Shanir, even if most of the latter, incredibly, didn't know it? How *dare* she make reference to Karidia's own mock-berserk fits in adolescence? When the Coman captain had protested Karidia's dismissal of the Shanir alarm, she had told the Kendar to go help the Ardeth herself, if she was so concerned, and to take her precious guard with her. *Now*.

Reluctantly, the Kendar had obeyed.

The disturbance had started almost immediately afterward. First, there had been that unearthly racket in the hallways—shouts, whistles, wails, and a sound like a dozen cats being boiled alive. Then the pounding had begun on doors. Objects flew. People were literally thrown out of bed. And in the midst of this were the shadows, sliding over floors and walls, terrifying the inmates, throwing those whom they touched into convulsions. In short order, the entire Highborn segment of the household had been roused, driven out of their rooms and herded into the great hall, from which they were now afraid to stir.

"Listen," said someone by the fire-pit. "It's stopped."

The uproar had been continuing in far corners of the compound, moving systematically from room to room, seeming to grow more violent as the invaders had run out of places to search. Now, however, the loudest sound was the wind as it threw itself against the hall's shuttered windows and rattled the smoke-trap above the pit. It had been considered bad luck to shut out the Tishooo, Karidia remembered, ever since the Knorth ladies had died in their snug quarters while the wind howled futilely outside.

A fine time to think of *that*.

"Look!" said the same voice again.

Three shadows had come into the hall. They lay on the floor, man-shaped, but cast by no readily seen forms. Karidia quickly circled to stand between them and the women huddled by the fire. She thought she could almost hear the intruders, almost understand their whispered council, although she would furiously have denied that it was her own Shanir gift which allowed her to do so.

"That settles it," one of them was saying in Bashti. "She isn't here. Now what?"

"Go on hunting. D'you want to tell the Guild Master that we failed?"

All three shadows on the floor wavered, as if touched with sudden cold.

" 's not fair!" burst out the third angrily. "A place this farking large, the prey not where we were told to look, nor yet this farking book we were supposed to steal . . . and then the Master's got to screw up even our blooding by limiting who else we *can* kill. You're in dead trouble for scragging that cadet, mate."

"Damned trick of the light," muttered the first. "Her eyes *did* look red."

"*And* she was too farking young, meat-brain. We were told to look for a matriarch."

"It's *got* to be a test of wits," the second protested. "*Any* eye will be red, if you pop it out properly."

"Farking right," said the third. "My turn to try."

His shadow slid over the flags toward Karidia. She stood her ground, glaring.

"You foulmouthed little boy," she said.

The ghost of a chuckle answered her—or was it only the rustle of dust on stone? The wind continued futilely to batter against the shutters, but here in the still hall motes of grit were rattling out of corners, out of cracks. First to its knees, then to its feet, a form compounded of dust and darkness rose between stalker and prey. It cast no shadow. Rather, it *was* a shadow, upright, aware. It turned toward Karidia. Why, the impudent thing: it was *bowing* to her.

Something long and limp twitched feebly in its hand. Turning back to the three intruders, it held the thing up . . . by the hair. It was like the flayed skin of a shadow, all essence sucked out of it but for that last flicker which kept it, horribly, alive. Its throat had been cut. Its captor slid a tenebrous finger into this slash and slowly drew it downward, ripping. The shadow-skin jerked. A long sliver of it came away in the other's hand and was tossed into the dying flames of the fire-pit, where it kindled with a thin shriek and was consumed. In that sudden blaze of light, Karidia saw the three assassins clearly, transfixed. Obviously, it had never occurred to them that someday they might encounter shadows more frightening than their own.

For some time, Karidia had been dimly aware of a disturbance going on more or less under her feet. She was still surprised, though, when the flagstone on which she stood began to tilt and she was obliged to hop quickly to one side. The counterbalanced stone overturned with a crash as a ragged figure scrambled up the stair beneath from the cellar.

"Shit on a half-shell," it said, stopping dead on the top step and regarding the shadow-man with dismay. "It must be 'later.'"

The shadowy figure dropped what was left of its victim on the floor (where that agonized face, sinking into the grain, was afterward found to have left a permanent image), bowed again as if to say, "The stage is yours," and melted back into the cracks.

By now, Karidia had recognized the errant Knorth—not by her face, which the matriarch had never before seen naked, but by the gloves and tattered remains of Aerulan's gown.

"*Well!*" she said, in a tone of high, moral outrage.

The Knorth gave her a quick, rueful look.

Footsteps rang on the steps behind her. She bolted up into the hall, turned, and kicked the first of her pursuers back into the arms of his fellows.

The three assassins above converged on her.

Not since the Fall had it been customary to teach Highborn women the Senethar; consequently, the Coman by the fire had never before seen one of their own fight, much less against invisible opponents. The effect was both startling and spectacular, a death-dance tracing its *kantirs* across the floor between firelight and shadow, fierce and beautiful. On the hall's far side, the Knorth lunged for the door and threw it open. The wind swept in around her in a triumphant whoop.

"Alli-alli-all-after-me!" she cried over her shoulder, and plunged out into the night, closely pursued.

The younger girls burst into applause.

"Quiet!" snapped Karidia. She stalked over and slammed the door.

No mask. Not even the vestige of one.

"Shameless," the Coman Matriarch muttered to herself. "Utterly shameless."

V

THE TISHOOO HAD GROWN in strength over the past hour. Now it was snatching up slates, casting down chimneys, and generally wreaking gleeful havoc in the upper air.

Jame skimmed along on its wings. She had come out on the south side of the Coman near its eastern end and had turned right because a gust of wind had pushed her that way. Before her lay a series of interconnected courtyards leading toward the Randir compound and the Forecourt. It suited her to be outside, where the Tishooo blew too hard for her pursuers to try their shadow-casting tricks. Let the bastards catch her if they could. Over the wind's roar she heard the brazen bellow of a horn as someone finally sounded the alarm. With luck, it was the Brandan captain, the only person she had met all night who might know what she should do next.

The Randir loomed before her. She dodged right into the covered passageway that separated it from the western end of the Coman. Ahead lay the Forecourt, with the old keep in its midst and the Brandan compound on the far side. Running feet echoed in the passage behind her. Then she was out under open sky again, racing over grass. Ahead, the Brandan horn boomed again, at last drawing together its scattered garrison. Presumably, the captured assassin was also on his reluctant way to that muster.

In that, however, she was wrong. As if by thinking of him she had conjured up his ghost, the blond boy's pale face rose in the arcade, disembodied. White ribbons fluttered down—the last of the petticoat bonds. Then he was over the low wall and coming at her. How in Perimal's name had he gotten loose? She had relieved him of both his knife and hood, although not managing to hang on to either herself. That blade in his hand—not steel: ivory. Sweet Trinity, he'd had it all the time, before she had known that it was stolen and had thought to search him for it: The Ivory Knife, whose least scratch meant death.

Jame swerved wildly, and her foot slipped on the new grass.

The blond assassin loomed over her. This close, in bright moon light, she could see him as a flaw in the rushing air, the Knife white in his *mere*-gloved hand. He had her cold—but he had stopped to stare in disbelief at the Knife, then at her unmasked face, then back.

Jame kicked his feet out from under him. As he fell, the Knife flew out of his grasp to land a dozen feet away. Of the three aspects carved on its pommel—hag, lady, and maiden—the third smiled back at her with a face so nearly her own. Under it, the grass began to die.

She scrambled after it, but it seemed to leap out from under her hand, kicked by a *mere*-shod foot. Damnation. At least one of the other ten had overtaken her. She rolled to her feet to find herself ringed by black shadows on the pewter gray grass.

At least, when still attached, their shadows were no more dangerous than her own; but there were eleven of them now, ten armed. She thought they would try to make a quick end of her. After all, this was no private place, and the alarm continued to blare out overhead. But it had been too long and frustrating a hunt to end so tamely.

"Mousie," breathed one, and darted at her.

She didn't see his knife flash until the last moment. Cloth ripped. Damn again. She'd forgotten that she wasn't wearing her knife-fighter's *d'hen* with its reinforced sleeve. Air wavered as the boy dodged back.

"Mousie," whispered someone behind her.

Whipping around, she felt a line like fire across her shoulder and saw the fabric darken. First blood.

"Mousie, mousie, mou . . . ."

Jame turned toward that last mocking whisper, caught the assassin's knife hand as it flashed past, and jerked him into a fire-leaping elbow strike to the chin.

"Tag!" she said.

His head snapped back and his hood flew off. The next moment he was airborne as she used earth-moving leverage to hurl him into the colleague who had just started his run at her.

Cat-and-mouse became free-for-all. The assassins hadn't trained for this sort of scuffle and couldn't see each other any better than Jame could, to judge from the curses and collisions. The latter as much as windblowing and water-flowing helped her to glide through their confusion. Nonetheless, she knew that her luck was wearing as thin as Aerulan's dress. The Ivory Knife had disappeared, picked up or kicked into deeper shadows. With or without it, they must try to kill her quickly now. The horn had stopped blowing. Each garrison would secure its own compound before converging here, but they would come soon.

Then she saw dark figures in the Randir arcade, silent and motionless, watching her. How long had they been there? Why didn't they help? Who were they, anyway —Randir, or some other house guard answering the

alarm, struck dumb at the sight of the mad Knorth capering in the moonlight? How their eyes glowed. Couldn't
they at least see the heads of the two assassins whom
she had unmasked, bobbing about apparently on their
own? Maybe, if she could snatch off a few more
hoods . . . .

At that moment, the Tishooo intervened. It had been
careening around the courtyard, indiscriminately trying
to brain people with flying shingles; but suddenly it
indulged in a violent updraft, taking with it torn grass,
bits of Aerulan's dress, and nine hoods.

In the moment of windless calm which followed, Jame
saw three shadows streak across the grass toward her.
She leaped back—not quite in time. One of them clipped
the shadow cast by her left arm, and her whole left side
went numb. She staggered, but it was the assassins who
fell as their shadows collided on the spot where hers
had lain. Other boys, darting forward, tripped over their
mere-clad colleagues and went down in a heap of swearing heads. Turning, fighting to keep her balance, Jame
found herself face to face with the only assassin between
her and the keep door. Stripped of his anonymity along
with his hood, he looked very young and very scared.

"Move!" she snapped at him.

He moved.

She lurched past, threw open the door and pitched
head first into the dark interior. The Tishooo, returning
belatedly with a roar, slammed the door shut behind her.
She pulled herself to her feet, hanging onto the door
handle. Extending a nail, she fumbled about inside the
ancient lock. The bolt creaked home just as a weight hit
the outer panels. The door was made of well-seasoned
ironwood, proof even against a battering ram, but the
lock was old and rusty. It wouldn't hold long.

It wouldn't have to, thought Jame, leaning against the door. Surely now those guards in the arcade would realize that something was wrong and come to the rescue.

The door shuddered again and again. Something inside the lock groaned. Dammit, where were . . . .

They weren't coming.

Jame knew that as suddenly and surely as she had that the assassins had been told exactly where to find her room. She kept forgetting that someone in Gothregor wanted her dead.

So. There wouldn't be any rescue after all. Well, there seldom was.

She pushed herself away from the door, groped for a candle, and lit it. Stumbling, she crossed the death banner hall to the door which would have opened into the inner ward, except that it was secured by a lock which would take more time than she had to pick. She made for the northwest spiral stair, saluting Aerulan as she passed.

Her left foot hit the risers as she climbed, but she could only tell because she kept tripping. She was tempted to slam her left hand into the wall to try to wake it. The Bashtiri had made her a prisoner in her own body, as surely as if she had been stricken with apoplexy.

Below, the door crashed open.

On all fours, Jame scrambled up into the third story chamber of the High Council. Ah, this was no use: they could run her down with ease now, however high she climbed.

Don't panic, she told herself, pausing to gulp down air. *Think. If they have tricks, so do you, and knowledge, and the will to use it.*

The judgment of the Arrin-ken came back to her: *Child, you have perverted the Great Dance and misused a master rune, a darkling in training if not in blood, reckless to the point of madness . . . .*

"Shut up," she muttered, hearing the slur in her voice from a half-frozen mouth, hating it. "Shut up, shut up! You ran away, left us all to make our *own* judgments. I'll do whatever I damn well have to, to survive."

And yet . . . and yet . . . they had given her an idea.

In the middle of the chamber stood a massive ebony table. Jame dripped wax on the western end of it and fixed the burning candle upright in it. Then she clambered up to stand on the smooth, black surface. Those gorgeous stained glass windows soared up thirty feet all around her with moonlight streaming through them. Three of the walls displayed the crests of the nine major houses, separated by stone tracery. On the fourth, facing eastward, was a map of Rathillien, jewel-colored even in this light, if with subtler hues.

A thin breath of air had followed her up the stair to ruffle the candle's flame, but now the breeze abruptly died. They had closed the lower door. Stealthy footsteps sounded in the stairwell behind her, climbing slowly, cautiously. Jame smiled. At least she had finally taught them to respect their prey, and so bought herself a few precious minutes.

She cleared her mind.

What she needed was a certain master rune; but no one could carry any of them for long in memory and she didn't have the Book Bound in Pale Leather for reference. She thought, though, that given its nature she might be able to reconstruct this one from the Senetha's more esoteric *kantirs*. If only she could have danced them . . . but not in this lead-footed state. Instead, she stood there, filling her mind with their airy movements as her body would have traced them, waiting for the rune to emerge from the dance.

A face floated up the dark stairwell, looking first wary, then confused. Whatever the assassin had expected, it wasn't this motionless figure standing on a table with its back to him, black against the amber gold of the map's Southern Wastes. Nonetheless, he ascended to the hall. Ten pale faces came hesitantly after him, splitting to right and left, blocking the entrances to all four towers, surrounding their prey. A moment's uncertainty followed, with a rapid exchange of glances.

This wasn't the hunt which they had been led to expect—a soft kill like the others here thirty-odd years ago and the glory of closing the Guild's second oldest contract. Through all their minds were running other stories, told of the only open contract older than this, which also involved a Kencyr Highborn, if of a different house. How many of their fellows had vanished utterly over the years while trying to close that account? The Guild shouldn't have accepted a second contract against the Kencyrath, however lucrative. It would never take a third.

Then they tensed, thinking that their prey had begun to move; but it was only her hair, stirring slightly about her face and shoulders. Loose strands of it flexed in the air. The braid started to unravel, as if combed out by invisible fingers. A slashed sleeve suddenly flared wide. The ribbons of her skirt began to plait themselves about her bare legs. It looked for all the world as if she stood in a rising wind . . . but at the other end of the table, the candle flame rose without a tremor in the still air.

The blond boy made a strange sound in his throat, turned, and bolted down the stair. They heard his feet slap on the steps in panic-stricken flight.

With a sharp gesture, the oldest stopped the others
from following. He had to signal twice more, though,
before their shadow-souls detached and flowed—across
the floor, up the table legs, onto its top . . . .

Jame didn't notice. Her mind was full of a great wind,
on which her soul balanced precariously like a fledgling
on the storm blast. To this stage the dance had come.
She hadn't yet the skill to pursue it further, or the immediate need. The master rune had come to her piece by
piece in patterns drawn on the air. She wouldn't be able
to hold it long, though. Her thoughts plummeted to
earth. She found that all this time she had been staring
blindly up at the stained glass map, at the spot where
the artisan had depicted a storm of black wings over the
mountains of Nekrien. How appropriate: the Witch King
of that southern land was said to have ruled the winds
for more than a thousand years. Still looking up at the
map, she brought the rune hovering to the tip of her
tongue, wrapped in the words which would unbind it.
Then, because the last time, in the Ebonbane, the result
had exceeded expectations, she barely whispered:

"*Wind, blow.*"

There was a frozen moment, then a gigantic inhalation
outside. The windows exploded, jewel-bright slivers
scything outward. Ten wisps of darkness were snatched
off the table and sucked, wailing, into the night. Inside,
ten bodies crumpled to the floor. The Tishooo kept inhaling. Jame dropped flat and clung to the table top as half
of the roof disappeared with a death shriek of timber.
The wind roared up through the gap. Shapes like great,
soft-winged bats swarmed up the four stairwells from the
lower hall, pale faces flashing past, white hands flailing,
as the death banners took flight. The air was full of them,

caught in the swift, upward spiral of the wind, a storm of ancestors ascending.

One of the ancient tapestries had snagged on the corner of the table, held by a disintegrating weft while its upper warp strings flew bare. They seemed to be weaving into a new shape in midair, or rather weaving *around* something. String ligaments gave form to the shadow of an arm, a shoulder, a face with the deep glimmer of eyes. Bane looked at her through the web of another man's death. The threads of his mouth shifted. He was smiling at her.

Then his head tilted back as he followed the other banners' flight, and the smile died.

These were the honorable dead. He had staked everything on death restoring his own lost honor, squandered in games of cruelty and despair. That gamble might have won, if not for Ishtier's treachery and Jame's bungling. How much did he blame her for that failure? Why was he here now, if not to collect his own blood-price? Some of the threads had worked free of the corner. They streamed up between shadow fingers as he reached for her.

"Don't!" she cried.

A moment later, without thinking, she had grabbed for that phantom hand as the rest of the anchoring weft gave way, but caught only a tangle of flying threads. The thing that had given them shape was gone, sucked upward with the rest of the dead into the beating darkness.

Beating?

Jame twisted to peer upward. Her own loosened, flying hair half-obscured her view, but through it she thought she saw the air above the keep full of vast black wings flailing against the moon. In their midst, far up, an old man fell and fell, never to reach the ground.

Then the man, the wings, and the wind all vanished, as suddenly as if some door in heaven had slammed shut.

Jame lay still for a moment, hardly believing that it was over—but what in Perimal's name had she seen, there, above the keep? It *must* have been an afterimage, brought on by staring too long and hard at what flew above the mountains of Nekrien on the map.

Oh, hell. The map. The windows. She sat up to gaze in dismay at the broken traceries, empty of glass, and the hole in the roof, with a few banners snagged on the shattered beams.

Tori was not going to be pleased.

Then she heard voices below, speaking softly in Kens. At last, the guard had begun to take an interest . . . unless these were the strangers with glowing eyes whom she had seen in the Randir arcade, come to see how the Shadow Guild had fared. Jame slid hastily down off the table, noting that her foot could almost feel the floor although otherwise her left side remained numb. She located the first assassin by falling over him. He was dead. So were the other nine. That surprised her: she had thought that they couldn't die when separated from their shadow-souls, but this separation had apparently been so abrupt that not one of them had survived the shock. Worse, none of them had the Ivory Knife. Also missing was the blond boy.

A Brandan cadet paused on the final turning of the stair, clearly startled to find the missing Knorth in such a place. More guards of her house came up behind her. Their captain staggered up the steps after them, leaning heavily on a cadet.

"Some fox hunt," she muttered, as disconcerted guards stumbled about the chamber, tripping over invisible bodies. Then she caught sight of Jame's bare face, and quickly looked away.

All winter, people had been lecturing Jame about the impropriety of going unmasked, but she had never really understood how they felt—until now.

"What took you so long?" she demanded, her voice sharp with sudden embarrassment.

The cadet had helped her captain over to the ebony table and left her leaning against it. "Lady," she said, still not looking at Jame, speaking very low, "it was a right mess. That maid you sent for help managed to knock herself silly falling downstairs. It took me nearly an hour to haul myself down to the guardroom."

"And then you had them sound the alarm."

"Yes. Trinity!" Her gaze, turning upward, had seen the moon through shattered rafters. "D'you always have this drastic an effect on architecture?"

"Fairly often," said Jame with a sigh, remembering the state in which she had left Tai-tastigon and a certain palace in Karkinaroth. "But what about Brenwyr? Why didn't she raise the alarm much earlier?"

The captain didn't know. Jame remembered her last glimpse of the Iron Matriarch, standing motionless over the captured assassin, that strange red light simmering in her eyes. Had Brenwyr moved at all until the alarm had broken in on her, just before Jame's arrival in the Forecourt?

An irate voice sounded in the lower hall, then in the echoing throat of the southeast stairwell. The Caineron captain. Damn.

"Look," Jame said hastily to the Brandan. "Are you sure there are always thirteen assassins in a casting? I only count one dead in the nursery, ten here, and a twelfth who, I think, ran away."

"For a blooding, the thirteenth would be a guild master." This time she did look at Jame, sharply. "D'you mean to say that he's still on the loose?"

The Caineron captain stalked into the hall, her cadet guards trailing cautiously after her. "So, lady, here you are at last," she said to Jame. "The next time you're scared by a little wind, try to show some gumption instead of scuttling off."

Jame opened her mouth, then shut it again.

The captain had already turned away with a startled oath, having just seen the pile of naked, white bodies which the Brandan cadets had begun to collect and strip.

Let her think what she liked. Explanations would hardly help.

Suddenly, Jame felt the hair prickle on her scalp. Brenwyr stood at the mouth of the northwest tower, staring at her with eyes as red as a cat's by fire light. Sweet Trinity, now what?

"Pardon, lady," someone mumbled at her elbow.

The next moment, two Caineron cadets had seized her arms, in the manner of hastily securing a fugitive. The reason was Kallystine, who had just entered the chamber.

Her guard must think it worth their lives to let me slip away again, Jame thought, watching Caldane's daughter sweep across the floor toward her as if they were the only two people in the room.

Instead of her usual daring mask, Kallystine wore a heavy veil, which her rapid progress flattened against her hidden features. Jame stared. Those lines of cheek and chin of which M'lady was so proud—could they possibly be . . . sagging?

"Lady," she blurted out, "what's happened to your face?"

Kallystine slapped her.

Jame saw the blow coming, with something in the other's hand that flashed cold in the moon light; but the cadets' grip held her fast, so that she could neither block nor dodge. It struck her numb left cheek, hard enough to jolt back her head. She heard the others gasp. Belatedly, the cadets released her and backed away, looking shocked.

"There," said Kallystine's honeyed voice, the smile audible in it. "Now you also know what it feels like, to lose face."

Jame touched her cheek. There was still no sensation in it, but to her finger tips it felt . . . odd, like a mask of soft leather with a great tear in it. Through the tear, she felt something hard and wet. Then she knew. That flash in Kallystine's hand had been the blade of a razor-ring. The wetness was blood; the hard thing under her finger tips, her own cheekbone, laid bare.

As that afternoon a slap had made her berserker blood flare, so it did now. Jame fought it. Her nails were out, sheathed in the palms of her clenched fists, and everyone was backing away. Not long ago, she had spoken a master rune. Now she again felt the power rise, seeking a half-remembered form—something from the last pages of the Book, to rip apart the senses of all who heard it, to rupture ears and burst eyes. It clawed its way up her throat like a live thing as she struggled to master it, half-succeeding at the last moment. Still, it burst out with terrible, wordless force.

The first thing the Kendar heard afterward, when their ears stopped ringing, was Kallystine's babbled complaints and orders. When their eyes had cleared sufficiently and the worst nosebleeds had been checked, a

Caineron guard bundled her lady off to her quarters with far less ceremony than she was accustomed to.

The Brandan Matriarch sat on a step with her head on her hands.

The Knorth had disappeared.

"Oh no," said a voice among the remaining Caineron. "Not again."

 **VI**

THIS TIME, however, there was a trail of blood.

A still shaken group of cadets followed it up the northwest tower stair to the apartment called Gothregor and there lost it, in the middle of the Highlord's small study. They looked behind chairs, out windows, under the table, and up the chimney, without success. Then someone remembered the catwalk to the other tower and, for her pains, was sent across to check.

"Nothing," she reported back, bright green with height-sickness, and lost her dinner behind the Highlord's chair.

Nonetheless, it was decided that the Knorth must also have crossed over and then gone down the southwest stair, while no one below had been in a fit state to notice. In that case, she could be anywhere in the greater fortress by now. The cadets were dispatched to search there, with orders from the Caineron captain not to tell anyone anything. When she included the Brandan cadets in this charge, their captain raised her brows, but didn't comment until they had gone.

"Two *are* missing," she said, as the Caineron tossed *mere* clothing over the bodies, temporarily concealing them. "One is almost certainly a guild master."

"No need to cause more panic. They'll be long gone by now."

"They came back after all these years, apparently as soon as word reached them that a young Knorth was in these halls again and spring weather permitted travel. They don't give up that easily."

"Look," said the Caineron impatiently. "It will be dawn soon. *Mere* or not, they aren't day hunters. By night, we'll have that wretched girl in our hands again, bound and gagged, if necessary, and the halls totally secured."

"As, perhaps, they should have been ever since she arrived."

The Caineron shook her head like a baited bear. She knew she had handled this badly, but be damned if she would admit it. "How could we guess that the contract was still active, thirty-odd years later? I know, I know: they've been after the so-called Randir Heir longer than that, but this is different. Anyway, the brat has scuttled again. If we can't find her, on our home ground, how d'you think the Guild will?"

"Gone back into hiding, yes. And hurt. With all due respect, how could your lady have been so *stupid*? We may have war over this."

"Over what?" asked the young Danior captain, emerging from the stairwell with her Edirr counterpart on her heels. "Trinity! Old Man Tishooo really took a dislike to this place, didn't he?"

"Never mind that damned wind," snapped the Coman captain, coming in with the Ardeth. "What in Perimal's name was that cry? *That's* what scared my ladies out of the few wits they had left."

"You're lucky," said the Ardeth soberly. "It reduced our Shanir to convulsions." She glanced at Brenwyr's huddled figure on the stair, and shot the Brandan captain a questioning look.

The latter replied with a flick of her hand: *I don't know.*

The Jaran captain had arrived during this exchange. "Well," she said, surveying the damage. "I see that someone got in the Knorth's way after all."

"Don't be an idiot!" the Caineron almost shouted. "A freak wind did this! Don't you farking know what the Tishooo is like?"

"All right, all right," said the Jaran pacifically. "Just tell me this, then: whose blood is that, on the floor?"

The Caineron shuffled her feet. If it had been left to her, the others would never have known. As it was, the Brandan told them.

The randon looked at each other with dismay. There hadn't been anything like this in the Women's Halls since the quarrel between Kinzi and the Randir Matriarch Rawneth, and even that hadn't come to blows, if only because the Shadow Guild had struck first.

"At least it's only a lady," said the Coman. "Think how much worse it would be if this had happened to someone important."

"Right," the Danior said drily. "It's only the Highlord's sister, his sole surviving blood-kin. Quiet as the man is, I don't see him letting this pass without comment. You were right," she said to the Brandan. "This could mean war."

"Not necessarily."

They all turned at the sound of this new voice. The Randir captain had entered the chamber some time during the past few minutes and stood in the shadows, hidden by her dress grays, listening. Now she came forward, half out of darkness. Moon light caught the thin gold lines embroidered on her shoulder and the white teeth of a smile which never quite reached her eyes.

"If the damage is repaired before the Highlord returns, how much complaint can he make, even if the girl is so ill-bred as to tell him? At the Priests' College, we have a healer so powerful that he once nearly restored life to a sheepskin coat. Shall I send to Wilden for him?"

The Brandan's brows rose again. "A Randir, prescribing for a Knorth? Shouldn't we at least consult Rowan, Torisen's steward? After all, this did happen in the old Knorth keep, not in the halls."

"Keep or not," said the Caineron, glowering, "the matriarchs made me responsible for the brat, and the only other death tonight in the halls was one of my own cadets. This is *my* business. Hell, yes: send for the healer! Should we risk civil war over a scratched face?"

The Brandan touched the marks around her own eyes, made with her own nails in the night nursery.

"There's something else you should see."

For a moment, it seemed that the Caineron would stop her, but then she stepped aside with poor grace. In an apparently empty corner, the Brandan bent to flick something away. A pale, tangled patch appeared, seeming to float a foot off the floor. In it was a confusion of thin arms, parts of two torsos, and a boy's head, lolling, dead eyes wide open in disbelief.

"Damnation," said the Jaran softly, after a moment. "They came back. And I was right: someone *did* get in the Knorth's way."

The others paid no attention to that. Taking the Caineron at her word that the missing Knorth was her responsibility, they disbanded in haste, each to secure her own compound against the two intruders still at large.

The Brandan stayed to help her matriarch. This time, Brenwyr rose at a touch on her shoulder. Blood had run down from her ears and red-flecked eyes, like scarlet tears.

"Save your questions," she said harshly. "I can't hear them anyway. And if you're staring at me, don't."

Descending step by blind step to the lower hall, she put up her hand to confirm what she had seen earlier. Among the night's other casualties were all the death banners on the west wall. Aerulan was gone.

A maledight curse—half pure malison, half prophecy —began to form below the level of Brenwyr's conscious mind. She felt it quicken, as always not knowing what shape it would take. Then it rose like a sickness which must be spat out or swallowed back. All the darkness of that long winter, all the misery and madness . . . She spat:

"Roofless and rootless, blood and bone, cursed be and cast out!"

No light, no relief, no sound, even, of her own voice in her stricken silence.

"Oh, Aerulan!" she cried.

The captain led her away.

 **VII**

BRENWYR'S WORDS CARRIED, as such curses do, until they reached the one for whom they were intended. Four flights up, a sigh answered them:

" '*Roofless and rootless*'? The same to you, Brandan. '*Cursed be*.'"

The door leading from the tower out onto the platform of the catwalk had been left open. Now it swung back. No one had stopped to think that a flat door is not going to lie absolutely flush with a curved wall. The jagged hole in the council chamber roof gaped beneath. Jame had heard every word spoken there. In fact, she had felt inclined to tumble down on the captains' heads, if they didn't shut up soon and go away. Oh God, was this faintness only shock, or had Kallystine doctored her blade?

They *had* gone, cursing her.

She stumbled back into her brother's study and collapsed into his chair. Senethar techniques had stopped the bleeding. Similar measures to control pain hadn't yet been necessary, but soon would be as the numbness wore off. Her front teeth felt loose from half-swallowing a master rune and her throat raw. As for her cheek, the pulse there was already beginning to throb. She touched it gingerly. No doubt about it: M'lady Kallystine had done her a serious mischief. Sweet Trinity, talk about losing face . . . .

But she needn't. The Randir captain had spoken of someone who might set all right. A healer from Wilden. A priest.

There was the rub.

No Kencyr liked or trusted his own priests, anymore than he did the god whom they served. Both were ignored as much as possible by the rest of the Kencyrath, except when a house wanted to get rid of a Shanir boy. The unforeseen result was that the Priests' College had accumulated most of the curative Shanir, who tended to mature too late for their families to realize what they were throwing away. Lords sometimes bargained to get their healers back, but they never really regained control of them. Being a novice changed a boy. Being a priest warped him utterly.

So, at least, Jame believed, judging by Ishtier.

Moreover, the very thought of deep healing made her skin crawl. Buried deep in every individual's mind was a soul-image—a metaphor for his or her essence in which illness and injury were also reflected. Repairing the image healed the body. A Shanir healer entered the collective soul-scape to do this, in perhaps the most intimate experience known to the Kencyrath.

Be damned if she was going to let anyone that close to her now, Jame thought, even if it meant wearing a mask the rest of her life. It wasn't as if her face had ever amounted to much, anyway.

Here, her thoughts began to blur, perhaps influenced by the healing techniques which normally ended in *dwar* sleep, perhaps by whatever-it-was which Kallystine might have put on her razor's edge. She slept fitfully for a time, in and out of dreams. A terror of helplessness kept her from the deeper reaches of *dwar*, which would have speeded the healing process but which also would have set the scar. Awake or dreaming, she stared up at the warped, bronze mirror over the mantle, in which her ghostlike image sat in her brother's chair.

More shadowy still was the reflection of the two figures who stood behind her, backs turned, on a balcony over a moonlit waste. From a great distance, she seemed to hear their voices.

"... *my boy, it's almost dawn,*" one was saying. "*Don't you mean to sleep at all?*"

"*I will,*" replied her brother, dogged, "*when the chair behind me is empty.*"

Dammit, he was blaming her again. Somehow, everything out of his control must be her fault, as their father Ganth Gray Lord had taught him.

... Ganth's hoarse, mad voice dripping poison in her brother's ear: "*You were all right until she came back, your darkling half ....*"

"Father, no!" she protested thickly, rousing. "*You drove me out, into shadows. It isn't fair to blame me. It ....*"

"*...'s no good whining,*" someone else seemed to answer her.

Jame cringed back again in the chair. That voice, with its pretended sophistication, its underlying power and cruelty, which she had last heard as a prisoner in his tent at the Cataracts ... Caldane, Lord Caineron. The reflected scene behind her had darkened into a different prison, where torch light glowered on dank stone walls.

Sounds answered Caldane: the rustle of befouled straw, harsh breathing, mumbled words.

"*Done enough to you already? Oh no. You betrayed me, Gricki. No one does that, least of all my own misbegotten bastard. I'll find a use for you yet—in a few days, when I've thought of something ... special.*"

"No!" Jame cried again, struggling against the grip of nightmare to rise and turn. "Caldane, don't you dare ...."

But the effort made her wits whirl. She thought, dazed, that she must have fallen, but didn't remember hitting the ground. Her angle of vision was ... odd. Askew. Instead of Restormir's dungeon, she glimpsed Gothregor across the Silver, shadowy ruins, and the blond boy-assassin, looking terrified. Then, very, very close, a pair of yellow eyes glittered down at her, with no face behind them. Not just *mere* clothes, but *mere* tattooing—the mark of a guild master. Invisible lips drew back from rotten teeth.

"You were sent to find a pale book," tongue and ulcerated throat said harshly from midair. *"Instead, you bring me this strange knife."* Trinity. She must be seeing him through the eyes of the Maiden, the third face carved on the pommel of the Ivory Knife. *"You were sent to kill a girl. Instead, you tell me that all your brothers are dead. That is ... unsatisfactory. Oh, I'm so glad that you agree, boy, because this isn't over yet ...."*

No, not yet. Not alive, not dead either. Just lost, bewildered, and very, very frightened.

Brothers, where are you? Where am I? What happened to us? There was a great wind, full of wings, and in its midst the Old Man snatched us up. Flying, flying, falling ... ah! Dead branches against the moon, catching us, but we can not catch them. Where are my hands?

On an ironwood floor, beside an ebony table, growing cold, growing stiff ....

No. Here. Not dead ... but not alive either.

The other is here too, snagged out of the air by the tree's bleached fingers, a darkness that flows down the white wood, stronger than we are, older and more cruel, a shadow with hungry, silver eyes. Run, hide!

... but we are growing cold and stiff.

"You can't run from me forever," it whispers, smiling. *"Blood binds."*

Jame sprang to her feet. For a moment, the suddenness of her rise struck her blind. *Dreams*, she thought, breathing hard, forcing herself to stand still. *Nothing but damned dreams* . . . .

"No," said Torisen's half-choked voice. "I refuse to dream this!"

Her eyes cleared. She was staring directly into the bronze mirror and a warped version of her own face seemed to stare back at her in horror. It had the same Knorth features, at least, even the blood across one high cheekbone. But it wasn't her.

"Tori?" she whispered. "Tori, wait!"

A hasty step forward had turned into a lunge as her legs failed her, and his image had recoiled. She clung to the mantle for support, her breath clouding the cold bronze.

"Dammit, where are you? Come to me, brother. Come!"

The metal cleared. Reflected in it, behind her, she saw the tower room and Torisen's chair, over which her shadow lay. No. Something sat there, spun of nightmares, silver-eyed. It rose, smiling. The wrong brother had answered, her darkling shadow-bane . . . .

Run. Hide.

Images blurred into a nightmare of flight. Underfoot, stairs, ironwood floors, grass, flagstones, get away get away get away . . . .

A stab of pain brought Jame up short. She blinked and found herself, breathless, in the ruins of her tiny room in the Caineron quarter. She sat abruptly on the bed and was enveloped in down from the slashed mattress.

Sweet Trinity, was this another dream? *Not with feathers in it*, she thought, sneezing. *Nothing so innocent.* As for the rest . . . .

. . . Torisen and Ardeth on the balcony; Caineron and Graykin; the Ivory Knife in a guild master's invisible hand; the souls of the boy-assassins hunted by Bane; *Blood binds* . . . .

All phantasms of a possibly drugged mind? Perhaps. Earlier, she had refused to believe that she might farsee anything—what did she want with another Shanir curse?—but these images rang all too true, all but the last. Bane was *not* her shadow. Darkling she might be, but unfallen, her soul and honor still her own.

Besides, the bastard was up a tree somewhere, breakfasting on nasty little boys. What would *their* souls taste like—sticky fingers and snot?

But then, if not Bane, what had her brother seen, to react with such horror? The room's broken mirror told her, over and over in a dozen shattered planes. Oh God.

Another flare of pain. Sensation was returning in ragged waves, in between which she hastily applied the appropriate technique. Ironic, that she had learned it here at Gothregor. Because of childbirth, the Women's World knew more ways to control pain than even her Senethari, Tirandys, had been able to teach her.

Then she looked again, and saw by her reflection to her surprise that she was wearing travel clothes—black boots and pants, black knife-fighter's *d'hen* jacket with its tight right sleeve and full, reinforced left—with no memory of having put them on.

Roofless and rootless . . . .

So, she hadn't come back here to hide. Well, they would have found her eventually anyway, wherever in

Gothregor she had gone to earth. Then there would have been a forced healing as subtle as a rape and a lunatic's confinement, with Kallystine gloating through the keyhole. And all that time, Graykin would have been in Caldane's hands where service to her had landed him, because she did believe that part of her dreams, if nothing else.

So she was running: North, to Caldane's Restormir, to the rescue, if she could manage it . . . with a face that could start a war?

Blood and bone . . . .

At least, Tori would never believe what he had farseen in his mirror. She wondered bitterly if he would even remember it, having seen him wipe far more important things completely out of his mind when they touched on the Shanir.

As for the rest of the Kencyrath, if it disliked unmasked females so much, it need never look on her face again. In her hand was a strip of clean linen, ripped from the hem of a spare underskirt. She wrapped it around her head, over the bridge of her nose and across both cheekbones, binding up the injury. A half mask covered the whole neatly—not that it made her a proper lady, she thought, scowling at her visored image in the broken glass, any more than skirts had made her Aerulan. Damn all mirrors, anyway. No more trying to see herself as others wished her to be, no more useless reflections.

She left the room without a backward glance.

The compound seemed abandoned, except around Kallystine's quarters. At a guess, the Caineron guard had searched their own territory while she had slept in Tori's chair and were now out combing the rest of Gothregor for her. The other compounds proved to be locked tight and fully garrisoned. Jame therefore had no trouble raiding the communal kitchen for provisions or making her way westward through the empty corridors north of the Brandan.

From the top of the wall that separated the Women's World from the inner ward, she saw her brother's scar-faced steward Rowan arguing with the hall guards at the gate, demanding information and entry, getting neither, while the fortress's regular garrison gathered behind her.

No one noticed the slight, dark-clad figure who slipped down off the wall into the shadows on their left and then walked around behind them toward the subterranean stable. The thieves of Tai-tastigon could have taught the Shadow Guild something about passing unseen through a crowd. That the Knorth Kendar failed to notice the same figure a few minutes later, going in the opposite direction with an ounce trotting beside it, reflected more poorly on their powers of observation, but it was a very confusing night.

The post-rider, dispatched in haste for the Priests' College, nearly trampled someone under the North Gate. Swearing, she wrenched her horse to one side and thundered past.

Fifty miles to Wilden. Four hours riding flat out with a remount at Falkirr, Jame thought, watching the messenger plunge down through the steep middle ward and across the broad outer. The healer priest could return just as quickly, if he hurried. She and Jorin were getting out none too soon. They followed the rider down through the wards to the curtain wall and the northern barbican, passing out under the latter unchallenged into the apple orchard beyond.

Overhead, the gibbous moon shone bright at zenith while the stars sank into the deep blue of a predawn sky. The air was giddy with apple blossoms. Looking up through their white glimmer at Gothregor's looming darkness, Jame experienced a moment of bleak clarity.

What she did next, she had to do, for honor's sake as much as for her servant's life; but it would end her chance of acceptance by the Kencyrath in any role which it had been prepared to offer her. So this was the end of the long, bleak winter, turned into empty spring. Driven from the heart, where was there left to go?

Cursed be and cast . . . .

Stop it, stop it. Brenwyr's curse buzzed in her mind like bees in the night's carcass. What would Marc say, if only he were here to ask?

Perhaps, again, *"Stop hiding. Follow honor and forget the rest."*

Wise, wise Marc.

Dawn birds were chirping sleepily as they left the orchard, bound northward for Restormir, forty leagues away.

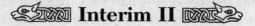

Interim II

Kothifir Encampment: 55th of Spring

"MY BOY, it's almost dawn," said Lord Ardeth. "Don't you mean to sleep at all?"

"I will, when the chair behind me is empty."

Torisen saw the old lord's worried look. The chair in question *was* empty, now that Harn had reluctantly left to do the rounds of the watch. He knew that. And yet ... and yet ... moments ago, something *had* sat down in it.

Think of something else. Burr.

"I hope," he said, "that there was nothing worse in that wine than a sedative."

Ardeth shrugged. "An infusion of black nightshade never hurt any Highborn. The dose wasn't measured for a Kendar, though. You should never have made him drink it."

Torisen winced. He should have asked about the wine's composition earlier, too. Pieces of the night kept slipping away from him. He forced himself to half-turn, his back still toward the empty chair. His servant slumped on the other side of the table, his head in a pool of wine as red as spilt blood. He touched Burr's broad shoulder. The bond between them told him that the Kendar only slept, but was beginning to breathe with difficulty. Face down in narcotic wine ....

Torisen carefully turned the man's head to one side, clearing nose and mouth. His hands had begun to shake again. Sixteen years together, through a dozen hells not even counting Urakarn, and he had almost let Burr quietly suffocate within arm's reach.

"You and your damned drugs," he said to Ardeth unsteadily. "Have you ever tried to live without them?"

"Why should I? My boy, can't I persuade you . . . ."

"No!"

Ardeth's pharmacopoeia might do no harm in itself—after all, Highborn were almost impossible to poison—but it could rob Torisen of the few defenses which his lack of sleep had left him. The old terror returned like a hand closing on his throat: not only to dream such horrible things but to be trapped in one of his nightmares, unable to wake. This whole night had begun to feel that way, but dawn was almost here.

Hold on, just hold on . . . .

He found himself again in front of Pereden's ornate mirror. His pale face seemed to float in the glass, black coat and hair casting almost no reflection. The room behind him was dim, lit only by gray light seeping through unshuttered windows. At his back was a chair—his, he realized, from his tower room at Gothregor—and in it sat an indistinct form. He must be dreaming, but he couldn't wake . . . .

Movement in the back shadows of the mirror: the ghostly reflection of the Wolver Grimly entering the commander's quarters in Kothifir, stopping short.

"I smell blood," he said.

Torisen looked blankly down at his left hand, at red running along the white scars on his palm. His grip on Kin-Slayer had cracked the hilt emblem.

Ardeth came forward at once, fussing. "Let me see." He took Torisen's thin, elegant hand and turned it palm up. "You are so hard on yourself, my boy. More scars . . ."

"That's enough," said Torisen thickly, detaching the other's grip with a strength that made the old lord blink. "That's more than enough."

"My boy . . . ?"

"I'm not. That was Pereden, and he's dead. Remember?" He jerked the emerald signet ring off his left hand and held it up. "I'm Ganth Gray Lord's son, former commander of the Southern Host, present Highlord of the Kencyrath, and I will *not* be condescended to or spied on. *Understand*?"

Ardeth fell back a step.

"My . . . lord," he said, shaken. "I understand that you are tired and ill. I will leave you to rest." With a formal salute he departed, deliberately not glancing at the Wolver who remained crouched in the shadows, on guard.

Torisen looked at Ganth's ring for a moment, then slipped it onto a finger of his right hand. Was this how Pereden had felt, trying to exorcize his pain by inflicting it on others? In another moment, he would have accomplished that wretched boy's revenge by telling Ardeth the truth about his son, after all he had done to protect the old man from it. Torisen put both hands over his face, heedless of the blood which still trickled down between his fingers.

Sweet Trinity. He *must* be going mad.

"*And whose fault is that?*" Ganth's voice asked. "*You were all right until she came back, your darkling half. Now you will never be right again until she is . . . .*"

What? wondered the Wolver Grimly, ears twitching.

But Torisen's hands had slid from his eyes to cover his mouth, stopping the words. The fur slowly rose down Grimly's spine. Did his friend know that he had been speaking out-loud? The "darkling half" must be Tori's new-found sister, whom Grimly had met at the Cataracts the previous winter and liked very much.

Until she is . . . what?

In turning away from Ardeth, the Highlord had brought himself again face to face with the mirror. Now he froze, staring into it. All Grimly could see was Torisen's reflection, a smear of blood down one cheek from his cut hand. The Highborn made a half-choked sound:

"No. I refuse to dream this. I refuse . . . . No!"

"Don't!" yelped the Wolver.

Too late. Kin-Slayer was out of its sheath, hissing through the air. Glass shattered. Grimly threw the unconscious Burr to the floor and shielded him with his body as razor-edged shards scythed overhead. Wood shrieked. Clay dust filled the air. For an endless moment, Grimly was sneezing too hard to wonder what had happened. Then he looked up. The mirror had disintegrated. So had the foot-thick wall behind it where blade and brick had met. A shaft of gray dawn light lanced through the ragged hole into the dusty murk of the room. Outside, dogs had begun to howl.

"Son of a bitch," said Grimly reverently. "You finally made the damn thing work. Tori . . . where are you?"

Dust began to settle. The room was empty except for the Wolver and Burr's sprawling figure. Below, hooves rang on stone. Grimly leaned out the ragged hole in time to see Torisen bareback on Storm, his quarter-blood Whinno-hir, bolting out of the courtyard, Kin-Slayer still naked in his hand.

Grimly remembered the old songs. You didn't unsheathe a battle-blade, especially that one, unless you meant to kill someone.

You will never be right again until she is . . . .

Dead?

"Oh, no," said the Wolver. "Oh, Tori, no." He dropped to all fours and ran out of the room yelping, "Tori, Tori, wait for me!"

PART

III

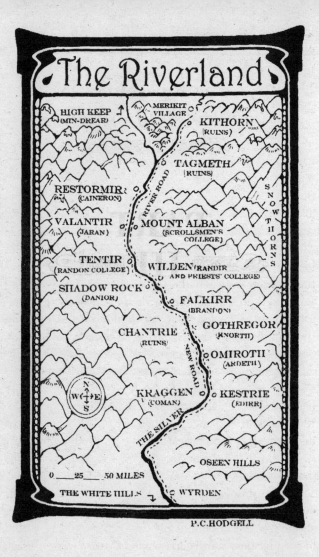

The Riverland

HIGH KEEP
(MIN-DRAER)

MERIKIT VILLAGE

KITHORN
(RUINS)

TAGMETH
(RUINS)

RESTORMIR
(CAINERON)

RIVER ROAD

VALANTIR
(JARAN)

MOUNT ALBAN
(SCROLLSMEN'S COLLEGE)

S N O W T H O R N S

TENTIR
(RANDON COLLEGE)

WILDEN (RANDIR AND PRIESTS' COLLEGE)

SHADOW ROCK
(DANIOR)

FALKIRR
(BRANDON)

CHANTRIE
(RUINS)

GOTHREGOR
(KNORTH)

NEW ROAD

OMIROTH
(ARDETH)

N
W E
S

KRAGGEN
(COMAN)

KESTRIE
(EDIRR)

THE SILVER

OSEEN HILLS

0   25   50 MILES

THE WHITE HILLS

WYRDEN

P.C. HODGELL

The Riverland:
55th–58th of Spring

I

THE RIVERLAND stretched out along the upper reaches of the Silver, bracketed by the Snowthorn Mountains—a rugged country, over two hundred miles long but scarcely ten across at its widest. The Silver was the frontier between those two giants of the Central Lands, Bashti and Hathir. At the height of their power, a thousand years ago, they had built rival fortresses up the length of the river from the Cataracts to Kithorn. Supplying the northern garrisons had always been difficult, however. After a massive earthquake disrupted the Silver from end to end, destroying all travel on it, they had given up and ceded their mountain keeps to the Kencyrath in exchange for military aid. Kencyr troops had served as mercenaries in the Central Lands ever since, the Riverland having proved too poor to support them either.

Meager strips of arable land surrounded Gothregor, most of them lying fallow. Thanks to Torisen's long absence with the bulk of his troops, it would be a thin harvest for the Knorth garrison and a worse winter. Black cattle grazed between the furrows. A bull stamped at the smell of strangers, but more to be feared were the horns of the cow suckling her calf behind him.

Beyond, the land was almost untouched except for the ancient River Road running along the Silver's east bank and the New Road occasionally glimpsed through trees on the west. To leave either was said to be dangerous. No reliable map existed of the reaches between the keeps—because all cartographers were incompetent, the lords said. The scrollsmen themselves simply couldn't agree on details, leaving some to complain in disgust that the terrain must differ for each traveler who crossed it.

Nonetheless, not wishing to be overtaken, two fugitives followed a hunter's path about a quarter of a mile up the mountain side with trees above them and a sweep of wild flowers below. So far, though, no one had passed by on the River Road, coming or going.

Odd, thought Jame. Maybe the priests weren't going to send their precious healer after all.

Morning slid into afternoon. The sun was in decline when they came to a brook plunging down through trees into the steep meadow below. While Jorin lapped avidly, Jame sat back on her heels with a sigh, feeling the pull of tired muscles. A winter of roaming halls had ill-prepared her to tackle mountains. Still, she should grow accustomed to it quickly. The same, alas, could not be said for Kallystine's handiwork. Gingerly, she touched her face. Beneath the mask, her cheek felt swollen and hot. At least it didn't hurt, the numbness of the assassin's touch having long since merged into her own pain control. It was hard, though, to keep the wits clear during such a sustained effort. Lulled by the stream's voice, she let her senses drift.

The day turned luminous around her. High overhead, snow blew off the western peaks in sparkling veils. Below, set against the darkness of pine forests, panicles of meadow grass floated in a golden shimmer. Down on the valley floor, birds flew up in a wave along the River Road, as if disturbed by someone passing by, northward bound. White wings gleamed in the upper air.

"Wah!" said Jorin, and dropped a half-eaten fish in her lap.

The sight reminded Jame that her own last meal had been sometime the previous day. However, she wasn't hungry. Damn Kallystine anyway, if this light-headedness was in part her fault. It was difficult to poison or infect a Highborn, but M'lady could be counted on to have tried her best.

Wait a minute. Those disturbed birds. *Had* someone passed by below?

She didn't think so, but couldn't be sure. At least, no one could have seen her as she knelt behind this waving screen of grass. Anyway, it was time to move on—higher up the slope, if she couldn't trust herself within sight of the road. She drank deep, splashing icy water on her flushed face below the mask, then rose and left the path for the trees above, Jorin bounding on ahead.

They found themselves in a forest of straight, pale trunks, floored with silver-edged ferns, roofed by spring foliage. Unseen doves were calling at a distance. A breath of air ruffled frond and leaf.

It was beautiful, Jame thought, but in an odd way it reminded her of the Anarchies or the Heart of the Woods at Hurlen—both areas of native power, intolerant of any alien presence. Marc had told her that his old home was much like that too—but Kithorn Keep lay nearly sixty leagues to the north, in Merikit hands. Here, she was still in the heart of the Riverland, which the Kencyr lords had claimed as their own for a thousand years.

Roofless and rootless . . . .

Now, there was a thought not without irony: suppose the Kencyrath itself had none too secure a grip on this land which it called home? After all, her people were alien to this world despite their long sojourn here. What if it saw them as invaders, as unwelcome as Perimal Darkling had been to the entire series of overlapping universes which made up the Chain of Creation? What had the Earth Wife of Peshtar called her and Marc?

"Stepchildren, if even that."

The loamy smell of the forest reminded her of Mother Ragga's low-beamed lodge and of the Earth Wife herself, that fat, old woman stuck together like a jackdaw's nest. On the floor of her house had been a map composed of dirt and rocks brought from all over Rathillien. By pressing her ear to this ridge or that hollow, she could hear what was happening on a mountain or in a valley half a world away. Listening to Marc's little bag of Kithorn soil, she had even heard the weightless feet of his long dead sister running across the keep's abandoned courtyard.

Kithorn . . . from whose ruined battlements Torisen had seen the Burnt Man hunt a kin-slayer with his pack of Burning Ones. Now some claimed to have heard the latter in the Riverland itself. Easy enough, safe within Kencyr walls, to dismiss them as bogies to frighten Merikit children. Not so here, under green leaves. Presumably, the Wilden priests should keep such things off Kencyr territory, including Old Man Tishooo from the south and weirding from the north. Patently, they had not.

This land is unguarded, Jame thought with a sudden shiver. *Anything can happen here.*

The light changed as the sun set. All shadows merged into a misty twilight, with a gilt glimmer edging each leaf. One by one, the birds fell silent. The wood seemed to hold its breath, then let it out in a long sigh as the wind passed between the trees. So like the Anarchies . . . but there she had been protected by the Earth Wife's *imu* medallion, which now lay shattered in the hollow at the Heart of the Woods near the Cataracts. A shiver slid down her spine. They were absolutely alone, and yet they were being watched.

Jorin's ears pricked. The faintest of sighs, somewhere above . . . .

Pale faces stared down at them through the foliage; white hands hovered as though in precarious benediction. The Knorth death banners hung there in rows on twig and bough, arranged just as they had been in the lower hall of the old keep. A breath of wind stirred them, so that for a moment the dead seemed to move restlessly in their tapestry webs. Then all was still again.

"Old Man, Old Man," said Jame softly, admiring the Tishooo's parting prank.

She could see, though, that for some of the banners this had been no joke: those too old for such a flight hung in shivering knots of warp threads, the identifying woof stripped away. Who would remember those Knorth dead now? Would Torisen know what names to chant on Autumn Eve to the empty places where their banners had hung?

"There are fewer of us left than I realized," said Jame to Jorin.

But as always she only looked for one, there, on the western side of this airy gallery. The familiar face smiled ruefully down at her through the fading light.

"Hello again, cousin," she said to it.

All the banners would eventually have to be rescued like so many treed cats, but only Aerulan was her immediate concern. How to get her down, though? Her banner hung on a small branch some thirty feet up, nothing between it and the ground but slick bark and air.

Hmmm . . . . Treed cats. Cats climbed trees. With claws.

Jame looked at her hands. She loathed even the sight of the ivory nails beneath those black gloves, the most obvious of her Shanir traits and the source of so much past grief. Moreover, she had been taught that to use them in any way whatsoever strengthened her bond to the third face of God: Regonereth, That-Which-Destroys. As when faced with a locked door at Gothregor, however, practicality won.

"Right," she said, stripping off her gloves and tucking them into her belt. "Here goes."

Soon she was well off the ground and climbing. How much farther? Tilting back her head to look, she saw Aerulan about ten feet above her . . . no, closer: the branch was bending, the banner's cord slipping.

"Aerulan, no!" she cried up at it. "Don't jump!"

The death banner plunged down on top of her. She scrabbled at its blinding folds with one hand, trying to hang on with the other, but the impact had jarred her loose. The next moment, she was slithering down the trunk with bark shredding under her nails, then in the air, falling, crashing through the silvery undergrowth, hitting the ground.

Darkness.

Well, that's it, thought Jame, *I'm dead.*

Then she realized that the tapestry still covered her face. Pushing it aside, she found herself nose to nose with an anxious ounce.

Rolled up, the banner made a long, surprisingly heavy bundle, which Jame slung across her back by its cord, shifting the food sack's strap so that the latter rode on her hip. She always seemed to be carrying around relics of the dead—although not as ostentatiously as her brother who, the previous fall, had ridden all the way to the Cataracts with the bones of Marc's sister in his saddlebag. Maybe no one could escape the past, but most people didn't get stuck with such tangible fragments of it. Still, this time Jame was glad of the company.

By now, dusk was falling. The air thickened with shadows which cloaked the color of the forest and hid whatever paths might run through it. With difficulty, Jame chewed a handful of dried fruit while Jorin grumbled over cheese rinds. Then she curled up among the roots of an oak and fell into a troubled sleep, the death banner spread over her for warmth, the ounce in her arms.

Dwar sleep would have been natural now. By fleeing the healer, she had tacitly decided to live with the face which Kallystine had given her. Still, every time the velvet dark yawned, she jerked back from it, half into the waking world. Confusedly, she remembered the last time she had fled injured, southward from her old home, the poison of a haunt's bite already at work in her savaged arm.

Poison: *Had* Kallystine's blade been tainted?

Betrayal: Who had sent the shadow assassins after her?

The moon rose, on the wane toward the quarter, faintly aglow through night mist in a cage of white branches. Dead wood against the lunar disc, white on white . . . she had dreamed of such a thing, sitting in her brother's chair. Darkness had flowed down those pale limbs, was there still, leaning against the trunk. No. That was only the last of the tree's bark. Where it had peeled away at eye level, however, two points of light glimmered mockingly.

Luminous moss, she told herself. *It feeds on decay.*

However, moss seldom has a face.

Out of the shadows, Bane smiled at her.

She knew she should be frightened, but Aerulan held her. Their eyes met over her head, Bane's silver-gray and Aerulan's too, like her own. It was, after all, a family trait. The shadow-man sketched an ironic bow, as if to say:

"If not now, later. I can wait."

The patches of light that had been his eyes seemed to blink. Then they fluttered away. Not moss. Moths.

"Later, what?" she cried after him. "Dammit, Bane, you're my b . . . ."

But the word died on her lips. She had evoked him by it before, but did he truly know that they were half-siblings? She had only guessed it herself during her last confrontation with Ishtier, after the mob had taken Bane off to the Mercy Seat.

"He trusted you!" she had shouted at the priest. *"Because you brought his mother, the Gray Lord's mistress, down out of the Haunted Lands, because he thought—and you let him think—that you were his father. But Ganth Gray Lord was alive when you deserted him, wasn't he? You're betrayed not only Bane but your lord as well. Coward, lack-faith, renegade . . . ."*

"And who are you to pronounce sentence on me?" the skull-faced priest had spat at her. *"Thief, whore, outcast . . . ."*

"The lord you betrayed was my father, the man consigned by you to torture on the Mercy Seat, my half-brother, and I—I am Jamethiel Priest's-Bane . . . ."

". . . WHO SHALL YET BE THY DOOM."

Somehow, for the second time, she had caused the God-voice which never lies to speak through the false priest's mouth, against his will. The boom of it filled her head. What had it called her?

"CHAMPION, FRATRICIDE, TYR-RIDAN."

. . . no, no, no . . . .

Then memory merged into nightmare as she slid uneasily back into sleep.

In the grip of his god, Ishtier had lost control of his temple. The power, set loose, spiralled outward, spreading fire and madness. Everything was burning—houses, people, the very air. In Judgment Square, the holocaust wind blew away piles of ash—all that remained of the mob that had stormed the Thieves' Guild palace in search of Dally's murderer. On the Mercy Seat sat a figure, charred black, the greasy smoke still seeping out of fissures in its skin. Its cinder-lump of a head was cocked as if listening.

From the hills about the immolated city came a yelping cry: "*Wha, wha, wha?*"

"*HA!*" boomed back the answer—and the thing on the Mercy Seat, the Burnt Man, rose to summon his pack of the burning damned so that they might hunt down one more to join their number, while the fratricide's blood trail was still fresh.

"No!" Jame gasped, waking with a start.

Aerulan's death banner, wrapped warmly about her, was covered with a dusting of snow which the wan sun had already begun to melt.

It was morning.

 **II**

THE HAZE of the previous day lingered, turning the sky the color of thin milk with the sun a dim opal afloat in it. By the latter at her back, seen intermittently through leaves, Jame knew that they were still going north. Soon high clouds swallowed it, however, and she was no longer certain.

The forest floor had leveled off. Upper foliage and undergrowth made the mountains' contours difficult to guess. At first, Jame thought that this wouldn't present a problem: after all, they had only to turn left and keep going eventually to hit the River Road. At some point between Gothregor and Falkirr, though, the Silver bent sharply westward, and then again before Wilden. To miss either turn would set them adrift in the folds of the hills. Ganth was said to have gotten lost within a mile of Gothregor on the night of the massacre. The Tishooo had brought him the screams, but he hadn't been able to find his way home until dawn. She was much farther into the wilderness now than he had been then.

They came out of the trees at last, opposite the rock face of a cliff crowned with flowering laurel. A self-important brook chattered over stones at its foot. Jame stopped in dismay. She had expected a clear path ahead with the mountain slope falling away to the left. They must have overshot the first turn. They were lost.

Then she focussed on the cliff face opposite. Stronger sunlight would have thrown its details into greater relief, but even so she thought she could trace an image: the front of a house, so low set that it seemed half-sunken

into the ground. Carved on its walls were a series of ovals
with circles in them—that crude, face-like symbol of
ancient power known as the *imu*. Serpentine forms in
stone rioted up the jambs and over the lintel.

It looked exactly like the Earth Wife's lodge in Peshtar.

When Jame took a step toward it, however, its details
changed with her new perspective, becoming merely
those of a weathered rock face. She had been thinking
about Mother Ragga only a moment ago. Her imagination must have supplied the rest. When she retreated,
however, there it was again—but not exactly as it had
been before: now, the rock slab of a door stood ajar.

It had been obvious in Peshtar that Mother Ragga had
special talents. Beyond her far-hearing, the *imu* medallion which her half-feral girl had given Jame had the
power to strip the skin from the face of a darkling
changer and to protect her in the Anarchies. However,
Jame had only thought of the Earth Wife herself as a
local wise-woman. To find the image of her lodge here
in the wilderness was . . . unsettling. She didn't think she
would investigate that door, or wait to see what might
emerge from it.

Anyway, the sight of the busy stream on its threshold
had given her an idea. This world might have some odd
aquatic conditions, from the great Chaos Maw, a whirlpool miles across on the edge of the Eastern Sea, to
patches of dead water off the Cape of the Lost where
ships sank like bricks; but one natural principle usually
applied: water descends. Eventually, this brook should
led them to the Silver.

They followed it well into the afternoon as it wound
downhill in a series of rapids, strengthened by freshets.
On its bank, Jorin surprised a woodchuck still groggy

with its winter's sleep and made quick work of it. Cheese rinds, it seemed, were not enough. At last, though a break in the trees, Jame saw a sprawling mass of stone below which she at first took for a natural formation. It wasn't. They had come out above and slightly north of Falkirr, the Brandan keep.

Jame had met Brant, Lord Brandan, at a memorial feast given by her brother after the battle at the Cataracts.

"The High Council needs to see you," Tori had said, *"to reassure themselves that, despite your bloodlines, you're only a pawn, not some dangerous new player entering their game of lineage and power."*

Since many people believed that she had appeared on the edge of the Escarpment with a flash and a loud bang, Jame supposed that reassurances were in order. Nonetheless, the dinner had been a disaster. She'd had to sit there in that hideous pink dress, not permitted to eat, drink, or (ancestors forbid) talk, while the lords had discussed her as if she were a prize filly about to turn brood mare and Torisen's responses had grown more and more curt as he realized, apparently for the first time, what they were both in for.

He might at least have been grateful, Jame thought, that (thanks to her) Lord Caineron had been off in his tent "not quite feeling in touch with things" and that none of those present had identified her hastily procured gown as having formerly belonged to an overweight Hurlen street-walker.

About the only thing Jame had to be thankful for during that endless dinner had been Lord Brandan's consideration. Not that he had ever spoken to her directly —that would have been the height of bad manners—but his remarks to the others had shown a respect for her feelings quite startling in that context. Of course, he could intend to press his own strong claim for her first contract: thirty-four years ago, he had begun to pay the enormous price demanded by Ganth for Aerulan's contract in perpetuity.

Be that as it may, the dip of his banner told her that Brandan hadn't yet returned from Kothifir.

Then too, she and his sister Brenwyr had parted damning each other.

Cursed be and cast out . . . .

She was out of Gothregor, all right, but cast how far? Under that kind of a malison, did one ever stop running?

No. She wouldn't think about that now. She would *not*.

They started down toward the Silver, quickly losing sight of Falkirr behind trees. The brook, now a tumultuous young river, tumbled beside them over stone ledges and around large, flat slabs. Curiously, when the latter diverted the water's course, the direct route was marked across their white surfaces as though some giant had flicked them with dripping hair. Along the wet lines, cracks had formed.

A scurfy little pine was using these fissures to cross the rock, its gnarled roots probing blindly ahead with the concentration of a mountaineer negotiating a sheer cliff-face. It looked like the desperate sort of shrub that finds itself seeded in shade, on the thinnest of soil, which now was using the first chance offered to escape. At the rock's edge it paused, roots like many jointed, arthritic toes flexing stiffly in the air; then it toppled over into the stream and was swept away, tumbling crown over root.

It occurred to Jame that she had just witnessed her first case of arboreal drift.

"Wha," said a voice behind her, barely audible above the water's roar. "Wha . . . wha . . . ."

For a moment, Jame froze. Then she hastily withdrew into the south bank trees, pulling Jorin with her.

No, it wasn't the Burning Ones of her dream but something almost as bad. Two men had emerged upstream on the water's far side—a Randir officer and a priest. The latter, very upset, was yapping questions at the former. The words carried imperfectly to the hidden listeners:

Why had the randon allowed . . . to escape? Did he realize *where* they were? . . . Brandan . . . trespassing . . . What would . . . say? *Where* were the dogs? *Wha . . . wha . . . wha . . .*

Jame shrank back. They must be hunting her. But how in Perimal's name had they known she was no longer at Gothregor, much less anywhere near here?

"*Woo! Woo!*"—baying now, deep-throated, bone-rattling.

Jorin began to growl, his fur rising in her grip.

Three hounds had come out of the trees opposite, straining on their leashes. Two were tall, black-coated lymers—loosely muzzled tracking dogs which seemed already to have caught the scent. Dwarfing them was the third, a steel-gray Molocar bitch, four feet high at the shoulder, of a battle breed whose jaws could shatter tempered spear-shafts. It was she who bayed, like a great bell tolling war. Hindered by the lymers and unhelped by the rest of the company (which kept well clear), the handler awkwardly tried to strap an iron muzzle on her. The Molocar flung it away and, with a contemptuous, sideways snap, crushed his skull. Baying, she plunged across the stream in a storm of spray, pursued by the freed lymers and Randirs' alarmed shouts.

Jorin bolted, with Jame a step behind. They cut westward through the trees, hoping to drown their scent in shallows downstream; but when they emerged below on a rocky overhang, the current beneath ran too fierce to risk. Damnation. They would have to make for Falkirr. From what the priest had said, the Brandan garrison wouldn't welcome Randir hunters on their land—but neither would they let her go her way after the intruders had been chased off.

As she hesitated, loath even now to give up her freedom, movement caught her eye. Down the rapids came a tall, golden willow.

At first, remembering the scrub pine, Jame thought that this much larger tree had also been swept away by the spring runoff. Then she saw that, ever so cautiously, it was walking down the steps. The bulk of its roots formed a fibrous mass which cushioned its descent. Pulling it along were its long fringe roots. The caps of the latter glistened with some kind of secretion which ate into whatever it touched, giving the tree innumerable toeholds. Its crown swayed with each step. Wands and narrow, shining leaves undulated like curtains of gold in the last direct sunlight of the day.

Something came crashing through the woods toward her. To her surprise, out of the undergrowth burst not one of the dogs but a young man.

He stopped short, panting, staring at her with wild, pale eyes set in a thin, white face. His hair was also white: A Shanir, wearing the brown robe of an acolyte.

"Highlord?" he whispered.

"No!" said Jame, remembering even as she spoke how on the battlefield at the Cataracts she had been repeatedly mistaken for her brother.

With a moan, the Shanir fell to his knees and began to beat his head against the stone. For a moment, Jame simply stared. She had never before seen someone deliberately try to brain himself. Then realization dawned.

"*You're* the one they're after!" she exclaimed. "Here, now: stop that!"

When he didn't, she seized his shoulders and forced him back on his heels. He swayed in her grasp, blinking blood out of unfocused eyes.

"You owe me no debt," he mumbled, "if you aren't willing to pay."

Sweet Trinity, now what? She ought to run, to leave this fugitive priestling to his own people—if he survived the dogs.

"Give me your robe," she snapped.

When he only gaped at her, she seized the shoulders of his garment and hauled it off over his head. He sprawled forward as it came free. For a moment she stared down at his emaciated back, the prominent ribs crisscrossed with welts. Then she jerked him to his feet and shoved him toward the curtain of golden leaves swaying past the cliff's edge.

"Get aboard. Try to find a dead branch to hang onto and watch out for those wands. It may not care for passengers. Move!"

Some of the glaze left his eyes and the corner of his mouth twitched. "Yes, sir."

"You too," said Jame to Jorin. "Go."

The hounds were in the woods, the two lymers perforce running silent, the Molocar bell-mouthed on the Shanir's trail. Jame backtracked some fifty feet, then darted off at a right angle due south, dragging the robe. Plunging down a steep slope with stones turning underfoot, clutching at bushes to slow her descent, she looked

back to see Jorin bounding over shrubbery after her. Try
telling a cat to do anything . . . !

At that moment, still looking backward, she collided
with someone, hard, and fell. They rolled down the slope,
tangled blind in the gown, bouncing over rocks and grap-
pling ineffectually with each other. At the bottom, she
kicked free. The garment floundered back, seeming to
wrestle with itself, and produced a tousled blond head,
apparently without a body.

"Right," Jame breathed to herself.

She should have guessed what had frightened the
birds along the River Road the previous day, passing by
unseen. At least the blade which the young assassin
waved nervously in her face was steel, not ivory. His
whistled summons wobbling shrilly, again and again; but
if the Guild Master heard, he didn't respond. After all,
this was still supposed to be a ritual blooding.

"Right," said Jame again, louder.

"P-please," the boy stammered in accented Kens.
"Please!"

Don't let me fail, he was really begging. *Let me make
this kill*.

Journeyman thief stared at apprentice assassin.
"Please? *Please?* You want it, you earn it!"

The boy lunged, desperate, inept. Hindered by Aerulan's banner slung across her back and the food sack on
her hip, she still caught his blade with ease in her *d'hen's*
full, reinforced sleeve and whipped it away. A water-
flowing move sent him head over heels after it, into a
cloud-of-thorn bush. There he floundered, *mere* cloth
ripping on barbs sharper than the blade after which he
frantically groped, pale skin turning red.

"*Dammit!*" said Jame, exasperated. "Didn't your precious master teach you *anything?*"

Jorin had been slinking around them, chirping anxiously at the copper smell of blood. When a muzzled lymer erupted from the undergrowth behind him, he rose on his toes and bounced into the hound's face through sheer fright. The beast retreated, trying to shake him off, uttering muffled yelps as feline claws raked his eyes.

Down the slope charged the second lymer, the Molocar bitch roaring on his heels like an avalanche.

With a cry to Jorin to follow, Jame bolted toward the stream. She heard the assassin thrash panic-stricken in the thorns, where he hadn't the sense to lie still, then his scream cut short by the crunch of jaws.

She burst out on a cliff's lip. The river curved beneath in a gorge, its northward course obscured by an opposite rock spur crowned with undergrowth.

Where was that willow? The air had thickened with twilight, all edges blurring, all colors melting in a molten haze. Downstream to the west, nothing. How fast could the damn thing travel, anyway? When she turned again to look eastward, the tree loomed over her like a shimmering hillock. An upper branch swooped over her head. Its trailing leafage swung into her. She found herself tangled up in it, off her feet, off the cliff. Golden leaves flattened against her eyes; supple wands fumbled about her throat.

Something crashed though them, knocking her free. Jorin. Falling, she grabbed for the ounce but caught a bough instead and clung to it for a moment, breathless. Then she scrambled inward to throw her arms around the trunk as to a mast, just out of the wands' hissing reach, as the tree swayed again like a ship in stormy seas. Looking down, she saw that the pale Shanir clung to a section of trunk well below her while Jorin balanced on a branch near him, wailing. Below, the burnished bole plunged down to the writhing serpent's knot of its roots.

Someone had scored the golden bark at eye-level—to mark this tree for spring harvest? Such resilient wood must be much prized. It would probably long since have been cut if the Riverland weren't so stripped of workers. Small wonder, then, that when the sap had begun to run, so had the tree, hell-bent on escape. The creek bed must simply have provided the easiest route.

The willow's draperies swung forward, then back, far enough to give Jame a glimpse ahead. She saw the Silver a bare sixty feet away and something else, much closer.

"Oh, my God," she breathed, and then shouted in warning to those beneath her, "Low bridge!"

The willow swayed forward again, more violently, gaining momentum. Its upper wands cracked against the water's surface like whips. It reared back, trunk groaning, foliage a golden blur, over and down.

The second forward swing had nearly dislodged Jame, who had only kept her grip by wrapping her legs around the trunk and sinking her nails into its sensitive bark. When the upper boughs crashed over backward, she was pinned beneath them, under water whose coldness shocked out her breath.

The trunk quivered against her like a bent bow, its water-laden foliage keeping its crown submerged. The bridge which spanned the creek's mouth, carrying the River Road on its back, must be overhead by now. Yes. Here came the swift current of the Silver, striking her from the right, nearly plucking her loose. Above, the water glowed with the molten light of the sky, willow wands streaming black against it. Below, leaves shone gold against the pebbled darkness of the river bed.

Don't panic! she told herself, fighting the desperate compulsion to breathe. *It* can't *stay bent like this for long . . . !*

Under those pebbles seemed to be a pattern as if of overlapping shields. A trick of light and water? They *couldn't* be rising and falling as though with some monstrous, slow respiration.

Then suddenly she was flying upward, through water, through leaves, through air, flung by the tree's recoil across the river—straight into the boughs of a giant white cedar which leaned out from the opposite bank.

Her impression afterward was that the evergreen had carefully rolled her from branch to branch down to the ground. At least, that was where she found herself an unguessed-at time later, sitting on a bed of pine needles, looking at her hands. Half-frozen fingers stung as sensation returned to them and the nails ached. The stitching at the gloves' tips had been ripped out.

A slope of feathery ferns stretched from the river's edge up to a band of sumac, a wide swath of churned earth cut through it by the willow's passage. Something was coming down toward her under the fronds. Jorin's head popped up, all long neck, pricked ears, and wide, anxious eyes. The moment she saw him, he gave an excited bleat and bounded down to her. She hugged him, noting that his silver-gilt fur was barely damp. Presumably, the lower section of the willow's trunk had remained in an arch above the water. Her own god might not give a damn about her, but something in the universe apparently looked after cats and idiots.

Speaking of the latter, where was that pale, young man?

They found him a few minutes later, in some difficulty. Dismounting from the willow, he had stepped into its

muddy wake and was now being slowly carried off by
the sumac as it took advantage of the disturbed earth to
seek sunnier slopes.

"I had no idea that the Riverland could be so lively,"
said Jame, regarding him across the crawling belt of
trees. "Not taking root, are you?"

"I-it's more a case of the roots taking me. I sank in a-
and they wrapped around my ankles."

He tottered, waving thin arms to keep his balance,
a half-naked scarecrow all bones and pale skin with a
preternaturally white thatch of hair.

A Shanir. A priestling. She ought to let him drift on
with the arboreal tide until his own people fished him
out—but if she had understood correctly, what debt
could her brother owe such flotsam as this which he
hadn't been willing to pay?

Jame sighed. "Hold on a minute."

The hillside was studded with large rocks, some of
which had been thrust aside by the willow and were now
slowly sinking in its wake. The sumacs' runners snaked
around them. Jame began to thread her way through the
maze of slender trunks, jumping from stone to stone.
Forgetting Aerulan's extra width on her back, she
became wedged between close-set trees and freed herself by pricking their thin bark. As they recoiled, the
runners of the whole clump writhed like serpents in the
earth. The Shanir bit back a cry of pain.

"I'd come to think," said Jame sourly, "that my house
had first claim to any situation this absurd. Who are you,
priest-bait, to trespass?"

The pale young man flushed.

"Kindrie," he blurted out defiantly. "My name is
Kindrie."

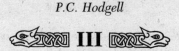

III

THE MOMENT he had spoken, Kindrie felt the heat in his face chill with dismay. Anonymity had been his last defense. But then he had felt perilously off balance ever since encountering this masked stranger, in a way which had nothing to do with subsequently being tossed into a tree, swept across a river, and dumped in a bog. His first impression that he had run into the Highlord was, of course, ridiculous. Somewhere, though, he *had* met this peculiar boy before, under alarming circumstances.

"Kindrie," the other repeated, as if he too were fishing for memories. "I've heard of you. You were with the Kencyr Host at the Cataracts. What in Perimal's name are you doing here?"

"Sinking."

"Uh . . . yes." The stranger glanced down at the rock on which he stood. "So am I, if not quite as fast. Look, I think I can pull you up here with me, and then it's an easy jump to the far side. Give me your hand."

Kindrie hesitated. Under the split tips of the other's glove, something glowered bone-white. Reluctantly, he reached out, and was caught in a grip like sheathed ice.

The shock of it made his senses lurch.

Cold. So cold . . . and dark.

Overhead, not the canopy of sumac leaves but far, far up, a fire-broken roof with verdigris lightning lacing the sky's greater darkness above. Beneath, a vast hall, paved with stone whose green veins pulsed cold with each sullen, silent flash. Death banners lined its walls, rank after rank. Threadbare hands clutched together tattered clothing; slashed, disintegrating faces regarded him slyly askance, snickering against cold stone.

Got you now, healer . . . .

Ancestors preserve him. The touch of those bare finger tips had plunged him straight into the other's soul . . . but he hadn't the strength to deal with an image so complex, so foul. He hadn't the courage. He must get out. Now.

The flash of something white . . . .

CRACK.

He found himself lying on the ground a dozen feet beyond the willow's wake, staring up at cracks of twilight between black oak leaves. His jaw throbbed. The stranger was staring at him, fists still clenched but forgotten.

"Sweet Trinity. I can't have hit you *that* hard."

Kindrie struggled up on an elbow. He saw that he had not only been knocked across a clearing but clean out of his boots, which the sumac had kept.

"You didn't," he said confusedly. "That is, you did, but . . . ." How to explain the tremendous power of that soul-image to protect itself, or his own involuntary response, as though to a lightning strike? "God, you've got strong defences!"

"I should hope so. Touch me like that again, priest, and I'll knock you half way to the Cataracts!"

"I am *not* a priest . . . and what's the matter with your face?"

They stared at each other.

"You're the healer that the Priests' College was sending to Gothregor."

"And you're the mad girl I was sent to heal."

"Mad? God's claws, I begin to think so! Here I am, on the run from a Wilden healer, and he runs bang into me. Likewise an incompetent assassin, a wandering death banner, a shadow demon, a Randir search party, and a walking tree. What *is* this place—the crossroad of the worlds?"

Kindrie didn't know what she was raving about, or care. It was the rising level of her voice which scared him. "Oh, please!" he cried. "We aren't far from the river. They'll hear you!"

That sobered her instantly. "I doubt they'll guess that we forded by tree, but still . . . ." She hesitated, then said grudgingly, "It will be dark soon. You can make camp with me tonight, if you like, as far from here as possible."

Kindrie's impulse was to run until he dropped, away from both his pursuers and this unnatural female; but daylight *was* fading rapidly, and this wilderness terrified him. He gave a small, reluctant nod.

"All right, then," said the other, and jumped to solid ground.

The ounce had been waiting with growing impatience on the far side of the drifting grove. He didn't attempt to cross, however, until his mistress turned to look at him . . . no, at the tricky path which he must negotiate. Kindrie suddenly realized that the beast was blind, that he was using the girl's eyes to see his way. He was *bound* to her. Of all the damning things which Kindrie had been told at Wilden about the Highlord's sister, no one had mentioned that, like Kindrie himself, she was Shanir.

Above the willow's path, they struck the west bank's New Road and followed it northward until a ravine opening above it provided shelter sufficient to hide a fire.

While Kindrie held thin hands out to the small blaze which she had kindled, the Knorth draped her sodden jacket over a nearby rock. Then, to his surprise, she unrolled a death banner and also spread it out to dry, its gently smiling face turned toward the warmth. It seemed to watch them benignly as they sat on opposite sides of the fire, regarding each other warily over the flames and eating winter-shrivelled apples. The ounce, offered cheese, scratched the ground around it and trotted purposefully off into the dark. Watching the cat's mistress gingerly chew her own dinner, Kindrie remembered the host of disfigured dead in her soul-image and shivered.

"I heard about you at the Cataracts," she said, so suddenly that he jumped. "You grew up in the Priests' College at Wilden, but ran away to serve first Lord Caineron and then Ardeth. You were free. Why did you go back?"

"It wasn't my idea," snapped Kindrie, despite his resolve to keep quiet. "Tending the wounded, I-I overtired myself and collapsed. When I woke, I was back at Wilden. It seems that Ardeth's people didn't know what else to do, with their lord off bone-hunting in the Southern Wastes and a sick healer on their hands."

"And Ardeth let you stay there all winter?"

Kindrie winced. "H-he had other concerns, I suppose. His dead son Pereden, your brother, and Kothifir is so far away . . . ."

"Awkward to apply pressure at a distance, I agree, but still . . . ! And Tori had nothing to say about this either?"

"The Highlord owes me no debts if he isn't willing to pay!"

"Proud," she said, considering him, "and devious, to imply and deny a debt in the same breath. Whatever he owes you, priestling, he owes. But that's his business. So. Winter passes, a call comes to Wilden for a healer, and you take the opportunity to bolt."

For a moment, she was silent, absently combing out tangled hair with long, black-sheathed fingers. One hand stole to her injured cheek.

Don't ask me to heal you, he silently pled. *Don't, for both our sakes!*

The hand dropped.

"So. You're free again. What next?"

"I . . . don't know."

From that terrible waking in Wilden the previous winter, he had fled to the most secret corner of his soul-image to hide, to wait for the rescue which had never come. Three years ago, the priests would have left him alone, mistaking his blank stare for that of the half-wit which they had always believed him to be. Now they knew better. Was it only yesterday that they had finally tricked him into emerging? And then . . . and then . . . .

Yes, he was out of their hands, but free? Not after what they had done to him. Perhaps never again.

"Stop that!"

He blinked, surprised to find the Knorth kneeling in front of him, gripping his clenched fists through the protection of the food sack. His head hurt.

"God's teeth and toenails. I've never met anyone so determined to beat in his own brains. What is wrong with you?"

"Leave me alone!"

He wrenched free, lashed out at her clumsily, and fell on his face as she slipped aside.

"Leave me alone," he said again, his voice muffled, and began to cry.

"Sweet Trinity," he heard her mutter. "And I thought *I* was a mess." A moment later, she dropped her still damp jacket over his bare shoulders.

Kindness, he thought. *If I accept that, I'll break down completely.*

He rolled over to look up at the Knorth. "How does your brother feel," he said, "about you being Shanir?"

Silver flared in the gray eyes above him. Kindrie flinched, guessing too late that the ability to mind-bond with an ounce might be the least of the other's Shanir attributes. If her powers were great, however, so was her control. Silver tarnished to gray.

"What do *you* think?" she said flatly, and returned to her side of the fire.

Kindrie answered her silently, in the darkness behind his squeezed shut eyes: *I think it may kill him.*

FRATRICIDE.

The God-voice had broken its silence of over two thousand years to call the Highlord's sister that, or so the priest with the skull-like face and the maimed hand had told Kindrie yesterday. Kindrie hadn't disbelieved it—how could one doubt the Voice of God when it burned its way like acid out of some unwilling throat?—but now . . . !

On the march to the Cataracts, Torisen had fallen into one of his mysterious nightmares and no one had been able to wake him from it. At Ardeth's insistence, Kindrie had entered the Highlord's sleeping mind to try to help. There he had stumbled across the soul-image of the blighted house with the vast death banner hall which he now realized had not been Torisen's at all but his sister's. It had apparently been poisoning the sleeping man. Kindrie had exorcised it, but he didn't trust his power to banish such a thing indefinitely. Given Torisen's violent antipathy to all Shanir, he might have been stricken by the mere knowledge that his sister was one. That prejudice, after all, was what prevented him from honoring his debts to Kindrie. Those he might shrug off, but not a sister's claims. And then . . . and then . . . .

"*She will destroy him,*" that death's-head Ishtier had hissed, leaning close, breathing the dregs of his winter-long sickness into Kindrie's face, "*unless you . . . er . . . render her harmless, shall we say? Yes, you, boy. No one else had been able to get close enough. But a healer's touch, ah, nothing comes closer than that.*"

B-but he *was* a healer. How could he ever hurt someone the way he himself had been hurt?

"*Just a little change in your soul-image, boy. It was clever of you to choose the Priests' College itself as the external metaphor of your soul. My colleagues thought they had you locked up here, mind as well as body. They didn't know about that image hidden within an image, that secret garden where Lady Rawneth confined you most of your childhood when the rest of us thought you lack-witted, But now m'lady has traded that secret to me. I could destroy your pathetic little bolt-hole—uproot the comfrey and heart's-ease, sow the ground with salt. Instead, I will give you a chance to regain it. We have taught you how to read soul-images, boy. Read the Knorth's to learn where she has hidden the thing which she stole from me, and then deal with her as she deserves, or you will never be at peace again.*"

Then they had sent him out with an escort of priests and Randir guards, bound for Gothregor, so confident he was broken that they hadn't bothered to watch him. What that skull-faced Ishtier had done to him was obscene, but so was what the priest wanted him to do. So he had run—straight into the very person he had been trying to avoid just as she, for some reason, had been fleeing him.

In his mind, he was still running. The outer dimension of his soul was that long corridor which spiraled down into the subterranean Priests' College, past dim classrooms where masters had beaten him, past dank dormitories where he had learned all shades of violation but one. None of that had mattered, though, while his inner spirit remained a refuge, inviolate. Behind one of the imagined doors was the secret room where the Randir Matriarch had confined him as a lesser woman might have locked a child in a dark closet. Where he had gotten the idea for the moon garden which had transformed Rawneth's prison into a sanctuary and the source of his strength, he didn't know. He might gladly have stayed there forever, even after his jailer stopped bothering to lock him in. However, three years ago he had overheard angry voices outside the door of his secret soul, saying that a Knorth was Highlord again.

"But I'm part Knorth too," he had said, blinking at the astonished priests.

Now Ishtier had hidden that door, and he was trapped in the outer dimension of his soul, in that corridor with its stale stench of warped, wasted lives down which he endlessly ran, pursued by the fear that to save Torisen he might have to do the terrible thing demanded of him, beating his fists against locked door after door as he passed, searching for the one that opened into peace.

Let me in, let me in, let me in . . . .

 **IV**

THE PRIESTLING had begun feebly to strike his head again, although he was asleep. Jame tossed aside all the rocks within his reach, then picked up the empty food sack. At least she had guessed right there: only direct contact with the Shanir triggered that horror which she had felt in the sumac grove, as if she were being turned inside out. Like most people, she had no idea what her own soul-image was, nor did she care to, when a mere touch of it left such a foulness in her mind, like the foretaste of vomit.

You've lived in ignorance so far, she told herself. *This is no time to stop.*

Scattered provisions rolled about underfoot. Apples, dried fruit . . . cheese.

Blind Jorin had never had much luck hunting prey which she couldn't see, except when the Arrin-ken Immalai had helped him. She would keep these despised rinds against his return, hoping that he at least wouldn't get lost.

Their meager rations regathered, Jame sat down again on her side of the fire, took a small sewing kit from an inner pocket of her *d'hen*, and began awkwardly to stitch up her split gloves, while still wearing them. A quarter inch at the tips, however, she left open. Marc had suggested that once. Only an idiot would forgo any advantage now, the cost be damned.

Nonetheless, her bare nails must never touch that damn Shanir again.

Jame swore as the needle slipped, pricking her finger.

The Old Blood, she thought sourly, licking a drop of it. *The God-chosen, the Shanir.*

How could one hate what one oneself was? Easily. Look at Torisen—except he didn't know he was a Shanir blood-binder and far-seer. Look at this healer, then, who kept trying to hurt himself. As far back as the Cataracts, hadn't he worked himself into a coma trying to help the wounded?

Help . . . .

Sore as her face still was, she no longer felt that trace of heat which could either have been infection or Kallystine's parting gift. Could that be the healer's work? She could ask him to do more. Even now, she didn't have to be scarred for life . . . .

No. He was priest-trained and she was Priest's-bane.

"Your name is an omen in itself," Marc had once said. *"Servants of God, any god, will be bad luck to you, and you to them."*

True enough. She remembered Ishtier, gibbering, trying to gnaw off the hand with which he had touched the Book Bound in Pale Leather. Some people deserved all the bad luck they got.

Did this young man, though? Her brother would hardly tell her what debt he owed to another Shanir. He had let one thing slip, though: Kindrie had a Knorth grandmother. Tori hadn't asked her name. The very idea must have made his skin crawl, as it did Jame's now—not that such distant, bone-kinship could matter much. If it had, prejudice aside, Tori would have extended the protection of their house to the healer long ago.

But with Tori hiding in Kothifir, Kindrie was her problem. Left on his own, he would surely be recaptured by the priests, whom he would tell about her. Every day that folk assumed she was still hiding in Gothregor increased her chance of success at Restormir.

To travel with a priest, though, past Wilden . . .

Wha . . . ooo, said the wind, keening down the ravine, making the little fire dance. *Wha . . . wha . . . oooo*.

No. It wasn't those others, flame-mouthed Merikit avengers of the dead, on her trail from Tai-tastigon.

Fratricide.

No.

The wind died and the fire sank. Jame sat beside it, waiting for her heart to stop pounding. It seemed to her, though, that she could still hear fragments of sound—*singing*—close by. Trinity. Could their pursuers have camped almost on top of them?

Thinking that they were probably at the mouth of the ravine, just off the road, she climbed to the pine coppice above. With the stars overcast and the moon not yet risen, it was too dark under the trees even for her excellent night-vision. Oh, for Jorin's keen nose and ears, although her use of both had been limited recently. She crept forward through crusts of sheltered snow toward the rocky beak which overhung the road, then lay flat on an aromatic bed of needles at the edge of the trees to wait for her eyes to adjust.

The only sound now was the wind soughing through the branches overhead. The only light came from below. Down the New Road drifted faintly glowing forms which Jame recognized as ghost-walkers, man-shaped patches of weirding mist which were said to precede a weirdingstrom. She herself had never seen weirding before, but had heard of its strange properties. Travellers caught in it had been known to emerge hundreds of miles away, if at all. Singers claimed that the ghost-walkers were those whom the mist had trapped, doomed to wander forever in its clammy clutch like the souls of the unburnt dead.

The wind momentarily died. The ghostly procession drifted to a stop.

In that lull, Jame smelled the unmistakable reek of human sweat.

A sudden, rasping snore made her jump nearly out of her boots. It ended with a loud snort. Not a dozen feet away, a dark shape which she had taken for a boulder rose, stretched, and scratched itself. It was a large, naked Merikit, a senior of his tribe to judge by the profusion of his braids, but so smeared with charcoal as to be almost one with the night. At his bare feet was a small, ceremonial fire, set but not lit. He muttered rapidly through the chant which she had heard before, as if his unintended nap had made him lose his place, then in ringing tones addressed the final lines to the fire, which made no discernible response. Satisfied nonetheless, the big man shouldered his sack with a grunt and scrambled down to the road. The wind had picked up again, the ghost-walkers resuming their southward drift. Catching up with one, he disappeared into it.

Jame blinked. Was she dreaming? In the morning, she might think so, unless . . . . In among the fire's pale kindling was an cinder shaped like a charred, human finger bone.

Proof, she thought, and pocketed it.

 **V**

MORNING DAWNED gray and chill, the fifty-seventh of spring, three days before Summer Eve.

"I had such a strange dream last night," said Jame, sleepily, to Aerulan.

As usual, her cousin didn't answer, but her warm arms gave a questioning hug.

"Well, first there was this hairy, naked man, covered with charcoal as if he'd fallen into a fire. He turned. His face had been burnt off and his eyes had boiled away. Then his charred flesh crumbled and his black bones clattered down at my feet. A cold wind scattered fragments of skin like black moths. I couldn't get the taste of them off my lips. But then I forgot about that, because there was something behind me. Such a chill darkness, big as a mountain, eyes like caverns . . . . No. Like the empty sockets of an Arrin-ken blinded with live coals in the Master's hall, somehow escaped alive. The whole Snowthorn range was one huge, crouching cat, and I was under its paw.

"*In the Ebonbane, by the chasm, you escaped my judgment*, it said in my mind. So cold. So desperately bitter, like a winter wind flecked with burning. *But these mountains are mine.*

"I wanted to argue as I did with Immalai, to say that I act only as I must to survive with honor, with precious little help from any of his kind . . . .

"But Graykin kept distracting me. All this time, you see, I could hear him whimpering. I know he's in desperate trouble and that it's my duty to get him out, but he nags and nags and nags until I could hit him! At least, though, he's still alive . . . .

"Oh. I forgot: you aren't, are you?"

Remembering that, she woke, to the warm embrace of Aerulan's death banner and an aching sense of loss.

There are so few of us left . . . .

Sometime during the night, Jorin had crept under the tapestry and now slept curled up as close to her as he could, his head tucked under her chin. Stroking him, she noted by the tight swell of his stomach that he had eaten well. Her hand disturbed a strange scent on his fur, musky and wild, like the Arrin-ken Immalai but with a faint reek of singed hair.

The burnt cat . . . had that been a dream, or the brush of her sleeping mind against Jorin's as the blind taught the blind to hunt? An Arrin-ken might well help a "little brother"—it had happened before—but not all those great, immortal beasts were as well disposed toward her as Immalai had been, nor was she still in his territory. More than one voice in that chorus by the Ebonbane chasm had wanted her to jump.

Jorin began to growl in his sleep.

"Hey!" said Jame.

The ounce snapped at her. She lay very still with his teeth through the collar of her woolen shirt, his breath hot against her throat. His eyes, seen aslant, looked as black as holes in rotten ice.

"Heyyyy," she said again, half crooning.

Jorin shivered, let go, and began apologetically to lick her chin. His tongue was very rough.

"Kitten," she said, fending him off, "you've been in bad company."

Throughout this, the Shanir hadn't stirred although his pale eyes were open. When urged, he sat up listlessly.

Was this despair, or an inward-turning so complete that it left no attention to spare? Goosebumps marched unheeded up his thin arms. She pulled off her outer shirt with its torn collar and put it on him, taking care to touch his bare skin only with her gloves. Linen undershirt and flash-blade's *d'hen* would do for her. The latter, especially, she had no intention of putting aside while the master assassin might still be after her, slight protection as it would be against the Ivory Knife.

As for her dreams, Graykin's crying had at least convinced her that if she arrived at Restormir with a healer in tow, so much the better. Luckily, getting Kindrie to return the way he had come proved easy: When she turned him left onto the New Road and gave him a push, he stumbled northward without seeming to notice which way he went or to care.

Patches of mist still drifted down the valley, but without the ghost-walkers' definition. Had that been a dream too? In Jame's pocket, though, was the odd-shaped cinder. She would keep it, she thought, to remind herself that in this wilderness the strangest of things might be real.

By day, at least, her sense of Bane and the blind Arrinken waned. After all, they were both Kencyr, as alien to this world as she herself, even if the latter marked this whole mountain range for his own as Immalai had the Ebonbane or the lords this valley. The land might not be theirs to claim. Anyway, thought Jame, the burnt cat probably didn't even exist. Dreams had played tricks on her before.

So had her imagination, come to that, and so it might be now: throughout the day, she kept catching half-glimpses of the Earth Wife's lodge. Never again did it appear as clearly as it had on the cliff-face. An arrangement of leaves, or bark, or shadow seen askance would merely suggest its carved lintel or *imu* decked walls, gone when regarded directly. It was only her nerves, Jame decided. How likely was it, after all, that a house should be keeping pace with her through this wilderness? In that case, though, she wished her imagination were less vivid: with each imagined glimpse, that shadowed door had crept farther open.

For the most part, the roadway was set well back from the river so that trees and undergrowth hid it from the opposite bank. Nonetheless, Jame would again have sought a higher, more obscure path if she hadn't been traveling with someone whose boots had been eaten the previous day by a grove of trees. Presumably, the healer could repair his own injuries. That didn't prevent him from sustaining them first, though, nor did it help that he paid no attention where he was stepping. Regarding the trail of bloody footprints behind them, Jame wondered if she would have the heart to drag him all the way to Restormir.

The New Road connected Kraggen, Shadow Rock, Valantir, and Restormir, the home keeps respectively of the Coman, Danior, Jaran, and Caineron. Shadow Rock, sister keep to Wilden, couldn't be far ahead. The east bank was already stripped of trees by Randir foragers and scored with erosion. Still, because of the Shanir's shambling pace they were forced at nightfall to made camp short of the Danior fortress.

Kindrie fell asleep at once, wrapped in Aerulan's banner. Jame sat up to tend the fire and wait for Jorin, who had again scorned the cheese rinds and slipped away when her back was turned. If he learned more self-reliance, she told herself, that was good, regardless of who taught him.

The thought of such dark instruction reminded her of Bane.

"*For such a clever person,*" he had said to her, moments before the mob had come to get him, "*you are remarkably ignorant. What a pity I shall never have the chance to educate you.*"

He might try yet.

Memories: his shadowy figure watching from an upper window as the half-flayed body of a child was pulled from the River Tone below. Later: "*There's a rumor that since you joined the Thieves' Guild Bane has given up young boys.*" Later still, Bane at the Res aB'tyrr, extolling the freedom of the abyss while his bullies held the inn's staff captive: "*The weight of honor twists us,*" he had said. "*Better to let it go, to fall away from all restraint . . . that is the course for you, as for me.*"

"*I don't understand you at all!*" she had cried, and he had answered with that slow, secret smile of his:

"*You know me as well as you know yourself.*"

Wind ruffled the horse-chestnuts above the hollow where they had camped. Rising sap traced the leaves' primary veins with faint luminescence, so that each defined its movements in the dark by a ghostly, seven-fingered dance.

"Ssssaaa . . ." breathed the wind, and the trees fluttered their innumerable hands. "Ssssssaaaaa . . ."

—or was that "*Thaaaa . . . ?*"

No.

Thoughts of the Burning Ones, Bane, or the blind Arrin-ken were all dangerous, apt like the smell of blood to draw that which she most feared.

Jame leaned forward to put more wood on the fire. Across the sinking flames, she looked directly into the cool silver of Bane's eyes.

He lay stretched out on the ground, propped lazily on an elbow. Firelight caught the dark bronze of scale armor made of last season's oak leaves. They rustled as he breathed.

"*Thaaaaa . . .*" sighed something under the trees which was not the wind.

The half-burnt sticks of the fire scattered as something thrust up through them. Jame stared at what, for an instant, she took to be an overbalanced log. But logs don't have fingers, charred black as these were, and logs don't grab wrists. It jerked her hand downward. She could feel the heat of the quickening flames through her glove, as well as the crushing pressure of the Burnt Man's grip. Kin-slayers were his special prey, and this time she was without Aerulan's protection. Her finger tips began to smolder. She remembered the story of a Merikit fratricide who had been pulled through a campfire into the ground beneath. All his companions could save had been a boot, with his foot still in it.

Bane watched, expressionless now, his eyes reflecting only fire. Had none of his dubious humanity survived? Was he now purely the demon which Ishtier had sought to create? But he had crossed the running water of the Silver, as no demon could have done. Perhaps he could still be reached.

"Your choice, b-brother."

An absolute stillness came over the figure opposite. He hadn't known, hadn't even guessed, but Jame could feel the conviction of it sink in, as it had with her in the Tastigon temple. For a moment, they stared at each other. Then he threw back his head and began silently to laugh.

The chestnuts cast up their hands—*aahhhh*!—as a gust of wind swept into the hollow, fanning flames, rattling dry leaves. Fragments of Bane's armor whirled into the fire. The chestnuts beat at the ascending sparks. Jame was still braced against the Burnt Man's pull, with fiery tongues leaping up toward her sleeve. Bane continued to laugh, even as the wind began to scatter him like autumn's memory.

"Choose, dammit!"

His laughter died. He looked at her, expressionless again, and then leaned forward. Between the flares of firelight, his face dissolved into shadow, but she could read his lips:

"... *my choice, then: no blood-price, sister* ...."

At his touch, the charred thing gripping her wrist crumbled and a quick leap of flame kindled the remains of his leaf shell. Suddenly released, Jame caught only the glimpse of a man-shape in flames, rising, as she went over backward.

"Ssssaaa ...." said the wind, and departed with leaf ash on its breath.

Beyond the fire, no one watched.

Sweet Trinity. Thought Jame, sitting up, dazed. *Did I fall asleep after all?*

But her wrist still hurt. On the black leather of the glove were the ashy prints of four fingers and a thumb.

VI

JORIN TROTTED BACK into camp just before dawn, smelling of nothing worse than catmint and bringing the conciliatory gift of a dead vole.

Day broke, with no visible sunrise. Clouds cut short the mountains, pushed along by a steady wind from the north. White birds ghosted southward under the overcast and deer drifted after them across the upper meadows, in and out of clouds. At some point, morning became afternoon. Day had begun almost imperceptibly to wane when veils of luminous mist came sailing down the valley, some low enough to brush along its floor.

"That's weirding," said Kindrie nervously. "You don't want to touch it."

A bank drifted past, leaving empty a bush which a moment before had been raucous with quarreling blue jays.

"Uh, right," said Jame.

She was glad that the healer was taking notice again, if only because his sleepwalker's pace had driven her half wild. Graykin's crying had haunted her dreams again last night, as forlorn as that of a lost child. Time was running out. Therefore, when Kindrie stumbled back toward somnambulance, she ruthlessly prodded him awake again with questions.

"You told the Highlord that you had a Knorth grandmother. What was her name?"

"Telarien, I think," he said vaguely.

"You *think*?" she demanded, silently swearing: The name meant nothing to her.

Kindrie flushed. "Lady Rawneth said that once, when she didn't know I could hear her."

Now, *that* name made Jame's eyebrows rise under her mask. Rawneth: the Randir Matriarch, Kallystine's great-aunt, the so-called Witch of Wilden. High company for a lowly acolyte.

"Did she name anyone else? Mother, father, family cat?"

"No! You aren't supposed to have any kin at all when you're a b-b . . . ."

"A bastard?"

Kindrie turned and limped hastily away, the tips of his ears scarlet through the white thatch of his hair.

Hmmmm, thought Jame, following him. That was the second case of bastardy she had heard about in the past four days, among a people who rarely misbred. Wouldn't it be curious if *he* were Tieri's unfortunate child, the Knorth Bastard? But no: one maternal grandmother didn't make a Knorth. Fortunately. The last thing she wanted, less even than a semi-demonic half-brother, was a priestling first cousin.

Still, she wondered briefly who Tieri's mother had been.

Ugh. Tori was right: better not to know. Change the topic.

To her own surprise, she heard herself ask, "What can you tell me about the God-voice?"

The Shanir turned and stared at her. "Why should you ask about *that*?"

Why indeed? Because . . . because sometime since Ishtier had passed on the Voice's judgment to her in Tai-tastigon, she had heard something like it again. Recently. But what . . . and where?

"All right," she said, dodging his question, "this is what I do know: It's the Voice of God—supposedly; it speaks through whomever it pleases, often in riddles; it never lies. What else, priest?"

"I am *not* a priest!"

"D'you mean, then, that you don't know anything?"

"I bet I know more than you do!" Kindrie snapped.

That might even be true, he thought. Locked in the garden of his soul, listening at the door, he had eavesdropped not only on Rawneth but on the priests as they discussed secrets which they never dreamed he overheard, much less understood. Suddenly, he couldn't bear that this hateful Knorth should think him as stupid as the Priests' College had.

"Of course," he said, trying to sound superior, "we've always had indirect contact with our god through the Shanir. Oracles, maledights, berserkers . . . ."

"Healers?"

"Er . . . yes, I suppose. But the first time the God-voice spoke was on this world, just after the Fall. The Arrin-ken had made Glendar Highlord in place of his brother Gerridon, Master of Knorth. The priests dissented. They claimed that all the lords had failed in their duty by letting such a disaster happen and that we should start afresh on Rathillien, as a hierocracy."

"Ancestors forbid!"

"It might not have been so bad a thing. Whatever the priests are like now, on other threshold worlds they used the power of the temples to help the Shanir defend our people. They were champions."

"Ha!"

"You've got to understand," he heard himself plead, as if defending his tormentors somehow made bearable when they had done to him. "Once it was a noble thing to be a priest. They performed a vital service, without which we would long since have been destroyed. Then came the Fall and flight to this world, with the lords blaming all Shanir, hieratic and secular, because Gerridon and the Dream-weaver were of the Old Blood. Worse, every other time we've had to retreat, we've found the Kencyr temples waiting for us on the next threshold world. This time, for some reason, their construction was incomplete. So the priests found themselves not only under attack by the High Council, which had always wanted them out of politics, but also cut off from the full power of their god. How were they supposed to defend themselves?"

"Apparently, by trying to replace the Highlord with a High Priest. Your people have never lacked nerve."

"*My* people . . . ! Well, nerve was no defense against the Voice, which spoke for the first time through the High Priest to denounce his ambitions, destroying him in the process. The College thinks that since this world's temples were never finished, the god-power found a different channel—one that, for a time, actually listened and gave judgments wrapped in riddles, which the Arrinken tried to solve. Then came one that they couldn't: '*Fear the One, await the Three, seek the Four.*'"

"Oh, that's helpful," said Jame. "Nearly everything in the Kencyrath comes in threes: The faces of God, the Tyr-ridan, the three times three major houses and temples."

The One might conceivably be Gerridon, she thought, under pressure to become the Voice of Perimal Darkling, darkness articulate, as the Tyr-ridan might ultimately become that of the Three-Faced God.

"But what on earth," she wondered out-loud, "comes in fours?"

"That's the big mystery. The Arrin-ken set out to solve it two thousand years ago, and haven't been heard from since. Neither has the Voice, until recently."

"I thought they left out of disgust with the Highborn."

"That was part of it. The God-voice offered an excuse to decamp, but they also took it as an order. Two thousand years without justice . . . . I wish they would come back."

Someday, Immalai had said, *someone will call us. It might even be you.*

Jame thought of the blind Arrin-ken, and shivered. Some judgements were best deferred.

"The One, the Three, and the Four," she repeated. "What comes in fours, besides the Senetha and Senethar?"

"The elements," Kindrie suggested. "The seasons, the phases of the moon from full to dark, the fingers on Lord Ishtier's left hand . . . ."

"*What?*"

He flinched away, as if from a blow.

"Look, I apologize for shouting more or less in your ear, but what in Perimal's name do you know about that forsworn renegade, Ishtier?"

"L-lord Ishtier has been at the Priests' College all winter, ever since the mission returned from Tai-tastigon with him. H-he was ill until recently. D-did you say 'renegade?' "

"Sweet Trinity, yes. Don't the other priests know?"

They don't, Jame thought, reading Kindrie's confused expression. Ishtier must have regained sufficient wits to lie to them. The mind boggled at that. The loss of honor

was in itself so unthinkable that one forgot how dangerous a thorough rogue like Ishtier could be.

Kindrie regarded her askance. "Did you . . . er . . .
abstract something from Lord Ishtier?"

"Steal it, d'you mean? No. He . . . er . . . abstracted
something from me. The last I saw of him, he was trying
to gnaw off his own hand after having touched this thing,
which must be how he lost the finger. A pity he stopped
short of the elbow. Sweet Trinity. You said that the God-
voice spoke again recently, for the first time since the
Arrin-ken left. Was that through Ishtier in Tai-tastigon?"

From his expression, she knew that it had been. Oh,
lord. Now she was really in the dunghill, neck deep.
What the Voice had said to her was alarming enough,
without whatever frills Ishtier might add. The other
priests must think that, in her, they had a real monster
on their hands, against whom all measures were justified.

But was it really their god who had spoken through
the renegade priest after so long a silence? Where *had*
she heard something like the Voice since, not obviously,
perhaps, but in its under-notes? If the Tastigon oracle
proved false, what happened to its dire prophecies then?

Eh, this was hopeless. After all, Ishtier had accepted
the Voice as genuine, and he was the poor goop through
whom it had chosen to speak.

Stop clutching at straws, she told herself. *Whatever
is, is, and you've got to live with it.*

But oh, lord—FRATRICIDE . . . and TYR-RIDAN.

It began to rain.

VII

COLD DROPS STUNG Jame's face, while Kindrie hunched thin shoulders under the rain-darkening cloth of his borrowed shirt. Only Jorin seemed unperturbed. He was taking this wretched weather unexpectedly well, Jame thought as she watched him trot on ahead. Some ounces enjoyed getting wet, but the blind Royal Gold had hated water ever since his breeder had tried to drown him as a kitten.

Strange. He didn't even look damp now.

When he returned, grumbling, at her call, she found that his coat was quite dry. So was the road ahead, and the leaves of trees a dozen feet away weren't dripping. The rain, it seemed, was exclusively for her benefit.

It came down harder, laced with hail. No. With tiny, green frogs.

"Do you mind?" she demanded, extracting a wriggling froglet from deep inside her shirt. It clung to her finger tip with anxious toes.

"Geep, *geep*, *GEEP!*" cried a growing chorus, doing agitated push-ups on her shoulders; but if they were trying to tell her something, Jame wasn't interested.

"Will you *stop* that?" she shouted up at the roiling clouds.

The shower of frogs stopped. A moment later, rain began again—in a circle around them.

"This place has the damnedest weather," Jame muttered, flicking off her clothes and proceeding, carefully, over the lively ground, with Jorin bouncing like a wound-up toy at her heels.

Kindrie stared after her. She *was* mad—and so was he, to be following her. His experience with Highborn women was limited to the Randir, whom he thought abominable, but at least they didn't wander about the countryside being rained on by frogs.

Why was he still in this lunatic's company? The last thing he remembered, before that suddenly silent bush, was challenging the Knorth about her Shanir blood. Then had followed the long nightmare of running, running . . . . No. Walking, stumbling . . . how far? His feet throbbed and he felt a sickening fatigue alien to his healer's nature. Where in all the names of God were they?

The naked slopes across the river were ominously familiar. So was the roof of a watch tower glimpsed ahead over trees on the west bank.

"That's Shadow Rock," he said in a stifled voice. "Wilden . . . . You've lured me back to Wilden!"

He turned and fled, blindly, blundering, only to trip and crash down on the New Road's hard stones.

"Steady," said the Knorth, over him. "What *is* all this? Surely you realized that we were going north."

"No! I-I didn't notice."

"Huh. I should have let you go on sleepwalking. Listen: we're going farther north still, all the way to Restormir."

"*Restormir!* Why?"

"Because a friend of mine has fallen into Lord Cainer-on's hands. He needs rescuing. He'll need a healer too, if dear Caldane starts on him."

As simple, as insane as that.

For a moment Kindrie lay speechless, shaken like a cage by his own heartbeat.

Only someone who had never seen Restormir would propose such a thing. He remembered his brief time there the previous autumn, after his initial flight from Wilden, when he had taken service with the first Highborn he had met, needing protection from the priests, naively hoping it would lead to contact with the lord whom he really wished to serve, not knowing that Torisen and Caineron were mortal enemies. He had tried to help the Highlord anyway, and Caineron had repaid him for it. Remembering that, Kindrie shook even harder. His back still bore the marks of the corrector's scourge because he couldn't forget.

No one had come to his rescue then, anymore than over this past winter.

Torisen couldn't have, he told himself. Either time. Otherwise, it would have been the natural thing for a Knorth to do—as it was now? No. Not for a female, however wellborn. Yet this unnatural creature would have led him in a daze all the way to Restormir.

She sat on her heels two paces away, regarding him scornfully, expecting him to refuse. That stung. Dammit, wasn't he part Knorth too?

"All right," he heard himself say.

"You're sure?"

"*Yes!*"

He rose, stiffly. Flesh and bone, but he ached, with a sudden copper taste in his mouth. His nose had started to bleed. That shouldn't be. He was a healer, whose first subject was his own body—except that he was shut out of his own soul-image. He could still enter the soulscapes of others to help as far as his limited strength allowed, but as for healing himself . . . . Frail as he had always been, for the first time he tasted his own mortality.

No. Don't think about that. Don't think.

Stiff-shouldered, trying not to snuffle, he limped past the Knorth toward the two places which he least wished ever to see again.

Jame rose and followed him, frowning. Pleased as she was that the healer had decided to go, she didn't understand why. In the last few minutes, she had watched him flip through a dozen emotions, frantically, like a gambler with a losing hand. This bravado probably wouldn't last long either.

Priests! she thought. You couldn't depend on them for anything.

They were close to Shadow Rock now, the home keep of Hollens, Lord Danior. Although only a bone relative, Cousin Holly was the closest kin Torisen had on the High Council and therefore his heir presumptive—not that the young man relished that distinction. Lord of the poorest house in the Riverland, he could barely maintain his own council seat, much less hope to occupy the Highlord's for long, should Torisen's death put him there.

Jame had met him at the Cataracts' dinner party. A nice boy, she had thought, if rather too much in awe of her brother.

More of Shadow Rock came into view. The original keep had only been a Bashtiri outpost, built to keep an eye on the much larger Hathiri fortress across the river. The Danior had marginally expanded it, limited by the defile which it occupied under the shadow of a balanced rock which someday would probably smash it flat. Today, its lord absent in Kothifir, it looked abandoned—the outer gate locked and all its windows tight shuttered except for one high up in the watch tower, which stood open.

Out of this last, a little girl leaned to peer across the river. Then someone pulled her back in and closed the shutter, quickly but quietly.

So Shadow Rock was garrisoned after all, by people in hiding. From what?

They rounded a corner and, for the first time, saw Wilden on the opposite bank.

It filled a valley much larger than its sister keep's, widened farther by quarry-work which had left sheer, surrounding walls of live granite. These the low clouds cut short. Judging from a distant rumble, the overcast also hid a considerable waterfall at the valley's upper end. Streams plunged down on either side of Wilden between the mountains' granite flanks and the inner walls of the fortress. Wilden itself angled down the valley's floor, presenting tier after jagged tier of its internal structure, tower after terrace after tower. Between the trapezoidal jaws of its double outer walls, it looked like a mouth full of sharp, ragged teeth. The streams had been dammed before it to form a brimming moat. From this, runoff driveled down the steep outer ward toward the curtain wall that sealed off the valley, toward the River Road and the Silver below.

As they crept past, Jame saw that the doors of the upper gatehouse stood open. Through them, white glimmered in the premature twilight: the ruins of the hill fort around which Wilden had been built, carefully preserved on a tiny hillock in an inner courtyard like white bones cradled in Randir jaws.

The Priests' College was somewhere in there too.

"Is there a temple in the College?" she asked Kindrie.

"Of course not. That much raw power would burn out the novices' minds."

"But they *are* drawing power in, from Tai-tastigon and beyond. I can feel it. A cesspool of divinity . . . . How many priests in residence, priestling?"

"I am *not* . . . . *Nine* of the first rank, when I left. Maybe a score of others, as well as acolytes and novices. Oh, my God. Look."

Although it had stopped raining, heavy clouds roofed Wilden's valley in a ponderous eddy. The hub of their slow circling was the fortress's farthest tower, whose heights they obscured. Above that hidden summit, a sulfurous yellow light grew, glowering down through the wrack's thinner patches. It spread. The moat reflected its progress, then the rivulets, then the Silver itself. The water smoked sullenly in its wake.

"The weather around here may be peculiar," said Jame softly, "but this is getting downright spooky. What in Perimal's name have we walked into?"

"Lady Rawneth is conjuring," the Shanir said in a taut voice.

Jame stared at the approaching light. As Kindrie had said, Kencyr power came indirectly from their god through the temples and the Shanir. This felt . . . different. She knew that some of Rathillien's so-called magics were accessible to anyone who knew the proper formulae, while others required the catalyst of faith. The latter was impossible for the average Kencyr, compelled to believe solely in his own absent god. However, she herself had accomplished two acts of it in Tai-tastigon, saving one native godling and killing another, through her faith in the truth of her own research. That had been nothing, though, compared to the natural forces unleashed here.

"But what do the priests think of Rawneth conjuring on their doorstep?"

"Knowledge is knowledge," said Kindrie, as if quoting hieratic dogma. "Besides, s-sometimes they trade information. She told Lord Ishtier h-how she kept me locked in my own soul-image m-most of my childhood."

"*What?*"

"Her revenge, she called it, although I never knew for what. S-sometimes she let me out, when she wanted s-someone to try her spells on who wasn't apt to die of them."

Jame remembered Ishtier's experiment with Bane's soul which had resulted in the Lower Town Monster. Perhaps it hadn't been as freakish as she had supposed—except that Ishtier had been trying to break the Kencyrath's monotheism by creating a genuine god.

I bet he hasn't shared that *bit of failed research with his peers*, she thought.

Kindrie started. "What was *that?*"

Something very close and, for the sound of it, very large, had just said, "*Quonk!*"

Out of the corner of her eye, Jame saw a green lump flash by in the river. That wailing, honking roar drifted back up-stream, sounding quite distraught: "*Quoooooonk . . . !*"

If the unknown lump had been upset, however, Kindrie was beside himself.

"She's really done it!" he babbled. "W-we've got to get away from here! It will do whatever she commands a-and then it will please itself . . ."

Jame caught his arm. "What are you talking about?"

"A demon! Ishtier told her how to conjure it. That was the price he paid to learn how to bar me from my soul-image."

"*Quonk!*" boomed that strange voice again, this time with an air of self-encouragement. "*Quok, quok, quok . . .*"

Each grunting "*quok*" sounded closer than the last. Jame could have sworn that it had somehow gotten ahead of them again. However, she wasn't as scared as Kindrie. For one thing, she'd had some practical experience with demons; for another, it was hard to take one seriously which talked to itself, much less in that tone. The Shanir was right, though: this was no place to linger.

However, their way was barred by a pool of rain water collected in a dip of the road. Something huge was rising out of it. Two bulging eyes emerged first, round as soup plates and about the same size, with slit pupils and irises each like a golden lattice crossing a rose colored ground. An expanse of bright green forehead followed, then a broad snout circled by an even broader mouth. The snowy vocal sac inflated like a lesser moon.

"*QUONK!*" said this apparition, eyeing the white haired healer with evident satisfaction.

Kindrie fainted.

Jame, on the other hand, nearly jumped into the pool to throw her arms around that vast, green neck—not that they would have reached.

"Why, Gorgo, you've grown!"

Gorgo, formerly the Lugubrious, switched his goggle-eyed gaze to her, and immediately looked apprehensive. The previous year, Jame's own experiments with the so-called gods of Tai-tastigon had first gotten him killed and then resurrected in his current (although much smaller) shape. Neither, obviously, was an experience which Gorgo would soon forget.

"*. . . quonk . . . .*" he said feebly, gulping.

Another sound came out of his closed mouth. It sounded suspiciously like muffled cursing. Gorgo yawned, wide, wider, like a toad beginning its molt, and there, snuggled in the pit of his throat, was a human face.

"I *hate* it when he does that," said Loogan. " '*Quonk*'! What a sound, *and* it nearly blows out my eardrums."

Jame stared at the Tastigon priest. "Sweet Trinity. Did Gorgo swallow you, or are you wearing him?"

"I don't know *what's* going on," said Loogan crossly. "We were both in the temple, preparing for the evening rites, when *this* happened. In fact, if I squint, I can still see the sanctuary. I don't think we're really here at all—wherever 'here' is."

Gorgo gurgled.

"Ah. He says we've been sent to fetch someone—that fellow on the ground, I think. A lady wants him."

"Sorry. He's under my protection."

"Oh. Well, that's that. Overreached herself, she did, trying to snag us in the first place. We're already slipping free, none too soon."

Gorgo's attention had strayed to a flight of dragonflies hovering about a nearby clump of reeds. He turned his massive head. Loogan's tongue shot out—all three feet of it—and snapped an insect out of the air.

"Gaaah!" he said, around a mouthful of shimmering wings. "I *hate* this. We're going home. Now. Before he finds out that it's the m-a-t-i-n-g season."

"Loogan, wait! Is everyone all right in Tai-tastigon?"

"Hardly everyone. Men-dalis has got troubles, but I expect you'll hear about that sooner or later. All your friends at the Res aB'tyrr are fine. Goodbye."

"*Wait*! What happened to Bane?"

"Believe me, you don't want to know."

As he spoke, the priest's round face had been fading. Only his voice now emerged from Gorgo's throat, as if from a growing distance: "Bye-bye, duckie. Keep your feet dr . . . ."

Gorgo's mouth still gaped wide open, frozen in what appeared to be astonishment. An iridescent sheen had come over him.

"*Quo . . . ?*" he said tentatively, and burst with a faint pop, like a soap bubble.

All that remained was the puddle, with a rumpled dragonfly floating in the middle of it.

 VIII

LOOGAN AND GORGO weren't the only ones who had disappeared. So had Kindrie and Jorin. The healer must have woken in time to hear Jame conversing familiarly with a "demon" and bolted, the ounce scampering after him.

Damnation.

Wet weather had somehow allowed the Wilden Witch to snatch an Old Pantheon rain god and his priest in the midst of their ritual lavations. She hadn't been able to hold them, but with that sort of power she was bound to try again, this time maybe conjuring something less ambitious but more effective—like a real demon. And it would be after Kindrie, whom Jame had just sworn to protect.

"*It never rains,*" as Loogan might say, "*without drowning someone.*"

At least the tracks of both Shanir and ounce showed clearly in the soft earth, heading upward from the road. Jame followed at a trot. Overhead, the clouds went from gray to black, edged by that unearthly yellow light which still spread out from the towers of Wilden. The weirding mist trailed down in darkening veils.

At first, Jame thought that the diminishing light was to blame when the prints of Kindrie's bare feet seemed to distort. She crouched, peering. No. The outer toes *did* splay at right angles to elongated feet, with indentations at the end of each toe that suggested claws.

Something ran after the Shanir, treading in his footprints step by step.

As she rose to follow, the back of her head seemed to explode.

Ancestors be praised for long hair was her first dazed thought thereafter. Once again, the thick, coiled braid under her cap had saved her skull from fracture or worse.

Then she became aware of weight, pinning her to the ground, and of cool air, moving across her face. Someone had removed her mask. She rather thought, too, that she was being sat on.

All she saw at first, though, through cautious, slitted eyes, was the nearly empty food sack bobbing over her. Withered apples flew out of it as if by themselves. Above and behind it hovered angry eyes without a face— bloodshot whites, yellow irises, hardly ever blinking. When they did, the pressure on her eased and the food bag sagged, as if for a moment her assailant became the shadow after which his guild was named.

The empty sack went flying. Crooked, yellow teeth bared at her in a snarl, which she smashed with a handy rock.

Free. On her feet. Running, closely pursued.

Tripped by a root, Jame turned her stumble into a lunge for the nearest sapling, bearing it down with her weight, then rolling off to let it whip back. Yellow eyes hastily shut. The slender trunk passed between where they had been. She tried to rise, but a freezing numbness had seized her legs. The assassin's shadow swarmed up her body, ending in two very real if invisible hands about her throat. Yellow eyes glared down at her, unblinking.

"Where is it?" a thick tongue hissed in midair, like an adder in a cage of rotten ivory, spitting blood and fragments of broken teeth in her face. "The book, you witch, the Book Bound in Pale Leather. Where?"

"I-I don't have it." Sweet Trinity, who had told him about that? Marc, Graykin, Kindrie . . . . "Ishtier?"

The grip on her throat tightened. "That priest-spawn! What has he told you, bitch? What?"

What *could* Ishtier have told her, except perhaps how he had forced a master assassin to attempt theft for him? If the guilds of the Central Lands were like their eastern counterparts, the Bashti thieves would howl over this.

Broken teeth sneered. "Bluffing, weren't you? As if a whore's-daughter ever knew anything."

White flashed. The Ivory Knife. Oh lord, where had he found to hide that?

"Guild Master," she heard herself croak. "I know this much: why the blooding at Gothregor failed."

The Knife hesitated. Her neck felt cold, where the blade so nearly touched it.

"Why, bint?"

"The 'prentices were unprepared and under-trained."

He slapped her, hard, across her injured cheek. "One of them gave you that, at least."

"No," said Jame, through sudden pain, tasting blood.

"Then not. Kencyr are too stupid to lie. Under-trained, how?"

"Not enough fighting experience." Amazing, how she found herself reporting as a journeyman to a master, if of different disciplines. "Too much dependence on shadow-casting techniques, under adverse conditions."

"Unprepared for what?"

"Partly, for me."

He struck again, harder. She almost lunged upward into the sharp ivory, a risk she might have taken with any other knife.

"Why don't you put that thing away, master, and try your own luck with me?"

He gave a sharp bark of laughter. "I tested your sort thirty-four years ago, sow. Soft throats and soft kills—except for the one who led me such a chase and the other one who cursed. Red-eyed whore . . . !"

A red-eyed maledight . . . .

"Brenwyr?" Jame said, stupidly.

"*That* was the name. Unprepared for what else, slut?"

"For Old Man Tishooo, who blew away their souls, and for a shadow-demon named Bane, who fed on them. In fact," she added, carefully, "if you were to look above you now . . . ."

He laughed again, harshly. "Kencyr never lie, but 'if' cuts no bread."

"This time," said Jame, "it does."

Bane dropped on the assassin out of a tree, like a coat of shadows. The guild master gasped. His frantic efforts to shrug off his tenebrous assailant became the jerky movements of a man being clothed against his will. His shoulders twitched as the other settled over them. His arms stretched and his hands flexed into gloves of living shadow. The Ivory Knife wobbled in his loosened grip, directly over Jame's face.

"Watch it!" she said.

Bane looked down at her. What Jame saw was the shadowy mask of his features, through which the assassin's eyes stared wildly. What he saw, for the first time, was her injured face, freshly bloodied. His grip on the guild master tightened. The man shrieked, and dropped the Ivory Knife.

"Eeee!" said Jame.

How she managed it, she never knew. A moment later, though, Jame found herself sprawling a dozen feet from where the Knife quivered upright in the sod, the grass dying around it.

Something unseen was blundering away through the trees, trailing a thin wail as much of rage as fear. The master assassin had bolted. Now there was a mount which would need some taming, even for such a rider. With luck, they would break each other's neck, Jame thought sourly, wiping her face. So much for Kindrie's first aid.

Sweet Trinity. Kindrie.

She snatched up the Ivory Knife and ran back the way she had come. Here was the clearing where the assassin had jumped her, her mask, cap, and linen bandage laying where he had dropped them. Beyond, those curious, composite footprints led on upslope. She followed, toward the sound of raised voices.

IX

"IT'S WEIRDING UP something fierce, Ten," the cadet on point called back, a plaintive, disembodied voice out of the dark, dripping forest. Muffled thunder rolled down the valley like a boulder wrapped in flannel. "And I think it's going to rain again."

"We should have turned back two days ago, when the ghost-walkers passed," the tall cadet in Five's rear-guard position muttered. "All patrols should, when it starts to weird up like this."

His voice carried, as he meant it to. The new ten-commander turned to look back at him over the seven intervening heads.

"Standing orders," he muttered defiantly, but his eyes fell.

Brier Iron-thorn could almost smell the slow burn of his resentment. Before her arrival at the college, a new Knorth cadet with a battlefield appointment, he had been provisional Ten.

In fact, none of the young cadets looked happy. All but one of them Riverland bred, of old Knorth stock, they had come to Tentir that spring thinking themselves the cream of its new crop, only to find how hard it was to serve the Highlord in a college dominated by his enemies. Worse, older cadets looked down on them both for having missed the great blooding at the Cataracts and for taking the place of friends killed there. Then, in the crowning insult, they had been put under the command of an upstart Southie of Caineron *yondri* stock.

To Brier, their discontent looked like the pout of spoiled children.

How old were they? Fifteen? Sixteen? At their age, she had already been in the field with the Southern Host for years, first with her mother, then on her own after Rose Iron-thorn's death in the Wastes after the debacle at Urakarn. Life was hard for the many Kendar who had lost their natural lord and must seek a new one. Nicknamed *yondri-gon* or threshold-dwellers, they could serve a house for generations before its master deigned to take them into regular service, especially if that house was the Caineron and its lord Caldane, who deliberately swelled his ranks with the desperate displaced who would do anything to gain his favor. Two years ago, when she had turned seventeen, he had at last given Brier her chance as a randon candidate—if she passed his private initiation.

The cadets, watching, were suddenly still. Under the helm of mahogany hair, the Southie's expression hadn't changed: as always, that hard, handsome face might have been carved from teak and those green eyes from the same malachite as the stud in her left earlobe. But for a moment the cadets had seen something there which had frightened them very much indeed.

Brier turned away. "Point, wait there. We're coming down to you."

Near mutiny returned to the ranks. "Down" meant farther south. Their assignment had been to check out the rumor of a naked Merikit seen near the college—just another dirt job for the Knorth rookies, they had thought, as well as an oblique insult to their new leader, since only Caineron hunted Merikit for sport and were said to treat them no better than wild animals when they caught one. This Merikit would, of course, long since have gone, assuming he had existed in the first place. They had expected to cover their assigned territory in time for supper. Instead, Iron-thorn had led them out of it, southward.

Now it was dusk two days later, under dark trees and a weirding overcast, with no food, no Merikit, and the prospect of more rain.

They were long overdue at Tentir. Commandant Sheth, no friend to the Knorth, could have their token scarves for this as it was. Had that, perhaps, been his purpose in assigning them to a former Caineron? What *was* the Southie playing at, anyway?

It would not have reassured them that Brier herself didn't know. She only sensed that something was tugging her. It felt like her new bond to the Highlord, but how could that be when he was still in Kothifir, over four hundred leagues away? Normally, Torisen's grip on his Kendar was so light-handed that her former mates dismissed it scornfully as limp. But how could Brier know what he might be capable of? The Knorth were so different from the Caineron, upon whom all her previous experience was based.

Different, and mad.

She had been brought up to believe that, too. Hadn't Ganth Gray Lord's insanity infected the entire Host, leading to its near massacre in the White Hills? Didn't his son sometimes shun sleep until his wits half turned? What was she to think of a Highborn who at the Cataracts had offered her sanctuary from Lord Caineron's wrath as if he actually cared what happened to her? That show of concern was only the Knorth glamor, she told herself, useful for binding gullible randon like Harn Grip-hard as tightly as blood could have done. Her own decision to change houses had been based entirely on ambition, since she could now never hope for advancement under the Caineron. She would use Knorth influence and the Knorth would use her ability. Pure self-interest, on both sides. It was mad to think that Highborn and Kendar could deal with each other on any other basis.

And madness was contagious.

Is that what pulls me southward? she wondered. *Have I gone mad too?*

The scout suddenly reappeared, with an urgent gesture for silence. Whatever he had found, though, defied his ability to describe by sign. Brier cut short his efforts with a brusque °*Show me,*° then followed him down to the edge of the trees, the squad close on their heels.

They emerged under black clouds so low here that they seemed to tangle in the branches overhead. An unearthly yellow light filtered down through them. Below, the river's pale breath was slowly flooding the valley to the height of the lowest trees. Between roof and floor of mist lay a slope strewn with large boulders, knee deep in grass, across which veils of weirding silently drifted. It was this middle ground to which the scout pointed.

A Randir ten-command was playing hide-and-seek among the boulders—if "play" was the right word for that silent, furtive activity. The strange cadets seemed almost to slither through the grass, supple as serpents, long-skulled heads and many jointed hands weaving as though in quest for a scent. Flushed from cover, a white haired Shanir stumbled into the open. The seekers surrounded him. They began to play him back and forth, still in that unnerving silence, as he floundered with exhaustion in their midst.

It was no affair of hers, Brier told herself. As a Cain-eron, the first lesson she had learned was to mind her own business.

The Shanir tripped and fell. The Randir crouched in a circle around him. One drew a fingertip delicately down his cheek, leaving a thin, red line.

"Stop that!" Brier Iron-thorn roared.

Her own cadets jumped, then nervously followed as she strode down the slope. Below, ten pale, blank faces turned toward her, ten pairs of ghost-lit, glimmering eyes, but still no one spoke.

"What in Perimal's name d'you think you're doing?" she demanded of them, then stopped short.

A Randir captain had stepped between her and the group crouching around the fallen Shanir. Brier blinked. She didn't recognize any of the ten-command, but this gaunt woman was a Tentir instructor, currently posted to the Gothregor Women's Halls and still wearing her dress grays with gold striped shoulder embroidery. What in hell was she doing here?

"Minding our own business, cadet," said the captain, smiling. The other Randir rose and silently ranged them-selves behind her, still surrounding the Shanir. "We sug-gest that you do the same."

Brier blinked again. To hear her unspoken thoughts answered was unnerving. Worse, she suddenly realized that whatever was going on here, she couldn't just walk away from it. The rules she had followed as a Caineron no longer seemed to apply, but how was a Knorth sup-posed to react? For the first time in her life, she didn't know what to do.

"Randir business, on Danior land, with someone under Knorth protection. Interesting."

The new voice made them all turn sharply. A slim, dark-clad figure stood on top of a white boulder, looking down at them. For a moment, impossibly, Brier thought it was Torisen Black Lord. Then she saw the other's mask. She had indeed been drawn southward by her bond to the Knorth, she realized, but not to the Highlord.

"Don't move, Kindrie," said Torisen's mad sister. "I think you've landed in a nest of bogles."

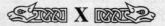

JAME HAD immediately recognized the Randir captain from Gothregor, or at least her semblance. That the woman herself should be here was quite possible: Wilden was her home keep, after all; and, given their crawling pace, she could easily have beaten the fugitives to it—but in such company?

From the boulder's height, Jame could see Kindrie's track beaten through the tall grass as he had fled from cover to cover. The ten Randir cadets, however, had left no trails at all, while their officer still stood as if by chance in the Shanir's footsteps, her own feet sunk into them to the ankles. It was too dark to see if, like Bane, she cast no shadow. If she *was* the demon whom Lady Rawneth had conjured, that would explain the ten others as bogles, mindless projections of her power. Yes: *if.*

" 'Knorth protection,' " the randon repeated, smiling up at Jame. "Now, who are you, girl, to confer that?"

One point to me, thought Jame.

The real captain had never seen her dressed like this, but she would have guessed after that slip about the Knorth. A demon concentrated the worst attributes of its host soul, without always gaining its knowledge. Unfortunately, she didn't know the Randir's true name either, which would have helped if this creature was indeed constructed around her soul the way the Lower Town Monster had been around Bane's.

The other's smile peeled back into a broad grin, baring very white, distinctly human teeth whose incisors had been chipped to form points, so recently that they still bled. Behind her, ten faces broke into empty smiles, luminous eyes devoid of pupil, iris, and life.

The glowing eyes of the strange cadets in the Randir arcade at Gothregor . . . these?

"Why don't you come down and play, little girl?" crooned their captain. "Or shall we amuse ourselves elsewhere?"

As one, the ten turned their gleaming gaze on Kindrie.

The dark randon on the upper slope moved as if to protest but checked herself. What in Perimal's name were Knorth cadets doing here anyway, Jame wondered, distracting her at such a moment?

"Your mistress won't thank you for hurting this boy," she said quickly to the face smiling up at her. "She must want him back alive."

"But not necessarily intact. Healers are such fun."

White hands reached out toward Kindrie. Long nails rattled together over him like thorns in a winter wind. Where they brushed his skin, red lines appeared and began to drip.

That did it.

For some time, thunder had been grumbling closer. Now the yellow light above flared briefly as lightning gave an oddly muffled crack. To destroy a demon, Ishtier had once told her, you needed first its true name and then lots of fire or water. True, she didn't know what to call the creature gloating up at her, but by God, maybe she could still wipe that damn grin off its face. No time to conjure up the proper master rune, but Gorgo still owed her at least one favor.

"All right," she said to the lowering sky, "*Now*."

A raindrop struck her upturned face, then another and another, hard. One moment she could see all the way upslope, where the red-haired Kendar had barked an order at her command and was starting down with the cadets scrambling into formation behind her. The next second, the rain had drawn a hissing, gray veil across everything. A wail of protest came from the grass below where Jorin lay hidden.

Something was climbing the rock. For a moment, Jame looked into a face from which all features had been washed except the sharp-toothed grin. Fingers webbed with melting flesh groped for her. She launched herself over the creature's head, as much through water as air, to land hard on the flattened grass beyond. Wet fur brushed against her, chirping anxiously. Jorin. She stumbled toward where she had last seen Kindrie. There he was, a pale, huddled blur on the ground, ringed by cloud-of-thorn brambles. She slashed through them with the Ivory Knife and hauled the Shanir out.

Suddenly, the air around them changed. The rain was replaced by a glowing mist so dense that Jame couldn't see or hear anything at all. She tightened her grip on Kindrie's arm while a frightened ounce pressed so close that he stood on her foot. Those two points of contact were all she could feel. Beyond them, all of Rathillien might have melted into chaos.

Then Jame realized what had happened: under cover of the storm, a bank of weirding had swept down on them.

Sweet Trinity, now what? Weird-walking had occasionally been practiced in the past, with mixed results. A walker might cover great distances, but he also might end up one place and his feet another. Still, the naked Merikit had risked it. This mist-bank was traveling southward. Would it roll past or was it already taking them with it? Since Jame neither wanted to stay where she was nor find herself at the Cataracts, much less both places simultaneously, she stumbled on in the direction which she had been going, hoping it was northward, dragging Kindrie and Jorin with her.

Time seemed to dissolve along with everything else. Past and future melted into a present that stretched on and on until it was hard to imagine anything but mist.

Then, between one step and the next, the world returned.

The mist rolled away southward, leaving them under a dusky sky fretted with stars, on the crest of a ridge. Some distance below, stretching from the river bank back until the western hills swallowed it, was the largest fortress which Jame had ever seen. Actually, it looked more like a city with many walled districts. A castle keep built on a towering mound dominated the whole, separated from it, moat-like, by the split waters of a tributary rushing down to join the Silver.

Jame only had a moment to stare, though, before someone behind her gave a startled exclamation. She and Jorin leaped aside as a number of people plunged out of the retreating mist, hanging on to each other. The lot of them tumbled off the ridge, taking Kindrie with them, to fetch up in a pine spinney a little way down the slope. Jame was left facing the dark cadet, who had emerged last and least precipitously from the mist.

"If it's any consolation," she said to the Kendar, glancing at the muddle below as it began to sort itself out with dolorous cries, "the one on the bottom is a healer. Who *are* you people, anyway, and where have we all landed?"

The tall randon was staring down at the mass of buildings, in patent disbelief.

"Restormir," she said softly. "*Restormir.*"

🐉 Interim III 🐉
The River Road: 58th of Spring

SOMETHING BAD WAS COMING.

The Wolver Grimly had sensed it all day in the prickling of his fur. He had seen it, too, in the animals he had passed—roe deer standing in tight knots in meadows by the River Road, wild cats wailing in the hills, field mice, snakes and even worms crawling out of their holes onto the road's surface.

He knew from the procession of ghost-walkers which had drifted past two nights ago that serious weirding was on the way. Worse, a really bad weirdingstrom could trigger earthquakes, the mere thought of which made the fur down his spine rise.

His mount jibbed, snatching for its bit as Grimly fumbled with the reins. Wolvers seldom rode, nor did any horse care to be ridden by them. Damn. There went a stirrup. He scrabbled for it, not realizing until the reins slipped through his paws that in his bone-deep fatigue he had reverted to wolver shape. The horse squealed, bounced sideways, and threw its rider in a convenient thorn bush. As Grimly extricated himself, swearing, it bolted back the way they had come. On foot again, dammit—falling behind, and he the only one on the right trail.

As far as anyone else knew, Torisen had simply disappeared after charging out of the courtyard in Kothifir.

"You don't see me," he had said to the guard at the gate, and the man hadn't. Quite possibly, he would never see anything again.

Simultaneously, a kind of selective blindness had raced through the entire encampment. Grimly hadn't understood how that could happen until he had heard shaken men comparing it to the effect of Ganth's madness on the Northern Host thirty-four years ago. That was something out of an old song to Grimly. He had never imagined that Ganth's son might also have such power over his followers, much less be ruthless enough to use it.

However, in the faces of Ardeth, Harn, and Burr (groggy, but recovering), he had seen that this was what they feared. They had decided to keep as much from the Highlord's enemies as possible, while they themselves set out to find him. Harn and Burr thought he had disappeared into the back streets of Kothifir. Ardeth was sure that he had fled into the Wastes, as he had done once before, and proposed to search for him there.

Listening, Grimly had realized that none of Torisen's friends expected to recover him sane. What chance did Tori stand against such a consensus? Far less than he deserved, the Wolver had thought, so he hadn't told them about Kin-Slayer or the distant, endangered sister. Instead, he had claimed that the upcoming Summer Eve rites required his presence at home in the Grimly Holt—which happened to be just over half way to the Riverland by the River Road. Harn and Burr hadn't thought much of him for that, but he told himself that he didn't care as long as it kept them looking for Tori in the wrong direction.

He had wondered if he himself might be wrong, though, when the first three post stations on the way to

Hurlen reported that the Highlord hadn't passed them. Then again, no one had seen him ride out of the encampment in any direction whatsoever. At the fourth station, a hundred miles east of Kothifir, Kendar spoke of hearing someone gallop past, but not being able to see who it was. The fifth station recognized Storm; the sixth, finally, identified his rider.

Grimly had begun to worry about Storm. The quarter-blood Whinno-hir had unusual stamina, but this pace would eventually kill even him. Sleep-starved, fleeing nightmares, Torisen had ridden a horse to death once before, on his mad dash into the Wastes four years ago. It would upset him horribly if he did it again. Half way to the Cataracts, however, Grimly found the black stallion exhausted but safe at a post station. Torisen had gone on by post horse. Grimly couldn't run down a succession of fresh mounts so he too, reluctantly, had taken to the saddle.

That had been two days ago. Now it was dusk, the fifty-eighth of spring, and he was close enough to home to smell it.

The road rolled northward over gentle hills. To the left lay a wild meadow with nightjars skimming over it and luminous mist collecting in its hollows. To the right ran the Silver, swift and chuckling. Glowing witchweed bent in its margin. Grimly found himself trotting, eager despite his fatigue. From the top of the next rise, he would be able to see home. Here was the hill's crest. Ahead, the main road swung to the right, following the river's curve, while a spur of it ran straight on into the lowering shadows of the Grimly Holt.

Just short of the fork, a dark-clad figure trudged northward, leading a lame post horse. Grimly recognized the

black coat, dusty and travel stained as it now was. He
also caught the cold gleam of Kin-Slayer.

"Tori!"

The Highlord plodded on, unheeding. When the
Wolver caught up with him, he blinked as if just waking
and regarded his friend without surprise.

"Oh. Hello, Grimly. Going home for Summer Eve?"

Bloodshot eyes, disheveled hair, four days' growth of
beard, and yet that unassuming elegance clung to the
Highborn which Grimly thought he would probably still
possess half way through his own cremation. What
unnerved the Wolver, though, was that dead calm tone.

"Er . . . actually, Tori, I was trying to catch up with
you."

"Really? That's kind, but I don't know what good you
can do. Better, perhaps, that you should go home. That's
it, isn't it, just ahead?"

"Yes," said Grimly.

He glanced surreptitiously at Torisen's nearest hand,
his left, which held the post horse on a loose rein. It
seemed to have nearly recovered from the cut which
Kin-Slayer's cracked emblem had given it. Kencyr could
shrug off much worse than that, he reminded himself. A
Highborn, especially a Knorth, could look as haggard as
a haunt and yet keep going days after a more sensible
person would have dropped dead.

"Yes," he said again, more confidently. "That's the
Grimly Holt."

"Good. When I blink, I see something so different—a
huge fortress with seven, no, eight walled districts surrounding a tower on a high mound . . . Restormir? But
that's ridiculous. I'm all muddled, Grimly."

"That's lack of sleep," said the Wolver, beginning to
be frightened again.

Tori *never* spoke about such things. He was an intensely private person, whose secrets the Wolver had no wish to know. Now they might both have been caught in the same nightmare, where barriers fell and anything might happen.

Then he caught sight of Torisen's right hand, which still gripped Kin-Slayer's hilt. It was swollen, especially around the emerald signet ring which appeared to be almost sunken into the finger wearing it. Burst blisters showed around the edge of the white knuckled grip. Red lines radiated out from them. Only the worst neglect could have brought such infection to a Kencyr—such as clutching the hilt of that malignant sword constantly for four days?

"Tori, come home with me. Please. You can rest there. The whole pack will keep watch over you."

"And what will they protect me from, when I don't know myself? You see, that's what I'm going back to the Riverland to find out. Either my Shanir twin is doing this to me, as Father claims, or I've gone mad."

Father? Grimly thought, confused. *Twin?*

"All right," he said, trying to match his friend's calm. "We'll find out when we get there. In the meantime, though, why don't you at least sheathe the sword?"

"Oh, I can't do that. Not until it kills someone."

Grimly was staring at him, speechless, when crows swarmed above the Holt in a black, raucous mob. Their uproar masked the oncoming rumble until it was almost underfoot. Then the earth began to quiver like a piece of fresh-killed beef, making Torisen stagger and Grimly crouch low. The lame horse threw up its head, jerking free, and plunged off the road into a patch of mist. It didn't come out the other side.

"Oh no," said Grimly, as the rumble faded. "That's weirding. Tori, listen to me: the wolvers' keep will protect us if we can reach it before the weirdingstrom hits. You've *got* to come with me now, if you don't want to be swept all the way back to the Cataracts, if not beyond. Tori, please!"

Torisen blinked. "It looks so much like Restormir," he said in wonder. "Caldane will just have arrived home. We mustn't go there, Grimly."

"We won't," said the Wolver, taking his arm. "I promise. Now come along. We're almost home."

PART
 IV

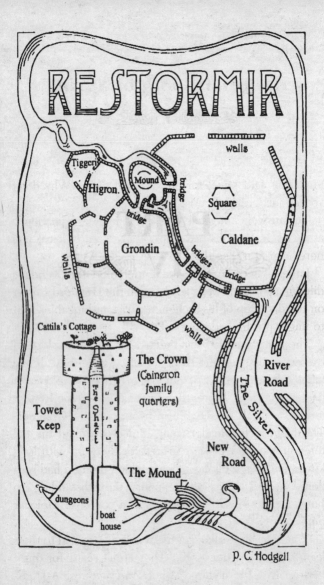

Restormir: 58th of Spring

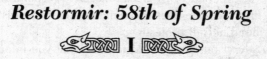 **I**

"LOOK," said Jame, for the dozenth time. "Why don't you all just go home? We'll be fine."

The answer came back with the same dogged patience as on each previous occasion: "Lady, I can't leave you here. You must see that."

Jame sighed. In fact, she understood the Kendar's dilemma perfectly well. To abandon the Highlord's sister on the doorstep of his archenemy was unthinkable—but to linger put his cadets at risk.

The latter huddled together on the southern slope of the ridge, six male and three female, where they all had taken refuge from sharp Caineron eyes. Only one, a cadet named Rue, was shorter than Jame, although the Kendar girl outweighed the Highborn by a good thirty pounds. The biggest, five-leader Vant, almost matched his tall ten-commander. All were armed for the hunt with long knives and short, elk horn bows, which the rain had rendered useless. Size and weaponry notwithstanding, to Jame they looked as bedraggled as a parcel of Molocar pups.

"For ancestors' sake, get them away!" she said to their leader, dropping her voice. "They aren't ready for this."

Brier Iron-thorn stared at her. *And you are?* A Highborn girl, sequestered and cosseted all her life . . . but this one spoke so disconcertingly, as if from her own store of experience. Brier had meant to respond slowly and firmly, as one does to a child or a half-wit. Instead, she found herself protesting:

"Lady, if only you would tell me what you intend to do!"

Jame hesitated. The cadet would think she was crazy but, dammit, this stalemate was wasting time. "All right," she said, and told her.

Brier blinked, twice. The Knorth *was* mad. Kendar at the Cataracts had whispered it when she had suddenly appeared in the middle of the battle and afterward been confined by the Highlord to the inner chamber of his tent until he could discreetly bundle her home by closed litter. *How sad*, the Caineron had said to each other, smiling.

"Don't interfere, cadet," the escaped lunatic said, looking hard at her. "This is honor—and obligation."

For a long moment, Kendar regarded Highborn without expression, then made a brusque gesture of acknowledgment. "Honor is honor, and obligation is unarguable. I can't stop you, lady, so I'll have to go with you."

"Lady," Vant burst out, "you should know: Ten is a Caineron herself."

"Was!" Rue snapped.

Ah, thought Jame. She had wondered why this tall cadet sounded so familiar. Confined to her brother's tent at the Cataracts, she had perforce overheard him outside, binding new Kendar to his service. One of them had spoken in just such a voice, rich but nearly inflectionless, a Caineron schooled to concealment.

"Raiding another house's Kendar," Harn Grip-hard had said afterward to Torisen. *"You won't hear the end of this in a hurry."*

"It can't be helped. I'll be damned if I'll let Caldane ruin someone like that—for her mother's sake, if nothing else."

"Huh. Old debts aside, you've snatched a real prize. M'lord Caineron is going to be furious."

Jame's curiosity had set Jorin's whiskers twitching then, as it did again now. One thing at least was obvious: after Graykin and herself, the last person who should visit Restormir uninvited was this erstwhile Caineron. She said as much.

"Nonetheless," the Kendar replied, in a voice like ironwood.

". . . in trouble enough as it is," Vant was protesting to the other cadets in a low, urgent voice. "The Highlord won't thank us for encouraging this . . . this . . . ."

He felt the eyes of the Highlord's sister on him, and stuttered to a halt. What word was there, anyway, both diplomatic and strong enough to describe so absurd a predicament? He lived to serve the Highborn, of course. Any ambitious Kendar did. But they in turn should behave as befit both their dignity and his. He had sneered at the Southie Ten at every opportunity. Now, however, he resented that she so obviously was not up to the situation.

"We're already days overdue at Tentir," he argued doggedly, not meeting anyone's eyes. "D'you *want* to make the Commandant a present of our scarves?"

"If Ten goes," said Rue stubbornly, "so should we."

"No!" said Brier and Jame simultaneously.

"I agree with Rue," another cadet said, with wriggle that might have been deference to his superiors or a digging in of heels. "If we stay behind, that's what people will remember about us for the rest of our lives. Anyway, think what an opportunity this is! We didn't have a chance to prove ourselves at the Cataracts, but a raid on Restormir . . . they'll talk about that at Tentir for the next fifty years!"

"Oh, at least," said Jame dryly. "Especially if you get skinned alive in the process. D'you really want to risk a blooding like that?"

"Well, lady, you know what they say: true tests are sent, not sought."

Brier and Jame looked at each other. Both knew that maxim's corollary: refuse such a test and risk never being sent another. Put that way, it would be as serious to interfere with such a matter as with honor itself.

Nonetheless, Vant made one last try. "Ten, I'm warning you. This may not ruin us"—not if *he* could help it, anyway—"but it certainly will you."

"In that case," said Brier Iron-thorn, rising and towering over him so that, big as he was, he shrank from her, "you have something to look forward to, don't you?"

HALF AN HOUR LATER, a ten-command in close formation trotted toward Restormir as if eager to take shelter for the night. Their way was lit by innumerable stars except to the far north, where darkness blotted them out. A faint grinding noise came from that direction, and the earth occasionally shivered underfoot.

More strangeness on the way, Jame thought.

She stepped on the heel of the cadet in front of her and would have fallen if hands hadn't caught her. Brier had tucked her in the middle of the formation, where her dark clothes rendered her almost invisible. By contrast, Kindrie's white hair shone in the front rank like a beacon. The cadets on either side gripped his arms tightly, as though to hustle along a prisoner, when in fact they were supporting most of his weight so that his bare feet hardly touched the ground.

They came to a small, half-built compound on the tributary's southern bank, at the fortress's western end, which belonged to Tiggeri, Caineron's youngest established son, still in Kothifir in disfavor.

"Not too deep, I hope," Jame had said. "Not if you intend to pass yourselves off as his retainers."

"Tiggeri's practical jokes never quite bury him, lady, but sometimes he makes his Kendar very nervous. If on their way home they found this healer wandering, they would bring him along as a peace offering to M'lord."

A peace offering. Jame glanced at Kindrie again, this time with a twinge of unease. The Shanir had served Caldane briefly. She had heard that they had parted with no love lost. Perhaps Restormir was dangerous for him too—but he was a healer, dammit. What risk, ultimately, could he run? Anyway, too late for second thoughts: here was the gate, and now they were through it into Tiggeri's compound, unchallenged.

Only the rathorn crest stitched in white on their black token scarves marked them as Knorth. Easy enough to fold the needlework inward and to turn the scarf knot to the front in the style which Tiggeri favored. Jame had been afraid at first that Iron-thorn would balk at this stratagem, which her own knowledge as a former Caineron had suggested. Something about the big Kendar made subterfuge seem impossible. However, she had apparently decided that on this mad night anything might happen—not that "anything" included lying about their identity if directly challenged.

It was a relief, therefore, to find Tiggeri's compound virtually empty. His people must still be with him in Kothifir, where perhaps he had managed to stay by design. Only established since the previous summer, he and his retainers still lived in half-constructed quarters which would have been cruelly cold that winter. Still, huge piles of fire wood showed that they would rather have kept these stark lodgings than give up the morsel of independence which their lord had granted them. How important it was to be established, given permission to bind Kendar in one's own right.

If he ever found out about Graykin, Tori would have a fit.

The squad slowed, for the first time hearing the sound of the greater fortress as it lapped about this silent compound. Ahead loomed the castle keep on its high hill. The lower, older portion of the tower was dark, but on top of that like some fantastic crown sat the family quarters. There all windows stood open and lit. Snatches of song and laughter fell from them, disjointed by the height, and the quarters below gave back echoes, laugh for broken laugh, cry for cry.

"Passwords!"

The challenge fell suddenly on them from a guard-box perched on top of the wall which they were approaching. Under the box, sputtering torches bracketed the closed gate leading to the next compound.

"Passwords!" the guard demanded again, with a curious, high-pitched giggle. "C'mon. *You* know!"

"I *don't* know," Brier shouted back. "We just got here."

"Atta girl." The gate creaked open. " 'I-don't-know.' Tomorrow's watchwords, if you're interested, are 'I-don't-care.' "

Brier waved the squad through. "Are you drunk?" she demanded of the guard, who was now leaning perilously far out of the box to watch them pass.

"*I'm* not. *They* are." With a giddy sweep of his arm, he indicated the lit windows of the keep high above. "Five days and five nights, ever since M'lord got home. All the sons are up there too, except yours. Think what fun you're missing, cadet! If Kencyr weren't so hard to poison, we'd all be dead by now. What've y'got there?"

He was peering down at Kindrie, trying to focus.

"Something M'lord lost awhile ago."

"His Shanir toy, is it? Good, good. That Southron play-thing he brought back with him won't last the night. Distract 'im, thassa idea. We've had about all the fun here we can stand."

He gagged briefly, but there was nothing in his stomach to bring up nor had there been, probably, for the better part of five days. They heard him begin to giggle again as they pressed on, his voice a shaky echo of his master's, carousing in the high keep above.

That shrill titter followed them all the way through the quarter belonging to Higron, Caldane's sixth estab-lished son. They heard it in raucous guard-halls, in shad-owy side-streets, in the darkened bedrooms of children, once even burbling in a rain barrel where a burly Kendar was trying to drown himself.

Jame fell in beside Iron-thorn, a nervous Jorin trotting close at her heels. "You know," she said, "this isn't partic-ularly funny. I had no idea that the bond between High-born and Kendar could work this way."

"A lord's health always affects his people, lady, depending on how tightly he grips them. All the Caineron hold very tight. Then too, excessive wine can . . . complicate matters."

Jame shot her a sidelong glance. "You feel it too, don't you?"

"I'm sworn to your brother now, lady," the other said stiffly. "But my family has been Caineron *yondri* for generations. I feel enough to remember why I seldom drink."

They were approaching the gate of Grondin, Caldane's oldest son and the frequent butt of Tiggeri's practical jokes. Once, Brier could have judged to a hair how matters stood between the brothers. Not now. But to reach Caldane's citadel they must pass this way.

Grondin's district was the largest in Restormir except for M'lord's on the far side of the river. Two bridges spanned the latter, the farther to the east, leading to Caldane's general compound; the closer to the north, connecting by a side door to the castle mound itself. Brier proposed to use this latter route, if she could get her squad past Grondin's watchmen.

This proved easy.

Once the guard had locked the gate behind them, however, he gleefully whistled up his cronies to harry the "Tiggie" cadets like so many stray dogs.

Brier hurried her squad on. Tiggeri notwithstanding, she had seen Grondin drunk. To fall into his people's hands just now would be more than unpleasant. Damn. It sounded as if the entire district was rousing to join in the fun. Drunken halloos echoed from street to street to mark the twisting course of the chase.

"We're going in a circle," said the Knorth.

Brier almost demanded how she knew, but then glimpsed the tower looming over roof tops to her right. She had only been in Restormir briefly two years ago and never in this quarter, which was laid out with as little foresight as everything else that Grondin did. Moreover, her sense of direction was even worse than her head for heights. Perhaps this narrow way cut back to the main thoroughfare. No. Windowless walls rose on three sides, close and dank. A dead end.

The uproar approached. Torchlight washed across the blind alley's mouth. Then someone seemingly overhead cried:

"Haloo-loo-loo! *This* way!"

Torchlight withdrew as the hunt followed that insistent voice, now crying in the upper distance:

"Kalli-kalli-catch-'em-if-you-can!"

Brier's relief was short-lived, however; when she turned back to her small command, the Knorth was gone.

She might have asked herself, *where?* Only a drainpipe to the roof broke that blank expanse of discolored brick. Instead, all she could think was that the girl had bolted. Knorth or Caineron, all Highborn were alike after all.

However, nothing her superiors did diminished her own responsibility. She must get these cadets safely away.

At the alley's mouth they turned left—toward the relative safety of Higron's gigglers, Brier thought. But soon afterward she realized that she had gotten turned completely around when they came to a wall with the sound of swift water beyond it. Left again . . . and here was the eastern bridge leading to Caldane's compound.

"Well, it isn't exactly the back door," said the Knorth, breathless at her elbow, "but I take it we can still reach the citadel by this route. You didn't think I'd run out, did you? Sweet Trinity. You did. Cadet, listen: you can expect some fairly strange behavior from me, off and on, but never that. Understand?"

The Kendar simply stared at her.

"Right," said Jame. "I'll just have to prove myself as we go, won't I?"

And she would, she swore to herself, just as she had to Marc—but not by telling this wooden-faced cadet how she had spent the last half hour scrambling about on the roof tops with a death banner slung across her back, playing hare-and-hounds for the third time that week.

"After you," she said, indicating the bridge with a sweep of her hand.

Water plunged under the span, snow-fed, raging between the close-set walls of the two compounds. The noise made ears ring. On the far side, after they had slipped through Caldane's gate and closed it behind them against the river's roar, Jame repeated the question which she had tried to ask half way across.

"You must have lived in this quarter when you served at Restormir. How well d'they know you here?"

"Well enough," said the cadet shortly. "It can't be helped." She gave Jame a sharp look. "How did you know I'd done a home tour?"

"I . . . er . . . must have heard it somewhere," Jame said, embarrassed.

In fact, she had overheard it from inside the Highlord's tent.

"*Ancestors know what that Kendar did to make Caldane so angry,*" Torisen had said and paused—in question, Jame had thought.

The quality of Harn's silence in response, however, had said as plainly as words, *There are some things Highborn shouldn't ask.*

"Odd that there's no guard here," she said, hastily changing the topic and backing up for a look at the sentry box perched over the gate.

Her foot hit a trip-wire. She went over backward, nearly landing on Jorin, who sprang aside with an affronted exclamation. Affront turned to a terrified squawk at a tremendous crash. Shards of crockery flew out of the shadows.

"Clumsy lot, you cadets," said a calm voice overhead.

A gray-haired man sat on the edge of the box. Propped against its corner support, legs dangling, he looked more like a discarded puppet than the veteran randon officer which his token scarf declared him to be.

"Well, well," he said, smiling down at the big Kendar. "Welcome back to Restormir, Brier Iron-thorn."

Brier answered in a language which Jame didn't understand, but the man interrupted her.

"Use common Kens, child," he said gently. "You don't have a right to Caineron battle-speech anymore."

"As you say, Randon Quick-foot. Are you going to raise the guard?"

"I just did, or tried to," he said, with a curious roll of his head toward the makeshift alarm. "Why are you here?"

"Private business, ran. Nothing that should endanger the Caineron or Restormir, as far as I can see."

She wouldn't have come, Jame realized, if she had thought that it did. It wasn't easy, after all, to change the allegiance of generations.

"Fair enough," said Randon Quick-foot. "You're hardly the one for whom the watch was set, anyway.

Most of our people are out chasing reports of Merikit at large in the valley. No one here has forgotten Kithorn."

"That was our mission too, randon, out of Tentir. We were about to call it off due to serious weirding."

"Weirding." His eyes flickered in his slack face. "Not that too. Still, our randon can go to earth, the Merikit way. Away from Restormir, their wits should at least be clear enough for that."

"Yes, randon. Without help."

The officer's mouth twisted in acknowledgment of some point which Jame didn't catch. "True, child, true. 'Help' can be costly. Advice is cheaper, so I'll offer you that, for old time's sake: whatever your business, stay out of M'lord's way. He's initiating a randon candidate tonight."

"I . . . see. Good-bye, Ran Quick-foot, and thank you."

"That was quite a crash," said Jame as they went on. "Why aren't we up to our necks in guards by now—and what was wrong with your friend?"

"My friend, lady? Yes, I suppose he was. He's been chewing black-root. A bit of it keeps the head clear. More leads to progressive paralysis, like a series of self-induced strokes. Five days of it . . . . At best, he'll never be quick footed again."

"And that's what's happening to randon all over this compound tonight? For a toad like Caldane?"

"No, lady. For the same reasons you invoked earlier: honor and obligation."

One of the cadets gave a startled exclamation, and Jame turned quickly to find a stranger in their midst. By her clothes, she was a common Kendar, perhaps a baker. She had come up behind the squad and then, because her pace was faster, walked straight into their ranks. Eyes wide but unseeing, she passed between Jame and Brier. They stared after her. She was walking on her toes, as if lifted by the scruff of the neck and hauled forward.

More sleepwalkers overtook and bore them along, as if caught in waters running rapidly downhill. All flowed into Restormir's main square. The large, open space was already full of people—men, women, and children —moving in unison as if to the steps of some strange dance. If one turned, all did; if another gestured, a thousand hands followed suit. Expressions crossed their sleeping faces like windflaws over water: anger, arrogance, and something very like fear. Some were mouthing words, others mumbling them, so that a low murmur filled the square from side to side.

"Wait here," whispered the Knorth.

Before Brier could stop her, she had slipped into the crowd and begun to winnow through it, apparently in search of the most articulate sleep-talker. No one paid any attention to her. Nonetheless, the walkers were becoming more agitated. Now it looked as if each one of them was circling something, or someone. The Knorth walked backward in front of a large Kendar, face to face, perhaps the better to hear him. A thousand hands swung in a sudden, vicious slap, but only one struck home.

Brier swore. Ducking into the crowd, she snatched the Highborn out from under the Kendar's feet while he and a thousand others went on kicking thin air. Back on the square's edge, she propped her against a wall.

"Did you hear that cry?" the latter asked, dazed.

"No, lady. You didn't make a sound." Brier's attention sharpened. "You're bleeding. Healer . . . ."

"No!" The Knorth straightened, hastily drawing a sleeve across her face. "Don't fuss. I'm all right."

In the square, the sleepers stumbled and for a moment fought to regain their balance, again on tiptoe. The sight of all those wind-milling arms would have been funny, if not for the sudden terror on their faces.

"It's never been this bad before," Brier muttered. "Never. What in Perimal's name is M'lord drinking?"

"It may be as much a matter of what he drank," said the Knorth under her breath. "*Damn.* C'mon, then."

III

JAME WAS STILL silently cursing herself as they left the square. It seemed that the bond between lord and Kendar was so cruelly tight here that those poor people, reduced to near stupor by Caldane's excesses, were unconsciously mirroring his actions and mumbling his thoughts. If so, under all his bully bluster Caldane was scared sick about something. And he was taking it out on that poor bastard whose cry she had so distinctly heard, if no one else had. It was Graykin whom Caldane was abusing, she was almost certain . . . because he couldn't get his hands on the Southron's new mistress? Could all this somehow be the result of that little trick which she had played on Caldane in his tent at the Cataracts?

They were drawing near the two arms of the river that surrounded the castle mound like a moat. More Kendar drifted past them, but no one tried again to raise the alarm. Two randon sprawled at the gate-posts of the moat bridge. One watched them approach but didn't speak, perhaps because she no longer could. The other was dead. Brier saluted both.

"This way," she said, and led her small command over the bridge and around to a lesser door which opened directly into the mound.

Inside, they descended a ramp of weeping stone, lined with doors. The dank, mildewed air made Jame's nose twitch and Jorin sneeze. At its foot the decline sank into black water, lapping against weed crusted lintels.

"Here," said the Kendar, and put her shoulder to the last unsubmerged door.

The shriek of its rusted hinges made Jame flinch, but no guard appeared. Beyond, a corridor lined with more stout doors stretched out ahead of them, its far end curving out of sight. The Kendar looked at Jame expectantly. All she remembered from her dream about Graykin's prison, though, was this stink of decay and Caldane's voice echoing off stone walls.

There was no sound of M'lord now, as surely there would be if he were still kicking Graykin around a cell. Had she been wrong, or were they both somewhere else?

"We'll have to search," she said. "How big is this place?"

"On this level, perhaps two hundred cells, opening off a series of concentric corridors like this one. You pass from one hall to the next through short passageways which double as guardrooms. There are at least a dozen levels above this, extending up into the mound. Below, who knows."

Oh, lord. "We'll have to separate, then."

"Lady, are you sure?"

Jame sighed. "Hardly ever, about anything."

But she didn't call off the hunt, to the cadets' delight and their commander's disgust. The latter sent the former off in pairs, herself going with Rue. That left the two Highborn. Kindrie hadn't spoken since his encounter with the bogles. Jame wondered if he was having second thoughts—much good they would do anyone now.

Jorin was snuffing around the corridor. Unfortunately, he had never met Graykin nor did Jame still have any of the spy's clothes. But she remembered their slightly sour smell. The ounce sneezed twice, then trotted off down the hall. She followed, Kindrie trailing after her.

They went down one curving hall after another, cutting between them by way of the numbered doors, moving toward the core. The whole dungeon seemed to be empty. Caldane must have cleaned it out the previous winter and not yet gotten around to restocking it with prisoners or guards. Cadets began to call back and forth to each other, as if this were all a game. Brier Iron-thorn must be having a fit. But they were out of Jame's way for the moment, which was what she had intended in splitting them up. The fewer to witness her first meeting with Graykin, the better.

However, the cell to which Jorin led them was empty.

Damnation, Jame thought, standing in the middle of it. Now what?

Of course, there was that thread of contact which had first warned her, back in Gothregor, that her servant was in trouble. She hadn't touched it since. After all, sharing awareness with Jorin was one thing, but with this scruffy little half-breed whom she barely knew? Ugh.

Don't be so damn squeamish, she told herself sharply. *Why did you come, if not to rescue him?* The image of

Graykin's thin face rose in her mind's eye. *Where are you?* she silently asked it. *What do you see? What do you feel?*

Pain. Intense, obscene, wrenching at shoulders as though to tear the flesh off of them, dragging the skin up around the throat . . . . Hard . . . to breathe. Underfoot, nothing, down and down and down . . . . But to the side, two faces staring, a young Kendar in the background, sick-eyed, eclipsed by Caineron's full moon gloat:

". . . *told you I would think of something special. Now dance, puppet, dance . . . .*"

Oh god, his fat hands on the wires, jerking them . . . .

Far below, down in the dungeons among the rats, someone screamed.

Jame woke to the echo, cracking off the stone walls around her. She was curled up in a ball on the floor. Her throat hurt.

Kindrie and Jorin had backed away from her into the far corner.

"Backlash," said the healer hoarsely. "Whoever this man is, he's bound to you, isn't he? *Isn't he?*"

Before she could answer, Brier Iron-thorn came swiftly into the cell, very large and controlled, prepared to be very dangerous. The sheer force of her presence brought Jame lurching to her feet.

"S-scream?" she stammered, in response to the Kendar's sharp question. "What scream? Oh"—remembering the echoes—"*that* scream."

Now she's going to think I'm a fool, as well as mad. But Graykin . . . .

"He's not here anymore," she said, not very coherently. "Caldane has him up in the tower."

A buzz of excitement rose from the hall, where more cadets had arrived in time to overhear her.

"I *can't* take you up there," said Jame desperately. "Any of you. This isn't hide-and-seek in the dark anymore. This is Highborn against Kendar . . . and if these innocents don't know what that means, Brier Iron-thorn, I'll bet my boots you do. Think! Torisen doesn't know where we are. If Caldane gets his hands on any of us, he can do anything he wants, and get away with it!"

"Are you going on, lady?"

"I have to."

"Then so do we."

Jame ran a distraught hand through her hair, forgetting that it was under a cap. "My brother is going to skin us all. You know that, don't you? Oh, hell. Caldane will probably beat him to it, anyway."

 IV

THE HEART OF RESTORMIR proved to be hollow. At the bottom were the flooded levels of the dungeon, a black, noisome well in which floated debris and drowned rats. The innermost of the concentric halls overlooked it, ring on ring of them connected by iron stairs, extending upward to the top of the mound.

The Knorth raiders climbed out of the prison pit as though into a different although no less deserted world, over a stained alabaster rim into a court paved with white marble across which dried leaves rattled. All around reared up the inner walls of Caldane's tower keep. On the court level, tall glass doors opening into reception halls, in whose dusty depths a wealth of mirrors and diamantine panels gave back the soft glow of stolen sunlight.

Jame caught her breath. For a moment, she had thought that the rooms were full of motionless giants. Now, however, she saw that they were gilded statues, multiplied by reflection. Portly figures, arrogant faces . . . they all looked like Caldane, larger than life, striking various heroic poses.

Snatches of discordant music and laughter echoed hollowly down the throat of the tower. The man himself was above in the Crown—carousing with how many of his kin? The Caineron was the largest house in the Kencyrath, and Caldane easily the most prolific lord. Aside from his numerous progeny, there must be several hundred Caineron Highborn, not that all lived at Restormir, much less in this tower. Of those who did, hopefully many besides Tiggeri had elected to stay in Kothifir.

Shouts above, and a jeering chant: "Go, go, go . . . !"

A golden shower rained down, mostly into the pit but some spattering the rim and the last cadet over it. He and the others hastily drew back. Either someone had a phenomenal bladder, Jame thought, or . . . how much water, from what height, equaled how many Caineron? No equation came to mind.

The cadets stared upward, eyes widening with their own calculations.

Ancestors be praised, thought Jame. *Now they understand*.

As if in answer, their gaze returned expectantly to her. Innocents these children might be, but not cowards.

Their commander had been watching her throughout, stone-faced as if to say: *This madness begins and ends with you*.

True, but not very helpful.

A regal stair swept up around the inner walls, fit for the ascension of kings although strewn with a winter's dirt. Jame began to climb, Jorin bouncing on ahead, the others following close behind.

Balconies studded the walls seemingly at random, decked with winter-worn finery—here a torn banner of silver and gold, there cat bone chimes clattering in the errant breeze. Inside, one glimpsed quarters left in disarray, presumably, by the Cainerons' hasty departure for the Cataracts the previous winter. Overhead, the Crown cantilevered out in nine tiers around the top of the shaft, leaving some twenty feet at the center open to the night sky. Stars shone there, eclipsed by small, swift shapes and one larger than they, which hung slowly swaying.

Jame was leaning over the balustrade, trying to see what the latter was, when a harsh sound made her turn quickly. One of the cadets had doubled up on the steps, down which he would have surely rolled if Brier Ironthorn hadn't stopped him.

"Height-sickness," said the Kendar tersely, steadying the boy.

For a moment, Jame was puzzled. A hundred feet to the courtyard, as much again to the floor of the pit . . . . Not bad. Then again, the only height that bothered her was from the back of a tall horse. Kendar, however, were prone to acrophobia.

So was Caldane.

"Why would a man afraid of heights live at the top of a tower?" she wondered out-loud.

"M'lord? If he thought that fear was common knowledge, he'd spit blood. Besides, the Crown was his father's work."

Of course, thought Jame. No one as vain as Caldane would admit any weakness, to others or to himself—nor, from what she had heard, would the Caineron Matriarch let him fall short of his father's measure.

Then she recoiled. Blackness like a piece of flapping cloth had swooped in front of her face and hovered there on furry wings. Wide, quizzical eyes in a velvet fox-mask; delicate, cupped ears; a long, flat brush . . . .

"*Quipp?*" said the foxkin, and dove inside her jacket.

"Healer, get down here," Iron-thorn said, impatient, preoccupied; then, as an afterthought: "Ignore it, lady. It's harmless."

Easy for her to say. Jame wriggled, trying to reach the furry body as it clambered up the curve of her ribs toward the spine.

Kindrie bent over the cadet.

"Can you help him?"

"*Quipp!*" said the foxkin in Jame's ear, and scuttled back down her collar.

"With the nausea, yes; not with the vertigo. His entire soul-scape is reeling." The healer himself suddenly staggered, his bare foot sliding off the step. The Kendar caught his arm.

"Don't tell me it's contagious," said Jame sarcastically, but she was perplexed: a Shanir healer should draw more stability than that from his own soul-image.

Ah. The foxkin had gotten into her *d'hen* sleeve—the full left one, fortunately. She shook it gingerly. A darkness with luminous eyes gathered at the cuff, then shot off. Jorin nearly sprang over the balustrade after it.

"Life out here is just too exciting," said Jame. "Let's go inside."

They had almost run out of staircase, anyway. It ended in a landing under the first of the nine tiers, with a door opening into what had been the old keep's ramparts. Now, off the main corridor, the level was divided into tiny rooms which probably housed the Crown's Kendar servants. If so, however, none were there now.

Feet tramped overhead. Objects thudded. Then there was a crash, an oath, and a sound like the spring migration of the bison, fading into the distance.

"What on earth is above us?" Jame asked.

"Kitchens," said ten-commander and healer simultaneously.

"I forgot that you both were here before. How well d'you know the layout?"

"Not very . . . ." they began, and stopped short, eyeing each other warily.

"M'lord insisted that I stay within earshot," said Kindrie.

"And I was only crown-side once, lady." The bronze planes of the Kendar's face seemed to clamp shut on the words.

Whatever happened between her and Caldane, happened there, Jame thought, warning herself, *That's her business. Just this once, mind your own.*

They found a minor flight of stairs and mounted it cautiously.

The room into which they emerged was indeed a kitchen, given over primarily to stewing. Fireplaces lined the walls, each with a waist-high, three legged cauldron sitting in it. The nearest was full of water, in which bobbed whole carrots, discolored parsnips, and onions still in their outer skins. Other pots and pans hung from the low rafters, except for those piled dirty on the floor. Parsley, figs, and raisins were strewn about an overturned chopping block. Grapes rolled underfoot. The strong licorice smell of half-crushed anise and fennel rose from a mortar.

"Hotchpotch, or an attempt at it," said Jame, drawing on memories of the kitchen at the Res aB'tyrr, and remembering that she hadn't eaten all day. This broth really needed some meat, though—mutton, or pheasant, or chicken.

From out in the hall came a rapidly approaching storm of feet, cries, and clucking. A white hen ran past the door, closely pursued by a dozen Highborn men in their finest if rather soiled clothes, brandishing knives, cleavers, and slotted spoons. No one glanced into the stewry—fortunately, because the sight and sound of them had frozen the cadets open-mouthed where they stood. Peering cautiously around the door's edge, Jame saw the pursuit plunge off down the curving hall, on its second lap of the tower. From somewhere above came a muffled chant:

"Food, food, food . . . !"

Then Jame realized that the door opposite had opened and someone was leaning out of it, just as she was from hers, to stare after the vanishing hunt. A girl, maybe sixteen, wearing a tight, pearl-strewn bodice and a flame-colored skirt . . . .

Behind masks, their eyes met.

"Why, lady!" the younger Highborn gasped.

Jame plunged across the corridor and shoved the girl back into what proved to be a pantry.

"Stay!" she snapped over her shoulder at the startled Kendar and slammed the door in their faces.

Surrounded by strings of onions, garlic, and mandrake, she faced this young Highborn whom she had first met in the royal apartments of a Karkinoran palace, the nominal consort of its prince.

"Well, Lyra. Now what?"

Caldane's daughter stared at her. "It *is* you! Oh, how splendid! Maybe now things will start happening again!"

"'Things'? *What* 'things'?"

"*Anything!* It's been so dull here, since Karkinaroth and the Cataracts. We did have fun on that barge ride in between, didn't we?"

"You did, anyway," said Jame, remembering their flight after the prince's death and the collapse of his palace. She had never considered what effect all that excitement might have had on a girl like Lyra, whom she had always thought the model of filial obedience, and not really bright besides.

"Oh, yes!"—with great enthusiasm, plunging immediately to despair—"but just look at me now, reduced to scrounging food like a . . . a menial! At the palace, I at least had Gricki to fetch for me. And that's another thing! If that wretched Southron has done something wrong, *I* should punish him, not Father. He was *my* servant, after all. It isn't fair!"

"Er . . . " said Jame. "Did you know that Graykin is in my service now?"

"Oh, *that's* all right, then," said Lyra, beaming at her. "We're sisters, or as good as. In that case, *you* should be punishing him."

"I've got to find him first."

"He's up in Father's private quarters." Her expression changed suddenly. "I heard him scream. No one should have to scream like that. Come on. I'll take you to him."

"Well, I'll be damned. That is . . . er . . . splendid. Lead on."

She threw open the door. The cadets jumped back, looking startled, curious, and vaguely disappointed. They had, she realized, been expecting a royal cat-fight. She introduced Lyra to them but not to Brier Iron-thorn, whose expression stopped her. Clearly, Caineron foibles didn't amuse the big Kendar.

Blast the woman, Jame thought. *She turns everything into a test, and I keep failing.*

"*Awk!*" said the hen, and dodged between her feet into the pantry.

"Stop!" cried the pursuing Highborn, rounding the hall's curve.

"Inside!" hissed Lyra.

The Knorth all piled into the pantry, slammed the door shut, and tipped a flour bin over in front of it. Fists beat on its outer panels. From the hall rose a vengeful, hungry cry:

"Give us back our chicken!"

Too drunk to realize what they've seen, Jame thought, backing away from the door. *That's something, anyway*—she turned to met Iron-thorn's stony look—*but not enough.*

"Back here!" Lyra called.

She had retreated to the far wall and now ducked out of sight through a low door, concealed behind a massive bin mounted on rollers. Jame and Jorin followed, emerging in a dark, intramural passage.

"Gran told me about this," Lyra whispered with a giggle. "Father has no idea it's here."

The cadets entered hastily, shoving Kindrie in ahead of them. Their officers, Ten and five, pulled the bin back over the entrance just as the outer door gave way. They heard confusion beyond the wall, a protesting squawk, and the sound of triumphant retreat.

Lyra tugged Jame's sleeve. "This way."

IT WAS VERY DARK between the walls of Restormir, with air as stale as the husks of memory. Sometimes the passage expanded as though into unseen rooms; sometimes it contracted so that one must pass along it edgewise, scraping. The stone brain within that proud Crown might have been half consumed by earwigs, so full of tunnels and blind pockets did it seem.

Jame spat out a clot of spider web, with the distinct impression that she had swallowed its occupant. Forgetting the extra width of Aerulan's banner across her back, she had almost gotten stuck more than once. All she could see was the slightly blacker patch which, presumably, was Lyra, rustling ahead of her. The patch rose. A moment later her foot hit a step. She climbed the invisible stair after her guide, the others on her heels.

Six more flights, almost to the top of the Crown.

From ahead, ever closer, came a stone-muffled chant: "Food, *food*, *FOOD!*" until the walls seemed to vibrate with it. Opening off the stair shaft was a sort of blind gallery, broached with many peepholes through which spears of red light lanced. Below lay Caldane's great hall.

It was two tiers high, its roof supported by stone columns carved in the likeness of tree trunks. Fireplaces roared down one side, making the air before them ripple with heat and the cold walls sweat. Opposite, tall, arched windows stood open to the darkness of the shaft. Between, a hundred Highborn men sat at table, chanting and banging flagons.

"*Food*, FOOD, *FOOD!*"

Empty plates bounced. So did the heads of those who had passed out.

Masked, skirted figures ran between the long boards, carrying wine ewers with which they tried to keep full the flailing cups—not women but young, Highborn boys, Jame saw, as one was suddenly tripped and jerked beneath a table. The men on either side leaned drunkenly down to watch. Above the salt, Caldane's six established sons roared approval. Down in the compounds, their followers must be shouting themselves bloody raw.

All this for one pot of inedible soup, Jame thought. *Maybe that will teach Caldane not to incapacitate his entire Kendar staff.*

—or maybe not: M'lord was not the sort to admit mistakes, much less learn from them.

The man himself lounged in a golden chair on a dais at the upper end of the hall, wrapped in a peacock blue robe, negligently holding a wine glass. Unlike his flushed, sweating followers, he looked sleek and smug. Sated. Now and again, he glanced out the windows, at something which Jame couldn't see. She recognized that cream-fed smirk, though. It had been on his fat face when he had held her captive in his tent at the Cataracts, and in Kallystine's voice after M'lady had slapped her.

Kindrie had been watching through a different hole. When he turned toward Jame, the spot of light moving from faded eye to pale cheek to white hair, she wondered if he had also seen such a smile, that night at Tentir.

"Are we too late?" he asked in a husky voice, and she knew that he had.

This time, Graykin's pain come to her muted through barriers warily half raised. Worse, though, was that choking hold on her/his throat, through which breath barely wheezed.

"He isn't dead," she said, gulping air, realizing that even so she might not have answered the healer's question.

They climbed again, up to the ninth tier. At the stair's head, Lyra cautiously opened a panel and slipped through. A moment later, she had swung it wide and was beckoning them into Lord Caineron's private quarters.

Jame stopped short on the threshold. For a moment, she was back in her room at Gothregor, staring at her fragmented features in a broken mirror. But these mirrors were whole and the face reflected in them visored, retreating. From behind came a muffled exclamation as her booted heel came down on Kindrie's bare toes.

This is ridiculous, she thought, and entered.

Easy to see where Kallystine had gotten the idea for her chambers at Gothregor, pale reflection that they were of this mirrored wilderness where wall reflected wall and room melted into room. Rich hangings and curious statuary marched off in all directions, over inlaid floors strewn ankle deep with rare furs. A haze of incense drifted under the low, mirrored ceiling. In the midst of such bewildering opulence floated the cadets' faces, seen from every angle as they stared about them.

"We mustn't separate," Jame said, and found that she spoke to reflections.

Had Lyra led them into a trap? Did Caldane know reflective magic? There was a bricked-up house in Tai-tastigon where the owner's first wife had wandered inside one mirror after another for twenty years, searching for the reflection of an open door . . . .

Then Jame looked again, harder. Since when had she been so tall, so . . . busty? All the mirrors were subtly distorted. Caldane *did* practice magic, but only to reshape his own portly image. Between these flattering glasses and those heroic statues in the reception halls below, perhaps he had well and truly convinced himself that illusion was truth.

"Here I am."

"Where are you?" reflected faces whispered, turning to look in the wrong direction, echo answering echo. "Five? Ten?"

Iron-thorn's dark visage and the Shanir's pallor moved silently among the silvered planes, caught for a moment and then gone.

"Gricki?" Lyra's light voice called off in the distance. "Gricki!"

The floor vibrated with the clamor from the hall below, muted by stone and fur. Mirrors seemed to ripple in their frames. So very hot and close . . . .

Statuary like the death-molds of men and women, cruelly altered; wolver pelts and mock Arrin-ken; a two-headed ape, stuffed; a great green parrot nailed to its perch, alive; potbellied bronze burners, belching clouds of incense to make the mind reel; Caldane's smell of rich perfume underlain with stale sweat, to make the stomach seethe . . . .

A vast bed, and under its counterpane, face covered, a still form.

"G-Graykin?"

But no. What strange figure was this, its body laid open and velvet coils of intestine spilling out, liver and lights strewn about the bed like stuffed toys? A doll, designed to be nightly disemboweled . . . and it had her face.

Jame threw the cover back over it.

Standing almost on her foot, Jorin sniffed and cowered. She smelled it too: the faint stench of burned flesh. The ounce slinking unhappily on her heels, she followed her nose.

Ahead, she thought she saw Graykin's face, oddly stiff and distorted. Another damned reflection . . . but this time it was that of a death banner, which she tracked from mirror to mirror back to a small room illuminated like a shrine by innumerable candles. Brier Iron-thorn stood staring at the tapestry, oblivious to the overturned incense pots at her feet whose hot coals were singeing the pelts of mottled leather which covered the floor.

"Genjar," she said, without turning.

Jame regarded that sharp face, caught forever by Kendar weavers in a sneer which the wavering smoke turned almost into a snarl. So this was Caldane's favorite son, who had led the Southern Host to slaughter at Urakarn, where a young Torisen had been taken prisoner and tortured. Hadn't there been some mystery about Genjar's death afterward?

"*A damned strange way to commit suicide*," she had heard somebody say.

Caldane had never forgiven Tori, although for what, exactly, no one seemed to know.

Iron-thorn was staring at the tapestry face with that particular woodenness which, for her, indicated strong emotion.

"Surely you were too young to have served at Urakarn," Jame said involuntarily.

"I was. My mother wasn't. She died escaping."

With that, the Kendar turned abruptly on her heel and stalked away.

Oh, lord. What have I put my foot in now? Jame wondered.

The pelts still smoldered in spots, between blue and black markings which looked almost deliberate. Jame had no objection to burning Caldane's roof over his head, except that she was under it too. She beat out the coals with gloved hands. The hides hadn't been entirely scraped bare, as she had thought at first. Each still had a mop of black, braided hair . . . .

Jame rose abruptly and backed to the door where Jorin waited, having refused to enter. She had been standing on the flayed, tattooed skins of Merikit hillmen.

Outside, the stink of burning grew stronger.

"Here!" Lyra was calling. "Here! Oh, hurry!"

Jame arrived last, still following her nose, to find her way blocked by the broad backs of the cadets. Water-flowing between them, she emerged in the cooler air of a balcony overhanging the shaft. To one side was a small furnace, sullenly aglow, in a litter of tools, bits of wire, and hooks. Several feet away, a Kendar stood on the very edge of the abyss, looking down. In his hand, forgotten, he held an awl from which wisps of rank smoke still rose.

"Well, candidate," said Brier Iron-thorn.

The man looked up. He was very young, hardly more than a boy, and would have been handsome if not for his haggard face and bloodshot eyes.

"Well, cadet," he said, with a rictus smile. "Is Tentir worth M'lord's price?"

"I refused to pay."

He blinked, refocusing. "So you did"—with a sneer that didn't quite stick. "Went the soft way through the little High-lord, didn't you? Solved Honor's Paradox by turning your back on it." He glanced again over the edge and swayed, gulping.

Not just height-sickness, Jame thought, going forward a step, stopped by Iron-thorn's back-flung, restraining hand. *A grisly hangover. Caldane, you son of a . . . .*

"It *is* a paradox, isn't it?" the boy said, with a cracked laugh. "Where does obedience end and personal honor begin? Nowhere, M'lord wanted me to say. Obedience *is* honor. Then he ordered me to do *that*." He gestured helplessly toward the shaft, realized that he still held the awl, and threw it away. "I was drunk. I did his bidding. And it broke the bond between us. No more lord. No more honor."

"And now?"

"Why," he said, again with that terrible smile. "I redeem honor, of course. I was only waiting for a witness."

With that, he stepped over the edge and fell without a sound.

"My God!" said Jame, and started forward; but Brier stood in her way.

"Better not to look, lady."

Jame slipped around her. "Honestly, Ten, I probably have a better head for heights than you do . . . ."

From below, the figure hanging in the shaft had seemed only a blot against the stars. From here above, it appeared violently foreshortened, the thin, naked body dwindling to invisible feet, the whole swaying fish-pale in the light spilling from Caldane's hall. Peaks rose from each shoulder where hooks took the body's weight, stretching the skin upward. More fleshhooks pierced ears, and wrists, and knees, to make the puppet dance. Oh, Graykin . . . .

Jame struggled to breathe, to stay calm. *It won't help to flare. Caldane is right below us, looking out his window at his toy, smiling . . . it won't help anyone if I flare . . . .*

Someone touched her shoulder. She felt the berserker rage leap down her nerve-ends, through flesh and fabric, lightning in search of the ground. In its sudden glare, to her amazement, she saw the white flowers of the tapestry which hung outside Gothregor's secret garden. The thunderclap made her gasp, but it cleared her head. The rage was gone. She hadn't moved, but Kindrie had been hurled backward into the cadets, two of whom he had knocked down. His white hair stood on end. Ball lightning rolled off his shoulders like hail to bounce crackling on the floor.

"I did warn you, priest," she said, shaken.

"How many casualties d'you want up here?" demanded Iron-thorn. "Behave . . . lady."

"Y-yes, ran. B-but my friend . . . he's choking."

A boom had been swung out over the shaft and lowered, with a makeshift puppeteer's crosspiece fixed to it. The two support wires were secured to the former. Control wires ran up through the latter, back ready for the puppet-master's hands. Cadets raised the boom and gingerly swung the dangling figure back over the balcony, wincing with every jolt for fear that it would tear loose. There was little blood: the hooks, inserted red hot, had finished the cauterizing begun by the heated awl. Nor need they have worried about ripping flesh: muscle as well as skin had been pierced. But between shock and near-strangulation by his own drawn-up skin, the Southron was in uncertain shape.

"Help him!" Jame said to Kindrie.

The healer had been hanging back, random sparks still snapping in his hair. "I'm not sure I can," he said unhappily. "He looks enough like a Caineron to be Genjar's younger brother—but he isn't pure Kencyr, is he?"

"He's a Kencyr-Southron half-breed," Lyra chimed in. "His name is Gricki."

" 'Gricki,' " muttered Brier, translating the Southron word: " 'filth.' D'you mean we've gone through all this for some Southland's mongrel?"

The Knorth shot her an impatient look. "We can't pick and choose with whom to keep faith."

Brier blinked. A Caineron would have laughed at such a naive statement: there was always some way consonant with honor to avoid such inconveniences. And yet . . . and yet . . . .

Values, Caineron and Knorth, shifted under her feet until with a jolt she landed on something solid: *Keep faith.*

Yes. Perhaps she could make a stand on that.

"Of course I don't object to his bloodlines," Kindrie was saying to Jame. "Who am I, to do that? But I've never dealt with a non-Kencyr's soul-image before, assuming he has one. A-and besides . . . ." He gulped, looking suddenly both miserable and desperate. "L-Lord Ishtier has barred me from my own. Just now . . . the door behind the tapestry . . . . You almost smashed through it, almost got me back into my garden. C-Can't you try again? Please?"

"You mean you can't heal anyone? But you helped that cadet on the stair!"

"A bit. As much as I dared. Don't you see? I-I can't draw on my own soul for strength, or retreat into it to heal myself."

"Sweet Trinity," said Jame, blankly.

Back at Wilden, he had told her how the Randir Matri-arch had bartered that knowledge to Ishtier. She should have realized that the priest had made use of it. Instead, she had brought the healer into this danger blithely assuming that he was, essentially, indestructible. And he had come without complaint, knowing that he wasn't. Who, therefore, had kept faith with whom? Just the same, should she try to help him as he asked? Did she dare?

"I can't," she said, helplessly. "The last person you should consort with just now is someone who keeps knocking you across rooms by sheer, bloody reflex. Next time, it will probably be through a wall. Just do what you can, as quickly as possible. Any minute now, M'lord is going to miss his plaything.

"We're lucky he didn't see that boy fall," she said in an undertone to Brier Iron-thorn, as Kindrie gingerly bent over his charge.

"He was probably expecting it."

"Ugh. Trust Caldane to test Honor's Paradox with the moral equivalent of a meat axe. Does he put all randon candidates through ordeals like this?"

"Only the best—to prove their loyalty to him, he says. And to see how strong their stomachs are. 'That boy' failed. Sometimes, doing counts less than living with the consequences."

Jame regarded her curiously. "If he had given you such an order, cadet, would you have obeyed?"

Green eyes turned to her, malachite set in ironwood.

"That," said the Kendar, "was not my test."

Behind them, someone gave a startled exclamation. They turned in time to see a Caineron Highborn bolt back through the apartment, throwing aside the jewelled slippers which he had apparently been sent to fetch.

"Yours," Ten snapped at Five, and was off in pursuit faster than seemed possible for someone so big.

"Right," said Vant with satisfaction, assuming command. "Up gear, Kennies. We're going."

"Where?" Jame asked.

The other cadets hesitated, obviously feeling that this was a good question.

"Er . . . ." said Vant, not looking at her. "Somebody, wrap that Southie up in something."

"Who?" demanded Rue, pugnacious. "In what?"

"*Anything*, dammit! Here." He tore down a silken hanging and threw it at her.

Jame helped bundle up her unconscious servant. He looked awful, marked not only with his fresh injuries but with the blackened eyes and broken teeth of a previous beating while his bruised ribs stood out like those of a half-starved dog. A hard winter he must have had of it.

"Father will kill me!" Lyra wailed.

"Calm down!" said Jame over her shoulder. "You're probably the only one of us that he won't."

"He will, he will! Listen . . . they're on the stair! Gran, help!"

With that, she snatched up her hem, betraying no underskirt whatsoever, and fled down the long balcony.

"Follow her!" Jame snapped at the others.

"Er . . . ." said Vant again, to the air above her head. "That isn't such a good idea, lady."

Jame sat back on her heels, regarding him. He was trying to put her in her place, as he saw it, as tactfully as he knew how. She remembered the battle of wills between Kallystine and her captain, Highborn power against randon discipline. "Perhaps your ten-commander could override me," she said, "but not you. Ever. Now go."

Not waiting to see if he obeyed, not needing to, she and Jorin went in search of Brier Iron-thorn, whom they found at the head of the main stairs, outrun by the fleeing Highborn. Nonetheless, Lyra had been premature: no one was yet on the steps. Nearby, multiple reflections gave back the image of the secret passage, open for a hasty exit. The Kendar glanced at her, then past, impatiently, for the cadets.

"I sent them after Lyra," said Jame. "She's run back to Gran—whoever *that* is—so there's another way out of here—presumably."

No need to be told that she had made a mistake.

Brier turned back to the stair, grim-faced. *Trust a Highborn to muck up.* "Then, lady, you had better go with them."

"You're drunk!" said someone at the foot of steps.

"I tell you, I saw them!"

"Didn't."

"Did."

"Didn't!"

"*Did!*"

Now the speakers were coming up, followed by a crowd loudly making bets.

"*Go,*" said the Kendar, with such force that Jame fell back a step, treading on Jorin's toes.

Trinity, but that was power, and in one who had barely begun her training. The feeling almost overwhelmed Jame that it *wasn't* her place to interfere in randon affairs. Tori would hardly think so. Neither would any other Highborn whom she had ever met. But Marc would understand. Very well: If she couldn't coerce, she would blackmail.

"I won't leave," she said, "without you."

Brier gave the Highborn a hard look. She had been prepared to fall into Caldane's hands herself to delay pursuit, to keep faith with her new lord—a bitter but simple choice. A premonition touched her now, though, regarding her lord's sister, that nothing from now on would be so straightforward. Stepping back, she closed the panel leading to the hidden stair.

After you, the ironic sweep of her hand said.

They went quickly back through Caldane's quarters, drunken voices slurring on their heels. At the end of the balcony, a stair spiraled upward. They climbed, petals drifting down the open well to meet them.

VI

THE OTHERS WAITED for them on top of the Crown. A grove of dwarf cherry trees hung with lanterns sheltered them to one side. On the other gaped the mouth of the shaft. Foxkin rode its feverish exhalation, light from the hall striking blue on the undersides of their black wings. Drunken argument sounded on the balcony below, then receded.

Jame sighed with relief. Turning, she found an anxious Kindrie at her elbow.

"We shouldn't be here," he said urgently to her in a low voice. "Can't you feel it? This is women's land."

He was shivering—from the cool air, perhaps, after the overheated rooms below, or from the memory of Wilden halls under their matriarch's cold hand.

"Huh," said Jame with a shudder of her own, remembering Gothregor. "Forbidden territory. At least no man will think of this as a hiding place. With luck, they'll decide that their friend really was drunk. We've only got to wait, then sneak back down by the secret stair."

"Here you are at last!" cried Lyra happily, sweeping down on them through a storm of cherry blossoms. "Gran wants to see you!"

Oh, lord. After a winter of Kallystine, Jame was as well acquainted with the Caineron ladies as she ever wanted to be. Moreover, mask aside, she was hardly dressed for a social call. But go she must, or "Gran" might raise the alarm through sheer pique.

Brier Iron-thorn was regarding her without expression, perhaps remembering how she had slipped away earlier to confer with Lyra.

"Oh, all right," she snapped. "Come along, then, if you want."

The Kendar gave her a brief, hard stare and then a curt nod, judgment suspended.

They followed Lyra through the grove, ducking under low branches, half-blinded by falling blossoms. Jame stopped suddenly. Ahead, through a moving screen of petals, she thought she saw familiar low walls, down which *imus* marched, and a door gaping third-quarters open. The Earth Wife's lodge? Here? No. Emerging from the trees, she saw a cottage set as though in a mountain-top garden, covered with climbing roses. As they approached, the whitewashed walls revealed themselves to be marble and the blossoms clustered about the windows rose quartz, aglow with warm light from within. More light spilled out the front door, which stood nearly open as though in invitation.

"Come *on*," said Lyra, tugging her sleeve.

The door opened onto the black and white parquet floor of a surprisingly large hall. On its far side was a fireplace with two high-backed chairs drawn cozily up to it. One had its back turned toward the door. From its hidden depths came the click of knitting needles. In the other chair sat a very old woman shaped like a slightly squashed apple dumpling, dressed in many layers of clothes. Her white hair was wrapped around her head in a twig-thin braid and her round face puckered inward around a mouth that had long since outlived its ability to grow new teeth. A black foxkin perched on the chair back over her. In her gnarled hands was the end of a knitted scarf, which stretched back to the busy needles opposite.

Jame realized that she had been slow-witted. "Greetings, Matriarch," she said, with the appropriate salute.

Age-gummed eyes fixed on her. The toothless mouth mumbled on its own gums, then opened. "So. You're Ganth Gray Lord's girl, are you? Got his temper, I hear. A touch of his madness too, eh? I never did find out if he was ticklish, though—which you aren't, particularly."

Jame blinked. "What?"

The Caineron Matriarch Cattila peered at her, wheezing slightly.

"Go to bed," she said abruptly to Lyra.

"Oh, but Gran . . . "

"Now, missy. And no eavesdropping, either. I'd know."

"Yes, Gran. You always do. I never have any fun anymore. Good night, sister!"

As Lyra reluctantly departed, Jame wondered if the old woman would also dismiss Brier Iron-thorn. On second thought, she didn't think that Cattila could see the tall Kendar as she stood respectfully in the shadows by the door. But then Jame couldn't see the occupant of the other chair, either. Through Jorin, though, she smelled something vaguely familiar, something . . . loamy?

"Scatterbrained," the Matriarch was muttering. "Just like her mother. Speaking of dams, what's this about you refusing to name yours? Ashamed?"

"No."

This old woman was beginning to rattle Jame. No one in the Women's Halls had questioned her so bluntly. Rudeness was the prerogative of great age, perhaps: Caldane's great-grandmother must be nearly two centuries old and none the duller for it, despite her mumble-gums.

Cattila gave a snort which might have been laughter. "Good. A waste of time, that sort of shame. So's regret, rose blight, and great-grandsons. You've got the air of a Knorth purebred, though, as Adiraina says. Now, Kallystine's mother was Randir, a niece of the Wilden Witch. Bad blood there. Very bad. Just what did darling Kally do to your face?"

How did she know that Kallystine had done anything, three days ago and over forty leagues away? By postrider, maybe. One could travel that distance in twelve hours with frequent remounts, bringing the Ear's message-scarf—perhaps the very one which the Matriarch's fingers were now reading.

Someone still worked on the other end of it. A lace section, so much faster to knit than straight work, edged toward Cattila's gnarled hands, a message in transit.

Then Jame placed that smell, last encountered in Kallystine's chambers. Cattila's other visitor was the Ear herself.

"Tell me this much, at least," the Matriarch demanded: "Will this business cause trouble between our houses?"

It would be sweet to pay Kallystine back, but Jame hesitated, remembering the Caineron captain's mention of a possible civil war. She kept forgetting the wider stage on which she now acted.

"No," she said slowly. "Not if I can help it."

Cattila grunted. "Just as well. You Knorth wouldn't've stood a chance. You may not anyway, but that's another matter."

Again came that vast grinding noise, closer than before, like mountains shifting in their beds. A shiver passed through the fabric of the tower. Jorin and the foxkin stirred uneasily.

"What *is* that?" Jame said.

The old woman had clutched the scarf to her chest, flinching as if between lightning flash and thunder clap. Her movement jerked into sight the knitter's hands, old and strong, with very dirty nails. The Ear jerked them back, so that for a moment the two of them seemed to be playing tug of war.

"That's a weirdingstrom," said Cattila, glaring at the again invisible Ear. "A bad one. I sent one of my pets to investigate, but she never came back, did she, Precious?"

This last was addressed to the foxkin, who "quipped" unhappily.

Why, she's bound to that creature, Jame realized, *perhaps to the entire colony. So that's how she learned that I'm not ticklish.*

"I've seen patches of weirding," she said. "Is this so much worse?"

"Is a cataract worse than a raindrop? What do they *teach* you girls at Gothregor these days? Listen: the Three-Faced God created the Chain of Creation out of the chaos of Perimal Darkling, yes?"

"Er . . . ." said Jame, startled. She had always understood that the Enemy was an invader from outside the Chain.

"Listen! The Merikit say that this world rests on the back of a great chaos serpent, left over from the beginning. Its mouth is the great maelstrom called the Maw, that drinks the Eastern Sea. Its offspring run like veins under the earth and water. Some call weirding the Serpent's breath. When it passes over the land, the Serpent's brood awakes, and that includes the River Snake, which lies under the Silver. The first time that happened, the Merikit sent down a hero to subdue the monster. They'll be preparing to dispatch another one now, none too soon. Hear that rumble? North of here, the very face of the earth is changing."

Did the old woman really believe such superstition? But then again, was it? As she had traveled the Riverland's wilderness, stranger thoughts had occurred to Jame. What *was* it which she herself seen on the river bottom when the willow had dunked her?

"If there's going to be an earthquake that bad," she said, "not to mention a weirdingstrom, this tower can't be very safe."

"The quake we'll have to risk. Worse, to be caught out in the weirding. The oldest buildings like this will be all right in the storm: they're built on hill fort ruins, and those ancestors of the Merikit knew how to stay put. But any additions may be swept away. Good riddance, too! A trap and a snare, this valley has been to us all. Without it, we'll have to resettle the border keeps where we should have been all along, guarding against the shadows."

"But what about your Kendar?"

"Safe in the tower, aren't they?"

"Well, no. They're all out sleepwalking in the square."

The old woman stared at her, toothless mouth opening, closing, opening again. "Well! Got 'em drunk, has he? The lord of this house, not man enough to hold his own hangover. Oh, how could he have been so careless, tonight of all nights?"

"I think," said Jame slowly, "that I know."

She would rather have kept quiet—it would certainly have been safer—but she felt that she owed an explanation to someone. So, haltingly, she told the story: how Caldane had taken her prisoner at the Cataracts, how she had slipped something into the wine which he had offered her and tricked him into drinking, how that "something," mysterious crystals taken from a Builder's house in the Anarchies, had affected M'lord:

"He started to hiccup and then to float, this, with only a canvas roof between him and open sky. He's terrified of heights. Imagine, drifting up and away, higher and higher and higher . . . . When would he come down again, and how fast? Matriarch, what can I say? He panicked."

"When?" demanded Brier suddenly emerging from the shadows.

"Er . . . that would have been the thirtieth of winter. He was still 'not quite feeling in touch with things' on the thirty-first, nor probably for some time after that. Why?"

Cattila had been peering at the big Kendar, smacking her gums thoughtfully. "Brier Iron-thingie, isn't it? I never forget a voice."

"But . . . . Matriarch, we've never met."

"We needn't have. I sit in my garden at the shaft's mouth. Nothing goes on below that I don't overhear."

A dull glow kindled in the Kendar's brown face. "Well, then. You know how angry Lord Caineron was with me, how he swore he would never let me either progress in his service or leave it. His grip is . . . very strong. I didn't think anyone could break it."

"But you must have," Jame protested. "At the Cataracts."

"Yes, lady. Now I understand how. He was . . . distracted."

"Meaning he was probably tethered to the floor having hysterics," said Jame. Then her amusement died. "Matriarch, I listened to his Kendar in the square tonight, unconsciously mouthing his hidden thoughts. He tells himself over and over that he's recovered, that it will never happen again—but underneath he's terrified that it will, and he's trying to bury that fear under excess. That's the reason for his carelessness, and for your danger. I'm sorry for the latter, but by God I had cause for what I did and if need be, I'd do it again."

She stopped, defiant, braced for the old woman's wrath.

Cattila had been making noises like a tea kettle coming to a boil.

"Heh!" she said now, with an explosive venting of stream which made her bob in her chair. "Heh, heh! 'Not quite feeling in touch with things,' eh? Bouncing around the rafters, more likely. Heh, heh, heh! Face like a dinner plate with frog eyes, I beg. Heh, ha, ho . . . hiccupping . . . *hooo!*"

"I'm glad it amuses you," said Jame weakly, as the Caineron Matriarch beat the arm of her chair with a puffball fist and crowed like a cockerel. "I wish it helped."

Cattila snuffled into the end of the message scarf and blew her nose on it to regain self-control. "Maybe it does, girl. It shows again, as with that boy who jumped, that the bond between Caldane and his Kendar can only take so much strain. T'cha. That idiot won't raise a fat finger to protect his people tonight. They must be free, to save themselves."

"But Brier wanted to break away," Jame protested. "The Kendar below don't."

"That's why they've held on this long. If my darling Caldane were to lose control again, though, and push them too far . . . ."

"Many might wrench free despite themselves."

"Or go mad," said Brier Iron-thorn grimly, "or die."

"It would take a genuine, destructive influence to bring that about," Cattila said, no longer laughing. "A nemesis."

Jame gaped at her. *The* Nemesis, of course, was That-Which-Destroys, the third face of Kencyr god. *A* nemesis was a Shanir who didn't quite make the apotheosis, apparently because the other two aspects of the Tyr-ridan, Creation and Preservation, hadn't yet manifested themselves.

"Now wait a minute . . . ."

A low rumble interrupted her.

"*Queee!*" said the foxkin, and streaked out an open window, Jorin crouched flat, ears back. Below in the compounds, dogs began to howl.

Then, ever so slightly, the tower started to sway.

Jame staggered. For one appalling moment, she knew exactly what terror Caldane had felt, so high up, with such a distance to fall. Behind her, she heard Brier swear.

The swaying stopped. The rumble faded to no more than an echo in the bones.

Cattila had hunched down in her chair, eyes screwed shut. "A nemesis," she repeated. One eye popped open to regard Jame balefully. "If I were you, girl, I'd get on with it."

What could one say to that? Jame bowed and turned to leave, but on the threshold the matriarch's voice stopped her:

"Why, it's for you!"

Cattila was holding up the lace section, which had at last reached her fingers. " 'Don't walk,' " she read out-loud. " 'Run. My turn comes next. You shouldn't have stolen my *imu.*' "

Jame boggled. "*Imu*? Your . . . ?" The earthy smell, the dirty nails, the proclivity to eavesdrop . . . . "M-mother Ragga? Is that you?"

" 'Step-mother to you, if that,' " Cattila read, from stitches knit half an hour before.

Jame shook her head as though to clear it. To imagine that the Earth Wife's lodge was following her was one thing: but what in Perimal's name was its mistress doing in the service of a matriarch, much less serving as her Ear on the very Council of Matriarchs?

"Earth-wife, listen: I did *not* steal . . . ."

" 'Don't talk. Run. Here I come.' "

Jame bolted outside, followed by Brier and no one else.

Dammit, she thought, stopping, feeling profoundly foolish. Those two old women had really spooked her, and for what? The night seemed normal again, the tower rock steady. Foxkin still flitted nervously around the shaft's mouth, but the dogs had stopped howling. A babble of voices floated up from the hall below:

"You're drunk."

"I tell you, it moved!"

"Didn't."

"Did."

"*Didn't.*"

"DID!"

"Look," said Brier.

She was pointing toward the roofline of Cattila's cottage, black against a faint glow beyond. Dawn? But it was far too early, and in the wrong direction.

They circled the building.

From this height, one should have seen the northern reaches of the Silver, a glinting, sinuous ribbon threading back into the dark hills. Instead, a vast river of luminous mist flowed down the valley, filling it from slope to slope. Ruined Tagmeth showed black against it for a moment, as small with distance as a toy, and then was swallowed. Farther back, against a pitch-black sky, peaks emerged like islands in a slowly boiling sea. A continuous grinding noise came from its hidden depths—faint, distant, ominous.

"Is it moon-dark?" the Kendar asked. "Has this world fallen into shadows at last?"

The weirdingstrom must be loosening knots of tension in the ground as it came, Jame thought, sending tremors on ahead of it. As good an explanation as any for the River Snake's writhing.

"It's more a case of Rathillien rising," she said, "which isn't good news for us either. And that tidal wave of mist is coming fast. Damn! If it isn't one thing, it's another. C'mon."

"Take the boat!" Cattila called after them. "God's teeth and toenails, Knorth, Lyra Lack-wit was right: things *do* happen around you!"

 **VII**

THE TEN-COMMAND waited uneasily where it had been left, under drifting petals.

Jame knelt beside Graykin. Difficult, in this light, to see if he had regained any color, but his breathing was more regular than it had been and his skin less clammy to the touch. After all, she reminded herself, he was half-Kencyr; the shock once past, his recovery should be rapid.

"Good work," she said, grudgingly, to Kindrie, who looked startled at the compliment.

As for the cadets, however, the boy taken ill on the stair had been sick again with the tower's movement and several others looked distinctly unwell. Mistrusting their stomachs if not their nerves, Brier stopped them at the stair-head and descended alone, cautiously, into chambers of her former lord.

The Kendar moved well for someone so large, Jame thought, leaning over the upper rail to listen, but not as quietly as she herself would have done—not that Ironthorn obviously thought her capable of anything but causing trouble. Odd, to be considered inferior and superior simultaneously. It reminded her, with a painful jolt, how she and Marc had parted without finding a balance between her new-found Highborn blood and his Kendar, after all they had been through together.

Roofless and rootless . . . how *could* she live among her own people—or anywhere else—without equals, without friends?

Iron-thorn reached the foot of the stair, turned toward the balcony, and froze.

"Well, well, well," said Lord Caineron's voice.

Jame leaned farther over the rail, holding her breath, gesturing urgently for the cadets behind her to keep back. The burnished crown of the Kendar's head was a dozen feet below her. Caldane remained out of sight, but he must be very close.

"Brier Iron-thorn," purred his hated voice. "How kind of you to drop in, just when another randon candidate has . . . er . . . dropped out. But I forgot. Pretending to be a Knorth now, aren't you? Not easy, is it, with Caineron blood in your veins? Not possible, I should think. Come, girl: we both know where the real power lies."

His voice had grown thick and deep. Jame's skin crawled. There *was* real power here, stripped to its ruthless core by days of self-indulgence, enough to shake even those of a different lineage. For the first time, she understood how Caldane could have ordered that young man to do what he had done to Graykin and be obeyed.

"Shall we resume where we left off?" Lord Caineron was saying. "Would you like to reapply as a Caineron candidate? Let's see your obedience, girl. ON YOUR KNEES."

Brier Iron-thorn made a choking noise. She crashed down as though the legs had been chopped out from under her.

"Kendar are bound by mind or by blood. Such a handsome woman as you, though, deserves to be bound more . . . pleasurably. By seed . . . ."

Cloth rustled.

This is obscene, Jame thought, and shouted, "Ironthorn, *move!*"

Brier looked up with a start, and threw herself aside barely in time. Jame landed where she had knelt.

"BOO!" she shouted in Lord Caineron's face.

"Hic!" he said, recoiling.

Jewelled slippers flew off as he thrashed, hiccupping, inches above the floor. Peacock blue sleeves flapped like broken wings on wind-milling arms.

"*Hic!*"

Pudgy hands leaped up to clamp futilely over his mouth. Small eyes boggled over ring-encrusted fingers.

Highborn, thought Jame, and prodded him in the stomach with a long, black-sheathed finger.

"HIC!"

He bobbed helplessly away from her, beginning to tilt sideways. A sudden stench filled the air as fear-twisted bowels let go.

Rotten, stinking Highborn.

Behind her, she heard Brier say hoarsely, "Don't . . . ." but ignored her.

"Make sport of decent Kendar, will you?" she demanded, following Caldane, jabbing at him. "Play God almighty in your high tower, huh? Well, the next time the urge takes you, remember me. And this. And keep looking down."

Caldane looked, and screamed. He was over the balcony rail. Under his feet was nothing but empty space—all the way to the foul waters of the pit some two hundred feet below.

Jame watched, savoring every detail: the gaudy, flailing figure; the inarticulate cries; the loosened, befouled trousers tangling around plump ankles, falling off. She didn't at first recognize her berserker flare, pure, cold, and deadly as it was, like the chill bite of poisoned wine. This wasn't the brute rage which she had previously known. Use had refined it, could refine it further still, she realized, into an instrument of terrible power. Was this intoxication what it felt like to be truly herself . . . a nemesis? Very well.

Or perhaps not: in Brier's face she saw her enemy's terror reflected and heard his screams echo from other throats in the hall below. Ancestors only knew what was going on among his Kendar, down in the square. Damn all Highborn anyway, herself most of all. What right did any of them have to respect, much less to friendship?

White knuckled, Brier gripped the rail to anchor herself. Caldane's panic had plunged her into the reeling world of a height-sickness which she hadn't known she possessed.

I am not *a Caineron*, she told herself, gulping down nausea, clutching at control. *I am* not.

A cold hand caught her chin and turned her head, neck muscles creaking like ironwood in winter's grip. Gray eyes shaded with silver smiled into her own.

"You don't know what you've done," she heard herself croak.

"I seldom do," said that husky voice, burred with destruction. "But I do it anyway. This is what I am, Brier Iron-thorn. Remember that."

The silver stare held her a moment more, then let go as the other turned.

Brier stumbled back a step, catching the rail, braced for nausea. Caldane had begun to turn bare bottom up despite frantic efforts to snag him from the balcony below, but the world didn't spin with him. That slim, cold hand had wrenched her free of the Caineron, perhaps forever.

Dammit, Brier thought. She should have been able to do that herself, as she had at the Cataracts . . . .

No. Even there, it seemed, she'd had help. It hadn't been her own strength at all, of which she had been so proud after so many humiliations. Damn all Highborn anyway, who could jerk her about like . . . like that Southland's bastard, a puppet on strings.

Out in the shaft, the foxkin had found a new playmate.

"Ticklish," said the Knorth, watching. "Good. Now, what's this about a boat?"

VIII

CALDANE'S BOATHOUSE was a chamber hollowed out of the mound at its base, dimly lit by diamantine panels. In the black water of the slip floated a ceremonial barge, some fifty feet long by twelve wide, with six oars to a side, fixed upright at rest. A small head on a long, serpentine neck arched over its prow. Its sides were figured with wings, which swept upward at the stern. Between the wing-tips, on the poop, was a raised dais and on this, a throne under a velvet canopy. Ripples of light danced on the ebon waters; shadows lay across the shining gunwales and deck. The entire craft, from avian figurehead to rudder oar, was sheathed in gold.

"Trust Caldane," said Jame, "to gild a swan."

"But what does Lord Caineron do with a boat like this?" a cadet wondered out-loud.

"Sits in it . . . ." said Kindrie.

". . . pretending to be Highlord," Jame finished.

The Shanir stared at her. "How did you know that?"

She gestured toward an embroidery worked in silver gilt on the black velvet behind the throne. It looked like a crown, but she had recognized it as a representation of the Kenthiar, a collar of ancient and mysterious origin which supposedly only the true Highlord could wear in safety. All others who donned it risked their necks. Literally.

"He must be mad!" Vant exclaimed. "To put that emblem on a boat like this, on the edge of a river that isn't even navigable . . . !"

"*What?*"

He shot her a sidelong glance. "Why, lady, *everyone* knows that river travel in the north ended a thousand years ago, after a great weirdingstrom changed the Silver's course from one end to the other. Back then, there were lots of trade cities on both banks of the Central Lands. One night, all the dogs started to make such a racket that orders were given to strangle them. After the din stopped, people could hear the earth growl. A red fog came down the Silver. It kindled lights in the air, and on the water, and under it, like whole weed forests burning."

"Catfish jumped out of the river," another cadet chimed in. To all of them except their Southron ten-commander, obviously, this was an old, favorite story. "Then the water leaped up—whoosh!—like a fountain. It swallowed its islands, jumped its banks, and flooded its cities. Whole populations disappeared—drowned, the survivors thought, although no bodies were ever found."

"Bashti and Hathir never recovered," Vant broke back in, glowering at the cadet, talking fast. "That was when they gave the Riverland to us, because they couldn't bring garrison supplies upriver by barge anymore, because it got so strange here that none of their people would stay anyway, but our priests settled it down . . ."

"Huh," said Rue. "Not so's you'd notice it. The Merikit say that the River Snake caused it all. Its tail reaches to the Eastern Sea, its heart lies at Hurlen, and its head is under the well at Kithorn keep. When it writhes, the Silver goes mad."

The others laughed.

"Stick to facts, shortie, not singers' fancies," said Vant scornfully. "Or do you Highkeepers really believe that tripe?"

Rue glared up at him. "We border brats face facts every day that would make a Riverlander like you shit in your boots. Anyway, your stories are as much hearsay as mine. Red fogs, jumping catfish, fire under the water . . . *all* singers' stuff, I bet. All we know for certain is that to this day any boat risking the river north of Hurlen tends to arrive without its crew, if at all . . . and no bodies are ever found."

Wonderful, thought Jame. Cattila couldn't ask for a neater way to dispose of awkward guests, if that had been her intention. She was a Caineron, after all, and a matriarch.

The rumble began again, closer, louder. Paving stones rippled underfoot; the water in the slip seethed.

On the cadets' upturned faces, Jame saw the same dread which she herself felt, not so much of the unstable earth as of the massive weight poised overhead, mound and tower and crown.

The earth bucked, throwing them all off their feet.

The back wall had split open. Rats swarmed through the fissure from the dungeons, over those Kendar not quick enough to get out of their way. Jorin squawked and bounced like a wound-up toy as they darted across his toes. Oblivious, they plunged past, into the slip, swimming frantically out toward the open river where they would surely drown.

Debris began to fall.

"Get on board!" snapped Brier.

The cadets vaulted down into the barge. Jame was poised to leap after them when without ceremony Brier picked her up and tossed her into the boat's stern. She landed awkwardly. Jorin did better despite also having been thrown—the only way to get him onto any boat.

The cadets' first action on boarding was to pitch Caldane's throne over the side and to tear down the canopy with its offending emblem. On the dais, Kindrie struggled to cushion Graykin's limp form with the velvet sway. Jame went to help, for once intending to keep out of the Kendars' way. However, as she watched the cadets plunge about in the waist, she realized that none of them had crewed a barge before or perhaps even been on one. Going down the Tardy to Hurlen, she had pestered those Southron bargees with so many questions. Why couldn't she remember any of their answers?

Because you're scared half witless, she told herself, and took a deep breath.

"First," she said, to no one in particular, "we have to cast off."

Brier gave her a black look. "Throw off the front moorings!" she shouted to the cadet nearest the prow, and turned aft to deal with stern lines herself.

The barge had begun to roll with the water's surge, snubbing itself sharply again and again. Left, right, left . . . .

"Wait," said Jame, but the Kendar brushed past her.

"Too . . . damn . . . tight," she grunted, working her thumbs between the two inch thick port hawser and its cleat.

Rolling to the right again, the heavy rope coming taut . . . .

It parted with a bass twang under the Ivory Knife. Half-freed aft but not fore, the barge swung its stern with a crash into the right hand pier, snapping oars, throwing everyone from their feet except Jame, who hung on to the cleat, hacking at the slack, starboard hawser. It gave way as Brier lurched to her feet, staring.

"What . . . ?"

"I do have my uses," said Jame, sheathing the knife. "You might remember that."

Meanwhile, someone had taken an axe to the prow lines.

The tremor subsided. The barge, freed, rocked uneasily in its berth. Into that taut silence came the crack of stone overhead, giving way.

Cadets grabbed the surviving oars and half-rowed, half-poled the boat forward. The slip gave way to a tunnel bearing left, fed through gates to the right by the river. As darkness and the current seized them, they heard the crash behind them of the ceiling giving way.

Something overhead chittered and whirred. They burst out of the tunnel under a roof of bats in panic-stricken flight.

Jame had a moment to note that they had emerged on the mound's southeastern side, just short of where the encircling arms of the river moat rejoined. Then the reunited might of the tributary seized them and they hurtled down it between Grotley's compound on the right and M'lord's on the left.

They shot under the bridge which they had crossed earlier, barely clearing it with their swan's head prow and the helmsman's crows-nest in the stern. Jame thought she glimpsed Ran Quickfoot's broken-doll figure. The water beneath glinted and flashed. Overhead hung a midnight sky tinged with an opalescence not that of dawn.

The roar of the swollen stream redoubled between the high, narrow walls. Over it, though, Jame thought she heard cries. Some of Caldane's people must have woken up—enough, she hoped, to anchor Restormir against the coming storm. As to Caldane himself, the foxkin wouldn't let him float away altogether—worse luck. Still, perhaps this hadn't turned out so badly, she thought, shooting a defiant look up at Brier Iron-thorn in the crows-nest as the Kendar clung to the rudder oar.

Brier was staring up at the wall which bounded M'lord's compound, at the fresh cracks which laced it. The sound coming from the other side was shriller than Jame had at first realized, disturbingly like an echo of Caldane's screams. Ahead, the wall bulged outward, fragments of it tumbling into the water. Suddenly the whole gave way. People fell with the masonry, clinging to it and to each other as though to anchor themselves even as they were dragged down. The barge plowed into them and over. As it plunged past the breached wall, its riders glimpsed a street within whose buildings seethed like kicked ant nests as desperate hands clung to walls and doors to stop their lord's tumbling world. The uproar leaped outward at the Knorth. Its madness stared blindly up from the white faces caught in the gold-plated welter of their oars.

Ahead raced the Silver. The barge plunged out into an eddy and was spun around by it, dipping and careening. The white faces in the water disappeared in rapid secession, mouths still agape, as if jerked down. Then the boat shot on its way again, going downstream stern-first.

Bits of barge-lore were coming back to Jame.

"It's no use trying to steer backward," she shouted up at Brier. "Better ship the rudder oar before it gets broken. We need people on the stern with poles to ward off obstacles—not that there are any at the moment," she added, glancing at the broad stretch of river which they had entered after the eddy, "but there will be. Then too, this boat may only have a three or four foot draft, but it will ride deeper as we pick up speed, so watch out for shallows that may rip the bottom out of her."

Brier stared down at her from the crows-nest, set high enough to have had a clear view over the canopy before it had been torn down. Spray plastered dark red hair to the strong bones of her face and clothes to the lines of her powerful body. As a figurehead, she was much more impressive than the one on the boat's other end.

"Anything else, lady?"

"Yes," said Jame. "Never, ever spit into the wind."

"You *are* mad!" Kindrie burst out. "D'you realize we're heading back toward Wilden, not to mention Falkirr, Gothregor, and half a dozen other keeps we weirdwalked past on the way north? What are we going to *do*?"

What, indeed? At Gothregor, her future had looked bleak enough. Now she was going back not only with a

clear case of Knorth lunacy but also with a face that
could start a war. Then too, there was Graykin. Madness,
war, *and* scandal, if word of his bonding got out.

She looked down at the Southron. A scruffy, little half-
breed, and the Kencyr half of that pure Caineron. At the
Cataracts, his desperate need to belong had bridged the
gap between them like a spark, surprising both. He was
the last person on earth she would have chosen deliberately. And now that she had him, what next, when she
couldn't even provide for herself? Perhaps she should
break the bond, let him go free . . . .

He began to moan.

"Do something!" she said to Kindrie.

But the healer shook his head. "I've done all I can.
His soul-image is . . . odd. He's like a—a ghost, haunting
someone else's soul-scape."

"Whose?"

"You should know."

Graykin's eyes fluttered open, then widened as much
as his puffy, bruised face would allow. He stared up at
Jame, bewildered, close to panic.

"W-who . . . ?"

Her mask confused him, Jame thought. "Do I have
to undress?" she demanded, with a sidelong glower at
Kindrie's expression. Be damned if she was going to
explain that the first time she and Graykin had met, she
hadn't been wearing so much as a pleasant expression.

Graykin was still staring. "It *is* you! B-but where are
we?"

"In a stolen barge, going down the Silver
backwards—which is fairly typical of any rescue I under-
take. You might remember that, the next time you
need one."

But Graykin had stopped listening. "I w-waited," he stammered. "In Hurlen, all winter, cold and hungry, guarding It, a-and you didn't come. Caineron's agents caught me, dragged me north to Restormir. Caldane t-tortured me, and you didn't come. I could have told him where I hid It, could have brought his favor again, but I didn't tell . . . I didn't tell . . . and you didn't come!"

His voice had risen to a thin wail.

"Stop that!" said Jame, exasperated, and slapped him.

He crumpled back onto the velvet.

Kindrie bent over his still form. "Why did you do that?" he demanded of Jame; then, in perplexity, "*What* did you do?"

Why and what indeed. It had felt like the edge of a berserker flare, not a tool or intoxication this time but an arrogance, to hurt because she could. And she didn't yet know if she was sorry.

The rumble began again, behind them. Birds rose in flocks from the wooded crest of the east bank, black against the milky haze which now permeated the sky. Jorin scuttled under the velvet swag.

"Why, we're slowing down," someone in the waist exclaimed.

They were. The shore had been sliding by as quickly as a horse might trot; now, walking, a rider would have passed them. The water was rising. It topped the low right bank and spread out over the meadow beyond, a sheet of glass under which grass floated. Ripples from the slowing hull broke it, kindling red witchweed beneath the surface. At the meadow's far edge, trees began ever so gently to sway.

"We've stopped," said someone. "No . . . we're going backward!"

And so they were. Waves began to slap against their stern. The current had turned, so that the river seemed to be pushing them back toward Restormir and the coming storm.

"The Snake is drinking up the river," Rue said, awed.

More likely the cause was quake-sunken lands to the north, Jame thought.

Beyond the gilded swan's head, the northern sky glowed. Then, around the valley's curve, came the vanguard of the storm: spheres of flickering light, yards wide, rolling down the Silver toward them.

Jame leaned over the gunwale. "This is the Earth Wife's turn, not yours!" she shouted down at the racing water. "River Snake, River Snake, let us GO!"

The waves subsided. The barge stopped, then began to move southward again as the current turned.

Jame shrugged, shamefaced. "Whatever works," she said.

This may have worked too well. They moved faster and faster, from a walk to a trot to a gallop. Jame clapped a hand to her cap to keep it from blowing off.

"Waah!" said Jorin, under the billowing velvet.

The east bank collapsed, casting down its crest of pine trees like spears. Spray drenched them all. The cadets rowed furiously to keep in the center of the channel—no easy matter without the rudder oar, which Brier had out of its lock to fend off debris. At this pace, thought Jame, they would reach the other keeps much faster than expected, if they didn't come to grief first.

The barge careened around a point.

Ahead, a rocky islet abruptly sank, swallowed whole by a fissure in the river bed. Water roared into the chasm. The barge swung around its rim. The velvet slid off the dais into the waist, taking with it healer, patient, and bitterly protesting ounce. The same lurch sent Jame reeling toward the side. Something flew in her face. She threw up a hand to ward it off, and found herself gripping the end of a crows-nest guy rope, torn loose from its mooring. The next moment, she was over the gunwale, swinging out above the whirlpool. Water thundered down into it over what looked like stone teeth, into an earthen gullet twisting down out of sight.

"River Snake!" she shouted down into it, her voice swallowed by the roar. "Behave!"

The barge swung and so did she, back onto the dais. Brier stared down first at her, then at the hole in the river, as if unsure which she found more preposterous. The barge plunged on downstream, prow first.

"Better?" Jame shouted up at the Kendar.

Brier had turned to look back. "No."

Behind them, the fissure closed. A great gout of water and red mud vomited up from the river bed. Its wave hurtled the barge on, out of control.

As the Silver had descended, its gorge had cut deeper and deeper into the mountain granite so that now they were careening down rapids between high cliff walls. Oars smashed on rocks, knocking cadets to the deck. Catfish fell on them. To either side, bewhiskered shapes were leaping as if in flight from the water to the rock face, where some of them stuck and clung. Looking over the side, Jame saw red, mud-stained water, with flashes of white under it—rock slabs, or scales? Were they sliding down the River Snake's back?

The Silver widened as another stream joined it from the right, the confluence a boiling cauldron. Jame thought she glimpsed keep walls up the stream's gorge.

The Jarans' Valantir already? Ahead, the river split around a wooded island much larger than the last. They were swept to its left into the narrower channel.

From her vantage point, Brier bellowed down at them, *"Falls!"*

The swan barge leaped out over the first drop as if trying to take wing. The dais fell out from under Jame's feet. The waist seemed to leap up at her. Velvet, cadets, and fish broke her fall. The deck tilted again. This time she didn't leave it, but everything else seemed to, all coming down on top of her. Stunned, she lay on the bottom of the boat, under sodden cloth. Something scraped along the hull on both sides. People were shouting and stepping on her. Then all sounds grew strangely distant.

Something wet tickled her ear. *You're drowning*, said a whiskery voice in her mind. *Get up. This isn't my turn.*

Jame gasped and choked. Her face was under water, pressed down by the masses of wet velvet. The bottom of the barge was awash. Sputtering, she clawed her way free, and found that she had not been alone: beside her lay an enormous catfish, its whiskers rasping against the planks, its thick-lipped mouth agape.

From the other end of the barge, near the prow, Brier Iron-thorn stared at her. "I thought you'd been thrown out," she said.

Everyone else was gaping at her from the shore. The rocks on which the boat was snagged had provided easy stepping stones to the east bank. Brier apparently had stayed behind to gather discarded backpacks, which now dangled in clusters from her big hands.

The barge teetered, groaning. Jame scrambled back onto the dais, fetching up as far astern as she could go.

They were balanced again, but precariously. Any moment, the rush of water from behind would dislodge them. Jame didn't dare move to look, but from the way the land fell away before them, she guessed that they were on the edge of at least a twenty foot drop.

"Get off the boat," said Brier.

The deck shifted slightly forward, making Jame press back against the foot of the crows-nest. "You first," she said.

"Get off," the Kendar repeated, implacable. "*Now*."

The iron will in her voice almost made Jame obey; but if she did, both barge and cadet would go over the falls, and where would a Southie like Brier ever have learned how to swim?

Dammit, they hadn't time for games. In exasperation and anxiety, she reached for an overriding tone of command such as she had never used before. It rose, compounded of innate Highborn power and something utterly ruthless, like the edge of a master rune.

"COME HERE," she said—and realized with horror, the moment she spoke, whose voice she had unconsciously imitated.

The Kendar's eyes went blank. As in the Crown at Restormir, she started to obey, but then staggered.

"No!" she said hoarsely, and lurched backward.

With a screech, the barge fell.

Jame was thrown off the tilting deck, the catfish flying beside her. She slammed into water as hard as she had half-expected to hit rock. Deep, dark, very, very cold. The weight of Aerulan's banner slung across her back pulled her down. There would be blood in the water if all of this had reopened Kallystine's handiwork. Cold, hard lips pressed briefly against her own. Whiskers tickled. Her thrashing feet hit bottom, kicked off from it. An endless moment later Jame surfaced, sputtering.

Kissed by a catfish. Sweet Trinity, what next?

She yelped as a golden, serpentine neck reared up beside her, then splashed over on its side. The swan figurehead. Other fragments of the barge bobbed up all around her, their gilding too thin to hold them down. This was a small backwater, she saw, blocked off from the Silver's main current by a beaver dam.

But where was Brier?

Near the shore, a dark head broke the surface. The big Kendar was still carrying the cadets' heavy packs, as well as wearing her own.

"They took me straight to the bottom," she was saying to Vant as Jame floundered up on the bank beside her. "From there, I simply walked ashore."

Jame couldn't meet her cold stare. That she, who hated her Highborn blood so much, should have used such a voice on someone like Brier . . . . What difference was there, after all, between her and a pig like Caldane, if they were both capable of such a thing?

"Look!" said cadet, pointing.

The trees on the island stood black against the light growing behind them. Then fingers of luminous mist crept down the stepped falls, tentatively, as if feeling their way. Their tips fumbled around the figurehead, which vanished soundlessly. They groped on toward the shore.

"Climb," said Brier to the cadets. "You too, lady."

The Knorth didn't move. "The Earth Wife wants her *imu,*" she said, without turning. "Perhaps she'll settle for me instead."

Brier swore under her breath. This was too much. She grabbed the Highborn's arm and started to swing her into a slap which would knock this latest idiocy out of her with a vengeance.

The blow never fell. Brier's hand was channeled aside in a perfect waterflowing move that ended abruptly in an earth-moving thumb-lock. Surprise more than pain shocked her into an off-balanced immobility.

"Someone slapped me not long ago," said the Knorth in a distant voice. "Never again."

Brier glared at her sideways, through the wet fringe of her hair. "Then stop asking for it . . . lady."

She was released so suddenly that she nearly fell into the river. The Knorth was laughing. "Wise Brier-rose. You and Marc should get along splendidly. C'mon."

They scrambled up to join the others on the River Road, fingers of mist combing through the trees after them. Beside the road ran fragments of an ancient wall. Clearly, the same hands had built both, but only the foundations remained of the latter like old, worn teeth fused into their sockets. Beyond them, the land rose in terraced foothills to the base of the cliffs. One towering white rock face stood out from the others. Many windows were cut into it, all dark and shuttered, but on top perched a keep blazing with light.

Mount Alban, the Scrollsmen's College. It must be.

"We've got to take refuge," Jame said, looking up. Underfoot, the earth shivered.

"Lady, you don't go indoors during a quake."

"And you don't stay outside in weirding. Take your choice."

Brier looked down at the mist tendrils that had begun to twine about her boots. "Up," she said to the cadets.

The ruins of a hill fort lay scattered at the cliff's foot, before Mount Alban's main door. Closer at hand was a sturdy wooden building set into the northwest side of the hill. It was locked. Brier and Vant put their shoulders to the door. Looking back, Jame saw mist well up against the broken wall, higher than it now stood, respecting its ancient dimensions, and she remembered what Cattila had said about the resistance of such work to the weirding effect. If they had stayed on the River Road, they might have been perfectly safe.

Mist rolled over the top of the wall which was no longer there. Behind it, mountains high, came the weirdingstrom.

The door suddenly gave way.

Brier rolled to her feet inside, but Vant sprawled, tripping his comrades as they rushed in on his heels. Last over the threshold, Jame hesitated, still looking back. A wizened scrollsman stood beside her—the same, apparently, who had unlocked the door. Now he jerked her back and slammed it, in the very face of the mist.

With a sigh, the weirdingstrom swept over them.

The wooden floor lurched. Dried herbs hanging from the low beams swayed while down one long wall hundreds of jars rattled on their shelves and many fell off. All the walls groaned. Clay seemed to melt out of their chinks, leaving each board outlined with light. Jame staggered. It felt for all the world as if she stood in the hold of a ship launched into heavy seas.

The old scrollsman had been darting up and down the long wall, catching jars as they fell, bleating with distress at each one missed. Now he stopped, arms full, listening.

"Why, we're adrift," he said.

The next moment he had shoved his burden at the nearest cadet and bolted to the back of the room, where he threw open a door and plunged through it, up stairs. They heard his voice, first in the passageway, then in some echoing open space beyond, shouting:

"We're adrift, everybody, we're adrift! Hurray!"

✿ Interim IV ✿

The Grimly Holt:
59th of Spring

IN THE NORTHERN REACHES of Bashti, south of
the White Hills, lies a great forest, deep and dark and
full of strange things. Men call it the Weald when they
speak of it at all. Few enter. Fewer still emerge.

Its eastern corner, the Grimly Holt, is just as feared by
ignorant people, although its folk are shy and courteous,
much different in manners if not in blood from their
wild cousins of the deep wood. The wolvers' keep is
another of those ancient ruins which line the Silver, this
one smaller than most and unreclaimed by later builders.
Its walls lie tumbled around the forest floor like so many
half-sunken boulders velvet with moss and a stream runs
down the glade which had been its great hall. The loam
of countless seasons obscures floor and hearth except
where skullcap mushrooms grow along buried veins of
ancient mortar mixed with blood.

Tonight, however, the weirding had restored to the
keep a ghostly shell of its former self. Glowing mist
sculpted itself against low walls long since fallen and
pressed down on the thatch of an invisible roof. Wisps
trickled in through narrow windows which had admitted
no light of sun or moon or star for time out of mind.

This was an opportunity not to be missed.

Since the storm had rolled over them hours ago, the wolvers had been trying to record every detail of their ancient home which the weirding revealed. Long, communal howls slid down the length of beam and stone. Modulated yips described the cunning fit of joints and hunting scenes carved over the outer lintels, seen in reverse as though from inside a glowing mold. As they sang, the mist pressed closer, taking more clearly the long vanished forms, and misty wraiths drifted down the hall to the sound of music lost in a dream.

The song snarled in snapping argument. There was a small structure attached to the rear wall which none of the singers understood.

"It's a privy," said the Wolver Grimly, and explained.

The word meant nothing in their tongue, so they settled for a description: the hole that all men mark but none claim.

Obviously, thought Grimly, they had never been in Kothifir during an outbreak of dysentery.

In fact, few of his kin ever left the holt at all or spent much time in man-shape except during adolescence, when each generation in turn discovered that humans have no set mating time. Here on the edge of the great, dark Weald, there were few true humans to imitate in other matters. Torisen's visit the previous winter was still avidly discussed, not only because he was an accepted wolf-friend but because he had marched the entire Kencyr Host through the Holt on a shortcut to the Cataracts.

Only once before in living memory had the forest been so invaded, by a much less courteous party, when King Kruin of Kothifir had descended on it to hunt wolver.

Grimly well remembered his first sight of humankind. Kruin had taken over the old keep as his base camp, never guessing how closely he was watched by his curious, would-be prey. Creeping close to listen, Grimly had heard a court poet declaim *rendish* verse to a bored monarch waiting impatiently for the dawn hunt. But one wolver cub had already been captured in a net of words. The poet had seen but not betrayed him, his vanity revenged for regal yawns.

No other prey was taken. The Holt is a dangerous place in its own right, the deep Weald even more so. Kruin lost most of his party before the wolvers tired of watching men die and led him out. He wasn't pleased to have his royal hunt ruined, but in fairness he offered any wolver who cared to come a place in his court. That "place," most wolvers assumed, would be on his trophy wall. However, the poet's words still sang in Grimly's mind. When he came of age, years later, he took the River Road south and presented himself to Kruin's son and successor, Krothen.

What days those had been, what pleasure and pain.

He had indeed learned *rendish*, from the very poet who had come with Kruin to the Holt. Oh, the intoxication of the words, winding through the rhythms of his native forest . . . .

And oh, the humiliation when his audience had howled back at him with laughter. It wasn't the would-be artist they came to hear, he quickly learned, but the freak with whom the old poet had bought his way back into court favor, as he might have done with a dancing bear or a singing pig. So Grimly had become "the Wild Man of the Woods," a caricature of what he wanted to be, usually drunk in order to stand himself, a sorry thing who had forgotten the dignity of the wolf and not yet learned that of a man.

"*Why are you doing this?*"

Sharp words, in an exasperated voice, from a young one-hundred commander with haunted eyes and bandaged hands.

Twelve years ago.

Grimly looked down the hall at the black-clad figure sitting hunched on a fallen block: Torisen, his first friend, then barely recovered from Urakarn and marked for death by his Caineron enemies, now the leader of his people.

And still a mystery.

Look at him, rocking back and forth, that damned sword still clutched in his swollen hand and his dark head bent as though listening to it, although the only words came from his own lips, lost under the wild poetry of the wood.

Grimly rubbed his tired eyes. No. They hadn't deceived him: weirding lit the ghostly hall and glowered back from the serpentine patterns forged into Kin-Slayer's blade, but his friend sat in deepening shadows as though they flowed off his black garments like murky waters. At his feet lay fire-scarred stone—a different floor, a different place. The fur slowly rose down Grimly's spine. Behind him, a new note entered his people's song as they felt their control slip.

"Tori . . ."

He found himself padding down the hall, then dropping to all fours and creeping. The air seemed to thicken around him. It stank of old burning, and sickness, and fear.

". . . a circular hall," Torisen was crooning, in counterpoint to the wolvers' song, "with two recessed windows to the north and south. Broken benches. Collapsed tables. A private dining room on the other side of the open hearth.

A scorched door leading up to the battlements, closed but not locked . . . oh God, not locked . . . ."

Grimly crept to his friend's feet over grating cinders as Torisen's voice built reality around him detail by detail. The song of his kin faded to the keening of wind through shattered walls. His paws ached on cold stone.

"Tori . . . ?"

The other's rocking stopped, then began again as he hunched lower.

"Shhh . . . . I'm hiding. I said I would never come back here, but I had to. I had to. This is the only place she won't look."

"B-but where are we?"

"Why, in the Haunted Lands keep where I—we—grew up. Oh, I burned down the real one last year, but this is a dream, isn't it? I burned the dead, too, haunts that they had become. Gave them to the pyre. That should have satisfied honor, shouldn't it? But they keep coming back. Listen to them in the shadows. Listen . . . ."

The wind keened through the narrow windows, thin and sour with ash, rank soot on the fur, the lips, the taste of forbidden flesh . . . .

Were those still shapes standing to either side of the embrasures and those murky points of light, two by two by two—clinks in the wall or unblinking eyes giving back the glow of the sword's malignant blade?

Run. Out of this nightmare, back to his own simple, sane world only feet away, to his own people, crying for him on the wind . . . .

But he couldn't leave his friend.

Shivering, Grimly crouched at Torisen's feet, to bare his teeth at shadows and bite them if he could, caught in a dream which might never end.

PART

V

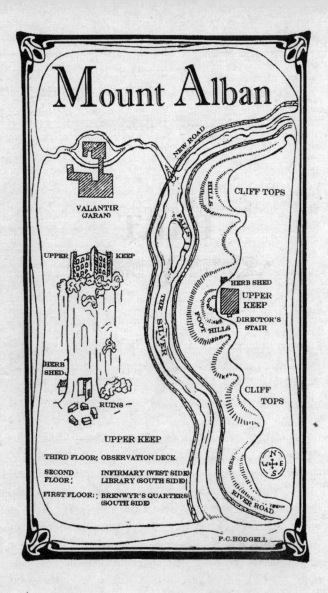

Mount Alban

VALANTIR
(JARAN)

NEW ROAD

HILLS

CLIFF TOPS

FALLS

UPPER KEEP

HERB SHED

UPPER KEEP

THE SILVER

DIRECTOR'S STAIR

FOOT HILLS

HERB SHED

RUINS

CLIFF TOPS

UPPER KEEP

THIRD FLOOR: OBSERVATION DECK

SECOND FLOOR: INFIRMARY (WEST SIDE)
LIBRARY (SOUTH SIDE)

FIRST FLOOR: BRENWYR'S QUARTERS
(SOUTH SIDE)

RIVER ROAD

P.C. HODGELL

Mount Alban: 59th of Spring

JAME PACED THE INFIRMARY, watched warily by
Kindrie and benevolently by Aerulan, laid out to dry over
the back of a chair. Having given up begging to be let
out, Jorin was curled up on the foot of Graykin's pallet,
ostentatiously ignoring everyone. Still, his ears twitched
at every tantalizing noise out in the hall. Jame twitched
too. Running feet, thumps, curses . . . all the sounds of
departure. But where on earth were they going, and
how?

Curtains of oiled cloth across the arched windows had
kept out the initial surge of weirding. Now the mist had
subsided to a flat, glowing sea, level with the cliff-top,
under a ribbed ceiling of clouds which dimly reflected
its light. The infirmary had none of the ship-board
motion that had almost made Jame sea-sick in the
wooden herb-shed below. Still, the floor did vibrate.

Out in the hall, people were approaching.

". . . shift more supplies to the top floor," said a crisp,
deep voice. "The entire core of the college is adrift, as
well as the upper keep, as the scrollsmen predicted; but
we may still lose the lower hall or more if the main door
gives way. Has our newest guest been made comfortable? God's teeth, a lady of that stature, to descend on
us at a time like this . . . !"

"She was caught out in the storm, Director," said someone soothingly. "It was pure luck that she found our front door at all, swept as far north as she had been, or that the singer sent down to fetch Index heard her escort hammering on it."

Jame frowned. That didn't sound like her own arrival.

Brier Iron-thorn's voice sounded outside. "The cadets have brought up all the supplies they could find, Director. Have you further orders?"

"Not at present, ten-commander."

Footsteps and voices receded down the hall, but the door knob quivered in Jame's grasp, as though at someone else's touch on the other side.

"Ten!" Vant's voice, approaching. "Captain Hawthorn wants you. Now."

"I . . . see," said Brier, just outside the door. The knob became suddenly inert as she let go of it. "Yes, of course."

"I did warn you," said Vant, smugly.

Two sets of feet retreated down the corridor.

Jame sighed, half relieved that Brier hadn't entered, half disappointed. She was still embarrassed by what she had tried to do to the Kendar at the falls. Sweet Trinity, in effect to have used Caldane's voice on someone who equated domination with violation . . . ! Iron-thorn's trust in the Knorth had been fragile to begin with. If Jame shattered it, Tori would kill her. He might anyway, on general principles.

But what lady of stature, what Captain Hawthorn, and what had Vant warned Brier about? She wouldn't find out here . . . but she didn't dare go out, either.

Brier wasn't the only person she was avoiding. In the confusion of their arrival, someone had mentioned that

Kirien, the Jaran Heir, was also in Mount Alban. He hadn't attended Torisen's memorable dinner at the Cataracts, so Jame hadn't met him. She had heard that he was a scrollsman engaged in studies of the Fall until, coming of age, he took his place as head of the Jaran. The last thing Jame wanted just now was to expose her conduct and damaged face to Highborn criticism.

She found that she was touching her cheek, and jerked her hand down. The impression lingered, however, of a developing scar bad enough to be felt through both mask and gloves. Whatever it had been like after the first injury, the repeated blows to the face which she had taken since couldn't have helped.

Damn.

But she wasn't the only one in trouble here. The Southron hadn't yet retained consciousness. His breathing didn't have the deep regularity of *dwar*, either; in fact, she could barely hear it.

"He was going to be all right, wasn't he?" she demanded of the healer. "Somehow I could sense that when I touched him, back in Cattila's garden. But not now. What happened? I didn't hit him that hard."

The Shanir sat on the far side of Graykin's pallet, back to the wall, head drooping with fatigue. Her voice jerked him awake.

"I think it has something to do with the bond between you," he said, marshalling his wits. "Why does it mean so much to him?"

"I suppose because he's a bastard, born without a name or a place. I seem to have given him both. He had an identity before we met, though. I'm not totally responsible for who or what he is. I don't even want his service. He's just a . . . stray dog I accidentally picked up."

"You made that pretty clear, when you slapped him."

"Sweet Trinity. What's been the point of this whole expedition, if not his rescue?"—and perhaps to make her forget her own problems. "I've never meant him any harm!"

"Maybe destructive Shanir can't help but destroy, however good their intentions. Maybe innocence isn't enough." He looked up at her askance, through the white fringe of his hair. "If you have this effect on a servant who needs you, what will you do to a brother who fears you?"

"He has no reason to. I love him."

"That makes it worse."

FRATRICIDE, the God-voice had called her. Bane . . . or Tori?

Jame looked down at Graykin's still form. "Is he going to die?"

Without thinking, Kindrie reached toward the unconscious man, then stopped. His fingers curled into a fist, which he drew back to cradle against his chest like a broken bird. "Find out for yourself," he muttered, no longer meeting her eyes. "He's your responsibility."

Jame regarded him for a moment with raised eyebrows, then sighed. To date, she had done a poor job of being a Highborn. This was one duty, though, which she could no longer shirk. She knelt and touched Graykin's face gingerly.

A momentary dizziness made her squeeze shut her eyes. In the darkness behind the lids, she felt as if she were falling, except for her fingertips on the Southron's forehead. It felt odd. She blinked away darkness and looked down into a face half human, half canine, wholly mongrel, like the dog in the old song after whom she had renamed this wretched boy. Under him, through him, she could see the cold hearth stone on which he lay. A ghost, Kindrie, had called him, haunting someone else's soul-scape. Whose?

Her hand had ivory plates across its back so on up her arm. On her face, the weight of an ivory skull mask. She raised her head with difficulty to look over her shoulder, down the sweep of a vast hall paved with green-veined stone, hung with death banners. Silver Knorth eyes watched her through the bars of their warp threads; the woof on each cheek bunched like an ugly scar.

The Master's hall in Perimal Darkling . . . her soul-scape?

"No!" Jame cried, leaping to her feet.

The darkness swarmed back, although this time her eyes were wide open.

Got up too fast, she thought, swaying, clutching at composure. Wait for the blood to rise, wait . . . .

Her sight cleared. Kindrie was staring at her open-mouthed. "What happened?"

"I . . . need some air. I'm going for a walk."

At the door, she turned. "All right! I came back for you after all, I've accepted responsibility, and now you can keep watch on that damned cold hearth until your tail freezes off. Satisfied?"

The door slammed. The ounce (who hadn't quite gotten through in time) squawked. The Knorth departed, swearing. Graykin's breath deepened into the slow, healing rhythm of *dwar*.

"B-but what happened?" Kindrie repeated, bewildered, to the silent room.

 **II**

OUT IN THE HALL, Jame turned left—away from the direction in which Brier had gone—and stormed off.

All these years of trying to escape her childhood in the Master's House by flight, amnesia, and arson (having left the upper stories in flames behind her) ... could she still be carrying the image of that foul place in her very soul?

Those disfigured banners, her scarred face . . . .

No, no, no . . . .

"Forget what you can't help," the Women's World taught.

She had smiled at that behind the mask which they had made her wear, thinking, How convenient: What one forgets, one needn't face or try to change.

Now the instructress's voice droned in her mind as it had in that winter-bound classroom, where little girls were taught how to forget some minor thing so that later they might dismiss much greater, inconvenient facts:

"Forget, forget . . . ."

A minute passed, or perhaps ten.

Jame found herself staring down the crooked stairwell which opened up before her. What had she been thinking about? It was still there, buried none too deeply. Let it lie. Now, where was she?

The upper keep was relatively new in construction and regular in design, built of ironwood and oak. Below it, however, the cave-riddled cliff had long ago been hollowed out and filled with a wooden maze in which all the rooms seemed to be on different levels with ceilings of different heights. Erratic steps connected them, and halls that moved by fits and starts; stairs plunged down dark wells, some slippery with moss, others turned into minor cascades by recent rains.

So much Jame had noted as she and the others had climbed to the upper keep. Now here she was back at an entrance to those interior regions. Well, why not? With Jorin on her heels, she descended to explore.

Below were the quarters and studies where most of Mount Alban's scholars lived. Signs staked out territories, here the prehistorians, there the epic poets, elsewhere the anthropologists and linguists.

"Serious scholarship in progress," read one notice. "Singers keep out."

"Facts please small minds," declared another.

So the old rivalry between the scrollsmen and the singers still flourished, as it had since the Fall, when the few surviving scrolls had gotten so mixed up that no one knew which was fact and which, fantasy. The singers' cherished prerogative, the Lawful Lie, hadn't helped, as their colleagues never failed to point out.

Everything here, though, had an air of abandonment several months old at least. Most of the scrollsmen and singers had marched out with the Host the previous winter and were now enjoying Kothifir's sunny clime. Those left had been the old, the infirm, and the indispensable. After a winter in this dank, drafty chimney of a college, no wonder they were also eager to travel, especially if they could take the dubious comforts of home with them.

The whole thing sounded pretty implausible, though. Did they really expect this massive pile to drift about the countryside, scaring the natives? Still . . . . Not only were the lower windows shuttered but the inner wall was panelled with wood, around which weirding light seeped.

The outer rock face should have blocked that out. Was the cliff still there at all? Maybe Mount Alban truly had been cast adrift, like a wooden boat, leaking.

Here was a more recently built stair, cutting down through the chaotic levels with welcome decision. From the depths of the square well came a groaning as if of ship's timbers in a heavy sea; and closer at hand, a different sound: quick, light foot-steps descending. Some fifty feet below, a robed figure scurried across a landing. It was the old scrollsman who had let them into Mount Alban, bound . . . where?

"Well, why not?" Jame said to Jorin.

They followed.

The farther down, the more the wood around them protested. At least, Jame thought, the principal supports must be ironwood, which virtually nothing could break. It wouldn't even catch fire unless exposed to hot coals for several months, and then a good-sized beam would burn for generations. The effect on it of weirding might be another matter. Given the centuries-old levels through which they were now descending, the newness of this stair might be more of a protection against being left behind.

At the stair's foot lay the lower hall. As Kendar had hollowed out the upper reaches of the cliff, so before them Hathiri masons had enlarged the caverns at ground level into high vaulted chambers. Before that, those same caves had been used by the ancestors of the Merikit, whose fort ruins still lay on Mount Alban's doorstep.

Jame paused at the foot of the stair, looking left down the long main hall to the door at its western end. The posts of the latter loomed some forty feet high and its leaves were secured by the counter-balanced trunk of a tree. Into the left leaf was cut a smaller door, cart-sized, and into that, a smaller door still, the height of a man. Each was outlined with weirding light, as were the wooden panels to either side.

Across the hall, the door to the herb shed stood open. Out of it came the chant of an ancient voice. The words became clearer as Jame approached, if not more comprehensible.

"Loosestrife kills flies," the old man was half-singing. "Loose lips tell lies. Parsley makes piss; so does a linguist."

A flight of wooden stairs led down to the shed floor. Jame sat on the fifth step from the bottom, low enough to see into the room below without venturing down onto its still unsteady floor. Jorin draped himself across her knees and fell asleep.

Below, the old scrollsman was sorting out the damage done to the wall of herb jars. As Jame watched, he picked leaves out of the glass shards, bundled them together, and put them in new container, all the time crooning bits of doggerel. These last seemed to consist of herbs' virtues (medicinal, culinary, or otherwise) linked often in scatological terms with the names of colleagues, historical facts, or old songs. Which herbs went into which container seemed very important to him, as did the latter's position on the shelves. Jame listened, trying to make sense of it all. The old man's voice rose and fell. Lamps swayed and wood creaked.

A kind of song began to weave in and out of Jame's mind, not words this time but sounds, rising and falling, wild and beautiful. The Wolver Grimly, she thought, half-asleep, serenading her outside the tent at the Cataracts where Torisen kept her a virtual prisoner. Any moment now would come her brother's exasperated cry:

"Grimly, do you mind?"

She jerked awake. No one had shouted. Below, the old man still crooned nonsense; somewhere above and behind her, wolvers still sang.

This is very strange, she thought and rose, pushing Jorin off her lap, to investigate.

The music came from outside Mount Alban's triple front door. Wisps of weirding trickled around jambs and lintel like smoke, but the surface was cool under her gloved hands. Then it grew colder still as a shadow fell outside, as stealthy and massive as an eclipse. Mist and song dissolved into a chill wind blowing through the cracks. Behind her, Jorin began to growl. Jame felt her own hair stir under her cap. Impossible . . . but she knew the stench born on that dark breath, the exhalation of a tainted land where deformed roots cried as they were wrenched from the ground and the unburnt dead always came crawling back. Incredible to think that once she had thought that loathsome smell only natural, as one does the air into which one is born. Awake or asleep, if she had any sense, she would turn and walk (run) away again, as she had twice before.

Yes . . . if.

Huh.

The smallest of the three doors opened at a touch . . . into another hall.

It was darker than Mount Alban's had been, lit only by the cold glow of a naked sword. Jame knew that bale-blade. In a moment, she also knew the man clad in dusty-black who sat with his back to her, holding it.

"Tori?"

Her brother stiffened, but didn't turn. "So you've tracked me down after all," he said dully. "No more hide and seek. Not from you, not from them. Don't you hear them in the shadows? They're all returning, the Kendar we knew, who ransomed me out of darkness with their souls. Returning, but so horribly changed, and it's all my fault. Listen . . . ."

Was she still asleep on the stairs to the herb shed? Had Tori dragged her into one of his nightmares as he so often had in their childhood?

Scratch, rustle, scrape . . . the stealthy sounds of the haunts that had been her childhood friends, waking to a nightmare of their own . . . .

"He's here too, you know," said Torisen, whispering now. "Father. Dead on the battlements with three arrows in his chest—no, half-dead on the stair, coming down . . . can't you hear him? His voice goes on and on, telling me to kill . . . to kill . . . ."

"You tell him," hissed Grimly, "to let go of that damned sword!"

His voice made her start: she hadn't distinguished the Wolver's dark form, crouching at Torisen's feet. Now she looked at her brother's right hand, lit by the hilt which it gripped, and winced. The thin, elegant fingers had swollen to nearly twice their normal size, knuckles and signet ring sunk into puffy flesh, tight skin marked by dark lines radiating out from burst, seeping blisters. She remembered how painfully that sword had blistered her fingers at the Cataracts, and she had only wielded it long enough to get across the battlefield. Tori had obviously been clutching it much, much longer than that.

Torisen put his free hand on the Wolver's head. "Go back to sleep," he said gently. "This isn't your dream. Anyway, I can't sheathe Kin-Slayer until it's killed someone."

Damn, thought Jame, dismayed. That's a new twist.

Or was it? Crossing the field at the Cataracts, she had spilled enough blood to glut a dozen swords. Of course, it could also be a thirst which the blade had developed after being reforged in Perimal Darkling. She should have warned Tori about that, or at least about the advantage and danger of wearing Ganth's ring on the same hand that wielded his sword.

"Why did you follow me?" he demanded in sudden, almost petulant exasperation. "Don't you see how dangerous we are to each other? I keep thinking that there should only be one of us, but which? Kin-Slayer may have to decide. Father says that you were a mistake, that you're too dangerous to live . . . ."

"Damn Father, Kin-Slayer, and the horse they rode in on!"

It came out almost in a shout. The wind faltered, then blew more strongly, the wolvers' voices all but lost on its foul, rushing wings.

"Please!" breathed Grimly, flat to the ground.

"I haven't come all this way," said Jame, trying to speak more softly, sounding half-strangled, "through fire, water, and darkling shadow, to play victim again to that man's madness. Anyway, he's dead. It's your responsibility now. You decide."

". . . oh, please. We're losing the song . . . ."

"Or should I just drop out of your life again?" She had come up behind him now, wanting to grab those hunched shoulders and shake them but somehow not daring to touch. "You can't bear to look at my face, can you? It's the price I've already paid for your cowardice. So, dammit, decide!"

Looking down, she saw how unkempt his dark hair was, how threaded with silver. What price had he paid, she suddenly wondered, over that long, bleak winter? What price was he paying still?

His head jerked toward the scorched door which led up to the battlements.

"Listen: he's on the stair. All winter, each night, coming one step farther down . . . until now. How can I decide anything with him at the door, listening? Listen. His hand is on the latch. He's fumbling with it, muttering. Is it bolted? I-I can't move . . . I can't . . . ."

The door was rattling. It was opening.

Jame threw herself at it, slamming it shut against resistance.

"Dammit, leave him alone!" she cried, and shot the bolt.

She found herself leaning breathlessly against the outside of Mount Alban's smallest front door. What in Perimal's name . . . ?

Abruptly, the next larger door swung open, taking the smaller one and Jame with it. She stumbled into the college's main hall, to be grabbed by a furious, white-haired figure. The second door slammed shut behind them, locking, as she was thrown backward against it.

"What do you mean, 'Leave him alone'?" demanded Kindrie. His anger shook him, shook her through his grip on her *d'hen*. "You're the danger here, not me! I followed you down because I couldn't understand how you could have helped Graykin without manipulating his soul-image, and now I've caught you tampering with your brother's. What did you do to it?"

"I-I don't understand. What soul-image? Whose?"

"The Highlord's! That awful keep in the Haunted Lands. Y-you got into it without even touching him. Don't you realize what harm you may have done to him . . . and what can a nemesis like you do anyone but harm? You a-and that vile Ishtier . . . . What did you do after you slammed that door in my face? What?"

"B-bolted it . . . b-but it was only a dream, wasn't it?"

"Dream? Dream? I'll show you how much of a dream that was!"

He dropped her. Jame hadn't realized, until she hit the floor, how far off the ground that slight Shanir had been holding her. He had a Knorth temper, all right, she thought bemusedly, and wondered if it had ever been roused in him before.

Grating sounds came from the shadows. Unable to open the smaller two doors, Kindrie was working the massive counter-weight which secured the double leaves of the largest. Jame looked up. Tendrils of weirding again snaked around all the edges. She scrambled to her feet.

"Kindrie, no . . . !"

The weight sank. Groaning, the tree trunk rose out of its brackets and the enormous doors yawned open. Weirding billowed into the hall.

Kindrie gaped up at it. "But . . . but . . . but . . . ."

Jame grabbed his arm and pulled him down the hall with Jorin bounding on ahead. "We'll sort it out later," she said. "Now, run for the main stair, d'you hear? Run!"

She herself made for the steps descending to the herb shed.

"Sir!" she cried down to the swaying lanterns and groaning timber. "Abandon ship: the hall is sinking!"

The old man appeared at the foot of the steps, staring up at her open-mouthed, then darted out of sight.

Jame swore and shot a glance back at the door. Mist rolled down the hall like a tidal wave but slower and more silent.

A clatter on the steps made her jump. It was the scrollsman scurrying up toward her. At the stair-head, he slammed the door behind him, locked it, and tied a rope to the handle.

"Well?" he demanded, turning to her. "What are you waiting for?"

They ran across the hall, the old man paying the line out behind him, and reached the stair just as the rolling mist engulfed them.

For an endless moment, everything was obscured. Then the weirding lifted.

Jame found herself crouching breathless, one hand locked on Jorin's ruff, the other gripping the edge of a wooden tread with sufficient force to drive splinters under her nails. Kindrie and the old man were clinging to the stair's rails with equal determination, the latter with his eyes screwed tight shut.

The mist formed a ceiling close overhead, but rising. Under it was a hall sculpted of glowing mist—scuffed floor, massive columns, panelled walls—like a chamber in the clouds. Opposite, the herb shed's door looked almost black set in such luminescence, as did the rope stretching across the shining floor. The old man pulled in its slack and secured it to the rail.

"There," he said. "That shed is new built. It should travel with us now, perhaps even longer than the stair does, if the rope holds."

"You mean we'll be trailing it behind us like the . . . the bait on a troll line?" Jame asked, bemused. Her voice sounded muffled, as had his, both half swallowed by the mist. More glowing details of the hall emerged over them as the white ceiling silently rose. "D'you think we'll catch anything?"

The old scrollsman had already started up the stair.

"Lots of old wood in the lower maze," he was muttering to himself as his head disappeared into the mist. "It won't travel far, whatever happens to the stair. Best to get above."

Abruptly he stopped and ducked back into sight, glaring at Jame. "What in Perimal's name d'you mean, 'we'?"

III

THE TOP FLOOR of Mount Alban's upper keep was an observation deck, open on all sides except for a low wall and the arches which supported the roof. Some two dozen scrollsmen and singers milled excitedly about on it, trying to see something—anything—above the sea of glowing mist which stretched featureless to the horizon under a clouded night sky with a hint of dawn to the east. Every few minutes, someone would cry, "Look!" and there would be a stampede from one side of the tower to the other, back and forth, back and forth.

If this really were a boat, Jame thought, standing well clear, it would long since have capsized.

As the old man had predicted, the new stair had kept them safe through the layer of weirding, which had continued to rise after them sending tendrils of mist before it to lace walls and beams, floors and ceilings. Below, all must now be like the lower hall, ghost-like, its reality left somewhere behind.

Her new acquaintance, Jame discovered, was the mysterious and much sought after Index, his nickname quickly explained as the others crowded around him demanding the location of such diverse information as the history of the late Hathiri empire and the average rate of arboreal drift. Many sources, inconveniently, had gone south for the winter; others were on shelves below in the library. Index had little respect for the latter. Memory, not writing, was the true scholar's way, the title of "scrollsman" notwithstanding. Like most traditional Kencyr, he had probably never learned how to read.

Jame stood beside the southwest corner stairwell, looking warily for the Jaran Heir, ready if necessary to bolt below to the infirmary where she had left Kindrie. What she saw were Highborn and Kendar so intermixed that it was hard to tell which was which. All dressed in scholars' robes belted over skirts or trousers, worn impartially by men and women. The woolen robes themselves varied in color but not in cut, each having many deep pockets inside and out in which might be stored memoranda or lunch. Some were brightly dyed and elaborately embroidered around collars and cuffs—more a singer's flourish, apparently, than an indication of wealth or race. The singers in general seemed a more flamboyant, mischievous lot. Jame noted that it was two of them, stationed on opposite sides of the tower, whose turnabout cries of "Look!" were making their usually sedate, quite elderly colleagues run back and forth like overexcited children.

Not so the Director, however, who stood as solid as a mountain peak in the center of the deck while his people ebbed and flowed around him, occasionally bouncing off. He, without a doubt, was Kendar, and probably a former randon officer as well, judging by the savage scars about his face. Many took the scrollsman's robe when their fighting days were done. But that tall scholar meekly accepting orders from him looked very like a Highborn. Interesting.

More interesting still was the only other person on the deck under seventy—a young woman, Jame thought, although that cropped hair and profile might as easily belong to a handsome boy. Moreover, he (or she) wore no mask. When Jame had arrived on Index's heels, the other youth had given her a quick, startled look, then turned politely away when Jame had retreated into such shadows as she could find. However, curiosity prevailed.

"Excuse me," she said tentatively, approaching. "Could you tell me what's going on?"

The other turned and smiled. Yes, definitely a woman, a few years older than Jame herself. "Where shall I start? To begin with, we're successfully launched on the crest of a weirdingstrom . . . ."

"How can you tell?"

"Observation and deduction." With a sweep of her arm, she indicated the expanse of mist, cloud, and milky night sky. "What do you see—or rather, what don't you?"

Jame surveyed the unmarked cloud-scape dubiously, then said, "Ah. The surrounding peaks of the Snowthorns. Left behind?"

"Yes, presumably. How far we'll go, though, no one is sure, or how long it will take to get there. In the past, individuals have been displaced more or less instantaneously as far as the Cataracts."

"You really think that the whole keep is moving?"

"Oh, not all of it. The hill fort ruins should act as our storm anchor—an advantage we have over individual weird-walkers. From what Index reports, we've already left behind the cliff face and the lower hall, as well as half the living quarters."

"The mist level inside is still rising, like water in the hold."

"Hmmm. That could be a problem if it reaches this high, but I expect it will begin to subside before that. This upper keep should travel the farthest, being the most recently built. We think Mount Alban will come apart like a . . . a puzzle-box, and then back together again as the anchor eventually drags us home from weirding patch to patch when the storm is spent."

Jame reflected that Mount Alban might have an affinity for ruins besides its own, considering how easily the wolvers' keep had snagged it. Perhaps that was how it traveled, from shattered foundation to foundation.

"But what supports us," she wondered out-loud, "if the cliff really has been left behind?"

"The weirding itself, I suppose, and our inner wooden shell. At a guess, we aren't any closer to the ground than when we started. It's all guesswork, though. We've done our research, of course, back to the last really bad storm that changed the course of the Silver for hundreds of miles. The Bashtiri and Hathiri keeps traveled some then, which is one reason why the old empire garrisons were scared out of the Riverland. It seemed likely that the same thing would happen again some day, so we kept that in mind while rebuilding Mount Alban. I gather that the stair to the main hall has come with us. So too has this one."

She gestured over the wall nearest to hand. Looking down, Jame saw an extremely improvised affair clinging precariously to the keep's southern face, disappearing into the mist at the cliff top.

"How far down does it go?"

"Nearly to the ground, with a rope ladder reaching the rest of the way. At the last moment, the Director insisted on the equivalent of a sally port. The point is, though, that no one knows how all this theory will work out in practice. Why, we could even end up stranded in the Southern Wastes. Exciting, isn't it?"

"Very," said Jame wryly.

The scrollswoman had been glancing at her askance. "Pardon me," she said abruptly, "but I have to ask: you are the Highlord's sister, aren't you?"

Jame felt her mouth go dry. Behind her, Index stammered to a halt.

He's overheard, she thought with dismay, but then realized that the old man had simply bogged down in his own material.

"Tansy tea, tansy tea . . . ." he was muttering over and over, as if trying to get himself started again.

" 'Gerridon's knee,' " she said over her shoulder. She didn't remember hearing that particular nonsense couplet, but must have as she dozed on the stair, and probably a lot more beside.

The old man stared at her. "Tansy tea; Gerridon's knee," he repeated, and was off again, only to be interrupted by another cry of "Look!" and another stampede.

"This is hardly the place for a private conversation," said the young woman. "Let's go below."

Jame's impulse was to bolt down the outside stair and keep going. Instead, she descended with the other, feeling trapped.

"What was that about Gerridon's knee?"

"Oh, just something I heard somewhere." She had apparently stumbled onto another secret, but it wasn't hers to spread, at least not until she knew for certain what it meant.

"Index is a bit eccentric, even for a scrollsman. Most of us here have at least two jobs: one manual and one academic. He tends the herb shed and does research on the Merikit. It's been nearly eighty years, though, since the north was closed to us after the Kithorn massacre. A scrollsman without an active field is like a snake without a tail. So Index started collecting facts about facts—where to find them, who knows what, that sort of thing. It's made him invaluable, and powerful. A word of warning: many scholars exchange information on a barter basis. Index may look as if he's answering questions indiscriminately, but he's keeping close track of debts and credits. At the moment, I suspect he owes you one answer at least."

"I'll try not to waste it," said Jame. Lucky for her that this young scrollswoman apparently didn't play the barter game unless, like Index, she was keeping score. Just the same, "Er . . . getting back to what you said before: why should you think that I'm Torisen's sister?"

"You're very much like him. Enough to have given me quite a start when you first came up onto the observation deck. But he's still at Kothifir, as far as I know, whereas Jameth . . . ."

"Jame."

". . . whereas Jame is (or was) at Gothregor. Aunt Trishien tells me that the Women's World has been rattled to the back teeth over your disappearance."

Jame remembered the Jaran Matriarch, serenely greeting her on her dash through the Gothregor basements. That was whom this self-possessed young woman reminded her of.

"Aunt?" she repeated tentatively, thinking, I'm missing something here. Who is this person?

"Great-great-aunt, actually."

She opened a door and gestured Jame into a high vaulted room lined with shelves. On them rested such scraps of scroll and manuscript as the scholars had managed to snatch up in their flight from the Master's House on the night of the Fall. A greater treasure saved, however, had been the memories of the scrollsmen and singers themselves, since each of them had memorized a master text to earn his or her robe. That practice still continued. Many of the scholars forced to remain here last winter were those who hadn't yet found someone to whom to pass on their knowledge.

Jorin began to growl. First through his senses, then through her own, Jame smelled something sickly sweet, something rotting.

At the far end of the room, black against the weirding glow of a window, stood a table and a chair. From them, a dark shape rose stiffly and bowed.

"Lordan . . . ." said a croaking whisper.

The scrollswoman returned the salute. "Singer Ashe."

Jame had backed up against the closed door. She knew that smell now.

The other was staring at her. "Why, what's the matter?"

"She was savaged . . . by a haunt . . . just as I was," said that hoarse voice from the shadows. "But she didn't . . . die of it."

Jame jerked her hand away from her forearm, which bore the scar marks of human teeth. "How did you know that?"

"Haunts know . . . what concerns . . . haunts."

"I'm sorry," said the young woman to Jame. "We've gotten so used to Ashe that it didn't occur to me that she might disturb you."

We're in the room with a talking cadaver, Jame thought, *and I'm not supposed to be disturbed?*

Perhaps she shouldn't have been, though. Everyone had heard about Singer Ashe, who had helped Torisen escape Caineron's trap at Tentir and then had marched south with him and the Host. An infected haunt bite, taken in the White Hills, had killed her three days before anyone had realized how seriously she had been hurt. If not for that, she surely would have died covering Harn Grip-hard's back at the Cataracts. The battle song she had composed afterward, from the viewpoint of the dead and dying, was something only whispered about in the Women's Halls.

Jame knew all that. Just the same, haunts came from those parts of Rathillien like the Haunted Lands where Perimal Darkling lay just beneath the surface. Their very nature reflected that shadow realm, where animate and inanimate, life and death, obscenely merged. How could you trust anything that tainted?

Then her mind skipped back to something that Ashe had said.

"The singer called you 'Lordan,'" she said, turning to the young woman. "But isn't that what they call the heir of a house?"

"That's right," said the other, smiling. "I haven't introduced myself, have I? My name is Kirien."

KIRIEN'S SMILE deepened. The Knorth looked like an illustration of the infinitive, "to boggle."

"But ... but ... but you can't be! You're a woman!"

"As I told your brother: technically, not until I come of age. Then, nothing in the Law prevents me from taking power, if my house and the Highlord consent. Torisen hasn't agreed yet, but I think he may. As for the Jaran, Uncle Kedan is fed up with playing interim lord and counting the days until he can get back to his own research."

The Knorth shook her head as if to clear it. "I'm confused. If the four duties of a Highborn lady are obedience, self-restraint, endurance, and silence, how does ruling fit in?"

"There's Law," said Kirien lightly, "and then there's custom."

Ashe stirred. Kirien could almost hear her old friend thinking: Be careful what you say.

But the Knorth was already working it out.

"If the Law doesn't prevent you from ruling, then maybe it doesn't demand all those other things from any of us. Are you saying that I've half-killed myself all winter trying merely to be conventional? Is that what all those girls in the Women's Halls are doing? In Perimal's name, why?"

"It would take a matriarch to explain that," said Kirien, thinking, Aūnt Trishien is right: she does have a mind. "What little I know comes from independent research. I'm not privy to the secrets of the Women's World."

"Those damned secrets!" said the Knorth explosively. "I bet they don't tell this one about law versus custom to the children until they're so trained that they can't imagine any other way of life. I had a sewing teacher like that at Gothregor. Oh, that's clever, to catch them so young. How old d'you think I would have been before anyone would have told me—or is that a level of secrecy they would never have let me reach?"

Kirien thought that she was probably right. It would be dangerous to the Women's World to have someone so independent possessed of such knowledge—but now she was, with only half a clue from Kirien. Scholar that she was, the Jaran Matriarch was not apt to be pleased.

"Aunt warned me that you were a born puzzle-breaker," she said ruefully.

The Knorth glowered. "Some things need to be broken."

Ashe stirred again. Kirien would almost have thought the singer was fidgeting except, of course, that she was dead.

"Not . . . everything," came that creaking voice. "Not even . . . all customs."

The Knorth shot her a baleful look. "You've broken a whole slew of them," she said in challenge to Kirien.

Kirien shrugged. "I'm Jaran. We have our own customs, which include not putting girls through the women's school at Gothregor unless they want to go. The curriculum sounded to me like a dead bore. Then too, since my Randir mother died bearing me, I've been suspect breeding stock. The Jaran aren't much sought after by other houses anyway. We're too . . . unconventional. So the Matriarchs let me go my own way. That may change now that my house has chosen me as lordan. But you're Knorth, with binding customs of your own. Hasn't anyone told you what they are?"

"The Women's World told me as little as they could about my house," said the other bitterly. "Not even the names of the death banners in the old hall so that I could pay proper respects to my ancestors. They said it was the Knorth Matriarch's role to instruct me, but the last one was assassinated thirty-four years ago. That was Kinzi, my great-grandmother. I have found out a bit, you see, despite the Women's World."

More than a bit, Kirien thought wryly.

Ignorance is weakness. She understood why the Matriarchs hadn't wanted to strengthen a girl whose bloodlines they intended to manipulate for their own purposes. In principle, she didn't believe that people should be used or knowledge withheld, any more than she believed in the barter game which her elders so much enjoyed playing. In practice, though, how safe was it to be totally candid with someone so sharp at drawing inferences —someone who, she sensed, was not being completely open with her?

"What . . . has your brother . . . told you?" Ashe abruptly demanded.

"Precious little."

"Perhaps . . . he has reason."

"Meaning?"

Until now, the Knorth had tried to ignore the haunt singer. Now they faced each other, one a black outline against the growing light of dawn, the other black clothed and masked, two shapes of darkness. Kirien suddenly felt caught between forces she didn't understand. She noticed that even the ounce had backed away.

"Ashe," she said uncomfortably, "this is a guest. Don't you think . . . ."

"Show the Lordan . . . the knife . . . which you carry . . . in your boot."

Behind the mask, silver eyes blinked. Then thin lips tightened. The Knorth drew a white knife from a boot sheath and defiantly offered it, hilt first, to Kirien, who took it.

"Why, how odd," she said, examining the blade. "And how cold . . . ."

She was suddenly aware of a dark figure close by on either side, without having heard either of them move. Ashe's cold grasp gently but firmly closed around her wrist and drew downward the hand on whose palm she had been about to rest the knife's point. The Knorth's black gloved fingers carefully detached the blade from her grip. Then they both stepped back, and it was possible again to breathe.

The Knorth saluted her with stiff formality. "My thanks for your hospitality, Lordan," she said, her voice very slightly shaking. "I will no longer detain you from your studies."

Then she was gone, the cat slipping out in her shadow, the door closing gently after them.

"I don't understand," said Kirien, "What happened?"

"Describe . . . that knife," said Ashe.

Kirien looked at her, puzzled, but obediently began the familiar exercise of description: "Item: one weapon, classified knife or dagger; approximately twelve inches long; double edged; composition: ivory . . . ."

She faltered, eyes widening.

"Go on," said Ashe.

". . . ivory," Kirien repeated, and continued, now quoting, " 'carved all of one piece, blade, guard, and pommel; and on that last shall you see the three faces of Regonereth—maiden, lady, hag—and know what you hold by its coldness. The very tooth of death . . . .'"

"Ashe, that was it, wasn't it? The Ivory Knife, one of the three great objects of power lost in the Fall, whose least scratch means death . . . and I wanted to see how sharp it was."

 V

OUT IN THE HALL, Jame leaned against the door, shaking.

You just *gave* it to her, she thought, appalled. And she was about to test its point. Some guardian you are. Throw the damn thing into the weirding; sink it in an ocean, if you can find one . . . .

Yes, and into whose hands would it fall then, for there *would* be someone else. It was an object of power, like the Book Bound in Pale Leather. It would go where it wished, although it took a millennium to arrive.

That last thought made Jame almost dizzy. Her life was tangled up in so many things the scope of which boggled the imagination. Usually, she tried to ignore them. Hard enough, living a day at a time. Eventually, though, she would have to come to grips with them all, or there would be real trouble.

But oh lord—nemesis, fratricide . . . and Tyr-ridan?

"Are you all right?"

The voice made Jame start. Before her stood a randon whose concerned, pleasantly ugly features gave her a second shock greater than the first.

"Captain!" she gasped, and hastily slipped the knife out of sight in its boot sheath.

The Brandan captain frowned, then also looked amazed as she recognized this masked, boy-clad figure. "Lady? What are you doing here?"

"I might ask the same of you. Shouldn't you be on duty in the Women's Halls at Gothregor?"

"Should, yes, but when my lady Brenwyr needs must leave for Falkirr, blind as she still is, with weirding coming on, how could I or her guard let her go alone?"

Brenwyr. She must be the "lady of stature" whose arrival had caught the Director so much on the hop. Ask for a matriarch to question and one appears . . . except that Jame didn't want so much as to see this particular Highborn, much less demand answers of her. Still . . . .

"Did you say 'blind'?"

"Aye. It was that shout of yours that did it, lady, if you'll recall. It shocked her deaf too, but that passed off more quickly. Not that I blame you for popping off with such a noise. That was a shocking thing which M'lady Kallystine did to you."

She was regarding Jame, trying to assess the remaining damage, but the mask thwarted her. Ironic, thought Jame, that if she had been bare faced the Kendar would have been too embarrassed to look at all. As it was, the Highborn turned away first.

"I should pay my respects to the Matriarch, I suppose."

"That's as you decide, lady, of course, but she's none too pleased with you."

"That I can believe," said Jame ruefully.

After all, the last words the Matriarch had addressed to her had been a curse. Memory set it rankling again:

Roofless and rootless, blood and bone, cursed be and cast out.

It had never been entirely out of her mind, she realized, like a burr that sticks and frets. Somehow, being under a Kencyr roof again made the irritation worse. In Brenwyr, had she really run afoul of a Shanir maledight? There were old songs about such people. They usually died young, though, killed by their families in self-defense, if they didn't wish themselves dead first. The cursing talent sounded akin to the God-voice, but with only That-Which-Destroys speaking—a frightening thought. Still, it didn't seem likely that Brenwyr could be one since it would take phenomenal self-control to hide such a thing and so-called Iron Matriarch didn't seem very controlled at all, at least around Jame.

"Nonetheless," she said, thinking out-loud, "I hurt her. That requires an apology, even if she bashes me over the head half way through it."

"That isn't very good sense," said the captain, "but it is good manners and good will. I'll stand by to see fair play. This way, lady."

Brenwyr had been allotted quarters on the third floor down, against the southern wall. As the captain and Jame approached, they found the escort—a cadet ten-command, late of the Gothregor guard—gathered out in the hall, speaking together in low, worried voices. Jame recognized one of them as the cadet who had failed to stop her escape with Jorin from the Brandan compound . . . could it only be six days ago?

"She's in a queer mood," the ten-commander reported. "Still of a stew to be on her way. When I told her that the weirding had closed in, she made a strange sound, like choking, and ordered us all out."

"She was too on edge to stay at Gothregor either," mused the captain. "A strong-willed lady, that. When her sight returns, as the Ardeth Matriarch assures me it soon should, she's apt to bolt, mist or no, unless we look sharp. Lady?"

Jame closed her mouth with a snap. What had she said when the Iron Matriarch had cursed her? The same to you, Brandan—and now Brenwyr was also too restless to stay under a Kencyr roof? Sweet Trinity.

"I'd still like to see her, captain." Now, more than ever.

"All right, lady. On your head be it."

She knocked. There was no answer, but they could hear footsteps inside, pacing back and forth, back and forth. Jame pushed open the door.

The large room beyond was a study, full of work tables and scroll shelves. Arched windows lined the far wall, the Director's stair spidering past outside against the growing light of day. Brenwyr's dark form stalked past it, up the room and down, up and down. Her boots intermittently rang against the oak floor and thudded as dust swirled up around the hem of her divided skirt. Her grim, blind way led through mounds of crumbling furniture, as if she had cleared a path for herself by cursing anything that got in her way.

Jame cleared her throat. "Matriarch?" Crack, crack, thud went the boots without pause. "Lady?" Thud, thud, crack . . . . "Brenwyr?"

The Highborn stopped short, not turning. "Aerulan?" she whispered.

"No, lady," said Jame, taken aback. "It's only me."

"You." The tone was almost a curse in itself. "The Knorth mountebank."

"Careful," said the randon softly, to either or both of them.

Whatever clever questions Jame had planned to ask went straight out of her head. "I-I came to apologize," she stammered.

"What good is that?" said the other harshly. "It won't bring her back."

"W-who? Aerulan? B-but Matriarch, she's dead . . . ."

Brenwyr took a fierce stride toward her and fetched up hard against a work table. Jame found that, without thinking, she had backed into the randon. Behind them, Jorin was digging frantically at the door. The matriarch leaned over the table, fighting to control herself, red sparking in her blind, blood-shot eyes. A choked sound came out of her throat through bared teeth, curses half-swallowed.

"Dead . . . ." she repeated thickly, and gave a terrible laugh that was half sob. "Don't you think I know that? Get out, Knorth. Now. Before I hurt you." Her fist crashed down on the table. "Rot you!" she cried at it, with all her thwarted grief and rage.

The table sagged. Dry rot dust rattled down from it as its legs started to crumble.

Jame heard the door open behind her and Jorin scramble out. The next moment she was through it herself, shoved so hard by the randon that she bounced off the corridor's far wall. The captain shut the study door behind them. Her short, sandy hair was bristling, like Jorin's tail. They heard a curiously soft, slithering, rotten sound inside as the table collapsed.

That could have been me, Jame thought.

The cadets were staring at them. They had probably never seen a Kendar manhandle a lady before.

"Stay out of there," the captain told them. "If she calls, I'll go in, but no one else. Understand?"

When she turned, Jame saw worry and more than a touch of fear in her blue eyes. She hadn't known what her matriarch was. She still wasn't sure. A maledight with berserker tendencies, so high in the power of her house . . . . The suspicion alone was the stuff of nightmares.

"She did stop with the table," said Jame.

"Next time, she probably won't. You'd better leave, lady. Now."

There was no answer to that but to sketch a salute and go, so Jame did, wondering.

Was she to blame for Brenwyr's state? It was hard to see how, considering that Aerulan had been dead nearly twice as long as Jame had been alive. She felt as if she had wandered into an old song of passion and loss, but one as yet without an ending. It was that which might yet drive Brenwyr mad. If it did, she could do hideous damage, and stopping her could be just as costly. But that really wasn't Jame's business . . . was it? Anyway, how could one destructive Shanir help another? Being so ignorant made her feel stupid and weak. Worst thought of all, was she fated to end like Brenwyr, a curse to everyone she loved? Tori thought so already.

". . . a mistake, too dangerous to live . . . ."

Eh, enough of that. Since she had made such a mess of apologizing for something that wasn't her fault, she should find Brier Iron-thorn and try again for something that was.

Only then did she realize that Jorin was gone. Lady Brenwyr, it seemed, had been one too many for him. His disappearance didn't worry Jame too much, though: blind as he was, the ounce could usually find his way in any area which he had previously seen through her eyes. She would look for him as she did for Brier.

The morning passed, however, with no sign of either. Noon came and went.

Mount Alban's upper keep floated on over a weirding sea as its inmates set to their experiments, trying to direct their wandering home in one direction or another. As usual, the singers and scrollsmen competed. The former stationed themselves along the western edge of the observation deck and in unison chanted any song they could think of that referred to the Western Sea. (A fine thing, thought Jame, if Mount Alban should land in the middle of it.) Below, the latter engaged in more individual efforts, aiming for landfalls as diverse as Kothifir and the Isles of the Dead, using methods which ranged from solemn appeals to the masonry to one ancient scholar playing hopscotch in a corner.

Jame fell in with Index as the old man bustled about the upper keep and what remained of the lower, dispensing information and counting up his barter-profits with a miser's glee. Sometime, though, he faltered. A doggerel couplet would start him off again if he could remember it or if Jame could supply it from those she had overheard in the herb shed. Index apparently used the wall of herb jars as a mnemonic device, with nonsense verse as its key, a clever solution for an old man with a failing memory and no trust in the written word—except that he had begun to forget the key. Jame remembered it for him when she could, and kept her own barter score for later use.

While she saved her questions with Index, however, she asked them whenever she ran into one of the Knorth cadets. Considerably junior to the Brandan honor guard, they had been scattered throughout the keep, told to make themselves useful or at least to keep out from under foot. None of them had seen Brier in hours, and all found excuses not to talk about her.

"Vant's orders," said Rue, glowering. "We're in trouble enough as it is, he says."

"What trouble?" Jame demanded.

Rue fidgeted with the sack of chicken feathers which she was carrying in aid, ancestors only knew, of what arcane experiment. As much as she disliked him, Vant was Five, with an authority over her more immediate than that of her lord's runagate sister. Suddenly she stiffened, listening.

"Did someone say, 'Land ho'?"

"Don't change the topic . . . ." said Jame, exasperated, then broke off as the cry came again. "Not 'Land ho.' 'Sand ho.'"

Rue dropped her sack and sprinted for the nearest stairs leading upward, hard on Jame's heels.

Hot, crimson light flooded down to meet them. Up on the observation deck, figures lined the western rail, black against the glare, singers and scrollsmen both. Beyond them, a setting sun hung low and swollen in the sky. Jame looked sideways down the line of scholars, blinking away black after-images from sun-shocked eyes. Not far away stood Brier Iron-thorn, red hair sullenly ablaze. As usual, her dark face revealed nothing, but the tense lines of her body suggested someone leaning hard against a short leash. Jame looked west again, following the Kendar's stare. A vast plain stretched out before them, seemingly endless, so absolutely flat as to look unreal. A hot breath of wind blew in her face. With it came a distant, empty keening and the dry incense of desert places.

"All right," said someone, breaking the awed silence. "What clown aimed for the Southern Wastes?"

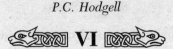

VI

"THIS," said the Director, "is serious."

A subdued knot of scholars had gathered around him, away from those who still lined the rail chattering like excited children. Kirien and Ashe had joined the circle, the latter hooded, an iron-shod staff in her hand. Listening from the rail, hoping to escape notice, Jame flinched as the Director turned his scarred face toward her; however, when he stared over her head, unblinking, full into the sun, she suddenly realized that he was blind.

"Ashe tells me that we're in the middle of the Dry Salt Sea," he said. "Urakarn is west of us, below the horizon but still dangerously close. I needn't remind you what happened the last time Kencyr fell into Karnid hands."

The group stirred uneasily, remembering. It had only been some dozen years ago, after all, during the long confusion after Ganth's fall. Without a Knorth Heir to lead the Southern Host, Caineron had secured the post for his favorite son, Genjar, who in turn had tried to further his own political ambitions by attacking the Karnid stronghold.

" 'Black rock on the dry sea's edge,' " Ashe suddenly chanted, her harsh voice like stones grating together.

" 'How many your dungeons swallowed. How few came out again.' "

Tori went in, Jame thought, and came out, with the marks of Karnid torture on his hands and soul. He must have been about her age then, if not younger. Strange. She remembered so clearly the child he had been and had met him again now as a man; but what had that boy been like, who had faced the horrors of Urakarn and barely survived them?

Ashe's song had stilled the chatter by the rail. What if the weirding stranded them here? They could see it stretching away to the east and north, a great cloud plain rosy with sunset light. Clearly, it had reached its farthest mark and now must either dissipate or withdraw. Which, and how soon? No one knew.

Jame slipped down the southeast corner stair, hopefully on Brier's heels. At least, when she had turned again to look, the Kendar had disappeared, and there weren't all that many ways for her to go.

High time that she also found Jorin. It occurred to her now that she hadn't looked for the ounce in the most obvious place. Sure enough, there in the infirmary he was, curled up asleep on Aerulan's tapestry lap. There too was Graykin, fretfully awake.

"Yellow isn't exactly your color," she said, regarding the half-healed bruises on his face, "but it's better than black and blue. Kindrie tells me that you may even have enough Kencyr blood to grow some new teeth."

"Fine," muttered the Southron, without looking at her.

Behind the mask, Jame's eyebrows rose. "If you're having second thoughts about serving me . . . ."

"It isn't that! You gave me a job to do, something to guard . . . and I failed."

"Oh." She sat down on the foot of his pallet. "Listen, Gray: it isn't important. I don't want that damned book anyway. If it wants me, it will find some way to come crawling back. I never meant to saddle you with it all winter, in any event."

He was glaring at her now. "Oh, so it's not important, is it? How nice to know that I starved, froze, and got beaten up by Caineron's thugs for no good reason. But that doesn't matter. What does is that you gave me an assignment—however stupid—and I failed."

"I see. What we're really talking about here is your pride."

"My pride?" He drew himself up, indignant, clutching the blanket to his bony chest. "How about yours? You're a great lady, aren't you? The Highlord's own sister! You shouldn't run around dressed like a . . . a Tastigon flash-blade. You've got me now . . . ."

". . . to keep my hands clean," Jame finished. "You've said that before. Let's get something clear, here and now: if you do serve me, my hands are only as clean as yours. I'm serious, Gray. Too many of my house have tried to hide behind Honor's Paradox, from Master Gerridon on down. But you should be serious too. Look: I'm in no position to offer you security, protection, or even a crust of bread every other week. The way things are going, I probably never will be."

But Graykin was shaking his head. "You'll have power," he said stubbornly. "You must. Nothing stops you."

There was a scratch on the door and Rue entered, scowling. "You were asking about Ten," she said in her abrupt way. "Well, it's not right. Someone's got to be told, orders or no."

Jame stood up, a ripple of apprehension down her spine. "You said before that there was trouble. What?"

"Nothing, at first. The captain thought we'd been caught out in the weirding and carried along with it, the same as she was. Then someone says something to her

Ten—I think it was Vant—and the next thing we know our Ten is on the mat . . . ."

"Wait a minute. This would be Captain Hawthorn, correct? Who is she, anyway?"

"You know," said Rue, impatiently. "You were talking to her outside the library."

"I was?" Light dawned. "She's the Brandan captain, with her cadet ten-command, escorting Lady Brenwyr. All right, Rue. I just didn't know her name before now. So, Brier is on the mat . . . ."

". . . and the captain asks her, flat out, if she ignored standing orders to take us back to Tentir when it started to weird up. 'Yes, Ran,' says Ten, wooden-like. You know her way. Did she in fact take us south, away from safety? 'Yes, Ran.' Why? 'No excuse, Ran.' "

"She didn't say anything about me or Restormir?"

"Not a word. Maybe we cadets should have, but like Vant says, we're already midden-deep in trouble, and how will it help Ten anyway? So Hawthorn says, 'You've endangered your squad, apparently without reason. You're relieved of command.' Ten's an outsider, like me. This will ruin her, and it's not fair!"

"It damn well isn't," said Jame. "Hawthorn is a reasonable woman, though. She'll understand if I explain, if she isn't still too mad at me to listen."

"She may understand," said Rue, sounding doubtful, "but it may not help. You didn't see, did you? When Ten left the deck, she went down the outer stair to the desert. I don't think she means to come back."

After that Rue left, relieved at having vented her feelings to someone, although plainly not expecting Jame to do anything but listen.

"Thought a lot of herself, that Iron-thorn did," said Graykin, with ill-concealed satisfaction. "And she was a

Caineron born and bred, whatever oaths she's sworn since. You don't need the likes of her, lady."

"Jealous, Gray?" Jame asked absent-mindedly, not noticing him flinch.

She was wondering if she should leave her heavy *d'hen* behind. No. Without its protection, she felt naked; and besides, the sun was setting. Water? A good drink should suffice. The Southron watched with growing alarm as she drained a flask left for his use.

"What are you doing?" he demanded. "You don't . . . you can't intend to go after her!"

"Don't I?" said Jame. "Can't I?"

She regarded Jorin and Aerulan. Blind ounce and dead girl seemed to look back at her hopefully.

"I think not. Still . . . . Down, kitten."

Shooed off the banner, Jorin stood by making sounds of protest as she rolled it up and slung it across her back.

"You can't!" said Graykin again, more shrilly. "Any minute now, this floating mad-house is going to snap back toward the Riverland. I over heard people up on the deck say so! I-I won't let you go. I'll call Captain Hawthorn . . . ."

The next moment he had curled back like a frightened spider, all knees and elbows, as the other bent over him. The back of one black sheathed finger lightly traced the line of his jaw and hooked under his chin, jarring it back with sudden pain. Silver eyes locked with his own.

"Oh no, little man, oh no. Never come between me and my honor. Never. Understand?"

"Y-yes . . . ."

The gloved hand patted his bruised cheek lightly, a panther's tap. "Good boy. Now sleep for awhile."

The door opened, closed. Graykin drew a deep, shuddering breath in the humming silence. "Be damned if I will," he muttered, shaken but defiant, trying to rally. "Be damned . . . ."

. . . and toppled over sideways, asleep before he hit the floor.

 **VII**

JAME CLOSED THE DOOR behind her quickly, before Jorin could dash through it. Power still sang in her blood, another berserker flare successfully controlled. This could get to be a habit.

Yes: a dangerous one. If each use of her claws brought her closer to the Third Face of God, wouldn't this too? On the other hand, what she had just done to Graykin also savored of the use to which such talents were put under shadow's eaves. It was damnable, to be caught balancing between her Shanir blood and the darkling training to which the Master had subjected it—and perhaps double damned in that she understood what had been done to her.

You may still be innocent, the Arrin-ken Immalai had said, *but not ignorant. If you do eventually fall, it will be as the Master fell, knowing the evil you do, welcoming it. The abuse of power will push you in that direction. On the other hand, its mere use may drive you the other way, toward our god. That is what it means to be a Shanir, to walk the knife's edge.*

"But I don't want to fall either way!" she had cried, and that rich, ironic voice had answered her, chuckling deep in her mind:

Which one of us does? For us, alas, good is no less terrible than evil.

No less terrible. What a choice.

And how seductive power was. It was her birthright, no less than Ganth's tangled legacy and no easier to deny. But how long could she master it before, like wine, it mastered her? Now, there would be a terrible intoxication indeed. It had already made her hasty and cruel. What choice, though, had Graykin given her?

Trust honor, Immalai had said.

Yes. For her, balanced on the knife's edge, honor was more than life, its loss infinitely worse than death. And part of honor was taking responsibility for one's actions and choices, over and over, as long as one acted or chose. If she had to accept Gray as her servant, he must learn to understand that.

Huh. Knorth or Caineron, honor should be the same: Kencyr. But that didn't suit Caldane's ambition. Honor restricted his power. He would reshape it, if he could, to mean unquestioning obedience from his servants, while he used their services to keep his own hands clean. Honor's Paradox suggested that, ultimately, no one was responsible for anything. It was the knife's edge which Caldane would make all his people walk, if he could, hoping that when they fell (as they must, if only he pushed hard enough) this uncomfortable world would be remade in his image.

Come to think of it, that was exactly what Gerridon had done.

And there were other Kencyr, today, who winced at the choices which honor demanded, who would abjure all responsibility if they could.

"A lady's honor is obedience," the sewing instructress had so vehemently claimed. Don't ask questions. Don't even speak. Just obey.

Of course, that young teacher was very low in the Women's World, down where secrecy starved the mind as a seeker's mask did the senses. How clever of the Matriarchs to realize that the most may be written on the blankest slate. To what degree, though, did they carry obedience to their lords?

Jame shivered, the elation of the flare draining away. The Three Faced God had apparently abandoned his people. The great mission which he had given them seemed more impossible year by year. The Arrin-ken had left. The women and Shanir were powerless, the priests treacherous, the lords merciless, and her brother was taking advice from a dead mad-man. What was left except honor—and how many secret fingers there were, picking at that last knot which held the Kencyrath together.

She had been going down the corridor glancing into each southward facing room as she passed. Outside a window, finally, was the silhouette of the Director's stair.

For the first time, Jame saw how jury-rigged it was. The steps descended in a tight spiral of narrow treads and uneven risers, precariously braced against the outer wall, held together by a pine trunk newel. Branch stumps were their main supports. Whose work was this, anyway—that gabble of ancient scholars? If Brier had come this way, though, it ought at least to support Jame. She stepped out onto it, and clutched the rough barked newel as a tread tilted under her weight.

Gingerly, she descended several feet, then bent to peer into the room below. Sunset lay in fading rose rhomboids on the floor by the windows, roughed by mounds of dust. Farther in, light edged the broken lines of furniture. All the tables but one had collapsed. The floor was rotting too. Jame's foot sank into it, unnervingly, as she stepped down from the window ledge. Dust billowed up. One loud noise, she thought, choking back a sneeze, and she would find herself suddenly one story down. One soft curse might get her there even faster.

She had started quietly across the floor, watching for soft spots, unslinging the banner as she went, when she realized that she wasn't alone.

A dark shape sat on the far side of the table, slumped forward over it.

Brenwyr.

When Jame had decided to leave Aerulan in safe hands, the Iron Matriarch had come immediately to mind. This room, patently, was far from safe, Brenwyr even less so. Still, Jame trusted her impulse. She hung the banner on the wall behind the Brandan's chair and retreated on noiseless feet.

The window sill crumbled under her weight.

"Aerulan!" exclaimed Brenwyr's voice behind her.

The Matriarch had started upright at the crash, staring blindly before her. Behind, in the shadows, stood Aerulan.

It's only the banner, Jame told herself; but then she saw Aerulan's hand resting on Brenwyr's shoulder and met the dead girl's smiling, silver eyes.

Out the window, down the stair, run away, run . . . .

. . . until a step turned underfoot, and Jame found herself again clutching the shaggy newel, all nails out, staring at a drop below her of several hundred feet.

A trick of the light, she told herself, thinking of the room above. Then, *Sweet Trinity, what have I done now?*

Whatever it had been, though, for good or ill, Aerulan was no longer her responsibility.

But Brier Iron-thorn still was.

The plain spread out below her, utterly flat to the southern horizon. Across the western prospect, half obscured by Mount Alban's bulk, stretched a range of purple clouds like distant mountains, veined with fire as the sun sank behind it. Red sand muted to rose and coral. Dusk flooded the desert land, beautiful, unearthly . . . lifeless? Had Rue been mistaken, or perhaps had Brier changed her mind? Somehow, Jame didn't think so.

The climb down seemed endless, one newel-trunk succeeding another, a denuded forest laid end to end. At first, the stair descended past the wooden walls of the upper keep. Below that, as Kirien had guessed, was weirding mist where the cliff-face should have been. yet the cliff hardly seemed absent, so exactly had the weirding taken its form. Sculpted cloud gave the illusion of rock grain and feathery fern. Windows opened into vanished rooms, furnished with fog, waiting for ghosts, all aglow with pale weirding light.

The stair ended in a rope ladder dangling some nine feet short of the ground. Jame hesitated, then dropped. She would have trouble getting back without help, but then she didn't intend to return alone. Her own falling weight barely disturbed the sand crust. Beside her feet, though, were the prints of someone much larger and heavier, tiger tread to her hunting ounce. Ah.

Down the mist flank of a Mount Alban that wasn't there, out free of its phantom western side . . . .

Voices?

Jame paused, listening. The cadence of human speech, at least, if not words, threading in and out of the desert

silence. The weirding-strom stretched obliquely back
from Mount Alban's northwest corner, a billowing tidal
wave held restlessly in check. The cliff's ghost shape
strained forward out of it like a figurehead . . . anchored?
Were there ruins here that could snag them as the wolvers' keep had in the Grimly Holt? She had heard of the
deserted cities of the Wastes, constantly appearing and
disappearing at the whim of wind and sand. If so, it must
be back under the weirding mass. Was Index's herb shed
still there too, trolling on its long line, catching . . . what,
or whom?

A hum rose again as if of voices, faded, was gone.

It was no business of hers, Jame thought, turning away.
She couldn't do anything about it anyway, while the shed
remained weird-bound and unreachable.

Brier's tracks led due west, when Jame could find
them. At first there were none except where the Kendar
had walked across one of the glittering mineral deposits
that laced the plain, leaving a trail of powdered crystal.
She couldn't be far ahead—walking, with not that much
of a head start—but Jame couldn't see her.

Sink-sand? Surely no Southron would accidentally
blunder into that, not that Jame herself knew what it
looked like on the surface, much less what other traps
the Wastes might set.

Underfoot now, the sand crust had developed corruga-
tions like frozen ripples. It was softer too, Brier's footprints showing clearly. The ridges got bigger, their
purple shadows striping the plain. Soon she could feel
the pull in her muscles as she climbed them. Dunes?
How could she have missed seeing these from the ladder,
when everything below had looked so flat?

Then, over the crest of one, suddenly, she found Brier
Iron-thorn.

The Kendar knelt, sunset light threading her dark auburn hair with fire. White grains shifted through the fingers of her raised, clenched fist, spilling back into the desert.

"Sand," she said. "Nothing but sand."

Jame stopped on the crest, feeling awkward. "Did you expect something else?" she asked, diffident.

"Expect? No. Hope . . . for what? This isn't even the right place."

"What place?"

"Maybe the sink-trap, where she died; maybe at the stone boat, where she returned."

"Who?"

For a long moment, Brier was silent, staring blindly at the far horizon. The purple clouds were closer, larger. The sun, shifting down behind them, traced their edges with gold, while inside tarnished silver lights flickered and distant thunder rumbled. A breath of wind rustled the raw silk of the Kendar's hair. Then, in a low voice, as if talking to herself, she said:

"They had escaped from the dungeons of Urakarn and were fleeing across the Dry Salt Sea. Rose stumbled into sink-sand. He tried to hold onto her, but Karnid torture had half-crippled his hands. All that long, terrible day, staggering northward, afraid to stop for fear of pursuit, he kept thinking that she was somehow still alive down there, under the sand. At dusk, they found the petrified remains of a boat and collapsed into it. In the night, feverish, he thought he saw the water return . . . all that flat sand plain changing back to the sea it had been, and the stone boat afloat on it. Under the surface, he saw Rose and reached down to her. She took his hand, pulled it down into the stinging salt water, pulled the whole boat across the sea . . . in a dream, he thought, born of fever; but in the morning there they were safe on the northern shore, with nothing behind them but sand . . . .

"Sand," she repeated, again regarding the grains which trickled through her fingers.

"Torisen told you that story, didn't he?" When? Jame wanted to ask. Why? Instead, she heard herself say, "How did he look?"

"Dazed. Sick. The Karnids and infection had almost cost him his hands; but he said he couldn't sleep until he had told me how my mother died."

For her mother's sake, Tori had said, accepting Brier's bond.

Jame had wondered what her brother had been like at her age. Now she had a sudden, vivid image of him, young and haggard, wondering if Rose Iron-thorn's impassive, red-haired child understood the news he had brought, not guessing that she would never forget a word of it.

"I suppose he thought you had a right to know."

"That's what he said."

Brier let the remaining sand fall and stood up. The quickening wind lifted her hair at the temples in glowing, short-pinioned wings. Thunder growled closer.

"Storm's coming, lady," she said. "Time to be getting back."

The Kendar had always meant to return, Jame thought, humbled, as she turned to follow. Not for Rose Iron-thorn's daughter, the self-destructive, almost petulant gesture which Jame herself had made all too often. Brier was tougher than that, too professional simply to give up. Likewise, apologies meant nothing to her. If Jame's presence here didn't convey her regret, words wouldn't help. Whether the gesture itself had, she couldn't tell.

Strange. Instead of diminishing, the dunes were growing bigger and softer the farther east they went. All Jame could see now from their troughs was the darkening sky above. On the crests, a rising wind had begun to whip sand from rise to rise. It stung her face as she glanced back. The storm-rack rolled close on their heels, black against the sky's deepening blue, blotting out the stars. Bolts of searing white leaped between it and the ground. Ahead, the faint glow of the weirding cliff seemed farther away than ever.

At the foot of a slope Jame tripped over a stone . . . no, over the top of a shattered wall, scoured clean by the swooping wind. All around, masonry fragments jutted out of the sand like so many decayed teeth. If these were the ruins on which Mount Alban had snagged, the oncoming storm must have dislodged it. If so, not only did it seem farther away, it was.

"Run," said Brier.

Jame tried. The dunes were mountainous now, though, and her feet sank into them to the ankles. For all her weight, Brier was well ahead of her, travelling fast.

Be damned if I'll call for help, Jame thought, struggling to catch up. Be damned . . . .

Salt stung her eyes like sea spray. Across her shoulders, her jacket felt heavy and damp with sweat. She floundered up the highest range of drifts yet and saw the weirding beyond like a glowing cliff against which the dune was poised to break. High above glowed the lights of the scrollsmen's keep. Below, the rope ladder swung wildly in the wind. Brier had almost reached it.

"Don't stop!" she called back sharply.

But Jame already had, panting. The slanted edge of the storm had overtaken her to the north. As it closed with the weirding, lightning leaped between them, flash on booming flash. The shock rolled southward toward the keep. In the flickering glare, the far end of the ridge on which she stood seemed to be cresting like a wave and crashing down in salt white.

"Move!" shouted Brier.

Jame took an almost involuntary step forward, and sank up to her knees. She could feel sand melting away under her. Up to her thighs, her waist . . . .

"Brier . . . ." she heard herself cry, in a voice so thin with fear that she scarcely recognized it. Up to her chest . . . .

. . . and down, mouth and eyes closed barely in time, sand pressing in on them, stopping ears suddenly against the thunder's boom. Her up-thrown hands writhed free for a moment—*Here I am, here . . . .*—then the earth gripped them. Squeezed, the breath trapped burning in her lungs as she was in this sandy grave, buried alive . . . . How deep did Rose sink? How long did she live?

Got you now, thief, Ragga's voice seemed to grate in her mind.

But the sand was changing. Her frantic hands moved again, as if through mud, then water. Eyes opened, shut again hastily against the saline sting. Then suddenly she was tumbling forward in darkness, over and over, hammered by a muted roar. No air. Which way was up? Drowning . . . .

Cold hands seized her, shoved her . . . downward, she thought, and struggled feebly. Cold words bubbled in her ear: *Don't, you fool. For your brother's sake . . . .*

The roar burst full-throated around her. Air, thick with salt spray; waves, throwing her up against the glowing cliff. Underwater again, then shoved back to the surface where a strong hand grabbed her by the collar and jerked her upward. Her fingers closed on shaggy wood. She clung, gasping, still in Brier's powerful grasp. On the Director's fragile stair, in the tumultuous darkness, they listened to the boom and crash below them of the returning salt sea.

The Grimly Holt: 60th of Spring

THE FOREST keep lay drowned in mist as though at the bottom of a luminous sea. Difficult to say in that glowing twilight when dawn came, or noon, or setting sun.

The shadow of that other, darker keep had long since faded like a bad dream, taking with it the stench of sickness and burning. The wolvers had not discussed it, afraid that words would bring it back. There were some things about humankind, after all, which few of them wished to know. Besides, there was so much else about which to sing.

Abandoning the outer walls of the keep to the weirding's care, the wolvers happily speculated about its interior. How thick had been the walls, how patterned the roof beams and floor, and where (whined hungry cubs) had food been stored? As debate rose and fell, weirding trickled in the long-gone windows to take the hazy shape of each detail, building its reality, a fragile shell crafted of song, cupped in a hollow of mist.

By the hearth, Torisen stirred in his sleep and mumbled incoherent words of distress. Not long ago, his breathing had changed from the deep, slow rhythm of *dwar*. Now he was beginning to surface, through the level of dreams. His hands twitched, as if clutching at something or trying to pull away.

". . . hurting me," he muttered. "Let go, let . . . ah!"

His eyes flickered open. He blinked, confused, then focussed on the worried face bending over him.

"Oh. Hello, Grimly." His right hand hurt. He frowned at swollen, splinted fingers. Kin-Slayer lay across the nearby hearth, sullenly reflecting the pale flames which danced in the grate. "W-Where am I? What happened?"

"How much do you remember?"

The Wolver's careful tone chilled him. The last thing which he recalled clearly was trying to last out the night awake in his Kothifir quarters. Obviously, he hadn't succeeded. After that? Snatches of memory, as broken as the dreams which they might in fact be. His breath caught.

"Grimly, did I kill Burr?"

"No, no. You haven't killed anyone this time, not even a horse."

Torisen looked at Kin-Slayer, confused. "But I was supposed to . . . . Father said . . . ."

But then Jame had shot the bolt. He could still feel Ganth's madness pressing hard against that locked door in his soul, but as long as the bolt held . . . .

He shook himself. Just another stupid dream. Absurd, to think that it had anything to do with this blessed return to sanity . . . assuming he was sane.

He looked at the surrounding walls of glowing mist, at the semblance of smoking torches and the phantom flames on the hearth. It might have been a hall hollowed out of living cloud. More mist drifted over the ground, or was it a floor? He lay on something ill-defined and yielding, yet substantial enough to support his weight. A muffled chuckling came from underneath. His fingers gingerly probing downward, touched water so cold that it seemed to burn. It was a . . . a brook, swift with melted

snow, running down the length of a ruined hall. This was
the wolvers' keep, where he had often been a guest
before; and there at its far end were his hosts: dark,
lupine shapes with glowing eyes regarding him shyly
askance. Their song rose and fell. The misty floor seemed
to firm. He jerked up his hand before it could become
trapped, then lay it wonderingly down again on a surface
textured like that of worn stone paving, almost gritty to
the touch.

"I was northward bound on the River Road." he said
slowly, remembering. "Just short of the holt, you and a
weirdingstrom overtook me. And then . . . and then . . . ."

"We took refuge here," said Grimly, still with great
care. "You looked at the sword in your hand and said,
'There's more than one way to break a grip.' Remember?
Then you pried loose your fingers one by one. Three
broke. Then, finally, you slept."

"How long?"

Grimly glanced up at the nebulous beams supporting
the roof of mist. "Hard to say. Fourteen hours, at least."

Torisen nodded. Even that much *dwar* sleep would
hardly set all to right, but he knew by the deep itch in
flesh and bone that healing had begun. He wouldn't lose
his right hand this time, as he so nearly had at Urakarn.

"What is it?" the Wolver asked sharply.

The old terror of mutilation had leaped on Torisen
suddenly, and with it the memory of that last true dream
before his present waking.

"I-I was in the Southern Wastes, trying to pull Rose
Iron-thorn out of sinksand . . . ."

But then it hadn't been Rose at all but his sister Jame,
sinking, pulling him down with her. "You can't bear to
look at my face, can you?" she had jeered up at him.
"It's the price I've already paid for your cowardice."

She wouldn't let go. Her nails were tearing the flesh off his hands . . . .

"Let go, let go . . . ." he gasped, and found himself struggling against Grimly's restraining grip. "Let go, dammit! I've got to leave for Gothregor. Now."

"You can't," said Grimly, holding him down. "Not in this weather. Be sensible, Tori! The Riverland is over four hundred miles away."

"Then I'll weird-walk. It's been done before."

"D'you want to arrive piece-meal over the next ten years? That's been known to happen too!"

By now, they were nearly shouting. Furry ears flicked in their direction. The wolvers had chosen the wrong moment, though, to let their attention wander. The weirding outside the keep had been stationary for some time. Now it stirred with a sigh and began to flow—northward, as if at the turning of a tide. The song-crafted inner shell shifted with it, away from the shadow of the brook under the floor, away from the old ruins, taking its crafters with it.

"Now what?" Torisen asked.

Grimly had leaped to his feet, all four of them. His hackles had risen.

"Damned if I know. We're adrift, in a cockleshell of song. This has never happened before . . . but then you've never been our guest during a weirdingstrom before, either, have you?" He showed sharp teeth in a nervous grin. "I've noticed, Torisen Black Lord, that what you want, you usually get. Maybe we're bound for Gothregor after all."

PART

VI

UPPER KEEP

HERB
SHED

RUINS —

UPPER KEEP

THIRD FLOOR: OBSERVATION DECK

SECOND   INFIRMARY (WEST SIDE)
FLOOR: LIBRARY (SOUTH SIDE)

FIRST FLOOR: : BRENWYR'S QUARTERS
                (SOUTH SIDE)

Mount Alban: 60th of Spring

THE CONFERENCE was held in the library. Outside its southward facing windows, lightning intermittently lit the storm-maddened Salt Sea, patently no longer dry. In the claps of darkness between, waves crested and crashed against Mount Alban's phantom foundation. Each time, the ironwood walls of the keep shivered and lamps swayed.

Singers, scrollsmen and randon cadets crowded into the room listening as Brier Iron-thorn made her report to the Director and Captain Hawthorn. Scholarly heads nodded. They had all heard rumors of this rare Southron phenomenon, the alluvial transformation, now demonstrated to be scrollsman's fact rather than singer's fancy. What an opportunity to investigate, even for those Kendar prone to sea-sickness.

Kirien stood near the edge of the crowd, taking notes in her spiky script which Aunt Trishien's hand would also be recording in far off Gothregor. Singer Ashe, hooded and dark, stood behind her like a shadow. Both looked up sharply when Brier described in her flat voice how the Knorth had been swallowed up by the sand and spat out by the sea. Everyone turned to regard the wet, bedraggled figure in the corner, but it kept its silence. No matter. They would barter for details later.

Jame was grateful not to be questioned, especially by Brier. The sea had returned. Brier must wonder if her mother had too. Jame hadn't told her about those cold hands, that salt-chilled voice. *For your brother's sake* .... Perhaps she had imagined it, and that other voice as well, the Earth Wife's gloat. Probably. But still she couldn't stop shivering.

"So it comes to this," said the Director, when Brier had finished. "If the storm flays away enough of our weirding support before we regain the rest of Mount Alban, this college will fall. Literally. The question is, can we do anything to prevent it?"

"It depends on will-power," said Index. "Either ours, or someone else's. Nothing happens by chance on this world."

That raised a fury of protest. Was he suggesting some sort of divine interference? From their god?

"Isn't that what we've been waiting for all these millennia?" snapped the old man. "But why only look within the Kencyrath? We're newcomers on an ancient world . . . ."

" 'Step-children,' " said the Knorth suddenly.

Index glared at her. "Whatever. The point is, there are forces on Rathillien about which we know virtually nothing. Now, among the Merikit . . . ."

Groans drown him out, the loudest from those the most in his debt. "Old facts, cold facts!"

"Stick to remembering ours—while you still can!"

"How long, Index, since you last discovered something for yourself?"

"Order," said the Director, cutting them short. "If willing ourselves not to fall can help, do it. In the meantime, bail out the lower rooms."

As the library cleared, Jame stopped Hawthorn. "About Cadet Brier. Rue tells me that you relieved her of command for endangering her squad. Well, she came south to help me, and then . . . ."

The captain raised a hand in warning. "This sounds like house business. Tell your lord brother, not me. So, you were acting as your lady's escort?" she asked, stopping Brier at the door.

The Kendar gave Jame a brief, unreadable look. "I . . . suppose so, ran."

"Why didn't you say so before? That puts your actions on equal footing with mine, escorting the Brandan Matriarch—for which, ancestors have mercy on us both. Take back your command."

That's one thing set right, at least, Jame thought as Brier acknowledged, expressionless, while Rue grinned at Vant's sour face.

As for telling Torisen, though . . . First, let him damn well ask.

IT WAS A LONG NIGHT.

Hour after hour, the sea broke against Mount Alban, each blow making the wooden walls shudder while moisture ran down them like cold sweat. Everything got wet except the precious scrolls, hastily wrapped in oiled silk. Soon the highest waves threatened the keep's lowest rooms—because of a rising sea or a sinking fortress, no one could say. Scholars scrambled to save their possessions until a wave surging into one room nearly swept a clutch of singers out with it. Upstairs, Kindrie and the infirmarian already had their hands full with a host of minor injuries. Finally, Hawthorn ordered the academic community out from under foot and the randon settled down to cope.

Jame stayed out of their way. She knew she should use this opportunity to rest, if not sleep, but she was far too unsettled. Index's words haunted her: "there are forces on Rathillien about which we know virtually nothing." Sweet Trinity, yes. The terror of those moments under the sand caught her again by the throat, stopping her breath.

Got you now, thief . . . .

Despite everything, she had only taken Mother Ragga half in earnest. Now how could she set foot on the earth again, anywhere, when at any moment it might open and swallow her? Had she forfeited her right not only to be among her own people but on this world altogether?

. . . *a mistake, too dangerous to live, cursed be and cast out* . . . .

So she wandered on about the lower rooms, aimlessly, a wet, unhappy ounce creeping on her heels and standing disconsolately on her toes whenever she stopped. If the sheer will not to drown could help, Jorin was doing his part. Then his ears flicked: they were being followed. Jame turned a corner, reversed sharply, and found herself holding an indignant Graykin at knife point.

The Southron still looked shaky, she thought, but much improved. Perhaps when she had ordered him to sleep, she had accidentally plunged him into his first experience with *dwar*. At any rate, the infirmarian had judged him fit enough to make room for more recent casualties.

"I'm your sneak," he said when she demanded to know why he was following her. "Just tell me who else I should sneak after and I'll get on with it. You know," he added impatiently, as if to someone slow witted. "Who's your worst enemy here? The Director? That Brandan captain?"

"Hawthorn? Sweet Trinity, why?"

He shot her a sly, side-long look. "They're in command, aren't they? But you should be. The Highlord's closest blood-kin, aren't you?"

"Yes, but . . . ."

Jame stopped, perplexed. If only custom, not law, had kept her subservient in the Women's Hall, she had no idea what her true status was. Graykin might even conceivably be right.

"Be that as it may, I can't do a better job just now than they can, so the question is moot. This is survival, Gray, not politics."

"Politics are survival," the Southron muttered, but she had already turned away.

At last the wind dropped, and then the waves. As quiet returned to the shaken keep, a stealthy rattling could be heard as all the salt water soaking walls, furnishings, and clothes changed back to glistening salt sand. Jame shook about a pound of it out of her boots, then went up to the observation deck with ounce and spy trailing after her.

The old scrollsman Index acknowledged her with a grunt as she joined him at the rail. They looked out over a featureless expanse of weirding mist level with the lowest rooms, faintly luminous under a predawn sky.

"Where do you suppose we are?" Jame asked.

"How should I know?" the old man snapped. "This whole junket wasn't my idea."

"But you think it was someone's?"

"Or something's. There are reasons for everything. Most people are just too lazy or stupid to figure them out. Which are you?"

"Uh . . . ignorant, I hope, rather than stupid. Afraid rather than lazy. About what you said in the library . . . what forces?"

"Among the Merikit? The Burnt Man, for one. Ha! Heard of him, have you?"

Jame had shivered, remembering nightmares of pursuit, a charred hand thrust up through campfire debris, a charcoal-smeared man laying fires in the wilderness. Out of her pocket she drew the cinder shaped like a phalange. Index snatched it.

"A Burnt Man's bone," he said gleefully, turning it over in his own bony fingers. "Bonfire, bone-fire. Tell you about that, shall I?"

"Please."

"On Midwinter's Day the Merikit burn the biggest log they can find, then bury whatever remains of it along with everyone's hearth ashes. 'Burying winter,' they call it, or 'burning the Burnt Man.' It's meant to hurry on spring, you see. Then these cinders start to turn up in their fireplaces. Not just finger bones; all different sorts. They collect 'em until they have about two hundred, a complete skeleton. Just before Summer Eve, fires are laid along the borders of the land which the Merikit claim, each with a 'bone' in it. During the festival, the chief strips naked and smears himself with charcoal to personify the Burnt Man. When he jumps over the first fire, the 'bone' in it bursts into flame. All the 'bones' in all the fires ignite at the same time. The shaman-elders claim that he passes over the whole lot simultaneously."

"This would be to draw death out of the ground, I suppose, in preparation for summer."

The old man made a face, not pleased to be anticipated. "For that, and something else besides."

"What?"

"Ha! Used up all your credit and then some, haven't you?" He pocketed the bone, looking smug. "Always keep count, my girl, and a question in reserve."

Damn. Index was a bastard and a crank, Jame decided, but not as much of the latter as his colleagues supposed. His nothing-by-chance theory paralleled her own determination to learn the rules of any game which she found herself playing. Like Index, she wanted facts, so as to understand cause and thus (hopefully) avoid being whacked on the head by effect. She had thought, after a year's research in Tai-tastigon, that she could safely dismiss all native godlings as mere by-blows of her own god. That still was true of the so-called New Pantheon. Clearly, though, Index was right that there were other powers on Rathillien of which the Kencyrath chose to remain ignorant. Tai-tastigon's Old Pantheon, now—had it evolved from something more native to this world and not limited to the Eastern Lands, something more . . . elemental?

The Burnt Man and the Earth Wife, fire and earth. The Tishooo and the River Snake, air and water.

Seek the Four, the God-voice had said.

No. It couldn't be that simple—and yet not really simple at all. If the Snake was a left-over bit of Perimal Darkling, as Cattila claimed, it wasn't really part of this world either. That catfish, though—what had spoken to her through it? And how was it that, according to Kindrie, the Arrin-ken had sought the Four presumably without success for centuries while she seemed to attract them like flies to honey? It was one thing to imagine oneself the center of the world, another to find that it might be true.

Rathillien is watching me, she thought, with a shiver. Why?

"As it happens," said Index, regarding her askance, "tonight is Summer Eve. Odd things always happen in the Riverland then, and nothing by chance, there or here. Keep track of where we stop on the way home. There'll be a pattern, you wait and see."

"Fine," said Jame wryly, looking down at the anonymous cloud-plain below them. "Just tell me where to look."

"There," said Graykin, pointing southward.

Emerging from the mist was a scrap of red cloth tied to a stick. At first Jame thought that someone was thrusting up this jaunty, improvised banner, but then she realized that rather than it rising, the mist around it was slowly sinking. An upright board appeared, to which the stick was fixed, then several bits of lumber haphazardly nailed together, and so on down, a rickety tower of debris.

"That," said Graykin proudly, "is the tallest structure in Hurlen. The tower waifs erected it last winter so that for once they could look down on everyone else. I . . . er . . . suggested it."

Jame grinned. How like Graykin, incurably ambitious.

"Hurlen?" Index demanded. "It can't be. We only snag on ruins."

So he had thought of that too.

"It's no ruin," Jame agreed, "but its island foundations are very, very old. Maybe that's the attraction."

Or maybe it was something else, not in the city but close by, one of the last places on Rathillien she had ever wanted to revisit, now shoved practically under her nose. *Nothing happens by chance . . . .*

"I left some things in Hurlen when M'lord's thugs snatched me," said Graykin. "Maybe the waifs still have them." Before anyone could stop him, he had turned and darted down the southwest corner stair.

Jame started after him.

Index grabbed her arm. "Where d'you think you're going, missy?"

"Sorry, no credit," she said, wriggled free, and ran.

III

AS THE WEIRDING SANK, it left behind the upper portions of the cliff upon which the scrollsmen's keep normally sat. Jame ran down the main stair with Jorin on her heels, through the restored levels of the wooden maze. She could hear Graykin's feet on the treads below, but he didn't answer her call. How stupid to risk the weirding for odd bits of gear. Bad enough that she was launched on what was probably a fool's errand. Bad enough, indeed.

Below, gray mist drifted across the stair, obscuring it. Jame descended with caution, blindly, through a clammy brume more like fog than weirding, on slippery steps.

Through Jorin's senses, she smelled damp earth, wet wool, and fresh dung. A muffled bleating rose to meet them. Then they were under the cloud-ceiling, looking down into the soil-filled hollow of Grand Hurlen, normally a park, now packed wall to wall with unhappy sheep. So it had been last winter too, when the city islands had braced for a possible siege by the Waster Horde. This time, the flock must have been brought in to shelter from the storm.

Looking up, she could see nothing of the scholars' college. Presumably it was still there; but when the morning sun burned off this fog, instinct told her that it would be gone. Once again she would have to scramble not to be left behind, with much farther to go than Graykin did.

Hurlen consisted of some thirty islands at the confluence of the Silver and the Tardy, not far upstream from the Cataracts. Each isle, from Grand Hurlen down to a rock barely ten feet across, had been hollowed out millennia ago and built up ever since, into a community of towers linked by cat-walks over swift water. Normally, the town would be astir by now, from the elegant confectioners on the main island down to the rowdy bargees on the wharfs at Tardy-mouth. This morning, however, the citizenry was still behind closed doors, waiting for the last storm trace to blow over. Jame and Jorin thus had the passages and catwalks to themselves, likewise the bridge over the smoking Silver to its west bank.

Jame hesitated at the bridge's end. The Upper Meadow stretched out before her to the trees at the foot of the bluff on its far side. Wisps of river fog drifted across it wraith-like under a low, gray sky. The luminescence filtering through from above was still weirding-glow, but soon it would be morning light.

Get on with it, Jame told herself, dry-mouthed, and stepped to the ground.

It didn't open under her feet. So far, so good.

She and Jorin went down the sloping field, over the stone steps called the Lower Hurdles and into the Middle Meadow. No bird sang or hare grazed. How many animals the weirdingstrom must have swept away, who would never see home again. Patches of weirding glided past, northward bound. Perhaps, though, some wildlife would be able to weird-walk back, as so few men had been known to do.

Her foot slipped on the wet grass and her heart lurched; but it was only dew. The last time she had been here, the whole dark meadow had been greased and stinking with blood, like the floor of a slaughterhouse. Hard, now, to believe that so many had died on this gentle slope, where the Kencyr Host and the army of Karkinaroth had meet the vanguard of the Waster Horde; and terrible to think that, in a way, all that carnage had been incidental. Few realized that the decisive battle had taken place elsewhere, on a far more intimate scale.

They turned right into the trees. It had been almost this dark and silent that night, despite the battle raging so close by, as she had run through this forest with Kin-Slayer in one hand and the *imu* medallion in the other, pulling her on, toward the sound of someone calling her brother's name and then the crash of single combat.

Here was the foot of the bluff, as before, and here the remembered host tree. Pale green leaves flexed on its boughs, filling their veins with golden sap in preparation for the spring migration to their northern host. A dead branch cracked under Jame's foot. The leaves sprang into the air, blades flashing, and disappeared into the low clouds. Beyond the now bare tree, the cliff face curved inward to enclose the Heart of the Woods.

Jame paused on the hollow's threshold. It was larger than she remembered—an oval perhaps a hundred feet wide and somewhat longer. Waist high ferns carpeted its floor. Spring run-off had transformed the encircling cliffs into a hanging garden of columbine and lace frond, gilt-edged pink and trembling green. Through the vines which obscured the heights came the soft glow of diamantine. Blocks of that precious, crystalline stone crowned the bluff, each weathered into a crude, gap-mouthed *imu* face. Ancient power slept here, none too deeply.

Jame left Jorin crouching under the host tree, blind eyes wide with worry. That cat had good instincts. Someday she would learn to follow them.

Entering the Heart was like walking into a green sea. Dense, dripping ferns swallowed her to the waist as she waded through them, trying not to trip over their tough stems. Last winter she had entered crawling under these fronds toward the sound of her brother and Ardeth's rogue son Pereden locked in battle. Then through clearing mist she had seen the eight darkling changers who ringed the combatants. Pereden had only been the bait. They were the jaws of the trap which had been set for the Highlord from the very beginning.

The rustle of her passage was echoed by the resonant *imus* above.

Shhh, they hissed through their vines, as if in warning. *Ssshhhh*.

Pereden had been no match for her brother nor he for the changers, even with a sword reforged in Perimal

Darkling, proof against the corrosive blood of its servants. Disarmed, he had been seized in a changer's crushing embrace. Jame remembered her scream, which the *imus* had caught and echoed from wall to wall, shattering Mother Ragga's clay medallion in her hand, striking down all who heard it.

Here was the center of the Heart and, to her surprise, a raw, burned patch. The charred fragments of a platform suggested a pyre. Among the debris were blackened bones—not the Burnt Man's this time, but spongy, like misshapen fungi feeding off the hollow's floor. Only the remains of a changer or a haunt could be so obscenely tenacious of life. Jame did a quick count in her mind: Five of the eight changers and the severed head of a sixth had been removed by Ardeth's people, but they had not immediately found the other three bodies. Of these, one had been truly dead, slain by the Ivory Knife. The second, driven mad by the *imus'* scream, must perforce have been consigned alive to this pyre, to leave behind these hungry bones. The third, decapitated by Kin-Slayer, had crawled away.

He might still be here.

Jame tried not to think about that. She had come to retrieve the *imu* medallion, or rather its clay shards, hoping to make peace with the Earth Wife. And there wasn't much time.

Now, where had she stood when it shattered? In the area since burned, she thought, or close to it. There wouldn't be much to find after two wet seasons, except for one possibility: back in Peshtar, the *imu* had acquired a mask of living skin by ripping it off of a changer's face. If the pieces were still so encased, they would at least be together. She ducked under the fronds to search, in dim light, beneath a second, lower level of plants. Her gloved hands, questing, found only root-laced soil. Dammit, this was impossible.

Shhhh . . . shhhh . . ..

She reared up through the leafy ceiling, heart pounding. The rustling hiss went on and on, from all sides. It was nothing, she told herself; the upper *imus* were simply echoing her. No need to conjure that image of a second searcher, drawn by vibrations in the earth, headless, mindless, crawling toward her under the ferns . . . .

sssshhhHHH.

A breeze had entered the Heart. It circled the hollow, ruffling ferns, swaying vines across the *imu* mouths. Now everything was in motion, rustling, echoing. Was it all the wind, or were any of those cats-paws across this leafy sea the wake of a hidden stalker? Beneath the undulating leaves, something fumbled at Jame's ankle. She sprang backward with a cry, tripped, fell, was up again in a moment and plunging out of the Heart. The green sea tossed behind her.

SSSHhhhhhh . . . breathed the *imus.*

Then, with the dying of the wind, they were still.

Jame stood panting on the threshold. "All right, all right," she said to Jorin as he crept to her feet. "You warned me. It was a stupid idea anyway."

The light in the woods seemed stronger. Out in the meadow, it lit the fog from above, beginning to burn it off. Patches of mist rose up from the wet grass like the ghosts of the slain and drifted northward. Out of one, suddenly, trotted a weary, blackened, naked figure. In a moment, it had plunged into the next patch of weirding and disappeared.

Jame remembered to breathe. It was the man whom she had seen laying fires in the Riverland, Index's Merikit chief, carried south with the storm and now doggedly making his way home. So should she, with little time to waste.

But as she neared the bridge back to Hurlen, she found herself slowing.

Wherever else Mount Alban might stop, it was on its way back to the Riverland. Was there anything there for her but trouble? So much unresolved business, so little she seemed able to do about any of it. Why go back at all?

. . . roofless and rootless . . . .

Tori clearly didn't want her. Besides, she was dangerous to him, if there was any truth in what Kindrie had said at the wolvers' keep. Perhaps she should simply drop out of his life again.

. . . blood and bone . . . .

To be free again, ah . . . but to go where, to do what? All roads from this place would be long and lonely, to uncertain ends.

. . . cursed be and cast out . . . .

But Brier Iron-thorn hadn't run away or given up.

Jame shook herself. Brenwyr's damned curse had crept up on her again, trying to drag her down with its sink-sand grip. Interesting, that the thought of Brier seemed a talisman against it, as that of Marc had against despair in the past. The Kendar might save her from herself yet, if not perhaps from whatever waited in the Riverland.

 **IV**

MORNING LIGHT spilled obliquely into the library, spreading like a cloth of beaten gold across the table. Rending it in two, however, was a shadow. The haunt singer Ashe sat with her back to the windows, a lump of obdurate darkness defying day.

"We need," she said in her hoarse, halting voice, "to make . . . some decisions."

Seated at the table's end, Kirien recorded the statement on her tablet, then added under it something in a rounded script not her own. "Aunt Trishien agrees," she said, reading the note, then looking up. "Myself, I don't entirely understand."

"Neither do I," snapped the Brandan Matriarch, glowering across the table at Ashe.

Brenwyr's sight had at last returned, although the bright light made her squint behind her mask. She kept her hand on a rolled tapestry which lay across the chair to her right, her fingers moving constantly against its nap with subtle changes of pressure.

"Jameth must go back to the Women's Halls to continue her training," she said impatiently. "No other course is open to a Highborn."

Kirien smiled. "No?"

"What a Jaran does concerns only the Jaran. This is a Knorth."

"Ah, but the Knorth aren't quite like any other house either, are they? Torisen certainly isn't much like any other lord."

"Thank . . . the Kendar for that."

"That's right," said Kirien thoughtfully. "He's served with randon all his life, many of them women like his steward Rowan or you, Ashe, before you took the singer's robe. More of his senior officers are female than in any other house. I wonder. Do you suppose that's why he didn't foam at the mouth when the Jaran proposed me as Lordan?"

Brenwyr made an impatient noise. "The other houses will never agree, once they realize that you are a woman. God's claws, to have kept it secret this long . . . !"

"No secret," said Kirien lightly, but with a slight hardening of her fine eyes. "Are we to blame that the lords can't see beyond their own misconceptions? Anyway, their agreement doesn't matter, as long as we have the Highlord's consent."

"Do you suppose that he'll give it now, with his sister to dispose of? If he empowers you, think of the precedent."

Kirien looked startled, then respectful. "You do have a brain, matriarch, don't you?"

Ashe made the rasping noise which for her was a chuckle. ". . . manners, child, manners . . . ."

The rasp became a deep, barking cough. One livid hand reached up, removed a tooth that had been jarred loose, and put it in a pocket.

"However," she continued, more seriously, "Torisen loathes . . . the Shanir."

Kirien frowned. "Who's Shanir? His sister? How do you know that?"

"The haunt that savaged her . . . she ripped off its face . . . with claws."

"Ancestors preserve us. Those gloves."

"And that sampler," added Brenwyr grimly. Adiraina had told her about the sewing teacher's slashed cloth, back in those dark, silent days at Gothregor when her only contact with the world had been the old woman's touch. "The Knorth is also a true berserker."

"And she carries . . . the Ivory Knife."

Brenwyr stared. "There really is such a thing? I thought it was only a Lawful Lie—no offense, singer."

"None taken. But much . . . thought to be myth . . . may come true . . . in the latter days, including Nemesis . . . That-Which-Destroys . . . the Third Face of God."

"The Tyr-ridan? After so long, to come in our lifetime . . . . And you think that this girl . . . . No. It can't be. Where are the other two, then? Answer me that!"

"Not yet matured," Kirien suggested. "Oh, perhaps come of age in the normal way, but unaware of what they are, much less ready to accept it. Nemesis would come first, in any event. Perimal Darkling has to be defeated before anything else can happen."

Her hand changed script. "Aunt Trishien says, 'Remember, the whole purpose of the Kencyrath may be to produce the Tyr-ridan and then not destroy them before they apotheosize. If so, everything else is incidental.'"

"Everything?" The Brandan Matriarch rose and began to pace. "All our long history, our trials and disasters, to no other end but that?"

"No one ever said . . . our god . . . was fair."

"I still don't understand," said Kirien. "Even granted that it's true (and it does have that horrible ring, doesn't it?), what do the four of us have to decide?"

"There have been . . . false nemeses . . . before."

Brenwyr stopped short, staring. "What?"

"It's a theory, anyway," said Kirien, now watching the haunt singer, suddenly wary. "Especially destructive

Shanir have turned up before—spontaneous binders, soul-reapers, maledights—and some of them have done great harm, perhaps because no equally potent creative or curative Shanir were on hand to counter-balance them. I think that either Jamethiel Dream-Weaver or Gerridon was a nemesis, or maybe both. The latter's obsession with immortality—that is, with preservation—certainly suggests a personal imbalance. Incidentally, he also seems to have been unable to sire children, perhaps even impotent. Some historians argue that if his people had realized what he was and had dealt with him accordingly, the Fall never would have occurred."

Without thinking, Brenwyr had picked up the tapestry and was now cradling it in her arms. "Do you mean that false nemeses should be killed? If they mature before their curative and creative counterparts, though, how can you tell false from true?"

"A good question," said Kirien, still watching Ashe. "Perhaps our ordeal has gone on so long because we keep destroying the true as well as the false, assuming that there's been more than one potential Nemesis in our long history. Even if the Knorth is the one and only, though, she can only be a nemesis until the other two appear and so, by definition, out of balance. Like Gerridon, she may also try to balance herself with acts of preservation or creation, although I would be wary of the results. What exactly are you suggesting, Ashe?"

Again, the singer's answer was indirect. "According to legend . . . the true Nemesis can only be killed . . . by another Kencyr. Most dangerous of all . . . to him or her . . . are the other two potential Tyr-ridan. Other tests . . . may exist as well. I propose . . . to apply them."

"And if the Knorth proves false?" Brenwyr demanded.

Ashe didn't answer.

"Ancestors preserve us," said Kirien. "Why us? Why now?"

Her hand gave a jerk and wrote. " 'Because when Mount Alban returns home, the matter will be out of women's hands,' " she read. " 'Because men can't be trusted to make this decision.' "

Ashe nodded. "The Kendar would say . . . it was none of their business."

"And the Highborn would answer as you did earlier, matriarch. If the Knorth is Nemesis, she's the arch-iconoclast. The lords will try to destroy her out of sheer self-defense. By God, 'Some things need to be broken' in the Kencyrath all right, with a vengeance; but can't we at least trust Torisen?"

"No," wrote her hand.

Kirien frowned at its sudden vehemence, waiting for an explanation. Instead, after a long pause, she got a sort of doodle, made by someone with her attention elsewhere. Two words followed, immediately scratched out. Then came an emphatic command: "Stay out of his/her/their way," and the curt symbol that signals a message's end.

"Well!" said Kirien, letting the pen drop. "What was all that about?"

"Whatever, we appear . . . to be . . . on our own."

The haunt singer sounded almost pleased, Kirien thought. "Hmmm. With decisions to make, you say. I suspect, though, that you arrived at yours long ago. You mean to test the Knorth, don't you, and you don't expect her to pass. Why?"

Ashe hesitated. "That one . . . was bred to walk . . . in shadows," she said at last, in a low voice. "She has . . . the darkling glamor."

Brenwyr snorted. "Coming from you, haunt . . . ."

Ashe pushed back her hood. Snatches of yellowed hair went with it, still attached to bits of dried scalp. Sunlight, which threw her face into shadow, shone off patches of naked skull.

"Yes. Coming from me. Who . . . would know better?"

The matriarch turned sharply away, clutching the rolled tapestry as if to protect it. "Abomination!" she said thickly, and stalked out of the room.

Ashe resumed her hood.

"She will still make her own decision about the Knorth," remarked Kirien. "You can't shock her out of that, or me either."

"Do you decide . . . against me?"

Again, Kirien felt the pressure of darkness. Her childhood had ended when she had realized that such evil could befall such a person as her old friend. She didn't like to think about the shadows that would eventually, inevitably consume Ashe. Only remarkable strength—physical, mental, and moral—had kept so much of the singer intact this long. Kirien refused to believe that integrity had yet been compromised.

"Not against," she said slowly. "Test her, if you must. For my part, I'd rather deal with facts than theory. She's Shanir, you say. All right: I accept that. The rest is conjecture. Even for a Shanir Knorth, though, there must be other options than the matriarchs' hen coop. My decision is to research possibilities. Whatever Aunt Trishien says, surely Torisen won't object to a reasonable alternative."

But as she rose, her mind already on who owed her what in barter, her gaze fell uneasily on the tablet and on those two now obliterated words which the Jaran Matriarch must never have intended to write:

". . . Kin-Slayer unsheathed . . . ."

V

BRENWYR STALKED through the halls of Mount Alban with Aerulan in her arms. She was very upset, which upset her even more.

Since childhood she had known that she was a berserker and maledight, and had prided herself on having learned to control those traits. Only that cold pride, duty to her house, and Aerulan had allowed her to live with who she was and what as a child she had done. After Aerulan's death, her life had been achingly bleak but (thanks to Adiraina's training and her brother's compliance) still largely under her control.

Then the Knorth had reappeared.

And now this.

Brenwyr believed in the god of her people—how could she not?—but not as an active force in her world, much less in herself. Like many Kencyr, lacking proof to the contrary, she had almost convinced herself that the old prophecies were mere singers' tales, and been glad to think them so. In that case, to be a Shanir was like having a tendency to drop plates or walk off high buildings, awkward and potentially dangerous, but manageable. But "nemesis" implied the divine, working through her, using her . . . as perhaps it had always tried to do? Was that upstart Jaran right? Had she been straining all her life to control a force which, ultimately, would control her?

Moreover, if Kirien was right, it was also at work in the Knorth Jameth.

Brenwyr's grip on Aerulan tightened. She didn't want to share anything with that wretched girl. Damn her anyway, when the very thought of her existence made Brenwyr's temper threaten to flare. Why, why, why should any Knorth be alive when Aerulan was dead?

"Steady, steady," she could almost hear Adiraina say, as in lessons oft repeated long ago. "Remember that the loss of control is death."

Yes. Remember. Hadn't she killed two of the only four people she had ever loved? Rather than curse Adiraina or her brother that way, she would use the white-hilted suicide knife which she had carried in her boot since Aerulan's murder. Perhaps all nemeses should be killed, false and true. If only she'd had a knife that night, she might at least have used it on that yellow-eyed assassin, the custom be damned that Highborn women shouldn't fight. It could hardly have been less effective than the curse which she had spat at him—her only malediction ever apparently to fail.

She had cursed the Knorth Jameth too.

As if thinking of the girl conjured her up, Brenwyr heard her voice, enough like Aerulan's to make her heart jump. She was approaching the half-open door of the infirmary. Inside, the Knorth was saying:

". . . sorry not to appear more grateful. You see, I'd hoped that the filthy thing was out of my life for good. You were right, though, to fetch it from Hurlen: it's far too dangerous to be left to its own devices."

"I'm so glad you approve," answered a sharp voice, almost snarling. "Next time, think twice what job you give me."

"Maybe you should think again, too, about serving me at all."

"What else can I do—go back to Karkinaroth?"

"Even to Restormir, for all I care."

Brenwyr stood outside the door, transfixed by the tone of deep resentments seething up unexpectedly, perhaps disastrously. Then a moment's taut silence within was broken by an exclamation that made her jump:

"Spy on us, will you?"

No. He didn't mean her. Hasty footsteps had crossed the floor, away from the door.

"Who sent you? Tell me, you damned spook!"

"Graykin, stop shaking him. Damn. I should have warned the infirmarian not to let him over-tire himself. He's gone blank again, just as he must have done at the Cataracts."

Brenwyr suddenly realized whom they meant. She threw open the door. In one far corner, an ounce leaped off a cot and scuttled under it. In the other sat a white-haired Shanir, staring vacantly past the dark figure who bent over him.

"Bastard," she heard herself say harshly, feeling the power in her voice surge almost into a curse. "Go back where you belong."

The Shanir rose. Like a sleep-walker, pale eyes open but unfocused, he stumbled past her out of the room.

The room's third occupant had also shambled forward a step as if to follow; but his companion in black stopped him, saying softly in the Knorth's voice:

"She doesn't mean you, Graykin. Perhaps you should keep an eye on Kindrie, though."

Go, said her warning tone, anger forgotten. *Now. This is dangerous.*

Brenwyr snorted. She felt dangerous. She felt deadly.

The one called Graykin had started at the Knorth's touch, for a moment looking frightened and confused. Now he gave her a sharp glance, a half nod, and slipped sideways out of the infirmary, watching Brenwyr askance as he passed like a cur expecting a kick.

The Knorth remained, standing her ground. Only by her voice did Brenwyr recognize her, having still been blind the last time they had met. Black jacket with one tight sleeve and one full, slim waist tightly belted, black pants tucked into black boots, black gloves and mask . . . . Highborn girls sometimes had an unnatural craving to dress as boys, but they grew out of it just as they did out of mock berserker tendencies, at about the same time.

This girl has refused to grow up, thought Brenwyr with scorn, her own travelling gear not for a moment crossing her mind. *She's still a child, willful, spoiled, perverse.*

"Matriarch," said the child, saluting her, polite but wary. "Aerulan."

Brenwyr's grip on the banner tightened. Waking in the room below, for one aching moment she had felt Aerulan behind her, almost the touch of her hand. When she had turned, the first thing she had seen after a week of darkness had been Aerulan's face—woven of the clothes in which she had died. Dead, dead . . . but for the Knorth, somehow, still a living presence in this room.

"She's been with you, hasn't she?" Brenwyr heard herself demand hoarsely. "All this time, she's been with you."

"Er . . . yes. We kept each other company on the road."

She might as well have said "on the moon," for all the sense it made to Brenwyr for a moment. Highborn girls rarely travelled, except under heavy guard. Aerulan had never before left Gothregor. It simply hadn't occurred to the Council of Matriarchs that Jameth wasn't still hiding in the deserted halls, sulking over her scratched face.

Until this moment, Brenwyr had forgotten that the Knorth had been hurt, much less how or by whom. Adiraina had spoken slightingly of the "accident," not realizing that Brenwyr had seen the blow struck or that Hawthorn had told her of the slashed sampler which the Ardeth matriarch had ordered to be dipped in the Knorth's blood on the council chamber floor.

"Your face . . . ." she said involuntarily.

The Knorth stiffened. "Yes, matriarch?" she said with chilling courtesy, as if in rebuke to an equal.

"Don't you dare take that tone with me, girl!"

The other's mouth twitched, almost into Aerulan's smile. "I apologize—again. Truly, I don't mean to keep offending you. It just seems to be a talent. About Aerulan, though, I don't quite understand. I know that Lord Brandan pledged a huge sum for her contract in perpetuity, that Ganth was about to give up all rights to her forever. Your brother must have loved her very much . . . ."

"It had nothing to do with him!" Brenwyr burst out, then swore at herself and began incontinently to pace.

Her agitated path obliged the Knorth to dodge aside, swooping to snatch an old knapsack containing something pale out from under her very feet. One part of Brenwyr's mind told her that the Knorth was using wind-blowing kantirs to keep out of her way; another rejected the idea: Highborn girls were not taught the Senethar.

"Matriarch . . . ." said the Knorth, slipping aside yet again, "sometimes I'm very stupid. This concerns sister-kinship, doesn't it?"

Brenwyr spun around, almost pinning the girl between two cots, but she rolled over one and out of the way in an instinctive, flowing evasion as if from a physical attack.

That must be the Senethar, Brenwyr thought, or its dance form, the Senetha. More forbidden knowledge.

"What do you know about the sisterhood?" she demanded.

"Precious little. Only that there's much more to life in the Women's World than any man realizes."

"Be quiet! You have no right to speak of such things!"

"You did ask. All right, all right." The moving pattern of her black gloved hands seemed to deflect Brenwyr's anger. "I've offended you again. Again, I apologize. Are you going to curse me?"

"No! I can control . . . dammit, I could control myself before you . . . before you . . . ."

She stumbled to a halt, watching those hands weave before her, unable to look away. The quality of light in the room changed, thickening like honey. Lithe, black hands swam through its amber glow, deft fingers easing the knots of her rage and restraint, try as she would to keep them tight. As if in a dream, she heard herself speak:

"I've learned to control when I curse, but not what I say when I do. Then the words just come, and sometimes kill."

"You cursed me once. Will I die?"

"I don't know. I don't think so." Sinuous hands, charming her . . . . "Perhaps we're too much alike. Snakes with similar venom. Nemeses . . . ."

"Can you lift the curse you put on me?"

"No." Seducing . . . .

"Have you ever tried to raise a curse?"

No, no, no . . . .

"Yes. Once. When I was six."

The knots had given way. "Forget what you can't help," Adiraina had told her over and over, but now she remembered, oh, God, she remembered . . . .

"I borrowed my brother's clothes and dressed up in them. Mother caught me. She was furious, called me perverted, tore them off . . . . I-I was so angry. 'I hope you break your neck.' I said that. And she did, going down the stairs with her arms full of shirts, and pants, and boots . . . . Oh, Mother, don't! I take it back, I take it back . . . ."

She was kneeling on the floor, looking into her mother's terrified eyes, hearing the breath escape her paralyzed lungs and not return.

"I take it back . . . ."

Aerulan held her. "You were only a child. You didn't mean it. You weren't responsible!"

Aerulan, who also had died in her arms, gasping, with a severed throat . . . .

The white-hilted knife was in her hand. What right had she to live, whose curse had slain both blood—and sister-kin?

Someone was wrestling with her, saying breathlessly, "Oh, don't, don't, don't . . . ."

Then black gloves caught her wrist and twisted. Her fingers sprang open. The blade dropped with a deadly thunk, to quiver upright in the floor which began to rot at its cold touch. It wasn't her knife at all, although for a moment she thought that her own face stared back at her, naked and hag-like, from the carved ivory pommel.

"Can't I leave you alone for a minute?" demanded Graykin from the doorway.

"Apparently not." The Knorth's voice shook. So did her hand as she reclaimed and resheathed the Ivory Knife. "Matriarch?"

"Leave me alone," said Brenwyr thickly. She dragged herself to her feet and stumbled over to lean on the window sill. What had she been saying? What in ancestors' names had she been about to do?

"Forget what you can't help." *Forget, forget . . . .*

But the light was still strange. It had been bright morning when Brenwyr had entered the infirmary and must be morning still, but the air had taken a jaundiced tinge with an under-taint of sulfur. She looked down on the backs of slowly swirling clouds, bounded by mountain slopes, roofed by more clouds of a darker, more sullen hue. Clearly, Mount Alban had stopped again, but where? She felt she ought to know. If only this room faced east instead of west—what would she see? A side-valley of the Silver in the Riverland, the main fortress hidden by clouds but rising over them at the upper end of the gorge, the Witch's tower. The keep below: Wilden. This filthy light: Rawneth, conjuring.

Dammit. She had told that wretched Shanir to go back where he belonged, and he had taken Mount Alban with him.

But it wouldn't last. The college was only some fifty miles south of home now. The pull of its anchoring hill fort foundation would lift it off this reef with the next weirding touch. The important thing now was that no one else disembark, least of all the Knorth.

"I did keep an eye on him, just as you told me," Graykin was protesting, full of self-righteousness but with a wary edge. "Didn't I see him walk down straight into the priests' arms? Taken him back where he belongs, haven't they? Best to let him go. You can't tangle with them."

"Oh, can't I? Watch."

Brenwyr was across the floor, between the Knorth and the door, faster than she would have believed possible.

"You aren't to leave this room," she said sharply. "I forbid it."

"Matriarch, you don't understand. I dragged Kindrie into this. He's my responsibility."

"A bastard has no claims on anyone, least of all on you. I-it's indecent that you even met."

"Lady, I've led a less sheltered life than you can probably imagine. I don't shock easily. Why poor Kindrie 'least of all'? Who is he, anyway?"

"The shame of your house. Tieri's bastard, born in the moon garden at Gothregor where his mother's death banner still hangs in disgrace. There. Now are you satisfied?"

Jame stared. "He said his grandmother was named Telarien."

"Bastards don't have grandmothers. Telarien was Tieri's mother and Kinzi's daughter."

"If I had some chalk, I'd work this out on a wall, if I had a wall. Kinzi, the last Knorth Matriarch, was the mother of Telarien, who was the mother of Tieri, who was the mother of Kindrie. Tieri was my father's full sister. That makes Kinzi my great-grandmother, Telarien my grandmother, Tieri my aunt, and Kindrie my first cousin. Correct?"

"Yes. I mean, no! Bastards don't have cousins!"

"Be damned to that," Jame muttered.

She should have worked all of this out long ago. She would have, if the thought of priestling blood-kin hadn't so thoroughly appalled her. But Kindrie wasn't a priest, despite having been thrown repeatedly into their arms. There he would wake again, probably not even knowing how he had gotten there. Back in hell . . . .

"Matriarch, I've got to go after him. Think! This is Tieri's son, the child of the girl whom Aerulan died to save."

Brenwyr hadn't moved. "You can't go down to Wilden. There are . . . other reasons as well. Kinzi and the Randir Matriarch Rawneth . . . they quarreled."

"So?" Then behind the mask, gray eyes widened. "Are you saying that I've inherited a blood feud, and no one saw fit to tell me?"

"There was no need. Anyway, it never came to blows."

"Let me guess. Before anything so unladylike could happen, the Shadow Assassins slaughtered every Knorth woman at Gothregor except Tieri . . . and no one ever knew why."

This time, Brenwyr's jaw fell. "You don't mean . . . you can't think . . ."

"Don't I? Can't you? God's teeth and toenails, if it was even a possibility, why wasn't Ganth told? But that might have led to civil war, the Knorth and their allies against the Randir and theirs. Better to keep it a secret of the Women's World. Better to see my house destroyed than all the Kencyrath, except that the White Hills nearly did that anyway."

Brenwyr was backing away, hands over her ears. "I won't listen to this. I won't think about it. You're mad, Jameth. All the Knorth are. Everyone knows that."

"My name is not Jameth. It's Jamethiel."

Brenwyr made an incoherent sound and bolted out of the room, slamming and locking the door behind her. They could hear her in the hall, piling furniture against it.

"I think you rattled her," said Graykin.

"By God, she's floored me. Secrets! How many will it take to get us all killed?"

Secrets . . . .

She hadn't meant to pry any out of the matriarch with her hand-dance, much less something so raw. That poor woman. The soul-reaping Senetha she had learned in Perimal Darkling and practiced in Tai-tastigon to control rowdy taverners should never have been put to such a use—except that Brenwyr's combination of maledight and berserker tendencies terrified her.

Secrets.

Could what she had suggested to the matriarch possibly be true? All that death and destruction, to have grown out of some squabble in the cloistered halls of the Women's World? Surely not. And yet, who had told the assassins where to look for her five days ago? Who had stood by in the shadows of the Randir compound, watching while the killers nearly fulfilled their contract in the Forecourt? Whose soul had Rawneth used to make the demon which she had sent after Jame and Kindrie? Who wanted the last Knorth lady dead?

"I think I recognized that last crash," said Graykin. "If your matriarch has tipped over the wardrobe beside the door, we're trapped here until someone rescues us. Too bad about the healer."

He sounded pleased. So much for one more rival.

Jame put an arm around his thin shoulders. "Dear Graykin. For your future reference, a few points. First: to be served by you is an honor, but not my only obligation. Second: as you keep saying, very little stops me, common sense least of all. Third: as for being trapped anywhere . . . ."

She jerked a thumb over her shoulder. Graykin, following the gesture, blanched.

"Oh, no."

"Oh, but yes. Where there's a window, there's always a way."

BY THE DAWN of Summer Eve, the worst of the storm had passed. Lances of brilliant sunlight pierced the overcast, impaling wet leaves, sparkling on the Silver, warming the shattered stones of Chantrie and melting the shadowy image that had hung above them as if of the fortress's ancient walls restored.

But the danger had not entirely passed. A river of clouds still flowed northward up the valley, trailing veils of weirding mist. Steward Rowan watched them from the ramparts of Gothregor. Out of one flew a phalanx of swans, ghosting toward the high lakes that were their summer homes. Migratory birds loved weirding weather. Much of the Riverland's wild-life had also been swept southward with the storm, but would soon begin to weird-walk back—something apparently safer for beasts than humans.

Ancestors be praised that this happened in spring, thought Rowan. In midwinter, no one would have returned. As it was, she hoped for some exotic additions to the larder when it was safe to hunt again.

And perhaps a problem. At first light, she had glimpsed something in the woods that might have been a young rathorn, except that it was pure white. There had been none of those beasts of madness in the Riverland since Ganth's disastrous hunt thirty-four years ago. Rowan turned and limped down the stair, shaking her head. An ill-omen even to think that she had seen one now, given rumors of the Highlord's growing instability.

Down in the inner ward, the small Knorth garrison was combing through the grass in front of the old keep for shards of stained glass. In days of greater affluence, it had been imported in panes from the Eastern Lands, to be worked by Kendar artisans into those glorious third story windows, now shattered. More precious than gold, their fragments would be sorted and stored until the Knorth treasury could afford an eastern glass-master to recast them—unless some clever Kendar discovered the trick first. Rowan shook her head again, looking up at the devastation. Blackie would not be pleased.

" 'Ware weirding!" someone called sharply.

A mist veil trailed over the south wall, then dropped like a vaporous curtain to obscure part of it. Some twenty feet wide, it drifted across the inner ward with deceptive speed—as fast, perhaps, as a trotting horse. Kendar moved hastily out of its way.

It left behind a man, hairy, dirty, naked, staring about him in dismay. The weirding had almost reached the north wall. Meanwhile, a second, smaller veil had followed it over the south. Given a choice, the man bolted toward the latter, braids flying. Bemused Kendar let him pass. He stepped on broken glass, hopped howling on one foot, and pitched headfirst into the oncoming mist. It swallowed both him and his clamor like the shutting of a velvet door.

"Obviously," said a familiar voice behind Rowan, "I've been away far too long."

Ever since Urakarn, when the name rune of the Karnid god had been burned into her forehead, Rowan had learned to equate facial expression with pain. Therefore, although her heart had jumped like a startled frog, her face showed no surprise as she turned.

"Welcome home, my lord."

He looked haggard, she thought: travel-stained clothes, unkempt black hair with more white in it than she remembered, and several days' growth of beard; but large as those silver-gray eyes were in that thin face, they looked blessedly clear and, at the moment, clearly amused.

"Who was that naked man, anyway?"

Rowan shrugged. "A Merikit chief, by the braids, with many kills and many children. Beyond that . . . ."

Torisen had stepped forward and caught sight of the damaged keep. "What in Perimal's name . . . ?"

"We had a visit from Old Man Tishooo. That was before the earthquake, which was before the weirding-storm, all of which was after . . . well, never mind for the moment. About all we haven't had is an infestation of foot-eating trogs. But come inside. Rest. Eat."

"I'm not alone, Rowan."

Rowan looked into the darkness of the gatehouse arch. Some twenty or thirty pairs of eyes glowed back at her, some man-height, others only a foot or two above the ground. Grimly trotted out of the shadows, grinning.

"That's right, steward. You're stuck with the whole pack."

"In that case," said Rowan, "we'll cope. Be pleased to enter, Lord Wolver."

Soon afterward, everyone had adjourned to the garrison's main hall, hard by the southern gate. The wolver pack came shyly, unused to so much company. The adults had taken on their most human (if hairy) aspect as a mark of respect, while the adolescents padded in awkwardly with mixed attributes and pups gamboled about underfoot. If any of the Kendar remembered that some Kencyr hunted both wolver and Merikit for sport, they didn't mention it.

"That reminds me," said Torisen. "Your people aren't to start for home until I have an armed escort to send with them. D'you hear me, Grimly?"

"I hear you, Tori."

Rowan, serving her lord wine, noticed that he took it left handed. Torisen was as nearly ambidextrous as long practice could make him; however, unlike most Kencyr, he favored his right. Seeing the question in his steward's eyes, he defiantly held up his right hand. She stared at the splints and swollen fingers.

"Don't ask, Rowan, and don't fuss. They're mending."

She accepted that with a curt nod. In her mind's eye, though, she saw a boy fresh from the tortures of Urakarn, saying over and over, "I'm all right, I'm all right," while his burned hands festered and his mind slid toward fever-fed madness.

Torisen put down his cup with a sigh. "No use putting it off any longer. Where's my sister, Rowan?"

"I don't know, lord."

He frowned. "She did arrive safely. You sent a dispatch saying so."

"Yes, lord. I also told you that the Matriarchs had taken charge of her."

For a moment, Torisen looked confused, trying to remember. That dispatch had arrived after the lords had been at him all day to decide his sister's fate. Exhausted, he had read the first line of Rowan's message and put it aside, never to be picked up again.

"Send word to the Women's Halls, then."

"They may refuse to let you see her, lord. They did me. Odd things have been happening here. The night of the Tishooo, someone in the Halls sounded the alarm. We don't know why. We weren't allowed in. But the next day pyre smoke rose from an inner garden. Do you think . . . ?"

Torisen shook his head. "Wherever she is, she's alive, but where in Perimal's name is that?" He rose. "Time to find out."

Rowan had also risen. "You're going to ask the Matriarchs? Blackie, they won't let you in!"

He grinned at her use of his old nickname, looking suddenly as wolfish as any wolver. "Let them try to stop me."

At the gate, they tried. The guards called their captain, and she called her eight peers, while the Highlord stood outside, polite but implacable. While they were still telling him that he couldn't enter, he put his left hand on the door which everyone had thought safely locked and pushed it open. Rowan went in with him and so did Grimly in his complete furs, determined to miss none of the fun. Inside, ladies stared aghast before bolting out of sight. In a room above the Forecourt, a whole class of little girls ran from window to window crying "Oh look, oh look!" while their distraught teacher chased them.

"Where are we going?" Torisen asked Rowan out of the corner of his mouth.

"The Ardeth compound. If anyone governs the Council, it's Adiraina."

The Matriarchs were waiting for them in Adiraina's room. The blind Ardeth sat very straight in her chair, in her hands a piece of needlework oddly torn and partly eaten away by rust colored stains. The others ranged behind her except for the Jaran Matriarch who, as usual, kept to her writing desk, a tablet full of notes in diverse hands open before her. She was adding a new notation as Torisen walked in.

"My lord," said Adiraina stiffly, in High Kens. "This invasion is inexcusable. Withdraw at once."

"Point of law," Trishien said, looking up. "Torisen Black Lord is master of this place, and our host. He can go anywhere he pleases."

The others clearly felt this contribution to be unhelpful.

Torisen gave them a half bow. "My lady matriarchs, I have come to visit my sister for whom, I understand, you have made yourselves responsible."

"Jameth's training can not be interrupted," said Adiraina, in a tone fit to freeze ice. "Incredibly ignorant as she came to us, she has far too much to learn."

"I bet she's taught you a few things too," muttered Grimly, subsiding with a yelp as Torisen stepped on his paw.

"Nonetheless."

The Ardeth Matriarch twitched, as if something had given her attention an unexpected tug. Her hands closed on the stained sampler. "It's taken you long enough to show an interest," she said, answering, it seemed, almost at random. The Danior Dianthe put a hand on her shoulder. "No Knorth guard or quarters prepared, not even suitable clothes . . . ."

"I . . . see. And no word from you, either, that such things were required. So, if I failed to provide an adequate establishment, into whose was she placed?"

"Why, into the Caineron, of course," said the Coman Karidia, glowering. "Who had a better claim than darling Kallystine, your consort?"

Torisen blinked. In point of law, Karidia was right, but oh lord . . . !

"That contract," he said, without emphasis, "has nearly expired. Be that as it may, I still want to see my sister."

"Well, you can't!" snapped Karidia, discretion (as usual) failing her. "The silly twit is hiding."

"Is she indeed. Why?"

"A-a stupid spat," said Karidia, against the combined wills of all her peers except the one who could have stopped her. But Adiraina still seemed distracted, as if working out some puzzle of her own. "Dear Kallystine was obliged to slap her."

"Oh, was she. And did you sound the alarm six nights ago because of this . . . er . . . spat?"

"That concerns only the Women's World," snapped Dianthe, trying to regain control, her fingers pressing urgently on Adiraina's shoulder.

"I think not. It happened in my house."

Power stirred. They had forgotten, as so many did, that this quiet man came of a bloodline stretching back to the creation of the Kencyrath. They had not seen him below, pushing open a door which for anyone else would have been locked. But now they felt the lordship in his voice, to loose or bind at will within his own domain.

"The next day," he was saying, very quietly, "you gave someone to the pyre. Who?"

Adiraina answered, as if the words had been jerked out of her: "Eleven shadow assassins."

"What was their commission here?"

"We think . . . to kill Jameth. Instead . . . somehow . . . they were killed."

"And then Jame disappeared, presumably with two shadows out of a casting of thirteen still at large. Correct, matriarch?"

"C-correct, Highlord."

"You don't understand!" cried Dianthe. "It wasn't like that!"

"Like what, lady?" The deadly courtesy in his voice made her shrink back, clinging to the Ardeth's shoulder as to a rock. "That you didn't officiously remove my sister from my steward's care? That while in your charge she wasn't mistreated and then wantonly endangered? That my hospitality hasn't therefore been egregiously abused? I think, lady, that I understand very well indeed, all but what matters most: where is my sister now?"

The question hummed in the air, demanding reply, receiving none. Its weight pressed Grimly flat to the floor. In the preternatural silence, he heard a faint sound beside him, as if of a raindrop's fall, but the splash by his paw was red. Torisen's white-knuckled grip on Kin-Slayer's hilt had opened the cut on his left palm.

Trishien had been sitting with pen frozen in mid-air. Now she gave herself a shake and said, unsteadily, "Highlord, you have a right to know: your sister is at Mount Alban. Only you might not find it where it ought to be."

His eyebrows rose, but he acknowledged with a bow. "My thanks, Jaran. For this kindness, however cryptic, perhaps I won't evict the lot of you after all."

Trishien inclined her head. As her gaze dropped, she gave a half-stifled exclamation.

She's seen the blood, thought Grimly, then started, realizing what he himself had just seen: the sword's blade hanging free through its supporting belt loop, behind the scabbard. Kin-Slayer wasn't sheathed. It never had been.

Torisen had widened his salute, now half-ironic, to include the rest of the Council. Then he turned to leave, with Rowan and Grimly hard on his heels. They had almost reached the door when Adiraina suddenly shook off her friend and fell to her knees. She still clutched the stained sampler in one hand. The other swooped unerroringly to the red drops on the floor.

"Twins!" she exclaimed, astonished and triumphant, her puzzle at last solved with the touch of brother's and sister's blood on either hand. "You are twins after all!"

Torisen stared at her. "Mad!" he said, and hastily left.

Trotting to keep up as they turned onto the arcade fronting the Forecourt, Grimly said, "That was quite a trick with the questions. I thought only Shanir had that sort of power."

"What sort? I asked, they answered. That's all."

"Oh, but surely . . . ."

"I said, that's all!"

He had turned sharply on the Wolver, who instinctively crouched.

"Grimly, don't do that," said Torisen, exasperated. "I am not your pack leader."

Rowan touched his shoulder in warning, then stepped quickly aside as a shimmering vision glided down the arcade toward them. Full skirt iridescent with lizard scales; low cut bodice insecurely laced with gold; the white swell of breasts; ivory throat, fluttering mask of gold tissue, perhaps a shade more opaque than usual . . . they had hardly had time to take in her full glory before M'lady Kallystine had flung herself into Torisen's arms, jarring his splinted fingers.

"Oh, my dear lord, you've come home at last!"

Because he had involuntarily recoiled with pain at the impact, the little puff of powder from between her breasts missed Torisen's face. Nonetheless, he staggered, eyes momentarily blank. Tactfully looking out into the Forecourt, Rowan didn't notice. Still crouched on the floor, Grimly did. He growled as Caineron's daughter raised a hand as if to stroke the Highlord's face. Torisen caught her wrist.

"You slapped my sister," he said, as if just remembering. "Why?"

Kallystine drew back with a hiss, hatred stronger than policy. "Jameth, always Jameth . . . ."

He shook his head as if to clear it and put her aside. "Excuse me, lady."

She stared after him, incredulous, as he walked away, unsteady at first, then with growing assurance and speed.

A half-stifled cough made her look up. On the spiral stair to the upper classrooms crouched a little girl—the same Ardeth chit who had seen Jameth's hands bare. The child bolted back up the steps. The sorcery which Kallystine had just tried on Torisen had been expressly forbidden by the matriarchs. If that wretched brat told Adiraina what she had seen this time . . . .

Worse, if Caldane should learn that she had failed . . . .

"Get me a fast horse," Torisen was saying to Rowan as they turned into the Forecourt toward the gate.

"I'll saddle every brute in the stable. You aren't leaving us behind this time, Blackie."

"Or me, or me!" the Wolver cried, capering upright with excitement and trying to clap his paws.

"Or me," said M'lady Kallystine through her pretty, white teeth, watching them go. She hadn't lost. Not yet.

PART
VII

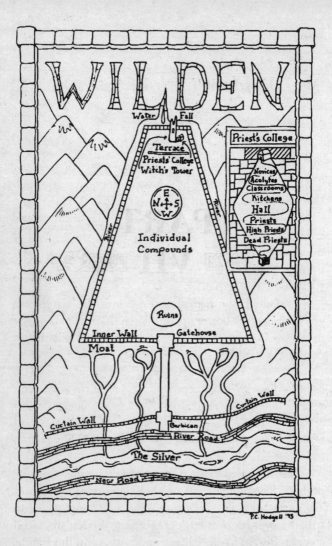

Wilden: 60th of Spring

I

THE PLATFORM DESCENDED, creaking, through the scholars' warren inside Mount Alban's cliff. Jame rode it alone. Climbing out the infirmary window and swinging in the one below had been easy for her, but impossible for blind Jorin. Graykin, sulking, had refused even to try.

Creak, creak, groan.

By accident, she had discovered how the scrollsmen got their ancient bones up and down the vertical college in relative comfort. Having set this wretched machine in motion, though, she wondered if she would be able to make it stop. Ropes snaked past, tied at intervals with esoteric knots. Kendar craftsmen were certainly clever. The older scholars must find such a convenience invaluable, but Jame was beginning to wish that she had walked. This ponderous descent was giving her far too much time to think.

Of all the stupid things she had ever done, this was perhaps the stupidest, far worse than raiding Restormir. There, at least, she'd had help and an enemy prone to tripping over his own fat feet. Here at Wilden she faced a very different foe in Ishtier, and perhaps in the Randir Matriarch as well.

Clearly, a feud could run three generations or more since Rawneth had told Kindrie that her revenge ran through him, whom she must have believed to be the last of Kinzi's blood.

Revenge for what?

As for Ishtier, what support did he have here? What had he told the other priests about her? She had called the Priests' College a cess-pool of divinity, but, after all, it didn't contain an active temple. Maybe there was nothing to worry about.

Maybe.

Still, the nervous tightening of her stomach said, "Dumb, *dumb*, DUMB."

The platform sank into a layer of mist and seemed to melt. Jame tumbled down worn stone steps, for the first time missing her voluminous overskirt, to fetch up breathless and bruised at their foot in deep grass.

"Watch out for the last step," Graykin had said. Huh.

Mount Alban loomed over her, covering the sky, yet as insubstantial as the moon at mid-day. The surrounding walls of Wilden looked just as ghostly, wooded slopes showing through them as if through a misty haze. Diffuse light bathed the grassy hillock on which she stood and warmed its crown of tumbled stones, relics of the ancient hill fort around which Wilden had been built. Gap-mouthed *imus* were carved on the fallen blocks. She traced one with a fingertip. At her feet, tiny star-shaped flowers sprang open in the deep grass.

This is the morn of Summer Eve, Jame thought. *Who knows what else may wake here before night-fall?*

As she walked down the hillock, Wilden redefined itself around her. The green knoll was girt with flagstones and granite walls pierced to east and west with arches. Above and beyond, where she had seen the wooded slopes of older days, were the valley's sheer, quarried sides, cut short by an overcast sky. Mount Alban all but disappeared as she stepped off the grass at the hillock's foot. A sulfurous light smoldered down through the steel gray clouds. Was the Wilden Witch conjuring again? What this time?

Faint cloud-shadows moved over the flags between her and the eastern arch. One of them, man-shaped, seemed to pause.

Jame felt her heart lurch. Sweet Trinity. How could she have forgotten? It was near Wilden that the master assassin had attacked her and been overwhelmed in turn by Bane. Was that *mere*-tattooed killer still Bane's prisoner and mount? Had they ridden out the weirdingstrom here, perhaps in the very ruins which she had just left?

The shadow melted back into the flow.

Jame let out her breath in a sigh. *Nerves*, she told herself—or, if not, one more element in a game already hopelessly beyond her control. She had no plan except to find Kindrie and, somehow, get him out. As for the rest—well, dammit, she couldn't worry about everything at once.

The road angled upward between tall, narrow buildings. Unlike Restormir with its cantons, here each house stood by itself, gates locked, windows barred, so many fortified camps. Jame saw no one, either of the garrison or of the college. The only sound was that of falling water, which grew louder the higher she climbed. Had Lord Randir taken all his people south with him to the Cataracts? He might have, to forestall trouble at home. Randir politics were said to rival those in the so-called poison courts of the Central Lands, tangled webs of intrigue, feud, and assassination—not that anyone outside Wilden ever learned the half of it. Above all else, the Randir was a house of secrets.

One secret, though, had slipped out. The wrong lord ruled here, women at Gothregor whispered (for one did whisper about the Randir, even in their absence). The old lord's choice had been one of those Shanir who, born apparently normal, change as they mature. By the time he had earned his randon's scarf at Tentir, the Randir Heir had changed too much. Rawneth had her own son Kenan declared lord. The whispers said that she had tried to kill the deposed Lordan and, failing that, had set assassins on his trail—much luck they'd had against a randon trained weapons-master. The contract was still said to be open, more than three decades later.

One more link between Wilden and the Bashtiri Shadow Guild, thought Jame, resisting the temptation to look behind her.

The road ended in a high terrace almost in the clouds, its flagstones wet with spray from the cataract which plunged down beyond the fortress's back wall to form the arms of its river moat. Earth and air shook with the continual roar. Puddles quivered. Black against this sheet of white water rose the Witch's tower. Glimmers above in the clouds suggested lit windows. Was Rawneth indeed at home, thinking what thoughts after her demon's failure to retrieve Kindrie? That pervading sulfurous light owed little to the rising sun, although it did throw the tower's shadow westward, almost to Jame's feet.

Huddled against the tower's southwest side as a plain, stone building, about the size of a modest stable: the Priests' College, Jame's sixth sense told her. Clever. Most people would walk straight past, while those who did know would find nothing threatening in so humble a structure. Away from their temple strongholds, in a society which tolerated them only as necessary evils, the priests were wise to take such precautions.

Why, then, had they left their door wide open?

With Ishtier involved and Kindrie in his hands to use as bait, it was very likely a trap. What choice did she have, though, except to bite?

Still, she hesitated.

Ishtier was only one member of this community, and a rogue at that. Jame didn't like the Three-Faced-God (what Kencyr did?), but he (or she, or it) *had* created the Kencyrath, and this was where Shanir trained to serve him. Likewise, she had always felt obscurely superior to his priests (what Kencyr didn't?); but what had her own half-remembered training in Perimal Darkling been but a perversion of the Great Dance which they did by right and necessity? Who was she to look down on them? Look what harm she had already done to Kindrie . . . through sheer prejudice? Had she been as irrational as . . . as Tori in his blind hatred of the Shanir?

No, she thought, not very clearly. *I'm better than that. I've got to be.*

Still, it was hard to cross that terrace under Rawneth's hidden eyes to that open door.

As her eyes adjusted to the darkness within, she saw a plainly appointed room, taking up apparently the whole interior. So, this wasn't one of those structures larger inside than out. Presumably a minor priest should be on duty to receive visitors and guard the inner door. However, neither priest nor door was in sight. Nor was anyone behind her, when she steeled herself to look—no foot prints across the terrace but her own, no empty man-shape by the balustrade defined by beads of mist, no glint of eyes, Bane's mocking silver or the assassin's cruel, bloodshot gold.

Jame stepped over the threshold and walked around the edge of the room, running her fingertips along the wall. At the back, her hand went through what had looked at a distance like rough stone. Instead, the bare warp threads of a tapestry hung there like a dense curtain. Anyone, slipping through it in the dim light, would seem to have walked through a solid wall. Clever, clever, clever.

She parted the threads, stepped inside and, for the second time that morning, fell down a flight of stairs.

Too damn much practice at Gothregor, she thought sourly, picking herself up at the bottom.

A corridor stretched away in front of her, curving downward into the earth, lit sporadically by guttering torches. Jame descended warily. As the curve widened into a spiral, doors began to open off its outer wall into what appeared to be novice dormitories, dark and dank, not much better than dungeon cells. Farther down, straw mattresses and dirt walls gave way to the cots and stone of the acolytes. Many of these cultivated mushrooms in far corners and multicolored molds on the walls, the latter forming intricate murals of unpleasant design. By their sickly glow alone, these chambers were lit. Doors began to open off the spiral's inner curve into claustrophobic classrooms. Below that was a dismal kitchen, moldy bread in discolored mounds on its tables. Under cauldrons of pale soup, its fires were all burnt out.

Dank, sour, mean. How could anything good come out of such a place?

But Kindrie had. True, he had made some spectacular mistakes since, and she had often wanted to kick him

out of his sudden trances. Still, from hints that he had
dropped, she gathered that he had as incomplete a memory of his childhood here as she did of hers in the Master's house. She should have remembered how many
false steps one could make, stumbling out of such darkness, what courage it took even to try.

I am as bad as Tori, she thought bitterly. *No, worse,
because I knew better.*

Where *was* Kindrie, though, not to mention everyone
else? The College had an air of arrested life, almost of
sudden disaster. It wasn't just the empty rooms and cold
soup, either. On the hall floor was a mosaic of colored
tiles, designed to help the downward spiral of power,
with tessellated eddies like catch-pools in each room.
She hadn't expected the savage current of a temple—as
Kindrie had said, constant exposure to that would erode
any half-trained mind. Even two days ago, though, standing on the far side of the Silver, she had sensed more
activity than this. Had something happened to the distant
temples, sources of their god's power on Rathillien, or
was the problem here in the Riverland, perhaps in the
College itself?

Still, there was something. As she had followed the
trickle of power through Wilden to find this place, so
now she felt drawn downward with it. The hall's spiral
widened. From below came a rhythmic shuffling sound,
massive, as if in its deep den some huge beast were
dancing. Before she was aware of it, her feet had caught
the pattern: step, turn, glide . . . down and down to
where the others wove the Great Dance, round and
round on the tessellated floor, straining to draw in power,
passing it down and down . . . .

Jame stopped short with a gasp. She stood on the threshold of the College's main hall, and she had found its community.

Innermost stood a high priest, still eye of the storm, yet its master. Around him like black clouds circled lesser priests, feet barely touching the floor, robes astream in wind-blowing Senetha. Water-flowing acolytes girt them with gray, and brown-clad novices with the *kantirs* of earth-moving. The whole wove a pattern of great power, each dancer caught in it, oblivious to all else.

His back to her, a young, white-clad scullion shuffled in step. His movements puzzled her until she recognized them as fire-leaping, consumed as it were to cinders by his exhaustion. How long had they all been at this, anyway?

The dance jerked the boy around. His eyelids dropped over burnt-out sockets. His gaping mouth was full of dried blood. He had been dead for days.

This isn't my business, Jame thought, sickened, backing away. *I can't let it be.*

But what about Kindrie? She could still feel the mindless pull of the dance which had sucked her down to fill the gap where that corpse jerked and twitched. Had the healer been snared before her? No. Of all the white-haired Shanir here, he was not one.

The stair led on, downward.

Below was the priests' domain. The lesser orders lived simply, if in cleaner, drier cells than the acolytes above. They also had better light, from diamantine panels glowing on the walls. In the high priests' quarters farther down, more diamantine filled all but the farthest corner with soft, stolen sunshine. It was as if the world had been turned upside down, the sun below and dank earth above. Jame passed austere but well-appointed rooms, many with scrolls piled high on tables. They reminded her of Ishtier's obsession with a certain pale book currently in her knapsack in the Mount Alban infirmary. These shelves weren't apt to contain anything half as priceless, but what she glimpsed looked valuable enough. She had never considered how the priesthood supported itself. An allowance from the Randir, perhaps. But that would hardly extend to this fortune in diamantine and arcane literature, or to the book chests faced with rathorn ivory which she noted many rooms. Clearly, the high priests had access to great wealth. Where did it come from, and on what else did they spend it?

Ever since the main hall, the corridor's spiral had been contracting. No more doors opened off of it, but still it continued to descend into dimmer light, past empty niches. A curious, musty smell rose from the depths, vaguely and disagreeably sweet.

Then came a niche which was not empty. Jame thought at first that a statue stood in it, clothed in crumpling finery, wearing a mask of beaten gold. Then she saw the white of bone under the cracked maroon flesh of long-dead fingers. On the lintel was carved an unfamiliar name, a date long past, and a rank: high priest. Each niche from then on had a similar inscription, and a similar inmate.

Jame had seen something like this, descending to the secret library under Gorgo's temple in Tai-tastigon. That had been distasteful. This was . . . obscene. Kencyr dead were given to the pyre. While one bone remained intact, the soul was believed to be trapped in it, naked before the three faces of God. To escape that hated divinity and the contract which it imposed was a Kencyr's last act of defiance, as honor was his first in life. The priests, it seemed, felt differently. Jame did note, however, as she gingerly descended between the grim ranks, that no one new had joined them in the past thirty or forty years.

The odor was getting stronger but, somehow, less disagreeable. That wasn't necessarily good. After sharing Jorin's senses intermittently for the past two years, Jame had begun to find the smell of some fairly nasty things quite appetizing. This was more of a green scent, though, as if of growing things. So far underground? Had the priests turned their world that much on its head?

Then she heard a slow, thumping sound and a voice, thick with exhaustion and hopelessness.

"Let me in," it was mumbling over and over. "Let me in."

A narrow hall curved left at the stair's foot. Around it shone a light. Jame advanced warily, then stopped, staring. At the hall's end, Kindrie huddled against a door, weakly beating against it with bloody knuckles. Above him hung a tapestry, aglow with flowers as white as the Shanir's hair. The light shone from it . . . no, *through* it. It wasn't fabric at all, Jame saw, but a window set in the door. On the other side, in full spring glory, was the secret moon garden at Gothregor.

Impossible, unless . . . unless . . . .

Tieri had died in that garden, where her tattered death banner still hung, and there the Knorth Bastard had been born. Kindrie had been locked out of his soul-image by Ishtier, hence his inability to heal those bleeding hands. Jame wasn't trained to enter others' soul-scapes, but she apparently had walked into her brother's at the wolvers' keep, perhaps because they were twins. Kindrie must also be very close to her in blood, as she had guessed, since here she was, uninvited, on the threshold of his soul.

"Please . . . ." the Shanir moaned, striking feebly at the closed door. Blood tricked down his thin wrist. "Oh, please . . . ."

Jame stepped forward, then froze as cracks radiated out from under her foot. They weren't real, she told herself, any more than that lightning flash had been in Caineron's tower which had first shown her a glimpse of Kindrie's soul-garden . . . and almost knocked the healer off the balcony.

Remember that, she warned herself, looking down at the broken floor.

Everything that happened on this level had repercussions in the physical world, hence a healer's power. But this was almost the opposite: some dangerous antipathy seemed to exist between her soul and Kindrie's, however good her intentions. She didn't dare go a step closer.

"If you want to reclaim that garden," she told him, "you've got to help yourself. Come on. Get up."

"Please, oh, please . . . ." he moaned again.

She could have shaken him. Always whining or retreating into trances . . . hadn't the idiot any pride at all? But the only thing which he thought he had to be proud of was his "trace" of Knorth blood. All right.

"Kindrie, tell me again the name of your grandmother."

His bloody hand wavered in mid-air. "T-telarien . . . her n-name was Telarien . . . ."

"Good. Now, who was her daughter? Go on. Ask me."

He frowned, muzzy, as if her voice had begun to drag him out of deep sleep. The light dimmed, no longer shining through the door but only from the tapestry which hung against it.

Damn, thought Jame.

As he roused, he was drawing them both from the metaphysical level back toward the real. Maybe this entrance to his soul would disappear altogether if he woke fully. Obviously, dream—and soul-scapes were closely related.

"Ask me!" she said again, with more urgency.

"W-who?"

"Tieri, your mother, who was also my aunt. And what does that make us?"

"F-first cousins," he stammered, sitting up, blinking at her. "Blood-kin. A-and the Highlord?"

"Him too."

And what would Tori think of that, or of her having told Kindrie? His skin was going to crawl off his bones. But that didn't change facts.

"You may be a bastard," she said, "and as wet as a fresh-dropped calf, but you're Knorth, all right, if ever there was one. So stop shaming our ancestors. Get up and open that damn door!"

He was looking full at her now, pale eyes at last focused behind white lashes. "Yes," he said, climbing stiffly to his feet. "Yes."

A tremor made Jame almost fall. She saw that the cracks underfoot now lay between mosaic tiles which shifted like the sullen mull of dammed waters, serpentine and lapis-lazuli, green and blue, fretted with foam-lines of ivory. Of course, the power gathered above must go somewhere. She had descended into a pool of it, channeled down to press impatiently against the sluice gate toward which Kindrie was now reaching. Couldn't he see that the only light now came from the molds which mottled its surface? Their spores burst, sickly luminous, under his hand. He was lifting the latch.

"No!" she cried, stumbling forward.

Too late.

II

THE DARK PRESSED IN ON ALL SIDES, loosening, tightening, like the guts of some great snake that feels the swallowed prey stir. Eaten alive . . . .

But I can still breathe, thought Jame. That terrified panting almost in her ear was her own. She fought to control it. *I can still move . . . .*

Just not very well. By the pain in her bruised knees, she located the floor. So that way was down. Her hands could feel it too, after a fashion. Now, get up. Slowly, slowly . . . .

The floor seemed to tilt. She hit it, sprawling, before her senses warned her that she had lost her balance. *Like being drunk,* she thought, remembering the last and only time.

What had happened? Kindrie had opened the door and then . . . and then . . . .

The force dammed outside had rushed in, taking them with it. Where? Clearly, not into the Shanir's moon garden. That had slipped back out of his reach, into some sealed off corner of his soul. In the priests' inverted world, this room was the deepest, the most secret and important, the very bowels of power. And it had swallowed her with one gulp.

Nearby, someone laughed softly.

"Who's there?" she demanded, trying again to rise, again falling. Her voice sounded flat and muffled. "Kindrie?"

"You suit me better," said a dry, thin voice, "on your knees. Greetings, thief."

"Ishtier." She must not show fear. She must not. "You suit *me* better trying to gnaw off your own hand. I hear, though, that you stopped short with a finger . . . ah!"

The darkness around her had seemed to constrict. For a moment, she couldn't breathe. No doubt about it: her old enemy had power in this place—not the mindless maelstrom of a temple but something more considered, perhaps more dangerous, with intelligence behind it. The other seven high priests must be close by, listening.

"Renegade," she said, raising her voice. "Have you told the College how you abandoned Ganth, your lord, in the Haunted Lands to die?"

"Priests have no lords, thief. Our houses abandon *us*, when they send us here. We owe them nothing."

The rancor in his voice scraped as though against raw flesh. Such bitterness, after so many years . . . . It must be true.

"B-but then why did you go with Ganth into exile?"

"Now, why would I tell you a thing like that? You used to be sharper witted, thief."

He was taunting her, but he was also right. Her mind seemed full of slow moving eels, brain-suckers, eating their way out . . . .

No, dammit. All these images of eat and be eaten . . . the priest was using the Great Dance to play games with her as she had earlier with Brenwyr. Knowing helped, some.

Don't be distracted. Attack.

"You betrayed Bane, when you used his soul to create the Lower Town Monster."

"Experimentation. You indulged in it too, theocide."

"Yes, I accidentally killed Gorgo, but I also helped his priest Loogan resurrect him afterward. That wasn't to disprove our own god's monotheism, though, as you tried to do with the Monster; and I never gave my allegiance to Perimal Darkling, as you did."

Darkness hummed. "That I deny."

"You boasted that you would bring down the Barriers and restore the Kencyrath to Gerridon, whom you called its rightful lord, under shadow's eaves."

"That I didn't."

"Liar."

The insult hung in the dark, throbbing air like a curse. Somewhere nearby, someone (probably Kindrie) gave a half-swallowed sob of fear. Jame held her breath. Despite all she knew about Ishtier, it unnerved her that he would lie so easily. In the back of her mind, thought, something whispered:

Idiot. He forced that charge out of you before you were ready. Now all your arrows are shot.

Darkness chuckled again, as dry and rustling as claws at work inside a shroud, as obscenely triumphant.

"Always nosing after the truth, aren't you, little thief? Like a bitch in heat. Shall we show everyone the truth about you? Yes, oh yessss . . . ."

Jame lurched to her feet. "Oh, no . . . oh, God!"

Intolerable dizziness had seized her. *He's turning me inside-out*, she thought wildly, then stumbled and fell again, retching, to the floor.

She could see it now, though the thin vomit of an empty stomach: dark stone, veined with green. Her hands shone white against it, fingers sheathed in articulated plates of ivory. Weight bowed her head, ivory helm and mask. So it had been when contact with the injured Graykin had jolted her into . . . into . . . .

"No," she said again, half moaning, as the memory surfaced. "Oh, no . . . ."

"Yessss . . . ."

The hiss brought her head up. Around her opened out Gerridon's monstrous hall in his house in Perimal Darkling, her soul-image. Thread-bare eyes watched her from the death banners of fallen Knorth; singed sockets from the pelts of Arrin-ken piled high on the hearth. The cold air stank. Always nosing after the truth . . . . This was what she had tried to forget, to deny, but could never escape: the abscess at her soul's core that made cruel mock of hope and honor. Bred to darkling service . . . . She wanted to curl into an ivory ball, to hide from herself forever and ever.

"So this is where you come from," breathed Ishtier. "So this is what you are."

His white face hovered over her, more skull-like than she remembered after his winter of illness, eyes alive with scorn in a death's-mask. "Listen to me, you abomination. You have something of mine. I sent the assassins to fetch it, but they failed. I sent that whey-faced healer, but he ran away. Nonetheless, I *will* have it. Where is my book, thief? My Book Bound in Pale Leather. Tell me, or as surely as I locked that cringing bastard out of his soul-image, I will lock you *into* yours. Think about it: your mind trapped here forever; your body mine, to do with what I will . . . ."

"No!"

She drew the Ivory Knife with clumsy, ivory-gloved fingers. He slapped it out of her hand. It clattered on stone into shadows by the door.

"Call *me* renegade, will you? Did you really think you could defy our master in his own hall? Swear allegiance where you please, Priest's-Bane, but this is where your soul lies and rots. Fool, to think that arms or armor can save you here!"

His second blow caught her on the side of the head, making her ears ring.

. . . the white rathorn colt, felled by her kick just where she herself had now been struck. Too immature, both of them, too unprepared . . . .

Blood splashed on the floor between her hands, Kallystine's cut reopened beneath the ivory mask. At its touch, the green marble veins began to pulse, cracks of verdigris light spreading out around her to the hearth's edge. The flayed paws of Arrin-ken flexed stiffly.

Screee . . . went their claws on the hearth-stone. *Screeeee . . . .*

Jame clapped hands over her ears. Inside her skull, panic babbled:

He'll let you out if you give him the Book. You never wanted to be the filthy thing's guardian, anyway. And this time, surely, it will kill him. Give him the Book.

Yes.

A ripple ran through the hall, like wind over water. Arrin-ken claws and rathorn ivory melted. Grimacing, the banners unraveled. Walls redefined themselves around her, closer than the hall's had been, under a low roof supported by massive, squat columns. Mosaic covered every surface, lapis-lazuli and ivory. Green serpentine throbbed like the veins of some great heart. No.

That was up in the hall, pounding itself to death with the exhaustion of its dancers. Here that gathered power was stored, in the bowels of the earth, the foul cloaca of divinity . . . .

A dark bundle with Kindrie's pale face stared at her across the tessellated floor. "What did you *do*?" he whispered, aghast.

What, indeed?

But the black clot of priests huddled by the far wall were staring over both the healer's head and her own. So was Ishtier. She hadn't admitted her defeat out-loud, Jame realized. Neither the priests nor her soul-image was responding to it. Someone had opened the door.

An indistinct figure stood on the threshold. Mold-glow glimmered on the gold mask which it held before its face. Rotting finery crumbled away from it. The unburnt dead always return . . . . But behind the mask as it fell, nothing . . . or was there? In the shadow of the hood, someone smiled at Jame, planes of darkness shifting around the eerie flash of stained teeth. Yellow eyes or silver, assassin's or Bane's? Whichever, they lifted, and the smile in them died.

"No . . . ." croaked Ishtier, recoiling. "You're dead on the Mercy Seat, flayed alive and crawling with flies . . . . No!"

His maimed hand rose. Fingernails scraped the low ceiling, raking together lines of power, jerking them down. A massive weight settled on the room. Walls groaned. Columns crumbled at the top. With a report like the earth's back breaking, the lintel cracked. The figure standing under it disintegrated in a puff of acrid dust.

"You'll bring the roof down on us all!" someone wailed.

Good idea, thought Jame.

After all, was anyone here worth saving? These fool priests, who had put such power in a madman's hands? The demon in the doorway or his half-sister, who had dreamed of walking in the light? Kindrie, who had deserved protection from so many and received it from no one?

Well, yes. Dammit.

She struggled to her feet, feeling as if the whole college rested on her shoulders. Once before, she had dealt with m'lord Ishtier, in his own temple, with an act of appalling recklessness. No helping that. Her black gloved hands were already rising, clenched in challenge not of the priest but of the god whom he feigned to serve.

"Lord," she cried, "a judgment!"

Ishtier's wild stare snapped to her face. Tendons stood out under the loose skin of his throat as he strained to keep his mouth shut. It opened anyway, muscles creaking. The God-voice boomed out through the nine spider-thin fingers which he clamped to his face, biting into them with each word:

"TRUST NOT IN PRIESTS . . . ."

What in Perimal's name?

". . . NOR YET IN ORACLES."

That *was* the Voice which she had evoked from Ishtier before, and yet not quite, as if some undernote in it now dominated. She hadn't thought before of her god's voice as a chorus, like . . . like . . . .

She seized the priest by the shoulders. He felt bird-fragile in her grasp. Sinking to his knees, he drew her down with him.

"Who's in there?" she demanded of his blank eyes, of pupils so huge with shock that they looked like holes burned in parchment. "Dammit, what game are you playing?"

. . . not eyes at all but scorched sockets fringed with burnt fur, opening into greater darkness . . . .

For a moment, Jame thought that she was back in her soul-image, that her spilt blood had animated an Arrinken pelt from the hearth to hood this wretched man, as Bane had the master assassin. Then a second possibility struck her: twice now, she had demanded a judgment and received it, perhaps not from her god at all but from his appointed judges, the Arrin-ken, whose plaited voices in the Ebonbane had also forced her to judge herself. There, Immalai's mercy had prevailed; but the Riverland was the blind cat's territory.

Ishtier grinned at her around his bleeding fingers. "*In the Ebonbane, by the chasm, you escaped my judgment,*" he said in a voice like a winter's pyre, frost and bitter ash, "*but these mountains are mine. Child of darkness, do you want my judgment now?*"

She recoiled. "No!"

A rush of priests thrust her aside to get at Ishtier. The oldest, smallest of them grabbed Jame by the arm.

"Do that again!" he cried, trying to shake her, only shaking himself. "Evoke the Voice!"

"N-not damned likely," said Jame, attempting to free herself. The little priest barely came to her shoulder and looked more frail than some of his late colleagues out in the hall, but he had a terrier's grip. "You want it, you talk to it."

"God's teeth and toenails. Don't you think we've tried? All winter, ever since we learned that the Voice had spoken again after all these years . . . . Oh, if only we weren't so starved of power, now, when we need it most!"

"Why? What's happened?"

"Too few of us here, too few Kencyr in the Riverland overall . . . who knows, except that we're being cut off from the temples. The closer to Summer Eve, the worse it gets. Not even the Great Dance is pulling in enough power to keep the valley ours."

"The Dance. You're killing your own people, priest."

"So? There are always more unwanted Shanir."

A harsh sound came from Ishtier.

The little man let go of Jame and darted over to join his peers, all shouting questions at the Voice which had just deigned for the third time to speak through the Tastigon priest. In their midst, Ishtier hunched jealously over his hands, tearing strips of flesh off them with his teeth and growling.

Jame pulled Kindrie to his feet. The healer's nose was bleeding freely, as surely it would not have if he had regained control of his soul-image. A fine pair of Knorth they were, or perhaps a trio. Discarded grave clothes lay strewn on the threshold, blind flies seething out of the eyes and mouth of the golden death mask. The pavement beneath had been smashed to powder. The assassin must have blinked in time for the shock to pass harmlessly through him. Was he still Bane's prisoner? Where in Perimal's name had they gone, anyway?

At least, there was no sign of them on the way up.

Kindrie faltered at the door of the main hall, staring at the carnage inside wrought by Ishtier's last, ruthless pulling down of power. Jame tugged him away.

"Think about it later," she said, herself white-faced beneath mask and drying blood. The Priests' College would need many new Shanir.

At the doorway of the little stone house, they paused to look warily out at the terrace. Judging from the growth of the puddles, it had rained. Now, however, the lower cloud level was beginning to dissipate.

Jame swore softly. "When this weirding haze lifts entirely, Mount Alban will be gone, if it isn't already. No time to lose."

But Kindrie caught her arm. "Wait."

The shadow of Rawneth's tower had moved since Jame had entered the College. Now it slanted southwestward, entirely across their way, where no northern sun would have thrown it.

"Don't tell me," said Jame. "The Wilden Witch can shadow-cast."

By the balustrade, a shaded puddle quivered. Out of it came groping something dark to fumble at the pool's rim and grip a flagstone's edge. A lumpish figure surfaced, out of water at most an inch deep. Gold embroidery glimmered on the muddy shoulders of dress grays. The lower half of its ruined face split into a white-toothed grin, framed by chipped, bleeding incisors.

Kindrie swayed.

"Don't faint!" Jame said sharply. "So the Witch's pet demon wasn't destroyed after all. So it still wants you. Things could be worse."

"H-how?"

"Bane could be behind us." She glanced over her shoulder. "Damn."

She had hoped that he had stayed below to deal with his betrayer—not that much more could be done to Ishtier, short of killing him. For that final mercy he could hardly depend on Bane, who in his darker days had flayed children alive for sport. Now his shadowy figure stood just behind the tapestry at the back of the room, watching her through its hanging warp threads.

Better the demon you know?

Kindrie gasped.

Still grinning, Rawneth's creature had heaved itself out of the puddle and was crawling toward them. Oily, black water streamed off its clothes, off the trailing, limp cuffs of its pants. It had no feet. The tower's shadow crept forward to give it cover, swinging in on the doorway where they stood like the closing of a massive gate.

"Quick," said Jame. "Its soul belongs to a Randir captain, late of Tentir, more recently assigned to Gothregor. What's her name? You used to live here. Tell me!"

"I-I don't know."

Jame swallowed her exasperation. After all, she had spent the entire winter in the same halls with the wretched woman without learning what she was called. Now she had made Kindrie feel as stupid and helpless as she did. Nonetheless, they must not be caught between two demons. As the shadow closed on them, she took a deep breath and shoved Kindrie out into it.

It was very cold under Rawneth's tower. They could see the white plumes of their breaths, the Shanir's so rapid that he was almost panting, her own hardly less so. Eerie twilight surrounded them like that of a solar eclipse. The splash of their feet, even the cataract's roar, sounded curiously muffled and far away. Jame wished that she were. The creeping figure had turned to follow them, sodden dress tunic bulging, pants legs now drained and flat. It left a foul, black trail behind it and sent a hideous stench on before. At least it would never overtake them before they reached the shadow's far side.

In the demon's path lay another puddle, beginning to mantle with frost. It pulled itself over the edge and sank, gurgling, through shattered panes of ice. Dark water closed over it.

Jame and Kindrie stopped, staring. Bubbles, then nothing.

"It's under the pavement," she said suddenly. "Run!"

Kindrie shot her a terrified look, then bolted. She floundered after him through such water as lay in her path, too much in haste to detour. The Shanir's bare feet scarcely cracked the growing sheet ice, but her boots crashed through it, sinking with each step from ankle to shin to knee.

Fifteen feet to the light, ten, five . . . .

Kindrie burst out into it.

Jame lunged to catch up and fell heavily, half on mist-chilled pavement, half up to the waist in freezing water. Something had grabbed her foot. Now it pulled. Her nails rasped on icy stone, clawing for a grip. Kindrie clutched her wrists. Behind her, something surfaced, stinking like a week old corpse, chuckling thickly.

"C-cum an' play, liddle girl . . . ."

Kindrie nearly let go. He was staring up at something, aghast. The grip on Jame's foot broke. She shot forward into the Shanir's arms, both of them going down in a heap.

Bane stood on the other side of the puddle into which she had nearly sunk. Out of it he had fished the demon, which he now held one-handed by the scruff of its dress gray neck, fastidiously, at arm's length, as it squirmed and mewled and stank. In his other hand was the Ivory Knife. With great care, he began to slit the uniform's seams. As each gave way, black liquid filth poured down. Those grinning teeth fell last, bloody at the roots as if just pulled. For a moment they floated white in the befouled pool, then sank. Bane held out the coat like a trophy skin and dropped it at Jame's feet.

She had risen and was standing just barely within the light, close enough to touch him or to be touched.

Not since that last night in Tai-tastigon had she seen him so clearly. Never before had she realized how much like Torisen he looked, especially in the elegant lines of his face and hands. But although his eyes mirrored the true Knorth silver, almost luminous in this half light, they hadn't the depth either of Tori's self-doubt or of his intrinsic strength. Bane had always believed that in the end he could defeat his own damnation, that an honorable death would wipe away stains even as black as his. How often she had seen the arrogance of that faith in his lazy, mocking smile.

He wasn't smiling now.

In his hand he held the Ivory Knife, gripped perilously by the flat between thumb and forefinger, its point resting lightly on his palm. He was offering it to her, hilt first.

Could the dead die? *Was* Bane dead? Perhaps he himself didn't know. A scratch from the Knife would make certain. It might even be the honorable death which he had sought, if given by her hand—or then again, it might not.

His voice didn't carry beyond the shadow's pall, but she saw his lips move: " . . . *your choice, sister* . . . "

Choice. She had been so proud of her ability to choose and to live with the consequences. That had been her honor, or rather her arrogance, more than a match for any of Bane's. But what did any choice matter when under it lay that cold, dark hall, that predestined damnation?

"Who am I," she said bitterly, "to judge you?"—and, with great care, she took the Knife from his hand. "Follow, if you choose."

Behind her, Kindrie caught his breath. He was staring up at the Witch's tower, at a low balcony just now cleared by the wispy, thinning clouds. Yellow light streamed from the interior, silhouetting the tall, slim figure motionless by the rail. Come out to see the fun, had she? Let her fish for her servant's teeth, then, in foul puddles and the rain which had again begun to fall. Jame sketched the proper salute—more insulting under the circumstances than a rude gesture—and turned her back on the Witch of Wilden.

"Time to go," she said.

They did.

III

THE PLATFORM ASCENDED, CREAKING.

Kindrie sat cross-legged on it, shoulders drooping with fatigue, a shock of white hair hanging down over his face. Jame wondered how much more of this he could take. True, the Knorth were tougher than they looked, but most of them hadn't depended all their lives on a healer's talents.

For that matter, how long had it been since she herself had last slept or eaten? About forty-eight hours in both cases—not that she hadn't often gone longer than that without sleep. As for food, sore as her face had been and now was again, thanks to Ishtier, the prospect didn't much appeal. Anyway, she wasn't tired or hungry, just numb.

Empty.

She seemed to remember, a life time ago, when her mind had teemed with plans. The narrow halls of Gothregor had taught her to think more . . . modestly, the Women's World would say. Since then, the world had seemed to close in on her, prospects slamming like doors along a dark corridor down which she had run, increasingly alone with that which followed. One could never out-run one's past. Now she couldn't seem to plan ahead at all. Tomorrow didn't exist; this afternoon, just barely. She supposed, making an effort, that they should sneak back into the infirmary before their absence caused a stir.

One thing at a time.

The platform stopped with a jolt in Mount Alban's upper reaches. Jame pulled Kindrie to his feet, then threw an arm around him as he staggered. She could count his ribs by touch.

Not until they had turned into the corridor did she remember that Brenwyr had toppled a wardrobe across the infirmary door. However, it had been removed. From within came voices, one patient, the other sharp with frustration. Both ten-commands had crowded inside to listen while Captain Hawthorn tried tactfully to learn from her matriarch why they should risk war by raiding Wilden.

Graykin stood by the door, biting his nails. He nearly bit off a finger when Jame spoke softly in his ear:

"What did you do, shout for help through the keyhole?"

"Someone had to be told," he muttered, regarding her askance.

"Huh," said Jame.

"Someone," apparently, had been Brenwyr, who must have summoned the guard posthaste but now couldn't bring herself to explain why the Knorth had gone down to Wilden, much less what specific danger she was in.

Women's secrets had some use after all.

Glancing back over the heads of her restive squad, Brier Iron-thorn met Jame's eyes. The Kendar's expression didn't change, but the sharpening of her attention made others turn as well, including the Brandan captain and her matriarch.

"Er . . ." said Jame, trying surreptitiously to shift Kindrie into Graykin's reluctant arms. "Is anything the matter?"

"Suppose, lady," said Hawthorn, sandy brows rising, "that you tell us."

Jame's mind went blank. Earlier, she had broken one of her own cardinal rules by making herself forget an unwelcome fact. Now her brain seemed to have closed shop altogether, lights out and nobody home. The truth wouldn't do nor would a lie, leaving . . . what? Twenty-four pairs of expectant eyes and the hiss of rain falling past the windows—except that part of that sound came from Jorin, followed by his low, throbbing growl.

The cadets had cleared a path between her and the two principal Brandan. In the shadows behind Brenwyr, Aerulan's banner lay unrolled across the seat and back of a chair. On her tapestry lap crouched the ounce, ears flat, fangs bared, moon opal eyes aglow . . . but what was he seeing, and through whose eyes? In the room's gray, rain-washed light, Aerulan's white hands glimmered, one clutching the cat's ruff, the other pressed against the crimson line across her throat. She was staring, transfixed, at something behind Jame.

Jame felt the hair on the back of her neck rise. Some-one stood behind her in the open doorway, so close that she smelled its rotten breath, but the cadets' fascinated gaze hadn't shifted from her face. Whoever—*what-ever*—it was, only the dead girl and the blind cat could see it.

A hoarse, mocking whisper breathed in her ear: " . . . *my choice, sister.*"

The master assassin's voice, Bane's words. "Follow, if you choose," she had said, and they had. Oh, lord. Now what?

First, clear the room.

"This is house business," she said to the infirmary at large. "Everyone, please leave."

Hawthorn's brows rose even farther, but she acknowl-edged with a wry salute and hustled her cadets out of the room. The Knorth cadets hesitated, hopeful, but Jame waved them out too, including Brier. The latter paused on the threshold.

"Lady, are you all right?"

Jame sighed. "Have I ever been?"

Only after the Kendar had gone did Jame realize what an insult she had just dealt her, now a Knorth herself, as good as told publicly that she wasn't trusted with fam-ily business.

Ishtier was right, thought Jame. *Where are my wits? Be damned if you must, but don't be stupid.*

However, this really didn't concern the ten-com-mander. Nor did it Graykin, who had slunk out with the greatest reluctance and would probably listen at the keyhole, if he could. Kindrie had tumbled over asleep on a pallet. What good that would do him without access to his soul-image, Jame didn't know, but still she hadn't the heart to wake him up.

"That was good thinking," said Brenwyr gruffly. "They won't challenge a house secret."

"Wait," said Jame as the matriarch started to pass her. She shut the door in Graykin's avid face. "I might as well have called this sister-kin business. About Aerulan . . . ."

Brenwyr stiffened, still facing the door. "She's yours again. What more do you want?"

Jame frowned. The matriarch *had* been about to leave without the banner . . . er . . . Aerulan, whom Jame could still plainly see, one hand on her throat, the other raised as if in supplication.

"But I gave her to you," she protested.

The Iron Matriarch turned on her. "One does *not* demean a lady by giving her away! Have you and your brother no decency at all?"

Her throttled rage drove Jame back a step. Then she thought, perhaps, she understood.

"Lord Brandan asked for Aerulan's banner," she said slowly, sorting it out, "and Torisen simply told him to take it."

Of course. Any other lord would have insisted on the fabulous price which Ganth had demanded for Aerulan's contract in perpetuity, paid in full. The Knorth were poor. Torisen could certainly use the money. But he had refused to profit from old grief and his father's rapacious bargain. Neither he nor, perhaps, Lord Brandan had realized what an insult this charity had dealt to the Women's World, where a lady's price confirmed her rank. Aerulan wouldn't have minded. Brenwyr did, terribly, for her sake.

A berserker and a maledight. Of all people to have enraged.

"We meant well," Jame said awkwardly, wanting very much to be believed. "We just didn't understand. I think, now, that I do. I'll explain it to my brother. There must be some way to send Aerulan home with honor . . . to you."

The older woman had turned away again, as if better to keep her precarious self-control. Without thinking, Jame put a hand on her arm. It felt as hard under her fingertips as the Iron Matriarch's nickname. A tremor passed through it.

"Adiraina said that you would instruct him."

For the first time, Brenwyr turned to look at the banner on its chair, and gave a sharp exclamation. A hasty stride took her out of Jame's reach, but then she stopped short, hands curling into fists at her side.

"Knorth, are you trying to drive me mad?"

Jame stared. "What?"

"Taunting me with glimpses of her, then snatching her away . . . . Traveling with her, sleeping with her . . . do you think I don't recognize seduction when I see it?"

God's teeth and toenails. She was jealous.

"Lady, I swear . . . ."

"*Liar!*"

Jame felt her hands go cold. A terrible clarity filled her mind—what she would do to this . . . this hag, with her disheveled hair and red eyes, who had dared to impugn the only thing of worth which she had left: her honor. She wanted the release of a flare, to feel its power burn away doubt and self-disgust. She craved its intoxication. Her claws were out through her glove tips, ready.

No.

This was the onset of a berserk seizure, against a woman striking out in pain, against another berserker. She must not, *not*, NOT.

Brenwyr was shouting unforgivable things in her face.

"Self-restraint, endurance, obedience-be-damned!" she shouted back as she retreated, to drown words which she must not hear. "Self-restraint-endurance-obedience-be-*damned*!"

Brenwyr grabbed her arm just as, groping behind her, she touched the death banner. The matriarch's other hand was poised to strike. Jame knew, with detached certainty, that if Brenwyr slapped her, Jame would kill her.

But another hand closed on the matriarch's raised fist. Joined by touch, the three of them stood frozen—two alive, panting, and one dead.

"Aerulan . . . ." said Brenwyr hoarsely. "Knorth, do you see her too?"

"Yes. I have off and on for days, but never so clearly as now. And no, you aren't going mad, unless I am too."

Thunder rolled, retreating. Gray rain fell, gray light in a gray room—but there the dead stood, smiling, in her rust-red gown.

"She was given to the pyre thirty-four years ago. How is this possible?"

"I'm not sure," said Jame.

Her left arm was going numb from the older woman's iron grip. Her right hand felt the rough tapestry nap, and beneath it a shoulder which flame had reduced to ash long before she herself had been born. *Had* they both gone mad?

Aerulan smiled past her, at Brenwyr.

"Perhaps," said Jame slowly, "the dead are more persistent than our priests have led us to believe." *The ranks of hieratic dead beneath the Wilden college.* "Perhaps the rules have changed here on Rathillien." *Bane, at her back, with his enigmatic smile. Where was* his *body?* "Or perhaps . . . ." *Aerulan's dress, woven of threads taken from the gown in which she had bled to death.* "Can blood trap the soul as well as flesh and bone?"

"If you say so," said Brenwyr, doubtfully.

Jame felt her scalp prickle. The matriarch had not been speaking to her.

Brenwyr stiffened. "He's *here*?" She spun about, her fierce gaze sweeping the room.

In the farthest corner, a flaw moved in the shadows, dropping the *mere*-tattooed hand with which it had hidden its eyes. The yellow irises were as blood-shot as fertilized egg yolks from being kept open so long and the spirit in them raged with impotent fury. Bane's features overlay the whole like a shadow-spun cowl, smiling.

Brenwyr rounded on Jame. "*You* brought him here!"

Jame recoiled, hands clenched behind her not this time to forestall a berserker response but to keep from dancing down the matriarch's rage. Ancestors only knew what she might unleash, trying *that* trick again.

"It's all right," she said hastily. "Aerulan's killer *is* in this room and I *did* more or less invite him here, but he's under control."

"Control? Yours? By God, Knorth, if you've sold your-self to the Bashtiri Shadow Guild . . . ."

"Oh, don't be silly."

Brenwyr boggled, suddenly deflated. "That's what Aerulan said."

"You can actually hear her? I can't, but then I don't know what her voice sounded like."

"That's something." The matriarch glanced back at the banner, mere tapestry again without Jame's touch to bridge the gap. "Then too, at last her blood-price will be paid."

"That isn't enough. I want to know who took out a contract on my whole family."

Brenwyr blinked. She had forgotten the larger massacre whose aftermath had almost destroyed the entire Kencyrath. Kinzi, Telarien, all those Knorth women dead and unavenged . . . . But what if the old quarrel between Kinzi and Rawneth *was* to blame? Could the Kencyrath survive such a terrible discovery?

"It was all so long ago," she said, hearing the echo of Adiraina's warning in her voice. "After all these years, is it wise to ask?"

"Vengeance aside, it isn't just ancient history. Everyone keeps telling me that the Shadow Guild never gives up. So why did the assassins let Tieri live, and will they keep coming after me?"

Brenwyr rubbed her temples, which had begun to throb. "Tieri lived because everyone except Adiraina thought she was dead."

"But this man knew better: he's the one from whom Aerulan hid Tieri. Why didn't he enlist the rest of the casting to help find her instead of leaving his precious contract unfulfilled? What happened? Bane, make him talk!"

Out of shadows, he looked at her unsmiling, as he had under the Witch's tower with what passed for his life balanced on the edge of the Ivory Knife. Choices . . . .

"Yes," said Jame unsteadily, meeting the yellow glare of the captive set unnervingly in his captor's face. "I choose this. It's necessary."

Bane nodded.

He seemed about to speak, but instead his mouth opened wide, wider, stained teeth and coated tongue shaping a mute shriek. The corner seemed full of writhing shadows, indistinctly at war like snakes in a bag. Then staring eyes and bared teeth lunged out into the room. The distortion of a *mere*-tattooed body showed against the windows, naked shoulders beaded with sweat and rain. Its faint shadow danced with it on the floor, all but consumed by the darker shape which clung to its back.

"Watch out!" Jame said sharply. "If he closes his eyes . . . ."

The yellow glint vanished. Rain drops spattered on the floor. Away from them streaked the guild master's living shadow, flat to the ground, free. If the Bashtiri had made straight for the closed door, blind, he would have slipped out under it. But at the last moment his nerve failed. He looked—and bounced off the panels with an oath back into his pursuer's grip.

The sound of struggle thrashed across the floor. Brenwyr snatched Aerulan's banner off the chair and Jorin scuttled out from under it a moment before it was smashed to pieces. The assassin's cursing changed to a cry of pain. One of his eyes filled with blood, then the other. Red brimmed over bony sockets and down hollow cheeks, defining their invisible planes with bloody tears.

"What's happening?" demanded Brenwyr.

"Bane has torn off his eyelids."

"Who in Perimal's name is Bane?"

The uproar abruptly stopped. Harsh panting came from amid the chair's wreckage, then a sharp gasp. A crimson line appeared beneath the grimacing face, following the winged arch of the collarbone. Blood trickled down the incline, down the sternum. Another cut traced the major pectoral of the right breast, then the left.

Brenwyr's fingers dug into Jame's shoulder. "What . . . ?"

"He's got the assassin's *mere*-knife and control of his hand. The pattern of cuts is called *kuth*. It's used in the public execution of child-killers." It might, Jame thought, have been the last thing which Bane himself had felt on the Tastigon Mercy Seat under the flayer's knife, unjustly accused of Dally's murder. "In the Eastern Lands, it would be considered just punishment for the assassination of Aerulan, her . . . blood-price."

With a deft flick, Bane cut off the assassin's right nipple. The bastard was enjoying himself. He would stop, though, if she asked.

The assassin spat out teeth, with fragments of gum attached. Demon-ridden for two days, he was doomed whatever she did. The left nipple . . . .

"This will only get worse," she said, hearing the truth in her voice, knowing how it was meant to mislead. "Talk, while you still can."

Yellow teeth bared in a ragged snarl. Parallel cuts marked prominent ribs as Bane continued to sketch in details of surface anatomy as if with a brush dripping red. A sinewy torso was taking shape in mid-air, slick with blood.

"Cut lower," said Brenwyr.

The assassin burst out cursing. The cut down his side skidded awry, into the fold of the groin.

"Bitch! Red-eyed, sodding whore . . . . D'you want to hear how I cut that one's white throat?"

"Yes," said Jame, reaching behind her to restrain Brenwyr. Her hand closed on Aerulan's cold fingers.

"Gaaah . . . . She came in with the little bint behind her, just when we'd finally pulled down the matriarch. 'Aerulan, Tieri, run!' she says—the old witch, brains half out on the floor and still squawking. They ran. I followed. Lost 'em both in that damned maze, then caught up with one again in the arcade. 'Brenwyr!' she was calling.

'Brenwyr!' You, huh, red-eyes? Came too late, though, didn't you . . . but still too soon for me, before I could make her tell me where she'd hidden t'other one. It should've been a double kill . . . ."

"What happened?" Jame demanded.

The bloody mask of a face worked. Bane never paused. Left ribs, external oblique . . . .

"Told the others both bints were dead, didn't I? The contract had been honored, I said. Get the hell out, get out, get out . . . ."

Abruptly, his voice sounded younger, the terror in it stark. Was Bane at work in his mind, slitting open the seams of memory as he did those of flesh?

" 'Shadow, by a shadow be exposed.' I *felt* that curse strike, sink in. Had to get away, contract be damned. Thirty-four years I waited for it to catch up with me, dreaming of red eyes, rising in the Guild. More rank, more tattoos . . . nothing is going to expose *me*. Then that dog-shit Ishtier sends word: The little bitch lived in hiding for years after our raid. *Years*! Says he'll tell the Grand Master that I lied, have me stripped of rank and tattoos . . . exposed . . . unless I do what he wants: steal a book (me, a *thief*!) and kill a sodding girl."

"So I didn't come under the terms of the original contract?"

The question jerked him back to the present. "Stupid cow. Had it down in blood how many to kill, didn't we? But I told the Grand Master that I wanted to go back anyway, to make a clean sweep. My turn to lead a blooding. My choice of target. Let the brats steal the book, kill the girl and all the red-eyed women they can find. No need to meet that cursing whore again, no need . . . ."

"But you have," said Brenwyr. "You son of a yellow bitch, who paid you to kill Aerulan?"

He knew where he was again, and who faced him. Bane brought him up short as he lunged forward. Jame slipped in front of the matriarch, drawing the Ivory Knife. The assassin strained inches from its point like a dog against its leash, attention fixed on Brenwyr.

"Curse *me*, will you?" he spat at her, spraying Jame with bloody froth. "Thirty-four years, snapping at my heels, ruining everything . . . *me*, the next grand master! Soil my hands with your sow's blood, should I? You should have been the brats' meat, but they failed. I won't!"

He strained forward, twisting to be free. The cuts opened red lips. Beneath, from collarbone to groin, muscles rotted by the Bane's touch tore like wet butcher's paper. Black intestines spilled out. His feet tangled in their coils, bursting them with a fecal stench. On his knees now, incredulous, he clutched at his abdomen as if somehow to cram back in its contents, but everything inside was tearing loose, falling. Then the aorta and femoral arteries ruptured. He collapsed, a look on his face of outraged disbelief. The red tide on the floor swelled twice with the failing heartbeat, then slowed to a spreading creep.

Out of the reeking cavity that had been his abdomen rose a miasma, a shadow. It stood over him, a mere thickening of the air against the windows' gray light. Then Bane raised his eyes. In their silver depths Jame saw mirrored her own pale face, her complicity. She looked away, back at the red ruin which lay at her feet.

"'*Shadow, by a shadow be exposed,*'" she quoted in an unsteady voice. "That's exposed, all right."

Brenwyr made a choking sound. The next moment, she had thrust Jame aside and thrown open the door.

Hawthorn and Brier Iron-thorn made way as she plunged blindly past them out into the hall, Aerulan's banner clutched to her breast.

Of course, the two Kendar would have waited beyond normal ear-shot to ensure family privacy, but not so far as to have missed the latter uproar. They entered in haste, probably expecting to find Jame reduced to chitterlings on the floor. Instead, there lay a complete stranger, completely disemboweled.

Hawthorn's sandy brows rose. "Lady?"

"Argh!" said Jame, snatched up her knapsack, and bolted out the door after Brenwyr, Jorin scrambling on her heels.

THE RAIN DECLINED into a gray drizzle as fine as the heart of a cloud. Impossible to see from one side of the observation deck to the other, much less down to the ground. Mount Alban might be anywhere. Jame thought, though, that it had probably returned home at last— everything back where it belonged except her. Appropriate, that she couldn't even see her feet as she sat on the deck's waist-high wall, legs dangling in space. What use were feet, anyway, with no place left to run?

Huh. There are always *options,* she told herself. *There have to be.*

From behind the wall came a low, reproachful cry. Jorin was not happy.

Still, thought Jame, she must be at least as wet as he, and as cold. At least her hands didn't feel the chill: the Ivory Knife had numbed them as she idly turned it over and over. Soon it would start to rot her already tattered gloves.

Someone stood behind her.

Bane, she thought, and said, without turning:

"So. Just what did we gain by that little exercise below? You, of course, enjoyed yourself. As for me, well, I already knew that Ishtier was behind this last raid on Gothregor. He bragged about it to me at Wilden. Presumably, he learned about Tieri from the Randir Matriarch when they traded information. A nice lever to use on an ambitious guild master, caught in a lie."

At a guess, she thought, *Rawneth didn't know that Tieri had survived until Adiraina was obliged to tell all the matriarchs after the poor girl's death. Some council meeting that must have been.*

"As for the original massacre, would we have found out who contracted for it even if Brenwyr hadn't precipitated matters? Now, I'm not so sure. That wretched man would only have been an apprentice then. He probably wasn't told. Perhaps he learned later, as he rose in the Guild—but 'perhaps' is a thin excuse for a death like that, Aerulan's blood-price notwithstanding."

A death you chose for him, she almost said. *Was I to blame for that?*

But she hadn't stopped him, and now she couldn't hide behind his actions. Honor's Paradox was a pretty thing in theory; in practice, it bit. Nor did recent revelations free her from it. Damned or not, she couldn't turn her world upside down the way the priests had their college. Honor was still honor.

"Wait a minute," she said. "Honor and obedience . . . ."

She had fled from Bane all winter, but what had he done except answer her summons? Now, down in the infirmary, he had obeyed her again, if in the most grue-some manner he could contrive. That was his style, after all—but since when had obedience been?

"Perhaps . . . ." said Ashe behind her, "since you blood-bound him."

Jame's start almost dislodged her from her perch. Unconsciously, she had depended on Jorin's senses for warning. What a time for the bond to fail. But Ashe was Torisen's friend, she told herself—and her enemy, instinct told her. In Kindrie's case, though, "instinct" had turned out to be another word for "prejudice." Maybe so again.

"Do you read minds, singer . . . and what in Perimal's name d'you mean, I bound him? I'm no blood-binder!"

Even as she spoke, though, she remembered Bane's mocking whisper: *"Blood binds,"* and felt her heart sink.

Could one be a binder and not know it? Her brother Torisen was, and didn't. The trait was said to run in particularly potent Shanir families. Like the Knorth. In the old days, before the Fall, it had allowed them to bind more Kendar more tightly than the mere mental discipline commonly practiced today. It had been the ruthless parallel to their god's binding of the Three Peo-ple as a whole to his service, the antithesis of honor because it was said to abolish choice.

"I don't think," she said mildly, "that I can stand much more of this. When did I blood-bind Bane? How?"

"To answer . . . first questions first, I don't read minds. But some thoughts . . . are louder than others. Then too

. . . haunt-sickness nearly killed you once. That forms . . . a bond. So did Bane's farewell kiss . . . in Tai-tastigon. Your blood in his mouth . . . his in yours. He was trying . . . to blood-bind *you*."

It was said to run in families. Of the three of them, only Bane had played with blood and knives enough to make such a discovery on his own.

Then the implication struck her.

"Why, you bastard!" she said, twisting about to search for his amused eyes in the shadows. "You wanted me any way you could get me, to the very last!"

The ghost of a chuckle answered her, from the opposite direction in which she had looked: . . . *worth a try* . . . .

"So the hunter got caught, uh? Like Tirandys with Torisen."

"Not quite," said Ashe. "Not between . . . two binders."

"*Snakes with similar venom,*" Brenwyr had called destructive Shanir, with limited or at least unpredictable responses to each other. Perhaps that was why she hadn't seen any sign of binding in Bane at the Sirdan's Palace. Even now, how affected was he, really?

"Wait a minute," she said again. "How do you know these things, Ashe? 'Haunts know what concerns haunts,' you said once. *Is* Bane dead?"

"His state is . . . peculiar. Did you know . . . that the Brandan Matriarch thinks he is . . . a projection of the nemesis in you?"

"Brenwyr. How is she?"

"Better. She is a strong woman . . . for all that you've seen her . . . only at her worst. She should be stronger still . . . if Aerulan stays with her."

"We'll work something out," said Jame, absently.

Stronger? Maybe. But Ashe didn't know that Brenwyr thought she had killed her own mother. The Brandan had learned to live with that, apparently, but if Jame were to dredge up her guilt again . . . .

A shiver ran up Jame's spine. For the first time, she knew exactly what spot to touch, to destroy someone.

"You *are* a nemesis . . . aren't you?" said Ashe softly. "But are you . . . the definite article?"

"*The* Nemesis, Regonereth, That-Which-Destroys?" Jame held up the Ivory Knife, the Maiden's cold, white face on the pommel so like her own under the mask, before Kallystine's handiwork. "You tell me."

"I can't. Not . . . without tests."

The shiver nestled between Jame's shoulder blades, light as the touch of a phantom hand.

"You're thinking about pushing me off this wall, aren't you, haunt? Why?"

"Because . . . I mistrust your blood. Because . . . you have the darkling glamor."

Bred to darkling service . . . .

Could that have been in Gerridon's mind when he sent the Dream-weaver across the Barrier to Ganth—to breed a nemesis, perhaps *the* Nemesis, bound to serve him? The abyss within her plunged down and down, to the cold hall, to the banners of the dishonored dead . . . .

Ashe caught her by the collar. "Not . . . yet."

Jame found herself leaning forward against the other's grip, staring down into milky nothingness. Almost over the edge . . . .

She reared back, appalled (how far to fall? a hundred feet? a thousand?), swung her legs inward over the wall, and stepped on her knapsack. The Book within shifted under her weight. She staggered, an inadvertent lunge with the Ivory Knife that sent Ashe hastily backward. The singer's iron-tipped staff swung up on guard. Bane rose behind her, a thing of clotted mist and cold eyes, reaching.

"No!" said Jame.

Haunt and demon stood still, the former almost enfolded in the latter's arms. Ashe could have been said to hold her breath, if she'd had any.

Let him take her, Jame thought. A crumbling dead thing, half sunk in shadows already . . . how could a haunt be anything but her mortal foe? Then she remembered the dead in the Haunted Lands keep, rustling. Which one of her childhood friends had attacked her outside the keep's broken walls, its mind decayed to gray scum, its rotting teeth buried in her arm?

"Haunt-sickness nearly killed you once," Ashe had said.

. . . the darkness of infection under her skin, in her blood, festering, undeserved . . . .

Who was she to judge Ashe, anymore than Bane?

"Let her go," she said. "D'you hear me? Now."

If Bane didn't agree, at least he obeyed, melting back into the mist with the ghost of a whisper: . . .*'s your pyre, lady* . . . .

Ashe leaned on her staff, the hood overshadowing her haggard face. In a mortal woman, the slump of her shoulders would have looked much like vast weariness.

"Whatever he could have done to me . . . perhaps would have been only a mercy. That too."

Jame realized that she was still clutching the Ivory Knife, that she had almost used it on Ashe—inadvertently? The damn thing had killed as if by accident before. It always had been and would be avid for death.

"Dammit," she burst out, "how can I survive Honor's Paradox saddled with things I can't control?"

Ashe straightened slowly. "What . . . things?"

"This." Jame held up the Knife. "And this."

A kick slid the knapsack within the singer's reach. Ashe flipped back its cover with her staff and stared at the contents.

"Ancestors preserve us. Carried around like a . . . change of underwear." She looked up sharply. Light caught her sunken, death-clouded eyes. "And the third object of power . . . the Serpent-skin Cloak?"

"Last seen slithering back into the Master's house. It didn't seen to fancy my company."

"No," said Ashe, as if to herself. "It wouldn't. Argentiel never favors Regonereth, preserver . . . against destroyer. See here. This is dangerous. Without the Cloak, the other two are seriously out of balance. The Knife . . . is bad enough, but the Book . . . ! You don't know how to read it, of course . . . but if it should fall into the wrong hands . . . ."

Jame turned away. The wretched creature was calling her ignorant and irresponsible—with reason. The Book *had* gone astray three times since she had become its guardian. Ishtier, the Sirdan Theocandi, and Graykin had all possessed it briefly, the first two with the knowledge to make fearful use of it. And she had almost given it back to Ishtier, to save herself. As for her own misuse of its master runes, the less said, the better. If the Book and the Knife *were* intended for her, patently she didn't yet have the wisdom or strength to wield them responsibly.

Jame sighed. "If I could safely put them aside, I would."

"I think," said the haunt singer, "that I know . . . a way."

V

ASHE'S WAY LED DOWN into the wooden labyrinth, almost to the lower hall.

At no level did Jame see any sign of weirding. Mount Alban must indeed have regained its foundation and encasing cliff face. So, at least, Index clearly believed, pattering past without seeing them, so eager to reclaim his beloved herb shed that he again scorned the slow-moving platform. Otherwise, the college rested except for the groan of settling timber. Most of its elderly inmates had at last put aside their experiments. Their voices murmured down the stair well, then faded as they retired to their diverse lodgings in the upper levels for a well-earned late afternoon nap.

Jame knew that she should also rest. Much longer without sleep would impair her judgment, if it hadn't already. Ashe's dark figure shambled ahead of her; behind crept Bane's shadow, almost but not quite treading on her own. This might have been the descent into some dark dream, except for the brush of Jorin's whiskers against her hand as the ounce trotted close at her side.

They came to an iron-bound door, set in the college's eastern wall, hard against the mountain face. The cool, dank breath of stone met them when Ashe unlocked it and darkness waited beyond. The haunt took a torch from a bracket and lit it, revealing a rough-hewn passage. Jame and Jorin followed the singer down it for some twenty feet before it ended at the edge of an abyss. Torchlight could reach neither the bottom, nor the top, nor even the far side of that great emptiness. The drip of water in its depths echoed upward, distorted.

"Is this what you brought me to see?" Jame asked.

No answer. No Ashe. Only her torch moving to the left, apparently along the sheer wall of the chasm. Then Jame saw a walkway carved out of the cavern's side and hurried to catch up with the light.

Sometimes the walk crept under low ceilings jagged with stalactites; sometimes it careened with a perilous slant along the chasm's sheer drop. Parts of it had been damaged by the recent tremors; parts, by quakes long past. A wonder, thought Jame, that the whole honey-combed mountain hadn't collapsed in on itself ages ago. Possibly Mount Alban's ironwood skeleton had fore-stalled that. The tips of her gloves began to soak through as she ran them along the wall to steady herself. The stones wept continuously, tears turning to drops of fire as they caught the torch light, tumbling past the black, crumpled forms of sleeping bats clustered in fissures. Blind, white crickets the size of her fist scuttled away from the brand's heat. What if there were trogs?

The light vanished.

Jame pressed back against the stone wall, blind in the sudden dark. The emptiness of the abyss seemed to tug at her. She remembered the chasm in the Ebonbane snow field, the terror of falling, the Arrin-Kens' sus-pended death sentence.

Dammit, no one is going to push me, if I don't want to jump . . . .

A few feet to the left, light glimmered. Jame edged toward it, and discovered a side-cave. Down three stone steps, there was a low-ceilinged antechamber cut from living rock and at its back, an iron door scabrous with rust. Ashe had laid down the torch and was struggling with a key. It turned, groaning, in the lock. She dragged opened the door.

Jame stopped at the foot of the steps. She didn't need Jorin's senses to hear the mad scurry within, as if of countless multi-segmented bodies seething away from the light. Through the crack, she saw a bare stretch of rough stone floor, the ruins of an iron chair, and a small iron table still half obscured. All the shadows' edges blurred with the torch's flare and furtive movement.

Ashe stepped aside. "Enter," she said.

For a moment, as clearly as she had felt the haunt's impulse to shove her off the wall, Jame saw the door slam shut—behind her. Her eyes filled with darkness; her ears, with the obscene in-rush of swarming life.

"Haunt," she said thickly, "you're joking."

"Afraid of shadows . . . darkling? I remember . . . what shadow stands guard . . . behind me. Put the Book and the Knife . . . on the table."

She could refuse. Leave. Back to the stalemate that had trapped her before? No. Wherever her way led now, it didn't retreat.

She ducked into the room. Good as her night vision was, she couldn't see its walls, nor did she wish to: that stealthy rustling surrounded her, all too close. It was a very small room, she sensed, and was glad for the cap that protected her hair. A tall man couldn't have stood upright, even if he had wished to. She put the Book Bound in Pale Leather on the lit side of the table. The darker half seemed surreptitiously to boil. When she placed the Ivory Knife next to the Book, however, the table top emptied with an unseen, verminous cascade off its far side.

"All right, haunt. Now what?"

"Now . . . leave."

"Just like that?" Jame turned to glare at her, surprised at how cheated she felt. This was no solution after all.

"Even locked, that door isn't going to keep out anyone determined. Believe me. I know."

"I didn't say . . . that there would be . . . no guard. Tell your pet demon . . . to stay."

A moment ago, disappointment had made Jame feel almost sick, but this was worse. "Ashe, no. I wouldn't confine my worst enemy here—well, maybe Ishtier, or Caineron, or Kallystine. Dammit, why does Mount Alban have a pest-hole like this, anyway?"

"Kendar builders discovered it. A secret Hathiri prison . . . perhaps for a secret prisoner. Who . . . we don't know."

"Well, I'm not going to order Bane to fill his place."

"Perhaps . . . you don't have to. Look."

He sat at ease in the rust-eaten chair, long, elegant legs stretched out before him. His black scale armor rustled with the overlapping wings of a million death's-head beetles. The spiders that had woven his fine gray boots hung inside them like ornaments. Silver wire-worms ringed his long, white fingers. All the finery of the tomb . . . .

But his smile jolted her back in memory to the night she had returned to find the Res aB'tyrr held hostage by his thugs and Bane himself waiting, just so, to welcome her home. Then as now, she had come from causing a man to be flayed alive—a hanger-on of Bane's, a miserable sneak-thief who had ambushed and nearly killed her friend Marc. Her revenge, like the smell of blood, had brought the thief's master down on her, not to claim vengeance in his turn but kinship.

They had talked of honor.

It wasn't his fault, he had said, that Marc had been hurt. Nothing was his fault. Forced into the Thieves'

Guild, hadn't he tried to protect his soul by entrusting
it to Ishtier? Wouldn't he redeem it and honor both in
the end by an honorable death? Until then:

*"Better to fall. Life loses all boundaries. No one can
tell you where to stop. Freedom . . . ."*

Jame shook herself back to the present. Here was the
dead, consumed with hunger for the living; the seducer,
seduced by his own argument; the man, whose soul she
had once offered to carry . . . and would again, if he
asked.

"Is that what you want me to do?" she demanded,
suddenly very angry. "To make myself answerable for
your soul? To tell you where to stop? To *order* you by the
blood-bond which you contrived between us? Dammit,
Bane, you always try to put responsibility off onto someone else! On Ishtier. On me. Without choice, there is no
honor, and I will *not* choose for you! If you want to sit
in this hell-hole, in the dark, ancestors only know for how
long, it has to be your decision. Well? D'you hear me?"

Only his smile answered her, enigmatic, infuriatingly
intimate.

"Fine. Stay, then, and be damned to you!"

She stalked out. The door shut behind her, with a
screech of rusty hinges cut short by a dead thud. She
pivoted, full of sudden misgivings, as Ashe with difficulty
turned the key in the lock. In her mind was an image
which she had been too late to see: Bane's sleeve trailing
across the Book Bound in Pale Leather, his fine-boned
hand at rest on the Ivory Knife. Shut away in the seething dark . . . .

"This isn't going to work," she said, dry-mouthed.
"Dead or not, he has to eat. We can't just let him starve."

"He won't." Ashe turned to face her, key in hand.
"The door will keep out . . . only the idly curious. Keep

it quiet as we may . . . word will spread of the treasure inside. From time to time . . . he will feed very well indeed."

Jame stared at her. "My God, you're cold-blooded."

"Of course. I'm dead."

She slipped the key through a slash in her robe, into the corresponding sword-cut underneath, as if into an inner pocket. The lips of the wound were shriveled and bloodless, the rib glimpsed through them, discolored white. The key's outline showed clearly through the skin, against the bone.

"Why don't you just swallow the damn thing?" Jame demanded.

"Because . . . it might fall through."

Jame sat down abruptly on the stone step. No sleep, no food, and now this.

"All right, kitten, all right," she said to Jorin, whose fore-paws were on her knee, his nose anxiously touching her own. But inside she was raging at herself.

How easily she had let Ashe and Bane manage her. Should she have given up the Book and Knife, when they had chosen her as their guardian over and over? Should she have agreed to Bane's living burial, assuming he was still alive? Only now did she realize how desperately she had wanted to be rid of both them and him—enough to have let herself be tricked into consent?

"That knife may have been given to me to use," she said. "What if I need it someday?"

"Then call. I think . . . he will bring it to you . . . with help."

Jame shuddered. Into her mind had come the image of that "help": a trail of disintegrating victims, chosen at random, ridden and discarded as Bane ate the soul out of each in turn.

"More guts on the floor," she said, shaken. "Perhaps across the breadth of Rathillien and beyond. Sweet Trinity. Whose responsibility will *that* be?"

"His, who feeds," said Ashe, clouded eyes merciless with the logic of honor. "And hers, who calls."

A rumbling tremor passed through the stones surrounding them, followed by a series of loud cracks and crashes outside.

"Bloody hell," said Jame. She found herself on her feet, without remembering having risen. With one hand she was steadying herself against the wall; with the other, clutching Jorin's bristling ruff as he stood on her toes. "Haven't we had enough of this?"

But she spoke to herself, in abrupt darkness. Ashe had snatched up the torch and darted out of the antechamber. Swearing, Jame scooped up Jorin and followed.

The brand already bobbed far ahead, throwing contorted, confusing shadows behind. Jame called on her trained memory to show her the way, but memory didn't encompass the changes wrought in the past few minutes. Echoes crashed farther and farther away, as if a dozen unseen cave-mouths had caught the sound and were gnashing it to pieces. Sections of the ledge had fallen. Others shifted, grating, under her feet as Jorin wriggled with fright in her arms. More light would have been welcome. Ashe might hesitate to push her, Jame thought grimly, but clearly wasn't above letting her fall.

The earth growled again deep in its throat, as though trying to clear it. Bats exploded from a crevice almost in her face, a black cataract ascending. Ten feet, five, and here, ancestors be praised, was the lip of the tunnel.

"Earth Wife, Earth Wife," she cried, turning, shouting into the abyss. "Leave us *alone!*"

"That," said Ashe, behind her, "was not helpful."

Darkness swallowed the haunt's hoarse voice, but Jame's still echoed from wall to wall, down to the depths, up to the heights. From far, far above came an answer—a crack like the splitting of worlds and then a massive downward rush. The wind of it threw Jame back into Ashe and sent the latter's torch flying, a moment before something smashed off the tunnel's shallow lip. Jame had the dazed impression of a giant's jaw full of ragged teeth, savagely biting down. No. A plummeting section of cave roof, studded with stalactites. The echo of its fall crashed off into the distance, starting more rock-falls farther and farther away. From above, light filtered down, full of dust and broken bat wings.

Jame disentangled herself from the haunt faster than was strictly polite.

"The tremor must have breached the cliff-top," she said, leaning perilously out to peer upward. "But why is it getting brighter?"

The answer came billowing down the opened shaft.

They bolted down the tunnel with weirding on their heels and tumbled into the college. Too late to shut the door. Mist rolled in after them, over them, a soft, sighing avalanche. Jame clung to the floor, all her nails out, Jorin pinned squawking under her. She could see and hear nothing else, except the pounding of her own heart.

Then the mist began to subside. It drained between floor boards into the supports beneath; it twined up load-bearing piers and across ceiling beams like tendrils of dry rot. Whatever ironwood it touched, it sank into and replaced. The bones of Mount Alban were becoming ghosts of their former selves which still, hesitantly, upheld the college's weight. The floor boards beneath

Jame shifted uneasily, like a raft launched on a troubled sea.

"Adrift . . . again," said Ashe.

She sounded pleased.

 **VI**

IT'S ALL COMING LOOSE, Jame thought as she followed Ashe through the maze toward the presumed safety of the main stair.

Underfoot, floor boards bobbed. Overhead, the ceiling rippled. Weirding glowed and smoked through every crack like cool fire smoldering inside the walls. Nothing was settled, after all, nothing finished. Was she disappointed, or relieved?

At least, Bane had definitely been left behind. And the Book. And the Knife. She had done without all three often enough before. Why did their absence now make her feel so vulnerable?

Having to trust a haunt didn't help, even in so small a matter as finding a flight of stairs. Moreover, it seemed to her that Ashe was deliberately going as slowly as she could.

Some thoughts are louder than others . . . .

Over her shoulder, the singer gave her a rictus grin. "D'you want . . . something to fall off me?"

The deceased she could deal with, thought Jame, or even the demented, but the decayed? Fragments of Ashe's thoughts crawled through her mind like maggots.

The haunt was glad not to see Mount Alban's journeys end with unfinished business, not when she still had the right test to find.

The right test for what?

More glowing beams, studs, and stanchions, their reality elsewhere, their boards left resting uneasily on weirding support. Before, the college's main framework had resisted much longer, the softer woods melting away first. If this replacement held true throughout, Mount Alban had been boned like a fish.

The rooms of the lower maze were mere attics for the Bashtiri halls below or cellars for the keep far above. At least, they seemed never to have been used for anything but storage. Strange shapes loomed out of corners. Rotting crates spilled their contents across the floor, centuries' worth of scholastic pack-rattery hidden under a gray pelt of dust.

But here was a room where the muddled stacks had been pulled apart—recently, by the torn webs still fluttering about them. Something in their disarray suggested curiosity rather than a deliberate search, and a certain amount of disinterested vandalism.

The dust on the floor was roiled with foot prints. Jame bent over them. In the soft light streaming through the door from the landing beyond, she saw that the feet that had made them were naked, one set huge, the other no bigger than a child's.

"Ashe," she called. No reply. "Ashe!"

The haunt singer stood looking up at the main stair. It glowed, treads, risers, supports, all sculpted in the finest detail in weirding mist. The spine of the college, gone too.

"We . . . are not alone," said Ashe.

The ghost of a snicker seemed to answer her.

Crooked halls opened off the landing in all directions. A murmur of approaching voices came from one, but which?

Kirien and Kindrie emerged from a doorway behind them.

"Ashe," said the former. "Ancestors be praised. Have you any idea where we are?"

"Dislodged from the Alban cliff. Upstream . . . given the weirding's northward flow. Probably caught . . . on the ruins opposite Restormir, or at Tagmeth beyond that. And the upper keep?"

"Left behind. We were on the stair coming down when the weirding surge rolled over the cliff top. The curtains weren't up to keep it out. It came down the stairs, sinking in and changing them. Brier Iron-thorn was right behind us, but before she could jump clear it lapped over her feet. Odd, but I could have sworn that I heard someone below call her name. Anyway, she set that ironwood jaw of hers and just kept walking down into it."

"L-like a ghost," said Kindrie, obviously still shaken. "More of her insubstantial with each step. T-then she just vanished. Ancestors only know where she is now."

"With the stair, presumably," said Jame, "wherever *that* is."

She spoke lightly, but her stomach had tensed. They had been incredibly lucky to weird-walk in one piece all the way north from Wilden to Restormir. Their sheer number—ten cadets, two Highborn, and a cat—might have helped. Now Brier was on her own in the mist, perhaps several places simultaneously if the stair had displaced in steps.

"What about you?" she demanded of the Shanir healer, dropping her voice. "You should still be safe in the infirmary, asleep."

"I woke up." Kindrie shot her a pale-eyed look, frightened but defiant. "Captain Hawthorn was trying to decide what to do with that . . . that mess you left behind. Brier said she had better go after you. I-I followed, and met the Lordan Kirien looking for Index. I thought . . . ." He swallowed and tried again. "I thought you might need me."

Jame bit back a sharp reply. In the past few hours, she'd had to acknowledge bonds with both a demon and a haunt. Now here was another connection, just as strong, twice as natural. All winter, searching for her dead family, and she couldn't stomach a live first cousin simply because he had fallen into the hands of priests?

"I did need you," she said, rubbing her tired face with a gloved hand, feeling the scar ridge like a knotted cord under the mask. "I still do. But I don't trust myself or my reflexes. I'll hurt you, Kindrie Soul-Walker. I can't help it. Stay away from me."

"This little side-trip may not amount to anything," Kirien was saying to Ashe. "My guess is that we well and truly hooked onto the Mount Alban fort ruins before the tremor and this last surge of weirding swept the college core temporarily northward. We're like a . . . a plucked bow string, vibrating, the middle out of line with both top and bottom—or the upper keep and the lower halls, in our case. Everything should snap back together again soon."

"Not soon enough to prevent visitors," said Jame.

She told them about the disarranged storage and the naked foot prints in the dust. For a moment, they looked at each other in dismay, then up, as someone above suddenly bellowed, in a voice trained to carry:

"If you lot of egg-heads can't sleep, we singers can. Shut *up!*"

For the first time in Mount Alban's travels, the academic community wasn't in the upper keep, prepared, safe—nor, apparently, did it realize that the college was on the move again.

"Where are the two randon ten-commands?" Jame asked.

"All in the upper keep, except Brier Iron-thorn," said Kirien, still looking upward, a frown drawing together her fine, dark brows. Her house was the protector of Mount Alban; its safety, her personal responsibility as the Jaran Heir.

"In that case," said Ashe, watching her, "we had better find out . . . where we are."

The main stair being unavailable, they used another, older one nearby, which cork-screwed drunkenly down a narrow shaft into what should have been a minor Bashtiri hall. Wooden treads gave way to fire-blackened stone. The well opened out. They were now descending a mural stair, circling a stone walled chamber some forty feet across past the charred stumps of floors. Mount Alban roofed them, its under-structure a seeming chaos of wooden planks and phantom, weirding beams.

More wood filled the bottom of this stone structure—logs, branches, brush, piled promiscuously together, red tinged by the light falling from narrow apertures above. Jame paused to look out one. The cloud ceiling had lowered again, almost to within reach of this third story window. A setting sun had kindled the weirding inside it, brightest above the hidden mountains to the west but already deepening to blood ruby with the fall of night. Crusts of snow sheltered under boughs on the opposite bank of the Silver. How far north had the weirding taken them? There was no sign on that dark slope of Restormir or the ruins opposite Tagmeth.

"This," said Ashe, looking over Jame's shoulder, "does not . . . bode well."

"What?" Kirien demanded, instinctively keeping her voice low. "You think you know where we are, don't you . . . . What's that?"

Ching! went a jangling bell-tone. *Ching, ching,* approaching from the left, passing by out of sight beneath the window. *Ching, ching, ching,* on to the right, northward and then east, circling the outer wall.

They followed its progress clockwise down to the tower's second story front door, which stood open. At the foot of a flight of stairs lay a flagstoned courtyard, an open well shaft gaping at its center. Most of the surrounding buildings, like the tower keep, had been touched by fire, rain, and long neglect. The barracks to the left in particular had been gutted, its roof collapsed, trees growing up through the ruins. Wild grape vines sighed against the wall behind it. Faint lines showed on the weathered stone, nearly washed away—a series of circles, each with three smaller circles inside, like so many round eyes and mouths gaping.

"Kithorn," said Ashe.

Then Jame recognized it too, not because she had ever seen this sad place before but because her Kendar friend Marc had described it to her so clearly—his childhood home, until Merikit had slaughtered everyone in it almost eighty years ago. That, and Marc's revenge, had closed these hills to the Kencyrath ever since, except for boys slipping up to these ruins on a dare to search for relics of its garrison. Last winter, her brother had come here on a similar mission and accidentally left the old tower in flames behind him.

A shiver ran down Jame's spine. From these walls, Tori had seen the Burnt Man face to face.

She ducked back. Seven figures had trotted into the courtyard through its eastern gate, one after another. Four of them were not the Burning Ones, as she had for a moment feared, but half-naked Merikit elders, smeared white with ash, each carrying a sack. Breasts made of goat udders swayed under gray hair loose to the waist.

Ching went the bells strapped to their ankles. *Ching, ching!*

Between them came three figures if possible even stranger: an overpadded parody of a woman with a hard, male face framed by a wig of straw; a dripping wet youth festooned with bladder weeds; an incredibly hairy man, aflutter with black feathers knotted to every elflock.

The whole procession jogged solemnly sunwise around the courtyard, *ching, ching, ching*.

"First close the outer circle," said Ashe softly, "then circle the inner square . . . to create sacred space. The summer rites begin."

"And we," said Kirien, "are inside the circle."

The first shaman-elder and the "woman" stopped at the eastern corner of the square which their perambulation had defined. The second elder halted with the feathered man to the south; the third with the wet boy, to the west; the fourth by himself to the north. While the three squatted patiently in their corners to wait, the four ash-smeared elders emptied their sacks respectively of clay, wicker, bucket, and kindling. Along with this last came tumbling out what appeared to be a crude, black skull. The solitary elder began to arrange the kindling around it, crooning softly in an age-cracked voice.

Jame recognized that chant. Four days ago, north of Falkirr, she had heard the charcoal-blackened Merikit sing it as he laid a Summer Eve bonfire. The Burnt Man's bone which she had taken from that site was no longer in her pocket. Now where . . . . Ah. She had forgotten to reclaim it from Index.

Index, who had come down here before them. Sweet Trinity, where was *he*?

Other Merikit emerged from the surrounding ruins—a good dozen of them half-naked like their elders and intricately tattooed. A nervous young man in green homespun appeared last, with obvious reluctance, gingerly holding an ivy crown.

Kindrie made a stifled sound. A huge, young Merikit stood close beside them, wearing scarlet drawers and nothing else. His long, fox-red hair was all combed to the left into a dozen or more braids. His heavy arms and chest were black with tattoos. He must have come down from Mount Alban, for surely those big, bare feet matched one set of the prints which Jame had seen above. Green, slightly crossed eyes widened in wonder as he touched the Shanir's white hair. He gave it a tug. Kindrie gasped, almost falling. The big man grinned and took a firmer grip.

"No," said Jame, as if to a large, chancy dog, and put her hand on the Merikit's elbow.

Her nails found the nerve. He let go of Kindrie with an exclamation, eyes bulging at first with astonishment, then with outrage. He was, thought Jame, looking up, very, very big.

Something crashed down the Mount Alban stairs: a storage crate, disintegrating as it fell. Butterflies caught perhaps a hundred summers ago shimmered azure and amethyst, gold-veined and bronze, their wings turning to dust with the first frantic beat. The crimson moss that had preserved them rained down like a shower of sparks. From above, quite clearly, came a snickering laugh.

The big Merikit laughed too, but the grin which he turned down on Jame was bright with malice. He juggled one of the moss clumps from hand to hand, as if it were as fiery as its color, then tossed it onto the jumble of dry branches below.

"Oh my God," breathed Kirien, staring down at the wood pile, then up at Mount Alban's vulnerable under-pinnings.

More bonfires than one had been laid for Summer Eve.

ᑳᔓᘏᓬ Interim VII ᘏᓬᑳᔓ

Mount Alban: 60th of Spring
I

"SO THIS," said Torisen, "is what the Jaran Matriarch meant about Mount Alban not being where it ought."

He was standing in the college's vaulted lower hall which looked perfectly normal, with one exception. So had the entire establishment as they had approached it, apparently untouched by the surge of weirding which had just rolled past at cliff-top level and the tremor which had run before it. He should have guessed, though, that the ghostly light spreading inside the cliff-face from window to window had had nothing to do with welcome. Now here was this ghostly stair molded in weirding mist and all the internal structure above too, as far as he could see, except for the shadowy lines of its ironwood skeleton.

"Hello?" he shouted up the glowing well. "Is anyone there?"

"They'll never hear you above," said Grimly.

The Wolver sat down on his haunches and began to lick a raw foot-pad. They had come over thirty leagues since sun-rise, exhausting several changes of mount, but he had insisted on running most of that distance. Better sore paws than more saddle sores. Now, however, he wasn't so sure.

Torisen had turned away, swearing under his breath. To have come so far, only to be thwarted again . . . . After a winter of hiding at Kothifir, this rush to reunion had caught him up like a spring thaw. He didn't know to what end he was hurtling, what would happen when, at last, he and his sister met, but meet they must. Soon.

Frustration sharpened by urgency turned him back to the stair's foot, set loose the innate power of a Highborn in his voice: "Dammit, COME DOWN!"

Grimly goggled, the fur slowly roaching up along his spine. Something *was* coming down the stair. At first, it seemed no more than wisps of smoke rising off each step in turn, then indistinct feet, legs, body, head—a complete ghost silently, steadily descending.

Torisen went back a step, almost tripping over the Wolver who had scuttled around behind him. His throat felt scraped raw by those ill-chosen words of command. What in Perimal's name had he summoned? Something in the set of those broad ghostly shoulders, that deliberate, grim tread . . . .

"Iron-thorn?" he breathed. "Brier? Dammit, Rowan, shut that door!"

Too late. A gust of wind swept into the hall around the steward's stocky form, rattling last autumn's leaves under her feet. The ghost on the stair faltered, then unraveled. Gone.

Rowan hadn't seen it. Expressionless as her scarred face always was, her tense carriage as she hurried down the hall betrayed a problem of her own.

"Don't tell me Kallystine has caught up with us!" Torisen exclaimed involuntarily.

Rowan almost smiled. "Not that. My lord . . . Blackie . . . we've found something you should see."

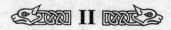

II

SOUTH OF MOUNT ALBAN, the damned horse slowed again, stumbling, ropes of bloody lather hanging from its lowered muzzle. Kallystine kicked at it savagely.

"Lady, ease up," warned the captain of her guard. "It's nearly spent."

M'lady cursed behind her mask. Damn Torisen anyway, for grabbing all the remounts between Gothregor and the scrollsmen's college, as if *that* would stop her. One by one as their horses failed, she had lost all her escort except its captain. She wouldn't catch the Highlord with a force behind her, but by God she *would* catch him, if she had to kill every horse in the valley.

A breath of wind teased her heavy travel mask awry. She jerked it back into place. Not since the assault by that Knorth bitch had she dared to look in a mirror, not that she had one left intact, but the potion's effect was only temporary. It *must* be.

. . . don't think about the maid's withered hand, clawing at the braid twisted around her neck, don't think . . . .

What did she have but her lovely, lovely face? What else was she? A glittering gown, a hollow mask . . . .

No. She was and always would be beautiful, *beautiful*—which was more than could be said, now or ever again, for the Knorth Jameth.

Remembering that, Kallystine smiled.

"Weirding coming up fast behind, lady," said the captain, looking back. "Another bank that should pass well overhead and a smaller patch at river level."

"Shut up. How far to Mount Alban now?"

"After the weirdingstrom, lady, that's hard to say. I haven't recognized half the land we've travelled through today."

"Damn you, how *far?*"

The randon sighed. "With luck, around the next bend."

Kallystine set her eyes on it and her heels to her horse.

Soon, she thought, with a hidden smile less pleasant even than the first. *Very, very soon.*

 **III**

THE GORGE NORTH OF MOUNT ALBAN echoed with the muted roar of the Silver. Overhanging trees dripped with spray and the stones of the River Road shone darkly. Bats flitted through shadows that had grown deep and cool with the sun's setting. Then larger shapes were among them, clowning in the spray, snapping bats out of mid-air and letting them drop, foxkin at play.

Their appearance preceded the clop of hooves, the jingle and groan of harnesses. Down the River Road came riders grimly upright in the saddle with the bloodshot eyes and strained faces of the hideously hung-over. One of them carried, drooping, a standard with the device of a serpent devouring its young, gold on black. A curtained horse litter followed. Beside it plodded an enormous draft-horse on whose back, hunched like a golden toad, rode Caldane, Lord Caineron.

His daughter Lyra followed him. Claiming that litter-travel made her sick (which it did, if she stuck a finger down her throat), she had been allowed to ride her little hill-pony. Consequently, at the end of this second day's travel, she was not only cold, tired, and hungry (as when was she not?) but also very saddle-sore. Nonetheless, how wonderful finally to be off on an adventure! She even took pleasure in feeling so much better, saddle-sores notwithstanding, than most of the Caineron Kendar. Once in Karkinaroth she had tried to pass on a stomach ache from too many sweets to her servant Gricki, without success. Father must know a very special trick to have so thoroughly inflicted the aftermath of his five day binge on his Kendar.

She bet that he wished he knew a trick as good, to get out of escorting Gran on this visit to the Women's Halls at Gothregor. He had better, Gran had said ominously, after incapacitating all her servants—except, of course, the Ear, whom nothing ever seemed to upset.

This would be their second night on the road, and they had come scarcely twenty-five miles south of Restormir. Gran complained of being jostled if they went faster. Besides, groggy Kendar kept falling out of the saddle, which Lyra had found hilarious, the first dozen or so times. By now, however, two-thirds of their company had been left behind and they had picked up a bare score of those Kendar who had been caught out on patrol when the weirdingstrom had swept down on them. The rest, it was hoped, would make their way home eventually. How long it would take some of those still at Restormir to recover from that terrible night's madness, no one could say. Lyra missed a dozen familiar faces in her father's retinue, without thinking much about it. She didn't know that they had quietly been slipped the white knife—and assisted in its use, if necessary.

Meanwhile, Gran had been hectoring Father for two days about the over-indulgence which had left them so short-handed, and about any other of his faults which she could bring to mind. Now, with sunset, she turned to his lack of foresight. If they had followed the New Road on the west bank, they would have been at the Jaran's Valantir by now, snug for the night. Did he *want* her to catch her death of cold out in this wilderness? Well? *Did* he?

Father hunched ever lower in the saddle, muttering.

Lyra nudged her pony closer, trying to eaves-drop, and ducked as Gran's foxkin Precious swooped close overhead, big ears cocked.

"*What* did you say, young man?" demanded Gran, peering at him through the leaf-patterned curtains of the litter. From behind her came the Ear's earthy chuckle. How *could* the two of them fit in so small a space? "You'd like to do *what?*"

Father started to answer, but a hiccup stopped him. He clutched wildly at his horse's mane, as if to anchor himself. Lyra wondered if that was also why he had put on every scrap of heavy gold he could wear. She knew for a fact, having seen it, that last night his servants had staked him down like a tent. His mount, the largest in the farm stable, laid back its ears, set its prognathous jaw, and plodded stolidly on.

They rounded a bend. The river divided around a wooded island, plunging down on either side in rapids and falls. Father straightened, staring from his superior height at something below still hidden from his daughter.

"My barge," he said thickly. "My beautiful barge," and spurred his mount into a heavy trot toward Mount Alban.

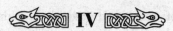 **IV**

ROWAN LED TORISEN OUT the smallest of the hall's three inset doors and through the old fort ruins beyond. Stones still rattled down from the cliff after the most recent tremor. Such after-shocks might be expected for days, Torisen had been told, assuming (dire thought) that they weren't instead a prelude to worse. No one knew yet what permanent changes so severe a weirdingstrom might have wrought down the entire length of the Silver. He noted, however, that not one leaning stone of the ancient fort had toppled. In their midst, ready for Summer Eve, someone had laid a small bonfire.

On the shoulder of the foothill where the fort stood, Torisen paused to look down the valley. The sun had just set over its western rim and purple shadows were lengthening down its slopes. The river threaded through them alight in the after-glow of sunset with that argent gleam which had given it its name. No sign yet of Kallystine. Good.

It was strange that he had ever felt attracted to that gilded lady or, for that matter, that he thought of her with such aversion now. Both emotions seemed unreasonably strong, especially in that he preferred not to feel strongly about anyone: it was too much like being in their power. He had long suspected Kallystine of trying to manipulate him through unnatural means. Soon their contract would expire, ancestors be praised—but Caineron had made it clear that he would consider failure to reinstate as a mortal insult. Oh, for an unequivocal excuse to break clean away.

Patches of weirding drifted by down by the Silver, tinged red by the setting sun. Their silent passage reminded him of Brier Iron-Thorn's ghost-like descent and disappearance . . . where? Northward, presumably, with the weirding-flow. That was probably where Mount Alban's innards had gone as well—taking Jame with them? Oh, to slip away like that, out of everyone's reach, as he used to do into the Southern Wastes . . . .

"This way, my lord," said Rowan impatiently. "Around on the south side."

The "something" which she wished to show him hung tangled in cloud-of-thorn bushes at the cliff's foot. It was a canvas sack, as long and thin as a rolled carpet, but disturbingly articulated. It must have fallen or been thrown from high above, to have smashed its way so far in among the tough branches before stopping, impaled. Blood ran down the long thorns from the punctured bag. The sodden ground beneath shimmered with the azure wings of feasting jewel-jaws.

Torisen realized why Rowan was watching him so anxiously.

"No doubt," he said, "someone will eventually stuff my sister in a sack and throw her off the highest cliff available, but not this time."

How he knew, as at Gothregor, that Jame still lived, he couldn't (wouldn't?) say, even to himself. Once again, Torisen was uneasily aware of questions unasked . . . of unwanted answers?

"Highlord!" said a voice overhead.

A randon officer dropped down beside them, seemingly out of the sky.

"Captain Hawthorn, isn't it?" Torisen looked up. Those naked trunks which he had taken for dead trees growing out of the cliff-face . . . . "Is that thing some sort of a ladder?"

"Yes, lord. 'Some sort' is about right, but it's come in handy despite itself. Not very good for carrying bodies down, though."

"So I noticed. Would it be tactless to inquire . . . ?"

"Who? Highlord, perhaps you can tell me."

Gingerly, the Brandan officer reached into the cloud-of-thorn and loosened the mouth of the sack. Out of it lolled a head. The Wolver growled. Those dead eyes seemed to stare at him, yellow irises and whites so suffused with blood as to be almost indistinguishable. The rest of the face, too, was blood-smeared—over skin that didn't seem to be there at all.

"*Mere*-tattooing?" he demanded.

Torisen nodded curtly. "A Bashtiri Shadow Master, unmasked."

The assassin's jaw fell open, as if about to answer, and then fell off. It rattled down through the branches to the ground, scattering the jewel-jaws, but only for a moment. The Brandan captain flipped the canvas back over that terrible face. As she withdrew her hand, a thorn laid open the back of it.

"Damn," she said mildly, brushing away eager azure wings.

"That's the last Kencyr blood he will ever cause to be spilled," said Torisen, hard-voiced. He had always known what misery the Shadow Guild had caused his house, but never before had it seemed . . . personal. So this was the creature who had come to kill Jame. "Shove kindling under these bushes. Burn the carrion where it hangs. Now, captain, will you please tell me where my sister is?"

Somehow, it didn't surprise him that the randon didn't know.

"She ought to be back soon, though," Hawthorn said, as if Jame had merely stepped out on an errand.

Both glanced up as two Brandan cadets dropped down from the hanging stair, followed by a scruffy young man. The latter slunk off to one side, trying not to catch anyone's eye.

Hawthorn shrugged, dismissing him. "At least," she said, "with the whole college as chaperon, the young lady can't get into too much trouble."

"Huh!" said Grimly.

Torisen had turned to look down the valley, which dusk was beginning to obscure. The Silver, tarnished, had lost its gleam except to the south, where it disappeared around a bend. There, the light on it grew, and on the cliffs facing it. A cloud billowed silently around the turn, its heart coolly on fire as if with continual heat lightning. It filled the valley from side to side, its raised skirts trailing over the top of the foothills, its crown just below the cliff summits.

It wasn't the approaching cloud, however, at which Torisen stared with such dismay. Under it came two riders on limping, lathered mounts—a randon officer incongruous in dress grays and a heavily masked lady. The randon's horse fell. Its rider jumped clear and reached for the lady's stirrup, either to stop her or to run along at her side. The slash of her riding crop made the randon spring back. Then the lady caught sight of the watchers on Mount Alban's hill. Her whip fell again, this time on her mount's bloody flanks. The beast tottered into a trot. Those above could hear the tortured wheeze of lungs long past healing.

"On to Tagmeth?" suggested Grimly.

"Good idea."

They started down the hill toward their own tethered horses, Hawthorn accompanying them to get safely below the on-coming mist; but here came one of the Knorth Kendar, anxious with news.

"Highlord, our scout to the north reports a company approaching on the River Road. She thinks Lord Caineron is leading it."

Damn. "How many troop?"

"Two one-hundred commands. My lord, we're outnumbered ten to one."

"I *can* still do simple arithmetic," said Torisen drily, but his heart had sunk. The last time Caldane had caught him at such a disadvantage, the previous winter at Tentir, he had almost ended up permanently confined as a dangerous lunatic. This time, the High Council wouldn't be so hard to convince.

"You still have nine cadets above, lord," said Hawthorn, "and I have eight more. Shall I call them all down?"

"Five to one, counting you. No, captain, I won't involve the Brandan."

Rowan appeared at his elbow, her expression as shocked as it ever got. "Blackie, in the herb-shed . . . you won't believe who we found . . . ."

"I don't care," said Torisen, "if it's the High Council, three ducks, and a goat." He was staring northward, at the huge horse which had just lumbered into sight on the River Road. "Sweet Trinity. Where d'you suppose it left its plow?"

"You could climb up to the cliff keep," suggested Grimly.

"Like a treed cat? Too late, anyway."

The leading edge of the mist passed overhead, obscuring the hill top and ruins. Its glow caught the silver in

Torisen's black hair, the fine bones in his face as he looked up at it speculatively.

"Oh no," said the Wolver, seeing him suddenly smile. "Oh, Tori, no."

 V

LYRA'S PONY SCAMPERED ON CALDANE'S HAIRY HEELS. The litter swayed wildly behind her, its postilion urged on by Gran's excited, bird-like cries from within. Foxkin dived around it. The Kendar vanguard kept pace, but didn't look as if they were much enjoying themselves.

They could all see Mount Alban now, over the broken wall that ran beside the road. Figures moved on the college's hill, under a passing mist bank. That slim one in black might be Jame, Lyra thought. Oh, splendid! Father seemed to think so too. He gave a hoarse shout and flailed his mount into an earth-shaking canter. Here was the front gate . . . .

. . . and suddenly from around the wall's southern curve came a masked lady on a blood-lathered horse. It skidded into Caldane's massive steed, staggered back, and stopped splay-legged, trembling.

Lyra almost didn't recognize her half-sister. She had always admired Kallystine's beauty and cool poise, both noticably lacking in this disheveled creature shrilly demanding that Father avenge slights which she had suffered at the Highlord's hands. There Torisen was now, going up the hill. Hadn't she followed him here all the way from Gothregor, he running before her like the yellow cur he was? Was she to be thwarted of her revenge at last by Caineron cowardice? No, dammit, that was *not* Jameth!

Father insisted that it was, so that he might finally have the pleasure of tearing the wretched brat limb from limb.

He and Kallystine were shouting at each other now. The raw, undisciplined power in their voices shoved the Kendar back as if from the heat of a pyre. The little postilion fell off his horse and lay motionless at its feet. Lyra retreated, frightened.

She glanced up the hill. The dark figure, whoever it had been, had disappeared into the glowing mist, followed by what looked like a huge dog. Other people were gathering around a man incongruously clad in desert gear who had just emerged from a wooden shed on the hill's north side. Why, that looked just like old Lord Ardeth. How very peculiar.

A stifled exclamation made Lyra look down. Out of the bushes growing by the front gate, a thin, familiar face stared up at her in horrified surprise.

"Why, Gricki!" she exclaimed, but softly: even as she had recognized her former servant, she had remembered what sport Father had made of him in the tower at Restormir—because he couldn't lay hands on Gricki's new mistress? Now Jame had escaped again. Father would want to make someone suffer for that, horribly, but what could she do?

"Psst!" hissed Gran through her leaf-patterned curtains. "Psst, boy! I *never* forget a voice. Get in."

Gricki shot her a doubtful look.

"Go *on!*" whispered Lyra, almost faint with this, the first time she had even obliquely defied her father. Nonetheless, it must be done. She might have treated Caldane's Southron bastard like the excrement after which she had named him, but he belonged to Jame now; and Jame, not Kallystine, was the sister of her choice. What had she renamed the wretched fellow? "Graykin, *go!*"

He looked up at her, astonished, then suddenly grinned. Her dancing pony gave him cover as he darted across to the litter and dived into it, head first. Lyra expected him to shoot straight through it, out the other side, but he didn't. He, Gran, and the Ear must be sitting on top of each other.

Kallystine gave a startled cry, abruptly cut off. Lyra looked up too late to see her vanish, but there went Father, swallowed whole by a rolling patch of mist. It billowed up over her like a cresting wave. As she stared, too frightened to move, the Ear's strong, grimy hands plucked her out of the saddle and pulled her into the litter.

She expected to fall on top of someone, but instead found herself sprawling on a cool, yielding surface, with loam under her hands. Weirding threw into relief the foliate pattern woven into the curtains. Foxkin dove in through the leaves. In the dim light, she saw them hanging upside down from the litter's framework . . . or were those branches? Graykin crouched near her, staring openmouthed about him. Gran sat on a puff of pillow moss, grinning toothlessly at their amazement. The other end of the litter was occupied by the Ear, on a throne of roots, canopied by leaves. She loomed as big as a bear, indistinct except for the gleam of her eyes. Weirding sighed around them. The foxkin rustled furry wings and then were still.

"All gathered up?" asked Gran.

"All," said the Ear's deep, gruff voice, a sound licked together out of darkness. "Now, let's go to a fire."

PART
 VIII

KITHORN

forge

Gate House

BONEFIRE

BASIN

WELL

LODGE

CAGE

Tower Keep

bluff

black walnut

Postern

spinney

N
W E
S

P.C.HODGELL

Kithorn: 60th of Spring

THE SUN HAD SET, but the lowered clouds still glowed with the sullen rubescence of banked coals. The air had grown very still. Its unseasonal warmth pressed down on the Merikit as they swept Kithorn's courtyard, renewed the *imus* drawn on its crumbling walls, and placed long-shafted torches in sockets around its inner square. These last hadn't yet been ignited. The shaman-elders continued their preparations under that flaming sky, watched by the three fantastically dressed Merikit squatting behind them and, less stoically, by Jame, through the smithy's barred window. She supposed that the intricate patterns which they had drawn on the four quarters of the square were the sigils of their gods. She also recognized the bone-fire being laid just outside at the square's northern corner. What was the purpose, though, of the box constructed of clay slabs to the east, or the wicker cage to the south, or the basin to the west?

This last had been revealed by the tipping back of a flagstone and appeared to be of great antiquity. Like the hill fort ruins to the south, Kithorn's court must be much older than the surrounding keep. Just look at that well at its center. Who in recent times would have dug so wide a shaft in such a remote place or rimmed it with what looked like serpentine marble? Damage to the stonework suggested that the Kencyr garrison had covered it with a more conventional hood and winch. The elder now straining to draw up a bucket of water must wish that the gear had been left in place. Feet braced, muscles quivering under age-loosened skin, he might be trying to reel in the River Snake itself.

Huh. *That* monster. Hadn't the cadet Rue said that its head lay under this very well and Cattila, that the Merikit would send down a hero to master it? Maybe they had already done so to stop the weirdingstrom —except that under this angry sky it hardly seemed over. Anyway, did she actually believe in the Snake, much less in the great Chaos Serpent that was said to have spawned it? More likely, such stories were only the Merikit version of a Lawful Lie. Rathillien couldn't be *that* much stranger than the Kencyrath thought—could it?

The shaman's bucket finally rose, full of shimmering silver. Over one side hung a great tail; over the other, a gap-mouthed head abristle with whiskers. The catfish flopped out onto the marble rim. For a moment, the elder goggled at it. Then he grabbed. Its barbed dorsal slashed his hand. He hastily bound up the cut with a switch of gray hair, but not before a drop of blood had fallen into the well.

From deep underground came a low rumble. The ground shuddered and flagstones ground together like teeth. Jame clutched the bars, feeling once again the terror of the living earth. How did one distinguish between fore—and after-shocks? What if all that had come so far had only been a prelude?

The tremor subsided. A vast sigh breathed up the well shaft, echoed by the catfish, which had crawled on its stubby pectoral fins over to the basin and gratefully plopped into it. The youth cast his mantle of weeds over the fish and hastily backed out of the square.

"*Bloop*," said the fish, spitting out a frond.

Jame remembered the catfish that had leaped out of the Silver during the last big quake and especially the one in the barge which had prevented her from drowning. This fellow looked not unlike the latter. Odd, how her encounters with the river seemed by turns primordial and personal.

Well, she wasn't on the Silver now and no fish was going to save her from her current predicament. Kirien had insisted that they not fight for fear of calling attention to Ashe, the Merikit having no tolerance at all for haunts. As a result, they had let themselves be made prisoners in this smithy, one of Kithorn's few intact buildings. Kirien, pacing back and forth behind her, clearly chafed at their helplessness even more than Jame did. Kindrie had retreated to a back corner with Jorin to keep out of her way. In the far shadows, Ashe and Index had resumed the discussion of Merikit fertility rites which the tremor had interrupted. The singer had pulled her hood well forward to hide her livid face. Perhaps Kencyr should learn from the Merikit, Jame thought, glowering at her. Why had she been so eager to put both the Book and Knife out of Jame's reach, just before they would have been really useful? Whose idea had it been, anyway, to trust a haunt?

Perhaps, at least, Mount Alban was safely away. But no. Moving to a chink in the western wall, Jame saw the panels which lined its inner wall still hovering ghost-like above the ruined tower, its upper reaches swallowed by low clouds red—lit as though already sullenly smoldering. Perhaps the weirding had already done its strange work there above. Perhaps the most valuable scholars in the college now slept in rooms detached from the fire-trap below. Perhaps. If not, they must be roused and brought down to safety.

Abruptly, her peephole was obscured. She jerked back as a stick was thrust through it. From outside came a hoot of laughter. That damned boy again. Tired of throwing boxes down Mount Alban's stair, he had descended to cause what trouble he could in the courtyard.

So had the large, young man in red, who was now swaggering around the square, trying to browbeat one elder after another, being waved away by each in turn. He looked like someone accustomed to getting his own way, unwilling to believe that this time he might not. The boy followed just out of reach, jeering. The big man stopped at the north corner and tried again.

Jame found Index at her elbow, listening avidly.

"Sonny-boy wants to play the Burnt Man," the old scrollsman said. "That's his father's role, Daddy being Chingetai, the tribal chief, but he's also not back yet from laying bone-fires around the Merikit borders for Summer Eve."

"I take it that there's to be a mummery," said Jame, who had seen such seasonal playlets often in the Old Pantheon section of Tai-tastigon's Temple District. New Pantheon priests sneered at their crudity, but they sometimes had surprising results, such as the year when all within earshot, including the men, had suddenly found themselves pregnant.

She understood now why the elders were so strangely attired. By the four-fold contradiction of male and female, human and animal, age and youth with unbound hair, life and ash-smeared death, they were trying to render themselves invisible to their gods. As important as they might be in the up-coming ceremony, they wished like puppet-masters to draw attention only to their puppets. But one of these, patently, was misbehaving.

"Hasn't . . . er . . . 'Sonny' already got a role? With those red pants, he's certainly dressed up for something."

"I told you she had a brain," said Kirien, coming up behind them.

Index sniffed. "Huh. But no more credit."

Kirien took a deep breath. "Index, I swear, if you withhold information now, with the entire college at hazard, I'll never barter with you again."

"Or I," said Jame. "Of course, if you don't *want* to be reminded how that precious herb shed of yours is arranged, or why . . . ."

Index glowered at her. "All right! Yes, Sonny has a role. Since last midsummer, he's been the Earth Wife's Favorite, the darling of the hills, although obviously not a very successful one."

"How can you tell?"

Index looked embarrassed. "For one thing, all his braids are on the left."

To signify the men Sonny had killed, Jame remembered. The absent right hand plaits would have been for children sired.

"Disappointing," she agreed solemnly.

"Er . . . yes. Also, it's dangerous. The Favorite's failure weakens the Earth, which consequently is less able to keep quiet the Chaos Serpent and its brood, including the River Snake. Hence this season of tremors. Therefore, the elders aren't waiting for Midsummer's Day, when the Favorite traditionally fights to retain his position. See that nervous fellow in green? That's the Challenger, already in possession of the ivy crown. The elders have told Sonny to lose."

"I can't see him liking that. If he obeys, though, what will happen to him?"

"In a quiet year, not much. To propitiate the River Snake, a goat would be thrown down the well in his place. This year, though, the Merikit believe that a hero has to be reborn in the Snake's belly so as to master it."

"An honor," said Ashe drily, "that most people . . . would rather decline."

"Including Sonny," said Jame, working it out. "Anyway, he'd prefer to play the Burnt Man—who, I gather, is always the chief. Would substituting for his father now give him a claim on the chiefdom afterward?"

"Yes. Which is something else the elders want to avoid. They'll keep the midsummer part of these rites as intact as they can, to please the Earth Wife, to quiet the Snake, and to provide the Burnt Man (that is, the chief) with this year's best choice of an heir."

"One out of three for Sonny," said Jame. "I wouldn't care to be snake-bait, either. Just the same, if we're dealing with real powers here, not just local politics, this is filthy dangerous. Not," she added, with a passing thought to Graykin, "that politics aren't. But with Earth and Fire involved, who knows what a mess Sonny may make of things? The elders must be worried sick."

"Index," said Kirien, looking out the front window, "when you studied the Merikit some eighty years ago, didn't you have a special crony among them? He was a shaman's son, I think."

"All right!" said Index again. "Yes, yes, yes! Tungit. That's the silly bugger out there now, singing to a pile of wood."

"Well, then, talk to him! He's been a guest at Mount Alban, he *can't* mean to incinerate all his former hosts."

But the old scrollsman was shaking his head. "We went through all that before you arrived. Tungit doesn't want to hurt anyone, but there's a Burnt Man's bone buried under the college as well as one out here. Both will kindle spontaneously if the rite succeeds. I'm telling you, a crisis like this supersedes the rules of hospitality, now, as it did eighty years ago. Bad enough that Sonny is playing the fool and we've stumbled in. Tungit won't even let the rest of the college come down for fear of upsetting things more."

"Wait a minute," said Jame. "Go back a bit. Are you saying that the Kithorn massacre was caused by a situation like this?"

"Very like." Index turned to her, eager to escape Kirien's insistence. "This courtyard has been a ceremonial site for time out of mind. The old lord who held this keep didn't mind. He even got his people out of the way so as to give the Merikit a free hand, so he didn't know about all the goats that'd been pitched down his well over the quiet years. The River Snake got 'em all, you see, so the water never suffered. But then there was a season of bad quakes and the Merikit planned to send down a hero. The lord got wind of it, though, and refused to have a corpse thrown down his only well. The Merikit were desperate. They thought, if they didn't do something, the Snake would destroy the entire Riverland. So they planned to seize Kithorn on Autumn's Eve and hold its garrison captive until their work was done. No one was supposed to be hurt."

"But the Merikit hall-guest who opened the gate cut the throat of the Kendar guarding it," Jame protested, remembering the story as Marc had told it to her.

Index nodded. "So he did. They knew that there would be a blood-price to pay for that, and they panicked. The barracks was sealed and set ablaze; the tower, stormed; the people—men, women, and children, Highborn and Kendar—slaughtered. Tungit wept when he told me, the last time we met before the hills were closed. And then, despite it all, the price fell due, because they'd missed someone."

"Marc."

"That's right." He gave Jame a sharp, surprised look. "A nice boy, that, despite everything. Big for his age."

"He still is."

"That's all ancient history," said Kirien impatiently. "Index, for the last time, *will* you ask your friend to stop this?"

"No! Dammit, I've done all I can!"

Jame wondered at his tone, at once exasperated and obscurely excited.

Even more, though, she wondered about the Merikits' purpose. There was something more to it than Sonny and the Snake, something that she should be able to guess, based on what she had seen and heard over the past few days. The Merikit were trying to combine two ceremonies this time, the first to quiet the Snake, the second . . . the second . . . .

She groped after the thought though a sudden haze of fatigue. The others' voices grew dim. Too damned long without sleep . . . . But then she was struggling back to the surface, away with a shudder from Ashe's cold, supporting hand.

"Trouble," said the haunt singer.

"You *want* this ceremony to continue, don't you?" Kirien was saying to Index, almost gently, but with a stir of power that made Jame's scalp crawl and Jorin growl in the corner where Kindrie held him. "You claim to be an authority on the Merikit, but the truth is that you have never before been permitted to witness a major seasonal mystery."

Index sputtered. "One needn't . . . Grindark rituals . . . Nekrien mythology . . . if one draws intelligent comparisons . . . ."

"But that isn't first hand experience, is it? For eighty years, since Kithorn fell and the hills were closed, you've been denied primary research, reduced to cataloging the details of others' work. Now comes this opportunity."

"*Nothing* happens by accident!" the old man cried. Before, he had sounded as defiant as a child trying to snatch a forbidden treat. Now he was backing away, as if from an assault for which his defences were proving unequal. "A chance like this . . . ."

" 'Chance' implies 'accident.' "

"Knowledge is everything!"

"Certainly, scrollsmen have died for it before, and killed."

So might this inexorable inquisition, slicing away the self-deceptions necessary to the old man's self-respect. At last Jame understood Ashe's concern: Anxiety had pushed the young scrollswoman into the academic equivalent of a berserker flare—a ruthless drive to lay bare the truth, regardless of the cost.

"Kiri . . . ." she said, awkwardly, out of her depth, "this isn't helping."

Cool, unblinking eyes turned on her. Their attention, focusing, drove her back a step. Too late, she realized that here lay the Shanir power not only to demand the truth, but to compel it.

"Helping what? Do you contend that self-knowledge is not of itself a worthy end?"

Jame winced, remembering the awful revelation of her own soul-image. "Perhaps," she said, "we can't endure to know ourselves too well. Perhaps . . . the truth can sometimes destroy."

"That which can be destroyed by the truth should be," said that implacable voice. Could any Arrin-ken have spoken with more authority? "Of what would you chose to remain in ignorance?"

Involuntarily, Jame started to answer, but then she stopped herself, swallowing hard. She felt a horrible sinking inside, as though fatigue had eaten out her heart and all was crumbling in toward darkness. Dammit, she would *not* be forced back into her own shadows. In a curiously detached way, she felt her anger try to spark an answering berserker flare, but exhaustion had dampened the tinder. She didn't even have the energy to argue, leaving . . . what?

"If I had a choice," she said, reaching up, "I would ignore this."

The mask came away in her gloved hands.

Kirien blinked. "Oh," she said, in a small voice.

"Effective," Ashe remarked. "As a point of debate, though . . . ."

"Agreed." Jame resumed the mask with fingers grown suddenly clumsy with fatigue. "It lacks subtlety. But then so did M'lady Kallystine."

Kirien had turned on Kindrie. "Healer, why haven't you done something about this?"

"Because I wouldn't let him," said Jame. "I may be a nemesis, Kiri, but I *won't* be his. Oh, hell . . . ."

She put a hand on the anvil to steady herself. Her reserves had been almost exhausted before. Resisting the Jaran had nearly finished her. Still, in justice to her cousin she must explain and did so, haltingly.

"When did you last rest?" Kirien demanded. "An injury like that requires *dwar* sleep. Lots of it."

"Not *dwar*. It'll set the scar."

"Oh, I suppose you'd rather just drop dead. Fools who won't sleep sometimes do. Listen. Nothing will happen here for . . . how long, Index?"

"An hour," said the old scrollsman sulkily. "Maybe two. *If* you'll accept a mere, informed guess."

"Very well. Until then, lady, you'll sleep, if I have to hit you over the head with a brick."

Jame laughed. "I have already been hit quite often enough, thank you," she said with careful enunciation. "Wake me when the fun starts."

She lowered herself stiffly to the floor by the west wall, finishing with a thump as her legs gave out. "Oh, my," she said, gathered Jorin in her arms, and tumbled over, fast asleep. The ounce licked her chin, then stretched out beside her with a deep sigh.

Ashe stood over them. " 'Nemesis,' " she repeated softly.

Kirien regarded her with alarm. "We still don't know that for certain, nor yet what kind, if it's true. For pity's sake, Ashe, if you still have tests in mind, postpone them. Haven't we enough trouble as it is?"

The haunt singer didn't reply.

"Ancestors know," said Kirien, after a pause, "*she's* got trouble enough. That face . . . ! Well, healer, what are you going to do about it?"

Kindrie's white head jerked up. "L-lordan, she told you . . . ."

"And I believe her. She was right to point out the risk. Now it's your decision whether to take it."

If Kindrie could have shrunk farther back into his corner, he would have, loathing himself all the more. After all, the young scrollswoman was only asking what he had already tacitly volunteered to do by coming down after the Knorth. Even then, though, he had doubted his ability to succeed, and been relieved to escape the test. Now it seemed that he hadn't. Dammit, what had happened to his nerves? Maybe he wasn't a hero like his two purebred cousins, but neither last winter had he been so very craven. No, just foolish, plunging into one misadventure after another through sheer ignorance, protected by the ability to heal himself of virtually anything. Now he knew where the risks lay, and, thanks to Ishtier, what their true costs were. Without the priest to unlock the way, perhaps he would never know the healing peace of his soul-image again.

If not, then what? Hide in dark corners the rest of your life?

No. Whatever he had lost, he had gained two things which he had never thought to have: a house and a name. He must try never again to be unworthy of either.

Get up, then, Kindrie Soul-Walker, and walk.

As he rose, his joints cracked like an old man's, full of shooting pains. This, too, was the mortality which Ishtier had made him taste. The others made way as he circled the anvil and crouched stiff-kneed by the Knorth. His hand, reaching out, shook. From her slow breath, she was already deep in *dwar* sleep. All barriers would be down. This was like standing on the edge of a precipice, all darkness below but in it lurking that monstrous house, that cold, blighted hall.

Take the plunge, Knorth. Go.

He touched her face.

THE RED CLOUDS began sluggishly to stir over the square, crimson patches silently appearing and disappearing, streaks of blood and fire swirling at the touch of no breeze felt below. The elders crouching each in his corner might have been so many fantastic statues, the "woman" and the feathered man hardly less so. Outside the square, the onlookers also stood motionless. All the workers had gathered at the southern corner, the challenger as if by chance keeping out of sight behind them. At the northern corner, in solitary splendor, even the big Merikit had lapsed into an expectant if morose silence.

Kirien wondered what they were waiting for. How much did any Kencyr, even Index, know about these wild hill-folk who had occupied the Riverland before the Kencyrath, before the old empires? If knowledge was power, surely this was its opposite. Therefore, she must also wait—for the Merikit to start, for Mount Alban (please, God) to escape, for the healing to finish.

"Why is it taking so long?" she burst out, speaking despite her anxiety barely above a whisper. "Obviously, no major muscles or arteries were cut. Early attention

would have healed it without a trace. Even now . . . !
How long does deep healing usually take?"

"How long . . . is a dream?"

"Ashe, please: no riddles."

"Rather, a metaphor . . . as are all dreams and soul-images. To a healer at work . . . time is subjective."

"Not entirely," said Index, screwing up his clever, monkey's face. "How long can a dream seem to last—a minute, a day, a lifetime? Sometimes, a healer ages accordingly. Why, I know one young chap who gained a century overnight."

As he spoke, he shot Kirien a malicious, sidelong look—his revenge, she thought, for having scared him so badly before. Not that she blamed him. What had possessed her, to have been so tactless? Oh, it had been exhilarating at the time, as debate so often was, but afterward . . . !

Still, the old bastard *would* raise a subject about which she had been trying very hard not to think.

Facts before theories, practical needs before specula-tion. She had said as much before to Ashe in conference, and had acted on it in pressing Kindrie to deal with Jame's injury. Still, a healer and a nemesis . . . .

Should she have forced two such people together, against the wills of both? What if they could only be mutually destructive? She wished she could see Kindrie's face, but his hair hung down over it, stained by the sullen light to a bloody fringe. His thin, sensitive fingers rested on the other's masked face with a moth's trembling touch. That fragile contact reminded her how precarious the balance between them must be. She flinched as Jorin whimpered and twitched, as if he were straining to plunge as deeply into sleep as his mistress. This time, however, she and the healer had gone where he could not follow.

"Listen," said Ashe softly.

Outside, at a distance, someone was shouting. That voice, although faint, carried as across a battlefield, an insistent rally-cry: "K-*north*! K-*north*!"

Back in the shadows, the breathing changed.

III

A thick, black thread stitched together a fold across the cheek of a death banner. Eye lid dragged down, mouth twisted up, that handsome, arrogant face seemed to sneer at its own deformity.

"Look at us, your precious ancestors. Are these honest faces? Are these kind?"

"Shut up," muttered Kindrie. "I'm not listening."

He shouldn't be talking, either. All that protected him was that his patient slept more deeply than he, although their *dwar* breathing matched. He must finish and extricate himself before she woke. He concentrated on ripping out that clumsy seam, one stitch at a time. How cruelly tight it was sewn. He worked a finger under the black thread and pulled. His nail split to the quick.

What is there here worth saving? We are a fallen house, a people utterly corrupt. Your house, your people . . . .

His torn nail caught on the tapestry's warp. The moldering strings broke and bled, like ruptured vessels, as he fumbled to retie them.

And what are you, who need us to prove your own worth?

. . . shut up, shut up . . . .

There. The warp stings were knotted back together and that damned black thread was free. It twisted like a whip-worm in his blood-slick hands, out of his grasp, up his sleeve. He felt it wriggle down to join the seething mass of scars already inside his jacket, inside the naked cage of his ribs. Fifty banners repaired. How many more to go? Row after row of disfigured faces lined the Master's cold hall, watching him askance, their rustle in the *dwar* wind snide with laughter.

You fatherless fool, you motherless bastard.

Kindrie slumped against the wall. He would never be able to mend them all, thereby restoring this soul-image to health. It had been mortally diseased to begin with. (*A fallen house, a corrupt people*—"I will *not* listen!") Perhaps a lifetime spent laboring here . . . but only a healer with access to his own soul would have the strength to attempt so epic a cure, though it might age and kill him in a night. Kindrie couldn't even control his own physical aspect on this level. That obscene roil eating out his guts—the symbolic equivalent of jewel-jaws in the stomach or of worms, feasting in the grave?

There it was again, that devouring fear of death which had made such a coward of him before. To enter this soul-scape, he'd had to match *dwar* breathing with his cousin. It still whistled in and out of him, his jacket acting as bellows to his fleshless ribs. He couldn't stop it. He couldn't wake. Without his soul's reserve, his real body would die of exhaustion in its sleep. At least it would go to a proper pyre. What if no such cleansing flames could reach here? Kindrie hugged himself, feeling the voracious churn within. His mind would be devoured inch by inch by his own fears, as real to him here as maggots in the flesh.

. . . crawling up his throat, about to spew out his mouth . . . .

"Stop it," he whispered behind clenched teeth. "*Stop it*, STOP IT!"

What allowed him to swallow that surge of panic, more than anything else, was a nagging doubt. He might not always like Jame, nor did he yet know quite what to make of her, but he no longer believed that she was the monster which Ishtier had claimed. If she really had come from such a vile place as this, it seemed to him that she had long since left it behind. How, then, could it still be the model of her soul? True, the death banners of these fallen Knorth accurately mirrored her injury. Any healer would look first for such a correspondence, and usually be right. They *might* represent her darkling fear of dishonor, but still . . . .

Had he been tricked into looking at the wrong thing? As his own soul-image consisted of an outer blind and an inner reality—the garden hidden within the priests' college—perhaps hers also was unexpectedly complex.

Think. Remember: that flash of white just before he had first been knocked out of this soul-scape and across a forest clearing—had it only been four days ago? What had struck him? What in this dark, accursed place was white?

One thing only, which he had deliberately avoided: an indistinct glimmer on the cold hearth at the far end of the hall. Graykin, he had thought, thankful that his fumblings hadn't brought that bitterly jealous spirit down on him. It occurred to him now, though, that four days ago Jame hadn't yet given Graykin's soul her grudging permission to occupy this place. What a maggot-seethe of fears that distant fireplace stirred between his ribs, the worse because he didn't know why.

Then find out, his training prompted him. *An unnamed fear is an unconquerable one.*

Disfigured faces grimaced at him through warp and woof as he passed. Whispers followed him down the hall: *. . . but what about me . . . and me . . . and me . . . ? Healer, kinsman, come back . . . !*

The walk seemed to take hours. Under his bare feet, the green-shot floor was numbing cold, but the wind that blew over it was the sirocco of human breath. Kindrie inhaled as it pushed at him, exhaled as it pulled, deep and slow. In his terror, he ached to breathe faster, but couldn't. The sense of suffocation fed his fears and had to be fought down, as did the gorge continually rising in his throat.

Three steps led up to the hearth. Over the top one hung the flayed paws and snarling masks of Arrin-ken pelts, some a ghostly silver gray, others iridescent as pearl.

That was what I saw, thought Kindrie. *I can turn back now.*

But he kept walking.

The black vault of the fireplace was full of charred, twisted limbs, fantastic in their deformity. The eye kept trying to make sense of them. They seemed to organized themselves around a pale block of ash and an ashy stick, lying flat as though on a table. A distorted figure as if of a man sat beside them, there one blink, gone the next as Kindrie drew closer and his perspective changed. He remembered that Ishtier had wanted him to learn from Jame's soul-image where she had hidden the Book

Bound in Pale Leather. Perhaps the strange, shifting image in the fireplace could have told him, except that, ironically, he had no idea what it meant.

If he found out and dealt with it as the priest had demanded, maybe he could still regain his own soul.

. . . do it, do it! the banners whispered.

Kindrie started to mount the steps.

A pale shape rose from among the furs and lunged at him. He was knocked back to sprawl in the floor, cringing as the other ravened over him on the end of its chain. It was naked except for a ridge of dark hair which ran from the head, down the curved spine, along the tail curled up between its legs as if for modesty. Its rear legs bent backward. Its dangling hands were half paws. The muzzle and barred teeth were also canine, but in those baleful eyes Kindrie recognized Jame's stray dog of a servant, chained to the hearth and starved by her reluctant acceptance, but grimly on guard as she had bidden him. The man-dog fell back into a crouch on the second step, slackening the chain, panting. Famine-gaunt, his bones seemed about to burst through the taut skin which covered them.

"Liddle man, liddle bass*stard!*" A thick growl, barely articulate, as few people are on the soul's level. "Go '*way! My* hearth. *My* lady!"

"B-but Graykin, she needs me . . . ."

"*No!*" Snaggle-teeth bared. "Needs *me.* No one else. *No* one needs you, no one wants you, 'cept *fed-chi* priests. Go back where you b'long, priest-*ling!*"

The Knorth had called him that at first, with no less scorn. Kindrie hunched over, gut-sick with the remembered sense of his own worthlessness, frantic to escape from it into the garden of his soul. How could he ever have hoped to out-grow Wilden? The priests had had him too long, made him too much their own—he, who had been nothing to begin with.

"Bassstard," the man-dog was crooning, eyes bright with hungry malice. "Worthless Shanir bassstard . . . ."

All this stress on bastardy, by someone more unfortunately bred even than himself . . . . Kindrie's training pricked him again into observation. The creature was actually salivating. A self-professed sneak and mongrel, Graykin fed on other's weaknesses to . . . to hide from his own devouring sense of worthlessness.

Understanding slowed Kindrie's panic. With a jolt, he realized that Lady Rawneth had played on him much the same way all his childhood, telling him over and over what trash he was, rubbing his nose in his misbirth until he could smell nothing else except in his garden where he had run to hide. From what weakness had *she* been trying to hide by demeaning him? What a fool he had been, to have let her do it for so long!

Indignant, Kindrie found himself on his feet without remembering having risen. He saw now what the man-dog had been trying both to guard and to hide: A second pale figure laying asleep in a nest of Arrin-ken furs, partly clad in rathorn armor. No, not armor exactly. Mask, gorget, breastplate, gauntlet and greaves all grew out of that slim white body in bands of ivory, as they would have on a young rathorn—and as on so immature a beast, not all the plates properly overlapped. Out of a gap over one cheekbone, thick blood welled. The ivory band across the small breasts rose and fell with the slow rhythm of *dwar*.

A-ha, thought Kindrie.

Through the halls came echoing a sound from beyond its walls, drawn out, distorted by echoes: "K . . . k . . . k . . ."

The sleeper's breathing changed. She had heard; she was beginning to wake.

The man-dog grinned wolfishly. "'s torn it. Get out while you can, white-hair!"

Louder, closer: "...*norrrRRR*...."

The quickening breath of wind pushed Kindrie back a step, then dragged him forward almost into Graykin's jaws. Behind him, banners clutched at the wall with thread-bare hands.

Rrrrun! their voices cried, with the sound of ripping cloth.

"Yesss," Kindrie breathed, pushed back again, perforce exhaling. What chance had he, half-trained, against a soul-scape so complex, so malignant?

But if he ran now, he would be running the rest of his life. Where was there a corner so dark that he could hide from himself? He had no garden to escape to now. Ishtier had cut off that retreat. Run, or advance. To do the latter, though, he must master his fears, or lose them.

Bastard, worthless....

No. Look at Graykin, a mongrel in his soul because he accepted that judgment in life. And he, Kindrie? A cringing coward with a belly full of death, disgracing his house, disgracing himself. The thought set his guts roiling, but this time he didn't swallow it back. He retched again and again. No more cossetting of weakness, no more excuses. Purge them all.

With a whine, the man-dog flung himself down the steps in a hunger-frenzy to snap at the seething mess. Kindrie edged past on unsteady legs.

"...*THHHHHH*...."

Sleeper's breath and the exhalation of sound matched in the wind hissing in his face, tearing at his hair. Arrinken fur rippled. Banners flailed. He touched the cool ivory of the cracked mask.

Nothing.

"... *HHHhhh* ...." The sound died with a sigh. Then, somewhere in the distance, it gathered itself again, faster this time, like a wave rushing for the shore: "... *k* ... *k* ... *knorrRR* ... "

Why hadn't his healing power engaged? What was he still doing wrong? Torn banners snickered against the wall: *failure, stupid failure* ....

Why should they be glad?

Then he thought he understood. Tricked again.

"Listen!" he cried, raising his voice against the approaching roar. "These banners aren't part of your soul-scape! Perhaps ... perhaps none of this hall is. It's a trap, to make you think that the shadows still own you, but here you are, in armor against them. Fight, d'you hear me? Fight!"

He had to shout, but he must have been heard. Under his hands the ivory was growing together again. Behind him, banners unraveled in the wind, swirling nets swept away even as they cast themselves to ensnare him. Green light laced the dark floor. Just another moment ....

"... *THHHHH!*"

The eyes behind the mask snapped open: mindless silver, the soul's pure reflection. A flash of white. Oh, no. Not again ....

CRACK!

Pain. Confusion. The blow of that ivory fist, lashing out by reflex, sent him flying sideways through a forest of charred limbs. No, into the fireplace. No, into a black room where a man with silver eyes looked up, smiling, from a pale book (—*welcome to the family, little cousin*—). Crashing into the iron fireback. No, through a hidden door into ... into ....

Green, and white self-heal. Wild heartsease drooping against the night, white herbs abloom, white moths dancing in the moon garden of his soul . . . .

Home. Safe. Sleep now. Sleep.

JAME FOUGHT HER WAY OUT OF SLEEP, crying, "Who calls the Knorth? Who? *Brier*?"

Cold hands held her down. Over her bent a livid face, leprous with death.

For a moment, she was back before the broken walls of her old home keep, under the dead weight of the haunt about to sink its rotting teeth into her arm.

"Don't," said Ashe.

Against every instinct, Jame sheathed her claws. But she *had* attacked someone, she thought, still half-dazed with sleep. Who?

Jorin stretched out limp beside her.

Oh, God, surely not.

The ounce twitched and began to snore. She remembered now, how he had tried to follow her into the depths of *dwar* and been left, crying, in its upper reaches. Obviously, he was still there.

A confusion of legs and hands moved toward the front of the smithy, taking with it a limp form.

She had struck . . . . Someone had staggered backward . . . .

Over the haunt's shoulder, Jame saw the anvil squat on its ironwood stump. One of the horns glistened darkly.

"Oh hell," she muttered, shaking off Ashe and rising unsteadily.

In the stripped light that fell through the barred window, Kirien bent over Kindrie. "I should never have forced this!" she was saying. "A healer and a nemesis . . . don't!"

Jame's hand stopped in mid-air.

Index shoved her aside and pressed a clot of cob-webs to the back of the Shanir's skull to staunch the blood.

Kiri was right, Jame thought, sitting back. It would be dangerous for her to touch the Shanir when he was so vulnerable. Damn her poisonous soul-image, anyway!

But someone (Kindrie?) had said something about it being a trap. What had he meant? She groped after the memory as if after a rapidly fading dream. The details were already gone, but the suggestion lingered. It implied a deception on the most intimate level, a deceiver closer to her than her own skin. Just the same, if she could disown any part of that ghastly hall . . . !

Steady, she warned herself. *Whatever the truth is, it won't be simple or perhaps so easily discovered.*

But still . . . !

Ashe stood behind her, a hooded death-mask hovering in the shadows. "Why . . . did you attack him?"

"I couldn't help it. He was too close."

"Huh," said Kirien. "Remind me to keep my distance. That's *dwar* breathing, at least."

So it was, deep and slow. Trinity. She had warned Kindrie that the next time she might knock him through a wall, and she had—back into the healing embrace of his soul-image.

Then she remembered: "*Did* someone call the Knorth?"

As if in answer, they became aware of an approaching disturbance outside. Struggling forms passed the window. The door was flung open and a large, gagged figure was thrown in, almost on top of them. It was Brier Iron-thorn.

"Ancestors be praised," said Jame.

The Kendar lurched to her feet and stood for a moment swaying. Muffled noises came from behind the gag, which she made no effort to remove despite her free hands. Breath smoked from her nostrils in faintly glowing plumes. Her eyes were screwed tightly shut. Oblivious to their questions, she set off across the room with a determined if unsteady stride and bounced off the far wall. Slipping up behind her, Ashe whipped off the gag.

". . . *north!*" the cadet was crying. "K-*north!*" Over and over.

Her voice seemed to come from a considerable distance. Its tone, however, was no less compelling than when it had reached Jame in the depths of *dwar* sleep. It conveyed no fear, only a grim determination to evoke an answer.

The old shaman called urgently from his corner of the square.

"If she won't shut up," Index translated, "they'll kill her."

Jame grabbed Brier's hand as it groped past her. "Cadet, stop it. *I'm* Knorth!"

Brier paused, head cocked to listen. "Lady?" she said in her far-away voice. Her glowing breath made Jame's face tingle. "Where are you?"

"At Kithorn. So are you. For pity's sake, *look* at me!"

The Kendar's eyes opened warily. Luminous mist filled the sockets, throwing into relief her high, strong cheekbones. "All I see is weirding," she said in a tight, slightly louder voice. "The Highlord called me down into it and now I'm lost. So is he."

Jame gave a stifled exclamation, involuntarily tightening her grip.

Brier's hand closed on hers. "I feel . . . something."

She was half-crushing Jame's fingers. Her voice seemed perhaps two rooms away now instead of half a field.

"Keep calling!" Kirien said.

"I . . . no. If my brother is lost in the weirding too, he needs help. A guide. Brier Iron-thorn, do you remember how your mother came back under the sand to bring Tori safely across the Dry Salt Sea?"

The Kendar's dark face hardened. "That story. A fever dream. A sop for an orphan."

"Maybe, maybe not. When the salt sea returned yesterday and I nearly drowned in it, I-I think Rose saved me too. It was wrong of me not to have told you before, but I was unsure, and scared."

Brier's face would never be good at showing emotion, whatever she felt. "What do you want me to do?" she asked at last, gruffly, almost in her normal tone.

"Will you go back into the weirding to find Tori? No, don't move." She pushed the Kendar down to sit against the west wall, next to Kindrie and the still sleeping Jorin, and knelt before her. "Just think about doing it. The Senetha can be done purely in the mind, perhaps this too. Will you try?"

Brier had squeezed her eyes shut again, like a child afraid to see. She *was* afraid. Jame could feel it through her grip. Never before had she been asked to do something so much on faith, for a girl whom she must think half-mad and a house which she had only begun to trust. Then she gave a curt nod and began again to call: "K-*north*, K-*north* . . . !"—each cry more faint than the last, as though she were resolutely walking back into the mist which enveloped her mind.

Kirien shivered. "I wouldn't care to do that, even with an anchor. For God's sake, don't let go!"

She had been stealing sidelong looks at Jame. Now, abruptly, she said, "Forgive the rudeness, but I have to know: would you please take off that mask?"

But Kiri had just seen her face, when she had used it to cut short the scrollswoman's berserker flare. It couldn't be such a treat as all that . . . .

Then Jame remembered. Kindrie had been in her soul-scape.

Not daring to think, much less to hope, she fumbled at the mask with her free hand. It came loose. She took a deep breath and turned to look at Kirien.

The Jaran regarded her critically. "A few minutes more would have been better. Still, not bad. Not bad at all."

Jame touched her cheek. Apprenticeship to the best thief in Tai-tastigon had trained her fingertips to abnormal sensitivity, even when gloved. As Kirien had said, a few moments more had been needed and lost, thanks to Brier's call. There was still a scar. It was so faint, though, that she could hardly feel it. Kindrie had done his work well enough: she was no longer disfigured.

Outside, someone cried in alarm, echoed by Index. Kirien hastily joined him by the front window, Ashe only a step behind her. Red light flared across their startled faces.

"Oh!" said Kirien, staring.

Jame tried to rise, but couldn't break Brier's grip. "What?" she demanded.

"The weeds in the courtyard's cracks . . . they're bursting into flames from the inner square out. Watch it!" She jerked Index back as lines of fire laced the windowsill, following the mossy cracks. In a moment, they had burned out, without spreading to the interior.

Outside, Sonny's voice rose again.

"Huh," said Index. "The fool acts as if he's never seen a purification before. He claims that the fires show the Burnt Man's disapproval. The chief isn't coming, he says, but *some*one's got to represent the Burnt Man here tonight, or the entire Riverland may be torn apart, Guess who volunteers."

"He may have a point," said Kirien. "Whatever they're up to, annoying the powers that be can't help. I wonder where that precious chief of theirs is, anyway."

"Four days ago," Jame said slowly, "he was near Falkirr, laying a bone-fire. Then he went on southward."

"Don't be a fool," snapped Index. "I told you: the silly bugger is off defining the Merikit borders for Summer Eve . . . ."

"Right down the Silver," Jame finished, as her wits finally woke. "He's preparing to reclaim the entire Riverland."

Index and Kirien stared at her. "Impossible!" they burst out. "The lords . . . the priests . . . ! They'd never permit . . . ."

"The lords have been gone all winter," said Jame. "So has most of the Kencyrath. You don't realize how empty and strange the valley has become. And the priests have been . . . preoccupied. Now they can barely draw in the power they need to maintain contact with their temples.

The Merikits' plan only takes things one step farther. They probably haven't had so good an opportunity since they closed these northern hills to us eighty years ago. How did they do that, Index?"

"My God." The old man stared at her. "With bone-fires."

It could have been more thoroughly done, Jame thought. After all, here she and others were. In her travels through Rathillien she had encountered areas such as the Anarchies so strong with native power that they could literally eat an unwary Kencyr alive. These hills were hardly as voracious, but she doubted that her people would ever live here again. And now that might become true for the rest of the Riverland as well? How ironic if the entire Kencyrath was about to become as roofless and rootless as she herself had been made to feel.

She remembered the dinner party at the Cataracts, those self-satisfied lords so sure that they had every right to dispose of her as they wished. The Kencyrath was theirs, wasn't it? Of course, they could do with it whatever they wanted. But what did they know about the blood feud between the Knorth and the Randir, still festering like an abscess after all these years, or the priesthood malignant in its foul hole, or the secret life of their own women? Nothing was as sure as they blandly assumed, not even their suzerainty over this northern land, perhaps about to be snatched away from them forever.

And these were the people who had told her that she could only belong to the Kencyrath if she played the role which they decreed, living in public and private behind the mask of their conventions.

And she had accepted that, even when she had fled Gothregor, just as she had been prepared to live with Kallystine's handiwork as the mark of her failure.

Jame looked at the mask still in her hand. *Seeker, seeker*... the children's taunt. That damned game of confusion and lost identity.

But the game's object wasn't to find out who you were. Rather, you escaped the eyeless mask by catching someone else and taking her name, which the next seeker might in turn take from you. Well, in trying to play by their rules she had damn near lost herself altogether.

No more of that, Jame thought, letting the mask drop. Thanks to Kindrie, she had her own face back again, and by God she was going to wear it.

"It could really happen," Index was saying. "We could really lose the Riverland. Sweet Trinity, what a catastrophe!"

"Why?" Jame asked.

They all turned to stare at her.

"I mean," she said slowly, thinking it out, "we've tried to make it home by ignoring its true nature, by... masking it, as it were. But it's always been a sort of trap, hasn't it? We can't support ourselves here, so we have to hire out our people as mercenaries—prostitute them, almost. Then too, it keeps the nine major houses preoccupied with the High Council's idiotic political games while isolated minor families near the Barrier guard against Perimal Darkling alone. If you look at it that way, life in the Riverland is perverting everything that makes us what we are, or should be."

Index snorted. "You sound like crazy old Cattila, always harping on how we're failing our trust, as if that damned god of ours hadn't failed us first."

"Does that change our responsibility? Why is it that no one can keep in mind what we Kencyr are supposed to be doing?"

"Perhaps," said Ashe, "because none of us . . . are as close to it . . . as you are, . . . nemesis."

"You might also consider this," said Kirien tartly: "To lose the Riverland now would tear the Kencyrath apart. I admire your brother. He's a far better man than we deserve, and the only one who could have held us together so far. But not in the face of this. Besides, remember that success for the Merikit tonight means the immolation of Mount Alban. Are you now in favor of *that*?"

Jame stared back at their suddenly hostile faces, dismayed. They were seeing her unmasked, the outsider, the potential destroyer. And so, perhaps, she might be. All the weaknesses which she kept uncovering among her people, all the secrets—for a moment, the whole Kencyrath seemed to lie in her gloved grasp, flawed and fragile.

Some things need to be broken . . . .

But it was Brier Iron-thorn's hand which she actually gripped, or rather which gripped her with a mute desperation that threatened to break her bones. She owed it to Brier, and Marc, and yes, even Tori, not to do anything stupid.

I will think first, and take responsibility afterward, she told herself, trying to ease her fingers in Brier's grip. *I will, I will, I will.*

Outside, there was a muffled *whoof* and a flare of blue light, then another and another. The moment's startled silence after the first broke with a babble of urgent voices, Sonny's rising above the others.

"What is it?" Jame demanded, then, getting no answer, "Scrollswoman, describe!"

"Spontaneous, sequential ignition of torches," Kirien reported, obedient to her training. "Cyanic flames and smoke, indicative of unknown properties. Conclusion .... Damn. Ready or not, here we go."

Index crowed with excitement. Whatever the outcome, he would have his treat after all. "The elders are ordering Sonny and the Challenger to get into the square before it closes. Green-britches looks ready to shit in 'em. Sonny is arguing. He's stripping naked. He's picked up a lump of charcoal . . . no, he's dropped it. Got his fingers singed, the idiot. Talk about the Burnt Man's disapproval! Tungit is pointing . . . ."

The three scholars watched with deep interest.

"What? What?"

Index cleared his throat. "It . . . er . . . has to do with those missing right hand braids."

The old fool. Whose innocence did he think he was protecting, anyway?

"D'you mean," said Jame, "that he's more impressive with his pants on?"

A shriek of laughter answered her. The ragged boy leaped up from beneath the window where he had lain eavesdropping and shouted to the big Merikit.

"Damn," said Kirien again. "D'you suppose that brat knows Kens?"

In answer, the smithy door crashed open. Sonny stood on the threshold, a naked, black hulk against the courtyard's glare. His head turned rapidly, searching. Before, a masked female had dared first to hurt him—*him*, the Earth Wife's Favorite—and now this . . . !

Only one mask was in sight. He lunged at Kirien.

Ashe stepped in front of the young scrollswoman. The Merikit elders had taken the singer's iron-shod staff, so she met the big man's charge with a water-flowing move that sent him careening into a dark, back corner. From the complicated crash which followed, he had blundered into the smithy's scrap heap. Yells of rage mingled with the clatter of rusty iron and the rip of rotten bellows. Any moment, though, he would extricate himself.

"You're the nemesis," Index shouted at Jame from across the room. "*Do* something!"

Jame growled. She would at least have liked the freedom to maneuver, but Brier still clung to her hand, so far into the weirding that only wisps of luminous mist came from her moving lips. How could Jame betray the Kendar's trust or, for that matter, break her grip?

Sonny emerged from the shadows and stumbled toward the front corner where Ashe stood guard before Kirien. The singer spoke a word in Merikit and pointed at Jame.

Damn all haunts anyway, teeth and toenails.

Jame pinched the nerve in Brier's elbow. The Kendar's grasp involuntarily loosened as her fingers went numb. Her unheard voice faltered. Jame pulled free and scooped up Kindrie's limp hand. Brier's grip clamped like a vice on the Shanir's thin wrist, with an audible crunch of bones. She began again soundlessly to call "K-*north*, K-*north*," but now sweat shone on her dark brow and weirding poured from her lips with each strong exhalation.

Sweet Trinity, thought Jame, recoiling. *What have I done now?*

No time, though, for second thoughts: Here came Sonny with a roar. He hadn't learned from Ashe's water-flowing move; possibly, he hadn't seen what had sent him flying into a far corner and now into a wall. Jame was out the door before the crash.

A row of torches burned blue down the northeast side of the square. Their pale, glowing smoke, drifting inward, filled the enclosed space like a box, from the bottom up. Blossoms of flame seen through the haze marked the progression of fire from torch to torch down the southeast side. Inside this closing perimeter stood the elders' indistinct figures. Their anxious voices sounded as thin and distant as Brier's in the weirding.

Hurry, they must be calling. *Hurry, hurry!*

Jame had paused for a moment to stare. Behind her, she heard big, bare feet slap on stone. The Merikit's arms swept over her head, snagging off her cap, as she ducked and kicked backward, as it were, at the bone of contention, connecting. Free, she bolted toward the court's eastern gate. If she left Kithorn, the outer circle would at least be broken. If Sonny followed, the rites might fail without him and Mount Alban be saved by default.

The ruddy light from above mixed with the blue glower of the torches to cast violet highlights on Kithorn's shattered timbers, shading to deep purple—a glowing world except in the velvet shadows under the gatehouse where indistinct shapes waited. Some rose at her approach to stand hunch-shouldered in the gloom. Others only gained knees and elbows, their feet and hands having long since fallen off. Blackened skin cracked with their movement. Red fissures opened in seams of blood and fire. From their huddled mass came a long, questioning sigh:

"*Whaaaaa . . . ?*"

Jame stopped. A breeze under the gatehouse brought to her the stench of burnt flesh and its taste on her lips in charred flecks.

"*Thaaaaa . . .*" breathed the Burning Ones, disappointed, settling back down outside the circle, like hounds at bay, to await their master.

A shuffling sound behind her and a furious curse. Here came Sonny, hopping on one foot as he pulled his red britches back on. Made him feel vulnerable, had she? Good. Oh, but what a fool, to be playing such games before such an audience . . . if he was aware of it. Ancestors knew, he was close enough now for the black specks of that terrible conflagration to freckle his fair-skinned face.

A thought struck her: Maybe he was one of those people who simply couldn't see certain things. She had met a few in Tai-tastigon, oblivious to its teeming supernatural community and contemptuous of their neighbors' belief in "such nonsense." If so, he literally couldn't see the reality behind the ceremony he was being compelled to perform.

Still, he wasn't the real problem. The ways north and east blocked, Jame veered southward along the square's southeast side, to gain time, to think.

The breeze followed her. Overhead, glowing clouds began slowly to wheel as though around the axis of the now invisible well. Blue smoke swelled up within the enclosure to met them, undisturbed by the wind except at the edges, where a few wisps were teased loose. One of these blew in Jame's face, and her senses lurched.

She was following the path which the elders had taken earlier, circling sunwise to close the square. Her feet fell with the remembered beat of theirs, the memory of their bells ring-ching-chinging in her mind—no, millennia of feet, and bells, and power called up from the earth, down from the sky. The Merikit clustered at the south corner stared but let her pass: they would as soon have stopped their own elders, treading the sun's path. It seemed to Jame that she was pursuing suns, one after another of them born in bursts of blue flame, one for each day of the summer to come.

Then she had out-paced them and was slowing, shaking her head to clear it. The wind seemed to keen in one ear and out the other. No. That whistling came from her right, inside the square, and the wind swerved inward at the west corner to answer it. What had she been doing, and where bound? In a damned circle, back to where she had started with nothing gained, nothing changed . . . .

But it had.

Ahead lay the smithy, with light streaming out of it. Index burst out the door, pulling Kirien with him. Jorin wobbled on their heels. A shape of darkness followed —Ashe, backing out. After her, billowing out the door, came weirding.

Jame stopped short. "My God," she said to the Challenger, who had just come up beside her. "Now what?"

In answer, the Merikit clapped the ivy crown on her head and shoved her between the torches, into the blue smoke of the square.

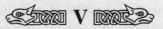

V

AT FIRST, Jame thought that she would die. Acrid smoke burned in her eyes, and throat, and lungs, inhaled all the more deeply with each racking attempt to cough it out. Kencyr might not poison easily, but they could certainly choke.

Bit by bit, however, breathing became easier. At last she was able to wipe her streaming eyes on a sleeve and look up.

Kithorn was gone.

Sacred space stretched out before her to horizons lost in a hazy distance, pale blue below, shading upward through lavender to mauve. Above, angry red clouds wheeled in a slow vortex, centered over the well. The latter's rim of dull green serpentine loomed in the middle of that interminable plain like a volcano's mouth, half-obscured by drifting smoke. A low, continual rumble came out of it, felt more than heard. The mottled veins of the marble rim extended into cracks and some of these into quake fissures. So far, however, the latter appeared to have been stopped by a network of dark lines lying across the granite-white plain. Ah. Those must the god-sigils which she had watched the shaman-elders draw in the square, the power of the Four still containing that of the River Snake's mouth.

While the sigil lines near the well looked spidery with distance, those close at hand lay in bold strokes across the plain. Jame had nearly fallen on top of one a good twelve feet wide . . . or would she have fallen into it? It was so impossibly black. When she tried to touch it, her hand disappeared as though into sunless water, feeling nothing.

A harsh sound came from the left. At a distance, beyond two more inky bands, the Favorite doubled over as racked with coughing as she had been a moment ago. He must have plunged into the square just before it closed, driven by his blind rage exactly where he had no wish to go. Jame reached up to remove the ivy crown. Whatever Sonny's role, she needn't play the one which the Challenger had thrust onto her . . . .

"BLOOP," said something behind her.

The basin, like the square, had grown. So had its inmate. A flat, fishy eye the size of a buckler gazed down at her dubiously. The huge head in which it was set seemed otherwise to be mostly mouth and whiskers. Four of the latter rasped on the basin's edge as the creature chinned itself there. Two more extended from its upper lip like downed spars, one passing almost over her head. The thick, wide lips parted. Out of them came a small, dreamy voice.

"There was a maid," it said. "Oh, so beautiful, so proud."

Jame stared. She almost thought that she knew that voice, sleepily gloating over its new secret.

"No chief's son would do for her, oh no. When the earth shook, what must she needs try but to seduce the River Snake itself."

The monster's maw gaped wider and wider. Deep inside that pink-ribbed gullet nestled something that glimmered like a viscid pearl. Jame had heard that some catfish carried fertilized eggs in their mouths to hatch them, but this "egg" had shadowy markings under its mucous sheath—no, features, as if under a caul: a face, which Jame knew only too well, despite never having seen it before without at least a tracery mask.

"M'lady? *Kallystine?*"

This was moderately strange, Jame thought, but perhaps no more so than Loogan stuck in Gorgo's craw. Did aquatic relationships always end in eat-or-be-eaten? So she asked again, only half in jest, "Did this fish swallow you, or are you wearing it?"

"Poor maid," said the voice, suddenly dolorous. "Poor, pretty maid. The Snake ate her all-l-l-l up."

The Caineron device was a serpent devouring its young, but that couldn't be what Kallystine was talking about, could it? Despite the similarities (pride, ambition—downfall?), this was someone else's story.

"Who *are* you?" Jame demanded, leaning into the creature's mouth, hands between teeth which, on a fish of normal size, would have been small. "*What* are you?"

A smile made the face under the membrane shift and flow, like a changeling fetus in its embryonic sack.

"The Eaten One," it said, in a different voice, in Merikit.

"I understood that!"—but then why shouldn't she? In this space sacred to gods not her own, ancestors only knew what might happen. Keep to essentials. "Why are you here?"

"To find a hero to feed the Snake to save the world."

"Oh, that's helpful. 'To feed' in what sense?"

"Pretty maid, guess."

That did it. What was this but another game of seeker's mask, one victim substituted for another? But when she tried to tear off the ivy crown, its leaves were so entangled in her hair that it might have sunk rootlets into her skull. Perhaps it had. No wonder the Challenger had been loath to put on the damn thing. Now, short of scalping herself, she was stuck with it—and with the victory which it implied?

Not if Sonny could help it. He had recovered from his coughing fit and was groping toward her, drawn by the sound of her voice. Whatever blindness had prevented him from seeing the Burning Ones now kept the blue smoke in his eyes. He came to a sigil stroke and stepped into it—except that for him it was still only a charcoal line drawn on the flagstones. On he came, stumbling across the abyss.

". . . such very, very good friends . . . " murmured Kallystine's silken voice.

Huge pectoral fins surged out of the water, hooked on the basin's rim, and pulled. The leviathan rose over Jame like a ship's prow about to dash itself on rocks, then crashed down. She found herself flat on her back, her head over the sigil's void, surprised not to be smashed flat. The darkened sky was vaulted with ribs, from which hung an improbable moon with Kallystine's distorted face.

". . . eat you all-l-l-l up," it crooned.

A rumble swallowed her voice. It came from behind, approaching fast, accompanied by a rending crack. Jame clutched the monster's chin whiskers for support as the stones beneath her back split and fell away. Looking down over her shoulder, she saw a seam of glowing red open deep in the darkness below. Then a rising wave of heat took away her breath.

"Let . . . me . . . up!" she gasped. "Dammit, it's . . . not . . . your turn!"

The moon-face shifted, pouting, and the great fish surged backward into the basin, hauling Jame with it and displacing a wave which almost swept her away. The vast mouth snapped shut: WHOMP. Steaming water seethed around it, red-lit from beneath. Looking behind her, Jame saw that a quake fissure had breached the sigil, running from the distant well-mouth almost up to the basin. The ground shook again.

"How do we *stop* this?" she demanded.

A sulky, Merikit voice answered from within. "I told you: feed the Snake."

"Ugh," said Jame. "There's *got* to be another way. Where can I find the Earth Wife?"

"In her lodge. Where else?"

"In *Peshtar?*"

"Dumb, dumb, dumb."

"Listen, chowder-head: *you're* the one in boiling water."

Or perhaps they both were. Here came Sonny, groping toward them through the steam. Damnation. Could he walk straight over fissures too?

The thick catfish lips parted slightly, the voice inside grumbling: "*Some*one has to feed that damn Snake. Here, boy, here, here!"

"Oh, go stew," said Jame, disgusted, then turned and fled.

On reflection, she thought she knew where to go, if not exactly how to get there.

The enormous sigils sprawling across this plain and complicating her route were made up of many lines, some connected, others not. Whatever their other properties, they clearly served as a series of entrenchments. The quake fissures must thus break through each in turn in order to breach the square, as one had already so nearly done in the western corner by the basin. Others had broken lines closer to the plain's well-mouth center and spewed into them the Serpent's hot blood. Rising heat met the cool breath of the sigils in smoke and stream, turning the expanse into the semblance of a burning battlefield—which, in fact, it was. The prospects south and west appeared only intermittently through a drifting haze. North and east had disappeared altogether.

Of course, it was some consolation that Sonny couldn't see anything at all; but then neither was he hindered by the sigil lines nor, much, by the fissures, which must be no more than cracks in the real courtyard. He was also stumbling around in an area only some fifty feet square, while the plain which Jame had seen before this last tremor had looked as if it would take days to cross, or months, or a life-time.

However, she'd had some experience in Tai-tastigon and the Anarchies with the quirks of distorted space, including their deceptive distances.

What she wanted lay to the east. She set off as nearly as she could in that direction, guided by her memory of the sigils' shapes and by the vortex flow of the clouds above, hoping for the best.

It was hard, hot going. A dozen fissures now laced the plain, reaching ahead through the branches of the sigil strokes which they had overwhelmed. Veils of smoke and wavering heat rose from the red fires in their depths. If they did indeed break open the square, would sacred space itself be breached? A cataclysmic thing, certainly. Perhaps this plain was Rathillien's soul-scape. In that case, events here might reverberate across an entire world.

She skirted yet another sigil line, trying to remember if one side or the other led to a dead-end. Another damn maze. Sometimes, her whole life seemed like one huge labyrinth whose key kept changing.

It was getting very warm. Oh, for a breath of wind.

One came, as if in answer to her wish, fretted with black feathers. Hundreds of these, the spoils of entire flocks, had been tied to the hairy Merikit. More fluttered past, many of them broken. She turned her face into the fitful breeze and followed it.

Ahead loomed a skeletal structure: the wicker cage, like the basin, grown huge. Loose feathers swirled inside it, vast, disorganized wings flailing at the bars. In their midst, an indistinct shape plummeted toward the earth . . . .

No. Jame's heart had leaped, anticipating the smash of flesh to bloody ruin on stone. Her nerves still flinched at the expected impact, but the figure seemed to fall on and on, as though through infinite space, without ever reaching the ground.

"Who are you?" she demanded.

A voice answered inside the cage, speaking a sing-song language which she had never heard before and yet, somehow, understood. "There was an old man," it said, "oh, so clever, so ambitious that he claimed to be a god. To prove it, his followers threw him from a high tower. Now he falls, forever and ever. He helped you at Gothregor, little girl. Help him now!"

Jame stared, remembering that storm of black wings above the old keep's broken roof at Gothregor. "Tishooo? Old Man, you nearly got me killed! What do you want?"

"Out, *out*, OUT!" Frenzied feathers beat against the bars, broke, and hurled their fragments forward again. "Oh, those foolish priests, to have whistled the wind into this cage when only he can blow away the Serpent's Breath! Oh, let him out of . . . HIC!"

The half-obscured figure began to rise, frantic, hiccuping. Hands thrust through the feathers to clutch at the bars, golden rings half-embedded in rolls of fat.

"No, *no*, NO!" babbled a different voice, in Kens. "Whoever you are—HIC!—out there, open that door and I'll have the living hide off of you!"

What door?

Going back a step, Jame saw a hinged panel on top of the cage, secured by a latch. From the latter, a string hung down outside the cage, swaying in an errant breeze. She caught it.

The plump hands tried to shake the bars, ineffectually since by now the other's heels had risen well above his head. "Answer me! Damn—HIC!—you, don't you know who I am?"

"Yes," said Jame, and pulled the string.

The trap door fell open. A riot of wind-born feathers streamed joyously out of the cage, in its midst a pudgy figure tumbling up into the sky. The angry red clouds swallowed them all. Caldane's wail, trailing after, faded into the distance.

"Damn," said Jame.

The overcast showed no sign of dispersing. So much for the Old Man's boast to blow away the Serpent's weirding breath and so, incidentally, to send Mount Alban home.

Time to move on, quickly, before M'lord's clamor brought Sonny down on her again.

More weaving through the maze, more fissures like ruinous, blind fingers groping outward. Finally, here was what she sought: the house of clay slabs.

At first, it seemed as small as when the shaman-elder had built it in the square's eastern corner, no more than a model. As Jame approached, however, it grew. The walls which had appeared so low were half sunken into the ground and lined by *imu* faces whose mouths gaped wide enough to swallow her whole. Serpentine forms rioted over the lintel and down the posts. For days, traveling northward up the Riverland, she had caught glimpses of that door standing farther and farther ajar. Now it loomed over her as though over the smallest of children, gaping wide open into darkness.

"E-earth Wife?" she called, flinching at the loudness of her own voice.

An earthy, musky smell flowed out into her face, as if of some animal's lair but massively, indefinably, female. If only Marc were here, as he had been at the lodge in Peshtar. Him, at least, the Earth Wife had liked.

"Mother Ragga?"

A faint voice answered, sounding incredulous: "L-lady?"

Jame frowned. Graykin? What in Perimal's name was *he* doing here? Eh, no helping it now: She entered.

 VI

IT TOOK JAME'S EYES a moment to adjust to the gloom.

Opposite the door, a fireplace smoked and flared, throwing a fan of uncertain light on the low beams and the sunken floor. Spread out on the latter was the earth map of Rathillien, composed of materials taken from the corresponding parts of that world—hills of rock, fertile plains of black soil, sandy wastes, river and sea beds of stone and coral. With her ear pressed to any of these features, the Earth Wife could hear what was happening far away, as she had the previous winter when Marc had consulted her about events in the Riverland.

The map looked much larger to Jame than it had that day in Peshtar, almost as though she might walk into it here at Kithorn and emerge wherever else on Rathillien she chose. Well, stranger things had happened. But it also looked less stable than it had then, with sections rawly altered—the weirdingstrom's work, perhaps, or the tremors' that had accompanied it.

"Lady!" said Graykin's voice again, almost whining.

A misshapen figure crouched to one side of the hearth, out of the fire's light.

Jame stepped down to the dirt floor and almost lost her balance. At the eastern edge of the map, sink-sand was pouring down as though through a hole in the floor. A nice pit-fall for the unwary, she thought. Side-stepping it, she began to circle a room which seemed to have no walls at all, only space opening out to the rim of night, crowded with motionless, watching shapes black against a scattering of stars.

Don't look at them, don't look . . . .

Two pairs of eyes, not one, waited for her by the hearth; not a single shape but two, clinging to each other. She indeed knew that thin, sharp face, although she had never seen it before with so long a nose.

"Why, Graykin," she said, staring. "Where did you get that muzzle, or that tail?"

The Southron showed sharp, white teeth in a snarl. "Don't ask!"

The thin girl with her arms around his neck hugged him tightly, as one would a trusted hound. Her eyes gleamed with a more feral light than his did, but she wasn't the Earth Wife's imp who had given Jame the *imu* medallion in Peshtar. Jame snapped her fingers in the girl's face.

"Lyra, do you hear me?"

Caldane's daughter blinked, and smiled. "Oh, here you are! Will things start happening now?"

"Very likely," rumbled a voice on the other side of the hearth.

Someone very large sat there in the shadows. Fire light caught the twisted lines of a chair like a tangle of oak roots. Bone white splinters flashed and clicked in hands scarcely less gnarled than the chair, or less strong. Jame couldn't yet see what was being knit, except that it appeared to be alive.

"Earth Wife," she said, rising and giving the seated figure her most formal if shaky salute. "Honor be to you and to your halls."

The Earth Wife grunted. "Very pretty. Think you can honey-talk your way out of anything, do you? Not yet caused enough trouble, hey? The map, girl. Look at it."

Jame looked, as another tremor rippled through the fabric of the lodge. On the floor, lengths of the Silver as far away as the Cataracts twitched and shifted. All across the map, seams of unrest stirred and sink-sand poured down into hungry maws as the Serpent's Brood awoke.

"This is trouble, all right," said Jame, "but I don't understand: are you saying that it's somehow my fault?"

"Had to look you over, didn't we?" the shadowy figure muttered. Her voice was a toothless mumble, but in it lay the strength to gum mountains to dust. "All four of us, here in the north, treading on the River Snake's back . . . woke him up, didn't we? He thought he'd blown you out of our reach with his weirding breath, down to the Wastes to feed his brothers under the sand, but back you came, *and* your people with you, just in time to muck up our ceremonies. Now his hunger rouses all the Brood, who may wake the Chaos Serpent itself and so end all. Of course it's your fault."

Jame shook her head to clear it. Index had said that there were reasons for everything, including Mount

Alban's journeys. The weirdingstrom—all to flush her out of the Riverland? And the sand which had swallowed her in the Wastes—pouring down some vast, subterranean gullet?

"No. It's too much. How can so many things hinge on me? Why *should* they?"

"As we are," that great voice grumbled, "so you may become. But there are three of you to our four, and different, so different! If I kill, I also give life, and I abide. That's balance. But you, what are you becoming? Pure destruction, Nemesis! Whose, girl?"

"If the Serpent and its brood belong to Perimal Darkling, perhaps we have the same foe. Is destruction always evil? Earth Wife, I know we haven't behaved well on this world. Our lords can be so arrogant and stupid . . . ! Trinity knows, I seldom act wisely myself. But if your enemy *is* ours as well, can't we also call Rathillien our home and you our mother?"

Stony silence, on which no seed grows.

"Why are you begging?" Graykin demanded in a low growl. "We're Kencyr, the Chosen!"

"Not this time," said Jame, chagrined. She felt like a whining child who had been pushed contemptuously away. This was so important, and she was handling it so badly.

"All right," she said, collecting herself. "You say this crisis is my fault. Help me to understand it. How can the River Snake be subdued?"

"Feed it."

Damn. "*Is* the hero at least reborn in its belly?"

"So the Eaten One says, but she seldom gives the same answer twice."

"And the Burnt Man—*must* he set all the bone-fires ablaze, including the one under Mount Alban?"

"Who knows what charred thoughts flake off that cinder of a brain, or what rules keep its fire banked?"

The Four didn't seem to know much about each other, Jame thought. What an odd way to run a world—if, indeed, that was what they did. Such almost human ignorance. Hmmmm. A maid eaten by the River Snake, an old man falling from a tower . . . .

"Earth Wife, tell us a story. 'There was an old woman . . . .' "

". . . who dug her son's grave. And when it was done, he buried her in it. Tcha . . . men!"

"But she didn't die. Neither did the Eaten One or the Tishooo or—ancestors preserve him—the Burnt Man, by water or wind or fire. Nor you, it seems, by earth. As I may become, so you were: a mortal, transformed. But when, and why? Did it have something to do with our temples suddenly appearing on this world? I know they raised hell with the Tastigon godlings. The New Pantheon arose, feeding off our temples' power, while the Old Pantheon of native forces declined. Was that when Rathillien's essential divinity was precipitated out into the four of you?"

Impatient huffs of wind had been coming down the chimney.

"*Hooom!*" it now said, as though the flue were clearing its throat, and exhaled a billow of smoke and ash into the room.

Jame slapped at a swarm of sparks determined to nest in her hair. The singed smell triggered a pang, almost, of guilt before the fact: sometime recently, she had overlooked something obvious, perhaps deadly, for someone —but who, and what?

"*Huh!*" said the wind in the chimney, a short, self-conscious cough that swept smoke from the hearth and made the flames there leap.

The Earth Wife's skirts rustled, or rather the ferns did, that cascaded over the cliff of her knees down to the floor. Between the fronds, as out of hidden caves, bright eyes caught the fire-light. Far above, dimly lit, was a face like a granite out-cropping with cavernous eyes and a bird's nest crown of twig-tangled braids.

"Ask a lot of questions, don't you, girl?"

"Uh . . . " said Jame. Her mind had gone blank. Who was she, anyway, to demand answers of this hanging garden that was Rathillien?

The tree-root hands turned their black knitting inside out, around the delicate bones that had served as needles.

"*Quip?*" said the knit-work, tentatively flexing dark, furry wings. "*Quip!*"—and scuttled down the Earth Wife's skirt to disappear within its leafy folds. A chorus of welcoming cries greeted it.

"Was that the foxkin that Cattila lost, investigating the weirdingstrom?" Jame asked. "She'll be glad to get it back."

"She is."

Jame shot Lyra a questioning look.

"Yes," whispered the girl. "That's Gran, or was before we got here. Isn't it exciting?"

Another substitution, the Caineron Matriarch for the Merikit "woman" who was to have played the Earth Wife, and now Ragga herself for Cattila. Puzzling was more the word, though, for the relationship between the matriarch and her sometime Ear.

"Does . . . er . . . Gran know with whom she's been dealing?"

"Yes," said Cattila, from the other side of the fire.

A log had burst into brief glory. In its glare, the Matriarch perched on the oak-root throne, blinking like a toad, tiny, arthritic feet dangling well above the ground.

"Well enough, anyway," she amended, gumming at the admission as though at something not quite palatable. "Ragga hears the most amazing things through earth and stone. Oh, what gossips we two old women have had! That fool Rawneth, trying to compel and control with her hedge sorcerers and rogue shamans, when all that's needed is a love of talk—oh, and a gift or two."

"What gift?" Jame asked, with deep misgivings.

Cattila glowered. "Think I'd do anything to harm our people, missy? The reverse, if anything. Ragga can only enter a Kencyr keep by invitation and me, I don't get around as much as I used to. So I made her my Ear, for both our sakes. That's all."

"All? To make an outsider privy to the Matriarchs' Council? You didn't even warn them, did you?"

The old woman squirmed. "As if they have much by way of secrets these days! Anyway, once she's inside, no tricks by earth or stone work, do they? Ragga has to use her own ears, like any silly maid, and maybe risk her own silly neck too. Hasn't figured a way around that one yet, has she? Well, for once she gets to listen through me."

"As the Eaten One does through Kallystine, the Falling Man through Caldane, and maybe the Earth Wife's imp through Lyra. Quite a family affair. I understand your involvement now, matriarch—more or less—but theirs?"

"Huh. Another damn trick of the weirding, to have put them in the right place at the wrong time. The Snake's meddling, I'd almost think, if it had the brains. How're Wind and Water supposed to think straight now?"

"They aren't," said Jame, remembering how both kept losing control of persona and power. "Your kin—our Kencyr people—have meddled with this world's balance and now we're confusing its soul. We don't belong on Rathillien, much less in its sacred space. Only you were invited, matriarch. Only you know how to play seeker's mask with a god. What are we going to do?"

The Earth Wife's rumble answered her like distant thunder: "What do you mean, girl, 'we'?"

The fire had sunk. Cattila had melted back into a shadow which had again become the substance, like a cliff upreared against the night. No. They were *circled* by cliffs with a glimmer at their heights, under a roof of southern stars. Ferns sighed. Jame, Lyra and Graykin stood on the pyre's blackened ground, beside a false-fire that was the efflorescence of spores on the bones of a darkling changer.

"Where *are* we?" demanded Lyra.

Her sharp voice echoed from cliff to cliff, a volley of blows rebounding from rock to flesh to bone.

Jame grabbed both girl and man-dog, a hand clamped over each mouth. "This is the Heart of the Woods at Hurlen," she breathed in their ears. "This is killing ground. For pity's sake, shut *up.*"

As debris rattled down from above, pale *imu* faces weathered out of diamantine emerged all around the summit, half obscured by vines as though by hanging hair. The Earth Wife's indignant voice muttered down from all their gaping mouths.

"Look at the mess you've made in my heart—just look! Fire and fungus, death and decay . . . Give me one reason, Nemesis, why I should let you leave this place alive."

"Well, there is this," said Jame, almost apologetically. "If you shout me to death, Lyra will die too, for which her Gran will hardly thank you."

"Ohhh!" Lyra said, not listening. She had picked something up from the ashes.

"Nice of you to remember me as well," Graykin snarled. "A fine lot you've involved me with!"

"And you such an innocent. I did warn you, Gray."

A tremor made them all stagger. If Ragga's heart lay here at the Cataracts, so did the River Snake's, in strong contention. The shaking had set loose spores like a cloud of sparks from the changer's bones, diminishing the false-fire glow. When it died, they might well find themselves stranded.

(But oh, what was it about bones and fire that she couldn't quite remember?)

"Look," she said, scrambling after her wits. "Here and now, I am *not* the problem."

"THIEF."

"Present," said the Earth Wife's imp, out of Lyra's mouth. Grinning, she thrust the ash-covered *imu* medallion into Jame's hand.

Jame stared at it. Her first thought when she had searched the Heart earlier had been right: the *imu had* fallen near the center of the hollow; but she hadn't considered that its sheath of changer's skin might resist the pyre's flames, much less that it would restore clay as it would have flesh. For whatever reason, the *imu* was whole again.

Lyra blinked, the feral light fading from her eyes.

"And that," said Jame, gesturing at her, "is exactly how I acquired the damned thing in the first place: as a gift from your imp. Here."

"You make me a present of my own property?" Despite everything, greed crept into that gravel voice, Ragga's master passion beneath the Earth Wife's stone. She leaned forward out of her root-chair, drawing them back to lodge and hearth-side by her covetousness. "If I give you Mother Ragga's favor, girl, what will you give me? Eh?"

"I-I don't know," said Jame. The Earth Wife might be offering her exactly what she had begged for before in vain, or "favor" might mean the medallion itself. Either way, she understood from Cattila the importance of exchanged gifts. "What do you want?"

"Mmmm. You left behind more than one mess, girl."

Ragga nodded toward the hearth, where a moment ago the darkling false-fire had danced at the Heart's core. They might almost still have been there: on the iron fire-back in high relief was wrought a pattern of fern fronds that seemed to wave in the flickering light. Among them, motionless, crouched a grotesque figure, without a head—the changer whom Kin-Slayer had decapitated.

"It's been long ages since I last had a pet. On the whole, though, I'd prefer one able to hear—say, a dog. Give me yours."

Graykin cringed.

Jame gulped. To lose the Earth Wife's favor in any sense of that word could be disastrous, for the entire Kencyrath. If Rathillien became actively hostile, they had no place to go except back into Perimal Darkling. And if they did finally defeat the shadows that lurked there, what was the point without a home to return to—for, as with the hills above Kithorn, she doubted that her people would ever live on the fallen worlds again. Compared to all that, what was the life of one scruffy half-breed?

Then she meet Graykin's scared eyes, and sighed.

"The only ears I have to offer," she said, turning to Ragga, "are my own. For whatever good *that* is to you."

But there was that nagging fear again: if she made a present of herself to the Earth Wife, she would be letting *some*one down (who?) by not warning him (of what?) Fire, bones . . . Sweet Trinity, Index! The old fool still had a Burnt Man's bone in his pocket.

"I'll be right back," she said, and ran for the door.

"The map!" cried Ragga behind her.

But Jame had already stepped on the nearest rocky ridge. A blast of cold air hit her in the face. Through watering eyes, she saw white peaks spread out before her under the sliver of a moon and under her leading foot, a sheer drop. Over and down, falling, stepping on a rocky slope among bitter scented flowers, floundering in a morass among flies, stumbling up a hill . . . .

" . . . sorry, sorry, sorry . . . ."

The Earth Wife's voice roared after her like an avalanche: "GirrRRLL . . . !"

. . . treading on the River Snake's back . . . .

Icy water up to the knee. The Silver's bed twisted under foot, throwing her sky high in a moon-spangled spray. Beneath, she saw another mountain chain, then plains, then the Eastern Sea, leaping up at her. At the water's edge, swallowing it, was the vast maelstrom known as the Maw, a hundred miles across—the mouth of the Chaos Serpent itself? For a moment, she thought that she would fall into it, but it was dirt onto which she crashed: the lodge floor beyond the eastern edge of the map, where sink-sand poured down as if into a hole. Still, the ground rippled under her like water, while the beams overhead groaned and the nearby steps cracked. Another tremor.

"*Woke the River Snake, didn't we?*"

If the Four hadn't, she now surely had.

"Nemesis," muttered Ragga, holding down her skirt as its hem seethed with the black wings of terrified foxkin.

"Sorry," said Jame again, staring at the five indentations her feet had left across west and central Rathillien, trying to remember if any cities had lain in her path.

She stumbled up the cracked steps and grabbed the door's edge for support as the lodge shook again. Chittering foxkin streamed into the square over her head. She leaned out after them.

"Index! Take the bone out of your poc . . . uh!"

A yelp of warning from Graykin, too late: a big hand closed on her collar.

VII

FAR AWAY, someone was shouting her name.

Jame tried to follow the voice out of the maze of pain throbbing inside her skull. She must have hit her head. No. Someone had struck it against . . . against a doorpost. Yes. Jerking her out of the Earth Wife's lodge. Now she was being dragged, her knees banging on uneven pavement. When she opened her eyes, though, the bruising abruptly stopped. Beneath her lay utter darkness. Had she been stricken not only numb but blind? No. Beneath her lay the abyss of a breached sigil, through whose depths even now a ribbon of fire was unrolling.

The moment she had seen it clearly, she was falling—only to be brought up short, half-choked, by the grip on her collar. Her captor jerked her impatiently out of the void and stalked on across pavement marked by charcoal lines which his bare feet scuffed and broke in passing.

"Lady!" Graykin howled somewhere off to the right. "Where *are* you?"

Obviously, in the square, being hauled by Sonny to the well to serve as snake-bait. Damn.

Jame twisted out of the Merikit's grip and rolled to her feet.

"Can't we discuss this?"

In answer, he lunged at the sound of her voice. She tripped him and ran.

By now, most of the sigils were breached and reeking, the angry pulse in their depths reflecting on the bellies of the low, sullen clouds, red on red. To keep track of where she was had taken a constant, conscious effort. Jame supposed that she must now be somewhere west of the well-mouth, unless Sonny had gotten lost. North was to the right, then. Best to get out of the square as quickly as possible, hoping that that in itself didn't rupture sacred space. Ancestors knew, she had done sufficient harm already.

Huh. Yes. Bad enough that she'd let herself get stuck in this mess as the most inadequate of Challengers, like a player in the seeker's mask when everyone else had run away. Since then, not only had she failed to win over any of the Four but she had wreaked havoc on the Earth Wife's map and, inadvertently, run off again with her precious medallion. Ragga probably even blamed her for the Caineron involvement, since neither Caldane nor his daughters would have been in the weirding's way if not for her. What rotten luck to have such a trio mixed up in this . . . .

But had it been pure chance? Cattila claimed that the Chaos Serpent and its brood were a primordial part of Perimal Darkling, which had also long sought to make that fallen highlord Gerridon its Voice. If he had become a part of it, perhaps it had gained not only his scheming mind but also his perverse desire to implicate his people in the fall of this world as he had in that of the previous one. What a tool stupid, ambitious Caldane would be in such a plan—and what a mess they all were in, Kencyr and Rathillien alike, if there truly was a link between Gerridon and the Chaos Serpent.

Ahead, beyond one of the last sigil lines, veils of smoke shifted around upthrust, blackened timbers that loomed like a pair of gigantic, knobby knees. Beneath them, the cinder skull of Tungit's bone-fire rested like a scorched boulder on a pelvic cradle of half-burnt beams.

A current of fresh, cool air stung Jame's eyes, just as the smoke had at first. Inhaling, she saw the quake-ravaged square, its pattern of charcoal lines nearly obliterated by cracks and Sonny's careless stumbling, Kithorn's broken tower still crowned with Mount Alban, and Tungit's small fire a bare twenty feet away. The old shaman himself crouched by his handiwork, a gray, shaggy gnome with anxious eyes. She had forgotten that he and his three colleagues were also in the square, as invisible to her as presumably to their gods.

More fresh air. Through shifting mist, she saw that the torches in the northern corner had been knocked over by the tremors and blue smoke was bleeding out through the gap. There stood the smithy, weirding boiling out of it like smoke from a house on fire. Kirien, Ashe, and Index watched with helpless fascination while a bundle of silver-gilt fur snored at their feet. Index held something black gingerly between forefinger and thumb—the Burnt Man's bone, Jame saw with relief. So, whether he had heard her or not, he'd had the sense to remove that potential inferno from his pocket, if not to let go of it altogether. The old miser.

But if scrollsmen weren't so tenacious, their knowledge would long since have turned to dusty rumor. Instead, Index clung to his morsel of primary research at the risk of his fingers, as single-mindedly as Kirien pursued truth or Ashe defended her humanity with songs full of terrible wisdom. Jame felt sudden gratitude to all three of them, for their basic worth. Perhaps there *was* a reason to go home after all, not to a place but to a people.

Or perhaps not.

Out of the mist rolling from the smithy's door walked Brier Iron-thorn, grim faced, carrying Kindrie's limp form. In her dire need she'd had the support of a Knorth, but not the one in whom she had put her trust.

I didn't keep faith, Jame thought. *Neither of us will ever forget that.*

At the Kendar's heels slunk a shaggy form: the Wolver Grimly, terrified, in his complete furs. After him came Torisen Black Lord.

Jame hadn't seen her brother's face at the wolvers' keep. How haggard he looked, shadows under his silver-gray eyes, black stubble blurring the sharp line of his jaw, white fretting his disordered hair. There was white, too, on his right hand. Bandages. Splints. But in his left hand shone bright, naked steel, stained with red light as though already dipped in blood: Kin-Slayer unsheathed.

Oh shit, thought Jame, stopping short.

The earth growled. Flagstones shifted uneasily in their beds, edges grinding together like teeth, pebbles spitting up from the cracks to dance around Jame's feet. The tremors were getting worse. Kithorn wavered in and out of sight as other torches fell to the east, confusing the currents within the square.

Then from the direction of the well came a disgusting noise, half scaly rasp, half wet slobber. Over her shoulder, Jame saw the well's lip rise. Under the green mottling of the serpentine rim was a band as pallid as an earthworm's belly. Then the well-mouth jammed back down again, hard.

The concussion sent an earth wave rolling outward. Flagstones tipped and shattered over it like thick ice, throwing Jame from her feet. On the shock surged, rapidly diminishing but still frightful, to scatter the bone-fire and crack the smithy wide open. Torisen tried to catch the doorjamb with his injured hand to steady himself, missed, and fell heavily. Jarred from his grasp, Kin-Slayer skidded into the square. His eyes, following it, met his sister's.

The currents shifted again. Back in sacred space, she saw Tungit's bone-fire overthrown, like the remains of some primordial giant strewn across the earth. Their fall had almost but not quite broken the last sigil, lying black between sacred space and ruin, between her and safety. Kin-Slayer flamed on the other side, out of both her reach and Tori's.

Jame lurched to her feet and turned to circle the obstacle—but here came Sonny stumbling toward her, huge and glowering. Reeking fissures cut her off to right and left. No breath of outside air disturbed the trap in which he had caught her.

Was it one, though? Before, she had only started to fall when she had clearly seen the abyss beneath her.

The Merikit advanced. Jame stepped backward without thinking. Her heel came down on empty space. She fell, mouth open in a yell of terror, eyes screwed shut. The yell became a startled grunt as the up-thrust edges of ancient paving knocked the breath out of her. She was back in real space.

No, don't look . . . . Run.

Impossible, over that shattered terrain. Jame dropped to all fours and scuttled, barking knuckles, banging knees, eyes screwed shut against the shock of each blow, against the urge to check her course. It was less than thirty feet to the north corner of the square. How far wrong could she go?

Far enough.

As she shifted her weight forward, her hand came down on air and she fell. Something stopped her with a blow to the stomach, jarring open her eyes. She was half over the edge of a broad pit. The ridge jammed into her middle was its rim, no longer smooth serpentine but green mottled and leathery. Just below her hand was a ring of yellowed spikes; below that, red, padded walls studded with down-turned, horny projections. Out of the depths came a rumble and then a hoarse sigh—*haaaah*—laced with wisps of weirding and an unholy stench.

Jame found herself on her feet, backing away from those scaly lips which had been the well's mouth. The River Snake's empty belly growled again, and the ground shivered.

Behind her, Sonny stumbled out of the smoke. His bare shins, seen through tattered red cloth, were bruised and bloody, likewise his feet. He kept tripping . . . on the patch of smooth plain between fissures which she saw? No. For him as for her moments ago, scrambling blind, this was Kithorn's quake-stricken courtyard. He was lurching across broken pavement which she now neither saw nor which would hinder her in a fight. For the first time, the advantage was hers.

But still something made her hesitate. She was remembering all the times in the past when she had been mistaken for easy prey. "A baited trap," her friend Darinby had once called her, too slight for some men to take seriously or to forgive when they found they were wrong. Unlike those bullies, though, Sonny was an over-grown, not very bright child. The scowl distorting his face squeezed all his features toward the center, like those of a small boy in a tantrum. He must have always gotten what he wanted through sheer size and strength. He was trying to bull his way through now, in near panic, against odds he couldn't begin to understand.

Just then, with a startled grunt, the big Merikit toppled forward.

A shift in the air revealed Tungit standing over him, the Burnt Man's cinder skull raised to strike again, if necessary. The other three shaman-elders flickered in and out of sight as they trotted up, goat-udder breasts swaying under gray hair. Jame heard their words in snatches.

"... too ambitious, too dangerous," Tungit was arguing. "... can't even walk the Way of the Four ... for the best."

"... you mad? ... will make the Challenger the new Favorite, and he isn't Merikit."

"... not even a 'he.'"

"Quiet! ... in trouble enough already? Only men ... allowed here, so he's a man."

"You *are* mad! What will Chingetai say? What about next year?"

Graykin would love this, Jame thought. Local politics at their most ruthless: the choosing of a scapegoat. Should she be glad that Tungit preferred to sacrifice Sonny? And what *about* next year?

Another hungry growl came from the River Snake's belly. The elders looked at each other. Then, with one accord, they grabbed the young man and dragged him, stumbling, dazed, toward the well. Jame found herself in their way.

"No," she said.

They had stopped, staring at her, when far off to the south the bone-fires began to ignite.

At first, Jame thought that they were only sparks. Everything was red—the clouds ribbed with flame, the conflagration in the ground, the tongues of lightning flickering between earth and sky—but those distant points of fire multiplied like glowing rubies added to a string, one after another, faster and faster, flashing up the Silver's curve.

The elders had dropped Sonny and were groping frantically for the bells which they had stowed in their goat-udder breasts. Out came the leather anklets, to be strapped in haste to skinny legs.

Ching! went the bells as the old men stomped, already far behind in the count, dancing like maniacs to catch up. *Ching, ching!* How many bones in all? One hundred? Two? All the Burnt Man's disjointed body, rising out of the earth in living flame, out of winter and night . . . . *Ching, ching, ching!*

Jame glanced up at Mount Alban, still hovering ghost-like above Kithorn's ruined tower which the quakes had not yet overthrown. All the old scholars sleeping above, the irreplaceable knowledge locked in their memories as in the most fragile of scrolls; and below, waiting for the first spark, the inferno . . . .

The bells jangled to an uncertain halt. The progress of the fires had stopped.

Why? thought Jame, peering southward. *Where?*

Somewhere between Falkirr and Wilden. Sweet Trinity. That was where she had removed the Burnt Man's bone from the Merikit's bonfire.

She found herself counting, as though between lightning and thunder, to gage the distance. *One, two, three* . . . . No more sparks appeared, but something still might be coming up the valley in a dark, vengeful rush. *Seven, eight, nine* . . . .

With a hollow boom, fragments of kindling blew out the doors and windows of Kithorn's tower to rain down on the square. Billowing smoke followed. Tungit yelped and kicked the cinder skull away, its eyes and mouth trailing fire. A faint cry from Index outside the square echoed him as the old scrollsman at last perforce gave up his prize.

Jame began to laugh. All that worry about Mount Alban and she had caused this debacle days ago, without even realizing it. How typical.

Then laughter died.

Black smoke had been pouring from the Burnt Man's skull. Now it stooped over them under the low, red sky. A sooty shape half-emerged, as confused as Tungit's scattered fire—the jut of a knee, a leg bone becoming the knotted ridge of a spine, smoke streaming down into ribs, gathering in a domed darkness which rose slowly on a disjointed neck, hollow sockets searching the ground beneath . . . .

From a world away, under the gatehouse, came the welcoming cry of the Burning Ones: *"Tha! Tha! Tha!"*

Tungit crouched, cowering. The other elders seemed to have melted into the ground. Jame wished she could.

"What next?" she hissed at the shaman, wondering if he could understand her as she had him. "It's all gone wrong, but there's got to be *something* we can do. Tungit?"

With the return of sacred space, he had disappeared.

Cattila hobbled out of the mist, supported by Lyra, surrounded by darting foxkin. When the latter saw what loomed over them, they dived inside the old woman's loose, outer vest. She approached, seething physically and mentally.

"A fine mess! Can't anyone do anything right these days?" The presence above had turned at the sound of her shrill voice, still blindly seeking. A muted growl as though of distant thunder came out of it. She glared up. "You—burnt-breath! Where's chief Chingetai?"

Lyra tugged at her sleeve. "Gran!"

"All right, all right. What's the point of a mummery, though, if the real thing barges in? Faugh! Now the Earth Wife is supposed to present her lover, the new Favorite, to her consort, the Burnt Man, as their son. Life out of winter and ashes, d'you see? Spring fertility and frolics. It's called 'fooling death.' Not too bright, our friend up there. Of course, once in a while he catches on and the Favorite spontaneously combusts. Charming, eh?"

"Very," said Jame, with another futile tug at the ivy crown.

"Oh!" said Lyra, staring upward.

Above them, the nebulous, smoky skull seemed to be emptying itself out through mouth, eyes, and nostrils. Fat, smudgy fingers drifted down. A wave of heat preceded them, fetid with the pyre's breath.

"It wasn't supposed to be like this," Catilla was complaining, oblivious. "We should have lost the Riverland, been forced to mind our own business for a change. Stop tugging at me, girl! Nothing less will save that idiot father of yours. Going to Perimal in a pushcart, that boy, and dragging his house after him . . . ."

The smoke fingers groped toward her rising voice. Foxkin, peeking out through the arm-holes of her vest, withdrew abruptly. Lyra buried her face in the old woman's gown as smoke brushed over Cattila's face, then slid past, leaving her in soot-smeared, sputtering outrage.

Sonny sprawled in the way. Smoke fumbled blindly around his fallen body, sparks scorching holes in his red pants, singeing his tattooed skin. He twitched. Loosened strands of his red hair rose in the heat's up-draft, crinkled, and stank. He would burn as though on his own pyre, alive.

"*Tha,*" breathed the murky air, a croon of hunger. "*Thaa, thaaaa . . .*"

"Matriarch," said Jame loudly. "I won the challenge. Present me as the new Favorite."

The smoke rose from Sonny's body and drifted toward her. She went back a step involuntarily but stopped, rigid, as her heel struck the well's rim.

The fingers closed loosely about her in a stifling wave of heat. She held her breath against their stench, as though pressed face to face against the dead. Through streaming eyes, she saw the sparks dance, two by two by two. Not sparks. Eyes: the Burning Ones unleashed and circling hungrily, waiting for the first flinch. She felt them brush against her. Their charred fingers rasped, crumbling, across her face.

Don't move. Don't even blink.

"Burnt Man!" she faintly heard Cattila cry. "Stop messing around! This is the Challenger, triumphant, your true child in destruction, if ever nemesis was. Now bugger off!"

Breath scorched Jame's ear in wordless protest. *A moment more*, must have been that hoarse plea; *just a moment more . . . .*

"*Thaaa-HA!*"

The command boomed like thunder too close to the lightning strike, a vast impact more felt than heard. The smoke shredded with a cry torn away into the distance: "*KI-Ki-ki-iiii . . . .*"

Jame gulped air a moment too soon and went off into a coughing fit. When her eyes cleared, she found herself tottering on the edge of the well, and the Burnt Man standing not a score of feet away with his head in his hands.

No.

That black thing was the cinder-skull, consumed to a brittle shell, already crumbling. The charcoal-smeared man let the pieces fall through his fingers. Through a profusion of singed braids, he was glaring at the erstwhile Favorite as the latter sat up with a groan.

"Somehow," Chingetai growled at his son, "this is all your fault."

What the Merikit chief meant by "all" he immediately made clear, from Sonny's failures as a mewling baby to his many short-comings as a man. It was an epic list, its details honed by repetition. Its subject rose and listened with a sullen scowl. The shaman-elders flickered in and out of sight beside their naked chief, reaching up to pat him as though to calm an enraged stallion.

"Even *that*," he roared, pointing at Jame, "would make me a better son!" Then he looked again. "By the Four, who *is* that?"

Tungit stood on tiptoe to whisper in his ear.

"My new *what?* The Burnt Man *approved?*" He made a half-choked protest as though at a world gone mad and tore at his hair. A scrawny right-hand braid, burned through near the root, came away in his grasp.

Out of the well rose a low, impatient growl, and the ground shivered. One rite might have failed, thought Jame, stepping hastily back from the quaking edge, but not the more important one. Not yet. The River Snake still hungered.

"You see?" Chingetai thundered at his son, brandishing the plait. "This was yours, started with four hairs on the day of your birth." He threw it into the shaft. The earth swallowed it, muttering, unappeased. "You're dead, boy, discarded by the Burnt Man and by me. Now do what you were born for: Jump down that damn well!"

In the midst of this denunciation, Graykin appeared breathless beside Lyra and Cattila, clutching Kin-Slayer. Jame was staring at him when Sonny grabbed her by the arms and swung her out over the well-mouth.

"No!" she and the Southron cried simultaneously, he at Sonny, she at him as he stumbled forward, swinging up the sword.

Too late. With a butcher's dull *thunk*, the war-blade sank into the Merikit's side. Sonny staggered, and dropped Jame.

She fell a dozen feet down the well's throat before her nails caught on its red wall. The surface shuddered and bled as she hung from it. Her boots skidded on its slime. From below came a swift up-rush of foul air—*haaaAAA* . . . —and a sense of something vast, rising fast.

Her foot gained purchase on a down-turned projection, then another. She clawed her way between the stained spikes, feeling the wall begin to bulge as its sheath of muscles contracted. Here at last was the lip . . .

And there stood Sonny, swaying, arms wrapped around himself to stop a tide of blood. Graykin had somehow disengaged Kin-Slayer and fallen back, aghast. From the dumbfounded look on the Merikit's face, he couldn't believe that such a thing had happened—to him, of all people. In shock, he hadn't yet felt the bite of his own death.

"*HaaAAAAA . . . !*" said the River Snake rising, ravenous, to the smell of blood.

The rim surged upward. Jame launched herself off of it, over Sonny's head, into Graykin's arms, nearly onto the sword. As they rolled, a terrible impact bounced them off the ground and down again, hard, in a cloud of dust. Into the ringing silence which followed came a shrill but oddly muffled sound: a scream that seemed to go on and on, until a rasping slurp cut it short.

All too close, something massive scraped over stones . . . questing? No. Receding, gone with a viscous gulp as the earth swallowed it back.

"Another fine lot . . . you've involved me with . . . ." Graykin gasped, choking on the dust-thick air.

"So quit! Or at least . . . get off of me. Matriarch? Lyra?"

Coughs answered her, then Lyra's voice, shaking and piteous: "Here, both of us. Will things *please* stop happening now?"

Perhaps they would. The last upheaval had overthrown all the remaining torches and the blue smoke had dispersed. The square was left quake-wracked, still partly obscured with dust, under red clouds beginning to unravel with dawn. Had everyone really come through this alive? No. Beside the well was a circular indentation as wide as the well-mouth and two spans deep. The pavement inside had been crushed almost to powder. At its center, however, in solitary splendor, were a pair of large, hairy feet, sheared raggedly off at the ankles.

A rumble not unlike a belch came from the depths. A hero had fed the Snake to save the world.

"I hope he gives you gas," said Jame.

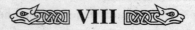

VIII

"FRIEND OR FOE?"

Jame's heart jumped at the sound of her brother's voice behind her. For a moment, she thought he meant her, but then she turned and saw that he was looking down at the orphaned feet.

"Neither, really. Just someone in the wrong place at the right time."

"Somehow, I'm not surprised." He surveyed the surrounding ruins. "Your friend Marc warned me that I would probably find the Riverland reduced to rubble and you in the midst of it, looking apologetic."

"Er . . . sorry."

A winter of things waiting to be said, and that was all she could manage before this cool, strangely elegant man who was her brother. She could feel him withdrawing into the mantle of the Highlord's power, out of reach.

Even now, he wouldn't deal with her twin to twin if he could help it.

Then he saw her face, and the mask of his expression slipped.

"Oh." Despite himself, he raised a splinted finger as if to touch her scarred cheek. "I dreamt . . . ."

A noise made him turn sharply, his uninjured hand leaping to the empty sheath at his side.

Graykin stumbled out of the dust. Narrow face set and ashen, he looked more like Genjar's death banner than ever—a bastard Caineron, clutching Kin-Slayer in his dirty hands.

Torisen went white under his dirt and stubble. "Treason!" he said, in a deep, hoarse voice. Terrified, the Southron fell back before him, unsteadily raising the sword's blood-stained point.

Jame slipped between them. "Tori, no!" She seized her brother's arms, feeling a strength in them far beyond her own. "The bolt is shot!"

He blinked at her, confused and suddenly—frighteningly—vulnerable. "What bolt?"

Impossible to explain, then or perhaps ever, that she had barred a door in his soul-image against their father's madness. Enough, that he had asked in his own voice, not in Ganth's.

Graykin had knelt, face averted but with a wary look askance, to offer Kin-Slayer hilt first—a dedicated sneak, embarrassed to find himself in so prominent a position.

"Company," said Jame softly.

On the far side of the indentation stood Chingetai. His shaman-elders huddled about him, their helpers including the erstwhile Challenger close behind them in a gray, wary clot. The chief was staring at Kin-Slayer.

The Knorth war-blade had come into these hills before, in different hands, to leave stories repeated for generations. Neither he nor his followers were armed at all except for Ashe's confiscated staff.

Still, they out-numbered the Kencyr more than two to one.

Torisen accepted Kin-Slayer and turned to face the Merikit, casually grounding the sword's point. Sonny's blood ran down its blade to form a small puddle at his feet. Jame had fallen back a step to his side. The brush of a furry shoulder against her leg heralded the arrival of the Wolver. The shift upward of the Merikits' eyes told her where Brier Iron-thorn had come to stand behind Torisen, and an unbreathing coldness at her back announced Ashe. Graykin scuttled to the rear, where Index and Kirien could be heard greeting him with surprise.

The two front lines regarded each other warily.

"All right," said Torisen quietly. "I'm open to suggestions."

"Can you use that thing one-handed?" Grimly muttered up at him out of the corner of his mouth.

"You've got Father's ring on your sword-hand," Jame said, "and Kin-Slayer has just tasted life's-blood. I'd be careful, if I were you, what you swing at."

He shot her an impatient look. "You can't mean that it's all a trick, as simple-minded as that. Anyway, how in Perimal's name would *you* know?"

Jame grimaced. "The same way as usual: trial and error."

Chingetai suddenly launched into a speech. At first, his attention still fixed on the sword, he inclined to preoccupation. Soon, however, he hit his normal, loud stride, with a piping echo from the back row where Index translated in paraphrase.

The Kithorn massacre of eighty years ago was mentioned, with the implication that it had been the fault of its misguided victims. Marc's collection of the resulting blood-price nearly side-tracked the Merikit, but after a brief boggle he plowed on, gaining vehemence.

"What *is* all this in aid of?" Torisen asked over his shoulder.

"Hush! He's finished with ancient history."

Chingetai jumped into the depression.

"It's all his fault!" he roared in Merikit, scooping up and brandishing his son's truncated remains.

What followed, up to a point, was the same denunciation as before, not at all hindered by Sonny's inability to hear it. Although sacred space had departed, Jame found that she didn't need Index's gleeful translation to understand; therefore, she knew what Chingetai was saying even when the old scrollsman broke off and began apparently to choke.

"No!" she cried, chagrined to discover that her new knowledge of Merikit didn't extend to speaking it. "Index, tell him that that's impossible!"

His indictment of Sonny's feet concluded, Chingetai seemed momentarily at a loss what to do with them. Then, with a shrug, he tossed them into the well and clambered out of the indentation. Jame fell back a step as he limped toward her, all fear of Kin-Slayer forgotten, a broad grin splitting his blackened face. She had barely time to note that under the charcoal much of his skin was tattooed when she found herself swept up in a bear hug that made her ribs creak.

"No, no, no!" Index was gabbling as he clung onto Tori's sword-arm.

Hearing Brier's quick footstep behind her and a growl from the Wolver, Jame made a flailing gesture for them to hold back. "It isn't—umph!—what you think!"

The next moment she had been dropped to regain her breath as best she could while the Merikit swept out of the courtyard after their chief. On the way, they nearly ran into Cattila and Lyra but skirted them, glaring. Jame remembered the Merikit trophy skins in Caldane's apartment.

Meanwhile, Index had collapsed into another coughing fit, which turned out to be laughter.

"A Kencyr girl, foisted on Chingetai as the new Favorite, his heir for the year! And what does that madman do to save face and get his people safely away? Declares her his new son, to take that young idiot's name and fill his boots—for which, ancestors know, he has no further use. What do you say to that, hey?"

"Only this," said Jame, glowering: "If that man expects me to earn any right-hand braids, he's in for a long wait."

"Hoo!" The old scrollsman wiped him eyes and nose, both of which had run copiously. "There is this, though: we're still on Merikit land. Chingetai has gone to raise his village. He'll be back as soon as he can with the whole tribe to kill us all—except you, of course, favorite son. Time we are leaving."

High time, thought Jame, looking up.

Mount Alban showed through rifts, its exposed inner walls glimmering ghostly silver in the gray dawn. The red-lit clouds had begun to disperse, the fire within them dying with the onset of summer's first day. The weirdingstrom was finally breaking up. The college was about to depart.

Below, glowing wisps trickled out of the broken shell of the smithy. In the back by the forge, where the chimney still upheld the rear wall and part of the roof, weirding light shone briefly as though seen through an open door. A dark figure moved against it, then came forward, brushing tendrils of mist from white, desert gear with a silken handkerchief.

"Well, *really!*" said Adric, Lord Ardeth, surveying the shattered courtyard with fastidious distaste.

IX

"MY BOY, are you quite sure that you're all right?"

"Yes, Adric," Torisen said patiently, for the third or fourth time in as many minutes. He wiped Kin-Slayer on Ardeth's proffered handkerchief and sheathed it, to everyone's ill-concealed relief. "You seem almost disappointed."

Shamelessly eavesdropping with Lyra at her elbow, Cattila chortled at Ardeth's protest. Even from the far side of the well, Jame had heard the wistful note in the old man's voice. A mad Highlord would have been easier to manage than her unpredictable brother, given his family penchant for absurd situations.

This time, though, it seemed to her that the Ardeth had rivaled the Knorth. Adric had been explaining, with a shade less than his usual aplomb, how he had been overtaken in the Southern Wastes by the weirdingstrom. Why he had been there in the first place, he hadn't cared to make quite clear, except that he had apparently expected to find Torisen there before him. Finding Index's herb shed instead had inclined him to question his own sanity, nor was he particularly grateful for the timely shelter which it had provided.

"I don't know how long we were storm-bound in that wretched little shack," he was saying peevishly, while Index sputtered with indignation in the background. "Two days, at least. As well to have been lost at sea in a closed dinghy, all groaning timbers and swaying herbs and seams leaking mist. My Kendar servants were hideously sick. Then we fetched up where Mount Alban should have been and I at last emerged, only to be swept up again by more weirding. Someone in it was calling your name, my boy. Such a forceful voice! I simply followed it here."

That would be Brier Iron-thorn, thought Jame, now with the Wolver on Kithorn's crumbling battlements, keeping watch northward for the Merikits' imminent return.

She wondered if she would ever win back the cadet's trust. After this, Brier would return to Tentir to resume her ten-command and training, no doubt glad to put this whole insane adventure behind her. Perhaps she would eventually become one of the great randon, whose memories live in song for generations. She had the potential. But she was also as much a prisoner of her past as Jame had been of hers—no, more, since Brier only knew how to fight what the Caineron had done to her with its own weapons of cold distrust.

What things we could teach each other, thought Jame.

Then with a jolt she remembered that Bane had once said something similar to her. What wisdom had she to impart less dark than his? The best thing she could do for Brier Iron-thorn, probably, was to leave the Kendar alone.

As for herself, though, what now?

Kirien and Ashe had withdrawn to the edge of the courtyard where Kindrie lay in *dwar* sleep with Jorin curled snoring in his arms. The scholars' low voices had half-woken the ounce, through whom Jame had overheard a conversation never meant for her.

"So you didn't try a test after all," the Jaran Lordan had said to the haunt singer. When the latter hadn't replied, Kirien had stared hard at her for a moment and then sworn under her breath. *"So that was it. According to the old songs, only a Kencyr can destroy a Tyr-ridan. When you pointed Jame out to Sonny, you thought that he would prove she was a false nemeis by killing her. Trinity, Ashe, that's cold-blooded . . . and lame-brained. His failure doesn't establish anything, except that she's damned lucky."*

"Next time," the haunt had muttered, *"I'll do better."*

Even her own people wanted her dead. No wonder she felt safer with the well-mouth between her and any of them.

Seeker, seeker . . . .

She had thought that it was enough to drop the mask, to be only herself. But who was she?

Maybe she should complete her withdrawal, run away to become the "son" that the Merikit Chingetai had proclaimed her, the first Kencyr in eighty years with free license to roam these hills. Jorin would love that.

Yes, but then what would she do about Graykin, now skulking around the edges of the courtyard as if afraid either to draw more attention to himself or to be left behind?

And if she did flee up into the hills, whom might she encounter there? According to Merikit beliefs, she was now also the Burnt Man's son, or was that the Earth Wife's lover, or both? This was getting not only complicated but potentially messy.

Anyway, Mother Ragga must still think of her as a thief. That damn *imu*. She took the medallion out of her pocket, as always feeling its power tingle unpleasantly through both her gloves and its covering of changer's skin. But this time something had been added to it. Eyes, mouth, ears . . . .

Ears, framing the crude *imu* face like bits of leathery, dried fruit.

"If I give you Mother Ragga's favor, girl, what will you give me?"

Not Graykin's ears or her own, after all, but the *imu*'s, to be carried into Kencyr houses where the Earth Wife feared to go, to listen for her as she had for Cattila at Gothregor . . . .

"Is that it, Ragga?" Jame whispered into one of the shivelled flaps. "Have I your favor after all?"

The *imu*'s lips moved against her face. She jerked the medallion away, unsure if it had meant to bite or kiss.

"We'll just have to see, then, won't we?" she muttered, slipping it back into her pocket.

A descending cry and a great splash drew all eyes to the basin at the square's western corner. In it floundered a great welter of wet skirts, making angry noises. Out of this confusion emerged Kallystine. Water weeds crowned her straggling hair and inch long catfishlings cascading from her clothes. She clawed a slimy caul from her face. Under it, her wet mask clung to her features with unbecoming fidelity.

Lyra, after a moment's open-mouthed gawk, burst out laughing.

By then, Kallystine had caught sight of Torisen. However, her half-sister's laughter made her pause, furious, to try ineffectually to set herself to rights.

Torisen had also recognized her, with difficulty and dismay.

His expression would have amused Ardeth, except that as the old lord's gaze had swept across the square toward the newcomer, he had for the first time noticed Jame on the other side of the well. Fifteen decades had made his far-sight unusually keen. Still, he hesitated to believe what he saw.

"My dear boy! That can't be . . . but the family resemblance . . . it *is*!"

"What?" said Torisen, his attention wrenched from the sight of his consort angrily shaking fish out of her bodice. "Oh. Yes, I'm afraid so."

"But . . . but this is appalling! A Highborn lady in this place, bare-faced, in that indecent garb . . . . See here, my boy, this must never become common knowledge! When I think how difficult it was to explain away your eccentric departure from Kothifir . . . ."

"How did you, by the way?"

"During my years as a diplomat, I earned a singer's right to the Lawful Lie. I told the High Council that trouble in the north demanded your immediate attention . . . which seems, after all, to have been no more than the truth. I tell you, though, your reputation won't survive another scandal!"

"But you just said that you successfully concealed my . . . er . . . eccentricity," said Torisen, a glint coming into his eyes which his old friend would have done well to notice. "As for our reputation, everyone knows we Knorth are as mad as a gelded rathorn, to use Harn's elegant phrase."

But Ardeth wasn't listening. The Highlord's affairs had obviously gotten out of hand, as he had always predicted they would, and must be saved by an older, wiser head. If he felt satisfaction that events could finally be turned to his own advantage, he dismissed the thought. After all, it only made sense that Knorth honor should be saved and his young friend's position strengthened by an alliance between their two houses. If his son Pereden wasn't alive to oblige, grandsons were. It only remained to decide which.

Torisen tried to stem this tide of plans, without so much as fully getting the old lord's attention. He himself impatiently brushed aside Kallystine when she swept down on him, her remaining charms in full if dank display.

"Lady, please. Not now."

Kallystine recoiled with a venomous hiss. "Jameth. Always Jameth . . . ."

She swung back her hand to slap him. In her palm, steel flashed.

"No!" Jame cried, starting forward, but she was much too far away.

Lyra caught her sister's back-flung arm, pulling her off-balance and bearing her to the ground. Kallystine's hand, striking the pavement, sprang wide open.

"Why," said Ardeth, staring, "that's a razor-ring."

"You slapped my sister," said Torisen slowly, "with *that*."

Lyra hastily rolled away. Kallystine was left crouching like a toad in her sodden finery, mask askew, perfect teeth bared behind wrinkled lips. The Highlord stood over her.

"Caineron," he said, in a voice through which the cords of his power ran like steel. "I curse you and cast you out. Never come near me or mine again."

His words drove her backward, yammering, on hands and knees. Then she was on her feet and would have bolted out of the courtyard if Cattila hadn't stood in her way. The Caineron Matriarch opened her voluminous vest, dislodging foxkin, and wrapped her great-great-granddaughter in it.

"There, there," she said as Kallystine buried her face against her ancient bosom and burst into tears. "There, there." Her rheumy eyes met Torisen's over the bowed head, power speaking to power. "A poor, disgraced thing, Highlord, but of my blood. I will care for her."

"That was well done," said Jame softly to Lyra. "You'll need a new title soon: 'Lack-wit' doesn't seem so appropriate anymore."

"Actually, it is," Lyra whispered back. "Tackling Kallystine like that . . . it wasn't exactly on purpose: I . . . sort of tripped."

"Huh. Just the same, in future I'd keep out of M'lady's way if I were you."

"*Now* what?" Torisen demanded.

They all heard it: another shriek that seemed to plummet out of the sky, although no one saw any falling body. It ended with a crash. At the southern corner of the square, the wicker cage which had held the Tishooo had been smashed flat. On its ruins sprawled a fat, glittering figure. Graykin ducked out of sight as Lord Caineron sat up with a groan. Ardeth went to help him rise under the weight of his golden accouterments which, nonetheless, had not prevented the Tishooo from carrying him off. He rewarded the old lord's assistance with a blurry snarl.

As the two made their way back across the broken pavement, Jame decided that shaken and confused as Caldane undoubtedly was, he would have been much more so if he'd had a clear memory of the past few hours. For him and Kallystine both, their possession respectively by the Falling Man and the Eaten One must now seem like bad dreams, rapidly fading.

Meanwhile, Ardeth was taking this opportunity to inform Caldane about the new alliance, making "Jameth" sound at best a poor bargain. If he hoped to slip this news past the lord of Restormir when he was in no state to protest, however, he underestimated the Caineron will, if not the wits.

"Wha' do you mean, a contract with your house?" Caldane demanded, stopping short. "The young fool's already contracted to my daughter, isn't he? Can't keep his hands off her."

"Not with Torisen. With his sister. Anyway, M'lady Kallystine has . . . er . . . rather badly disgraced herself. She just tried to slash the Highlord with a razor-ring. In front of witnesses. I'm afraid," Ardeth added smoothly, with no evident sorrow, "that he had quite sufficient grounds to cast her off."

"*What?*" Glaring around him, Caldane caught sight of his daughter cowering in Cattila's arms and advanced on her. "Here, girl, what's all this nonsense . . . and what in Perimal's name has happened to your face?"

"You, boy," said the Caineron Matriarch, stopping her great-grandson in his tracks. "Leave be. This business is mine."

Caldane turned, shaking his head like a bull that had charged a sapling and hit an oak. His blood-shot eyes fell on Lyra. He grabbed her arm. "Then here's younger meat, Knorth, good enough for the likes of you. She even comes to you unbroken. You laughed at me for contracting her to that Karkinorien princeling, but I wasn't fool enough to grant him full rights."

He shoved the terrified girl into the Highlord's arms, jarring the latter's splinted fingers. Torisen swallowed a grunt of pain. Over Lyra's head, his eyes met his sister's. It had come into both their minds simultaneously that Lyra didn't know what being "broken" meant.

"Don't be afraid," he said to the girl gently and put her aside.

"Not the Highlord," Ardeth repeated patiently, "*Jameth*."

Caldane, following his gaze, flinched. "Oh, my God! Not *her*." Then, in a surprising act of self-control, he pulled himself together. "That is to say, yes, of course she must be contracted out—to a Caineron. In my house, we know how to keep women in their place . . . ."

"Ha!" said Cattila.

". . . and believe me, that one needs it."

On this, the two lords agreed. Then they fell into a wrangle over Jame's disposition which, from its abbreviated points, must have summarized all their previous arguments.

Torisen rubbed his eyes, looking suddenly exhausted. Jame wondered why he didn't just tell them to mind their own business. Then she realized that it wasn't this squabble alone but a winter's worth of them which had wore him down and now threatened to grind out the sparks of his authority. Not knowing what to do about her, he couldn't fight them. At stake here was not only her fate but that of the Kencyrath: would its Highlord rule or be ruled by the self-interest of such men as these?

"Listen!" came the Wolver's yelp from the battlements.

His ears, keener than theirs, had caught the sound first, but in a moment they all heard it: a distant, bone-jarring throb of drums. The Merikit were coming.

"What these people do to captives," said Index, "you really don't want to know. Believe me, we need to get out of here."

"Well, I and mine won't," snarled Caineron. "Not without a decision! Knorth, you've danced around this long enough. To whose house do you send your sister?—and if it isn't to mine, be prepared for war!"

"Oh, really," said Ardeth. "Caldane, I keep telling you: It's already decided. My grandson Dari will probably be the best choice," he added, thinking out-loud. "His breath may smell like a rotten eel, but no woman ever contradicts him twice."

With that, they were off again, the chance of an imminent, messy death secondary to their winter-long obsession.

Graykin sidled up behind Jame. "*Let* them stay," he hissed in her ear. "*We* can go."

Then he ducked away again as Torisen shot him an annoyed glance.

"Who *is* that person anyway, and what does he mean, 'we'?"

"Gran?" said Lyra, in a small, frightened voice.

Cattila shook her head. Although she had faced Caldane down in a woman's matter, now they were bound by his word.

"We won't leave you," Torisen said, turning back to them.

Kirien cleared her throat. "Highlord, it sounds to me as if the Ardeth and the Caineron are deadlocked. May

I suggest an alternative? 'Lordan' is an ancient title applied to either the male or female heir of a lord. Nothing in the law forbids the latter, as I've told you before. Since then, my research has progressed. By ancient custom, the heir always has the status of a man, and 'he' doesn't form any contracts before coming of age at twenty-seven. Why don't you take a lesson from the Merikit Chingetai? He's made your sister his son; likewise, you can declare her your lordan."

Caineron gaped, then sputtered with laughter.

Ardeth smiled. "You academicians will have your little jokes."

"The joke," Index snapped, "is that we should be debating this now."

Indeed, they were all aware of the approaching uproar. "*Boom*-wah! *Boom*-wah!" The Merikit could hardly be accused of stealth.

"There are about two hundred of them," Brier reported, coming up with the Wolver close on her heels. "They're bringing fire. Highlord, this is not a defensible position."

From far above, in Mount Alban's tower, a voice trained to carry floated down: "Will you *please* stop that racket? People up here are trying to sleep!"

"That does it," said Torisen. "Kiri, I accept your suggestion."

"Mad!" Caldane exclaimed, staring. "D'you hear that? Raving mad!"

"Really, my boy, this farce has gone on long enough . . . ."

"There is this too," said Ashe. "Traditionally, the Knorth Lordan trains at Tentir to become a randon."

Was the haunt singer proposing another test? If so, the only way Jame saw to pass it was to get herself killed by some enraged randon. Or Tori might wring her neck on general principles. Instead, after a moment's blank surprise, he looked thoughtful. Sweet Trinity. Could he actually be considering the idea? It *would* buy time, and give him an excuse to drop her as his heir if she failed. It took Ardeth, however, to make up his mind.

"My dear, dear boy," said the old lord, with an air of much tried patience, "you simply can not . . . ."

"I can do anything which the law allows and custom approves. This seems to be covered by both. And I'm tired of you or anyone else trying to run my life. *Understood?*"

He looked at Jame, with a sudden, wry smile. "When I was a boy, serving the Ardeth, I would have given anything to become a cadet at Tentir. But Adric forbade it."

"You *know* it was impossible!" the old lord protested. "Why, if anyone had so much as suspected who you were before you came of age . . . ."

"So you told me, Adric, when you dismissed my request as if it were a child's whim. So I lost my chance. Now, it seems, my sister is to have hers—if she wants it. Do you?"

"Yes," said Jame. "Very, very much," and burst out laughing at Brier Iron-thorn's expression.

"Right. Then I assume that we can leave. Caldane?"

Caineron glowered at him. What an ugly face that man had when he was thwarted, Jame thought—or anytime else, for that matter. "No doubt, as always, you think you've been very clever. Well, Knorth, if your 'lordan' can enroll at Tentir, so can mine, and it's my war-chief's turn to serve as the college commandant. So we'll just see, won't we?"

Torisen sighed. "I suppose we will. About all sorts of things. In the meantime, if I've understood this correctly, our way home lies above Kithorn's tower. My lords and ladies, will it please you to climb? I shouldn't dawdle about it either, if I were you."

They didn't, taking Kindrie's limp form with them, Graykin skulking behind, with an anxious glance at his mistress as he sidled past her.

At Kithorn's front door, Jorin draped over her shoulder and snoring in her ear, Jame had paused to look northward over the battlements. The Merikit were flowing toward Kithorn between dark hills, torches flaring in the gloom beneath dawn-lit clouds. Drums echoed back from the mountain slopes above:

"*BOOM*-Wah-wah . . . *BOOM*-Wah-wah . . ."

It looked more like a procession than an attacking force.

The Merikit would undoubtedly kill any trespassers whom they caught, but Jame didn't think that their chief really wanted to catch anyone. Even someone so flamboyant must feel, as Lyra did, that Summer Eve had already provided enough excitement. If Chingetai had known that the Caineron lord was here as well as his womenfolk, he might have felt differently.

And how did *she* feel about all the strange things which she had learned concerning the Merikit gods (if that was what one called the Four) and Rathillien itself? If even half of it was true, the Kencyrath had totally misjudged this world and their relationship to it. Two years ago, in Tai-tastigon, the mere suggestion of such a thing would have half-panicked her. Now she felt an old, familiar excitement: There was so much to learn and, thanks to Chingetai, such a wonderful opportunity to do it.

Last up the steps, Torisen stopped beside her. "You can't go back to the Riverland wearing that." He disentangled the ivy crown from her hair and threw it away. "Next Midsummer Day, the Merikit will expect you to return here. Of course, you won't."

Jame didn't answer.

She had wondered what to tell her brother, about not only the Merikit but also the strange things going on among his own people. Nothing, she decided, unless he specifically asked. The scrollsmen were right: Knowledge was power. She would need much more of both to survive, lordan or not, as long as Torisen could reduce her to nothing again with a word if it suited him.

The clouds over Kithorn still simmered red, but they were beginning to lift and disperse. Soon the Tishooo would return to blow them away and Mount Alban southward with them. To the east, over the Snowthorns, a sickle thin crescent moon rose barely before the sun.

Torisen remembered how he and his sister had watched it rise over the trees at the Cataracts, the two of them reunited after so long and such strangers to each other.

"This is going to be hard," he had said. *"For both of us. But we'll find a way to make it work. We have to."*

That was still true, and no easier than it had been before. He felt as if events had out-paced him, too much happening too fast and he too little in control.

"The moon is waning toward the dark," he said somberly. "I should have known about Caldane's man being in charge of Tentir now. Did you know how our father came to power? His older brother, the Knorth Lordan, was killed in training at Tentir. The college has its own rules. If you're hurt there, I can't even demand your blood-price."

It was on the tip of his tongue to renounce his offer. What was it but madness to think that any Highborn girl could become a randon? At best, she would fail and make them both laughing stocks. At worst . . . . But he had proposed this before his oldest friend and worst enemy. To back down would look like weakness. He couldn't afford that, and his sister knew it. He heard it in her silent refusal to protest or point out the obvious. Her strength frightened him.

Your Shanir twin, boy, your darker half, returned to destroy you . . . .

No. He wouldn't listen. The bolt was shot.

The sun raised a blazing rim over the mountains' spine, striking him momentarily blind.

"The moon may wane," said the darkness beside him that was his sister, "but this is also sunrise on the first day of summer. Warm days and new life. You've earned that, and so have I. Let the bastards take them from us if they can."

Then she laughed and whistled, a clear, soaring note. The wind came as if in answer. Its wings brushed his face as he blinked to clear his tired eyes—or was that her finger-tips in a phantom caress?

"Here's Old Man Tishooo at last. Come on, brother. Let's go home."

TO RIDE
A RATHORN

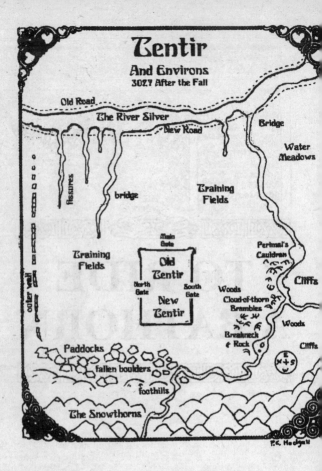

Tentir

And Environs
3027 After the Fall

Old Road

The River Silver

New Road

Bridge

Water
Meadows

fissures

bridge

Training
Fields

Training
Fields

Main
Gate

Old
Tentir

North
Gate

South
Gate

New
Tentir

Perimal's
Cauldron

Cliffs

Woods

Cloud-of-thorn
Brambles

Woods

Breakneck
Rock

Cliffs

outer wall

Paddocks

fallen boulders

foothills

The Snowthorns

P.C. Hodgell

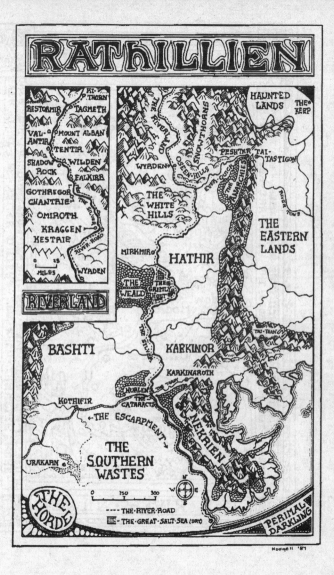

RATHILLIEN

RIVERLAND

FR-THORN
RESTORMIR   TAGMETH
VAL-   MOUNT ALBAN
ANTIR
          TENTIR
SHADOW   WILDEN
ROCK
               FALKIRR
GOTHREGOR
CHANTRIE
  OMIROTH
  KRAGGEN
  KESTRIE

0   25
    MILES
          RIVER-ROAD
               WYADEN

FR-THORN
CLAW THE RIVER
EVER-QUICK RIVER
SNOWTHORNS
HAUNTED LANDS   THE KEEP
WYADEN   OSSE-HILLS   PESHTAR   TAI-TASTIGON
THE WHITE HILLS   ANARCHIES   RIVER TONE
MIRKMIR   HATHIR
THE WEALD   TREB   GRIMLY HOLT
                              THE EASTERN LANDS

BASHTI   KARKINOR   TAI-THAN

KARKINAROTH
KOTHIFIR   HURLEN THE CATARACT   TAI-THAN
  ← THE ESCARPMENT →   NEKRIEN
URAKARN   THE SOUTHERN WASTES

0   150   300   N W·E S

THE HORDE

---- THE·RIVER·ROAD
▦ THE·GREAT·SALT·SEA (DRY)

PERIMAL DARKLING

Hodge II '87

THE · RIVERLAND

Kithorn

Restormir

Tagmeth

Mount Alban

Valantir

Wilden

Tentir

Falkirr

Shadow Rock

Gothregor

Chantrie

Omiroth

N W E S

25 miles

○ keeps
○ ruins

Kraggen

Kestrie

BY · ORDER · OF · THE · HIGH · COUNCIL · THE · SCROLLSMEN · OF · MT · ALBAN ·
PREPARED · THIS · MAP · DATED · 3026 : THE · LORDS · ARE · REMINDED · HOW ·

EVER · THAT · THE · VALLEY · DIFFERS · FOR · EACH · TRAVELER : MORE ·
OVER · THE · WEIRDINGSTROM · OF · 3027 · MAY · HAVE · SERIOUSLY · ALTERED · IT

THE · RIVER · SILVER

·The·Eastern·Lands·

THE KEEP

THE
HAUNTED LANDS

PERIMAL
DARKLING
THE BARRIER

SKYRR
TAI-TASTIGON

THE EBONBANE

METALONDAR

EAST
KENSHOLD

TAI-
TAROSOLOFF
(ruined)

BEN-AR
CONFEDERATION

EMMIS

RIVER TONE

END-
ISCAR

TONE
MOUTH
BAY

LEFY

TAI-ABENDRA

RIVER WEIR

TAI-WEIR

TAI-THAN
(ruined)

RIVER SONDRE

TAI-
SONDRE

THE EBONBANE

MILDARIEN PENINSULA

CAPE OF
THE LOST

THE
BAY OF
BENITAR

FAR
ISLES

N

Miles   50 100 150 200 250

HODGELL

⚜ CHAPTER I ⚜

An Unfortunate Arrival

1st of Summer

I

THE SUN'S descending rim touched the white peaks of the Snowthorns, kindling veins of fire down their shadowy slopes where traces of weirding lingered. Luminous mist, smoking out of high fissures, dimmed the setting sun. A premonitory chill of dusk rolled down toward the valley floor like the swift shadow of an eclipse. Leaves quivered as it passed and then were still. Birds stopped in mid-note. A moment of profound stillness fell over the Riverland, as if the wild valley had drawn in its breath.

Then, from up where the fringed darkness of the ironwoods met the stark heights, there came a long, wailing cry, starting high, sinking to a groan that shook snow from bough and withered the late wild flowers of spring in the upland meadows. Thus the Dark Judge greeted night after the first fair day of summer:

All things end, light, hope, and life. Come to judgment. Come!

On the New Road far below, a post horse clattered to a sudden stop while his rider dropped the reins and stuffed the hood of her forage jacket into her ears. It was said that anyone who heard the bleak cry of the blind Arrin-ken had no choice but to answer it. She had heard . . . but so had the rest of the valley. It probably wasn't a summons to her at all, the cadet named Rue told herself nervously. Surely, she had done nothing that required judgment, even at Restormir, even to Lord Caineron.

Just following orders, sir.

Sweat darkened her mount's flanks and he resentfully mouthed a lathered bit. They had come nearly thirty miles that day from the Scrollsmen's College at Mount Alban, a standard post run between keeps, but not so easy over a broken roadway strewn with fallen trees. They were near home now and the horse knew it, but still he hesitated, head high, ears flickering.

The earth grumbled fretfully and pebbles jittered underfoot. Rue snatched up the reins to keep her mount from bolting. The damn beast ought to know by now that he couldn't outrun an aftershock. Three days ago, a massive weirdingstrom had loosened the sinews of the earth from Kithorn to the Cataracts. The Riverland had been shaken by tremors ever since but, surely, they must end soon.

"Damn River Snake," she muttered, and spat into the water—a Merikit act of propitiation that the Kendar of her distant keep had adopted.

The hill tribes believed that all quakes were caused by vast Chaos Serpents beneath the earth who must occasionally either be fought or fed to be kept quiet. Rue found nothing strange in such an idea but had the sense—usually—not to say as much to her fellow cadets.

Memory made her wriggle in the saddle: "*Stick to facts, shortie, not singers' fancies.*"

That damned, smug Vant. Riverland Kendar thought that they were so superior, that they knew so much.

But only the night before on Summer's Eve, a Merikit princeling had descended, reluctantly, to placate the great snake that lay beneath the bed of the Silver. Rue had seen the pair of feet, neatly sheared off at the ankles, which he had left behind.

The horse jumped again as a silvery form tumbled down the bank and plopped onto the road almost under his nose. With a twist and a great wriggling of whiskers, the catfish righted itself on stubby pectoral fins and continued its river-ward trudge. If the fish were coming back down from the hills, thought Rue, the worst must be over.

She kicked her tired mount into a stiff-legged trot. The sun sank. Dusk pooled in the reeds by the River Silver, then over-flowed them in a rising tide of night. Shadows seemed to muffle the clop of hooves and the jingle of tack.

They crested yet another rise, and there before them lay Tentir, the randon college.

Rue stared. All along the river's curve, the bank had fallen in, taking trees, bridge, and road with it. Parallel to the river, fissures scored the lower end of the training fields, some only yards in length, others a hundred feet or more, all half full of water reflecting the red sky like so many bloody slashes.

Farther back, much of the outer curtain wall had been thrown down. The fields within lay empty and exposed.

The college itself stood well back on the stone toes of the Snowthorns. Old Tentir, the original fortress, looked as solid as ever. It was a massive three-story high block of gray stone, slotted with dark windows above the first floor, roofed with dark blue slate. As if as an afterthought, spindly watch towers poked up from each corner. To the outer view at least, it was arguably the least imaginative structure in the Riverland. Behind it, surrounding a hollow square, was New Tentir, the college proper. While the nine major houses had once dwelt in similar barracks, changes in house size and importance over the centuries had allowed some to seize space from their smaller neighbors. When they could no longer expand outward, they had built upward. The result from this vantage point was an uneven roofline of diverse heights and pitches, rather like a snaggle-toothed jaw. At least none of the "teeth" seemed to be missing, although some roofs showed gaping holes. Rue sighed with relief: she had expected worse.

But what was that, rising from the inner courtyard? Smoke?

Rue's heart clenched. For a moment, she might have been looking down on Kithorn, the bones of its slaughtered garrison lying unclaimed and dishonored in its smoldering ruins. None of her generation had been alive then, eighty years ago, but no one in the vulnerable border keeps ever forgot that terrible story or the cruel lesson it had taught.

To the Riverland Kencyr, however, it was only an old song of events far away and long ago. After all, no hill tribe would dare to try its strength against *them*.

No. Not smoke. Dust. What in Perimal's name . . . ?

The post horse stomped and jerked at the reins, impatient. Why were they standing here? Why indeed? From behind came the click of hooves and a murmur of voices. The main party had almost caught up.

Rue gave her mount its head. It took off at a fast, bone-jarring trot toward stable and home.

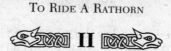

II

INSIDE OLD TENTIR, shafts of sunset lanced down through the high western windows and through holes in the roof. Dust motes danced in them like flecks of dying fire. The air seemed to quiver. A continuous rumble echoed in the near-empty great hall, punctuated by the crack of a single word shouted over and over, its sense lost in the general, muffled roar.

A Coman cadet stood at the foot of the hall, before one of the western doors beyond which lay the barracks and training ward of New Tentir, the randon college. His attention was fixed on the purposeful commotion outside and his hands gripped the latch, ready to jerk the door open. He didn't hear Rue knock on the front door at the other end of the long hall, then pound.

The unlocked door opened a crack, grating on debris, and Rue warily peered in, one hand on the hilt of the long knife sheathed at her belt. A quick glance told her that the hall was empty, or nearly so. Frowning, she pushed back the hood of her forage jacket from straw-colored hair as rough-cut as a badly thatched roof.

"Tentir, 'ware company!" she shouted down the hall. "Somebody, come take this nag!"

A moment later she had stumbled over the threshold, butted from behind by her horse. She caught him as he tried to shove past, then led him into the hall, needing all her strength to hold him in check. In response, he laid back his ears and arched his tail. Turds plopped, steaming, onto flagstones already littered with broken slates from the roof, downed beams, and fallen birds' nests.

Rue glanced around as she tramped on legs stiff from riding down the long hall that bisected Old Tentir. Disordered though it was, the wonder of it struck her anew. All her short life, she had dreamed of training at the randon college and now here she was, a cadet candidate sworn to the Highlord himself.

But for how long, whispered fear in the back of her mind, *given the events of the past week*. Rue set her jaw. Here she was and here she would stay. *Don't think of failure*, she told herself. *Don't think. Look.*

In the galleries of the second and third floors, rank on rank of silver collars seemed to float against the darkening walls. Suspended from each shining ring were the plaques that recorded the career of its owner—in what class graduated, what ranks and stations held, what honors won in which battles and in which slain: white edged for the debacle in the White Hills when Ganth Gray Lord had been overthrown, blue for the Cataracts early last winter when his son Torisen had stopped the Waster Horde, black for the misery of Urakarn in the Southern Wastes, from which so few had returned, and on, and on.

Along the lower walls hung the banners of the nine major Kencyr houses whom most of the randon served. Leaping flame, stooping hawk, and snarling wolf on the south wall: Brandan, Edirr, and Danior. Gauntleted fist, two-edged sword, and devouring serpent on the north: Randir, Coman, and Caineron. Over the two western doors that opened into New Tentir were the stricken tree and the full moon of the Jaran and the Ardeth. Between them, in pride of place over the massive fireplace, hung the rathorn crest of the Knorth, highlords of the Kencyrath for thirty millennia.

One tenth of that time had been spend here on Rathillien, the last in a series of threshold worlds held and subsequently lost in the Three People's long, bitter retreat from Perimal Darkling down the Chain of Creation.

The college at Tentir dated from the ceding of the Riverland forts to the Kencyrath nearly a thousand years ago. Since that time, every cadet had added his or her stitch to the appropriate banner, building it up even as its back decayed against the dank walls. Some, such as tiny Danior, showed patches of stone wall between bare upper threads. Others, especially the Caineron, looked like ungainly, pendulous growths.

Not unlike Caldane, Lord Caineron himself, thought Rue, grinning.

Her horse stopped and tossed back his head, nearly jerking her off her feet. A moment later, a faint rumble came from under the earth and the hall shivered. More slates fell. Birds fled out the holes in the roof. The horse backed, eyes rolling white, jerking the reins out of the cadet's hand. Before she could recapture them, he had bolted across the hall and down the side ramp to the subterranean stables. The frightened bugling of horses already in stall welcomed him.

Rue tramped up to the cadet by the door.

"Didn't you hear my hail?" she demanded, having to raise her voice over the rumpus. She also had to look up, the other being a good head taller than she as most Kendar her age were. "D'you know that the outer ward is unguarded and the hall door is unlocked? I thought for sure the hill tribes had broken in and sacked the place. Where *is* everyone?"

The Coman cadet shot her a distracted look, and winced: the young lord of his house, looking to his standard, had set the fashion of wearing a tiny, double-edged dagger as an earring, never mind that with any incautious move it stabbed its wearer. "I heard you, but this is my post. No, the guard isn't set. We aren't back to rights yet since the last big quake, nor yet since the one before that."

"Huh," said Rue.

As far as she could see, Tentir had gotten off easy. In contrast, sections of Mount Alban had been displaced all the way to the Southern Wastes, then north to Kithorn, before finally snapping back to their foundation. Parts were still missing. That morning, when Rue had left, the scrollsmen and women had been searching with increasing urgency for the upper levels' privy.

The Coman flinched as something overhead shifted. Grit rattled down into his upturned face.

"A week we spent," he said rapidly, "sweating in the fire timber hall below, expecting every minute for the whole keep to collapse on our heads. They said the old buildings were the safest and no one dared go out for fear of being swept away by the weirding, but still . . . all the new cadet candidates jostled together—Ardeth, Caineron, Knorth, the lot . . . No discipline. Fights. As for the Merikit, I wish they *would* come! Tentir is a proper hornet's nest, just waiting for some fool with a stick."

"Hall, there! *Hall*!" roared a stentorian voice outside, over the general tumult.

The Coman threw open the door. Cadets thundered past, rank on rank, feet booming on the boardwalk. They ran grimly in cadence to the now distinguishable shouts of the drill sargents standing in the middle of the training square:

"Run! *Run*! RUN!"

The Coman waited for a momentary break between squads, then darted out. Rue, craning out the door, saw him reach a cadet who had tripped, fallen, and been trampled before his mates could scoop him up.

"*Down!*" shouted the commander of the on-coming squad.

Rescuer and victim fell flat. The ten-command hurdled over them two by two, a ripple of heads rising and falling like water over a hidden rock, lucky that none of them tripped. Then they were past. The Coman lurched to his feet, supporting the fallen cadet. They flattened themselves against the wall as the next squad thundered by, then staggered back to the door. Rue reached out to pull them in. All three collapsed in a heap on the hall's flagstones.

"Get off me!" someone in the pile said thickly.

They sorted themselves out with much cursing and some flaying of fists, one of which caught Rue on the ear. She staggered backward, shaking her head to clear it.

"What's wrong with you people?" she demanded, but instinctively she knew: the former Lord Coman had been a staunch Caineron ally, but the new one, Korey, was wavering. Caldane was said to be furious about that, and the young cadet whom they had just rescued was a Caineron. Here, writ small, were all the tensions between their houses.

The Coman shook the smaller boy until he stopped trying to fight and the teeth rattled in his head. Then he propped him against the wall.

"This . . . has been going on . . . for hours," he panted, leaning against the doorpost. "Punishment run . . . ha! D'they want . . . to kill . . . us all?" For the first time, he regarded Rue closely. "You're that border brat . . . aren't

you? The one that came down . . . from the Min-drear
High Keep. One of Brier Iron-Thorn's ten-command."

"Bloody Thorn," muttered the Caineron. His nose had
begun to bleed. He groped for his token scarf and snuffled wetly into it. "Damn, bloody turn-collar. S'if M'lord
Caldane wasn't good enough for her . . . "

"He wasn't," said Rue, glaring. "Ten serves the Highlord now."

"Your ten-command was out Merikit-hunting and
went missing without leave during the storm." The
Coman regarded her speculatively. "We thought you'd
been swept away. Better if you had been. You're in dead
trouble now, brat."

Rue glowered. "We had things to do."

"Tell that to the Commandant. I reckon he's about
fed up with you Knorth. We all are. Crazy, the lot of
you. D'you still check under your bed every night for
Gerridon, or maybe for a darkling crawler like the one
your precious highlord claims to have seen here last
fall?"

Rue set a pugnacious jaw. She knew that he was bait-
ing her, that the Coman and the Knorth were on even
less easy terms than the Coman and the Caineron, but
this touched on her lord's honor.

"What d'you mean, 'claims'? D'you think it couldn't
happen? You Coman live at the southern end of the
Riverland. Here in the north, things happen. We're
closer to the Barrier than you seem to realize and what's
behind that, eh? Perimal Darkling itself! Some days at
High Keep, you can see Master Gerridon's House looming through the mist like it was about to push its way
right through."

Behind the now sodden scarf, the Caineron snorted.
In that muffled sound was all the contempt with which

his lord Caldane regarded all things darkling, or anything else not of immediate use to him.

"You don't believe me? Well then, who d'you think was behind the Waster Horde, pushing, when we fought it last winter at the Cataracts? Darkling changers, that's who. Our own kind, once—Kencyr, fallen with the Master, warped in the shadows of his house."

The Coman grinned. "So the singers of Mount Alban say, especially that creepy Ashe. If you want to label anyone 'darkling,' how about a dead woman who won't lie down, much less shut up? As for the rest, some people will swallow any singer's Lawful Lie. And I wouldn't brag about the Cataracts if I were you, brat: Folk may recall how the Highlord acquired a sister at the edge of the Escarpment—with a flash and a loud bang, apparently. He's the last pure-blooded Knorth, isn't he? So where did *she* come from? The whole thing's another Lawful Lie, if you ask me . . . and what are *you* smirking about?"

"Wait and see," said Rue.

The Caineron focused blurry eyes on her. For so young a boy, barely fifteen, he looked remarkably dissolute, like someone recovering from a vicious hangover. He might well be: two days ago Caldane had indulged in an epic drinking binge and passed the effects on to all the Kendar bound to him who hadn't yet learned how to defend themselves.

"Think you're so clever for getting out of this, eh, shaghead?" he said thickly, indicating the grim stream of exhausted cadets pounding past the door. "And you got out of High Keep too, didn't you? One more minor house dying on its feet, one more Kendar scuttling out before it falls . . ."

Rue's ill-cropped hair almost bristled. She had hacked it off to leave in her lord's cold hand in case she should never return—a poor substitute for her bones burnt to honorable ash on the pyre but better than nothing. If she had been glad to escape that grim place, guilt had made her chop all the more fiercely.

"I have my lord's permission to train with the Highlord's folk. Min-drear randon always do."

"Damn, bloody Min-drear, trotting after a crazy rat-horn . . ."

"That's *rath*-orn, moron." Rue glanced up at the Knorth house banner, at the fierce, horned beast embroidered on it, ivory armor agleam in the darkening hall. How could anyone make fun of a thing like that, except perhaps some idiot Riverlander who had never even seen one?

The Coman glanced out the door. "Here comes your house again, lad. Up and out."

The Caineron cadet lurched to his feet. At the door, he looked back at Rue. "I'll remember you, Mind-rear. And we Caineron all remember Brier bloody Ironthorn." For a moment Caldane seemed to leer out of the boy's heavy eyes. Rue fell back a step, making the Darkwyr sign against evil. He blinked, laughed uncertainly, and stumbled out to be swept up by his people as they thundered past.

The Coman stared after him. "Has everyone gone mad?" He looked at Rue as if tempted to make the warding sign against her. "Insanity is contagious. Ganth Gray Lord infected the entire Host in the White Hills and now Torisen Black Lord is doing it again!"

"If you want to complain to him," said Rue as the far door was forced open, screeching on bent hinges, "here's your chance."

Into the twilight of the hall came two riders, one on a tall black stallion, the other on a small, gray mare with an intricately braided white mane.

"That's Lord Ardeth," said the Coman, staring at the latter. "What in Perimal's name . . ." His voice trailed off and his jaw dropped.

The lord of Omiroth seemed to have brought a great light into the hall, as if at the rising of the full moon that was the emblem of his house. It shone bone-deep through his clothes, through his very flesh. But no, thought Rue, also staring: it must only be that snow-white hair. And yet, and yet . . .

The Ardeth were an arrogant lot, proud of their subtle lord who in his one hundred and fifty odd years had brought his house through so many disasters that even the scrollsmen of Mount Alban had lost count. The worst had been the thirty-one years of chaos after the White Hills when, without a highlord, the Kencyrath had nearly fallen apart. Only Ardeth had known that Ganth's heir lived: the boy Torisen, exile-born, who had come to him in secret and whom Ardeth had hidden among the random of the Southern Host. There, four years ago, Torisen had come of age and at last claimed his father's seat.

The Caineron claimed that he was still Ardeth's puppet, or worse.

At the Cataracts, others suspected that the Highlord was slipping through his mentor's fingers.

Since then, his friends had begun to wonder if, after all, Torisen needed Ardeth's influence to save him from himself.

Rue knew instinctively that the old lord was now trying to reassert control over the younger man.

Perhaps that was only right, she thought, half-dazed, drawn to the old Highborn as if to the sun after bitter cold. Perhaps here was the true heart of the Kencyrath, its secret master to whom all should yield as Torisen himself once had. Her own lord was a broken man, his sons ash before him, his Kendar loosely bound to him by his faltering will. Torisen Highlord held his own people almost as lightly—through weakness, sneered the Caineron, whose own lord gripped them like cruel death; through misplaced tact, said his allies, shrugging. Rue only knew that it made her nervous. What a splendid thing it would be, she now thought, to fall at Ardeth's feet, to put her life between those thin, strong hands and hear his murmured words of welcome.

Then she shook herself, silently cursing. Everyone knew that old Adric had a taste for the exotic drugs of the Poison Courts and had resorted to them for help before now, sometimes with unnerving results. Let him glow in the dark like a rotten eel. She was a Min-drear and would hold true to her bond, if not for her lord's sake then for her mother and her mother's mother before her.

Torisen Black Lord, Highlord of the Kencyrath, rode into Tentir on his war-horse Storm like the shadow cast by the other's brilliance. Dark clothing, dark ruffled hair shot with premature gray, both horse and rider seemed to melt into the hall's shadows except for the latter's face, pale with strain floating forward wraithlike—that, and his fine-boned left hand with its tracery of white scars, gripping the reins. His right hand he carried out of sight, thrust into a dusty coat.

A large, gray wolf slunk at his side as close as he could get without being stepped on, closer than Storm liked, judging by the roll of the stallion's eye. However, the Wolver Grimly only watched his old friend Torisen with unhappy concern.

If Ardeth's lunar glow seemed to promise safety, the Knorth appeared to be in obstinate self-eclipse, dark of the moon, when all things fall into doubt and danger. He neither looked at his old mentor nor seemed to listen to him. Nonetheless, he rode with all his weight on the outside stirrup, leaning away from that soft, insistent voice.

Rue got the Coman's attention by kicking him in the shin. "Go tell the Commandant we have company."

"Yes," he said, still staring, and then, belatedly, "ouch."

He stumbled out the door without looking, and brought down an entire Edirr squad.

"*Rest!*" roared a sargent.

All around the square, cadets collapsed, panting, on the boards.

Meanwhile, other riders had entered the hall at a wary distance from their lords, two columns of them, split by house. They ignored each other but their mounts, catching their mood, fidgeted and snapped.

Rue's attention leaped to the most reassuring face in the crowd, there, a respectful length behind the captain of Ardeth's guard. Teak brown from the southern sun, short cropped hair the smoldering red of mahogany, Brier Iron-thorn had come to Tentir by a long, hard road. She was older than most cadets, more experienced, and mistrusted by them for her sudden change of houses at the Cataracts. Before that, no one had believed that such a thing was possible. Not from the Caineron. Not against the will of its lord. But here she was, even more an outsider than Rue. If anyone could show these smug Riverlanders a thing or two, it was Rose Iron-thorn's hard, handsome daughter.

Oh, please, thought Rue, *let her start with him*.

Five-commander Vant rode glowering at Brier's back. They had all seethed with resentment when a former Caineron *yondri* had been put in charge over them, but none more so than Vant who had been forced to yield ten-command to her. If he kept in Brier's shadow now, it was because he hoped that she would draw the light-ning of whatever punishment they all have earned.

Hooves rattled on the flagstones. A bay gelding danced nervously, eyes rolling, between the two lords and their retinues. Everyone looked somewhere else except Rue, who stared open-mouthed despite herself.

Like her brother, the bay's rider wore black, but her jacket had an odd cut to it, one sleeve tight and the other full. Unlike Torisen, the slim hands that nervously gripped the reins were sheathed in black gloves. What she didn't wear—and this was why no one would look at her directly—was a mask. For a Highborn lady to show her face naked to the world was indecent, much less one marked across the cheek by a thin, straight, barely healed scar. That she looked so much like a younger version of her brother was, in contrast, merely disconcerting.

So was the thin, sharp face that peered warily over her shoulder. The bay bore two riders, the second Caineron's half-caste bastard son who, somehow, had become the first's servant.

As if to compound this strangeness, a Royal Gold hunt-ing ounce trotted after them into the hall. The cat, Jorin, was blind, which perhaps explained why he blithely plumped himself down in the path of the on-coming riders and began industriously to wash.

His tail twitched under a descending hoof. He leaped up, squalling, the bay shied, and both riders fell off.

The whole mixed retinue was suddenly in motion, horses separating by house and wheeling about to face each other, their riders' hands falling instinctively to sword hilts.

The bay, unheeded, tossed his head and trotted sedately off down the ramp.

Only the black stallion and the gray mare hadn't moved. Ardeth's voice murmured on, oblivious. Torisen stilled the commotion behind him with a raised hand—the right, its three broken fingers splinted and heavily bandaged. He looked past Rue, and his thin mouth twisted in a wry half-smile. She realized, with a start, that the Commandant had entered the hall during the confusion and was standing behind her.

She had to crane to see his face. Sheth Sharp-tongue was tall even for a Kendar, with a touch of Highborn subtlety in his features. Highborn and Kendar alike found him unnerving. Most believed, however, that he was the greatest randon of his generation. Rue remembered uneasily that Sheth was also a Caineron and that house's war-leader.

"My lords, welcome to Tentir," he said.

His gaze fell, speculatively, on the bedraggled figure in the middle of the hall, who had picked herself up and was slapping dust off her clothes. Her companion and cat both tried to hide behind her. Meeting the Commandant's eyes with a carefully blank stare, she swept up long, black hair that had tumbled down in her fall and twisted it back up under her cap.

"Who have we here?" he asked of no one in particular.

Rue couldn't help it. " 'Some fool with a stick,' " she muttered.

The Commandant glanced down at her. "I daresay," he said dryly. "My lords, welcome to Tentir."

Rue ducked hastily away from him to hold Storm. The tall stallion snorted down his nose at her and stood rock still as Torisen awkwardly dismounted, favoring his injured hand.

"Honor be to your halls," he responded, preoccupied, and touched the mare's shoulder with concern. Sweat had turned it pewter gray, and she was trembling with fatigue. "My lady? Adric, for Trinity's sake . . . ! Think of Brithany, if not of yourself."

Ardeth had also swung down and was drifting toward him like a sleep-walker, still murmuring. Sheth raised an eyebrow as both Grimly and the Highlord retreated behind Storm, the wolver keeping between the two Highborn, ignored by both. The stallion laid back his ears but subsided, grudgingly, at a sharp word from his master. Ardeth's power rippled out through the hall. The stitches on the nearest banner rustled as if trying to escape.

"You know," said the Commandant mildly, "each stitch represents a randon's bond the eternal fabric of his house. The cadet candidates here haven't yet formally earned their scarves nor set their marks, so they aren't as strongly anchored as their seniors."

"Tell him, not me!" Torisen snapped, circling behind his horse. "Adric, you should rest. Remember your heart."

"Yes, Grandfather. Please rest."

A handsome young man had slipped into the hall from the arcade. He wore a cadet's belted jacket, but of an elegant cut and material touched with embroidery as golden as his hair. Obviously, he hadn't taken part in the run. Rue's first indignant thought was that, Highborn or not, he should have. That conviction faded, however, in the presence of a glamour more subtle than his grandfather's, but still enough to make Rue stare. So did Torisen.

"Peri," he gasped.

"No," said the Commandant, giving him a brief, hard look. "His son, Timmon."

As Ardeth advanced smiling on the boy, his attention diverted, the whole room seemed to breathe for the first time since he had entered the hall. Torisen sagged against Storm's hindquarters, and not just with relief that the old lord was no longer focused on him. He looked like someone who had taken a hard, unexpected blow. The Wolver rose up on his hind legs and became a very hairy, very worried young man, reaching out to steady his friend.

"Look at you," Ardeth was saying fondly to his grandson. "All dressed up like a randon. Your father would be so proud."

Among the Kendar, someone turned a snort into a cough. Timmon's father Pereden had never trained at Tentir. Nonetheless, he had expected to lead the Southern Host and finally had gotten his chance after Torisen put down the commander's collar to become Highlord. On Pereden's orders, against the advice of his randon, the Host had marched to near ruin against the vastly larger Waster Horde. Pereden himself was believed to have died in the Wastes. A good thing too, many thought, but no one said so in his father's presence. Ardeth had spent the previous winter vainly searching the Southern Wastes for the bones of his beloved, heroic son.

Now, his mind momentarily off the Highlord, the old man sagged with exhaustion.

Timmon regarded him with growing alarm. "Please, Grandfather," he said again. "Come to my quarters and rest. Your business with the Highlord can wait."

Ardeth patted his grandson's arm absent-mindedly. There was a winning quality in the boy's voice that made even strangers eager to please him, but his words had set the old lord's thoughts wandering back to the real business at hand: convincing Torisen that his best interests, nay, his very survival, lay in putting his shaken fortunes in the hands of his former mentor. No one could doubt Ardeth's thoughts, because he spoke them out loud.

"You must remember, my dear boy," he added, with devastating candor, "that many believe you as prone to madness as your late, unlamented father." His pale blue eyes drifted to that second black-clad figure standing silent between the restless battle lines. "Indeed, once news of your latest scheme leaks out, even I may be unable to save you."

Torisen straightened with a jerk. "Young man," he said, forcing himself to look at Timmon, "if you will extend your hospitality to me and my friend Grimly, we will gladly drink the welcome cup in your quarters. Adric?"

Ardeth smiled, the drug-fired light again emerging from the cloud of his exhaustion. The hall shivered as his renewed power rippled through it. "But of course I will join you, dear boy. We have so much to discuss."

"Take care of your grand-dam," Torisen said to Storm, who snorted: *of course*. Avoiding the old man's extended hand, he slipped out of the hall into New Tentir with Grimly again on all fours trotting at his heel.

"Well done, my lord," murmured the Commandant as Torisen passed, adding blandly, "I believe I will join you." At the door, he turned.

"Conduct the Highlord's . . . er . . . guests to the Knorth quarters," he said to Rue. "As for you—" his hooded glance swooped back to the other uneasily waiting cadets "—I will have something to say to you later. In the meantime, tend to these horses. All of them."

Ardeth's guard gingerly skirted the Highlord's sister with eyes averted and thrust their reins into unwilling Knorth hands. The mutter of protest that followed them died under Iron-thorn's hard eyes. Tired and hungry, the Knorth cadets sullenly followed their Southron ten-commander down the ramp.

The Highlord's sister was left standing in the middle of the hall. She looked about her at the banners, the battle flags and, above, at the faint glimmer of randon collars hanging on the upper walls.

"So this is Tentir," said her other companion, looking down his sharp nose at the disheveled, darkening hall.

"Yes," said his mistress, in quite another tone. "This is Tentir."

Rue approached them, reminding herself that she had spoken to the Highborn before, but Jameth's face had been decently masked then. She looked quickly away as the other turned to her.

"If you'll follow me, lady."

As they climbed the stairs to the second story Knorth guest quarters, the relentless shout rose again from the training yard outside:

"All right, younglings, rest's over. Up and run, *run*, RUN!"

CHAPTER II

Wyrm Hunt

1st of Summer

I

"WE'RE LOST," said Graykin, glowering about the low, dusty corridor. "Three times now, I've trod on the same loose board. Here, you!"—this, to the straw-haired cadet who led them. "Do you even know where you're going?"

The young Kendar named Rue glanced back at them, then quickly away. "Where, yes; how, no. Most of the second and third floors are unused, except for guest quarters and the outermost rooms. We don't like coming up here. Besides, there are stories . . . ."

"Oh?" said Graykin with a nasty grin, baring still raw gaps where m'lord Caldane had knocked out some of his teeth. "More 'singers' fancies'?"

Jame recognized the line that Vant—never her favorite Kendar—had taken with the young border-lander. "What stories?" she asked.

"That something lives up here in a hidden room," Rue burst out defiantly. "That it has the paws of a bear and an axe buried in its head. That it growls and it prowls and it eats cadets who stumble into its lair."

Graykin hooted with laughter. Rue hunched her shoulders, the tips of her ears reddening. Jame considered. Through Jorin's senses, as they wandered, she had caught whiffs of something odd, something rank, something alive.

"The Lawful Lie notwithstanding, most songs have some element of truth in them."

"Hah!" said Graykin. "D'you hear that, brat? Just be careful what door you open. Ugh!" He swatted at the cobweb that he had just walked into and spat out the husk of a fly.

"Poor Gray," said his mistress. "Tentir isn't living up to your expectations, is it?"

"Is it to yours?"

"Oh well. This isn't the college proper. We'll see."

Still, thought Jame, this was not auspicious. Neither had been falling off a horse practically at the Commandant's feet. Then again, it was usually her departure —from anywhere—that caused the most damage. Tai-tastigon in flames, Karkinaroth in ruins, *The Riverland reduced to rubble, and you in the midst of it, looking apologetic . . . .*

What shape would Tentir be in when she left it?

Speaking of shapes, it was odd how every Riverland keep was so different, as if the original builders had made a point of it. Generations of Kencyr had brought their own personalities to the task but less so here, where commandants changed by rotation and no one house had power. From the outside, Old Tentir looked straightforward, even dull. Inside, it was . . . strange. Low halls melting into twilight, right angles that never brought one back to the same place—she was fairly sure that Graykin was wrong about it being the same squeaky board: they all squeaked—someone subtle and secretive had designed this place, disguising its nature behind a bland face.

"Jorin, stay in sight," she called to the ounce who was trotting ahead, eager to explore. Blind from birth, he only saw what she saw and remembered it, but this was all new to her.

Lost.

Would Tori be glad if she disappeared, gone from his life as suddenly as she had reentered it?

Run, she thought, *before he tells that alarming randon why he brought you here, before he proves himself as mad as they all fear—or hope—that he is.*

Graykin was grumbling again. "This is an insult!" he burst out. "You're the Highlord's sister, his only surviving blood-kin, but he pays more attention to that damned gray mare than to you!"

"Brithany is a Whinno-hir, a matriarch of the herd. She's at least as old as Ardeth, perhaps older than the Fall."

And smart. And brave. Imagine weird-walking all the way from the Southern Wastes to rejoin her chosen master, bringing her grand-colt with her. Storm, a quarter-blood Whinno-hir, was far more intelligent than the average horse, but still a moron compared to his grand-dam.

"Damn it!" Graykin burst out, flailing at more webs. "You don't belong here!"

Jame sighed. "That's the question, isn't it? Where do I belong?"

"If you were a man," said Graykin, regarding her slyly askance, "you would be Highlord. I don't care if your brother is older than you are. You're stronger than he is . . . and why are you fidgeting like that?"

"I'm saddle-sore. Don't laugh." She rubbed her buttocks, wincing. When there was time to check, she would probably find them black and blue. Her knees still felt unstrung. "Highlord, huh? Your ambition is showing, Gray, but I'm not a man and I don't want power, at least not that sort. Just give me a place to stand."

"You're a Highborn lady," said the Southron stubbornly. "Stand on that."

"I tried," she said, hearing the weary exasperation in her voice, trying to curb it. "All last winter, in the Women's Halls at Gothregor, I tried."

Masked, hobbled with a tight underskirt, told over and over what a proper lady did or did not do . . . all to what end? She gingerly touched the scar ridge across her cheek, a parting gift from the Women's World in the person of Kallystine, Caineron's daughter and Tori's erstwhile limited term consort.

"Gray, these days Highborn women are little better than fancy breeding stock, and I'm the last pure-blooded female in the Knorth stable, just as Tori is the last legitimate male. If any house gets a half-Knorth heir out of either one of us, how long d'you think we'll last?"

For that matter, how long could Tori stand up to Ardeth pressure? Why didn't he fight back? She understood that he owed a great deal to his former mentor, without whom he would never have survived to claim his father's seat nor held it during these first, turbulent years. Moreover, he didn't want to hurt the old man. For all his drug-enhanced strength, she could sense how fragile Ardeth was, how deep into his resources he was reaching. For her brother, loyalty—yes, even love—must be at war with resentment.

And he did resent the old lord.

"When I was a boy," he had said to her in the ruins of Kothifir—had it been only the day before?—"I would have given anything to become a cadet at Tentir. But Adric forbade it."

Ardeth had protested. It had been impossible. If anyone had guessed who Tori was before he came of age . . .

"So you told me, Adric, when you dismissed my request as if it were a child's whim. So I lost my chance."

Such bitterness, remembered and dismissed, but never forgotten or quite forgiven.

However, if Ardeth was vulnerable now, so was Tori, and not just with exhaustion. Something about that good-looking boy Timmon had hit him hard, something to do with the boy's father, Pereden.

Worse, something deep within Torisen himself was closed off, withdrawn . . . dead? His Kendar felt it. So did she, and it frightened her.

Graykin hunched his thin shoulders as if against a cold wind. If he could have run away from her words, he would have. He wasn't stupid. Far from it. However, bastard and half-Kencyr that he was, his need to belong consumed him like a ravening hunger. At the Cataracts she had accidentally bound him, mind to mind, her needs at that moment matching the strength of his. Now there was no easy way to shake him off, nor should she want to. Ancestors knew, over the past winter he had earned his place in her service with scars that he would bear to his pyre, and he hadn't yet begun to re-grow (assuming he had enough Kencyr blood to do so) his lost teeth. Things were going to be hard enough, though, without him clinging fiercely to her sleeve, measuring his importance by hers every step of the way.

One last try:

"Gray, listen. I can't promise you anything. Not even a crust of bread every other week. Least of all protection. And you're in danger here. M'lord Caineron doesn't give up his playthings easily, much less those he considers he owns by right of blood."

"You *are* strong," he muttered, not looking at her, repeating his one article of faith as if by itself it would protect him. "I've watched. I know. Nothing stops you."

She could have shaken him.

Jorin sniffed, then dug at the lower edge of a heavy oak door. Whatever he smelled was too faint to reach Jame's senses, but she felt his interest, and his unease.

"The right door at last," said Rue with relief and tried the handle. "Damn. It's locked, and I don't have a key."

"Let me try." Jame slid between the cadet and the door, screening the latter. She extended a claw and probed the ponderous lock.

Her gloves' slit fingertips had been Marc's idea. At first she had rejected it, not wanting to use her hated nails at all, for anything, but many pairs of ruined gloves later she had had to admit that the big Kendar was right.

It still amazed her how casually he took her deformity. When her nails had first emerged, betraying her Shanir blood, her father had cast her out into the Haunted Lands, with no place to go but across the Border. Into Perimal Darkling. Into the Master's House. She had been seven years old at the time.

Then again, pure-blooded Kendar like Marc were never Shanir. Perhaps that made them more tolerant than the vulnerable Highborn.

If only Marc were with her now rather than this opportunistic half-breed—but she wasn't in a position to provide for her old, dear friend any more than for Graykin.

Marc was better off with her brother. She wondered if Tori had yet offered the old warrior a place in his household. He had better, and no one deserved it more. But still . . .

Lost, she thought again, with a sudden wave of desolation. *I've lost Marc, and Tirandys, and Tai-tastigon, and now here I am where no one wants me.*

Then she gave herself a shake. Graykin was right, darkness take him. Nothing stopped her, not despair, not loss, least of all not common sense. This was a new life. She had started over before, many times, and would keep on doing so until she damn well got it right.

Tumbles ground in the lock. "There."

The portal swung slowly inward, grating on its hinges. From the darkness within came a breath of hot air—*Haaaaah* . . . —and streamers of cobweb floated out into the hall. With them came a sharp, acrid smell, intensified for Jame through Jorin's senses. She only realized that she had backed away when the other side of the hall stopped her. The ounce also retreated, then turned, crouched, and sprang into her arms. Her knees nearly buckled. Almost full grown, he was very heavy.

Rue and Graykin were staring at her.

"That smell . . . " Jame said, and sneezed violently.

"What smell?" asked Rue, too mystified for once to look away.

"The room is musty," said Graykin, impatiently. "That's all. You. Light my lady's chambers."

Rue made a face at him and disappeared inside.

"What's wrong?" hissed Graykin.

"I . . . don't know," said Jame, shifting the ounce's weight, and she didn't . . . quite.

Inside, steel rasped on flint, and candlelight danced out into the corridor. Rue gave a stifled exclamation.

Without thinking, Jame dropped an indignant ounce and brushed past Graykin, into the apartment.

The cadet stood in the first room of three, holding a candle, looking about her in amazement. The low-ceilinged chamber was full of heavy furniture indistinct and sulking under filmy shrouds: a massive chair beside the fireplace, a table, a glimpse into the next room of an enormous, shadowy bed, its counterpane disordered and bulging.

"... *haaahhh* ..." sighed the open vents to the fire timber hall three stories below. As the suite exhaled into the hall, its hot breath stirred walls and ceiling swathed in translucent, faintly glowing white.

"Ugh," said Graykin, peering in. "More spiders."

"I don't think so," said Jame.

She ducked, wary of the filaments that drifted down toward her as if blindly groping for her face. Not all of them were spun in single strands, she saw, but some in the round, like boneless fingers, merging higher up into flaccid sleeves. The walls and ceiling of the suite were festooned with intertwined, insubstantial shapes, afloat in the flickering light. Stirred by the hot breath of the vents and the draft from the door, they seemed languidly to grapple with each other about the room's upper margins.

"Careful," she said, touching Rue's arm to make the cadet hold the candle lower. "Let's only set fire to the keep as a last resort."

Graykin snorted.

They all felt the need to speak softly except for Jorin, who leaned in from the hall anxiously chirping at Jame to come out. When she didn't, he slunk in and crouched at her feet. A moment later Graykin nerved himself to join them in a rush that caused a momentary wake in the sea of ghosts overhead.

Jame loosened her collar, feeling sweat trickle down inside it. She didn't like heat. As for that smell . . . . Although it had faded somewhat with the influx of fresh air, she could still almost taste it in the back of her throat, like the sting of old grief. Then she knew what it was.

"Rue, how long has a darkling crawler been loose in Tentir?"

The cadet gaped at her. "How did you . . . who told you . . . "

Another hot room, another house where monstrous shadows crawled . . .

"Senethari, y-you've poisoned me."

No wonder Tirandys had been in her mind.

"Someone once gave me wine infused with wyrm's venom. I drank it. It had that same sharp smell and taste."

The cadet sighed, almost with relief. "Most don't believe it was ever here at all. How long? Since last fall, when m'lords Caineron and Knorth stopped here on their way to the mustering of the Host at Gothregor. A darkling changer came hunting the Highlord and would have killed him, sure, if Singer Ashe hadn't pushed the changer into a fire-pit down in the fire-timber hall. His blood kindled and he more or less exploded—a proper mess all around, or so I've heard. As for the wyrm, no one saw that but the Highlord, and afterward the Caineron claimed that he'd imagined it."

"The poor, mad Knorth."

"That's it . . . lady," she added, remembering herself and of whose house she spoke. "They tried to say the same about the changer, but too many had seen it including my cousin, who was on duty that night outside Commandant Harn's quarters. We border brats take these things seriously."

She said this so pugnaciously that Jame laughed. "I know. I'm a border brat myself and so is Tori, if he isn't too grand these days to have forgotten."

Her eyes kept drifting back to the ceiling. The figures that floated there were as empty as a spider's egg sack in the spring, but hot air from the vents breathed fitful definition into the flaccid forms. Here a head rose, inflating. For a moment there was the suggestion of a fine-drawn chin and an arched brow that seemed to frown. Then all features swelled grotesquely and the figure turned away with a sigh, deflating. Elsewhere limp gloves of web became elegant lace-work hands, became veined, translucent sausages, vented, and collapsed.

They were like the fitful images of a troubled dream, but whose?

Two figures emerged over and over, interacting at different points in what appeared to be a prolonged conflict. One, better defined than the other, was always turning away.

The other, more nebulous, kept changing as if trying to hold a true shape—any shape—while at the same time unraveling around the edges. Nonetheless it . . . no, *he* had the sharper presence of the two, a thing fiercely clung to even as errant drafts teased him apart. All over the room, his multitude of heads were turning toward her as if aware of her thoughts. Filaments floated around each like a cloud of wild, white hair.

Jame brushed a tendril of web from her neck. It left a thin, stinging line.

. . . are you the one?

"Careful," she said to the other two. "There's still a trace of venom in these threads."

There was also that ghost of words, echoing faintly with impotent rage.

. . . are you the one who made bitter ash of my life?

No, Jame wanted to say. *You did that to yourself and, thanks to Tori, you got what you deserved.*

She was stopped, however, by the memory of another pyre, another changer's shape melting into flame, and her eyes stung with remembered tears.

Ah, Tirandys, Senethari. Did you deserve what happened to you? Damn Master Gerridon, honor's paradox, and all three faces of our god, for giving us impossible choices, then damning us when we choose wrong.

"So the changer died," she said, collecting herself, "the wyrm fled, and everyone marched south to fight the Waster Horde which, incidentally, was led by other rebel changers. Meanwhile, the crawler spent the winter at Tentir, maybe in these rooms. Ancestors know, it's hot enough. Well insulated too. A proper nest."

Highborn and Kendar looked at each other.

"We should get out of here, lady."

"Good idea," said Graykin, starting for the outer door.

Jorin sat up, ears pricked. Then he jumped to his feet and trotted purposefully through the opposite door, into the bed-room. When he didn't return at Jame's call, she went after him. As they hesitated, Rue and Graykin heard an exclamation followed by a sharp summons: "Come see this, both of you."

The second room was hotter than the first, its ceiling a floating mass of loose filaments especially thick over the bed. Jame had thrown back the coverlet.

"I want witnesses to this," she said.

They stared at the bed's contents.

"A broken shell?" said Rue. She poked the pearly fragments gingerly. They dissolved with a faint hiss into a pool of viscous fluid.

"More likely a cocoon," said Jame, "or perhaps a molt. What do I know about the life cycle of a wyrm?"

The liquid began to eat its way through the sheets, then through the mattress.

"Ugh," said Graykin. "Whatever was in here must just have broken out—now, of all times. Why does everything always happen to me?"

Rue grinned. "Just lucky, I guess."

His indignant response turned into a stifled cry of alarm. They all stared at the clotted mass above the bed. A shape was emerging from it, as if a giant face was leaning down from the ceiling, itself a mere void but defined by the clinging web. The fading consciousness of the dead changer glared down at Jame through a silken mask already beginning to droop under its own weight.

. . . *are you the one who stole my Beauty?*

"What beauty?" she demanded out loud. "Whose beauty?"

"Bugger this," muttered Rue, and thrust her lit candle up into the sagging mass.

It ignited from within. In a moment, the threads had become a fiery mask distorted by rage and despair. The jaw blackened and dropped, disintegrating into a rain of ash. The rest followed, feature by feature. Fire spread in red-orange tendrils across the ceiling into the first room. Ghosts tumbled down in flames.

Driven back by the heat, they retreated into the third room. Jorin wasn't with them, but fresh tracks in the dust showed where he had gone, following a shallow groove in the floorboards worn not by use or weight but by the wyrm's corrosive passage. Both disappeared at the back wall. The stones there were slightly ajar, enough for the three to squeeze through one by one into the darkness beyond, Jame last.

Graykin's yelp of surprise receded downward.

"Stairs," said Rue succinctly.

All Jame could see at first was a fire-lit streak of the opposite stone wall, mere inches away. She put her hand on it and waited for her eyes to adjust, gratefully breathing the cool air.

"So this is how the Highlord escaped," said Rue in the dark, several steps down.

"Through a hole in the wall?" Graykin's voice came from much farther down, edged with hysteria. "I think I've broken my ankle," he added resentfully.

"Escaped?"

"Didn't you know, lady? The Caineron locked him in. He was raving." Jame could just make out the cadet's embarrassed wriggle. "Said the wyrm had bitten him."

Jame felt suddenly cold. "It *bit* him? Oh, sweet Trinity."

She could see the steps now, dimly, and went down them in a precipitous rush, past Rue, over Graykin who was sprawling where he had fallen. Their voices followed her, calling questions, but she didn't answer. What could she have said?

The wyrm bit my brother. My brother is a blood-binder, but he doesn't know it. To be a binder is to be Shanir, and Tori doesn't know that either. Our father taught us both to hate those of the Old Blood beyond

reason, as he hated me, as Tori does too when he remem-
bers what I am. If Tori finds out how alike we are, it will
destroy him.

No, she couldn't say that, not to anyone.

Venom had hollowed out the lips of the treads, render-
ing them treacherous. Her foot shot out from under her
and she bounced down the last, long stretch on her
already bruised tailbone, through a wyrm hole at the
bottom eaten through solid stone, into the straw bedding
of an empty box stall. Horses stirred nervously all around
her, the whites of their eyes flashing at her through the
wooden slats of adjacent stalls. Hooves danced.

Out in the aisle, Jame paused. Which way to go? The
stable was much larger than she had expected, underlying most of Old Tentir, a maze of moveable wooden
partitions between the massive stone arches that supported the fortress above. The air should have been
sweet with the breath of horses and ripe with their fresh
droppings. Instead, a sharp tang of fear overlaid all. A
tickling in her nose told her that Jorin was still on the
wyrm's scent somewhere in this restless labyrinth.

Cadets were shouting back and forth: "D'you see anything?"

"Not yet."

"That smell . . . what died in here?"

Following their voices, she came to an open arena
under the great hall. Secured to iron rings set in the
surrounding pillars, the new arrivals fretted in their full
tack. Vant was stalking back and forth behind them,
impatiently slapping a brush against his leg.

"I tell you, Iron-thorn," he shouted, "the horses are
spooked by that damn cat. That's all! Sweet Trinity, d'you
expect me to put up this lot by myself?"

This wasn't quite fair: across the arena another cadet was struggling to hold Storm. The black stallion danced in place, jerking the cadet back and forth in his attempt to follow Brithany as the gray mare trotted from stall to stall, whickering reassurances. The inmates quieted, but began to fret again as soon as the matriarch had passed. Their anxious calls to each other echoed off the low vault of the ceiling.

"What are you doing here, lady?"

Vant's voice next to her made Jame start. He didn't look at her directly, but his hand closed on her wrist as if to secure someone's runaway pet. On the perilous road they had all so recently trodden, he would never have dared to touch her, furious as he had been at her assumption of command. Highborn females didn't behave that way—sane ones, at least. How could he possibly have submitted to her will? How much had that weakness compromised not only his pride but also his honor? Now, however, he was in his proper place again, and all would be right.

"Listen," she said urgently to him. "There's a darkling crawler loose down here and I've got to catch it."

His grip tightened. In another moment, she thought, he would gladly slap her as a cure for hysteria, and she would try very hard not to kill him.

Then she saw Jorin. The ounce was in an empty stall directly across the arena, cautiously circling a big mound of straw. Vant saw him too. He gestured with his free hand for the nearest cadets to close in. Two of them began stealthily to climb the adjacent slat walls. Jorin daubed at the mound with a paw, and jumped back as it rustled. The wyrm's scent carried through his senses was so strong that Jame's eyes began to water.

The ounce crouched, hindquarters twitching.

"Jorin!" she shouted at him. "Don't!"

Vant glanced down at her with a kind of savage satisfaction. "Now, now," he said, grinning through clenched teeth. "No need for tears. Your pet will be returned to you . . . if you behave. Or maybe not."

Jorin pounced.

Something erupted from the stack in an explosion of straw. It hit the back wall and passed straight through it with Jorin in wild pursuit. The horse stabled beyond screamed and tried to jump out of its stall. Wooden slats splintered and fell. More partitions crashed down in a spreading wave of chaos. Cadets were shouting, "Stop them! Stop them!" But Brier's voice roared over theirs:

"Stop them, be damned! Get out of their way!"

Horses spilled into the arena, careening in mindless panic. Vant jumped back between the tethered mounts, dragging Jame with him, but they too had caught the madness and were plunging about in a nightmare of hooves, teeth, and eyes.

The stampede knocked Brithany off her feet, into a wall. As she struggled to rise, her forelegs tangled in the loop of her reins and she fell again. Storm screamed and reared, trying to reach her but cut off by the wild surge.

"Let me go," Jame said to Vant.

He looked at her as if she were mad and twisted her wrist. She reversed the lock on him and drove a nail into the nerve center at the crook of his arm. He swore, as much in astonishment as in pain, and she wrenched free from his suddenly nerveless grasp.

The loose horses wheeled and swerved wildly about the arena, each trying to lose itself in the safety of the herd. Jame dodged between them. Instinctively, she knew that they would trample her without a thought if she got in their way. The size, speed, and power of this living avalanche appalled her.

Here at last was the Whinno-hir, hopelessly entangled and thrashing. Jame ducked a small but lethally flailing hoof and put her hand on Brithany's shoulder. The mare instantly quieted, her large eyes bright with fear but also with that more than equine intelligence that can defy instinct. Jame drew her knife, a parting gift from the Jaran Lordan Kirien, and slashed the leather reins. She noted in passing that the Whinno-hir's bridle had no bit. Here was a creature the equal of any lord, who could only be ridden with her own consent.

Just as Brithany lurched to her feet, Storm came up roaring like his namesake, ready to kill someone. For a moment, Jame was afraid. For all she knew, this towering black stallion saw her as his master's enemy. So, for that matter, might the Whinno-hir.

Then Jorin pelted under the stallion's nose and leaped into Jame's arms, knocking her backward into Brithany and both of them nearly off their feet. Storm snorted, amused. A footstep sounded behind him, and he whirled on his hocks to find himself eye to eye with Brier Iron-thorn. Behind her Vant cradled his numb arm, looking murderous.

"Someone take that wretched cat out and drown it," he said.

The dark Southron turned to look at him. "Why?"

"Why? *Why?*" He indicated the scene behind him with a jerk of his head. "Just look!"

"I am looking."

So was Jame. The herd had slowed, their terror finally run out of them. Cadets were catching halters, soothing frightened beasts, and leading them back to whatever stalls remained intact.

"If the ounce's presence caused the panic," said Brier, "why are they calming down now? Whatever was here is gone now."

Then Jame remembered. "Sweet Trinity, the wyrm. Brier, I've got to reach Tori, to warn him."

"Not that again," said Vant, sounding thoroughly exasperated. "Haven't we had enough of this nonsense? Cadet, escort the Highborn back to her quarters."

Rue had come up, Graykin lagging warily behind her. "I can't, Five," said the cadet, with a self-conscious wriggle. "They're on fire."

"They're *what*?"

Brier looked at Jame. "Why am I not surprised."

Jame shrugged. "I didn't like the décor."

She caught a flicker of intense relief on Rue's face. Burning down the Highlord's apartment was not a good way to start anyone's life as a cadet.

"Ten, please. I've got to see my brother. This is deadly important. My word of honor on it."

The big cadet regarded her somberly. Abused by her former Caineron masters, she found it hard to trust any Highborn. They both knew that if she did as Jame asked and the mission turned out to be frivolous, it would be the end of her career.

"Very well, lady," she said. "Come with me."

II

IN THE GREAT HALL, a Coman cadet tried to stop
them. Brier brushed him aside and opened the door to
New Tentir, to a blur of runners and the thunder of
their passage.

The Coman turned to Jame. Clearly, he didn't know
what to make of her. Highborn, female, Knorth . . . for
him, she added up to a complete nonsense.

"Lady, d'you want to get yourself killed," he pleaded,
"or, worse, me expelled?"

"Relax," said Jame wearily. "You can claim that I
bewildered you."

She would have liked nothing better than to sit down,
right there in the midst of the quake debris. Every time
she stopped moving, her saddle-sore legs threatened to
fold under her. Her idea was to stick her head out the
door, shout "Rest!" and hope that the running cadets
obeyed.

Instead, Brier said, "*Now*," and plunged out into the
storm.

Jame was scrambling to catch up before she had time
to think.

They emerged on the arcade between squads,
between houses too, as it turned out, and the one hard
on their heels was Caineron. Caldane's cadets instantly
recognized Brier and surged to catch up. Here was their
former comrade, the *yondri* turn-collar, and they
wanted blood.

The Danior squad ahead glanced over their shoulders.
Their young lord was a Knorth ally, bone-kin to Torisen

and formerly his heir. They slowed and opened their ranks to admit the newcomers. Jame stumbled. Hands caught and bore her along, her feet off the ground, her shins repeatedly kicked to a muttered chorus of "Sorry, sorry, sorry . . . "

Meanwhile, the back rank of the Danior was trying to fend off the Caineron without catching the sargents' attention. That, luckily, had already been captured by growing ructions between the Ardeth and the Knorth on the other side of the square.

"Keep your order! Keep your order!" came their harried shouts.

"Where to?" grunted the Danior ten-commander to Brier.

"The Highlord."

"The Ardeth, then."

The running battle pounded down the northern side of the square, turned sharp left with the arcade, and thundered on. Just when Jame thought they were going to pull off her arms, Brier grabbed her by the jacket and lunged sideways into a door. It crashed open. Jame, pitched in headlong, rolled to her feet and then off of them again as much abused muscles rebelled. Dammit, if she never rode another horse as long as she lived, she would go to her pyre smiling.

Brier faced the door, which seethed with struggling cadets. Outraged yells to the rear announced the arrival of the Ardeth, who had seen their quarters presumably under attack. Behind them, someone gave the Knorth's rathorn war-cry, shrilly and somewhat wildly, in a voice not yet broken.

"Go," Brier said to Jame. "Now."

They had gate-crashed a lower reception hall, flanked with doors, a stair at its head.

Turning, Jame found herself face to face with Timmon. He gaped at her, then at the boiling mass of fighters at his door. Jorin squeezed between their legs and scuttled through the inner door from which the young Ardeth had emerged and which he still held open.

"Inside," he said to Jame. "Quick."

Beyond was a communal dining room, the long tables laid out for supper but no food on them.

Timmon slammed the door. "God's claws," he said, leaning against it. "Are all your entrances this dramatic?"

He was, she supposed, about her own age, twenty or twenty-one, mid-adolescence for a Highborn whose kind matured more slowly and lived longer than most Kendar. As she had noted in Tentir's great hall, he was also startlingly handsome, if now somewhat disheveled, his elegant jacket open at the throat, his golden hair ruffled. He also held a raw, half-eaten carrot.

"Where is my brother?"

"Up there." He indicated the chamber above their heads. "With my grandfather."

They stared up at the ceiling. Footsteps sounded above, circling, circling, and the floor groaned. Whorls in the wood grain shifted with each step. They might have been looking at the surface of a disturbed pool, from underneath. Timmon's hair bristled. Jame felt her own prickle all over her body.

"What are they *doing*?" whispered the Ardeth.

"Whatever it is, it's getting worse. Oh Tori," she said to herself, "how can I help you?"

Timmon stared at her. "You don't. You stay out of the way, my girl, and so do I. Sweet Trinity, don't you think I would help Grandfather if I could?"

Jame glanced at the carrot.

"I got hungry," he said defensively, and flicked the vegetable away.

Jame stifled a sneeze. Her nose was tickling with the wyrm smell again, and Jorin was nowhere in sight. Only one door stood open in the hall, leading downward. Of course.

"*Now* what are you doing?" Timmon called after her as she hastily descended. He followed, catching up at the foot of the stair. "Trinity, you Knorth are peculiar! Your brother tears apart my quarters, and now you want to start on the cellar?"

"Nothing that bad," said Jame, casting about for the scent. "I hope. I'm hunting a darkling crawler."

"Oh. Is that all?"

The basement of New Tentir must be roughly on the same level as Old Tentir's stable, a straight shot for a creature that could pass through wood and stone at will. And they were comfortingly dark. At first, the only light came from thick candles set in wall sconces, marked with the hours of the night, newly lit. Here, the cellar was divided into many small rooms—servants' quarters, mostly, all empty.

"Where is everyone?" asked Jame. She found that she was whispering.

"Your brother told all the Kendar to leave. *Our* Kendar, you'll notice. But the Commandant seconded him and they did."

Of course Tori would try to get the Kendar safely out of the way, never mind whose they were. She would have done the same.

However, instinct told her that her brother stood in greater danger now than anyone else. There was no doubt in her mind that the wyrm would seek him out.

His blood called to it, but was he its master now or was that still the dead changer? From what she had seen in the web-images festooning the guest quarters, it was one confused beastie. Of course, Tori might simply kill it, and that would be that. The last thing he needed right now, though, was such a distraction.

Here, down several steps, was the kitchen that served the Ardeth barracks, with the makings of dinner strewn about it—stew, judging by the heaps of raw vegetables and the vast cauldron on the central hearth, just coming to a boil. It all seemed very cheerful and ordinary, except that no one was there.

A loud crunch behind her made Jame jump. Timmon had found another carrot. "I'm still hungry," he said cheerfully. "What's wrong with your cat?"

Jorin stood in rigid silhouette against the flames, his back and tail arched. A singing whine came out of his throat, like a saw cutting live bone. But what did he sense? Jame edged closer, peering at the hearth, the fire, the cauldron, the water . . . nothing. Debris rattled down. She looked up.

"Timmon, your family crest is the full moon, isn't it? Then why is there a serpent rampant over your mantel-piece? Oh."

The wyrm lost its grip on the crumbling stones and fell. Jorin dodged behind Jame. Recoiling, she tripped over him and went down hard, cracking her head on the scoured flagstones. The crawler landed on top of her.

Knocked breathless, she barely had time to throw up an arm to protect her face. The wyrm twisted to right itself. Its sides were fringed not with legs but with fingers covered in a lacework of white scars. Her skin stung where the venom of its touch ate though her clothes; but the full sleeve of the knife-fighter's *d'hen* was reinforced to turn an attacker's blade, and so it did this creature's assault.

"*Are you the one?*"

Its features shifted inside the caul that enveloped its entire head except for a round mouth like a lamprey's. The dead changer glared at her and gnashed his ring of teeth.

"*Are you the one who stole my Beauty?*"

He thought she was Tori, Jame realized, and Beauty . - . . Trinity, Beauty was his name for the wyrm.

The face inside the membrane whipped back and forth, changing.

"*No, no, no . . . .*"

Tori's features emerged, haggard, desperate. "*Adric, don't . . . help me, help . . . .*"

"How?" cried Jame, lowering her arm. "Oh Tori, let me help!"

His fingers slid over her face, a touch as light as gossamer but it made her skin burn. She felt her body arch under his weight. *Oh, touch me again . . .*

"No!"

She was with her brother, circling, circling, the old lord's glamour beating against him/her/them like the desert sun, fifteen years' experience of each other all focused on this moment, on this issue: Who would be master?

Oh Adric, I don't want to fight. I'm tired. I hurt. And I don't want to hurt you . . .

Nowhere to hide. Be a rock, a black rock in the Southern Wastes, but what shadow lies behind it?

Adric searching for the bones of his son, which I ordered to be burned in secret on the common pyre at the Cataracts . . . .

(What?)

I promised to protect him, as he once protected me. If he knew what you had done, Peri, it would kill him. I couldn't let you tell him. I keep my promises. But oh Adric, don't!

"Don't what?" said Timmon.

He was wiping her face where Tori—no, where the wyrm had brushed it. Her skin burned as if with too much sun, but no worse. The creature's venom must almost have been spent.

"Nothing." She took a deep breath to collect herself and burst out coughing. The weakened fireplace had collapsed, overturning the cauldron onto the fire. Smoke still seeped out of the ruins, mixed with the gritty dust of stone and mortar. Jorin was sniffing at the mound of debris. Then he began to scratch around it as if trying to bury something. "What happened? Where's the wyrm?"

"Under there. It attacked you, I hit it with a shovel, and the mantel fell on it. I thought the whole wall was going to come down, maybe the whole barracks."

Both his voice and his hand shook slightly; he was not as calm as he wished to appear.

Neither was she. Just now, linked by the wyrm, she had been in that tent by the Cataracts, in her brother's mind and memory, when he had broken Pereden's neck. The feel, the *sound* of it . . . and here was Pereden's son who had probably just saved her life, trying to laugh off the terror that still quivered in his very bones.

If he knew what you had done . . .

What *had* Timmon's father done, to be killed in secret, his bones given to the pyre in stealth? She only knew that the sight of Pereden's son had stricken her brother in the great hall, and guilt now kept him from defending himself as he must in order to survive.

From overhead came the scuffle and thud of feet. Dust drifted down between the floorboards. Something fell with a crash.

Jame lurched to her feet, and her sight blurred. She waited for it to clear.

"How long has that been going on?"

"About as long as you were unconscious. A few minutes. Is your life usually like this?"

"More or less, and I still have to help my brother."

"Rest first. Stay with me."

She became aware of his arm around her waist, steadying her. It felt good to lean against someone.

Oh, touch me again . . .

"It's quiet here now," he said, "and safe, as long as the ceiling doesn't fall in. Stay. I've never met anyone like you before."

For a moment, she was tempted. She had never met anyone like him either, nor was she used to flattery. He certainly had a beguiling air, and he *was* very handsome.

Knorth and Ardeth, Ardeth and Knorth, circling, circling . . .

"No." She pulled free of his embrace. "Stay here if you want. I'm going."

"You can't help," he called after her.

She paused on the stair. "Then I'll hurt. I'm good at that."

Her first impression of the dining hall was of chaos. A mob of cadets had spilled in from the hallway, but no one seemed to be fighting now nor making much noise except for the scrape and shuffle of feet. She scrambled up on a table for a better look, catching her toe in the process and nearly falling flat among the crockery. It had been much too long a day. Knorth and Ardeth, Ardeth

and Knorth were circling each other as if in a macabre
dance, eyes glazed, faces twitching as if caught in a bad
dream. Overhead, the ceiling roiled and groaned in a
storm of wood. Jame cursed under her breath. She had
seen this sort of thing before, in Restormir's main square
during Caldane's epic drinking binge. When a lord let
things get out of hand, it went hard on the Kendar bound
to him, and these cadets were hardly more than children.
She stumbled down the length of the table, jumped to
the floor, and slipped out into the hall.

The Ardeth guards were pounding on the front door,
whose edges appeared to have grown shut. M'lord
Ardeth did not want to be disturbed.

Brier Iron-thorn was half way up the stair, hanging on
to the rail. Blood as dark red as her hair ran down her
face from a split lip, and someone had ripped the malachite stud out of her ear. She lurched around to block
Jame's way, her green eyes murky and half-focused.

"He saved me from the Caineron. Bound me. I am
his, although I trust no Highborn fool enough to trust
me. I don't trust you. You will only hurt him."

Jame blinked. "Now, listen," she began, then stopped.
There wasn't time. She ducked under Brier's arm and
went up the stairs.

At the top stood Sheth Sharp-tongue, the commandant
of Tentir, waiting.

"So, girl," he said, with a faint smile, "here we are.
My Lord Caineron fears you. I begin to see why. Are
you always this . . . er . . . disruptive?"

The door was behind him and behind that, her brother
fought for his life.

"Do something!" she cried.

"Why?"

Timmon came up behind her. The Commandant ignored him. So did Jame.

"You'd let them destroy each other?"

"Why not?"

For a moment, she saw him as a Caineron, the enemy of both her house and the Ardeth; but something else was at work here too, a cool assessment of power.

"Now, what kind of highlord would need my help?" the tall randon said gently to her. "If he is weak enough to fall, better for the Kencyrath that he should, don't you think?"

For a moment, she saw it: what chance did the Three People have if their highlord wasn't strong enough to lead them? Tori had weaknesses, no question about that. Suppose that in the end he wasn't able to surmount them. So the Kencyrath would fall and so would end their world.

No.

"Lord Caineron is strong," she said, "but strength isn't everything. There is also compassion, justice, and honor."

Behind her, Timmon turned a gasp into a cough.

The Commandant regarded her, eyes hooded and enigmatic. She glowered back. One didn't say such things to such a man as this, but she had, and damned if she would play rabbit to his hawk now.

He inclined his head and stepped aside.

"Let me," said Timmon, pushing past her. "These are my quarters, after all." But the door wouldn't open. "Locked," he said, with ill-concealed relief.

Jame put her hand on the latch. No, it wasn't locked. As below, the wood grain bound door, posts, and lintel together as if they had grown that way, with only a shallow crack between them.

Her fingertips tingled. An image began to form in her mind, intricate and verdant, deep green laced with pale gold on a bronze filigree. It was a master rune. The Book Bound in Pale Leather, that dire compendium of power, was no longer in her hands; Bane guarded it and the Ivory Knife in that pest-hole of a prison in the rock face behind Mount Alban. She had had mixed experiences with it anyway, having once accidentally set fire to a blizzard, and this rune wasn't familiar to her at all. But she could still unmake it. Already she was teasing it apart in her mind, line by line.

"What are you doing?" asked Timmon behind her.

She ignored him. It was harder to ignore the looming presence of the Commandant. Did he know what she was doing? That man had Shanir blood, although what sort she couldn't guess.

From inside came the murmur of Ardeth's voice: " . . . so like my dear son Pereden. Ah, what a lord he would have made. My heart breaks to think of it. You and he would have been like brothers and I a father to you both . . ."

Tori couldn't stand much more of this. In his place, she would long since have flared and brought down the roof, just to shut the old man up.

Jame backed away, then threw herself at the door.

It disintegrated.

She plunged into the room off balance, into a table laden with crystal, past it to the sound of shattering glass, into the folds of a curtain, through that with a mighty ripping of cloth, and onto a bed, which collapsed.

Fighting free, she saw her brother staring at her open-mouthed, as well he might. Behind him, Ardeth put his hand on his shoulder.

"My son . . ."

And, finally, the Highlord turned on him. "NO!"

The room shook. In all its corners, things broke, and the furniture lurched. Jame went over backward into the chasm between the bed and the wall, where she landed on top of something warm and furry that yelped.

As she struggled with whatever-it-was, both of them tangled in a winding sheet of linens, she could hear Ardeth's guard pouring into the lower hall and confused sounds from the dining room below as dazed cadets began to sort themselves out.

Closer at hand, her brother was speaking urgently. "Adric? Can you hear me? Damn, I was afraid of this. It's his heart. Commandant, does the college have a healer in residence?"

"Not at present. The Priest's College claims that we wear them out too quickly."

"Here's Grandfather's box of drugs. Which bottle?"

"The blue one, I think. Yes. Hemlock, in wine. Filthy stuff, but I've seen him drink it many times to calm himself. Damn. You pour it, boy. I'm no good one-handed. There. Is that better, Adric? That's right. Drink some more. Here's your grandson to look after you."

"Highlord, a word."

Torisen and the Commandant moved closer. Jame stopped floundering.

"Under other circumstances," panted the Wolver Grimly beneath her, "this would be fun."

"Quiet!"

She wished she could hide under the covers forever, but what would Ardeth think if he found her and Grimly there in the morning?

"Your pardon, my lord, but it would be best if you were not here when he awakes."

A deep, weary sigh answered him. "Yes. Yes, I see." Jame peeked out. Tori was rubbing his eyes. The dark circles under them looked like bruises, and the high cheekbones sharp enough to cut skin. He stood for a moment collecting his thoughts with an obvious effort. "Very well. I will ride on tonight, at least as far as Shadow Rock. As for my sister . . ."

Jame rose, half-sheepish, half-defiant. Grimly's furry ears pricked up beside her, just clearing the coverlet. Here it came.

" . . . she will be staying here as a cadet candidate and—" he paused to gulp "—as my heir, the Knorth Lordan."

From below came a crash and much shouting. The dining hall had just collapsed into the kitchen below.

⚔ CHAPTER III ⚔
Wine, Women, and Wolvers

2–3rd of Summer

I

HE LAY ON THE HARD COT in the big, dark room, pretending to sleep. From all around him came the deep breath of his fellow cadets, mixed with their occasional murmurs, sighs, and snores. It should have been a time of utter peace, of deep sleep after good, hard work remembered almost luxuriously in the fading ache of muscle and mind. He should have been intensely happy and so he was, he told himself. He had begged to attend the college, with little hope that Father would permit it, yet here he was, against all odds, on the threshold of a new life.

Why, then, did every nerve twang with tension?

Feet shuffled on the floor overhead. Two voices rose and fell. Then one exploded in a shout of drunken laughter.

The Lordan was carousing late again, probably with that sly-eyed Randir who would be drinking one cup to the other's three while seeming to keep pace.

That afternoon, at the pool, he had looked up and seen them staring contemptuously down at him from atop Breakneck Rock. Their gaze, especially the Lordan's, had made him feel not just naked, as all the swimmers were, but stripped down to his pitiful soul and left there exposed, for all to see.

He curled up shivering under the thin blanket. If only they would leave him alone . . .

A hand on his shoulder that made his heart leap like a startled frog. A soft, mocking voice in his ear: "The Lordan wants you. In his quarters. Now."

Torisen woke with a violent start, his heart pounding. Where was he? Not in the Knorth dormitory at Tentir. Tonight his sister Jame would be spending her first night there as a cadet candidate, as the Knorth Lordan. And he . . . he was on the run. From Ardeth. From her.

"Awake?"

A shimmer of starlight through an arched window caught the glow of eyes at his feet where Grimly curled up in his complete furs, muzzle across Torisen's ankles. The long jaw altered to a mouth still full of sharp teeth but capable of human speech. "Were you dreaming?"

He sounded both worried and wary, with good cause. In the past, Torisen had sometimes stayed awake for days, even weeks, pushing himself to the edge of madness, all to avoid certain dreams.

The Shanir dream, boy, his father had said. *Are you a filthy Shanir?*

No, he was not, and he now knew that everyone had dreams of some sort. Still, that last really bad one had been enough to send him storming out of Kothifir and up the length of the Silver with the sword Kin-Slayer naked in his hand and his dead father's voice in his mind inciting him to murder.

Your Shanir twin, boy, your darker half, returned to destroy you . . .

Overtaken by the weirdingstrom, he and Grimly had sought refuge in the wolver's native holt on the edge of the great Weald. Then had come dark dreams. In one of them, he had found himself clutching Kin-slayer, cowering in the hall of the Haunted Lands keep where he and his sister had been born. He was hiding from her, as he had been in Kothifir all winter, but she found him. She always did. Father was there too, dead on the battlements with three arrows in his chest. No, on the stair descending, step by step, muttering as he came, cursing him, telling him to kill, to kill.

The sword is in your hand, boy. You know that she is stronger than you. Save yourself. Strike!

But Jame *was* stronger. She had cursed their father and slammed the door in his dead face. Then she had shot the bolt against his madness.

When Torisen woke, his hand was already in splints.

"You looked at Kin-Slayer and said, 'There's more than one way to break a grip,'" Grimly had told him. "Then you pried loose your fingers one by one."

Had he really meant to kill Jame? Surely not. As children they had been as close as a single soul shared by two bodies. He had played in her dreams and she in his, until Father taught him to fear both dreams and her. Still, how he had missed her after Father had driven her out, and how he had blamed himself for letting her go. Now, miraculously, she had returned to him. He loved her, if "love" was the right word for this roil of emotions.

Father says destruction begins with love.

"Does it hurt?" Grimly asked.

It took Torisen a moment to realize that the wolver meant his broken fingers. Grimly knew all about Torisen's horror of becoming a cripple. When they had first met, the young Knorth had been fresh from the terrors of Urakarn where Karnid torture and infection had nearly cost him both hands. He still had the lacework of white scars as a reminder of the horrible vulnerability even of Kencyr flesh.

"Pain doesn't matter," he said, "as long as they heal. And they are. Yes, I was dreaming."

He coughed, his throat parched with the memory. Grimly rose, reverting easily to full if hairy man-shape, and padded across the floor to a table where a pitcher of water stood. He poured a cup full. Propping himself up on an elbow, Torisen accepted it gratefully and drank.

He remembered now: They were at Shadow Rock, the Danior keep, snatching a few hours of desperately needed rest before riding on to Gothregor. Across the river was the Randir fortress with Rawneth, the Witch of Wilden, in residence. Dangerous. They would have to be on their way soon, but not just yet.

"I dreamed," he repeated thoughtfully, frowning, "that I was at Tentir in the dormitory, and overhead the Lordan was getting drunk."

"She didn't invite you up?"

"That was the problem. He . . . no, she did, and I was afraid to go. Truly terrified. And I don't know why."

"That's bad," said the Wolver, now only half-joking. He partially resumed his furs and curled up beside the Highborn, a warm presence in the predawn chill. "You don't frighten easily."

Torisen laughed, tasting his bitter fear. "Many things scare me."

Odd, how easy it was to talk to Grimly, or perhaps not. Young and friendless in that strange city, Kothifir the Cruel, one formed alliances quickly or died. He had

had good reason at the time not to trust his own people. Among them, even now, only Harn, Burr and Rowan could guess his deepest thoughts. "Why do you think we're on the run now? What am I going to do without Ardeth's support and protection?"

"You really think you've lost it?"

"For now, at least. Adric has tried force. Now he will leave me to fend for myself, waiting for me to regain my senses and come crawling back."

He heard the bitterness in his voice. Up until three years ago he had been Ardeth's to command. No one but Adric had known who he was—it would have been suicide to announce himself before he came of age—but the old lord had also been both a mentor and a friend. Not to have him there now was like standing with his back to an open door, knowing his enemies were gathering in the dark beyond it.

I opened that door when I made my sister my heir, he thought. *I was a fool. Perhaps.*

"You're stronger than you think," said Grimly. "You must be, or the Caineron and Randir would have long since picked their teeth with your bones. Your sister is strong too."

Torisen considered this. "Yes. She's very strong. And dangerous." The word escaped him, flicking awake the terror he had felt in his dream at her summons.

Your Shanir twin . . .

By some weird quirk of fate, though, she was still only a half-grown girl while he was a man in his prime. Besides, he was Highlord, dammit, at no one's beck and call.

The Wolver grinned. "I'll tell you this: you may be my oldest friend, but it's a lot more fun wrestling with your sister."

A soft knock on the door made them both start. The Danior steward entered, shielding a candle with his hand. "M'lord," he said, "something is brewing across the river."

Torisen threw back the blanket and joined Grimly at the window.

Wilden lay across the Silver, slotted into its steep, narrow valley. A mountain stream divided at its head and hurtled, frothing, down either side into a brimming lower moat. Within its walls, the Randir fortress rose terrace on terrace, compound on compound, up to the Witch's tower glimmering white under the sliver of a crescent moon waning toward the dark. Mist was rolling out of the Witch's open door. It flowed down the empty streets, collecting at each corner, then rolling on in a slow, thickening tide, down toward the Silver's glint.

"Nice neighbors you've got," said Torisen as Grimly helped him pull on his boots. Otherwise, he had slept fully clothed. "How does she do that?"

"We have no idea. Remember, though, that the Priests' College lies literally in the shadow of her tower. Highlord, with m'lord Danior and most of our people still at Kothifir, there aren't enough of us here to protect you."

"Time we were gone anyway." Torisen rose and stomped home the boots. The steward's worried voice followed them down the stairs:

"If the mist catches you, there will be no one to rescue you."

"We'll risk it, thank you."

"And if you leave the road, odds are that you'll get lost in the hills. After the weirdingstrom, ancestors only know where anything is. Even our balancing rock is missing."

"If it falls on us, we'll let you know."

"Cheerful fellow," muttered Grimly as he held Storm's stirrup for Torisen to mount. "No wonder your lord cousin left him behind last fall."

They rode out into an increasingly hazy night. Mist mounted silently across the Silver, then overarched it. Tendrils, drifting too low, were carried away with the current. They had to go slow on the quake-broken road or risk their horses' legs. Soon, they rode in a tunnel of fog, cut off from moon or stars, their way lit with flaring torches, the clop of hooves muffled.

Trotting at Storm's side, Grimly noted uneasily how the mist opened before them and closed behind. They were on the west bank New Road, which offered less protection than the ancient stone-work of the opposite River Road. Moreover, both had been severely damaged. He didn't like the way white tendrils of mist quested blindly after Torisen like so many phantom snares cast after prey, but none of them quite managed to catch him. Even stranger, cracks seemed to half-close under Storm's hooves—either that, or the stallion had uncanny footing, but looking back Grimly saw that the paving had been subtly refitted. He had noticed odd, little things about his friend before of which Torisen seemed unaware and which upset him greatly when they were pointed out. The Wolver himself found them obscurely comforting.

Luckily, the Witch could only reach so far, and the sun was rising. After what seemed like hours, they emerged into a hazy dawn. Another hundred yards, and the mist burned off entirely, leaving a bright morning. It was the second of summer, and they were still some fifty miles from home.

Early afternoon found them opposite Falkirr, the Brandon keep. Brant, Lord Brandon, was also still with the Southern Host but his sister Brenwyr, the Brandon Matriarch, was said to be newly arrived home. Torisen decided not to pay his respects. In truth, he found Brenwyr almost as unnerving as Rawneth and preferred not to meet her without her brother on hand for protection.

They reached Gothregor, saddle-sore on tired mounts, at dusk. It, too, was held by a token garrison, but one overjoyed to see their erratic lord again. If they could have, Torisen thought, submitting reluctantly to their fervent greetings, they would have kept him wrapped in cotton, locked away somewhere secret and safe. Their god had played a vicious trick on the Kendar by making them only feel complete when they were bound to a Highborn. To lose one's lord was a terrible thing. He appreciated their concern, knowing how much they depended on him, but still . . .

If only they felt free to stay or go, he thought as he swung down from Storm and stood for a moment gripping the stallion's mane to steady himself, his legs quivering with fatigue, his splinted fingers throbbing. *If only they would leave me alone!*

Grimly snarled at the thicket of hands reaching out to support his friend, causing most of them to withdraw hastily. But the Kendar were also giving way to a newcomer invisible until she parted their towering ranks and glided through to face Torisen.

"Highlord, the Matriarch Adiraina wishes to speak to you."

He stared down at the small Ardeth lady, his mind going blank. Nothing could be read from her masked face, but every line of her trim, tightly laced form radiated determination.

"What, now?"

"Yes, my lord. Now."

The Wolver yelped in protest, and the lady's randon escort dropped hands to sword hilts to protect her. By now, however, Torisen had had time to think, and his thoughts appalled him.

"Grimly, no." He let go of Storm and stood, gathering his strength and wits. "This might be important. I'll see you later in the common room."

Torisen followed the Ardeth Highborn, with her guards striding behind him as if to prevent his escape. Something very like panic made his stomach clench. What if Adric's heart attack had proved fatal after all? Adiraina was not only an Ardeth but a Shanir. She might know if the lord of her house had suddenly died and by whose hand, for surely she would blame him for driving his old mentor to such extremes. He certainly would blame himself.

They crossed the broad inner ward, passing the original Old Keep on its hill fort foundation, incongruously small for such a mass of buildings to have grown up behind it. Foremost of these were the Women's Halls, into which he was led by the northern gate. As the scrollsmen had Mount Alban and the randon Tentir, the

Council of Matriarchs had claimed the westernmost halls of Gothregor for the training of Highborn girls of every house to become proper ladies. The womenfolk there far outnumbered Gothregor's small garrison, with the Highlord as their reluctant host. Nonetheless, neither he nor any other man usually came here, where even the randon guards were female.

Only days ago, however, Torisen had virtually stormed this forbidden domain in search of his sister, only to be told that she had vanished, with two shadow assassins on her trail. His encounter then with the Ardeth Matriarch had hardly been cordial. The thought of a second interview now made him shudder, no matter what she had to tell him.

His escort led him through the Brandon, Edirr, and Danior compounds, leaving behind a flutter of ladies who clearly hadn't expected to encounter a man, much less the Highlord, at this time of night. This was the long way around, avoiding the Coman and Randir. Torisen wondered why.

But here was the Ardeth.

The tiny Highborn bowed him into a room and firmly shut the door after him. He was relieved not to find the entire Council of Matriarchs waiting for him, as it had the last time. On the other hand, this small, candle-lit room appeared to be the antechamber to Adiraina's private quarters, unnervingly intimate with its delicately scented air, claustrophobic without windows.

Torisen knew a trap when he stepped into one, but step he must.

The Matriarch sat upright in a filigree chair beside the fireplace. When they had exchanged salutes—wary on his part, gracious on hers—she indicated a chair opposite her. All too aware of the slight tremor of fatigue in his legs, he sank into it, and kept on sinking as the tapestry back slid down under his weight.

"Such an interesting design, don't you think?" Adiraina smiled sweetly. "And so comfortable, I'm told. My old bones don't allow me such luxury."

Torisen stared owlishly back at her over his jutting knees. This was her revenge for his behavior the last time they had meet, when he had nearly thrown the entire Women's World out of Gothregor on their collective ear for their treatment of his sister. In retrospect, he had probably been rude, but if he had followed his instinct, he wouldn't now be perched on his tail-bone outside a lady's bedroom.

Between them was a delicate table bearing a glass of dark, red wine and a plate of sugar cakes sprinkled with what appeared to be cinnamon.

"Eat, drink," said the Matriarch with a graceful wave of her thin, white hand. "You have had a long, hard ride. You must be famished."

Torisen was, although nerves nearly killed his appetite. This wasn't the reception he had expected. Surely, if Adric were dead and his cousin knew it, she would be far less welcoming. But if not that, then why had she requested . . . no, demanded . . . to see him the moment he set foot inside his citadel?

As he strained forward to take a cake—Trinity, how was he going to get out of this diabolical chair without falling flat on his face?—he studied his hostess. Over one hundred and twenty years old, she was a study in subtle shades of gray from the dark pewter of her gown to lace-work trim tinted the rose blush of storm clouds at sunset. Her velvet half-mask had no eye-holes: she had been blind since adolescence—the cost, some said, for her awakening Shanir powers. Although immaculate in dress and regal in bearing, wisps of white hair escaped her coiffure and the toe of a bedroom slipper lurked in the folds of her skirt. So she hadn't expected his sudden return.

Her voice flowed over him in a stream of small talk about the weather, about the coming midsummer harvest, about mutual acquaintances and friends; but hidden in the stream were rocks. She bemoaned Adric's fragile health without mentioning his recent heart attack, of which she was apparently unaware.

So much for Shanir omniscience, thought Torisen, a bit smugly.

"He can't help but worry, you know," the matriarch was saying. "We all do. You haven't quite found your feet yet as highlord, have you, my dear? These past three years have been . . . interesting, occasionally verging on the catastrophic. You really must learn to take a stronger hand and to depend more on your own kind—not that the Kendar aren't useful, when kept in their place. If you had grown up among your peers, things would be different. However, you didn't, so I suppose we must make allowances. Of course, the battle at the Cataracts was a great victory, although also a terrible tragedy for our house with the loss of Pereden. Now Adric pins his hopes on Peri's son, Timmon. To my mind, the boy is a bit frivolous and his mother over-ambitious; however, we will see how he shapes up at Tentir.

"But you aren't eating. Please do. And drink, or I will be offended."

She laughed as she spoke, making light of it, but with a silvery ring to her voice like knife-play.

Blind she might be, but her hearing was acute.

Torisen nibbled the cake and found it sweet enough to hurt his teeth, with an odd after-taste. Then again, nothing tastes right to an exhausted man. It did, however, make him very thirsty. He surreptitiously discarded the pastry and, after a struggle to reach it, seized and sipped the wine. It was stronger than he liked and made his head spin, dangerous on an empty stomach. Nonetheless, under its influence he began to relax.

"By the way, did you ever find your sister Jameth?"

He noted that she couldn't say the name without a slight shudder, and at that she still hadn't quite gotten it right. Did the Matriarchs even know that they had been trifling with a second Jamethiel, perhaps even more dangerous than the first?

"Such an . . . unusual girl," Adiraina was saying, with an air of sweet forbearance. "So lively. And so inquisitive. However, she will settle down with the right consort. Have you picked one yet?"

"No." The wine was making Torisen drowsy and giving his voice a faint slur. He tried not to stare cross-eyed at his knees, which was hard since they were practically under his nose. "I made her my lordan and left her at Tentir to train as a randon cadet."

"Oh!"

He could almost see the Ardeth trying to decide if he had just made a joke in very bad taste, but that would imply a lie, which was unthinkable. He had, however, rattled her. Good.

"Well, of course we would never accept her back here after all the trouble she caused."

"What, fighting off shadow assassins? I understand there was a cast of twelve apprentices under the guidance of a master, out for a blooding. How many ladies were killed?"

"One, but that isn't the point."

"It is for the eleven who survived."

Adiraina gathered her wits and temper with an effort. "Still, you really should have consulted my lord Adric. It was hardly wise to set her up as your heir, much less to expose both her and you to ridicule over her inevitable failure at Tentir. You Knorth!"

Her tinkling laugh rang with indulgence. *How we humor you*, it said. Torisen gritted his teeth.

"For the moment, however," she continued, "we must reluctantly consider Jameth out of play. That leaves you, my dear. Have you considered whom to take as your next consort? No? You should. It is your duty."

She cocked her head, as if considering a new thought. "You know, my talent lies in sensing bloodlines. Our house is very pure in that respect, almost as much so as your own. That makes you and your sister all the more puzzling. It is so important to know which lines cross, don't you think? About some matches, the less said the better. You and your sister . . ."

"Jame," he said helpfully, to see her squirm. Slightly befuddled as he was, he could see where this conversation was going, and he didn't like it.

"Yes . . . er . . . dear Jameth. Both of you are pure-blooded Knorth. I know that. However, all the Knorth ladies died in the massacre except for poor Tieri, who died later giving birth to a bastard of unknown lineage."

Torisen blinked. "You mean Kindrie? He's my first cousin?"

Her thin lips tightened. "A bastard is kin to no one. Really, you sound like your wretched . . . er . . . dear sister, always asking such indelicate questions. The Priests' College has a place for such people. Tieri's brat never should have left it. But we were speaking of your mother."

"We were?"

"Neither you nor your sister look much like your father, or so I am told. Poor Ganth was always a bit unrefined—the result, no doubt, of his unfortunate childhood; even good blood can't surmount everything—but you are both pure, classic Knorth. Blind or not, I know that."

She wrapped her slim arms around herself and spoke so low that he could hardly hear.

"Sometimes, when either of you is present, my very bones shake. Did you know that, as a child, I spent hours studying the faces of your ancestors in the death banner hall? The Kendar played cruel tricks in portraying some of them but even then, such eyes, such hands, such power once flesh and blood! When your dear great grandmother Kinzi first spoke to me, I thought I would die. I hear echoes of her in your voice and in that of your sister, yet I know that both of you are closer heirs to the ancient glamour of your house even than my beloved Kinzi was. But how can that be? Tell me, boy: who was your mother?"

If Torisen had known, in his current state she might have made him answer; but he didn't, and preferred to keep any suspicions to himself.

"With all due respect, matriarch, I decline to answer."

"Will you answer this, then? I also sense that you and your sister are twins, but how can that be when she is at least ten years your junior? Where has she been all this time?"

"Again with respect, you will have to ask her."

"We did. She wouldn't tell us."

"Then neither will I."

If he could have seen her eyes, she would surely have been glaring at him. However, like her cousin Adric, she was adept at self-control.

"Please," she said, with an abrupt return to her earlier graciousness, "drink. It will do you good."

Torisen wasn't so sure about that. As a rule, he preferred cider to wine, and this was a strong, unfamiliar vintage, again with that peculiar after-taste. However, it did soothe the nerves. The matriarch's voice resumed its smooth, cool flow over his tired muscles and fretting thoughts.

"You must allow for an old woman's eccentricity. Bloodlines are rather an obsession of mine. All that really matters is that yours are pure. And they are. You really should ally yourself with our house, my dear. It would strengthen your position greatly and, if I might mention it, show cousin Adric that you truly do appreciate all that he has done for you. As it happens, the Ardeth have several young ladies currently in the Women's Halls who might suit you. May I introduce two of them?"

"I don't think . . . " began Torisen.

However, she had already turned to call forth the ladies in question from an inner room, where they must have been waiting for her summons.

Their entrance was preceded by a short scuffle in the dark—"You first."

"No, you."—before a short, plump girl emerged suddenly as if pushed from behind. Like her matriarch, she appeared to have thrown on her best dress in a hurry, its tight bodice straining against unmatched buttons. She was followed by a taller, older young woman whose gliding step would have been more impressive if she had remembered to put on her shoes.

Torisen struggled to his feet, wincing as he jostled his injured hand. More fervently than ever, he wished that he had thrown Adiraina out of Gothregor—no, into the river—when he had had the chance.

"After your unfortunate experience with dear Kallystine," the matriarch was saying, "it is only fair that you have a chance to inspect what you are being offered. Ladies, please. Unmask."

Both girls froze, eyes widening with horror. Torisen had always considered the masks a coy embellishment, probably because Kallystine had made a game out of wearing as little as possible in bed and out of it. However, these ladies were genuinely upset—more so, perhaps, than if Adiraina had asked them to strip naked.

"That isn't necessary," he said hastily.

"Oh, but I insist. This is Pentilla." She indicated the older girl. "She has already honored two contracts, one with male issue, the other without, as specified by the terms of each agreement. Her consorts both speak highly of her amicable nature and her willingness to please. Darlie, on the other hand, is a novice, but highly trained with exceptional bloodlines. We expect great things from her. Also, of course, if the terms of your contract with her allow, you can break her to your liking."

Torisen stared at the two Highborn, who stared back at him. The older was pretty in a polished, inhuman way, as if she had made her face as much a mask as that which she usually wore. However, there was something in the depths of her eyes that made him uneasy. What kind of a life had she led, to be described as "amicable" with all that hunger locked up inside? Her child, of course, being male, had stayed in his father's house, probably with a Kendar wet nurse, while she had returned here to be used over and over again, as her house saw fit.

The younger girl wore her innocence on her face, but also some hint of her ignorance, verging on stupidity. After all, what had she been taught but how to follow orders and, in theory, to please her future consorts?

Jame's face flickered across his mind, alive with quirky humor and sharp intelligence, always asking awkward questions, dropped into this nest of females blinded and gagged with convention. The wonder was not that the Women's Halls didn't want her back but that they had survived her at all.

The Ardeth Matriarch was waiting for him to say something.

Wine unlocked his tongue. It was also beginning to make him queasy. "You sound as if you're trying to sell me a horse," he heard himself say, "or rather, a brood mare."

Adiraina stiffened with outrage, but the older girl's perfect mask of a face twitched and the younger giggled outright. The matriarch clapped sharply to restore order. They ignored her, all their attention focused on him. The older ran the tip of a pink tongue over rouged lips. The younger stared at him like a greedy child at a box of candy.

"Oh dear," murmured Adiraina. "It wasn't supposed to work this way."

"What wasn't?" Then he remembered the odd taste of the refreshments offered to him with such persistence. "Lady," he said carefully, "as you well know, Highborn are very difficult to poison, but we do react to drugs in different ways. What did you put into the wine?"

She made a gesture as if to brush away both the topic and her embarrassment at having been caught in so crude a trick. "Only a sprinkle of love's-delight. I thought you might be too tired to make an . . . er . . . appropriate decision."

"So you gave me an aphrodisiac. On an empty stomach." He seriously considered up-heaving on her pretty carpet—it seemed the least he could do—but the girls were coyly advancing on him.

"Truly, my lord, you would like me better." The sudden, naked hunger in Pentilla's eyes appalled him. "A man like you, with mature tastes . . ."

Darlie elbowed her aside. "I know all the best tricks . . . in theory, anyway. Wouldn't you like to practice them with me?"

"Ladies, please!" Adiraina cried, but no one listened.

I'm the Highlord of the Kencyrath, dammit, Torisen thought as he backed away. *I will not be chased around the furniture*.

Ancestors be praised. No one had thought to lock the door. Torisen slid through and closed it behind him on the uproar within—"He wants me!"

"No, me!" "You hag!" "You snot-nosed baby!"—and turned to face a solid wall of women.

Most were Ardeth, these after all being their quarters, but mixed in were a few Danior, Coman, and Caineron, drawn from their own compounds in various states of dress or undress. Those farthest away could be heard demanding to know what was going on. Those closest had their eyes fixed on Torisen in a way that strongly reminded him of a mouse suddenly thrust into a calamity of cats.

Someone tugged his sleeve. He looked down into the serious face of a seven-year-old, in a nightgown, clutching a rag doll.

"Please, Highlord, will you marry me?"

He scooped her up with his good arm. "No, sweetheart. You're too young for me."

Her face lit with joy. "Then I'll wait for you!"

He tossed the child, squealing with laughter, into the arms of the nearest woman who looked strong enough to catch her.

"Put her to bed. For Trinity's sake, doesn't anyone sleep anymore? The rest of you, MOVE."

And they did, clearing a passage for him through the halls, all the way to the forecourt gate. There he was stopped by a Jaran captain.

"Highlord, my lady Trishien would like a word with you."

Torisen pulled up short, gulping. "My regards to your matriarch-*eeerrp*—but I think I'm about to be sick."

The randon regarded him curiously. Ancestors be praised again: the Ardeth's diabolical draft didn't apparently work on Kendar.

"Pass, my lord," she said solemnly, and opened the gate. As it closed behind him, he heard her defending it against a wave of females, but was too busy heaving his guts out into a bush to care.

Across the darkening, inner ward, the common room windows cast welcoming bars of light across the grass.

Sanctuary, thought Torisen, and made for it as quickly as his unsteady legs allowed.

 III

The common room seethed as the garrison threw together what food they could to welcome home their

lord. Grimly's pack was there too, having been stranded
at Gothregor some days before by the weirdingstrom,
all thirty-odd of them charging back and forth in their
complete furs. Pups bowled over each other. Adults
paused to offer Torisen shy greetings before rejoining
the wild chase under and over tables, between Kendar
who grinned or cursed according to their mood, but the
pack didn't care. Tomorrow they would set out for their
home in the Weald with an armed escort. Torisen was
taking no chances: Some Kencyr, especially, the Caineron, hunted the wolver for sport. Watching Grimly gam-
bol with a trio of pups on the hearth, he already missed
his old friend.

Supper arrived—stew, fresh bread and butter and, as
a treat, a plate of last season's apples. Clearly, the winter
larder was nearly exhausted. The cubes of meat floating
in the broth were unfamiliar.

"It tastes better than it looks," said one of the garrison,
noting Torisen involuntarily make a face at the musty
smell. "The weirdingstrom swept some odd game into
the Riverland. Desert crawlers, dire elk, rhi-sar—
Steward Rowan claims she even caught sight of a white
rathorn colt."

Queasy enough as he was, Torisen forbore to ask what
creature had made its way into the bowl before him. He
made a show of eating, meanwhile slipping lumps of the
spongy gray meat to a pup under the table, finding an
odd comfort in the small, rough tongue as it avidly licked
his fingertips clean.

Suddenly a fight erupted at his feet. The pups who
had been playing with Grimly tumbled out, snarling and
snapping at the one whom Torisen had been feeding.
This was no casual game; already there was blood on fur.

Luckily the young wolver with the cold, blue eyes and the enormous paws was a match for any two of her opponents.

Grimly quickly broke up the fray.

"She's a problem, that one," he said. "An orphan of the deep Weald and willing to submit to no one. We found her wandering. Of course, we couldn't let her starve. If we drove her back to her own pack now, though, after being with us, they would probably kill her."

Torisen regarded the orphan pup, who had withdrawn to a corner to lick her wounds. She was certainly much more feral than Grimly's people, who in their own way were remarkably civilized, with a strong sense both of ethics and of aesthetics. The deep Weald wolvers, on the other hand, were reputed to be savage beasts if, indeed, they were even of the same species.

A Kendar offered him a cup of mulled cider. Although his stomach revolted at the thought, he accepted it and started to thank the man, but couldn't recall his name. That had never happened before, not with someone bound to him. The other's smile faltered and his ruddy face paled in blotches as he felt the bond to his lord weaken.

Soon after Torisen slipped out of the hall into the moonless night.

What's wrong with me? he thought, leaning against the outer wall. *Am I finally losing my mind, or is this just exhaustion on top of Adiraina's filthy brew?*

Whichever, best to withdraw before he hurt someone else.

He crossed the inner ward to the old keep, that relic of ancient days around which the rest of Gothregor had been built. Like the larger fortress, it was rectangular with a drum tower on each corner. The first floor was low ceilinged, dark, and musty, its walls lined with half-seen Knorth death banners. Someone in the common room had mentioned having to rescue the lot of them from a grove of trees, of all places, where the southern wind, the Tishooo, had swept them on Jame's last night in residence here.

He saw more evidence of that night in the third floor Council Chamber. Here, tall stained glass windows had glowed with the crests of the major houses and, taking up the entire eastern wall, there had been a map of Rathillien glorious in jeweled light. Now, the ruins of the latter glittered in the starlight on the inner court below—the Tishooo's work again or Jame's, he wasn't sure which and didn't care to ask.

Up again into the southwest tower and here was the small, circular room that he had claimed as his bed-chamber, dusty and dank with a winter's neglect.

Home, he thought, with a sudden surge of depression as bitter as bile. No, it had never been that, only a place out of the way, hard for anyone else to reach, where he could hide.

"You haven't quite found your feet yet as highlord, have you, my dear?"

Damn and blast Adiraina. Blind as she was, she saw far too much. Was that what he really wanted—a home? A place to belong, to love and be loved?

Nonsense. He couldn't afford such luxuries when so many lives depended on him. These quarters only missed his servant Burr's touch. He could also have used help undressing around the bandages but wasn't going to ask it of some Kendar whose name he suddenly couldn't remember. Things would be better in the morning.

Fully clothed, Torisen lay down before the ash-choked hearth and there drifted into an uneasy dream. He and Jame were children again in the Haunted Lands, chasing each other turn and turn about over the gray, swooping hills under a leaden moon. Up and down, down and up...

She pounced him and drove her elbow into his face. He yelped in pain. They rolled down the slope, scrabbling and snapping at each other in the manner of dreams like wolver pups. At the bottom, she broke free and dashed up to the next crest. He joined her there, wiping a bloody nose on his sleeve.

"Why did you do that?"

"I wanted to see how you would block the blow. You didn't. I was trying to learn something."

"Father says it's dangerous to teach you anything. Will the things you learn always hurt people?"

She considered this, idly plucking blades of grass and letting them wriggle through her ragged black hair where they tried to take root. "Maybe. As long as I learn, does it matter?"

He snuffled loudly and wiped his nose again. "It does to me. I'm always the one who gets hurt."

"Crybaby."

"Little girl."

"Daddy's boy."

"Filthy Shanir."

She sprang to her feet and looked down at him. Her eyes were silver, frosted with blue, fey, wild, and alight with mocking challenge older than her years. "I am what I am, but what are you? You don't know, and you're afraid to find out. Come, then, let's play hide-and-seek. You be Father. I'll be Mother. Catch me if you can!"

And she was off, plunging down the hillside toward the keep in a swirl of flying hair, rags, and thin, pale limbs, going, gone.

This is wrong, he thought. *It didn't happen this way . . . did it?*

If he followed, he knew where he would find her, just where he had on that terrible day over two decades ago: in their parents' bedroom, standing before a mirror whose misty depths reflected not the keep's shabby chamber but a vast, dark hall; and the face staring back at her would not be her own but that of the mother they had lost, for whom their father still desperately searched. He would try (again) to reach through the glass for her and (again) Jame would stop him. She didn't understand. Unless Mother came back, Father would turn on her, their mother's Shanir mirror-image. But she would fight him as she always did, as if his life rather than hers depended on it. And perhaps, again, she would knock him backwards into their parents' bed, where they had been conceived and born, and it would collapse on him.

That was the last he remembered. When he woke, she would be gone, from the keep, from his life, and not even in dreams would he be able to find her.

Torisen blinked. That was then. This was now. Not gray hills but heaped ash on a dead hearth lay before him, and his sister had returned.

An open west window brought him cheerful sounds from the common room, then a sudden crash followed by the cook's exasperated shout: "All right, that's it! Out, out, out!"

The parcel of wolver pups spilled yipping onto the grass of the inner ward. Torisen could hear their joyful tussle, punctuated by yelps and mock growls. Then they began to keen in unison. Their shrill voices rose and fell, first together, then in counterpoint in imitation of their elders who could shape mist with their song and bring back the ghosts of winter.

Torisen smiled. They were serenading him.

He groped in the darkness, found an old boot, and tossed it overhand out the window. The chorus broke into yipping laughter. Claws scrabbled up the stone steps of the old keep. Moments later, a half dozen pups burst into the tower room and pounced on the Highlord as if they meant to tear him apart. He fended them off with his good hand, laughing, until they collapsed panting around him and began to snore. Lying under a blanket of small, furry bodies, he drifted off into blessedly dreamless sleep.

 **IV**

IN THE MORNING, the wolver pack left with its escort, the pups yipping goodbye and trotting off, eager to be home.

Grimly lingered. "Take care of yourself," he said. "This is a cold place. It doesn't love you. Your friends do, when you let them."

"And who are they?"

"You know. Harn, Burr, Rowan, maybe even your sister."

"Father always said, 'Destruction begins with love.'"

The Wolver curled a lip back over sharp teeth. "When you talk like that, I smell the dead on you. Be yourself,

Tori, not someone else. Especially not him. And give my love to your sister." He grinned, suddenly all wolf. "Tell her I enjoyed our time together under the bed."

Then he dropped to all fours and sprinted after his pack.

Only when all had left did Torisen realize that the ruddy-faced Kendar hadn't gone with them as part of their escort as ordered, and that he still couldn't remember the man's name.

CHAPTER IV

Testing

Summer 1–2

I

WHEN JAME WOKE early the next morning, on the floor under a pile of musty blankets, she didn't at first know where she was. At Tentir, of course, but beyond that . . .

She felt Jorin's warmth at her side and reached out to stroke his rich fur. He stretched full length, sighing, and snuggled his head into the crook of her arm. Eyes closed, she let her *dwar*-bemused memory drift over the previous evening.

The Commandant had taken Torisen's announcement that she was staying with raised eyebrows, but had only said, dryly, "I see. Very well."

Timmon, on the other hand, had gaped at her until she had snapped at him, "What are you staring at?"

"I'm not sure, but I think I like it." Then he had given her such a dazzling smile that she in turn had blinked. Dammit, what *was* it about that boy?

Tori had waited until Ardeth was resting quietly, one drug having counteracted the other, and then had called for his horse. Shadow Rock, the Danior keep, was a good twenty miles to the south. Neither he nor Storm would have much rest that night, but he was clearly anxious to be on his way before Ardeth woke.

"For Trinity's sake," he had muttered to her on his way out, "don't make fools of us both."

"No more than I can help," she had said, which was honest if hardly reassuring.

Jame considered her situation.

She hadn't known what to expect when she had rejoined her people the previous fall except to be reunited with her twin brother Tori. That he was now at least ten years her senior thanks to the slower passage of time in Perimal Darkling had come as an unpleasant surprise to them both, and would cause considerable complications if anyone found out.

Ever since her sudden appearance at the Cataracts, Tori had been under intense pressure to contract her to either the Caineron or the Ardeth, the two most powerful houses in contention for mastery of the Kencyrath after the Knorth. What she had told Graykin was true: thanks to Jamethiel Dream-weaver's role in the Fall, most lords considered the Highborn women of their houses only good for breeding and political alliances. For Jame, that was apt to mean either one of Caldane's vicious sons or the Ardeth Dari, he with the breath of a rotten eel (according to his father) whom no woman contradicted twice.

She hadn't spent most of her life trying to rejoin her people for that.

Moreover, if either she or Tori had a son by someone from another house, that boy would become the first highlord in Kencyr history not of pure Knorth blood.

The balance of power would shift irreparably, perhaps disastrously.

The Kencyrath was already perilously close to losing its identity. Some, like Lord Caineron, professed not even to believe the old stories. Singers' lies, he called them, and it was true that song and history, fiction and fact, had become intertwined over time. Only Kencyr on the Barrier with Perimal Darkling—the Min-drear of High Keep, for example, or Jame and Tori's own people in exile in the Haunted Lands—had no doubt whatsoever that their ancient enemy only bided its time.

Presumably, the Merikit hillmen also understood the danger since they lived closer to the Barrier than any Riverland Kencyr except the Min-drear.

Jame's thoughts drifted back to Summer Eve in the ruins of Kithorn—had it only been the night before last?—when she had found herself thrown into a Merikit rite to placate the vast River Snake whose waking had brought on the earthquakes and the weirdingstrom. Somehow, she had emerged as the Earth Wife's Favorite. So far so good, and no stranger than a dozen other things that had happened in her short but not uneventful life. She still carried Mother Ragga's "favor," the little clay face called the *imu*, in her pocket. However, the Favorite also played the Earth Wife's lover, to ensure the coming year's fertility. To save face, the Merikit chieftain had declared Jame his son and heir until the next ritual. Then, please God, she could pass on the role to someone better equipped to fulfill the Favorite's duties.

But all of this had given the Jaran Kirien an idea.

" 'Lordan' is an ancient title applied to either the male or female heir of a lord," she had told Lords Ardeth and

Caineron, breaking into their interminable wrangle over which house should have the newly discovered Knorth, Jameth. "Nothing in the law forbids a female heir."

Well, she should know. Hers was a house of scholars and she herself was its lordan, no one else having wanted to leave his studies to take on the job. Torisen knew that she was female. The other lords assumed otherwise, not that Kirien had ever deliberately set out to fool them. There would be hell to pay when she came of age and claimed power.

In the meantime, "By ancient custom, the heir always has the status of a man, and 'he' doesn't form any contracts before coming of age at twenty-seven."

Jame could see her brother's mind working; that would get them both out of the fire for several years at least.

"There is this, too," the haunt singer Ashe had added in her harsh, halting voice. "Traditionally . . . the Knorth Lordan trains . . . at Tentir to become . . . a randon."

So here she was, against all odds, against everyone's will but her brother's, and he was already beginning to have doubts.

"For Trinity's sake, don't make fools of us both . . . ."

Easier said than done.

At last, Jame opened her eyes.

Over her loomed the dawn-tipped peaks of the western Snowthorns, seen through a ragged hole in the roof where the weirdingstrom had carried off both slates and rafters. Birds flitted in and out. The air was crisp enough to turn her breath into puffs of mist. She was in the attic of the Knorth barracks.

First they had tried to put her back in the Knorth guest quarters in Old Tentir, only to find them charred beyond use. Luckily, the fire hadn't spread. Unluckily, it had also consumed all evidence of the wyrm. Then there had been the third floor apartment in the Knorth barracks, where she had had such bad dreams. Finally, she had come up here, to the top of the world, it had seemed, with only the mountains and star-frosted sky wheeling through the night above her.

In a corner, Graykin stirred fitfully in a nest of moth-eaten blankets. Even his snores resounded with discontent.

Jame, however, felt a surge of excitement. She might be adept at falling on her face, but then just as often she landed on her feet. Either way, nothing had ever stopped her from jumping. She stretched luxuriously, and Jorin stretched with her down the length of her body. The old, defiant chant rose in her mind:

If I want, I will learn.
If I want, I will fight.
If I want, I will live.
And I want.
And I will.

This was going to be fun.

Outside, a horn blared, and birds fled out the hole in the roof. Jame scrambled to her feet, tossing the blankets over a protesting ounce. Across the dusty floor, the windows of a dormer faced eastward towards Old Tentir. As she leaned out to look, in the training square below a sargent again raised his ram's horn and sounded its raucous note.

"All right, you slug-a-beds," he roared. "It's morning. Up, *up*, UP!"

In the second story dormitories below, bare feet hit the floor in a garble of *dwar*-slurred voices. The whole college must have been out cold last night, small wonder after the previous day's events.

Turning, Jame saw that Graykin was awake. He gave her one look, then hastily averted his eyes and began to search for his clothes. He at least had slept in his underwear—a Southron custom, perhaps. She didn't know if all naked bodies upset him or only hers, but that was his problem. Ancestors knew, the rigors of the past two weeks had left hardly enough flesh on her bones to offend anyone.

Suddenly, Jame was ravenous. Nobody had eaten the night before. When had been her own last meal? She couldn't remember.

Think of something else.

Rubbing her sore buttocks, she twisted around as far as she could to look. Yes, those shadows were bruises. Damn all horses anyway.

But Graykin had the right idea: she needed clothes.

Her pants, boots, cap, and gloves were all right, but the jacket would never do. Why could she never arrive anywhere appropriately dressed? The last time it had been a voluminous dress "borrowed" from a Hurlen prostitute. This time, it was a Tastigon flash-blade's *d'hen.* Sweet Trinity, what if someone last night had recognized it for what it was?

That apartment below—hadn't it been strewn with neglected garments?

A central, square stairwell reached from the attic to the second floor landing. Jame ran down the steps, the chill mountain air raising goose bumps on her bare skin. The third floor was divided between a long common room overlooking the square and the lordan's private suite facing outward and west toward the mountains. Only two rooms of the latter were accessible—a dusty reception chamber and the inner room beyond. Presumably the suite continued to the north and south, but walls of chests, layers thick, blocked it off in both directions.

Jame paused in the second room beside the cold fireplace on its raised hearth, where she had tried to sleep the night before. In her dream, the floor had been covered with rich, soiled clothing, left where a careless hand had dropped them. She remembered fur and silk, velvet and golden thread, all sunk in a miasma of stale sweat, but that hadn't concerned her then. She had been sitting beside a roaring fire, drinking and laughing so hard that wine spurted out her nose like blood onto her white shirt and richly embroidered coat. That had seemed hysterically funny at the time. Sitting opposite her, her companion had also laughed but more softly. She knew he was less drunk than she and in a fuzzy way resented his self control. Damn, superior Randir. She would impress him yet.

"No, truly," she heard herself cry in a hoarse, slurred voice not her own. "Such games we used to play, my brother and I! The things I made him do!"

"Did he enjoy them?"

"Now, if he had, where would have been the fun? Once the poor little fool even tried to tell Father, who called him a liar to his face for his pains."

She was leaning forward now, supporting herself with a thick hand studded with gold rings and coarse, black hair. Her voice dropped conspiratorially. "You don't believe me? Listen. This very minute, he sleeps below in his virtuous cot. Dear little Gangrene, all grown up and come to play soldier. Shall we have him up, eh? See if he remembers our old midnight game?"

If there had been more to the dream, Jame didn't remember it. She spat into the fireplace to clear the foul taste of that voice from her mouth. What in Perimal's name had it all been about anyway? Who was "dear little Gangrene"? Surely Father had never called her brother Torisen a liar, the worst of all possible insults. As for midnight games ....

Jame shrugged away the thought. It had only been a dream.

Or perhaps not.

Sprawling on the hearth like the flayed skin of a nightmare was the embroidered coat.

She picked it up. It was surprisingly heavy, its entire surface covered with thread in many colors, couched with stitches of tarnished gold. Here and there were stains as if of wine, or of blood.

It also stank.

She remembered now how she had wrapped it about her for warmth the previous night and tried to sleep in its noisome folds. Ugh. No wonder she had had bad dreams.

Jame dropped the coat and turned to the nearest wall of chests. When she dislodged and opened one, the smell was as she remembered it, with an added stale air of must and mold. Several layers down, she found a serviceable shirt and a belted jacket cut cadet style.

"Oh, very stylish," said Graykin from the doorway. "What's that stench?"

"History. Don't ask me whose."

She put on the clothes. Both shirt and coat were much too large for her, but they would do.

Below, the rumpus had subsided.

Good, thought Jame, turning up her sleeves and clinching the belt. She would slip down and keep out of sight until she knew what was expected of her.

"Try to stay out of trouble," she told Graykin as she passed him with Jorin at her heels. "Better yet, hide."

From either side of the second floor landing, stairs led down to the front and to the back halves of the ground floor, which itself was divided by the internal corridor that run all around the three sides of the square, cutting through every house barracks.

Jame bent down to peer below. To the front, nothing. That, as she vaguely remembered from the previous night, was a public area. From the back, however, came a stifled cough and a stealthy shifting of feet. Ten long tables had been set out and ten cadets lined each of them, five to a side, standing at attention. Bowls of porridge cooled before them. At the head table, one empty seat waited. Even as she realized that it was meant for her and that no one could eat until she sat in it, the horn sounded again and everyone bolted toward the square. Descending, Jame saw the Kendar pile through doors that opened onto the common corridor, cross that, stream through their own front hall, and so out into the morning light. She snatched up a hunk of bread, stuffed it into her mouth, and followed, with a wistful backward glance at the rest of the uneaten breakfast.

Cadet candidates were forming up in tens. Jame took a position behind Brier's squad, but hands reached back to draw her forward. She found herself pushed out in front, level with the other ten-commanders, all too conscious of her reeking, over-sized tunic. Timmon, also front and center before his own house, sketched her salute in greeting. Brier stood behind her and Vant parallel, before another squad.

She chewed hastily and swallowed. "What's going on?" she hissed at Rue, a pace behind her to her right, inadvertently spraying the cadet with crumbs.

"Iron-thorn was demoted to Five. You're Ten now, lady."

"The hell I am!" But she hardly needed Vant's side-long smirk to know that Rue spoke the truth.

"Hut!"

Everyone stiffened. Several cadets, let go by supporting hands, fell over, still lost in *dwar* sleep.

Flanked by his randon instructors, Commandant Sheth Sharp-tongue strolled into the yard from Old Tentir. He moved like an Arrin-ken, thought Jame, powerful, lithe, and subtly dangerous. Morning light caught the hawk lines of his face and cast his deep-set eyes into hooded shadow. He wore the white scarf of command as he did his authority, easily, as by birthright. Here were the makings of a lethal enemy. And he was a Caineron. She felt his eyes sweep over her and sensed Jorin cower at her side.

"Cadet candidates, I bid you welcome to Tentir."

His voice, light but resonant, carried easily to every corner of the square. No sound crossed it but the swish of his long coat and a breath of wind chasing last season's leaves across the tin roof of the arcade. Somewhere in a back row, a fallen cadet began to snore, grunted as a mate kicked him, and again fell silent.

"You come to us in unusual times. Last fall, almost the entire student body marched south with the Host to the Cataracts. Many died there. We honor their memory and will not forget their names. For the most part, those who survived were promoted on the battlefield and now serve with the Southern Host at Kothifir. As a result, we have very few second year cadets and no third years except for those who have returned to assist as master tens in charge of their respective house barracks.

"In addition, you may have noticed that we have several Highborn candidates, including Lord Ardeth's grandson Timmon. The Caineron Lordan is also expected momentarily."

Is he, by God, thought Jame. She wondered whom the prolific but fickle Caldane had picked for an heir this week, and how Sheth meant to introduce her, if at all.

At that moment, the hall door swung open and a burly, travel-stained randon stumped into the square. He stopped, blinked, and swore at the unexpected sight of the drawn up troops, who stared back at him.

"Ah," said the Commandant, smiling slightly. "My esteemed predecessor at the college and the Knorth warleader, Harn Grip-hard, and Steward Rowan," he added as a scar-faced woman appeared in the doorway, "and Sar Burr"—this last, to a third Kendar, who had stopped at pace behind the other two. "Goodness, nearly the Highlord's entire personal staff. Have you misplaced him again?" Someone in the Caineron ranks snickered. "How may we be of service, rans and sär?"

"We're looking for Blackie," the big randon said gruffly to the yard at large. His blood-shot eyes fell on Jame and widened. "Here, boy, what in Perimal's name are you playing at?"

Jame felt a powerful urge to withdraw into her oversized tunic like a turtle into its shell.

"If I may continue," the Commandant said smoothly, "I was just about to announce the presence among us, for the first time in forty-six years, of the Knorth Lordan . . . ah, Jameth, is it not?"

"Lordan?" Harn blurted out. "Has Blackie gone mad?"

More snickers, louder this time.

"As to that," said the Commandant with a smile, "you would know better than I. Torisen Black Lord rode on last night. You probably passed him in the dark. A moment, please," he said, as the three turned to go. "If you will stay for a bit, Rans Harn and Rowan, you can do the college a great service. Sar Burr, no doubt you will wish to retrieve . . . er . . . rejoin your wandering lord as quickly as possible."

He turned back to the cadets. "Our three lordans, of course, will serve as the master tens of their respective houses. You will also no doubt have noticed—especially those who had to sleep last night two or three to a bed—that there are nearly twice as many candidates here as usual. One thousand three hundred and ninety, to be exact. Death has greatly thinned our ranks. However, the college is only equipped to train some eight hundred cadets at a time. I speak, of course, of those who are still here at this time next summer. Between now and then, there will be three culls rather than the usual two. Over the next three days you will undergo a series of tests to determine who stays and who goes."

Tests.

Jame gulped. No one had said anything about that. She was certain that her brother hadn't known. No wonder Sheth had barely blinked when Tori had presented her as his heir. Neither the Commandant nor anyone else expected her to be here long enough to matter except as proof of the Highlord's lunacy.

"We have summoned every available randon officer, sargent, and senior cadet to oversee this . . . ah . . . winnowing process. Ran Harn, if you would be so kind as to stay and assist? Thank you. I expected no less.

"Good luck," said Sheth blandly, "to you all," and swept back into the shadows of Old Tentir.

A sargent stepped forward. "Tens," she cried. "Count off!"

II

BY THE END OF THE FIRST DAY, the randon were optimistic. There were many good candidates, judging by the first three tests, easily enough to fill the college's depleted ranks. Also, there were some promising young Shanir whose particular talents they would assess later.

As for the rest, those who couldn't wake in a timely fashion from *dwar* sleep had already been dismissed. Some of the Caineron were clearly hopeless. Caldane had over-filled his quota with every young Kendar he could lay his hands on, half of them still hung-over from their lord's excesses of the week before. Even the Caineron randon glumly agreed, more freely than they might have if the Commandant didn't habitually dine alone in his quarters. The rest, officers, sargents, and senior cadets, had gathered in the officers' mess in Old Tentir to share dinner and compare notes.

There was no sign yet of the Caineron Lordan. It didn't matter. By unspoken agreement, his place was secure at the college, whenever he deigned to arrive. After all, Sheth could hardly turn away his master's son.

"That Ardeth Timmon is shaping up surprisingly well," remarked a Danior randon, reaching for the salt. "Even if he does slide out of some things."

"Like the punishment run."

"Yes. But he clearly had good teachers at home and enjoys physical challenges. Not quite the spoiled brat we were expecting, eh? A little irresponsible and immature, though."

"I just hope he doesn't have his father's taste for the Kendar," a Coman sargent muttered to her Jaran counterpart. "That damned Pereden could charm his way into any bed, for the sheer deviltry of it."

"But this is only a boy."

"Not so young as all that, and the Ardeth start early." She raised her voice. "Did your lord get off safely, Aron?"

"Before dawn, ran," replied the Ardeth sargent. He looked exhausted. It had been a rough night, even without part of the dining hall collapsing into the cellar. "If his guard can keep him quiet with drafts of black nightshade, they hope to get him past Gothregor before he decides to tackle the Highlord again."

"Huh," said a young Coman randon. "More likely, he'll wait to see what happens here. There'll be no hiding it now. You didn't exactly help, Harn. D'you have to call your lord crazy in front of the whole college?"

Harn Grip-hard was morosely gnawing a mutton bone, his broad, stubbly face glistening with its fat. Rowan sat beside him, carefully expressionless as usual; fifteen years after the Karnides had burned the name-rune of their god into her forehead, the scar still hurt.

A Caineron laughed. "Yes. What will your precious Blackie say when he hears about that, eh?"

"Nothing," grunted the former commandant of Tentir. "The boy knows I have a big mouth, and I've known him since he was fifteen, so new to the Southern Wastes that he looked like a flayed tomato."

"What was he like then, ran?" asked a senior cadet. "Besides sun-burnt, I mean."

"Quiet. Wary. Determined. Not like his father Ganth Gray Lord at all, except in certain moods."

"It took Urakarn to unsheathe the steel in him," said Rowan. "I was there. I saw."

Harn thought for a moment, absentmindedly wiping greasy fingers on his jacket. "It's hard to explain. He isn't like most Highborn. Never has been."

"Obviously not," said a Randir, with a sidelong glance at her table-mates. Even in the close-knit world of the randon, the Randir held themselves subtly apart. There were also more female randon in that house than in any other. "To make that freak his heir and then to bring her here . . ."

The other randon stirred uneasily. They knew there was bad blood between the Randir and the Knorth, although not all knew why.

A senior cadet broke in, grinning broadly: "D'you see her this morning trying to wield a long sword? Trinity, I thought she was going to chop off her own toes, or maybe mine. That cadet Vant made a proper fool of her."

"Still," said an Ardeth thoughtfully, "she didn't do so badly with the short sword although I'll wager she'd never had one in her hands before. I've been watching her technique. That girl knows knife-craft, although I've never seen that particular style before. D'you see how she tried to block with her sleeve? The Commandant was watching too. 'I thought so,' he said."

"Thought what?"

"He didn't say. Still, what in Perimal's name are they teaching in the Women's Halls these days?"

"Quiet, wary, determined," repeated a Brandan thoughtfully. "What if there should be steel there too, underneath? We may be surprised yet."

This was met with general laughter and some flung hunks of bread, which the Brandan flicked away with careless, good-natured grace. "Just the same," he said, "talk to Hawthorn when she gets back from escorting M'lady Brenwyr home. I hear she had some odd experiences with the Knorth during the weirdingstrom."

"Yes, but did you see the plan she—the Knorth, that is—submitted for storming the citadel?" Like so many in his house, the Edirr cadet clearly found anything ridiculous irresistible. "I mean, a herd of goats disguised as priests?"

While he elaborated, gleefully, the older randon grumbled among themselves. It was a new idea that cadets should learn how to read and write rather than to depend, as for millennia past, solely on a well-trained memory. Things were changing. Not everyone approved.

". . . ending in a rain of frogs!" crowed the Edirr cadet, "and, you know, it just might work!"

The others exchanged looks and shook their heads.

 III

By the end of the second day, the randon were less easy. The competition was getting ugly, and candidates were beginning to get hurt. Worse, instructors had come across possible evidence of sabotage. A notched bow had snapped at the full draw, nearly taking out a cadet's eye. Swords mysteriously lost their baited points or acquired newly sharpened edges. Horses were found to have burrs under their saddles or cinches hooked by twists of tail hair to their privates.

Practical jokes, said the Randir, shrugging.

Others feared that it was only a matter of time before someone was seriously injured or killed. In the latter case, no blood price could be demanded by the cadet's house, but such things tended to fester, sometimes for generations. Again, some glanced from Randir to Knorth.

They also spoke, with increasing unease, about the Knorth Jameth.

Most had expected that by now she would have burst into tears and retreated to her proper place, namely the Women's Halls at Gothregor. Captain Hawthorn, newly returned from escorting her own matriarch home, rather thought that the Women's World would as soon welcome back a handful of burning coals.

The Highborn girls there had barely settled down and stopped (oh, horrors) asking questions when who should arrive but Lord Caineron's young daughter Lyra Lackwit, ostensibly to gain some polish in women's ways, actually to get her out of sister Kallystine's sight before the latter killed her. Various ladies had been heard to prophesy the end of the world, if only so that they might at last get some rest.

"However, they're apt to give the Highlord precious little of that," Hawthorn said, amused, pausing to drink from her mug of cider. "Now that his sister has slipped through their hands, I've heard that the Council of Matriarchs means to make a dead set at him for one of their own houses."

"But the Knorth Jameth. What d'you think of her?"

The Brandan captain considered for a moment. "Thoroughly unorthodox," she said, "but weirdly effective. Not unlike her brother."

The Caineron jeered at this. "What do *you* know? Your matriarch wears riding boots and a divided skirt. We've even heard that she sleeps with a death banner."

Hawthorn merely smiled. "She suits us. Perhaps we Brandan aren't all that orthodox either, anymore."

"What does Sheth intend?" one senior randon asked another quietly undercover of the above exchange. "Can he really mean to let this girl stay?"

"He accepted her into Tentir," said the other. "His honor is bound."

"Even against the will of his lord that she should fail?"

"Even so, unless he bows to that will."

"You speak of Honor's Paradox. Where does honor lie, in obedience to one's lord or in oneself?"

"Just so. The Commandant will have to decide. So will we all. But what d'you think of these sightings of the White Lady? Has the Shame of Tentir come back to haunt us?"

The other stirred uneasily. "With a Knorth Lordan here for the first time in forty-odd years . . . ah, I don't know. Certainly, the Lady has unfinished business with that house, if even half the stories are true."

"As to that, only the Randon Council knows. Maybe it *is* just a wandering rathorn, swept north by the weirding-gstrom. Cam did swear that he saw its horns. Still, a lone rathorn. A rogue. A death's-head. That's bad enough."

The Edirr cadet could no longer contain himself.

"Did you hear about her riding test?" he burst in, claiming the room's reluctant attention. "I'm waiting at the top of the training field when she and a Jaran ten come up. When she sees what's next, she stops dead (both squads piling up behind her, mind you), and says, 'Oh no. Horses.'

"So I get everyone including her mounted and in line. As you know, the test is to ride a circuit of the fortress keeping in formation, starting at a walk, ending in a full charge, over a variety of terrain. Well, from the first the horses are all in a fret, lunging, bucking, and then the Knorth's starts backing up. She's kicking it for all she's worth but it lays its ears flat and keeps going, right into one of those quake fissures, over and down, backward. It hits the bottom and bolts and so, if you please, do both ten commands.

"The next thing I know, we're thundering down the field with the Knorth keeping pace at the bottom of a ditch.

"Then up she comes, both stirrups ripped off, hanging on for dear life, and barges into the front line. Two horses go down, three more bolt off at a tangent straight through a quarter-staff practice—sorry about that, Aron; I hope none of your cadets were trampled.

"Passing the front door, we lose half a dozen more horses when they take bit in teeth and plunge inside, hell-bent for the safety of their stables.

"Then up the southern flank of the college over hill and dale, through wood and water, between archers and their targets, apparently, because suddenly arrows are whizzing past our ears. More horses shy. More riders fall.

"By now, there are only five of us including the Knorth and that big Southron Iron-thorn who's galloping beside her and holding her in the saddle by the scruff of her neck.

"Well, finally we stop and then, if you please, the Knorth falls off."

" 'Oh,' she says, looking up at me. 'Wasn't I supposed to do that? Everyone else did.' "

The Edirr burst into helpless laughter. As he beat his head on the table-top, the two senior randon exchanged glances.

"That's it," said one. "We're doomed."

CHAPTER V

A Length of Rope

Summer 4

I

IN HER DREAMS, Jame heard a voice:

Kinzi-kin, it was crying. Such a lost, plaintive sound, she thought, but fearful too, and hushed, as if afraid of being heard.

Kinzi Keen-eyed was her great-grandmother, slain some thirty-odd years ago in the massacre that had claimed all but one of the Knorth ladies at Gothregor. Who would call her by that long dead name?

She rose from her nest of blankets, went to the hole in the slanting roof, and looked down. It was early morning, barely light, with shreds of mist floating through the trees. A ghostly figure stood below, looking up. Again came that desolate cry:

Kinzi-kin!

Jame leaned out. "Here!" she called down.

The stranger appeared to be a woman clothed in filmy white, but the face raised to Jame was almost triangular, broad across the forehead, tapering down to a small mouth and chin. Ears pricked through the long, tangled

658

locks that veiled half her face. Her single, visible eye was large and dark.

Aahhh . . . she breathed, in a long shuddering sigh. *Nemesis*. Then, in a pale flicker, she was gone.

The morning horn sounded and below feet hit the floor. Jame stood by the window, wondering if it had been a dream. Below, however, were hoof-marks in the rain-softened earth.

So began the third day of tests.

Hastily dressing, Jame wondered if she had been insane to believe she could ever qualify as a cadet. The Kendar against whom she was competing had prepared all their lives for this. Her own training had been at once more intense than theirs and more limited, including precious few weapons. She had only scraped through sword practice because at first her opponents couldn't bring themselves to look her in the face. Vant had broken that with a set glare, and then had thoroughly trounced her into the bargain.

She had thought she was doing well with the knife, only to be penalized for her unfamiliar style.

True, she had enjoyed plotting the overthrow of a citadel, only to realize when she turned in her closely written five pages that most cadets were still laboriously scrawling their first paragraph. That was the first time she had ever seen Brier Iron-thorn sweat.

She also thought she might eventually get the hang of the quarter-staff and bow, but not in time to help now.

As for riding, the less said, the better. Several of the horses had been found to have burrs lodged under their tails, which accounted for a great deal. Her own mount had been clean except for strange scratches along his crest that looked almost like claw marks. Jame was hardly going to explain how *those* had come about.

There were nine tests in all, three or four a day, administered at random as far as Jame could tell. For each, her ten-command was paired with a ten of a different house, and the twenty of them were sent wherever the appropriate officer waited. With so many tests all conducted more or less at the same time, Tentir and its environs swarmed with sweating cadets and shouting randon. Each time, a candidate was ranked from first place to twentieth, and the scores added as he or she went. A perfect (but unlikely) over-all score would be nine; the worst, one hundred and eighty. No one knew for certain, but the cut-off for admission to the college was believed to be around one hundred and thirty. The Randon Council, comprised of past and present commandants of Tentir, would set the final mark when all scores were in.

After seven tests, Brier was leading Vant by thirteen to his twenty-one.

Jame, on the other hand, had already nearly accumulated the fatal number. To qualify as a cadet, she would have to do very well indeed on the last two tests.

One of them was bound to be unarmed combat, the Senethar.

Jame only knew that the other took place in the great hall of Old Tentir, and that cadets often emerged from it pale and shaking. A few didn't return at all. Those who had passed refused to say exactly what had happened, on orders of the randon. Each day left a smaller, increasingly apprehensive number of the uninitiated. Finally, among the Knorth only Jame's ten had yet to face the nameless ordeal.

"I've heard some candidates choose the white knife rather than do whatever-it-is," said one of her cadets at the breakfast table.

That was Quill, thought Jame, the one whose mother had wanted him to become a scrollsman, hence the name. It had suddenly struck her that despite all they had been through together—raiding Restormir, careening down the Silver in a stolen barge in the middle of an earthquake, riding Mount Alban all the way to the Southern Wastes and back—the only two of the ten whom she knew by name were Brier and Rue. But now they were her ten, her responsibility.

"If they killed themselves, where are the pyres?"

That was Erim, clumsy, beetle-browed, and slow of speech, who looked stupid but, she suspected, wasn't.

"Idiot, they would send the bodies home for the burning."

Mint. Pretty, with green eyes and a touch of Highborn refinement in her bones. A flirt who liked to set male and sometimes female Kendar against each other, just for fun.

"Or salt them for the winter larder," said Rue. "God's claws, I'm only joking! Five, what do you think?"

Brier Iron-thorn, as usual, had drawn her bench slightly back from the table and was taking no part in the nervous chatter. "I think the missing cadets failed the test and went home, all right, too embarrassed to stay."

"Or in disgrace." Vant flung this from the neighboring table. His ten had undergone the mysterious ordeal early and all had emerged unscathed, if shaken. "What will you tell your lord, shortie, when you come crawling back to him?"

Rue flushed. "I'd rather die, or be eaten."

"Maybe they'll give you a choice. Fried, broiled, jerked . . . you're about the right size for a roast suckling pig, though."

"Ten," said Jame, "shut up."

Vant sketched her a salute. "As you wish, lady."

His cadets tittered nervously, unsure if they should follow his lead. He believed he would be rid of her soon, Jame thought. He might be right.

In the square, the horn blared its summons and all rushed outside to take formation.

Although they had been half-expecting it, the order that the Knorth and a Danior ten should report to Old Tentir still came as an unpleasant shock.

Entering the dim great hall, Jame looked around. It didn't appear to be any more of a torture chamber than usual—less, in fact, now that its floor was clean and its roof mended. House banners still hung portentously against the lower walls and randon collars still winked farther up in the gloom. The only difference took a moment to spot: a rope, stretched from one side of the hall to the other from the third story railings.

Behind her, a cadet gagged. Jame turned to find them all staring up at that innocent length of hemp as if they expected momentarily to be hanged with it.

Then she understood. Many Kendar suffered intense vertigo and nausea when faced with heights—a potentially fatal drawback for a professional soldier. It made sense that any cadet who couldn't overcome this weakness had no place at the college. Still, what a test to set them so early in their careers!

A cold voice spoke from the upper gallery: "Come up."

Above, a gaunt Randir officer waited for them. "So you would be randon," she said, with a thin smile at their carefully blank faces. "And what is that, eh? Would you master others? Can you master yourselves? Here, we find out."

She began to pace slowly up and down their rigid line, from the Danior ten at one end to Jame at the other and back. Her long coat swished as she moved, like the dry hiss of scales on stone. Her arms folded tight across her chest seemed to hold in and concentrate her malice. In a soft, almost caressing tone she spoke of a randon's duties, harmless stuff often heard before, but beneath the surface ran another voice like the murmur of black water under ice. Jame heard it most clearly when the woman paused before her and fixed her with dark, unblinking eyes.

"Don't think you'll get away with it," came that subtle whisper inside her mind, echoing her fears and doubts.

The woman's eyes seemed to be almost all black pupil now, holes plunging into an abyss, and someone else watched through them.

"Fail one more test, and you are gone. Pass, and how long will it be before we drive you out? Fool. Abomination. Besides, you have hurt my cousin and crossed my lady, who is far from done with you. Run. Hide. But in the end, in the dark, she will find you."

Then she smiled. Her teeth were very white and the incisors chiseled to needle points. Then she passed on, leaving Jame as breathless as if those tightly clasped arms had crushed the air out of her.

What *was* she doing here? (*Fool.*) What could she expect to accomplish, except her brother's ruin and her own? (*Abomination.*) What place was there anywhere for such a creature as herself, bred to darkling service, in futile rebellion against her own nature?

Wait a minute, she thought. *I hurt her cousin? Who in Perimal's name was that . . . and of whom do those sharpened teeth remind me?*

Then she caught a fragment of what the randon was saying under her breath to Rue: "*Border brat. Runt. What made you think that you could fit in here, among your superiors? Give up. Go home. Die. No one cares which.*"

This randon's lady was Rawneth, the Randir Matriarch, the Witch of Wilden, who perhaps had been behind the slaughter of the Knorth women thirty-four years ago; and yes, Jame meant to cross her at every possible turn until she not only knew the truth but could prove it.

Now she recognized the power in the randon's voice. It was similar to that of Brenwyr, called the Iron Matriarch for her fierce self-control—a good thing, too, because she was a Shanir maledight who could kill with a curse.

"*Rootless and roofless . . .*"

No, Jame thought, pushing Brenwyr's words out of her mind. *I'll prove her wrong yet. I must.*

Another word floated up in her mind: tempter. That was this Randir's power, aligned with the third face of god, and that was her role: to taunt her victims to destruction, if they were weak enough to fall.

Beside her, Rue was shivering like a drenched puppy. In a moment, she would stumble forward to end this ordeal one way or another. Jame touched her arm as she moved, stopping her.

"Age before innocence."

The randon had reached the other end of the line, and so didn't see Jame step forward. A gasp from the cadets made her turn to find the Knorth already standing on the balcony rail. As they all watched, horrified, she spread her arms and stepped gracefully out onto the rope.

At last, thought Jame, something at which she was good. Not only had she no fear of heights, but a year of playing tag-you're-dead with the Cloudies across the rooftops of Tai-tastigon had given her considerable experience in such aerial sports.

She was half way across the hall when a choked exclamation from below broke both her concentration and her balance.

Jame recovered enough to part with the rope on her own terms and to catch it as she fell past. Swinging, looking down, she saw the violently foreshortened figure of Harn Grip-hard, who was staring aghast up at her.

"What in Perimal's name are you doing?" he demanded hoarsely.

"I was trying to pass a test. Sorry, ran," she added, seeing his stricken face.

"Come back." If a voice could have chipped stone, the Randir's would have.

Jame reversed and returned, hand over hand this time. She thought, as she neared the rail, that the rope gave slightly, but the stark face of the waiting randon held her attention. As she swung herself back over the rail into the gallery, she saw half the cadets bent over heaving up their breakfasts and the rest barely retaining theirs. One boy had fainted.

Kest, she thought. The cadet who had suffered so terribly from height-sickness on their climb up Lord Caldane's tower that even Kindrie couldn't help him.

Only Brier Iron-thorn watched her with cold detachment, as if the witness to a mountebank's failed trick.

"Now, why did you do that?" asked the Randir, very softly. Under her voice, the cold currents ran swift and deep. *"Did you think these brats would admire your*

*courage and skill? Do you need their approval so badly?
Just what were you trying to prove, and to whom?"*

Someone said, "Look!" and when they all did, there
was Rue, starting across the rope hand over hand, do or
die, her face white and sweating, her eyes screwed shut.

She was half way across when the rope groaned and
sagged. Rue's eyes snapped open. Paralyzed with fear,
she stared down at the cruel stones thirty feet below.

Her mates lined the rail, discipline forgotten.

"Come back!" some cried.

"Go on!" shouted others.

Below, Harn was roaring, "Where are the bloody
mats?"

The rope sagged again. It was parting, strand by
strand, some ten feet beyond the rail.

Brier started forward, but Jame stopped her. "I know
you've a good head for heights, Five, but you weigh half
again more than I do."

As she swung a leg over the rail, the Randir grabbed
her arm. "Stay here," she hissed. "Haven't you done
enough harm already?"

Jame broke the randon's grip. Black rage flared in her,
driving everyone back. "Never. Touch. Me. Again."

She wanted to keep her anger, to kindle it with all the
misery of the past three days into a full berserker flare
that would return to her all the power that others had
tried to strip away. What she really needed now, however, was self-control. She regained it with a fierce effort.
A moment to gauge distances, and out again over the
void.

Here was the weakened section of the rope, between
her hands. The outer strands had been pried apart and
the inner ones notched. To all but the closest scrutiny,

the rope would have appeared to be sound, and so it had proved under her slight weight. She swung past and on to where Rue helplessly dangled.

"Rue, move."

"Can't," said the cadet through clenched teeth.

"Must. Just a bit farther. Do it."

With a sob, Rue loosened the fingers of one hand, groped ahead, and clutched.

"Again. Good girl. And again."

The rope parted. Jame tightened her grip on it as it plunged away and wrapped her legs around Rue's body. They swung down with a heart-stopping rush toward the far wall and into the fibrous mass that was the Caineron banner. As Jame had hoped, it cushioned their impact nicely, if with a choking billow of dust. She let the rope slide through her gloved hands. They hit the floor harder than she would have liked, given her already sore bottom, but that was nothing compared to what it would have been like if Rue hadn't inched forward those last, vital few feet.

"Yow," said Jame, letting out her breath.

The shock-headed cadet gulped, turned, and cast herself into Jame's arms, bursting into tears. Jame held her, oddly touched. She looked up to see Sheth Sharp-tongue standing over them.

"All right, children?"

"Yes, ran," she answered for them both. "In a minute."

The other cadets came scrambling down the stair, slowing in a wary gaggle as they recognized the Commandant.

"Return to your barracks and rest," he said, addressing both squads. "You are excused this trial until later in the year, with a provisional pass for now. Your last test will take place this afternoon."

Harn reentered the hall, dragging a large, heavy floor mat. He dropped it, panting, when he saw that they were safe. "This was bundled up in a side room. And why was that rope slung three stories up instead of the usual two? What in Perimal's name is going on? Here, you!"

He stalked toward the Randir, who was descending the stair more slowly than the cadets into the hall. The Commandant sauntered over to join them.

"Take the squads back to their quarters," Jame told Brier. "I'll be along shortly."

The big Southron gave her an unreadable look, and a curt nod.

Jame was left irresolute, watching the three senior officers. Two of them were immortal in song and legend, the greatest randon of their generation. Who was she to interfere? However, she had stayed because Harn Griphard was her brother's oldest friend, and a berserker with reputedly failing self-control. She could easily guess what the Randir Tempter was saying to him under her soft voice, between those sharp, sharp teeth:

"Give in to your rage. Let it devour you. Become the beast that you know you are . . ."

And the Commandant merely watched, as he had when Tori had fought Ardeth for mastery of the Kencyrath's very soul.

"You say the hall was set up as you found it." Harn loomed over the smaller woman, his big fists clenched at his sides. "You say the rope appeared to be sound. But you know we don't set it that high this soon, much less without safeguards. And before that, arrows in the wood, as if anyone would conduct an archery trial there! What the hell are you Randir playing at?"

"Let go. Give in."

Harn shook. Veins stood out on his neck and burst in his eyes, turning them red. Sheth drew back a step, as if to enjoy a better view. The Randir woman smiled.

This was intolerable.

Jame slipped between the Knorth Kendar and the Randir. "Ran Harn," she said, raising her voice and her hands to stop him. He caught her by the wrists in a brutal grip. Bones ground together. Both Highborn and Kendar might be called berserkers, but with the former it was a colder, more considering thing. A Kendar like Harn could rip a foe limb from limb, only later realizing what he had done.

"Harn," she repeated, louder, trying not to wince, "Blackie trusts you."

Finally he looked down at her, blinking blood-shot eyes, then thrust her aside and blundered out of the hall.

Jame watched him go, rubbing her bruised wrists.

"If he should break," said the Commandant mildly, behind her, "better it be among his peers, who can defend themselves, than among his students, who cannot. You, perhaps, are an exception." She turned to find him regarding her speculatively. "I haven't quite figured you out yet, child."

"No, ran. Nor I, you."

He smiled and flicked her under the chin with a careless finger. "No doubt we will both eventually succeed." With that, he strolled away, his white scarf the last thing to melt into the shadows of Old Tentir.

Jame turned to confront the Randir. She put all the strength she had left into her voice, where it echoed hollowly. "Ropes and arrows, burrs and notched bows . . . whatever is going on, ran, it's between your precious Witch of Wilden and me. Leave my friends out of it."

The Randir raised an eyebrow. "You blame us? Why should we wish you to fail more than, oh, say a dozen others? You don't belong here, girl. Your mere presence tarnishes the honor of all randon, alive or dead, just as it calls into question the sanity of the brother who sent you. I, too, have reason to wish you ill, all the more so because the cause means so little to you that you can't even remember it. And who are these precious friends of yours? If they exist, which I doubt, point them out to me so that we may mark them too. Tentir has no place for fools."

Then she turned on her heel and was gone.

Alone at last, Jame sagged against the wall, feeling utterly spent. It had already been a very long morning, and quite likely it was only an hour past breakfast.

The Kendar had a phrase: to ride a rathorn. It meant to take on a task too dangerous to let go. Also, since the rathorn was a beast associated with madness, it implied that to ride one was to go insane.

Like father, like son, like daughter?

"Oh, Tori," she said, looking up at the Knorth banner with its double horned, rampant emblem. "We are truly riding the rathorn now."

MOMENTS LATER, it seemed, someone was shaking her awake.

Jame surged out of *dwar* sleep to find herself in the attic of the Knorth quarters. She noted, bemused, that someone had changed her mildewed blankets for clean bedding. Brier was bending over her. Then she came fully, horrifying awake.

"How did I get here?" she cried, struggling to rise. "What time is it? Have I missed the last test?"

"You walked in," said Brier, "it's early afternoon, and the only thing you've missed so far is the noon meal. Here." She indicated a slab of buttered bread and a jug of milk on a nearby tray. "Eat quickly. The rally will sound any minute now."

Jame gulped the milk and bolted the bread, all the time scrambling to collect her wits. She remembered now walking back into the barracks to find it full of both Knorth and Danior. The sudden silence that had greeted her entrance. The stairs. The nest of smelly blankets. And escape into *dwar* sleep.

That was an unusual reaction for her, even after such a morning. She suspected that the Randir had something to do with it. However, if that woman had said anything at the end in her soft, serpent's voice, Jame couldn't remember it.

She did, vaguely, remember something else from the depths of *dwar* sleep—another voice, other words: *"What is love, Jamie? What is honor?"*

Tirandys. Senethari.

But he was dead. She had stood beside his pyre, watched him burn. A darkling changer he may have been, but whatever good there was in her she owed to him. The rest of the dream was gone.

"Brier," she said abruptly, "I'm sorry about your demotion. That was the last thing I intended, coming here. And I'm sorry I showed off on the rope. I never meant to make light of the Kendars' fear of heights."

The big Southron regarded her, no expression at all on her sun-dark face. "You never intend, lady. That's the problem."

⬬⬯⬭ III ⬮⬰⬱

THE LAST TEST took place in the training square of New Tentir, under the Commandant's balcony. Cadet candidates knelt in a circle around the place of combat, ten Ardeth and ten Knorth, Timmon smiling on one side, Jame intent on the other.

She meant to be very proper and restrained this time. Remembering Tirandys had also reminded her of the dignity inherent in the Senethar, that first and most unique of the Kencyrath's unarmed fighting skills.

As with the other trials judged by single combat, two out of three contests determined victory. The winner went on to face a new challenger; the loser waited to confront whoever lost the ensuing match. After two defeats, a cadet's score was established and he or she retired to watch the superior fighters continue. Thus, at the least one fought two opponents, at the most all twenty, up to the coveted first rank.

Jame's chance came early, against a large, slow Ardeth who could hardly bear to look her in the face, much less lay hands on her. She tricked him off-balance and threw him with a crisp earth-moving maneuver that used his own size against him. The instructor, who had turned his head to speak to someone, looked back at the thud and blinked.

"Again," he said.

The second time took perhaps ten seconds longer, but with the same result.

After that, at first, things went quickly. The cautious tended to use earth-moving; the timid, water-flowing; the aggressive, fire-leaping; the ambitious, wind-blowing (usually poorly), all to the same effect or lack thereof. Their opponents had been very well trained.

"That's pure, classic Tirandys," said one senior randon quietly to another. "I haven't seen a move yet less than three thousand years old. Who in Perimal's name was her teacher?"

"Tirandys developed his form specifically for High-born women," said the other. "Some say it was a love gift to Jamethiel Dream-weaver, although she favored the Senetha version. What if they still teach it in the Women's Halls, and their lords none the wiser?"

"Now that," said the first, "is a truly frightening thought."

Jame was aware, as the trials continued, that more and more randon were coming up to watch, but she put them out of her mind. It was a long time since she had been in regular training and she felt the lack of it acutely. Moreover, few of her adversaries in recent years had been Kencyr. She needed all her wits about her now. As she met more and more skillful opponents, she began to lose the occasional fall, but still managed two out of three wins. The instructor called increasingly frequent rest breaks.

The sun set behind the Snowthorns and shadows rolled down into the valley. Torches were kindled around the square. By now, all the other contests had ended and Kendar were returning to quarters, some to settle in as cadets, others to pack and leave. As she knelt in a space of silence during a break, amidst a growing, chattering thong, Jame tried to add up her points but couldn't. At the moment, it didn't seem important. All that mattered now was that she do her best in the last two rounds.

The instructor clapped. Timmon rose and stepped into the ring to exchange salutes with her.

Not to Jame's surprise, he favored the showy aggression of fire-leaping. She countered with water-flowing which meets and turns aside attacks, all the time studying his technique. He could be made to lose patience, and soon did, over-extending in a kick that would have sent her flying if it had connected. Instead, she slid in under it and swept his foot out from under him.

"First win, Knorth," announced the instructor.

Timmon picked himself up, looking amazed. Then he grinned and came to attention, awaiting the second round.

This time he fought with more respect for his opponent, and finally caught her out with a slick, earth-moving wrist-lock.

"Second win, Ardeth."

By now, they had taken each other's measure and had found themselves well-matched. The third round moved smoothly from earth to fire to water, with a touch of wind-blowing, back and forth, give and take, though torchlight and shadow. Senethar flowed into Senetha. They no longer fought but moved together in the ancient patterns of the dance. All voices around them ceased as the glamour spread. Their movements mirrored each other. Hands moved, almost but not quite touching. Body slid by lithe body, each tracing the other's contours on the air, and the senses tinged as they passed.

Someone began softly to play a flute. It was a common exercise, by name the Sene, to alternate between fight and dance, changing instantly from the former to the latter when the music began, changing back when it stopped. The two dancers had shifted to wind blowing. They hardly touched the ground, almost weightless with balance and soaring poise. The Ardeth was good, but the Knorth . . .

Space seemed to open out around her. Instead of the practice square, she danced with golden-eyed shadows on a floor of cold marble shot with green. Darkness breathed around her:

"Ahhhh . . ."

The instructor shook himself and clapped twice, loudly.

The flute fell silent. Later, no one would admit to having played it, and some would claim to have heard nothing.

Jame started, suddenly awake, aware, and shaken to the core. Sweet Trinity, she had nearly reaped that boy's soul.

Timmon's hand moved past her face. She caught it, turned, and twisted. He seemed to whirl past, a sleep-dancer waking in mid-flight, too startled to break his own fall.

"Third win and match, Knorth."

"So," said the first senior randon to the second as a shaken Timmon rose, brushing himself off with unsteady hands. "Senethar and Senetha. Tirandys and the Dream-weaver both have come to Tentir, in one, small person, and with her more than a touch of their darkling glamour. What next, I wonder."

Next and last came Brier Iron-thorn.

Highborn and Southron Kendar saluted and began to circle each other. Somehow, Jame had never believed that things would go this far, nor did she know what to do now that they had. Dancing was out of the question, but she didn't want to fight Brier either. Cadets began to clap softly in unison to urge them on. This was ridiculous, she told herself. After all, it was only a contest.

She feigned a blow to draw the Kendar out. Brier slapped aside her hand, nearly snaring it in a water-flowing lock.

It occurred to Jame that she had never before seen the other fight. For such a large woman, Brier's reflexes were very fast, and she was undoubtedly much stronger than Jame. Still, this was the sort of unequal contest for which Jame had been trained.

Right, she thought, and settled down to it.

The first match was cautious on both sides, with a stress on defensive, water-flowing moves. The cadets clapped louder, an insistent, impatient beat. They wanted to see what these two champions could do. Jame caught Brier out and threw her.

"First win, ah . . . Highborn."

The second match went faster. They were striking at each other now, fire-leaping countered by wind-blowing, earth-moving against water-flowing. Brier caught Jame mid-leap and slammed her down, hard.

"Second win, Kendar."

Some cadets cheered.

Jame rose gingerly, shaken in every bone. If she had held back before, so had Brier. Now, she knew she was in trouble. Did the other's hard, green eyes see her at all, or only one of the hated Highborn? Here and now, did it matter? She tried to disable her adversary with a strike to the transverse crease of the wrist between the tendons, which should at least have numbed her hand, at best have made her knees buckle. Instead, Brier caught her wrist, pivoted and struck at Jame's ribcage with her heel. Only a quick water-flowing turn caused her to miss. Trinity, that blow could have broken Jame's ribs, even collapsed a lung. Was the Kendar trying to kill her?

"Only a Kencyr can destroy a Tyr-ridan," Kirien had told the haunt singer Ashe; and she, Jame, might one day become Nemesis, the personification of That-Which-Destroys, the Third Face of God.

Ironic, that an ally could kill her more easily than an enemy.

She knew she was almost spent. This kind of light-headedness only improved with rest, and the instructor just sat there stony-faced, waiting for the end. She didn't mind losing. She could simply fall down and lie there until Brier's win was called. It wasn't in her nature, however, to give up.

Dumb, stupid pride, she thought muzzily.

Then Brier moved—in a blur, it seemed to Jame—and she was on the ground.

"Third win and match . . . " began the instructor, but was cut off by a general uproar.

Jame felt hands supporting her. She spat and stared dully at the resulting spatter of blood, a tooth glimmering in the midst of in it.

Brier stood back, watching her with as white a face as her deep tan allowed.

"Careful," said Jame, thickly. "I may be a blood-binder."

Why did you say that? one part of her mind demanded as some Kendar recoiled. *Because they had to know,* said the other.

Meanwhile, the argument raged on:

". . . a fair win . . ."

". . . an unorthodox move . . ."

". . . but effective . . ."

". . . Kothifir street fighting . . ."

". . . preserve the purity of our traditions . . ."

"All right, all right!" said the instructor, throwing up his hands. "Third win and match, Highborn."

"Now wait a minute," said Jame thickly, but was drowned out with cries of delight. The Kendar, cheering her? Nothing made sense.

Rue hoisted her to her feet.

"Oh no," Timmon was saying in the background. "I'm not going to fight that giantess. I'm happy with third place. Let her have second."

"I'm confused," said Jame, whistling slightly through the gap where one of her front teeth had been. "But then I usually am."

"Just take the win, lady," hissed Rue. "You need it."

While Jame tried to sort this out, someone began to clap. All other noises died. Cadets backed away. A newcomer stood at the edge of the circle, striking his hands together with slow, heavy emphasis. He was only a few years older than the cadets around him, but his rich riding coat already strained to conceal the beginnings of a pouch. And he had his father's heavy, hooded eyes.

"Well, well, well," said the Caineron Lordan. "First blood already. This is going to be more amusing than I thought."

CHAPTER VI

The Lordan's Coat

Summer 4–5

I

SUPPER THAT NIGHT was painful.

Throbbing head and aching muscle aside, it didn't help that cadets kept darting incredulous looks at Jame—except for Brier Iron-thorn, who wouldn't meet her eyes at all.

"What a farce!" Vant proclaimed from the next table, making no effort to lower his voice. "For two ten-commands to rig a contest like that . . . well, how else d'you explain the final ranking? I tell you, it's a shame upon us all."

Rue bristled. "If you mean the last test, Ten, I took a fall from the lordan that taught me more than a dozen Senethari could have, and no holding back, either."

Vant laughed. "With you, Shortie, I believe it."

"Well then, d'you think Five pulled any strikes? Trinity, man, isn't m'lady's blood on the ground to prove it, aye, and her front tooth as well?"

Jame gave up trying to chew the hunk of bread that she had wedged into the back of her mouth. It kept snagging on the raw gap in her teeth. She was too tired to eat anyway.

"Oh, yes, our esteemed Five, hot from the Southern Wastes. So that's how they fight in the back alleys of Kothifir, is it? Rough and dirty. I guess you showed us untaught cubs something, Iron-thorn, didn't you?"

Brier got up without a word and left the hall. Vant laughed again, echoed by several other cadets.

"Let her go," said Jame to Rue, who had half-risen in protest. "Was that why she lost the last set? She used Kothifir street-fighting?"

Just as I lost for my Tastigon knife style, she thought, as Rue nodded. *Idiots. In a fight, what works, works.*

"Seriously, lady, who taught you?" asked another of her ten, leaning forward and dropping his voice. "The randon are wild to know."

Jame didn't answer. Of course they were. Someone had broken their precious rule that highborn women should not know how to defend themselves, Tirandys be damned—as, of course, they believed him to be.

Ah, Senethari, she thought gingerly sipping cider, wincing at its sting. *If the randon flinch at a few unorthodox moves, what would they make of me, your last pupil, who loved you?*

"At any rate," Vant was saying, with a smug sidelong glance at her, "it doesn't matter."

And it didn't, any of it: Despite her first place in the Senethar, she had come in one hundred thirty two over all in the tests. She had failed Tentir.

Soon after, Jame went up to the attic to bed.

However, exhausted as she was, sleep wouldn't come, nor could she bear to make plans for the morrow. The moon had fallen into the dark, she noted, staring up through the hole in the roof. Wonderful. Perhaps, if she was lucky, the world would end before morning.

Jorin grumbled at her restless tossing and finally stalked off to find a more peaceful bed.

At some point Graykin slipped in. From the noise he made, clearing his throat, deliberately tripping over things or dropping them, she guessed that he wanted to rub in the news of her failure. Finally he subsided fretfully into his corner and soon began to snore.

At last Jame also fell into a fitful sleep. In her dreams, she was dancing the Senetha with Timmon. "*I know a better dance than this,*" he murmured, brushing her face with his fingertips, sliding them through her hair. "*Stay with me. Stay.*"

She leaned her cheek against his warm touch. Perhaps, after all, life as a woman wouldn't be so bad. No cares, no responsibility except to please one's lord, no more knocked out front teeth . . . .

A roughness in the texture of his hand made her pull back. She saw the white lacework of scars, and then her brother's face as he recoiled from her. They stared at each other, frozen in the figures of the dance.

Somewhere, nowhere, a tiny disgruntled voice was muttering, " . . . not the way it's supposed to be. This has never happened before."

But Jame was distracted by the ruddy faced Kendar tugging at her sleeve.

"I am the Highlord's man!" he cried, his face fading in patches with distress. Through the holes she glimpsed the shadowy death banner hall at Gothregor. "In the morning, he will send me away to guard his wolver friends, but if I go, what if he forgets me forever? Oh please, lady, I served your father in the White Hills and would have followed him into exile if he hadn't driven me back in the passes of the Ebonbane, as he did so many others. Forty long years and more I waited for his return, and then came his son. Now am I to be cast off again? Lady, for pity's sake, remember me!"

But without his name, how could she? As far as she knew, they had never met. He melted in her grasp, crying, crying, as if at the loss of his very soul. She could have wept herself in frustration and distress.

Damn our blood anyway, and god-damn our god, who cursed us with it. Oh, Tori, between us what have we done?

"What is love, Jamie? What is honor?"

"Ah, Tirandys, Senethari . . ."

His voice came from somewhere behind her, at least as far away as the eastern window although it might have been farther still. The predawn glimmer cast his faint, attenuated shadow on the steep inner pitch of the roof. Her own darker shadow huddled, shapeless, at its feet. Try as she might, however, she could neither rise to embrace him nor even turn her head to see once again that beloved face, now lost forever.

Then she remembered what poor use she had made of his training.

"Tentir has rejected me. I have failed you, my teacher, my mother's half-brother, you who damned himself for her love and for mine."

"Ah, not so." On the wall, the shadow bent down. Jame could almost feel the phantom touch of his hand, stroking her hair, and her eyes stung with unshed tears. "Where I failed, you need not, nor have you yet. But oh, child, you may."

"Senethari, how? Please tell me!"

He laughed, and it was a sound to break the heart. "Who am I to judge you, child—I, whom honor's paradox destroyed? There is only this: Keep faith with those who keep faith with you. And beware: our house has failed in this before now. Already, your brother is in danger of failing again, however good his intentions. How can he not, as long as he denies his true nature? And you, who have long guessed what you may become, beware as well. Great power brings greater responsibility, and the greatest abuses. This place has unfinished business with those of our blood. I only tell you what you have already guessed. Some dreams do no more than that."

His voice faded as he spoke into a faint crackle as if of dried leaves or of fire. "Oh child, remember me."

"Senethari, wait!"

Jame struggled, hardly knowing if she wished to wake up or to sink deeper into sleep, even into death, if by doing so she could follow him, the only person who had ever accepted her knowing fully what she was.

His shadow faded as the light on the wall grew. He was returning to his pyre. Oh, not again the heat and stench and bitter taste of ashes on the wind . . .

Jame threw aside her blanket and jumped up, only to trip and fall over something that yelped. For a moment, struggling in folds of bedding that seemed to fight back, she was confused: *Which changer is burning? Whose beauty have I stolen? What am I becoming?*

Then her claws hooked on the cloth and ripped it away. Light blinded her. As she stood there panting, she realized that she was staring not into the flames of a pyre but directly into the newly risen sun.

"Do you mind?" said the roll of blankets at her feet. Graykin emerged from it, tousled and indignant. "The next time you have a nightmare, kindly leave me out of it."

Outside, the morning's ram's horn blared and in the dormitory two floors below, feet hit the floor.

Jame dressed quickly and went down the stair into the hall. Only when she met Vant's astonished gaze did she remember: she no longer belonged at Tentir. She sat down, feeling suddenly numb, and stared without seeing it at the bowl of porridge that a cadet thumped down before her.

Rootless and roofless . . .

So the Brandan Maledight Brenwyr had cursed her at Gothregor, within her family's own stronghold and under the eyes of its unforgiving dead.

Blood and bone . . .

She couldn't help what she was. Perhaps she couldn't live with it either.

Cursed be and cast out . . . .

But where did one go from here?

Dully, she became aware of a buzz spreading through the hall. Rue nudged her. "Lady, d'you hear? The Randon Council has finally set the mark!"

"Well, what is it?" others exclaimed eagerly, craning to hear.

"One hundred and forty!"

Jame looked up sharply. Around her, a few faces had blanched, but over all a sigh of relief echoed through the room.

I'm in, she thought blankly. *Brenwyr's curse has failed, at least for the minute.* Then she wondered, *Why am I in?*

They could easily have stuck to one hundred thirty and been rid of her. Everyone knew that the cut-off score was fluid, and she had missed the original mark by mere points. Perhaps, after all, Tentir was going to treat her like any other cadet-candidate, which was all she had asked, and more than she had hoped for.

Suddenly ravenous, she wolfed down the congealing porridge, and thought it the best thing she had ever tasted.

In the evening, the candidates would be initiated into the randon college as cadets. Until then, they were free to prepare.

Breakfast and morning assembly done, Rue hauled Jame up to the third story lordan's quarters in search of suitable clothing for her to wear for the ceremony. While the straw-haired cadet rummaged through the chests, Jame sat in shirtsleeves on the wide, raised hearth with needle and white thread, trying to knot stitch the rathorn emblem into her black token scarf.

Graykin prowled about the apartment waiting for Rue to leave, palpably jealous that she had claimed Jame's attention first. Jorin followed him, pouncing at a ribbon snagged and trailing unnoted from his boot.

"You should clean all of this out and move in." He glared at the walls of boxes blocking either end of the room. "There have got to be apartments behind all that junk. A master bedroom. Servants' quarters. Real beds."

"I like the attic," said Jame, frowning over her stitches. "It's airy."

"Oh, it's that, all right. The wind blows in one end and out the other. You just wait until winter. Sweet Trinity, part of it doesn't even have a roof."

Rootless and roofless . . .

"I don't like being confined, and I don't like this place." She sneezed into her scarf but, at a glare from

Graykin, forbore wiping her nose with it. "It smells. Besides, it gives me bad dreams. Who lived here anyway?"

"Your uncle, lady. The last Knorth Lordan."

"Ouch." Jame had stuck the needle into her thumb. "And who was that?"

Rue had turned aside to examine the shreds of a silk shirt. She didn't want to say the name, Jame realized. Interesting.

"Who?" she prompted, removing the needle.

The cadet tossed away the ruined shirt, and the name of its former owner with it. "Greshan, nick-named Greed-heart at least among his Kendar."

"Did you know how our father came to power?" Tori had asked Jame in the ruins of Kithorn. *"His older brother, the Knorth Lordan, was killed in training at Tentir."*

Something very bad had happened in this airless, windowless room. Jame regarded a large stain on the wooden floor. It was barely a shadow now, sunk deep into the grain, but someone had bled here, perhaps to death. She remembered her dream that first night at Tentir and shivered.

Dear little Gangrene.

Ugh.

In the past her sleep had sometimes been troubled, but rarely by dire visions. Tori was the far-seer, not her. Yet that last winter at Gothregor she had dreamed truly that Graykin had fallen into Caldane's hands and that Bane was on his way to the Riverland. It was less remarkable that she and Tori had shared certain dreams; as children, they had done so constantly, thinking nothing of it. Perhaps rejoining her people was waking dormant powers in her. If so, she didn't much care for them.

Graykin turned up his nose at the pile of clothes that Rue had set aside as potentially salvageable, the plainest and most practical among all that spoiled finery.

"You should at least dress according to your rank. How about this?"

He had picked up the embroidered jacket.

Rue stared. "Why, that must be the Lordan's Coat."

"What, my uncle's?"

"Not just his, lady. Every Knorth heir for generations has worn it, and generations of Knorth Kendar have mended it."

"Here," said Jame. "Let me see that."

Graykin gave it to her, reluctantly, and she spread it out on her knees.

Although dimmed by a half century of dust, the needlework was exquisite. Tiny stitches covered every inch of the surface in shades from the autumn gold of a birch leaf to the phantom blue of a shadow on snow, from the sharp green of spring grass to the deep crimson of heart's desire. Lines swooped and curved. Fantasies of shape and color swirled, blending into each other. Half-seen images came and went with every shift of light.

"Careful!" said Graykin sharply as threads snapped at her touch.

If the coat was truly as old as Tentir, Jame thought, gingerly turning it over, probably little of its original fabric remained. The earliest records must long since either have been repaired or stitched over, as with the house banners in the great hall. Nearly fifty years of neglect hadn't helped. Without thinking, she tugged at a hair caught in the threads, and jumped as the coat writhed on her knees as if in pain.

"Sweet Trinity. What's this?"

Rue bent to look. "Well, they do say that every lordan since the beginning has worn this coat, and that each of them has added something . . . er . . . personal to it."

"You mean," said Graykin, with a queasy smirk, "that this is not only an heirloom but also a 'hair-loom'?"

All three regarded the strand in question. It was short, coarse, and irrepressibly curly.

Rue clapped a hand over her mouth to stifle a giggle.

Graykin blushed.

"Hmm," said Jame, with a raised eyebrow. "The Kendar really hated my dear uncle, didn't they? I wonder why."

"I wonder . . ." began Rue, then stopped.

"What?"

"Well, just before your uncle died, the White Lady disappeared."

"Who?"

"The Knorth Matriarch's Whinno-hir mare, Bel-tairi, sister to Lord Ardeth's Brithany. She left Valentir, where she was visiting a new great-grand-foal among the herd, but she never reached Gothregor. There are rumors that m'lord Greshan met her in the wilderness and . . . well, did something to her. He and Lady Kinzi weren't on very good terms at the time. Then news came that the lordan was dead, and his father the Highlord soon after him. The whole thing was a right mess, by all accounts."

"The senior randon call her 'The Shame of Tentir,'" said Graykin. "Why, I don't know. So I listen," he added crossly, seeing Rue's expression. "Is it my fault that they talk and I hear things? They also say that she has unfinished business with the Knorth and that having you here as lordan may be stirring things up."

"Unfinished business," murmured Jame, turning over the coat. So Tirandys had said: *I only tell you what you have already guessed.* It seemed, since she had rejoined her people, that she kept stepping into one ancient mess after another. Trinity, didn't her family ever clean up after itself? Then too, what was she to make of the pale lady who had called her Kinzi-kin and vanished like a ghost, leaving hoof-prints in the turf? Unfinished business indeed, and here in her hands, perhaps, was another piece of it.

The coat's peacock blue silk lining had at some point been soaked with a dark fluid. It was also ripped.

"A knife in the back?" Jame asked, only half joking. However, the tear seemed too ragged, its edges frayed, and she found no corresponding slit in the outer fabric.

Rue added the coat to her armload of saved clothing. "At least we know now why it stinks. I'll try to clean these, m'lady, and hope they dry by tonight. In the fire-timber hall, they might. Then we'll see about cutting them down to your size and repairing the coat. After all," she added, seeing Jame's expression, "it's a piece of history."

"And, in its way, a masterpiece. All right, all right. As for the rest, I *have* mended my own clothes before, you know."

Being waited on made her nervous. In the Women's Halls of Gothregor, the petty tyranny of servants had made her feel ignorant and stupid. Now it was happening again.

"Oh." She ruefully regarded the scarf. Her attempt at the rathorn crest looked like an upside-down boot with two spikes growing out of its sole; and, as usual, she had managed to sew her gloved fingertips together.

Rue left, grinning.

"If you ever want a lock of my hair," Jame called after her, "just ask! And don't forget your own scarf."

The cadet had done her needlework the night before, and a very fine job of it too, but someone had stolen it. Jame hoped the barrack wasn't going to be plagued with a petty thief.

Graykin watched Rue's departure wistfully. "Smelly or not," he said, "there goes a royal coat."

His tone reminded Jame that, as Caldane's son, he was half Highborn. However, his illegitimacy and his mother's Southron blood barred him from even the trappings of that rank. She didn't think that he was missing much. Graykin, however, clearly felt otherwise.

"How you look and act reflects on the dignity of your house," he said stubbornly, with a discontented glance at her battered face and the purple bruises on her wrists where Harn had gripped them, all affronts to his own dignity as well. Fortunately, he had come in too late the night before to see what the rest of her looked like.

"Enough small talk," she said, gingerly biting off tangled threads, wincing as they caught on the raw gap in her front teeth. "Report."

As she had suspected, he had spent the past three days exploring the secret passages of Old Tentir, eavesdropping whenever possible.

"I would have told you last night that you'd qualified," he said with a sniff, "but you were pretending to be asleep. Anyway, the Randon Council set the mark at one hundred and forty, then waited for the Commandant to take them off the hook. But he didn't. Now they've got their breeches in a twist trying to decide how to deal with you. The Caineron claim that you've been kept on for the amusement of their lordan—his name is Gorbel, by the way."

"Gorbelly?"

"Close enough. Fun and games aside, they mean to humiliate your brother through you—and remember, the Highlord can't do anything about it short of jerking you out of here."

The college has its own rules, Torisen had told her at Kithorn. *If you're hurt there, I can't even demand your blood-price.*

"And that," Graykin was saying, "would be a victory for just about everyone except the Knorth. The general belief is that by admitting Gorbel without testing him, Sheth is tacitly saying that his master's son can get away with anything. The other randon aren't happy about that. They think it damages the college's integrity; but these are intensely political times."

"I have noticed," said Jame dryly.

"By the same token, although he let you in, they don't think Sheth will let you stay to the end. He's covering his ass with both lords, as it were, giving the Highlord's sister a chance but at the same time turning a blind eye to the Caineron lordan."

Sheth Sharp-tongue must be under intense pressure, Jame thought, to accept his lord's belief that honor meant nothing but obedience. Honor's Paradox had destroyed Tirandys. If Caineron could corrupt Tentir through its commander, what chance did the rest of the Kencyrath have?

"The consensus, though, is that you won't last. What Highborn girl could? The Randir called you a freak."

"Huh. They should talk. These passages in the old fortress must be giving you lots of chances to spy."

"I am your faithful sneak, mistress," he said with a mocking cringe.

"Don't call either of us that," she said sharply. "The Mistress was a different Jamethiel, and you're my . . . my loyal servant. Damn. That doesn't sound right either."

"Pretty titles, dirty hands."

His hands, she noticed, were remarkably dirty.

"Pick out some new clothes for yourself, while we're at it," she told him. "You look as if you've been dragged up a chimney backwards."

"Hand-me-downs," he said with disgust, kicking at a pile of moldy finery.

"I seldom wear anything else. These passages . . . what are they like?"

"Dark, narrow, filthy."

He wanted to keep them to himself, she thought. Knowledge was power, and the Caineron Bastard had precious little of either. Neither did she. "Once you said you would never deceive me, although there were many ways you could within the bounds of honor."

He glared at her, caught by his own pledge.

"All right, all right! From what I've seen so far, the hidden ways are much more direct than the public ones. I'll show you if you like," he added ungraciously. "I may . . . er . . . even have found the brat's hidden room. At least I thought, once, that something was keeping pace with me all down one wall, on the other side. I could hear it muttering and clawing at the stones. Then it started to pound on them. Whatever-it-is was big. And strong. The stones shook. And I'll tell you this too: The kitchen staff lays aside raw joints of meat for it. I saw them do it when I was . . . ah . . . borrowing some food. I have to eat too, you know."

"I know, I know. And so far I've been precious little good at providing for you. Well, see what else you can

find out, about anything, and watch out of the Caineron.
Caldane can't be happy that the Knorth have snatched
both you and Brier Iron-thorn away from him."

With Rue gone and Graykin departed to nose out more
secrets, Jame went looking for Brier.

She found the big Southron and five of her ten-command in the third story common room opposite the lordan's apartment. They were all bare foot, polishing a
seemingly endless row of boots.

"For tonight," said Brier. "And yes, these are every
pair in the Knorth barracks except for yours and Rue's,
who appears to have run off in hers. On your orders, I
take it."

"On my business, anyway. She seems to have
appointed herself my servant."

"Good," said Brier, giving her a sharp look. "You need
one." *Better yet, a keeper*, her tone said.

"But all these boots . . . why you?"

"Vant's orders."

"Huh. Vant's revenge, more likely. How much did you
outrank him in the trials?"

"Fifteen to thirty-six!" chorused the other cadets,
grinning.

At least Vant's petty tyranny seemed to have brought
the squad squarely behind their new Five. But two faces
were missing. Mint, Dar, Quill, Erim, Killy . . .

"Where are Kest and . . . and . . . " Damn. She hadn't learned the last cadet's name.

"Yel failed. And Kest left last night. The rope test broke him. He didn't even wait to hear his score."

"Oh," said Jame, blankly. She had been so relieved at breakfast to hear that she had qualified that she hadn't noticed who had not.

"The Knorth lost ten candidates in all," said Brier dispassionately, examining a scuffed toe. "That takes us down to ninety cadets, nearly a one-hundred command. Not bad. One of our provisional squads will be broken up to provide replacements to the others."

That reminded Jame that she was not only ten-commander of this particular group but—nominally, at least—master ten of the entire barracks.

"Wait a minute. Why is Vant giving you orders?"

"Of the ten-commanders, his score was the highest, so he stands second to you in authority. He will expect to have the day to day running of the barracks."

Damn. Jame would much rather have had Brier, and would have, too, if the Southron hadn't been demoted for breaking college rules on her behalf. She scowled at the formidable array of boots.

"I can countermand Vant."

"Don't," said Brier. "At least not until you've given your scarf to the Commandant and received it back from him through the hands of a Knorth senior randon. You aren't officially part of Tentir until then. None of us are, however some choose to act."

"Oh," said Jame, taken aback. She hadn't known.

"Anyway," the Southron added, following Jame's line of thought regarding her demotion, "the cadet body as a whole wouldn't have welcomed an outsider in charge over them."

"Well, they'll have to lump it, won't they? After all, they've got me."

Brier gave her another look, this one askance under the fringe of her dark red hair. Sunlight flooding in through the room's many windows gave her a fiery halo. "Sorry I knocked out your tooth," she said gruffly.

"Oh, it could as easily have been yours as mine. I think. A risk of the game. But that move you used against me . . . I've never seen anything like it before. Will you teach me how to fight Kothifir style?"

Brier looked up, startled. "Why?"

"It was effective, and it caught me totally off guard. I'd rather not have that happen again." She hesitated. "Just out of curiosity, were you trying to kill me?"

"Trinity, no. I'd never fought a Highborn before, much less a lady. I had no idea you were so fragile."

Jame blinked. Fragile? It had never occurred to her that she was. True, most of her adversaries in the past had been much stronger than she was, but untrained. She had usually beaten them easily. Here, that would no longer be the case.

"I've been a fool," she said, thoughtfully. "An arrogant one, at that. Thank you, Brier Iron-thorn. You've already taught me an invaluable lesson, and cheap at the price." She fingered her sore jaw. "Just the same, I've never had a tooth knocked out before. How long does it usually take to grow a new one?"

"About three weeks," said the Kendar. She picked up another boot—Vant's, perhaps—spat on it, and began to polish. "Find a twig to chew on or the teething itch will drive you crazy."

III

IN ANOTHER PART OF THE BARRACKS, Vant could be heard ordering someone else around. If she wasn't going to interfere, Jame didn't want to listen. She and Jorin slipped out the front door into the covered arcade, into the bright summer morning.

New Tentir was laid out in the same order as the house banners in the great hall: Randir, Coman, and Caineron from east to west along the north wing; Jaran, Knorth, and Ardeth along the west; Danior, Edirr and Brandan from west to east along the south. By chance or design, this arrangement grouped allies and enemies, with a scattering of neutrals between them. Jame turned southward.

For the first time, she seriously considered the physical dangers she faced at Tentir. The randon were the deadliest fighters on Rathillien, and she didn't know what rules bound them beyond the increasingly slippery concept of honor. These were her superiors, not her peers, except among the rawest recruits. Moreover, among them were bitter enemies of her house. Had she been a fool to come here? It had hardly been a considered decision, rather a spur-of-the-moment escape from an intolerable situation.

Yes, she told herself, but think of the other risks she had blithely taken in the past—the streets of Tai-tastigon, where she had stalked gods and in turn been stalked by them; the carnivorous hills of the Anarchies, where she had granted an aging rathorn mare her death wish and so gained the hatred of her death's-head foal; the Master's

House itself, with its layers of corrupt history, all the fallen worlds stacked one on top of the other—all undertaken with a child's careless arrogance.

If she had known what she was doing, would she have done it? Was she growing more cautious with age, or more cowardly?

And on top of that, she had just been handed responsibility for an entire barracks, containing all her brother's precious cadets. A loner by nature, what did she know about command? Should she—*could* she leave everything to Vant?

The arcade took her by the broad facade of the Ardeth, then turned a corner to head eastward toward Old Tentir. Jame noted that the Ardeth had appropriated not only the southwestern corner but a length of the south wing. Poor little Danior with its thirty cadets was so pinched by its larger neighbor that one half expected the building to squeak. The Edirr faired only slightly better, under pressure on the other side from the Brandan.

In front of the latter, Captain Hawthorn leaned on the arcade rail tranquilly smoking a long-stemmed, clay pipe. She raised a scar-broken eyebrow as Jame approached.

"We'd heard that you were gone, lady," she said. "Seemingly, you didn't sleep in your quarters last night, or at least not in the lordan's apartment."

Someone must have checked, thought Jame. Someone who didn't know she had shifted lodgings upward, into the attic. Vant. No wonder he had been surprised to see her at breakfast.

"Well, here I am." She sniffed her sleeve, which retained the stale reek of Greshan's jacket. "Like a bad smell, I linger."

The randon grinned. "So I perceive."

"Speaking of the lordan's suite, how is it that we can afford to leave it empty, given how full the college is? For that matter, we Knorth seem to have almost more space than we need."

"Hush, or your neighbors will hear. Actually, you can thank them, specifically your allies the Ardeth and the Jaran, that you have any quarters here at all." The randon drew on her pipe and exhaled a meditative plume of smoke. "I can remember when the Knorth barracks were nearly as full as our own. That was before your lord father fell, and nearly brought his house down with him. For more than thirty years, those rooms stood as empty as the Highlord's seat, for no one dared to seize either."

Jame gazed, frowning, back across the square at the Knorth facade. Vant could be seen intermittently as he paced the second floor, harrying a ten-command as it scrubbed the dormitory floor. Brier sat tranquilly on a third story window ledge polishing yet another boot. Heights didn't seem to bother her. Poor Kest. The Caineron barracks looming on the north side of the square were broad, five stories tall, and virtually windowless. Perhaps Lord Caldane's height-sickness ran throughout his house.

"So," said Jame, pulling her mind back to the matter at hand, "there have only been Knorth cadets at Tentir since my brother came to power? That was just three years ago."

"Aye." The randon puffed again. "Barely time for the first class to graduate, and many of those died at the Cataracts. You've much rebuilding yet to do, if your enemies give you time. Take care, lordan. Your brother can't protect you here."

Jame leaned against the rail as memory swept her back to a conversation with the Brandan Matriarch Brenwyr not long ago:

"Kinzi and the Randir Matriarch Rawneth . . . they quarreled."

"So? Are you saying that I've inherited an undeclared blood feud, and no one saw fit to tell me?"

"There was no need. Anyway, it never came to blows."

"Let me guess. Before anything so unladylike could happen, the Shadow Assassins slaughtered every Knorth woman at Gothregor except Tieri . . . and no one ever knew why."

It was still only a guess that Rawneth had been behind the Knorth massacre. Even if she was, Jame had no idea what quarrel could have led to such deadly consequences, yet she herself must still be part of it or the Shadow Assassins wouldn't have come for her that last night in Gothregor.

Huh. More unfinished business.

"Who are my enemies?" she asked Hawthorn.

The randon frowned, troubled. "I shouldn't have spoken. Not until you're a proper cadet under Tentir's protection, such as it is, and even then you should be told by a member of your own house. In a few hours, we will tell you all we know." She straightened and knocked out her pipe against the rail. "In the meantime, you'll be safe among your own people. Wait a minute while I tell my folk where I'm going and then, lady, I'll escort you back to your quarters."

When she returned, however, the Knorth was gone.

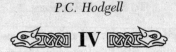

IV

THE GREAT HALL of Old Tentir hummed with activity. Kendar scoured the flagstones while others polished the randon collars hanging against the upper walls. Beams were being dusted and retouched with gold paint by those presumably least prone to height-sickness. The rope from the trials had been removed. Delicious smells drifted up from the fire timber hall below, where whole oxen were being slowly roasted over charcoal pits for the feast that would follow the cadets' initiation into Tentir.

Jame's stomach rumbled as she and Jorin stood in the shadows, watching. With luck, by evening, she would be able to chew again, if cautiously.

She knew that Hawthorn was right. It was foolish to take chances, but damned if she was going to be delivered back to the Knorth barracks like some willful, wandering child. In a minute, she would make her own way home. Now, she had to be sure of herself. That she hadn't lost her nerve. That she would take whatever risks she must to succeed at the college, while never forgetting that this was a dangerous place, full of dangerous people.

Jorin growled.

"Good morning," said the Randir Tempter, beside her. "Or perhaps I should say 'good afternoon.'"

"We . . . I didn't hear you, ran."

"Ah." The other smiled. "It occurred to us that you and the ounce might be bound. You are, of course, Shanir."

"As are you." Jame listened intently. The other didn't seem to be using her under-voice, but then it had slipped past her guard before. As for physical violence, *"Never touch me again,"* she had told this woman from the depths of her Shanir nature, and she suddenly knew that the Randir never would nor could. However, Jorin was still growling, which distracted her.

"Hush," she said to him.

"There are many Shanir here," said the Randir, "a few Highborn like you and the Ardeth brat, but mostly Kendar with a touch of the Old Blood. What is it, I wonder, that draws Highborn men to Kendar women? One rarely hears of the reverse. Among our own kind, we can control conception as well—or ill—as Highborn ladies. But not with Highborn lovers. They take us and use us and cast off our children as the whim takes them. They should not, for we are many and we are proud."

What a strange conversation, thought Jame.

She knew that the Randir was toying with her, deliberately holding her attention, but why? It was on the tip of her tongue to ask straight out what quarrel the Randir had with the Knorth, but Jorin's growl had risen to a singing whine.

As she turned to quiet him, a movement caught the corner of her eye. There was someone behind her . . . and a sudden blow fell on the back of her neck.

"Blood for blood, Knorth," she thought she heard the Randir Tempter say as she fell. Then darkness swallowed her.

CHAPTER VII

In the Bear's Den

Summer 5

I

JAME WOKE, still in darkness, to a savage headache. She thought at first, dazed, that she had lost her sight, but then realized that she was only blindfolded. And gagged. And bound hand and foot. This, on the whole, was not good. But where was she, besides on the floor?

Her other senses began, reluctantly, to function.

She could feel the coarse grain of wood under her cheek. It was damp, with a curiously heady tang. Other smells, less appealing, lurked behind it: unwashed flesh, rotting meat, human urine and feces. Unlike the ancient miasma of the lordan's apartment, this reek was fresh, a living stink. She had caught whiffs of it through Jorin's senses when they had been searching Old Tentir for the Knorth guest quarters.

Trinity. Jorin. Where was he? If they had hurt her cat, she would kill them.

Close behind her, something large stirred and groaned. Leather creaked. Something muttered, then began to breathe deeply again, with the hint of a snore.

So.

At a guess, she was in the lair of the mysterious monster who ate little children for lunch and raw joints of meat for dinner.

Also, it drank strong wine. She was lying in a spilt puddle of it. Perhaps its keepers periodically drugged it when they came to clean out its den—and they must, or the stench would be much worse. Her captors had apparently taken advantage of this to dump her here.

"Blood for blood," the Randir had said, but not on her hands.

Perhaps they expected the beast to rip her apart. All the more reason not to be here when it woke up. Besides, if its head hurt half as much as hers did, it would be in a truly foul mood.

Her hands were bound behind her. She curled into a tight ball and began to work them down her back. Cramped muscles threatened to spasm in revolt. Halfway through, she got stuck and lay panting around the gag, trying not to panic.

This was no good. Try again.

Suddenly her hands shot up over her bent knees and hit her in the nose. She fumbled at the blindfold with fingers numb for lack of blood, then at the gag. The former, she saw, was her own token scarf. The latter was Rue's. This had been planned well in advance. The Randir must have been waiting for her to stumble into their hands, and so she had. No one would accuse poor Rue of plotting her death, but the presence of two Knorth scarves would suggest that this was a house matter, best dealt with internally by its lord. Ancestors only knew what Tori would make of such a mess.

By now, her eyes had adjusted to the dim light, most of which came from a fireplace where embers winked and tinkled in the grate. It was very hot. Opposite the hearth was a heavy door, undoubtedly locked, with a narrow, hinged panel at the bottom. There were no windows, thus no way to tell how long she had been unconscious. Damnation. If they made her miss the evening ceremony as they almost had the final test . . . however, that seemed to be the Randir style: traps within traps within traps.

Another deep sigh behind her. Craning painfully to look over her shoulder, she saw a low bed with a large form huddled on it. The breathing had changed. He would wake soon. And her fingers were too numb to untie her ankles, much less her hands.

The rest of the apartment was comfortably furnished, but much disordered. A chair slumped before the fireplace, its arms and back hanging in flayed strips. In the corner, a gutted bookcase spilled its contents onto the carpet. The shredded fragments of books and scrolls littered the floor.

So did little wooden figures, cunningly carved.

A monster that played with toy warriors?

One of them held a little knife as if it were a sword, firelight flickering red on the blade. She wriggled across the floor as quietly as possible, picked it up, and fumbled to lay the edge against the rope securing her legs. She had almost sawed through when the figure on the bed yawned and stretched.

Jame rolled under the bed. Her legs came free as she moved, but she lost the little knife, and her hands were still bound. The leather web of straps above her groaned and sagged. Big, bare feet hit the floor in front of her face. Overgrown toenails extended and flexed, rasping against the wood. Trinity, now what? Could she hide here until someone came to feed the brute?

Now it . . . no, *he* was pissing in a nearby corner. Jame edged back from the spreading puddle. Did the man have a wine vat for a bladder?

At last, the waterfall ceased.

"Hmmm?" said a deep voice, rusty from lack of use. He was sniffing the air. Surely he couldn't smell her over the room's other assorted stinks.

"Huh!"

The bed upended against the wall with a crash. Jame rolled to her feet and plunged for the panel at the base of the door. It flipped open at her touch, but he caught her by the hair and jerked her back. She kicked at his face. He flicked aside her foot, grabbed her by the shirt, ripping it, and threw her into the wall.

Play dead, she thought, sliding down the wall and lying still. Indeed, she was too shaken to do much else.

Big hands picked her up and dropped her into the chair before the dying fire. The chair sagged, exhaling a sharp breath laced with dead mice. She curled up in its hollow, knees to chin, behind the veil of her long black hair. He bent and sniffed her all over, muttering deep in his throat. Instinctively, she raised her hands to protect her face.

There was a moment's silence.

She felt his hot breath snuffling on her wrists, and then his teeth bit down on the cords that bound them.

Jame opened her eyes.

He was kneeling before her, turning her freed hands over in his own. He had claws as big as a cave bear's, three inches long at least and too large to retract. Her own ivory nails, unsheathed, were delicate in contrast. She could make out little of his face in shadow, behind its wild mask of beard. He snuffled at her fingertips, then folded them in on themselves so that the nails were hidden and cupped within his own huge claws as if in a cage of polished bone. His touch was surprisingly gentle, almost protective.

"D-d-d-d . . ."

"Don't? Don't what?"

"T-t-t-t . . ."

"Tell? Don't tell?"

The door burst open. In a blaze of torchlight, Jame saw the man's face, the savage cleft in his skull into which his wild graying hair tumbled. Something long ago had cleaved him half way down to the eyebrows. No one should survive such a blow, but this man had. He sprang back as a swung torch roared past his face, over Jame's head. His beard sparked as if infested with fireflies. The room stank of burnt hair. As he backed away, beating at his face, a big hand reached over the chair's back, grabbed Jame by the arm, and jerked her up. The room seemed to be full of giants, although there were only two of them. The one with the torch propelled her out the door into the hall and slammed the door after them. Something very big hit it on the other side. The wood shook, but held.

Harn Grip-hard backed away. The torch, unnoticed, still flared in his hand. He was shaking, his broad face white beneath its perennial stubble. From inside the locked room came strange sounds. The captive was crying. Harn dropped the torch and blundered away. Jame picked it up before it could start a fire, noting that it was wet with blood where Harn had gripped it. With a last glance at the door, she followed him.

Someone rounded a corner, fast, and almost knocked her off her feet.

"Where have you been?" demanded Graykin fiercely, grabbing her by the shoulders. She noted that he was liberally festooned with cobwebs. He also looked angry enough to kill her, presumably for still being alive. "Everyone is looking for you!"

"Tell you later. Damn. Where did he go?"

They tracked Harn by the blood drops on the floor, Graykin hissing questions to which Jame had no answers. She was touched that her peculiar servant really had been worried about her, although he hid it well behind an affronted air: How dare she upset him like that? She had no idea at first where they were, the inner halls of Old Tentir being dark enough even by day to require candles.

"What time is it?" she asked Graykin abruptly.

"Late afternoon."

"Good. What day?"

He stared at her, then looked quickly away. She became aware that her shirt was hanging in tatters over bare skin.

"The same," he said, not very clearly, but she understood.

"Very good."

Here at last was a hall slotted on one side with narrow windows. They had emerged at the northeastern corner of the third floor, near a door that opened to one of Tentir's four watchtowers. Jame recalled hearing that during her stint as commandant Harn had made his quarters in this out-of-the-place. She set the torch in a wall sconce.

"I need clothes," she told Graykin. "Go back to the barracks and tell Rue. She'll find me something. Bring it here."

When he had gone, radiating irritation that his mistress needed help from anyone but him, Jame climbed into a rush of sweet air.

On the first of two levels, windows opened to the north and south onto the sweep of the Riverland. Below, the Silver threaded through gathering shadows under as yet sun-crowned heights. It took Jame a moment, blinking against the light, to make out two large chairs drawn up before a cold fireplace. Someone slumped in the one with its back to her.

"You stink," growled the unseen occupant, "like a tavern latrine. Bathe. There." A large hand waved toward the northern window, under which Jame now saw a large tub of rapidly cooling water, undoubtedly brought here for the randon's solitary ablutions. She hesitated only briefly, then stripped off what was left of her now decidedly rank clothing.

He threw her a sharp look, as if still not entirely convinced that she wasn't Blackie in disguise.

More like black and blue, she thought wryly, but bruises only hurt for a while, turned interesting colors, and then went away. She was used to them.

"How did you know where I was, ran?" she asked, gratefully sinking into the tub. Harn would have overlapped it on all sides, but it fit her slender limbs nicely.

He grunted. "I heard a rumor that you'd had the good sense to leave Tentir. I should have known better. Anyway, I went to check."

On the way, he had encountered the Randir Tempter helping a colleague back to their quarters.

"Proper shredded, his legs were. I knew your cat's work when I saw it."

Harn had found the ounce racing about the Knorth barracks, bouncing off walls, scratching anyone who tried to stop him. Vant was shouting that the cat had gone mad and calling for archers. When no one moved (except to get out of Jorin's way), he had grabbed a bow but then inexplicably tripped, nearly impaling himself on the arrow. By then, Captain Hawthorn had arrived, looking for Jame. She and Brier had thrown a blanket over the ounce as he hurtled past and bundled him off, all teeth and claws, to a vacant room. There they had left him, from the sound of it, careening off the walls, floor, and ceiling.

Harn had put together bloody legs, an hysterical cat, and a lost Knorth. Then he had gone off to storm the Randir quarters.

Here, he fell silent.

Jame ducked to rinse soap out of her hair, then rose and slid, dripping, into the enveloping folds of Harn's gray dress coat. She picked up a shirt to dry her hair, hoping belatedly that Harn hadn't meant to wear it that night, curled into the chair opposite him, and waited.

The burly randon slumped in the over-sized chair, staring blankly at the previous winter's ashes, his arms limp on the chair's rests. The knuckles of his left hand were broken and crusted with drying blood. Finally he spoke in a low, hoarse voice, as if to himself.

"So I go to the Randir. They know I'm coming, plain enough, because the door is shut. I knock. Inside, I think I hear someone snicker. Then they begin to chant, oh, so softly, 'Beast, beast, beast,' and I knock louder, to drown them out."

As he spoke, he began unconsciously to beat the wooden arm of his chair with his clenched fist, harder and harder, reopening the cuts on his battered knuckles.

Jame slipped out of her chair, knelt beside him, and wrapped her own hands around his fist as it descended.

She wondered, biting her lip, if she was about to add broken bones to the day's other mementos. Harn didn't seem to notice her grip, but his blows faltered and stopped. His fingers unclenched and his big hand, relaxing, hung over the chair's arm. Blood dripped from it onto the floor. Jame cleaned the cuts with the shirt, still damp from her hair.

"I think I must have beaten down the door," he said slowly, "because the next thing I know I'm inside, surrounded by a ring of spears. No one was laughing then.

"They say, 'Leave, or we'll kill you.'

"I say, 'Bring me your bitch temptress or you'll have to.'

"So finally she comes, and I ask her where the Highlord's sister is. She says . . . she says, 'Look in your future lodgings.' And smiles."

Jame considered this as she ripped strips of cloth to bandage his wounds. That done, she wadded up the torn, bloody shirt and threw it into the back of the cold grate. Then she resumed her seat across from him. Sunk deep in his chair, Harn reminded her of a large, wild animal flinching away from the light, drawing back into self-imposed, self-destructive isolation.

"Become the beast that you know you are . . ."

"The man in the locked room is definitely Shanir," she said, "but I don't think he's a berserker. That needn't happen to you. Who is he, ran? What happened to him?" A sudden thought struck her. "Don't tell me I've stumbled across the long-lost Randir Heir!"

"I won't because you haven't," snapped Harn, rousing. "Besides, Randiroc isn't lost. He just doesn't want to be found. Neither would you if the Witch of Wilden and Shadow Guild assassins were after you."

In fact they were, but she wasn't hiding. Yes, and look how *that* had worked out so far.

Harn raised a hand to rub his eyes and frowned at the bandages, clearly surprised to find them there. "We call him Bear," he said.

"'We'?"

"Every commandant knows about him and attends to his needs. Since we command Tentir by rotation, that means all the senior randon, not to mention the sargents and servants. He was one of us. The best. Until the White Hills when a war axe did . . . that."

Thirty-four years ago, thought Jame, just after the slaughter of the Knorth women when her father's misguided revenge against the Seven Kings of the Central Lands had led to such carnage and to his own exile. So much pain led back to that time, to those events.

"It must have been an awful wound," she said, involuntarily imagining it red and raw, white shards of skull and gray, spattered brain. "Why wasn't he offered the White Knife?"

"His lord lay dead on the field and his heirs were already squabbling over the spoils. No one had time for the dying."

Jame remembered Tori the previous autumn, wandering alone through the bloody shambles at the Cataracts, drawn by his Shanir power (if only he realized it) to those bound to him who lay mortally wounded, bringing them honorable release with a white-hilted suicide knife. A true lord cared for his own—in life, in death.

"There was so much loss, and confusion, and pain." Harn leaned forward, elbows on knees, big hands tightly clasped, fresh injuries forgotten for old. He spoke to the ashes as if to those distant dead, as if still trying to understand. "I was there. I saw it all, until the Highlord's madness took me, and then—ancestors only know what I did, and to whom. We fought our own kind, you know, Kencyr against Kencyr, the Host against our own kindred hired out as mercenaries to the Seven Kings. It was . . . terrible."

"And Bear?"

"His younger brother found him on the third day, under a pile of the slain. Oh, he was strong, was Bear, to have lived that long with blood and brains leaking onto ground already too sodden to drink in any more. At first we thought he was dead and put him on the pyre, but then he moved in the flames and we pulled him out. Better if we had let him burn alive. However, his brother wouldn't let him go. After all, our kind have recovered from worse and so did he—in body, at least. In mind—well, you saw. The new lord of his house didn't want him shambling around his precious keep, so the college took him in. After all, he was . . . is . . . one of us. For awhile, he even taught the Arrin-thar."

"The what?"

"A rare, armed combat discipline, based on clawed gauntlets. Originally, only Shanir like Bear practiced it. You saw his hands."

Jame folded her own into Harn's jacket. She had completely forgotten about them while tending to his injuries. Her gloves were with the rest of her clothes beside the tub.

"There are many Shanir here," the Randir had said.

Highborn Shanir like her cousin Kindrie were often sent off to the Priest's College at Wilden—in a sense, thrown away. It occurred to her now that Tentir would be a logical place for Kendar Shanir to gather.

"Are there other Shanir-based fighting skills, ran?"

"Many, but seldom practiced. Most Highborn don't approve of them."

That made sense. Given the disaster of the Fall and the Shanir role in it, Tori was hardly alone in his hatred of the Old Blood. Most lords didn't even know that they were Shanir. All must be, however, in order to bind Kendar to them. The greater their power, the larger their house, except that some like Caldane added the Kendar bound to their established sons. In the old days, these new lords would have gone off to set up their own minor houses as the Min-drear had, often near the Barrier. Now, however, all nine major houses held their people close, at the most sending them out as mercenaries to support those at home here in the barren Riverland.

"But why is Bear caged, ran? To be forced to live like that, even to spread rumors of a monster to keep cadets away . . . . It's cruel. It's intolerable."

Harn rounded on her, so fiercely that she shrank back into her chair. "Don't you think we know that? He was confined because he mauled a cadet to death. Never mind that the fool had been taunting him all winter, as we found out later."

He paused and gulped. "I . . . ripped the arm off someone once myself. One of Caldane's cousins. In a berserker fit. Because he taunted me. Blackie had moved north to the Highlord's seat by then. With him nearby, I can control myself. Without him . . . . I would have used the White Knife, but Blackie forbade it and sent me instead to Tentir as commandant. That's why I set up quarters here, to protect the rest of the college."

He shook himself. "Anyway, seclusion turned Bear even more savage. Somewhere in that broken head, he knows who he is and what honor is due him. We all know it. But what can we do? He can't be allowed to roam free, to savage the next cadet stupid enough to make fun of him. We gave him a White Knife. He picked his toe-nails with it. Some would poison his food or rush him with spears like a cornered boar, but God curse anyone who takes the life of such a man without a fair fight."

He beat the chair's arm again in time to his words, making Jame flinch: "We don't know what to do."

Jame had no idea either, but she was going to think about it.

"Tell me why the Randir hate the Knorth."

The question jolted him from his personal nightmare and reminded him to whom he spoke. "That's Tentir business."

"So, presumably, is Bear. That didn't stop the Randir from trying to feed me to him."

He looked hard at her. "You aren't going away, are you? You should. This making you lordan is madness. Blackie won't hold to it. He can't. One way or the other, it will destroy him."

Jame considered this. "It might. I'm not stupid, ran, nor am I some willful, spoiled brat hell-bent on playing soldier. You know that. You've watched me fight. I was blooded long before Brier Iron-thorn made me a present of my own front tooth, or M'lady Kallystine gave me this." She almost touched the scar on her cheek, but remembered in time to keep her hands hidden.

The burly randon regarded her almost with amuse-ment. "How long ago, then, child?"

Jame frowned, thinking. "Honestly, I don't remember. It feels as if I was born blooded, but then so is everyone. The point is, what I don't know, I will learn, whatever it costs. The one thing I can't afford is ignorance. So, tonight I become a cadet. Tell me what I need to survive until then."

He gave an explosive snort of laughter. "I think you'll survive us all. Whether we survive you is another matter. All right. When your father Ganth was a cadet here, he was present at the death of a Randir named Roane—a cousin and favorite of the Witch of Wilden, as it turned out."

Jame remembered the stain on the floor of the Knorth apartment. "Was this in Greshan's quarters?"

"It was." Harn looked at her under craggy, lowered brows. "What have you heard?"

"Nothing." In fact, she was surprised. How did this tie into anything that had happened since?

"Mind you, your father and I were nearly the same age, but I came to Tentir the year after he left, at the same time as Sheth Sharp-tongue. From what I heard, though, Greshan summoned Ganth to his quarters in the middle of the night. Roane was there. He and the lordan had been drinking. Greshan was his father's darling, but . . . well, as a Highlord, he would have been a disaster."

"Worse than Ganth Gray Lord?"

She heard the bitterness in her voice. After all, they were discussing the man who had led his people to disaster in the White Hills and later had driven his only daughter out into the Haunted Lands to seek whatever protection she could find, even in Perimal Darkling, even in the Master's House itself.

But Harn was shaking his massive head. "It isn't that simple. Nothing ever is that really matters. Parents, children, family . . . and we're talking about a boy here, younger than you are now. I meet Ganth Grayling once at Gothregor, before his brief career at Tentir. His lord father Gerraint treated him like shit. Called him a liar in front of us all, although we never knew why, while that damned Greshan stood by smirking. Ganth slunk off like a whipped puppy."

Jame stared. To her, Ganth Graylord had always been a monster. She could barely conceive of him as a helpless boy younger than herself, despised by his own father.

"What happened in the lordan's quarters?"

"No one knows exactly. When the randon broke in, Roane was dead, Greshan was fouling himself in a corner, and Roane's servant was floundering around on fire. Also, for some reason, Ganth was stark naked."

Jame caught her breath, remembering her foul dream, that first night at Tentir, when the Knorth lordan had suggested calling "Dear little Gangrene" up to his apartment for some "midnight games" to impress his Randir friend. Only she had been the lordan, inside Greshan's dirty coat, inside his stinking skin. The thought made her want to crawl back into the bath and shrub herself raw to remove even the memory of that tainted touch.

"Anyway," Harn was saying, "Ganth put on some clothes and walked out of Tentir without a word to anyone. That was the end of him as a randon. A year later, Gerraint and Greshan were both dead, and Ganth was Highlord."

"Trinity. Does Tori know all this?"

"Not about Roane. That secret belongs to Tentir and Blackie doesn't. Ardeth did him no service in forbidding him to train here."

"But the randon respect him, and he loves them. He said once that the Southern Host was his true family."

"Yes. In a sense we raised him and he's done us proud. We haven't had such a decent, competent Highlord in a long time—not that those are necessarily the qualities that we need just now. These are perilous times. To survive, should we side with the just or with the powerful? Well, I made my choice when I put my hands between his in this very room and swore to follow him to the death. It's life that scares me. We totter on a knife's edge. In these treacherous times, where does honor lie?"

Jame listened, a chill running up her spine. She had thought it was only her own weakness that made her doubt, but here was one of the foremost randon of his age asking the same questions.

"You've sworn loyalty to Torisen Black Lord. Don't you trust him to recognize honor when he sees it?"

"Yes. But he still isn't one of us."

Poor Tori, Jame thought.

It had occurred to her before that her brother must feel nearly as rootless here in the Riverland as she did, neither of them having grown up in the heart of the Kencyrath. Still, she had envied him his link with the randon of the Southern Host. Now it seemed that that might not be as strong as she had supposed, lacking the Tentir bond, and here he was giving her this precious chance which he himself had been denied . . . if she lived to take advantage of it.

"Are the Randir going to keep attacking me?"

"They mean all Knorth ill. Never forget that." He scratched his stubbly chin thoughtfully, with an audible rasp. "A strange house, the Randir. Secrets within secrets. Of course, it doesn't help that the Witch has chased out their natural lord and set her son in his place, which is enough in itself to set up some fierce cross-currents."

"How did that happen, anyway?"

"I dunno for sure. The old Randir lord died, and Rawneth put a contract with the Shadow Assassins on his heir, Randiroc. Your father Ganth was to have sorted out that mess, but then came the massacre of the Knorth ladies and the White Hills. With no highlord in power to stop her, Rawneth did as she pleased."

Another piece of the puzzle, thought Jame, *if only I knew where to place it.*

"A strange house it was then," Harn was saying, "and stranger still it's become. Some Randir never use their true name unless among themselves. Some don't seem to have names at all outside their own house."

"Like the Randir Tempter?"

"That one." He growled, almost like Bear. If he had had claws, he would have flexed them. "Aye."

"In the hall, during the rope test, she said that I had hurt her cousin. I don't know whom she meant."

"Huh. Roane, perhaps, if she was speaking to you as a Knorth. On the other hand, the Randir tend to call all their blood-kin 'cousin.'" He shook himself. "At any rate, those here won't have so free a hand once you're an acknowledged cadet. Randon discipline tries to transcend house politics, not that it isn't getting harder and harder with lords like Caldane stirring the pot. You watch out for that Gorbel too, girl."

"That's another thing, ran. Why Gorbel? He isn't one of Caldane's established sons, is he?"

Harn gave a snort of laughter. "I'd like to see any of that lot try to fit in here. I hear Grondin is so fat that he has to be moved around his own house in a wheel-barrow, and the rest are too old. I don't know this Gorbel, but he's probably the son closest to cadet quality that Caldane could dig up and, for his pains, he gets the title 'lordan' slapped on him, not that he's apt to keep it long. He's only here because you are, as long and probably no longer. I'm not saying the boy is smart enough to cause true mischief, but he's bound to try."

"I'll be careful, ran. At least it's only for a year."

He snorted again. "One year? Try three, if you do well, and not all will be spent here under the protection of the college. You really don't know what you're getting into, do you?"

"Er . . . apparently not. I seldom do. And Tori didn't have time to explain much. What happens after Tentir?"

"That will depend on your final ranking, assuming you survive the autumn and spring culls. Some people have to repeat Tentir as novice cadets. That's what you'll become tonight. You get two tries. Do better, and they send you out into the field—to the Southern Host at Kothifir if you're lucky, or as an honor guard attached to the Women's Halls at Gothregor. Some third year master cadets come back here to teach and to learn advanced techniques. Some finish up with their house's randon, wherever their lord sends them. One way or another, all have to prove themselves to the Randon Council. In the end, maybe one in ten win their collars."

They hadn't noticed as they spoke that the room was falling into shadow. Then from somewhere far below came the peremptory note of a horn.

Harn sprang up, aghast as a tardy schoolboy. "It's beginning, and I'm not even dressed!"

He was, in fact, a good deal more dressed than Jame. She stripped off his coat, threw it at him in passing as if at a distraught bull, and bolted down the stairs in a glimmer of white limbs and black, whipping hair with what was left of her own clothing bundled in her arms. Around the first turn, she ran full tilt into Graykin. They tumbled down the rest of the way together. At the bottom, Jame contrived to land on top.

"I'm dead," Graykin moaned.

"No." She rolled off of him onto her feet and began rapidly sorting through her salvaged clothes, discarding most of them. "With luck, I only broke your back. You deserve it. Spy on anyone else, Gray, but not on me."

" 's not fair. You never tell me anything. Look," he said, doing anything but, struggling to sit up. "They've already started. It's too late. Give up this madness, take up your proper rank, and for God's sake put on some clothes!"

"I'm trying," said Jame, hopping on one foot to pull on a boot. "Highborn I may be, worse luck. However, I am not"—hop—"nor will I ever be"—hop—"a lady. Damn. The wrong foot, or the wrong boot. But I swear, on my honor, I'll be initiated tonight as a cadet if I have to do it wearing nothing but gloves and a surly expression."

Rue appeared, panting, with an armload of clothes. "Why'd you try to lose me?" she demanded of Gray. "Here. Hurry." She thrust the still damp but blessedly clean garments into Jame's arms. The shirt, jacket, and pants—Greshan's, no doubt—were still much too big, but at least the cuffs had been basted up. Reminded, Jame fished in the pocket of her discarded coat, drew out the two scarves, and tossed one to Rue.

Rue caught and stared at the sodden black cloth with its finely worked rathorn crest. "Where d'you find it?"

"Stuffed half way down my throat." Jame knotted her own scarf haphazardly around her neck. "I'll explain later. Damn. Where's my cap?"

Above, they could hear Harn apparently tearing apart his quarters. An anguished cry rolled down the stair: "*Where's my damned shirt?*"

Rue tugged urgently at Jame's sleeve. "God's claws, he's coming. Run!"

Too late. They shrank back as the burly randon blundered past, trying to pull himself together.

Jame started in pursuit, but Rue stopped her.

"He'll be going to join the officers by the front door. We need to come in with our house by the back." She looked about frantically. "Trinity, don't let us get lost now!"

Jame advanced on her servant. "Graykin . . . ."

"Oh, all right."

With an ill grace, he led them through a maze of halls to an obscure, narrow stair that plunged straight down to the first floor, emerging in the short, blind corridor between Old Tentir and the Randir barracks. Smart and stiff with a sense of occasion, answering the imperious summons of drum and horn, cadets passed the corridor's open end on the boardwalk, wheeled right, then left into the great hall, stepping proudly into their future.

"Coman," Rue breathed with relief. "Next Caineron, Jaran, and then Knorth. The other houses will be entering by the south door. We're in time."

Jame waited, fiddling discontentedly with her loose, wet hair as it tumbled well below her waist like a rain of black, blue-shot silk. It was her only vanity, but she usually kept it up out of the way, under a cap. Wearing it down now made her feel disheveled and vulnerable.

"Let me," said Graykin with irritation, beginning to comb out its heavy fall with nimble fingers. Then he twisted it up into a knot and secured it with thin-bladed knife, almost a spike, produced from somewhere on his person. "Honestly, don't you know any feminine arts?"

"Caineron . . . Jaran . . . ." Rue was counting down. "Here we come."

Vant appeared, almost strutting, at the head of the Knorth cadets. He started violently as Jame slid in before him, followed by Rue. His ten wavered and fell back as Brier lead her grinning squad to the fore. If there had been room or time, there might have been a serious scuffle, but they were almost to the door and the drumbeat called them insistently on.

Inside, the massed torchlight was almost blinding. Jame stopped dead on the threshold, sure for a moment that the hall was on fire, nearly tripping up all those behind her. She had to advance before her eyes had adjusted and blundered into the rear rank of the Jaran, who fended her off with a ripple of nervous laughter. Here at last was her place, before the blazing western fireplace and under the rathorn banner, parallel to Timmon on her right and the Jaran master-ten on her left, with her house drawn up behind her. The drums in the upper gallery ended with a thunderous flourish and fell silent.

In their wake, one heard only the crackle of fire, the slough of wind through upper windows, and the breathing of nine hundred-odd younglings.

Opposite, by the front door, stood the senior randon in a dark mass. Firelight glinted off their silver collars and caught the weathered, sometimes scar-broken lines of their faces. A few were clearly Highborn, smaller and finer boned than the Kendar, but claiming no precedence over them. Here as at Mount Alban, the Scrollsmen's College, ability outranked both blood and gender:

at least a third of the senior randon were women, more than Jame had yet seen at Tentir. None of the latter, however, were Highborn.

Am I the first, ever, to come here? she wondered, and was suddenly, profoundly, grateful that she hadn't appeared in her uncle's stinking rags.

The Commandant stepped forward, his mix of blood clearer than ever in the keen lines of his face and in his tall, rangy form. He paced down the hall, his boots clicking on the flagstones in a measured tread. Around the high neck of his austere dress coat he wore a silver collar hung thick with plaques that chimed softly as he moved. So many battles. So much honor.

"Four long days ago," he said, "I welcomed you to Tentir as candidates. Now I do so again as novice cadets. Tonight you join our ranks and receive your scarves in token of the randon collars that you may someday earn. You have passed a time of testing, the first of many. Each day from now on will bring new challenges to surmount or to fail. A year hence, only the best of you will remain."

He regarded the cadets as he passed, as if already further thinning their ranks. It was hard not to cower under that ruthless, winnowing glance.

"As you progress, consider well your goals. This is no easy path to glory. It never has been. We buy our honor with blood, and scars, and pain."

Their eyes were drawn, with his, to the upper walls where the collars of the dead hung, glimmering down on this new, raw muster of children, many of whom had never seen death, much less the horrors of battle.

"Within our ranks, all of us have lost friends, family, beloved. Some we knowingly sent to their deaths and they willingly went, because it was necessary. We remember them always and honor their names. Death can be easier to bear than life. Oh, but it is sometimes hard. Very hard. Expect no soft choices here."

Gorbel yawned. Perhaps it was only nerves on his part, but it made Jame's jaw ache to imitate him. *Ancestors, please, not now!* she thought wildly as the Commandant stopped equidistant from the three Highborn cadets. He seemed now to speak directly to them.

"We randon think of ourselves as a breed apart, an amalgam of all that is best in the Kencyrath. Our ranks transcend politics, or should. Yes, we are loyal to our houses. Fiercely so. But also to each other. Note this and note it well: While you attend this college, it is your home and all within it are your family, wherever you were born, whomever you call 'enemy' outside these walls. Here we are all blood-kin. House and college, cadet and randon, Highborn and Kendar. Honor holds us in balance, but what is honor? Consider that too, as you progress, and remember that you are bound by whatever words you swear in this sacred hall, before your banners and under the insignia of our dead so, on peril of your souls, swear honestly or not at all." He turned, his coat swinging wide. "Officers, administer the oath."

Nine senior randon stepped forth, one from each house, and advanced on their respective body of cadets.

Harn Grip-hard stumped down the hall to the Knorth. He looked as if he had thrown on his dress clothes in the dark and not adjusted them since, which was probably true. The undershirt was the same that he had worn before, liberally spattered with grease. However, the honors suspended clanking from his massive collar outnumbered even the Commandant's. He stopped in front of Jame.

"Last chance to save yourself, girl."

"Now, ran, when have the Knorth ever showed that much sense?"

He gave a grunt of laughter. "Not in my lifetime, nor my father's before me. Give me your scarf."

She loosened the clumsy knot and handed it to him. He regarded her attempt at needlework with raised brows. "Perhaps better here than in the Women's Halls after all. Now for it. Do you swear to obey the rules of Tentir? To guard its honor as closely as you do your own? To go out and come in, to live or to die, as you are bid? To protect its secrets now and forever, from all and sundry, whatever should befall?"

As he spoke, she heard the murmur of oaths and answers, weaving the fabric of Tentir around her, each house fitting into the pattern, somber Brandan and bright Edirr, subtle Ardeth and gaudy Caineron, rough-spun Kendar and silken Highborn, the oaths like sinews binding all together.

Now I join this pattern, she thought, *this tapestry eternally renewed. Finally, the thread of my life will be racked into place, crossing the lives of others and crossed. Finally, I will belong.*

But then she hesitated, frowning. There was a flaw somewhere in that texture of oaths given and received. A snag. Someone was swearing falsely. How could they at such a time when it weakened the whole fabric, or was that the point? This was as bad, as treacherous, as the notched rope, waiting for the first strain to fail. She began seriously to hunt for the fatal flaw, fingering through the different textures with all her Shanir wits. If she could find the source, she knew instinctively that she could destroy it.

But what if doing so rips an even larger gap?

She became aware of Harn waiting for her response. Perhaps he thought she was losing her nerve. Behind her, the Knorth cadets stirred restively, waiting to take their oaths with hers. Everyone else had finished.

Jame took a deep breath and swore the strongest oath she could:

"Honor break me, darkness take me, now and forever, so I swear."

The first part she spoke alone into a startled silence. Then came a ragged echo, not just from behind her but also from all down the hall on both sides, and every massive banner shuddered where it hung:

"So I swear" . . . "So I swear" . . . "So I swear . . . ."

Jame knew she had struck hard at someone, but whom?

Gorbel stared at her with his mouth agape, no yawn this time. Then he laughed unsteadily and said something that made his cronies snicker.

At the far end of the hall, there was a sudden stir of consternation among the Randir.

"Indeed," said Sheth softly, looking at her. "So swear we all."

Harn blinked. "That," he said, "should do nicely."

As he tied her scarf back on, correctly this time, she took the opportunity to twitch his coat closed over a particularly large grease stain. At least the bandages still wrapped around his knuckles were clean.

"Salute!" came a collective roar from the sargents.

As one, except for Jame, the cadets wheeled to face their house banners.

Now what? she thought, belatedly turning, and then flinched as the Randir war cry ripped through the hall, discordant and shaken; but perhaps that was how it was supposed to sound.

The deep, sure note of the Brandan answered it from across the hall. Then the Coman, small and shrill, like their house; the Edirr, in a falcon's jeering shriek; the Danior's gleeful howl; the Jaran, a shouted phrase in High Kens: "The shadows are burning!"; the Ardeth, not loud, but with a swelling under-surge of Shanir power.

And now for us, thought Jame.

She took a deep breath, down to the pit of her soul, and let loose with the rathorn war cry.

It began as a scream, high and wild. She could hear each cadet's voice in it, tuning to her own, ripping the air. Rathorns were called "beasts of madness" for their effect on their prey. Their cry was an assault in itself, an incitement to panic. Then it sank to a bone-shaking roar.

Yells of consternation and outrage cut it short as if with a snap of teeth. Jame turned to see that every banner in the hall but her own had fallen, half on top of their assembled companies. Heavy tapestries heaved as indignant cadets fought their way out. Angry randon crowded around the Commandant, brandishing lengths of the banners' cords and crying foul, although clearly they had snapped by themselves, without external tampering.

And all this time that wild cry went on and on, under the floor, under the flagstones. In the subterranean stable, every horse was screaming.

"Truly," said Sheth, regarding Jame over the heads of his furious officers, "we live in interesting times." He clapped his hands. "And now, we feast."

The doors to New Tentir were flung open. Beyond, the training square blazed with light, falling on long tables loaded with food and drink. Roast ox and stag, stuffed stork and crisped carp; mawmenny stew boiled in wine, garnished with almonds; baked pears and apples swimming in caramel sauce. The cadets cheered, as much with relief as joy, and rushed out to drown the taste of fear with ale. Jame and Sheth were left, looking at each other.

"I think," said the Commandant, "that you may have broken the Randir Tempter. At least, they carried her off gagged to stop her raving. A pity, that. I would have liked to hear what she had to say. Nonetheless, if you please, don't make a practice of driving your instructors mad."

"N-no, ran. I'm sorry—I think."

"At the moment, that is all I require of you: think. Now go."

But on the threshold she hesitated, stopped between past and future by the sudden memory of something she had just heard but not immediately recognized. Over the cries of cadets and horses, out in the dark, in the night, a rathorn had answered her.

CHAPTER VIII

A Forgotten Name

Summer 5

I

GOTHREGOR'S HERBALIST stood over a simmering pot, stirring it. The cream-colored paste was almost ready. From a basket at his elbow, he picked out a large, hairy leaf of comfrey and added it to the mixture, making a face as its spines stung his fingers.

Afternoon light slanted into his workroom through its southern facing windows. It also shone through the pot's stream and the glass bottles arrayed on the sill with their tinctures of iodine, decoctions of agrimony, burdock juice, and spirit of camphor, among a score of others. The Kendar's hands moved through a haze of pale green, rose, and amber light as if he were also mixing them too into his healing art, as perhaps he was.

Outside lay the broad inner ward of the Knorth fortress, with the garrison's barracks in the outer wall to the right. To the left rose the Old Keep. If one craned out the window to look east, far back beyond the Women's Halls loomed the desolation of the Ghost Walks, where the Highlord and his family had lived until assassins had

729

slaughtered all but a handful and the rest had gone into exile with Ganth Gray Lord.

The physician sighed. He himself was a Knorth, as his family had been for generations. It grieved him that so few of his house were left. If . . . no, when its last two Highborn were gone, what would happen to their people?

A door opened in the wall beside the old keep. From it emerged a lady, followed by a randon guard. From their purposeful angle across the inner ward, they were headed straight for the infirmary.

"Company from the Women's Halls," remarked the herbalist, as if to himself. "I think . . . yes, they're Ardeth."

From behind him came a stifled exclamation from his waiting patient and a rustle of cloth. Then all was still again.

As he wrapped his apron around his hands and lifted the pot off its tripod, away from the fire beneath, the Highborn entered without knocking. He turned and saluted her respectfully.

"Lady, how may I serve you?"

The Ardeth swept into the cluttered room, black eyes darting about it behind her mask. Because of her tight under skirt, she moved in tiny steps converted by long practice into a smooth glide. However, her full outer skirt brushed against glasses, instruments, and furniture, knocking some over. As she pivoted, the belling garment toppled a chair. This, in turn, snagged the table's floor-length cover and would have pulled it off if the doctor hadn't hastily set the pot on it.

"Guard, tell this Knorth my business."

The randon sargent—a woman, as were all who protected the Women's Halls—returned the herbalist's salute. She would have been more deferential if he had been a Shanir healer or even a surgeon, but still as a soldier she had a healthy respect for anyone connected with the healing arts.

"My lady seeks the Highlord." She regarded the pot of steaming paste and raised an eyebrow, but didn't comment on it. "Matriarch Adiraina wishes to speak to him."

The herbalist bowed. "I will inform my lord when I see him. He has spent the morning searching for a missing Knorth Kendar. That, perhaps, is why you have failed as yet to . . . er . . . run him down."

"Perhaps," agreed the sargent. "Lady?"

The Ardeth had made a dart for the door leading to the infirmary. Inside, she bent down and peered under each bed in turn as if she expected to find the Highlord of the Kencyrath hiding beneath one of them. Disappointed, she returned to the workroom. There, the draped surgeon's table caught her eye. As she approached it, however, a low growl stopped her in her tracks and the guard's hand dropped to her sword. The cloth stirred. A sharp muzzle emerged, flat to the ground, followed by a pair of fierce, ice blue eyes set in creamy fur. The wolver pup glared at the two Ardeth and growled again, low in her throat, showing a dark, curled lip and the needles of her white teeth.

"Well!" said the lady. "I thought we had seen the last of these mangy creatures."

With that, she turned on her heel and glided away. The guard saluted, with an amused glance at those defiant, blue eyes, and followed.

The physician began to soak linen bandages in the cooling pot.

After a moment, the table cloth lifted and Torisen Black Lord crawled out from underneath.

"The Ardeth matriarch is looking for you, my lord," the Kendar reported dutifully.

Torisen righted the chair and sat down on it. The pup slunk out and crouched warily beneath, making herself as small as possible. The Highborn looked very tired and not a little dusty, with cobwebs adding more strands of white to his dark, ruffled hair. "If Burr asks," he said, with a wry smile, "you can tell him that I've already searched under the surgeon's table."

"And for whom are you searching, my lord?"

Torisen tried to meet the other's sober gaze, and failed. That was the trouble: as in the commons room that first night, he couldn't remember the ruddy-faced Kendar's name. And now the man was missing.

"My lord?" The herbalist was regarding him with concern, probably wondering if, like his father before him, he was coming unhinged.

Was he?

Then with a sick jolt, Torisen remembered why he had come to the infirmary in the first place. Reluctantly, not looking at it, he placed his injured hand on the table.

The herbalist loosened the bandages.

"Well now, that's not so bad," he said, examining the three broken fingers, splinted together to immobilize them.

His tone was so kind, so reassuring, that Torisen looked up sharply. Yes, this man knew his dread of becoming a cripple. Perhaps everyone did. Trinity.

"The swelling has gone down considerably. And this happened . . . when?"

"About six days ago."

The herbalist reset the splints and began to wrap his hand with paste-soaked cloth. "Another term for comfrey is 'bone-knit,' " he said. "I've heard that some such plants of great potency grew among the white flowers in your great-grandmother Kinzi's Moon Garden, along with many other special herbs; but the way into that place was lost long ago. In another week, barring accidents, you can have your hand back. There."

Torisen blankly regarded the neat, new bandage that imprisoned all but his thumb.

The herbalist turned to straightened his work area. "My lord . . . " he said over his shoulder.

"Yes?"

"The missing Kendar is named Mullen. Do you remember who I am?"

He asked it casually, without turning, but tension underlay his voice.

"I do. Thank you, Kells."

II

A HUNDRED OTHER KENDAR NAMES raced through Torisen's mind as he slipped out by way of the infirmary, the wolver pup following at a wary distance as if afraid he would chase her away. Harn, Burr, Rowan, Winter . . . no, she was long dead, cut nearly in two by his father's sword . . . Chen, Laurel, Rose Iron-thorn . . .

It was nothing, he told himself uneasily, to forget one out of so many. Yes, he was new at this, but surely such things happened all the time. Besides, this Kendar had been in his service less than a year.

The battle at the Cataracts the previous fall had opened gaping holes in the Knorth ranks which many were eager to fill. Torisen wasn't sure why, but he could only bind a certain number before he began to feel a distinct, distracting strain. At the Cataracts, he knew he had over-extended himself. Still, if he could, he would have taken in anybody who asked. One way or another, weren't they all Ganth's victims? However, as Burr had explained to him, the Knorth Kendar kept close track of status and resented any infringement of it, as many did his acceptance of that turn-collar, Brier Iron-thorn.

In their estimate, first came the Exiles, who had disappeared with Ganth into the Haunted Lands and paid for their loyalty with their lives. Of them, only Torisen, his sister and, it was rumored, a priest had survived—how, exactly, remained unclear.

Next were Those-Who-Returned, whom Ganth in his madness had driven back at the high passes of the Ebonbane.

Last came the Faith-breakers, who had chosen to stay with the Host after the White Hills when Ganth had thrown down his name and title. These Kendar had sought and for the most part had found places in other houses, whose ranks had also been thinned by battle. Torisen had heard rumors that some had gone into the Randir and remained there, implacable foes of the house that they believed had betrayed them.

At any rate, by the time Those-Who-Returned had limped back, the Kencyrath had had little room for them except as *yondri-gon*, threshold-dwellers, in whatever house would give them shelter. In token of their fervent hope that the Highlord would one day return, many had branded themselves with the Knorth sigil, the same highly stylized rathorn head used to mark the Knorth herd. It was Torisen's goal to reclaim these first, along with their families; but there were so many. It had been so much easier when he had been merely the commander of the Southern Host. Then he had been responsible for some twenty-five thousand lives, but for none of their souls. Now, two thousand-odd Knorth Kencyr, body *and* soul, laid claim to him, with many, many more still unredeemed. Sometimes he woke in the middle of the night, unable for a moment to breathe under the pressure of their need. At such times, floundering in the dark, he felt like a swimmer dragged down by a multitude of clutching hands, desperate to cast off every last one of them. Dammit, he couldn't save everybody.

Ha. You can't even save yourself, boy.

But he thought that he had at least rescued the missing Kendar—a middle-aged Danior *yondri*, he now remembered, One-Who-Had-Returned. When the man had knelt before him, he had seen the three wavy scar lines of the Knorth sigil branded on the back of the man's neck. *This is someone*, he had thought as he accepted those broad, worn hands between his own, *who knew my father's face*; and he had felt embarrassed by the glowing gratitude in that round, red face. No one should have such power to make or break, power that he often saw other lords abuse as his father had, power that he didn't really want.

Admit it, boy. You're weak and you know it, especially since your sister returned. She's gelded you, and you never even noticed.

Sometimes it was hard not to snap back at that voice in his mind, behind the locked door in his soul.

Oh yes, father? he wanted to say. *Was it better to give up, as you did, and let everything fall apart around you?*

And if my sister sometimes unnerves me, our mother unmanned you. Destruction begins with love, you said. Remember?

But he couldn't say that. Not yet. The image formed in his mind of the hall of the Haunted Lands' keep where he had grown up. He was sitting in it still, in the dust and dark, his back hunched against the voice behind the locked door.

Just ignore it, he told himself doggedly. *Father is dead. Sooner or later, he's got to shut up.*

Of course, not love but duty bound him to the forgotten Kendar. When he found what's-his-name, he would give him a good tongue-lash for neglecting his duty that morning and then reinstate him. That would show Kendar like Kells how foolish they were to have made such a fuss.

He had been headed for the garrison dormitory, meaning to search it, when a voice ahead stopped him. In the sharp diction of the Coman, a lady was demanding to know where the Highlord might be found.

Torisen turned and bolted for cover.

III

LATE THAT AFTERNOON, a tired post horse trotted through the north gate into Gothregor and stopped. Its rider swung stiffly down, staggering as her feet hit the earth. One leg nearly buckled. Steward Rowan hung on to the saddle, cursing softly, waiting for the old injury to release her cramped muscles. She owed those damn Karnids for more than the scars on her face.

Before her lay the broad, green inner ward, sliding into the shadow of the western mountains as the sun set behind them. At this hour, the Knorth garrison should have been settling down for the night. Instead, small, determined processions crisscrossed the darkening grass. Each was led by the gliding form of a lady followed, like a goose with her goslings, by a line of masked Highborn girls and a randon guard who brought up the rear. When two such lines meet, they cut through each other without a word in passing. Others were threading purposefully through the garrison's barracks, kitchens, and other domestic offices. A few Knorth Kendar could be seen whisking furtively in and out of sight, trying to keep out of the way.

As Rowan stood, staring, she was spotted. A small, plump lady turned abruptly and came at her as much at a run as her tight underskirt allowed. Her line of girls—by far the longest and most varied in the ward—swerved to follow her. Rowan saw as she approached that it was Karidia, the Coman Matriarch.

She saluted, one hand twisted in her horse's mane both to keep her balance and to prevent the animal from wandering off in search of its dinner.

"Matriarch, how may I serve you?"

Karidia glared at her, straining within her tight bodice to regain her breath. The garment creaked alarmingly. What could be seen of her face below the mask was bright red. "You can tell me . . . where that precious Torisen of yours . . . is hiding."

"Lady, I just got here. I don't know."

The Coman made a sound of disgust. "You Knorth! Always misplacing . . . your Highborn. Trinity! With only two . . . it shouldn't be that hard . . . to keep track of them."

She turned with a haughty toss of her head, but spoiled the effect by tripping over her own full hem and falling flat on her face. The girls squealed. The guard set her back on her feet and off she sailed for all the world like a righted clockwork toy, her exhausted retinue trailing after her.

Rowan sighed.

By now, the stables should have been moved from under the fortress into converted rooms set into the outer wall, opening onto the inner ward. However, given the past week's confusion, no one had had time. Rowan limped down the ramp to the winter stalls, found an empty box and, there being no one on duty to help her, put up the horse herself.

Down the row, she heard restless hooves. When she went to investigate, Storm lunged at her over the top of his open half-door, teeth snapping almost in her face. Then he recognized her and withdrew with a whick-ered apology.

Rowan found her lord in the neighboring tack-room, sitting on a bale of hay, trying one-handed to mend a broken stirrup leather. She sank down gratefully opposite him and stretched out her sore leg.

"I'm surprised you aren't hiding in Storm's box," she said, rubbing knotted muscles, "or under that nice big pile of manure around the corner."

"I'm keeping the latter in reserve. As for Storm, he'd keep them off all right, but he doesn't like my shadow. There," he added with a jerk of his head, seeing the question in her eyes.

In a dim far corner, now that she looked, Rowan could make out the curled shape of a pup. Blue eyes met hers defiantly over the white brush of a tail.

"Isn't that a wolver? Are Grimly's people still here?"

"No. They left this morning. We thought at first that she'd been left behind by accident, but now I think that she decided, ancestors know why, to stay. At any rate, no one can catch her and she follows me everywhere, just out of reach."

"Odd. How old d'you think she is?"

"I'm guessing about five years. Wolvers live longer than wolves and mature more slowly. Then again, she's from the deep Weald. Things may be different there."

"Yes. A lot more savage. And look at the size of those paws. If she grows into them . . ."

"She'll be enormous, and a shape-shifter by the time she reaches adolescence, if not before."

They regarded the pup thoughtfully. She glared back at them as is to demand, *So what?*

"Well," said Torisen, with the air of resolutely turning to business, "what news from Tentir? Burr told me about the qualifying tests."

Rowan nodded. "A nasty surprise, that. Usually, such things get sorted out before the cadet candidates arrive." She took a deep breath. "Well, when I left yesterday morning, your sister had one of the lowest scores in her class. Short of a miracle, and with a Caineron commandant in charge . . ."

"Trinity," said Torisen blankly. "I don't suppose I really expected her to make it through the whole year, but to have failed so quickly . . . . Damn. I thought I would have more time to make alternate plans. This puts us back to where we were last winter."

"Worse. I'd be no friend if I didn't tell you this, Blackie, but now the pressure is really going to be on for either you or your sister to form a contract with another house. True, the hunt going on now for you is a farce. At a guess, the Council of Matriarchs summoned you and you didn't respond fast enough."

"Not the Council," Torisen murmured, still fiddling with the broken strap. Even with two hands, he didn't think it could be fixed: there were too many other weakened patches. "Just Adiraina, trying to get a jump on the game. I suspect it's every matriarch for herself now."

"Huh. Well, it doesn't help that you've picked this of all times to fight with Adric."

"Not that, exactly, but close enough. It had to come some day."

Rowan snorted. "Yes, but *now*? Anyway, in case you haven't noticed, Gothregor is up to its turrets in hunting parties, each with a bevy of prospective consorts in tow. Yes, it's ridiculous, but I know these women. When today's ruckus dies down, they'll settle in for the long chase. And I have to tell you, Blackie, we'll need help getting through next winter. If not from the Ardeth, then where?"

Torisen had been worrying about that too, but now flicked it aside. "One disaster at a time, please."

"All right." Rowan leaned forward, steeling herself. "I do see a way out of at least one mess. Take your sister not as your lordan but—" she paused, with a gulp "—as your consort."

The strap slipped from Torisen's hand. Before it hit the floor, the pup snapped it up and retreated to her corner to gnaw it.

"Well, why not?" Rowan demanded. "If you were twins, it would only be natural. As it is . . . well, you *are* the last two pure-blooded Knorth. How better to re-establish the line and simultaneously take you both off the . . . er . . . market. The Matriarchs might even approve. I've heard rumors that they arranged similar matches in the past, brother to sister, uncle to niece, father to daughter, trying to create the Tyr-ridan."

"Ending up with monsters, more likely."

"Well, yes. Sometimes. Usually. Nonetheless, the basic idea is sound, and some matriarchs still carry far more weight with their lords than you might guess."

"Yes, but . . ."

The pup's ears pricked and she growled softly. Some-one was coming. Storm lunged, only to recoil at a sharp slap to the nose. A Jaran randon appeared at the tack room door.

"So here you are, my lord," she said with a smile and a salute.

They all started at a crash. Storm was trying to kick down the intervening wall. Torisen thumped on it with his good fist.

"Behave! Fair is fair. You've tracked me down, captain, and I owe you for covering my retreat that first night. How may I serve you?"

"M'lady Trishien asks if you can spare her a few minutes. She promises you safe conduct, at least where our people are concerned."

Torisen considered. He rather liked the scholarly Jaran Matriarch and, as far as he knew, none of the hunting parties above were hers. Besides, at some point he had to talk to someone on the Matriarchs' Council besides Adiraina.

"All right." He rose and stretched. "Since my work here seems to have been . . . er . . . devoured"—he glanced at the pup—"I am at your command."

Rowan watched them go, the wolver trotting a distance behind. She thought about what she had said concerning Jameth and wondered how many other Knorth Kendar had had the same idea. It might save them all, or the two Highborn in question might kill each other first.

"Just consider it," she muttered at the Highlord's receding back. "We can't go on like this much longer."

 **IV**

ABOVE THE STABLES lay the subterranean levels of the Women's Halls. As they threaded their way through dark corridors, Torisen thought about what Rowan had suggested. It had practically knocked the breath out of him. He still couldn't quite bring the idea into focus, any more than if someone had told him that the moon had turned backward in its course. Jame was his sister, ten years his junior, a Shanir, his twin . . . and she was Jame.

Images of her flickered through his mind: the half-feral child with ragged clothes and silver-gray eyes too large for her thin face; the girl on the edge of the Escarpment, crying for a dead darkling changer; the child-woman in the ruins of Kithorn, whistling up the south wind to take them home.

Then, last night, had come that strange dream that they were dancing. How she had moved, with such aching grace. Long, lovely hair had slid through his scarred fingers like black water over fissured rock, and he had hardly known if he wanted to let it glide free or to grip and wrench it out by the roots.

Let me not see . . .

Then the ruddy Kendar had interrupted them to beg that she, not he, remember his name. What business was that of hers?

Your Shanir twin, boy, your darker half, returned to destroy you . . .

No. The bolt was shot, whatever that meant.

THEY REACHED THE JARAN compound without incident and climbed to the matriarch's third story chambers.

At her bidding, Torisen entered and stopped short, blinded by the light streaming through the western windows. The forecourt below now lay deep in dusk, but up here the day was still dying.

"Step to the right, my lord."

When he did, the bulk of the old keep mercifully blocked the setting sun and, slowly, his sight returned. The Jaran Matriarch had risen from her writing table near the window to greet him. The lens sewn into her mask flashed fire as she returned his salute, but her voice was cool and lightly amused.

"Honor be to your halls, my lord. You're a hard man to find. My sister matriarchs have been complaining about it most bitterly."

She resumed her seat, sweeping her full skirt around the chair legs, and picked up her pen. Torisen noted that it had worn a permanent groove in her index finger and that her hands were ingrained with ink spots. He carefully moved a stack of manuscripts to the floor and perched on the window ledge.

"What do you write, my lady?" he asked as she dipped the quill and resumed her flowing, rounded script on the page before her.

"That you look tired, but far better than the last time we meet."

It was hard to remember that that had only been six days ago. So much had happened. "My thanks again, matriarch, for telling me where to find my sister. Without you, I probably still wouldn't know."

She smiled slightly. "Oh, I think Lady Jameth will always, eventually, make herself known. One might more easily conceal an earthquake. I also write that you seem to have acquired a new . . . er . . . pet? Dear me. One never quite knows how to refer to a wolver."

She regarded the pup thoughtfully, then extended a hand to her. Torisen held his breath. The pup crept forward, touched the matriarch's fingertips with a cold nose, and immediately retreated.

"Well," said Trishien. "That will do for a start. My greetings to you too, little one. Still, how very odd. Have you bound her to you, my lord?"

"No!"

"Would you know if you had?"

"I'm . . . not sure. I think so."

"Ah." Torisen wished that he could see the Jaran's eyes more clearly. Glassed over as they were and reflecting the sunset sky, it was impossible to guess her thoughts. "You came into your power late, my lord. We scrollsmen have wondered before now how well you understand it."

"Do you write that too?" Torisen asked, watching the quill move. He spoke more sharply than he had intended.

She might have read his mind; assuredly she did his tone. "My lord, when you assumed your father's seat, you took responsibility for your people and consequently opened wide tracts of your life to them. I speak here of the entire Kencyrath. Of course we discuss you. I am sorry if you find that offensive—and I can see that you do—but you must learn to accept it." Her lips twitched. "I also write that your hair is laced with cobwebs and straw, from which I deduce that you have recently been in a stable . . . and perhaps under various articles of furniture?"

Torisen relaxed with a wry laugh. "Your sister matriarchs press me hard although not," he added, thinking of the manure pile, "to the last extreme. Yet."

"I think you will find only the Ardeth, the Danior, and the Coman in hot pursuit. Yolindra of the Edirr may also try her hand, if only to tease Karidia. Luckily, the Caineron, Randir, and Brandan matriarchs are not currently in residence at Gothregor, although you may well hear from them."

"I've already heard from the Brandan, but not about my sister. Brant wants to conclude negotiations for my cousin Aerulan, but I don't understand. Aerulan died a long time ago."

Trishien put down her quill. "Thirty-four years ago, my lord, with all the other ladies of your house except for poor Tieri. It's Aerulan's death banner Lord Brandan wants. Before the massacre, he negotiated a contract with your father for her in perpetuity."

"Yes, for a huge sum of money not yet paid, but now he's dead and so is she." He grimaced and rubbed his temple.

"Are you unwell, my lord?"

"Not exactly." Dealing with the Women's World made his head ache. There were always things left unsaid that he was supposed to understand. "I told Brant last winter that he could keep the banner with my blessings. Sweet Trinity, how can I profit from so much grief?"

"I . . . see." She picked up the pen and resumed writing. "Your generosity does you credit, especially when you need funds so badly. Yes, yes, we all know about that. But here your tact may be misplaced."

There it is again: the unspoken message, this time unmistakably a warning, but he knew from experience that she would tell him nothing more.

Trishien sighed. "This would be so much easier if your house had a matriarch. Have you considered your sister . . . "

"No!"

"Very well. I will only say that it would be better if you let Lord Brandan pay the dowry in full, but I can see that telling you will do no good. You don't mean to profit from anything your father did if you can help it, beyond claiming his power."

This hit too close for comfort. Veer away.

"You mentioned four houses in pursuit," he said, attempting levity. "What, have the Jaran no taste for the hunt? I seem to remember that you also wanted to see me when I first arrived."

"That was only to tell you that Lord Ardeth has recovered from his illness and is on his way home, although in a fragile state of health. As to the other matter . . . ." Trishien sighed in vexation and rubbed the side of her nose, leaving an ink smudge. "I admit that I am tempted. After all, we have one lady who would suit you very well

whom you already like; but she would hardly thank me
for interrupting her scholarship."

"You mean Kirien."

He considered the Jaran Lordan with her intelligence,
good nature, and dry wit. Yes, if forced to it he could do
worse; but no, she would never leave her studies. He
wondered how she would find time for them when she
came of age and assumed control of her house, if as
Highlord he still permitted it. She might prefer that he
did not. As Kirien had explained it to him, the entire
Jaran had flipped a coin for lordship and she had lost.

"However," said the matriarch, resuming her usual
brisk manner, "I did ask you to come in part because of
her. Earlier today, Kirien sent this message."

She handed him a paper containing a half dozen lines
of Kirien's distinctive, spiky script.

He read quickly. "Jame has passed the tests after all,
but since then she has disappeared. Harn is searching
for her."

His hands felt cold, his mind an echoing vault. *I endangered my sister when I sent her here last winter without
protection. I didn't know. I didn't know. But this time
I've done it well aware of the risk she faces. Do I want
to see her dead?*

"Your pardon, lady," he said, rising quickly. "I must
leave for Tentir at once."

He was half way to the door when she called after
him: "Wait!"

Her hand was writing again, but the letters that
emerged jagged across the page, interrupting her normal, smooth flow. Kirien was sending another message.

The Matriarch is a Shanir, Torisen realized, and
despite himself drew back a step. *Perhaps Kirien is one*

too. At the same time, another, cooler part of his mind observed, *So that's why Trishien's news is so much more recent than Rowan's, although my steward half killed herself bringing it to me.*

Trishien read what she had written, and smiled. "Ah. The lost is found. Your war-leader Harn has rescued your sister from the bear's den—now what could that be? a metaphor perhaps?—and even now she is accepting her scarf as a cadet from his hands."

The sun set. Cool mountain shadow swept into the room with the first breath of night. Torisen shivered, then wondered why.

She is slipping out of your control, boy. I said she was too strong for you.

But Jame was safe . . . for the minute at least. Surely Harn could keep her out of future trouble.

And since when, boy, has anyone ever managed to do that?

A rap on the door made them both start. Outside, Karidia's voice rose over the captain's protests like the shrill yap of a lap dog out for blood: "Trishien, you open this door this minute! I know you're hiding him in there!"

"Oh dear," said Trishien as Torisen looked frantically for another way to out. "I'm afraid there's just the door. And the windows. I *am* sorry."

Plump little fists pounded on the door. "You selfish, glass-eyed, book-loving snob, let me in!"

"The window it is, then," said Torisen, and swung his legs over the sill.

The wall below was thick with ivy, but he was still three stories up, and he only had one good hand. His feet scrabbled for purchase in the tangle of tough vines.

Stiff leaves poked him in the eyes. The trick was to step down, secure a foot, then let go and grab a lower hand-hold, quickly, before gravity pulled him off the wall. Above, the pup leaned out the window yipping with distress. Torisen was about half way down when she lunched herself after him. Instinctively, he let go to catch her and they both fell, straight into Burr's arms. The burly Kendar set Torisen on his feet and the pup leaped to the ground.

Trishien laughed down at them. "I do believe that you and Lady Jameth are related after all. Now please excuse me, my lord. Someone is at the door."

"Run," said Torisen to Burr, and followed his own advice.

 VI

THEY STOPPED IN THE FORECOURT, hard against the stone flank of the old keep.

"Trinity," said Torisen, laughing, holding a stitch in his side. "I'll never regard a stag hunt the same way again." Then he saw Burr's expression. "What's the matter?"

"My lord, Steward Rowan has found the Kendar Mullen."

His formality set Torisen back. "Found who? Oh. Of course. Where?"

"In the death banner hall."

They were almost at its door. Torisen hesitated a moment, his hand on the latch, then entered, followed by Burr. They left the pup, forgotten and rigid, on the threshold.

The hall took up the old keep's first floor, a low-ceilinged, unfurnished, windowless chamber. A torch set in a bracket by the door brought flickers of false life to the gallery of faces crowding the walls. There hung the Knorth dead. Most were Highborn with the family's sharp, proud features, not a few of them betraying the mad twist that ran also through the Knorth blood. These were portrait banners, but also sometimes caricatures; in death if not in life, all Highborn faced the judgment of those over whom they had had power. Also among their serried ranks were a few Kendar, mostly noted randon, scrollsmen, or artisans. Every banner was woven out of threads unraveled from the clothes in which each, man, woman, or child, had died. The air stank of cold stone and old, moldering cloth, laced with the unexpected reek of fresh blood.

Rowan sat in the middle of the floor, cradling the head of a missing Kendar. When she looked up, her scarred face, never expressive, seemed less animate than the dead that surrounded her.

"I looked here first, my lord, and found him."

Torisen knelt beside her. It took a moment to realize what he was seeing.

The Kendar's broad face was relatively unmarked, but whatever ruddy color it still possessed now came from torchlight alone. Below that, the broad chest and gnarled arms seemed to hang in dark, clotted tatters, as if he had started cutting the wavy lines of the rathorn sigil into his clothes and gone on to the skin beneath, slicing deeper and deeper except where old battle scars had turned aside the blade. Much of the blood had long since dried.

Some still welled in sluggish surges from his throat, where the white hilted knife had at last cut too deep. The blood in which Torisen knelt was still warm. He could feel it seeping through his clothes.

The man was still breathing, but just barely. His eyes half opened like those of a tired child reluctant to wake. Then he saw who bent over him and smiled.

"My lord."

Torisen gripped the Kendar's worn hand. "Mullen. Welcome home."

The smile remained, but the eyes lost their focus and no breath returned.

Torisen sat back on his heels, feeling dazed. He stared at the pattern of blood, fresh and dried, spread out around him in a pool, then running dark into the flagstone's cracks. "This took time."

"Probably most of the day," Rowan agreed. She regarded her lord steadily. He could also feel Burr's eyes on him, and a weight as if all his dead ancestors lining the walls also watched in judgment.

"You want me to understand," he said to them all, "but I don't. Why here? Why like this?"

"D'you mean why'd he turn himself into the raw material of a death banner?" Burr asked gruffly. "To be remembered, of course, and what better place for it than this?"

"My lord . . . Blackie . . ." Rowan spoke gently, as if to a slow-witted child. "Did you have any sense that this was happening?"

"Of course not!"

"You would have if he had been one of your people dying at the Cataracts."

Torisen started to answer, then stopped. He remembered that restless and, to him, inexplicable urge that had driven him out after the battle to search through the carnage for the mortally wounded of his house, to bring them honorable death and release from pain by the white-hilted knife.

"Are you saying that he did this, and took so long about it, hoping that I would come to find him?" He looked from one impassive face to the other, appalled. "Trinity! You know I didn't cast him off on purpose!"

"We know," said Rowan. "You just forgot his name, and the bond broke. But you did remember him in the end." She paused, then asked carefully, "Will it happen again?"

Torisen rose, greatly perturbed. He started to run a hand through his hair, then stopped, seeing that it was still wet with Mullen's blood. "I don't know. I don't know why it happened this time, unless I took too many new Kendar into my service at the Cataracts and just couldn't hold on to them all."

But there was more to it than that. They all sensed it, without knowing what it was, much less what to do about it.

Ha, boy. I told you: you're weak.

Torisen looked from Burr to Rowan and back again. After everything the three of them had been through together, over nearly two decades, they trusted each other with their lives, their souls, and their honor. But then so did every Kendar sworn to him. Where was the flaw that had let this man slip away?

Didn't you abandon me, your father and lord, to my death? For that I died cursing you. Lack-faith, oath-breaker, do you wonder that your title rings false and your people fall away?

Words echoed in the hollow shell of his soul, and he still couldn't turn to answer them. The dead watched, their judgment hanging over him like the blade Kin-Slayer, bane of the unworthy.

I must find my own way, he thought, steeling himself. *For my people's sake if not for my own. The old times have passed, but not honor.*

"I swear to you," he said, swinging around to address all the watching faces, alive and dead, "I will find out why this happened and I will never let it happen again. My word on it."

A shiver went through the hall, as if all in it had been holding their breath.

"What of this man?" Rowan asked, Mullen still limp in her arms.

"He deserves to be remembered, as he wished. Let his body be given to the pyre and his clothes to the artisans, that his banner may hang here forever with his peers."

Noble words, Torisen thought as he watched Burr and Rowan gather up the corpse. With his broken hand, he couldn't help even if they had let him, nor would it have been his place to do so. Mullen had passed into the care of his own people. Noble words indeed, but with a muffled echo in this place of the dead that chilled his heart. If he couldn't make them good, the Third Face of God, Regonereth, would have precious little mercy on his soul.

Nor you either, he thought. *My sister. My nemesis.*

On the threshold, the wolver pup threw back her head and howled against the coming of the night.

CHAPTER IX

School Days

Summer 6–32

I

AND SO RANDON TRAINING began at Tentir.

After the first testing, roughly a thousand cadets were left at the college—still too many, but more were expected to fall prey to the autumn cull. As expected, the Caineron had lost the most candidates in the first few days, but with Lord Caldane's eight established sons adding their numbers of sworn Kendar to his, they were still the largest contingent at the college. Following them in numbers were the Ardeth, the Randir, and the Brandan, all houses with Kendar bound to more than one Highborn. Lord Hollen's little Danior could only muster three ten-commands. The Knorth mustered nine, just shy of a one-hundred command.

For the most part, school days followed the pattern established in the testing. The horn usually sounded at dawn, although sometimes earlier to surprise those who still depended too much on *dwar* sleep. Following breakfast and assembly, there were four two-hour lessons—half before lunch, half after—then a free period, then supper. Evenings were spent studying, mending gear, or attending to other house business.

Sometimes, after a particularly dismal lesson or because an instructor had had an especially bad day, a ten-command was obliged to repeat a class far into the night.

Often, depending on the season, cadets were called on to perform one of the thousand or so chores that the college needed done to function properly.

Every seventh day they were free to do whatever they pleased.

While each house ate and slept in its own hall, cadets continued to train together, two different ten-commands at a time under whatever randon or sargent was best suited to teach them. In this way, the college hoped to forge bonds between houses that even their lords could not easily break. Whether this stratagem would work or, indeed, ever had, was a subject of perennial debate in the officers' mess.

To Jame's relief, most of the classes began with reviews of the basics—to correct bad habits, the randon said, and they found much to criticize. However, she had no habits whatsoever in many disciplines and so was glad for the chance to learn whatever she could, as well as to regain the physical edge that a winter in the Women's Halls had badly dulled. It was hard, muscle-aching work, but she enjoyed it.

The situation in the Knorth barracks was less to her taste.

From the start, Vant barely consulted her in the running of her own house. He assumed she knew nothing about such matters, which was true, and proceeded to arrange things to suit himself. For the most part, Jame couldn't fault his competence. For example, it would never have occurred to her to detail cadets to guard the doors to the inner, common corridor when they stood open. Like any other house the Knorth could always gain access to either half of their first story by going up the stairs to the second floor landing (which straddled the corridor) and descending on the other side, but it was considered rude to seal off the barracks during the day and positively hostile to obstruct the corridor itself, as any house could by closing the great gates at either end of their section.

Other house duties included cooking, cleaning, and serving at table, done by rotation. Unlike the Caineron or the Ardeth, the Knorth had no Kendar servants, its lord having none to spare. Whatever needed to be done, the cadets had to do.

And then there was house discipline.

Vant could assign individuals or whole ten-commands such necessary but unpleasant chores as mucking out the Knorth stables, de-worming the hunting pack, and unclogging the kitchen well after a seething of eels set up residence in it.

The boot-polishing incident turned out to be the first of many for Jame's ten. Vant was always finding fault with one or another of them, for example when Erim tripped over his own feet and more or less threw a bowl of soup in Vant's face (Jame wondered about that: Erim might be clumsy, but he had very good aim), or when Niall, Kest's replacement, woke the whole barracks by screaming in his sleep.

Her own ten didn't want Jame involved in the punishments earned by these mishaps.

"Don't you come with us, lady," Rue insisted as the ten-command geared up during what should have been their free time to tackle a trog-infested latrine. "He's got it in for Five, sure, but he's also trying to get at you. He thinks if he makes things nasty enough, you'll give up and leave." She laughed. "Doesn't know you yet, does he?"

He knew her well enough to have put her in a fix, thought Jame glumly, watching her ten go. Whether she went with them or not, should she submit without comment to Vant's unfair punishments and look weak, or complain and look petulant, or pull rank and tell him to lay off them altogether? Being a master ten was awkward to begin with, not (presumably) like being a one-hundred commander with clear-cut lines of authority. If she hadn't come to Tentir as a lordan, Brier would be master now and Vant her second in command. Brier would know how to run the barracks. Jame didn't. If this was another test, to see how each master ten handled his or her house, she was failing miserably.

As it happened, that afternoon she couldn't have gone with them anyway. At breakfast, a sargent had arrived and called out a dozen names including Jame's with orders to report to various randon after classes. A bit nonplused (after all what had she ever had to do with birds?), Jame went off in search of the Falconer.

The mews occupied a long second story room in Old Tentir, overlooking the inner square. Half the windows were screened with oiled cloth to keep out drafts. Rank after rank of goshawks, peregrines, gyrfalcons and eagle owls rustled on their perches in the subdued light, the bells tied to their legs ringing softly. Their hooded heads jerking toward the door as Jame paused on the threshold, waiting for her eyes to adjust.

"Well, come in, come in!" a shrill voice called from the other end of the room. "D'you think we have all day?"

The far window was uncurtained. A misshapen figure stood black against it in a shaft of light smoky with dust. This half of the room seemed as messy as the other half was obsessively neat. As Jame made her way forward, stumbling over debris and colliding with work tables, she saw that a dozen cadets from various houses had arrived before her and were perched precariously on stools around the cold fireplace, watching her progress. She found an empty stool off to one side. It rocked under her on uneven, rickety legs.

The Falconer had spoken to her as sharply as to any tardy cadet. He must not know who she was. Good.

"Right," he said as she gingerly settled. "We were discussing how bonds form between Kencyr and animal."

Jame felt her tension ease. She had worried how Tentir would regard someone so clearly aligned with the Third Face of God, That-Which-Destroys, especially given the chaos her house had already caused along those lines. However, of all her Shanir traits, this surely was the one least apt to get her into trouble.

Seen momentarily in profile, the Falconer's hooked nose looked like a beak, and there was something strange about his eyes. His apparent hunchback consisted of a small, alert merlin and the padded shoulder that served as its perch. As the bird's head jerked to and fro, so did its master's.

"A select few," he was saying, "have always had this ability. Perhaps we all did, in the beginning, but lost it with the thinning of the Old Blood. You, sirrah!"

A Danior cadet straightened abruptly on his stool, nearly falling off of it.

"How did you and that beast come to be bound?"

Squinting against the light, Jame saw that the great, sprawling mass at the cadet's feet was alive. It raised a massive head, yawned with cavernous, nearly toothless jaws, and went back to sleep.

"W-we were born on the same day," the boy stammered, "and b-both our mothers died. The old lord valued his Molocar as much as his Kendar. Torvo and I were suckled by the same wet nurse."

That meant the hound was fifteen or sixteen years old, a great age for his breed. He began to snore in great, gusty sighs, with an unnerving catch between breaths.

"We've been together forever," said the boy, bending to stroke the gray muzzle.

"Well, now," said the Falconer, not unkindly. "You have the talent. There will be others."

"It won't be the same!"

"No. Alas, that we should out-live so many of those whom we love."

He ruffled the breast feathers of his pretty little merlin. The bird raised its tail and squirted a white stream of excrement out the window. Someone below cursed.

"And you, boy?"

The cadet addressed didn't answer, didn't seem to have heard. His dreamy face was turned toward the window, eyes unfocussed. The Falconer stalked over and slapped him. He came back to life slowly, like a sleeper waking, and sat there stupidly rubbing his cheek.

"Cast your mind after your companion, yes, but, never, ever, lose yourself! All of you, take note: some of us never come back.

"And you, girl?"

The Randir cadet whom he had addressed scowled sullenly at the floor. Like many of her house with some Highborn blood, she had thin, sharp features and hooded eyes. "I don't know what you mean, ran. I don't even know why I'm here wasting my time . . . and yours."

"The answer is up your sleeve." He whistled, a sweet, wavering sound that made the hound twitch in his sleep. "Ah. Here it comes."

The Randir's jacket bulged and rippled as if with new, strangely placed muscles. Something golden flowed out of her sleeve onto her lap. There it collected itself in thick, molten coils and raised a triangular head with glittering orange eyes. At its soft hiss, the others drew back and the merlin bated, screaming.

"It's a gilded swamp adder!" someone exclaimed.

Jame liked snakes, and this one fascinated her, being at once so beautiful and so grotesque. She leaned forward for a better look.

"Is it blood-bound to you?" she asked, genuinely curious.

Randir and serpent both hissed. The wicked little head wove back and forth, black tongue flickering.

Jame withdrew hastily.

"You Randir have odd tastes," the Falconer said dryly.

"It was a gift from my mistress."

"Dear Lady Rawneth. That explains everything. And you, girl? Where's that ounce of yours?"

He *did* know who she was. "Back in the Knorth quarters, ran."

"Sure of that, are you, or only guessing?"

Jame reached out to Jorin's senses. As a rule, he used hers much more easily than she did his.

"Well?" the Falconer demanded. "What d'you see?"

"Nothing, ran."

Or rather, only memory: she was on a ropewalk between Tai-tastigon's inner and outer walls. Below her, a man carried a wriggling sack. He threw it into the water.

. . . close, wet, and all those other weighted, pathetic sacks bobbing lifeless in the current . . .

She gulped, swallowing the sense of something so precious, so nearly lost forever.

"He's a Royal Gold," she heard herself say. "Extremely valuable, if sound, but Jorin has been blind since birth. His breeder ordered him to be destroyed. He was drowning when we bonded and I rescued him. Now I am his eyes and, sometimes, he is my nose."

"Ah," said the Falconer. "A spontaneous bond, and not one by blood. Interesting. Those in distress must be particularly vulnerable to you. Be careful whom you touch, and when."

Too late for Graykin, thought Jame, not that he seemed to mind except when she failed to live up to his grand expectations.

"And you, boy?"

He spoke to the shadows behind Jame. She had been aware for some time of the buzz of flies but had assumed that they were attracted to some bit of food left out too long in the general mess. Now, turning, she saw a Coman cadet hunched in the corner, surrounded by a blur of wings.

"It isn't always flies, ran," he said, with a lop-sided smile. "Sometimes it's wasps or moths or jewel-jaws. They don't bother me—much—because they never land, but they don't tell me anything either."

Jame reflected that insects seldom bothered her either, which was fortunate. The last thing she needed was a swarm of blood-bound mosquitoes.

"Hmm," said the Falconer, tapping his yellow teeth with a dirty fingernail. "You should talk to Randiroc, the next time he swings by. Then again, he doesn't talk much to anyone."

The name stirred Jame's memory. She sat up straight. "The missing Randir Heir?"

A stool crashed over. The Randir cadet had sprung to her feet. "There is no 'missing heir,' only a hunted renegade and traitor to his house!"

Jame recoiled, not so much at the finger thrust almost in her face as at the sinuous, golden form gliding down the other's arm toward her. Her stool broke. She turned a backward fall into a roll, fetching up on her feet in the corner with the Coman cadet. For a moment, she was surrounded by a sizzle of tiny wings.

Then the swarm launched itself at the Randir.

The latter backed away, flailing, tripped over the supine hound, and crashed into the Falconer.

Snake and merlin went up, the former inadvertently flung into the air, the latter launching itself after it. The bird caught the serpent behind its wicked little head and shot out the window clutching it.

Half the hooded hawks screamed and leaped to follow, but their jesses stopped them short in mid-air, leaving them to swing upside down from their perches, wings bating and beaks angrily panting.

The Randir lurched to her feet and fled the mews, pursued by a furious cloud of flies.

"Well!" said the Falconer as some cadets hauled him to his feet while the others rushed to help the frantic birds before they injured themselves. "At least we've discovered one thing your talent is good for, boy. Myself, I wouldn't care to be your enemy."

In the process of brushing him off, Jame saw his eyes clearly for the first time, or rather didn't: the sockets were sunken and the lids were sealed shut over them with tiny, neat stitches.

He groped for a chair and sat down. "Well, well, well. That's quite enough excitement for today. Come back next week and we will continue."

II

IT HAD BEEN A SHORT SESSION.

When Jame emerged from Old Tentir, a Jaran and an Edirr ten-command were still practicing swordplay on horseback in the training square. Timmon leaned on the rail before his compound, watching as if the display were being staged purely for his amusement.

He greeted Jame with a smile and a jerk of his chin toward second story window of the mews.

"Did you have fun up there? First a hawk with a snake in its beak and then a Randir with a ball of flies for a head. She half-drowned herself in the water trough getting rid of them."

"I think," said Jame ruefully, "that I've made another enemy. Why aren't you in class?"

"Oh, I didn't feel like hammering nails."

From behind them within the Ardeth quarters came the ruckus of reconstruction, where Timmon's ten-command (minus Timmon) was apparently being kept busy.

"I wish they'd finish," he said. "We haven't had a hot meal since you dropped the dining room into the kitchen."

"Sorry about that, but it wasn't entirely my fault. I mean, buildings don't necessarily fall down or burn up whenever I walk into them."

"Only on special occasions, I suppose. Speaking of which, have you ordered that gaping hole in your barracks' roof to be repaired yet?"

Jame grimaced. There it was again: the question of command, when she didn't even like telling Rue to clean her boots. Of course, Rue did it anyway, with the air of helping the helpless.

"I like to sleep under the open sky."

Timmon shot her a grin. "I was teasing. As the senior Knorth randon, Harn Grip-hard should tend to any structural repairs, now that he's decided to stay on for the term as an instructor."

"Is Harn also the Knorth one-hundred commander?" she asked hopefully.

"No, silly. In the barracks you are, in all but name, as I am in mine—although," he added with a note of complacence, "the Ardeth have twice as many cadets as you do. No, Harn Grip-hard will only intervene there if you make a real mess of things."

So it *was* a test of sorts. Damn, blast, and hell.

"Seriously, Timmon, how do you handle being a master ten?"

"Oh, I leave it all to my second ten-commander, of course. So does Gorbel, from what I hear. Why should we lordan be bothered with such mundane trifles?"

"Because we're training to become randon officers and the heads of our respective houses?"

Timmon laughed. "D'you really think the three of us will ever assume lordship? Gorbel is only at Tentir because you are. Why you're here, ancestors only know. I came because I enjoy sports and, frankly, to please my mother, who has ambitions for me. I may have older half-brothers, you see, but my parents were half-siblings, which counts for a lot in our house." He grinned. "Are you shocked? In the Knorth, don't twins often mate?"

"Not since Gerridon and Jamethiel Dream-weaver."

And if the High Council knew that Tori and I are twins, she thought uneasily, *what then? Would they throw us together or make sure that we never met again? Between them, the Master and the Dream-weaver bred the Fall. Between us, what might Tori and I produce?*

"Don't you have any ambitions of your own?" she asked Timmon.

"To enjoy myself, mainly. I wouldn't mind commanding the Southern Host as my father did, provided my staff did all the work. He was a great man, my father. But lordship sounds too much like hard work. Let cousin Dari have it if he wants it. Grandfather will probably live forever anyway, so why fret."

Before them, two horses collided and their riders tumbled, laughing, onto the ground. Jame flinched, then wondered why. The fall was nothing, given their training. What was it about horses in general that set her teeth on edge? Granted, her encounter last fall with the rathorn mare and her death's-head colt hadn't helped, but this—call it what it was: fear—predated that. Forgotten events still lurked like assassins in the shadowy pockets of her childhood. The ghost of one now rose—something about a dark gray stallion stained black with sweat and flecked with white foam . . . .

She remembered. It had been her father's warhorse Iron-jaw, the one that had turned into a haunt. The changer Keral had threatened to feed her to it.

Timmon was looking at her sideways.

"I have to ask: why *are* you at Tentir? What do you want?"

"A place to belong, I suppose. You wouldn't understand. Half of the time, I don't either."

"What a strange way to live. Don't you miss the Women's Halls?"

"No!"

He laughed. "I've heard something about your adventures there. No doubt they don't miss you either. My mother says Highborn girls often go through a hoyden stage. Obviously, you reached it later than most. You ran wild too long, she says, like a filly that's never been broken to ride. Someday, though, you'll settle down and realize what you really want."

"And what, pray, is that?"

"Why, what any woman wants: a good man, of course, or maybe several of them, preferably one at a time."

Jame grinned, showing the half-filled gap in her front teeth. Brier had been right both about the timing of regrowth and about the teething itch. "Like you? Like your grandfather, who worships tradition? Like Caineron, whose only god is power? Like Tori, who can't face who or what he is? The best man I know is a seven foot tall, ninety-five year old Kendar named Marcarn whom, ancestors know, I miss with all my heart."

"You," said Timmon, "are adorable. And more than a bit peculiar. I'd like to see you properly dressed or, better yet, undressed. We could have pleasant times together, you and I."

He wound a loose strand of her hair around his finger, using the excuse to trace the curve of her neck. Jame shivered and drew away.

"You'd only be disappointed," she said over her shoulder, turning to leave. "I've often been mistaken for a boy."

His voice, gay with laughter, followed her: "Now, where's the fun in that?"

III

THE DAYS PASSED, edging toward midsummer. Up and down the Riverland, the bad-tempered black cattle had been driven up into the mountain pastures to graze and the long horned sheep with them, shorn of their thick fleece. Flax was sown, cherries and strawberries picked. The apple crop was thinned to make the remaining fruit grow larger and swine feasted on the discards under drooping boughs. Grass grew thick toward hay-time, called the Minor Harvest, while oats, rye, and wheat ripened in the riverside flood-plains and water meadows for the Major Harvest at summer's end.

So far, so good, reported the Kendar harvest-master. Despite the previous year's neglect, when the Kencyr Host had marched south to fight the Horde rather than stay home to mind the fields, the Riverland might yet squeak through the next winter without famine.

Meanwhile, last year's stores were beginning to run out. Oatmeal, moldy cheese, and black bread hard enough to drive nails were supplemented by whatever forest, field, or sky could provide by way of fruit or game. Hart season would begin soon. Streams were eagerly fished or set with traps. The Silver itself, however, was left alone: anything hooked there was likely to snap the line or pull the fisherman in, never to be seen again.

Anyway, as Rue said, why risk offending the River Snake? Vant might laugh at that, but he didn't meddle with the Silver either.

The weirdingstrom had swept other, stranger game into the valley, both from the north and the south: black swans and fierce little hawks with pearly feathers shading to pale blue; dire elk whose eight foot antler-spans kept tangling in the undergrowth; lumpy desert creatures that caught cold in the crisp, mountain air and rent the night with their hacking coughs; flying frogs and things like black, leather kites that killed by wrapping themselves around the heads of their prey.

And there was something else.

One morning Jame and her ten went with the bow-legged horse-master to bring in fresh mounts from the upper field where the Knorth horses pastured.

It proved a frustrating task. The herd was on edge, easily spooked but unwilling to stray far from the paddock's lower fence.

"There's a predator somewhere about," said the master, peering up the slope from under his shaggy eyebrows and mopping his bald, perspiring head. He sniffed as if for a scent, but it would be a wonder, thought Jame, if he could smell anything, given that at some point long ago his nose had been smashed almost flat to his face.

At its top was a jumble of enormous boulders, many newly tumbled down from the mountains above.

Jame glimpsed a flicker of white among them and immediately thought of the phantom Whinno-hir Beltairi. As she shifted for a better look, however, the horses suddenly surged around her, all wild eyes and great, swinging flanks.

"Don't crowd the mares!" the horse-master was shouting. "They'll kick you if you get between them!"

Jame ducked under a gelding's belly and jumped for
the fence. What she hit, though, was the gate, which
swung open, taking her with it. It stopped with a jar that
sent her tumbling over its top rail, down between the
gate and the fence. The herd plunged through the opening and thundered off down the slope, pursued by sweating, shouting cadets. Brier gave Jame an unfathomable
look and then, more sedately, followed them as the whole
mob, equine and Kencyr, made for the underground
stables at a dead run.

"Perhaps in future, lady," said the master in his nasal
voice, eyeing her askance, "you should leave horse-wran-
gling to others."

Jame glanced again at the upper slope. Nothing white
showed now, but it had been there, and it hadn't been
a Whinno-hir.

A LUNCH OF BREAD, hard cheese, and milk followed,
with much subdued laughter and glances at the top table.
By then, everyone had heard about the stampede
through the great hall and the chaos it had caused below.

Afterward, Jame and her ten tried to stay awake during
an interminable lecture on strategy, delivered by a randon so battered that he appeared to have made every
mistake against which he was now warning them. When
he got excited, he pounded the desk with a wooden fist
or sometimes detached and threw it at a dozing cadet.

Their next class was held in the great hall of Old Tentir. They entered to find Senethar practice mats spread out on the flagstones and half a ten-command lounging on them. Jame slowed, recognizing Gorbel's heavy-lidded face, so like his father Caldane's that it set her teeth on edge. His four Highborn toadies eyed her askance as she approached and snickered among themselves. Behind them stood five young Caineron Kendar, their personal servants and cadets in their own right, watching Brier Iron-thorn with hard, set faces older than their years.

Gorbel rose casually to acknowledge the arrival of their instructor, a small, red-faced Coman sargent. His friends followed suit, waiting just long enough to make clear their opinion of a teacher so far beneath them in social rank and blood.

The lesson began with a demonstration of a simple water-flowing throw. One pulled an opponent off balance, pivoted back to belly, and threw him over one's hip. It didn't call for great strength, only good balance and proper leverage. As for falling, the mats were an unexpected luxury.

"Form a circle!" ordered the sargent and they did, one house taking the inner ring, the other the outer, face to face. "Salute and begin."

Jame's first opponent was a grinning Caineron Highborn who used the excuse to let his hands wander.

"I know a better game than this," he breathed in her ear.

"Perhaps, but can you play it without balls?"

She reached behind her, low, and squeezed. He gasped. As his grip involuntarily loosened, she threw him, hard.

The sargent frowned, knowing that something had happened but not what. He clapped. "Change!"

The pace quickened. Throw, fall, change; throw, fall, change, over and over. The cadets grimly settled down to the rhythmic thud of bodies hitting the mats. It seemed to go on forever, until breath burned in the lungs and sweat stung the eyes. Thirty minutes, sixty . . . sweet Trinity, did he mean to keep them at it the full two hours? However, if someone fell off onto the stone floor, he or she was permitted to quit. Jame saw first one, then another and another of Gorbel's cronies roll free and settle back to watch the fun. She was tempted to join them. This was the most sustained practice yet, worse than when she had tested in the Senethar because this time there were no rest breaks, or rather only one.

As he fell, a cadet grabbed both her cap and a handful of the hair coiled beneath.

The sargent glared as she interrupted the lesson's flow to disengage the other's grip. "You should cut that short, lady. Anyone who can grab it in a fight is going to have you at a disadvantage."

Grinning, the cadet tugged. Hard. Jame bent his wrist until he yelped with pain and let go. Then she twisted the black skein of hair back on top of her head and defiantly tugged the cap down over it. Other randon including Harn had said the same thing, admittedly with reason, but be damned if she was going to lose the only attractive feature she had left.

The lesson continued.

Throw, fall, change . . . and here was Gorbel.

This was the first time that the rotation of classes had brought them up against each other. He was younger than she had thought. Breathing hard, hair plastered with sweat to his bulging forehead, the Caineron lordan stared at her.

"You," he said heavily.

"Me," Jame agreed. She expected a sneer, but he looked merely exhausted and dogged. "Ready?"

In answer, he grabbed her jacket and threw her awkwardly. For a moment, she thought his legs were going to buckle under them both. On impulse, when her turn came, she threw him near the edge of the mat. His friends pulled him off, laughing at his half-hearted attempt to resist.

That left only a half dozen cadets in the game, Brier Iron-thorn among them. The Southron flowed through the moves, the only sign of effort a sheen of sweat that made her dark face gleam like polished wood. Her expression was calm and remote, as if her thoughts dwelt on the far side of the moon. It didn't change when one of the Caineron Kendar first threw, then kicked her viciously in the ribs.

Jame had heard that muffled thud before over the course of the practice without realizing what it was. Four times? Five? More? She should have recognized the hatred in the Kendars' eyes for one of their own who had escaped their lord's cruel grip. Their masters snickered. Her own ten stirred and muttered; they had seen what was happening long before she had. So must the instructor, but he had done nothing. Perhaps he felt that a turn-collar deserved no better. Brier picked herself up more slowly than before. That last kick had hurt.

Jame felt rage stir in her. *Careful*, she thought, as her current partner backed hastily away. *Don't over-react.* Then, *the hell I won't.*

She stalked across the mat toward the Kendar, who shrank back and looked quickly away. Here was one who either could not or would not met her eyes. They hadn't been matched before; he had been avoiding her. She clapped, and he jumped like a spooked horse.

He was taller than she was by at least a head. She had to reach up to touch his face and turn it, nails out only enough to prick although they still drew tiny drops of blood.

"Look at me." Her voice roughened with the undernote of a purr. "There. That's better. One should always meet one's enemies face to face, don't you think?"

He was a handsome, almost pretty boy, or would have been without terror distorting his face. A sudden stench announced that he had lost control of his bowels. She tapped him lightly on the cheek and let her hands slide down to grip his sleeves.

"Now, let's play. Throw me, or try."

Stiffly, he assumed the proper stance, took a deep breath, and turned to lift her over his hip. She leaned back and shifted her weight so that his buttocks shot past her. Nervous laughter rippled through the cadets. They had often played this trick on each other, but the Caineron was too rattled to counter it.

"Again."

White face beginning to blotch with red, he tried, and was caught off-balance, bent backward with her knee in the small of his back.

"Again."

This time she moved even as he did, rolling over his arm, landing on her feet in a crouch before him. Her grip shifted to a lock on his wrist. She twisted. He somersaulted over this fulcrum of pain and slammed down on the stone floor.

"There," said Jame, straightening up. "Isn't that better?"

The instructor clapped twice. "That's enough," he said. His voice shook and so did he. "Never, ever humiliate a fellow cadet that way."

"If not respect for one, then why for any?"

He gaped at her, mouth opening and closing. At another time, it would have been funny.

"Let it go," said Brier behind her.

Jame glanced at her. "If you wish. For now."

Dismissed, the rest of the command except Rue scattered to practice on their own until dinner.

Brier gave Jame an unreadable look. "What you did back there during the lesson, lady . . . it didn't help."

With that, she turned and walked away.

Jame stared after her. Dammit, the Southron was right. Terrorizing Kendar only made them more stubborn unless it broke them altogether, and what right had she to do either? Blood right, some would say. She was Highborn, and had just demonstrated everything that she hated about her own kind's casual abuse of power, to someone who had already suffered far too much from it.

"Has she had to put up with much more of this harassment?" Jame asked Rue.

The cadet squirmed. "A lot," she admitted, "usually not so obvious. She says she can deal with it. I wasn't supposed to tell you."

It seemed that either she scared people shitless or they thought she was too weak to protect her own. What a choice. Jame sighed. In every way, the road ahead was longer than she had realized.

CHAPTER X

Battles Old and New

Summer 41–2

I

SOMEONE SCREAMED.

For a blurry moment, half asleep and half awake, Jame thought it might have been herself.

She had dreamed again that she sat on the hearth of the over-heated Lordan's chambers, drinking and laughing drunkenly with that sly Randir, Roane. A servant had gone to fetch "dear little Gangrene" from the dormitory below. Anticipation stirred in her gut, and lower down. It was a long time since she had indulged in the old, sweet midnight games with her darling little brother. The poor fool probably thought he was safe here at the college.

Ha. You are my meat, boy, and Father has given you to me to devour, just as he will all the Kencyrath with his death. May it be soon. I am empty, and I hunger.

A hesitant footstep on the threshold and there he stood, flanked by two guards, the boy Ganth Grayling with sick terror on his face. Out of his eyes, however, stared someone else, as she did out of Greshan's. Sweet Trinity. Torisen.

Then had come the scream that had woken her, but not from either of them.

From below, Jame heard Vant's voice raised in a shout of exasperation. She grabbed the first clothing that came to hand, a long-tailed shirt, and pulled it on as she went quickly down the central stair to the second floor with Jorin dashing on ahead.

The dormitory was divided into two sections. To the left, as one faced the square, were the ten-commanders' individual rooms. To the right, each squad slept in a canvas cubicle rather like camping out inside, except that during the day the partitions were folded back against the walls. On a hot summer night like this, Jame would have expected them to be left open to catch any stray gasp of cool air. However, the Kendar apparently suffered less from extremes of temperature than the Highborn, for which she envied them. If only it would rain!

As she threaded through the canvas maze, pulling her long, black hair free of the shirt and letting it spill loose over her shoulders, Jame heard sleepy voices within raised in protest:

"Not again."

"Let us sleep, can't you?"

"Somebody, please, gag him with a dirty sock."

A scowling, tousled head popped out between canvas flaps. "Do you mind . . . oh!"

"Go back to sleep," Jame told him, and went on toward a murmur of voices. It came from the quarters closest to the southern fireplace, a position of honor held by her own ten.

"If you can't keep your filthy nightmares to yourself," Vant was saying with a kind of throttled fury, "go home. We don't need your sort here."

He spoke to the new cadet, Niall, who was sitting up in bed, knees clasped tightly under his chin. Thin and quiet by day, he looked gaunt and haunted by candle-light, and he was shivering. The rest of Jame's ten had gathered around him. Brier, as usual, held aloof but watchful in the background.

"You leave him alone, Ten," snapped Mint, to a mutter of agreement from the others. She sat on the edge of the cot and put an arm around the boy's hunched shoulders. "If you'd seen what he saw, you'd probably wet your bed every night."

Before Vant could answer, they all became aware of Jame.

"What's the matter?" she asked.

"Nothing that need concern you, lady." Vant gave her a smile that was mostly bared teeth. "Sorry you were disturbed." He turned back to Niall. "As for you . . ."

"This is my ten-command, you know." Jame slipped around him and perched on the chest at the foot of Niall's cot while Jorin dived under it and began happily to play with whatever he found there. "Now, what was it you saw?"

When the cadet only gawked at her, Mint answered.

"Lady, last winter while the rest of us stayed snug with the garrison at Gothregor (including you, Ten), Niall stowed away in a supply wagon and went south with the Host. He served as a messenger in the battle at the Cataracts. We don't know exactly what he saw there—he won't tell us—but it must have been awful. Now he's afraid that he'll fail Tentir because he can't stop the nightmares. He thinks only cowards have bad dreams."

Vant started to jeer, but Jame stopped him.

Not another Kest, she thought, *lost for lack of the right word.*

"I was at the Cataracts," she said. "It *was* terrible. The noise, the smell . . . the very ground shook. Then the Waster Horde came, wave on wave, breaking against the shield wall, until the grass was slimy with blood and all the horses screamed. The whole thing was a nightmare. Brier, you were there too, weren't you?"

In the shadows, the big Kendar stirred. "I was, but after the battle."

"So you missed the fun." Vant made it a sneer, as if glad at last to score a point against his rival.

"Fun?" Brier considered the word. "Not exactly. I was with the Southern Host when m'lord Pereden marched it out into the Wastes to meet the advancing Horde. Three million of them, some fifty thousand of us. Our center column clashed head on and was ripped apart. The sand drank our blood and the Wasters ate our flesh. I saw Commander Larch flayed and dismembered. It took her a long, long time to die. I was there when Pereden—" she paused, hunting for the right word, saying it at last with a curious twist—"fell. We didn't know that the left and right columns had survived. Those few of us who escaped joined one or the other of them and harried the Horde all the way to the Cataracts."

"Which is why," added Jame, "the Northern Host was able to reach the bottleneck at the Escarpment first. Otherwise, that would have been the end of us all."

There was silence for a moment as the three unlikely veterans remembered and the rest tried to imagine what horrors they had seen. For once, not even Vant could think of anything to say. Jame heard a murmur on the other side of the canvas wall and soft voices saying, "Hush!" The other ten-commands were listening.

Distant thunder grumbled and the air shifted restlessly. The walls stirred. Under the bed, Jorin engaged in mortal combat with a stray sock.

"Did you kill anyone in battle, lady?" asked Erim.

"Probably." Jame grimaced. "I had Kin-Slayer, y'see, and was trying to hack through the thick of things to give it to my brother. If ever a sword thirsted for blood, it's that one."

"And you actually managed to hang on to it?"

Vant, rallying, caused a ripple of nervous laughter. In practice, one way or another, Jame almost always managed to lose her weapon.

"This one I could barely get rid of," she answered grimly. "I tell you, that damn blade *likes* to kill, and it can cut through anything . . . if you know the trick."

The "trick" was to wear Father's emerald signet ring on one's sword-hand, as she had discovered by accident. She had tried to tell her brother, but didn't know if he had taken her seriously.

"Do you ever dream about it, lady?" asked Niall, looking at her askance. "The battle, I mean."

Jame considered. "Occasionally as a bloody muddle, which most of it was. Sometimes, though, it's all too clear. I have to get Kin-Slayer to my brother or he will die, but I don't know where he is and there are so many people in the way. Some of them are changers. They wear Tori's face and beg me to throw them the sword. When I don't, they change into my father and curse me: 'Child of darkness, filthy Shanir, die and be damned . . .'"

They were all staring at her.

"And then," she finished, somewhat lamely, "I wake up."

Quill's face had twisted with concentration. "Isn't there a song about a randon who shrieked all night long in his sleep before a battle, until his Kendar had to stuff tufts of wool in their ears? The next day he fought like a demon, but in silence because he was too hoarse to make a sound."

"I remember that one," said Killy eagerly. "He got behind the enemy and cut down a score of them before they even knew he was there. With everyone else roaring battle-cries, y'see, they didn't hear him until it was too late."

"Another Lawful Lie," said Vant scornfully.

"Maybe." Jame considered the story. "To me, though, it has the ring of truth."

"Then you don't think I'm a coward, lady?"

"Because you have nightmares? Of course not. Everyone has them. The more you see, the less these particular ones should bother you; but if you start running away from them, you may never stop."

Like Tori, in a way. He wasn't running now, but somehow he had been stopped dead in his tracks, and that wasn't good either.

She roused herself. "Enough. Go to sleep, all of you, and dream sweetly if you can. If you can't, well, it isn't the end of the world. And if you give Niall punishment duty for this," she added softly to Vant in passing, "you're a bigger fool than I thought . . . if that's possible."

A breath of fresh air met her on the stairs. As she reached the attic, the hole in the roof briefly flooded with light, followed at a slight interval by the thunder's growl. Jorin retreated to a corner; he disliked storms and hated getting wet. Jame crossed to the hole and leaned out of it.

The storm was approaching from the north, rumbling down the throat of the valley. Snake-tongues of lightning flickered across the sky, throwing the mountain sides into sharp relief and making the river gleam like its name.

Watching it come, Jame considered nightmares, specifically the one from which Niall's scream had woken her. No one now alive knew what had happened in that close, hot room, the night that Greshan had summoned his younger brother up to it; yet, somehow, the memory lingered, like the stink of the gorgeous coat that her uncle had worn, now resigned to a chest in his former apartment. Each dream brought her closer to some terrible truth. For herself, whatever it was, she felt she could endure it, but could Tori? It hadn't occurred to her until that night, when she had seen his eyes set in their father's terrified face, that it might also be dragging her brother along, one nightmare at a time, toward an ultimate horror.

Damn and blast. Tori was stronger than her in so many ways, but not in this.

The air fidgeted this way and that, now hot, now deliciously cool, lifting tendrils of Jame's loose hair. Leaves began to fret. Now came the wind, roaring in the tree tops, making boughs toss until the whole forest heaved like an ocean gone mad. A blinding flash, a boom like the end of time, and rain fell in a shower of icy arrows mixed with stinging hailstones.

Well, they would cope. Whatever haunted Tentir wasn't stronger than both of them, as long as they supported each other.

She stayed, drinking in the tumult, until at last the storm rumbled off down the Riverland, and one by one the stars crept out of hiding.

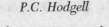 

II

AT BREAKFAST, Niall still looked haggard but more in control of himself, answering her raised eyebrow with a slight, shy duck of his head. Talk and laughter moved freely back and forth across the hall, as if the previous night's storm had broken more than the oppressive heat. Only Vant looked sour, as if he had swallowed something nasty. Jame sat at the head of her table and Brier at the foot. They both tended to be quiet in company, but for the first time Jame felt included in the group even while it respected her reserve. She wondered if Brier Ironthorn felt the same way.

Then she remembered: the Southron had said that she had been there when Pereden . . . fell. What an odd, ambiguous word. Did Timmon know? Should she tell him? Better not.

The day's first class—archery with a Jaran ten—passed without incident, except for Erim hitting the mark every time. His aim was indeed very good, almost uncanny, for someone who looked as if he shot at random from a truly awful pose.

Next came sword practice with the Danior, which again provided no surprises. As always, Jame was quickly disarmed.

"Next time maybe we should bind the hilt to your hand," said the randon in charge, not altogether joking.

After lunch came a work detail with an Edirr ten.

The largest of the quake fissures in the outer training field had been spanned half-way down with a wooden bridge. Normally, the steep ditch was dry, but the previous night's storm had sent a flash flood down it to the

Silver, piling debris against the bridge's footing. Until the mess was cleared away, it was impossible to know if the structure had been damaged. Consequently, the two tens were set to removing the tangle of broken branches under the guidance of a red-faced sargent.

It was hard, dirty work. Mud cemented the makeshift dam together and mud backed up against it, under a foot of murky water. Moreover, the sides of the fissure were slick with more of the same, where they weren't jagged with exposed boulders. Cadets kept slipping and falling while the sargent got redder and redder with shouting at them to watch what they were doing and to stop playing silly buggers, dammit.

Then he was called up-field to help the horse-master. A stallion had gotten loose among the mares and must be captured before they, not being in season, kicked their eager suitor to pieces.

Dar started to climb out of the ditch, but an Edirr cadet pushed him back in. When he had scrambled up the opposite side, outraged, the Knorth all found themselves on one side and the Edirr on the other. There was a moment's speculative silence, then a grin that seemed to spread from face to face.

"Red clover, red clover, send Rue over!"

Rue plunged down the slope, plowed through the muddy water, and scrambled up the opposite side. At the top, the Edirr girl who had called caught and flung her back down to land with a great splash at the fissure's bottom. She rejoined her own side, muddy from head to foot.

"Red clover, red clover, send Honey over!" she called back to her opponent in a kind of throttled shout, as none of them wanted to attract attention.

Honey, in turn, was sent flying to a chorus of muted Knorth jeers.

Then Erim bulled his way up and through the enemy line. "I capture you," he said to Honey, and bore her back to the Knorth side.

Jame, Brier, and the Edirr ten-commander watched from the bridge, or rather the Edirr kept watch against the sargent's return. If he had any hesitation about his role, it was only that he couldn't join in the fun.

Jame didn't know what to do. The cadets were clearly having a wonderful time, but they weren't doing the work assigned to them and would be in trouble if the sargent caught them at it. "I should stop this," she said, "or shouldn't I?"

Brier gave her an impassive look. "You are master ten of your house," she said—that, and no more.

It hadn't been fair to ask her, and Jame knew it. She had to start making her own command decisions.

Swearing under her breath, she approached her cadets from behind and touched Dar on the shoulder. Before she could speak, he reached back and seized her, apparently thinking that she was the captured Honey bent on escape. The next moment, she was in mid-air. Sky and earth wheeled past, dotted with startled faces, and then the brown water at the ditch's bottom leaped up to meet her.

Jame emerged sputtering, mud in her eyes, her hair, her mouth. A rock in the river bed shifted under her hand as she tried to rise and she lurched forward again into the mire, face first. The cadets on both banks were staring down at her, appalled. She sat in the filthy water, feeling it seep through her clothes, considering her situation,

For Trinity's sake, Tori had said, *don't make fools of us both*.

Had she come to Tentir for this? What hope was there that she would do any better in future? Maybe she should give up, go back to Gothregor, stop trying to accomplish the impossible.

But was this really that much worse than the Women's Halls? Jame thought about that for a moment, then burst into laughter.

"Knot stitches," she said.

The sargent returned, horrified to find his lord's sister sitting at the bottom of a muddy ditch, laughing like a lunatic. He didn't understand why she found a needlework phrase so funny. Neither did the cadets, but it was infectious. As they resumed work, one only had to catch another's eye and murmur "knot stitch" for them both to burst out in giggles.

It was in this high good humor and in wet, filthy clothes that the Knorth reported for the last lesson of the day. And that was where things began to go seriously wrong.

III

THEY SHOULD HAVE been bound for a reading lesson —hard work for most but a welcome rest for Jame. Instead, they were told to clean up as best they could and then to report to a third story room in Old Tentir where none of them had ever been before.

Their destination overlooked the inner square, high enough to make some of the cadets turn pale. Gorbel's ten-command waited for them. The Caineron were jeering at the Knorths' muddy clothes when the Commandant entered, followed by a richly dressed, unfamiliar Highborn.

A surprised murmur ran through the Caineron ranks: "Corrudin."

"It's Corrudin, Lord Caldane's uncle and chief advisor."

"What's he doing here?"

If Gorbel knew, he didn't say. Jame thought she saw a flicker of alarm in his eyes, but he instantly hooded them, his face becoming as expressionless and dull as a toad's.

"Sit down, all of you. I see that some of you recognize our guest."

The Commandant's manner was as suave as ever, his half-smile as elusive and ironic, but he was wary too, and watchful. He reminded Jame of Jorin, feigning nonchalance before the pounce.

"M'lord Corrudin has gifted us with his presence today in response a certain . . . er . . . incident that took place during a recent lesson."

It *was* about the Senethar class, thought Jame as she and the other cadets settled crossed-legged on the floor, furtively tugging at wet clothes to ease their cling. Could this elegant, elderly Highborn be here to lecture the Caineron about their harassment of Brier Iron-thorn? Then she caught a fleeting smirk on the face of the Kendar whom she in turn had humiliated. No. Justice for the Southron wasn't on anyone's mind.

"Normally," the Commandant was saying, "this subject arises later in your training. However, since there are no fewer than three lordan currently at Tentir and some of you have already experienced their . . . er . . . effect, it was thought wise to bring up the topic early. This is for the benefit of you, the Kendar who serve with them. M'lord, if you will . . . ?"

He invited the Highborn forward with a sweeping salute and withdrew to the shadows at the back of the room where he stood, a motionless, alert presence.

The Highborn advanced at his leisure, his dark purple robe, crusted with gold embroidery, swishing across the floor in the silence. His face was finer cut and more austere than most Caineron, his silvery hair slicked back from a sharp widow's peak. He looked far more like the leader of a house than his over-weight, over-bearing nephew. Jame wondered why Caldane was Lord Caineron and not his uncle, and whether Corrudin resented it. He didn't look like a man to suffer fools, gladly or otherwise.

"I thank Commandant Sharp-tongue for this opportunity," he said, "and for his faithful service to our house." His voice, smooth and melodious, made Jame twitch, as if at something just beyond her range of hearing. Out of the corner of her eye, she saw Gorbel's stubby hands tighten on his knees.

"As you Kendar know," he said, ignoring the two lordan, "you are bound by our god to obey the Highborn. Normally, you are given no choice in the matter just as, normally, you are given no choice in what house you serve. You stay where you are born." His gaze flickered over Brier, who returned it wooden-faced. "Now, it would follow, would it not, that you are bound to obey every command given to you—even if some are . . . ill-advised?"

Jame leaned forward, listening intently. Was Caldane's chief advisor about to warn them about Honor's Paradox, which Caldane himself was doing everything he could to circumvent?

"I do not speak of those orders issued by our liege lords, of course," Corrudin continued smoothly. "Who is the judge of honor, if not they? No, I refer to lesser Highborn, not so old or wise as their masters, whom they too must obey."

Cadets were nodding. Born to servitude, they liked to hear that all Highborn but a few also had limited power. Jame tried not to fidget. She suspected that this was all about her, but didn't yet see how.

"That said, it follows that as future randon, and as valuable assets to your respective houses, you must learn how to resist the folly, even the malice, of such minor Highborn as would misuse their power over you, as has recently occurred."

Ah, that was it. No wonder the Caineron boy had smirked.

"I believe a demonstration is in order." The Highborn turned suddenly to Gorbel. "Lordan, if you would oblige, give one of your comrades a foolish command."

Gorbel blinked and stirred, taken as much by surprise as Jame and the others, but hiding it better. For a moment he returned his great-uncle's sleek smile with a stony glower, and then he twisted around where he sat to regard his ten. His hooded eyes swept over them, and all but one failed to meet his stare. That one, a Highborn, grinned back at him, but his amusement quickly faltered.

"No," he said, with a laugh shaken by disbelief.

"Yes. Kibben, stand on your head."

The cadet gaped at him, then lurched to his feet, his face twisting between astonishment and horror. Jame recognized him as the master of the Kendar boy whom she had made pay for Brier's harassment. Neither master nor servant was smiling now.

"Resist," murmured Corrudin. It was more than encouragement.

"You heard me," said Gorbel. Sweat trickled down his face, channeled slantwise by the heavy lines of his scowl. "Do it."

The cadet staggered between the Cainerons' opposing wills. Both ten-commands had scrambled to their feet and were backing away from the conflict.

Also instinctively in retreat, Jame shot a glance at the silent figure at the back of the room. Why didn't the Commandant stop this? All three were Highborn of his house, and two were cadets presumably under his protection as the current master of the college.

Then she remembered Sheth standing outside the door that first night while within her brother fought with Lord Ardeth for his very soul, and again, in the hall when the Randir had tempted Harn Grip-hard to become the beast that he feared he was. Here again was that cool assessment of power, Lord Caineron's chief advisor against the Caineron's future lord. If either should break, better here, better now, than later when so many others might fall with them. Such had been the bitter lesson of the White Hills, when her own father's ruin had nearly brought down the entire Kencyrath.

Kibben made an odd, choking noise. He bent, put his hands and the top of his head on the floor, and swung up his legs. For a moment he tottered upside-down, the long tails of his foppish jacket falling into his face. Then he crashed over like a tree falling, all of a piece. The wooden floor shook.

Gorbel smiled. "Good boy," he said softly.

Suddenly Jame realized something that perhaps she should have guessed before: these Highborn cadets weren't Gorbel's friends. They were his father's spies. No wonder Caldane had received news so quickly of the training incident and sent his uncle to assess the situation.

Corrudin stood unmoved. He might never have exerted himself if not for the flicker of thwarted rage in his eyes, quickly masked. However, Jame had seen it. He hadn't expected to lose against his lumpish, despised grand-nephew. Now he knew, as did she, in whose blood the true power ran; and for all his smooth veneer, that knowledge infuriated him.

"Well," he said lightly, as Kibben's servant helped the shaken Highborn to his feet and tried to prevent him from again attempting a head-stand. "There you see a perfect example of misused authority. My thanks, lordan, for your assistance. However, we have yet to see how such abuse effects a Kendar. So, another demonstration. My lady, if you please."

He turned to Jame and drew her forward with languid wave of his hand. Then he did the same to Brier Ironthorn.

"I think this time I will propose the order," he said, slowly circling them, beginning again to enjoy himself.

Jame's skin crawled. This was going to be bad. She met Brier's eyes, as green and cool as pond moss, and as lacking in expression. Only weeks of observation told her that the Southron was braced to show no emotion, whatever happened.

"My," said the Highborn, still circling, looking them up and down. "How dirty you both are, but especially you, my lady." A ripple of nervous laughter went through the cadets. Under it, Corrudin's voice sank to a murmur. "Been playing in the mud, have we? How appropriate, given all that your house has dragged us through. I was in the White Hills. I saw. Blood, and mud, and more blood, pooling in the hollows where the wounded drown in it. There also the honor of your house died, as we see yet again in your presence here. And you, Iron-thorn, were once one of us. Your mother died in our service. You disgrace her memory."

The Kendar stirred, but silver-gray eyes locked and held jade green: *Look at me, not at him. Don't listen. Don't react. Don't give the bastard the satisfaction.*

Corrudin made a slight sound of annoyance.

"So you are theirs now, body and soul. Very well. It is only fitting, then, that you kiss their filthy boots. Girl, give this turn-collar the order."

Jame lurched as his will crushed down on her. Such power . . . ! How had Gorbel contested it? But then he hadn't been its primary target. As if from a great distance, she could hear the cadet Kibben struggling to obey Gorbel's last command, over and over again. Between them, grand-nephew and grand-uncle had broken him, perhaps beyond repair.

"You heard me," Corrudin whispered in her ear, a smile lurking in his voice. "Do it, you stupid little bitch."

She turned on him. "Back. Off."

The Highborn stiffened. His look of astonishment changed to utter horror as, step by step, he found himself retreating backward towards the window. The low sill caught him behind the knees. He flailed for a moment, trying to regain his balance, then fell. They heard him hit the tin roof of the arcade two flights below, then the ground.

Gorbel gave Jame a slow, sleepy smile. "Good girl," he said.

 **IV**

CONSIDERABLE CONFUSION ENSUED.

Cadets rushed to the window and those hardy enough to brave the height leaned out to gape down. Alarmed cries and questions rose from the square below. The cadets answered in a babble of shouts that enlightened no one and, in future days, gave rise to some truly startling rumors.

Meanwhile, freed from restraint, Kibben stood on his head in the corner.

Jame hadn't moved. She felt as if she had blown out her brains with one searing act of will power. Trinity, where had that come from . . . and was it apt to happen again? What she had done to the Randir Tempter was nothing compared to this. It had been like a berserker flare, but much more focused and ruthless. If she had ordered the very stones of Tentir to collapse on them all, perhaps they would have.

Brier held her elbow, steadying her.

"Lady, sometimes you worry me."

Jame gave a shaky laugh. "Not half as much as I worry myself."

The Commandant winnowed through the swarm of cadets, separating Caineron from Knorth—not that either stunned house had thought yet to turn on the other.

"This . . . er . . . lesson is concluded, and with it the class day. Dismissed. Someone, please escort Cadet Kibben to the infirmary, if you can get him upright. You," he said to Jame, "wait for me in my office."

Only then did the consequences of her act strike her. Sweet Trinity, he was going to expel her immediately. No, the entire Randon Council would set her up as the butt for archery practice and then award prizes for the best shots. Erim was a cinch to win that one, if they let him compete.

"All right?" asked Brier. It took Jame a moment to realize what she meant: *If I let go, will you fall over?*

"I think so," she said, somewhat confusedly, and the Southron withdrew her support.

The cadets filed out, shooting her stunned looks in passing. They took Kibben with them, horizontal, one cadet at his head, another at his feet, while he continued to grope desperately for the floor. Only when everyone had gone did Jame realize that she had no idea where the Commandant's office was.

Well, that wasn't quite true: he sometimes reviewed the cadets from a second story balcony. That might be attached either to his living quarters or to his office, or perhaps to both. In fact, leaning out the window, she could see it below, to the left. Until she meant to cap her day's exploits with a demonstration of wall-scaling, she needed a stair. That should be easy enough to find. After all, her ten had used one to reach the third floor.

However, she hadn't taken into account Old Tentir's confusing innards, or her own rattled wits. Once away from the windows and daylight, she quickly became lost in the maze of dusty corridors. This was ridiculous, she thought. After all, as the Talisman she had mastered the layout of an entire city. However, complex though it was, Tai-tastigon hadn't been deliberately built to bewilder. Here, even straight hallways seemed to take a perverse pleasure in wandering. Where was Graykin when she needed him? Dammit, she was going to be late for her own expulsion.

A dingy, long tailed rat made her jump as it broke cover and scurried down the passage away from her.

Suddenly, a great paw of a hand, all claws, shot out of a swinging panel down by the floor, seized the rat, and snatched it back inside. Jame hadn't realized where she was, much less that the feeding flap to Bear's prison was double-hinged. She knelt and cautiously pushed it open a crack. A gust of hot, foul air breathed through it into her face. She could see Bear's massive form hunched against the glow of the fireplace. He bent his shaggy head to what he held in his hands. The rat screamed once, and then was silent. Jame eased the panel shut on the sound of strong teeth ripping wetly at the small, furry carcass and crunching its bones.

Around the next corner came a glimmer of daylight. Jame followed it to a window which again overlooked the inner square. For all her wandering, she had ended up in the room next to the one where she had started out. On the other hand, the Commandant's balcony was now directly below her, one story down. She surveyed the square. In this, the free period before dinner, it was nearly empty.

The Coman cadet from the Falconer's class whom she now knew as Gari crossed the arena, surrounded to the waist by a swarm of bouncing grasshoppers. He didn't seem to have any control over what kind of insect he attracted, although they did seem in some way to reflect his current mood. A cry of dismay greeted him as he entered his barracks. They shouldn't complain, thought Jame. The last time, after a particularly miserable work-detail cleaning latrines, it had been a swarm of stink-beetles.

Swinging her legs over the window ledge, she dropped lightly onto the balcony.

"Most people use the door," said the Commandant's voice from inside.

"Sorry, ran." Jame brushed aside a filmy curtain and entered, wet boots squelching, leaving a trail of muddy prints. "I got lost."

It was a large room, indirectly lit by windows on either side of the balcony. These were shaded with taut, peach-colored cloth, probably old tent canvas, vertically slashed to allow the breeze to edge through. The filtered light cast a mellow glow over walls covered with exquisitely detailed murals.

The Commandant lounged in a chair slightly back from one of the windows, his long, elegantly booted legs stretched out before him and crossed at the ankles. Silver flashed: he was whittling a bit of wood with a small knife. Although it was hard to tell with his face in shadow, Jame thought that he sounded tired.

"This is the Map Room," he said, with a languid wave of his hand. "Here you see accurate depictions of all our major battles on Rathillien, and in the cabinets below are accounts of the participants. Yes, that one is the Cataracts."

The mural in question occupied a large portion of the northern wall. Jame recognized Hurlen, that town of wooden towers built on many islets at the convergence of the Silver and the Tardy. There was the Upper Meadow where the Host had camped; there, the Lower Huddles, along which she had been riding when the Caineron charge had come over the crest on top of her; there, off to the left, the mysterious, lethal Heart of the Woods where her brother and Pereden had fought.

Looking closer, she saw tiny figures including one in black, repeated at different places in the field. By their growing size, she could trace her brother's progress through the conflict, except that several times he appeared to be two places at once.

"That is one of the mysteries of the Cataracts," said the Commandant, watching her. "Who was the rider in black on a white horse who suddenly appeared in the midst of the battle? My lord Caldane claims that the High Lord sent a decoy into the field to lessen his own chances of being killed. Why, then, a white horse, when everyone knows Torisen's mount is black?"

"That was by accident," said Jame, still looking at the map. "So was my presence in the Caineron charge. I was just trying to get across the field. Also, I'm the one who . . . er . . . borrowed your warhorse later. Sorry, but it really was an emergency."

"I will take your word for it and not press to know why you, of all people, tried to ride Cloud bareback. Interesting. That answers quite a few questions, if not why you arrived there and again here wearing a Tastigon knife-fighter's jacket."

"It's called a *d'hen* and with due respect, ran, that's all I will tell you about it."

"I see." He leaned back, hands dropping with their work into his lap. "Now, did I or did I not request that you not break any more instructors?"

Jame swallowed. "You did, ran. Sorry. Is he badly hurt?"

"A cracked collarbone and many bruises. Worse, only by concentrating can he prevent himself from backing up, regardless of what lies behind him. I would say that Kibben is avenged, and then some. Out of curiosity, may I ask what happened?"

So he hadn't been close enough to hear. Jame told him what Corrudin had tried to make her do. "It would have destroyed Brier," she concluded, "and she's already been hurt far too much by my kind. It might also have destroyed me. I suddenly thought, maybe that's what he wants, and be damned if I'm going to be forced into it."

"A good instinct," murmured the randon. "It was his desire, no, his demand, that he be allowed to try. A powerful Shanir, that, and dangerous. After all, he brings out the worst in everyone. Truth for truth, Knorth. You would have done my house a service if you had broken his neck, but then we would probably have had civil war. There will be trouble enough as it is, but that needn't concern you. He may have also influenced the worst in me when I allowed the test; however, I had just heard that you were sitting in a mud puddle, having hysterics."

"And, as lordan, if I should break, better here than later."

He gave her a shadowy, fleeting smile. "I see you understand."

"But ran, what I did to Corrudin, whether he deserved it or not, wasn't that also a gross abuse of power? I can't seem to get it right. First I can't exert control over an arrogant twit like Vant; then I force a Shanir Highborn to commit defenestration. Maybe I don't belong here after all."

"With that power, where would you go?" He spoke softly, a voice out the gathering shadows, giving shape to her own fears. "Untrained as you are, who is safe against you? Not enemies, not friends, perhaps not even your own brother."

He shifted to prop his chin on his fist. She felt the pressure of his assessing eyes and the keen mind behind them at work on the problem. On her. "It seems to me," he said, "that you hate your own blood and its inherent power. Perhaps that mistrust is warranted. Dark things stir in you, girl. I sense them. But part of what you are is also the blessing, or the curse, of our god. Your position in the Kencyrath is unique. You are a Shanir, a Highborn, the Knorth Lordan, and a female. If you don't learn how to control your innate abilities, either they will destroy you or you will fall back into the trap that you came here to escape. Do you see another course?"

"N-no, ran." And she didn't, short of leaving her people behind forever. But if she returned to Tai-tastigon as the Talisman, she would still be herself. *If you start running away*, she had told Niall, speaking of nightmare, *you may never stop*. The same held true here, even more so.

He leaned back again, into shadow. "Tentir is a testing ground. If it eases your mind, I promise that by the time you leave, you will know beyond a doubt if you have succeeded or failed."

Jame's heart gave a leap.

"Then I'm not expelled, ran?"

"No. You are riding the rathorn now, to what fate I have no idea, but it would be unwise of me to interfere. I believe, however, that I should assign you extra duty for damaging the arcade roof, say, by repairing it. Please leave the normal way, through the door. The college has had enough excitement for the time being."

Her foot was on the threshold when he spoke again, out of the gathering darkness:

"By the way, you also should know that the Randir Tempter has returned to her duties at Tentir—prematurely, I would have thought, but here she is. Take care, Knorth. She has no love for your house or for you."

"Yes, ran. Thank you." She saluted him and left.

Only on the way out did she recognize what the Commandant had been carving. It was a little, wooden soldier.

This time, she found the stair easily and was descending to the main hall when a mound of dirty clothes on a pair of muddy legs entered from New Tentir. Jame wasn't sure about the legs, but she recognized the mud.

"Rue?"

The clothes dropped and there was the border cadet waist deep in them, gaping at her.

"Lady! You're still here!"

"Of course I am. Oh, you mean I haven't been kicked out yet. No, but we have to repair the roof."

"That's all?" A huge grin split the girl's face. "My, won't Vant be surprised."

"What's all this about?" Jame asked, indicating the sprawling heap.

Rue shrugged. "Vant gave our ten punishment duty for the mud fight. It's laundry day down in the fire timber hall, and we have to wash the entire barracks' dirty underwear."

At that moment, Vant himself entered the hall. "You, shortie, what're these clothes doing on the floor? Can't stay out of the dirt, eh?" Then he saw Jame, and turned his start into a sideways salute with eyes averted. "Your possessions are packed, lady. We can have you on the road to Gothregor before dinner."

"Oh, can you." Jame finished her descent at a leisurely stroll. She had no impulse whatsoever to lose her temper: after Corrudin, this seemed like a minor affair and Vant, for all his six feet of arrogant bluster, a bug not worth squashing. "Such unseemly haste, but then every time you turn around, you apparently expect to find me gone. Well, now you can relax. At least this side of the autumn cull, I'm not going anywhere."

Others of her ten had entered as she spoke, each with arms full of laundry. Vant was staring at her now, open-mouthed.

"You throw Lord Caineron's chief advisor out a third story window, and the Commandant doesn't expel you? Is he insane?"

"You may ask him that, with my blessing. In the meantime, I rescind your punishment order. Each ten will do its own washing, as usual. And in future you will clear any such order with me before you issue it. I'll be making a list"-*as soon as I can find a reliable master ten to consult*, she thought—"specifying what duties are yours and what are mine."

Vant stood rigid, staring straight ahead. "Lady, I can't read."

Jame remembered that he had indeed lost most of his points in the entry trials on that score.

"Learn," she said, and walked out.

Rue followed her, trailing clothes as she sorted out the muddiest of them. "What about yours, lady?"

Jame plucked at her shirt, feeling it unglue from her skin and bits of half-dry mud rattle down between her breasts. Head to foot, she was a mess.

"I need a bath," she said, "or better yet, a swim."

CHAPTER XI

The White Lady

Summer 42

I

NO ONE SWAM in the Silver by choice: those who did tended not to come out, nor were their bodies ever found. The Merikit blamed the River Snake. Jame believed them, having been dropped halfway down the Snake's gullet at Kithorn. However, the river's tributaries were generally considered to be safe.

South of Tentir, one such stream tumbled down through a series of falls, basins, and rapids. Jame heard the water's roar as she approached on a path hacked through rampant cloud-of-thorn bushes, also the laughter of cadets who had had the same idea and a head start on her. She stripped off her filthy clothing as she went, mindful of those reaching three-inch thorns.

Here a rock thrust up into the afternoon sun. Dropping her bundle of clothes at its base, she climbed toward the sound of water, untangling her mud-clotted hair as she went. At the top she was met by the delicious tingle of cold spray on her bare, hot skin and a cool breath that lifted sweaty tendrils from her face. Across the gorge, the stream plunged over boulders, half rapids, half falls, into a wide, oblong cauldron. The swiftest water flowed past on the far side of some large, flat-topped rocks into a stony bottleneck, then down into the next pool. The rest of the basin swirled slowly in an ever-renewing backwater. Heads bobbed in it, turned up open-mouthed to stare at her. Well, let them look. She poised defiantly on the brink for a moment, then dived.

It occurred to Jame in mid-air that jumping headfirst into unfamiliar water was not very smart and, sure enough, she barely missed a submerged ledge.

Fed by mountain snows, the water was cold enough to jolt the heart. It was also surprisingly deep once away from its treacherous margin. A chasm opened in its bed, gaping down below the reach of light—the work, surely, of the River Snake's writhing rather than of mere erosion. Fish hung over its terraces, motionless except for the shimmer of their scales in the mottled light. Then, in the flick of an eye, they were gone. Through the cloud of dirt drifting off of her skin, Jame thought she saw something below in the abyss, something that stirred and began slowly to rise.

A hand touched her shoulder. Jame lost her breath in a flurry of bubbles and surfaced, gasping. Timmon's golden head bobbed up beside her.

"You scared me," he said. "People don't usually dive off Breakneck Rock head first." He looked at her closely. "Your teeth are chattering and your lips are turning blue with the cold. Come on."

He swam to one of the flat midstream rocks and climbed up onto it. Turning, he offered her his hand. Mindful that her gloves were with the rest of her clothes, on shore, Jame scrambled up without his help and stretched out face down on the rock, hands tucked under her elbows. The stone was blessedly warm. Slowly, the memory faded of what she thought she had seen in the depths. A leviathan in a puddle indeed—not that it would have been the first time she had seen such a thing.

The other swimmers were slipping out of the pool and departing, either through tact or out of sheer embarrassment. At that moment, Jame didn't care which.

"Ah," she said with a contented sigh, relaxing. "This is nice."

Timmon cradled his head on folded arms, regarding her askance. She thought he was going to ask her about the defenestration of Corrudin, but word of that mishap apparently hadn't yet reached him.

Instead, he said, "No one would mistake you for a boy, but I can count every one of your ribs. You really should eat more."

"So everyone tells me, but I think my sense of taste was permanently damaged in the Haunted Lands. How would you like to dine day after day on whimpering vegetables?"

"Not much. Did they really?"

"When they weren't groaning or screaming, and the potatoes' eyes followed you reproachfully around the room. We won't even discuss the cabbage heads or what was in them."

"Thank you. I think I've already lost my taste for supper."

He, at least, needn't worry about starving, any more than about growing fat. Through streamers of wet, black hair, she regarded the slim, nicely muscled body stretched out beside her, alabaster white except for his tanned face where the sun had brought out an unexpected garnish of freckles. He grinned at her and she looked quickly away, surprised to discover by the heat in her own face that she was blushing.

They were lying close enough together to feel each other's warmth. Timmon ran a fingertip lightly over her skin. With an effort, Jame held still, although the hairs on her arm quivered and rose.

He smiled. "You aren't used to being touched, are you?"

Hit, pushed, kicked, occasionally thrown off high buildings, yes . . . but no, mere touching wasn't a common experience for Jame. Neither was being hit by rocks.

"Hey!" said Timmon, rousing, as a pebble bounced off his bare back.

Two figures stood on Breakneck Rock. For a moment, Jame had the strangest feeling that all of this had happened before, only that man in a bright coat had been someone else, and so had she. A scrap of dream, a bitter rind of helplessness and shame . . . or had it been she on the rock, looking down scornfully at a thin, naked boy trying futilely to cover himself?

But the newcomers proved to be only Gorbel, his scarlet coat aglow like a banked fire in the gathering twilight, and one of his friends. The latter leered down at them.

"Fast work, Ardeth!" he shouted over the waterfall's clamor. "At least save us a bit of Knorth thigh!"

As Timmon swore back good-naturedly, Jame regarded the Caineron Lordan, who stared back at her without expression. Clearly, he had been pleased by her handling of his grand-uncle, as had been the Commandant. Corrudin must normally keep well in the background for his name never to have come up before outside his own house. Was he the brains behind Caldane's otherwise mindless drive for power? Caineron politics obviously were far more complex than she had realized.

Someone was shouting. The words were broken by distance, water, and tree, but they were coming closer. Again came the cry, clearer now:

". . . rathorn! There's a rathorn in the woods!"

The second Caineron plunged out of sight—from the sound of it, into a thorn bush—but Gorbel had turned and now stood as if rooted to the spot. Then he began, slowly, to retreat backward toward the rock's slippery edge.

Jame and Timmon jumped to their feet.

"Watch out!" Timmon shouted, but too late: Gorbel's foot came down on vacant air. He tottered for a moment, arms wind-milling wildly, then fell. He landed with a great splash and immediately sank. The water turned red. Trinity, if he had hit the ledge . . .

Timmon dived in after him. On the verge of following, Jame froze.

Something white had emerged on top of the rock; something like a horse, but clad underneath in bands of ivory armor from throat to loins. Ivory also masked its face like a battle helm, and out of it grew two horns, the smaller between flared nasal pits, the larger, wickedly curved, between deep-set ruby eyes. It stared down at Jame, and bared its fangs with a long, soft hiss of satisfaction.

Jame felt her jaw drop. The last time she had seen the rathorn colt, it had only been a foal. Time passes: it had grown.

Timmon surfaced with a thrashing, sputtering Gorbel. The back-flop had apparently saved the latter's neck, but not taught him how to swim.

"Help!" Timmon shouted, and flinched as Gorbel's flailing fist caught him in the nose. Then the weight of sodden clothing dragged them both down again.

Rathorn be damned. Jame dived in.

Again, the shock of cold water, again the glimmering depths, with two figures sinking into them. Their struggle had taken them out beyond the ledge. Timmon was trying to strip off the deadly coat, which seemed to have developed a dozen extra arms, while Gorbel clutched at him with a drowning man's panic. Jame swam after them. Her ears throbbed in time to her heart-beat and her lungs ached by the time she caught up. The Caineron, mercifully, finally went limp. She hooked her nails in the coat and ripped, releasing a fresh cloud of red dye. They wrestled the remains off a now unconscious Gorbel and struck out for the surface, taking him with them.

Far below in the rock shadows, eyes as large and unblinking as dinner plates thoughtfully watched them go.

Gasping, Knorth and Ardeth dragged the Caineron ashore. Gorbel made a gurgling sound. Timmon turned him on his side as he began to vomit water and what was left of his lunch.

They were on a spit of rock between the upper basin and the first of a series below, with water thundering down through the narrow throat of a chasm at one end. The noise covered the sound of approaching hooves. Jame had no doubt, however, what had just breathed down the back of her neck. She turned and found herself eye to eye with the rathorn colt. His nasal tusk came up almost gently under her chin, lifting it, obliging her to rise or be impaled.

Something red flew out of the water with a wet sound—*p-toot!*—as if it had been spat. Gorbel's coat whacked the colt in the head and flung its dismembered arms around his neck. He squealed and reared, fore-hooves flailing, rear slipping on the wet rock. Over he went, backward, to a shout of alarm from Timmon and a squawk from Gorbel.

Jame ran.

Below Breakneck Rock, a wall of thorns kept her beside the river as it snaked down the mountain side from wide pool to narrow rapids, from outthrust rock spit to cleft gorge. The roar of water deepened as more streams joined it, covering any sound of pursuit, and she must watch where she placed her bare feet rather than look back. There was no turning to fight such a thing anyway, no chance at all except either to lose it or to reach safety before it caught her.

Jame paused on top of a boulder the size of a small house. Rubble spilled precipitously down its far side to a narrow rock ledge. Beyond that gaped the mouth of Perimal's Cauldron with the river thundering down into it and mist billowing out. From here, she could see no way out below. She was turning to back-track when a stone shifted under her foot and suddenly she was falling.

There are probably worse things than tumbling, naked, down a steep, rocky slope, but at the moment Jame couldn't think of any, unless it was the abrupt stop at the end. Bruised and breathless, she found herself sprawling on the stone ledge at the cauldron's smoking rim, amazed that she hadn't broken anything or gone over the edge.

But she wasn't alone.

Kinzi-kin.

On the far landward end of the ledge stood a figure wreathed in mist, haloed with thorns. Long white hair—or was it a mane?—stirred in the updraft. Ears pricked through it. Jame wondered if in her fall she had cracked her skull without noticing it. As the mist shifted, at one moment the other's form appeared to be that of a thin, pale woman; the next, that of a spectral horse, and yet not quite.

Trinity. Was it a Whinno-hir? A name came back to her: Bel-tairi. The missing White Lady.

One dark, liquid eye regarded her warily.

My lady Kinzi bade me find you.

Jame sat up, wincing.

"Your lady . . . my great-grandmother Kinzi . . . is dead. Sorry. It was a long time ago."

The dark eye showed a white rim.

How long?

Jame thought fast, doing sums. "Er . . . thirty-four years."

The other flinched. Jame saw her clearly for a moment as a small, painfully thin mare who pawed the ground in denial and tossed her head as if to dislodge those words that threatened to shatter her already tottering world. The hidden half of her face emerged briefly from the veil of silvery hair. Something about it was terribly wrong.

Then she was a woman again, with trembling hands clasped over her ears as if to hear nothing more.

No, no, no. Dead? And for so long? Oh, Kinzi, for me it was one endless night full of terrible dreams. Kinzi-kin, my lady bids me warn you . . . but my lady is dead, yet she summoned me, spoke to me. In a grove. Under the eyes of so many silent watchers.

That must have been the stand of trees where the Tishooo had left the Knorth death banners hung as if in some aerial hall, Jame thought.

"Kinzi's banner called to you, lady?" she asked, to make sure.

Yes, yes. Oh, her blood must have trapped her soul in the weave of her death.

Damn. Jame had suspected as much with Aerulan. The wider implications appalled her, but there was no time to consider them now.

"You said my great-grandmother sent you to warn me. About what?"

Rocks rattled down, followed a moment later by the rathorn like a bolt of white lightning, all horns, hooves, and fangs. The Whinno-hir screamed and vanished. Where she had stood was a gap in the cloud-of-thorn bushes. Jame bolted through it, the rathorn roaring on her heels. The path ended in a wall of thorns. Beneath them was a dark hole, a burrow leading to some animal's lair. Jame dived down it. Wet skin and damp soil turned it into a slick, muddy chute, with a quick glimpse at the bottom of furry hindquarters scuttling for dear life out the back door.

The rathorn crashed down on the bush. Thorn and dry branch snapped against his armor and between the twin scythes of his horns. Jame started up, but her loose hair caught on the brambles. Trapped, through a fretwork of thorns she saw something white eclipse the darkening sky like a falling moon. Then the rathorn smashed down again, and she scrambled free.

Her wild flight ended abruptly against a pair of legs. There was a crescent of them, and a spiked ring of spears leveled over her head at the bush. In its ruin, the rathorn reared and screamed his defiance. His sides and flanks were bloody from the bite of thorns and his red, red eyes glared into hers.

Come away from them, said his voice in her mind.
Come away with me and let us be done.

A hand on her shoulder stopped her.

The colt snorted. *If not today, then tomorrow, or next
week, or next year. Wait.* Then he turned and plunged
away.

Captain Hawthorn grounded her spear with a sigh.
"One thing about having you around, lady," she said to
Jame. "Life is never dull."

II

THEY ALL ENDED UP in the Commandant's office,
which turned out to be adjacent to the Map Room.

Timmon had found his pants. Jame was shivering
naked inside a borrowed jacket. Gorbel, in his pink-
stained shirt, was throwing a tantrum.

"You *have* to let me hunt it!" he raged, leaning over
the Commandant's desk and fairly shouting in his face.
"No one has ever bagged a rathorn before! When am I
ever likely to get another chance like this?"

Gorbel, obviously, was an avid hunter. Jame had never
seen him so animated or less like the miniature version
of his father that he always tried to be—not that Caldane
didn't hunt too, she thought, remembering the Merikit
skins, scalps still attached, strewn about his bedroom
at Restormir.

No one had mentioned the pale Whinno-hir. Jame
began to wonder if she had imagined their strange conversation. Great-grandmother Kinzi's soul trapped in the
web of her death? A warning never quite delivered?

"You've *got* to let me hunt him!" Gorbel cried, adding in a rising note of triumphant, "Father would insist!"

The Commandant regarded him thoughtfully.

"Something does have to be done about that beast, sir," said Hawthorn, regretfully. "I've never seen its like, all white and red eyed—magnificent, in a terrible way—but it's clearly a rogue. A death's-head. No rage will let it join, and they're social creatures, rathorns, for all their filthy tempers. On its own, it will go mad, if it hasn't already. It's dangerous."

The other randon murmured agreement.

"At least we know now why the herd has been acting up," said the horse-master. "Of course it would, with something like that on the prowl."

"Yes, but why here? True, some of them are man-eaters, but to attack so close to a keep and with such determination . . ."

Everyone looked at Jame.

She glared back through a tangle of wet, muddy hair with enough broken thorns in it to build a respectable bird's nest and wished she could stop shivering. It wasn't just that she was cold and wet, or that under the coat her body was laced with stinging scratches. The colt had been inside her mind. She could still taste his fury, but beneath that the grief and aching loneliness. She had taken away the only thing he had ever loved. Now she was all he had left, and he wanted her dead only a shade more fiercely than he wished for his own death.

"Indeed," said the Commandant, "something must be done. But not by cadets."

Gorbel looked stunned, then furious. The Commandant ignored him.

"Organize a hunt. Take randon and sargents, war-hounds and hawks. The Falconer will be our eyes, as usual. See to it. Dismissed."

And they all found themselves trooping outside, including a stunned, stammering Gorbel. "B-b-b-but the Commandant is a Caineron!" he said with genuine, almost hurt bewilderment.

Timmon shrugged. "Perhaps Daddy's reach isn't as long as you supposed. Perhaps Sheth will let you kill something later. Something small."

"Ah!" Gorbel snarled and stalked off, squelching loudly in his wet boots.

"I'll see you back to your quarters," said Timmon to Jame, sounding a shade too pleased with the situation.

"No, you won't," she snapped, shrugging off his solicitous arm.

"Don't you at least want this?" he called after her, holding up the borrowed coat which had come off in his hand.

"No!"

Cadets stared, aghast, or dived for cover as she stormed down the arcade. One, his arms full of armor to be cleaned, fell with a great clatter head first over the rail into the training square.

Rue met Jame at the Knorth door. The cadet's jaw fell. "Lady, you . . . you're . . ."

"Wet, cold, muddy, and in a foul temper. Just get me some hot water before I kill somebody. And stop staring at my ribs!"

CHAPTER XII

Unsheathed

Summer 43–44

I

JAME WOKE WITH A START, heart pounding, tangled in sweat soaked bedding. Trinity, when would these nightmares stop? But this one had been different. No hot, close room, no drunken laughter or unholy hunger. They had been chasing . . . someone. Her, she thought. In pain. In despair. How her face had throbbed.

Was that me? Jame wondered, touching her cheek, surprised to find the scar so slight.

In her dream, it had sprawled across half her face, and she had been running very fast on all fours.

There had also been terror.

They would finish what he (who?) had started or, worse, they would give her back to him.

Oh, Kinzi, is this all that honor has come to mean?

And he hunted with them in his gilded armor, as avid for blood as the hounds that bayed on her trail.

"Ho! So ho! Hark, hark, hark!"

There *were* voices below in the training square, in the predawn glimmer.

Jame scrambled out of her disordered bed and crossed to the inner window, snatching up clothes as she went. The square seethed with subdued, purposeful activity. Horses, dogs, randon and sargents . . . of course. This morning they would set out to kill the rathorn colt.

Downstairs, she found most of the college's cadets lining the rail, watching and chattering excitedly.

"I reckon they've called up every hound in the college except Gorbel's private pack and Tarn's old Molocar," Dar was saying as Jame slipped between Brier and Vant to a place at the rail.

"Tarn is as mad as fire about that," remarked someone from Vant's ten. "He won't admit that old Torvo isn't up to it. Anyway, the lymers are already out casting for the scent."

"They'll start at the pool," said Quill wisely. "I hear it crashed through the thorns, so there'll be a blood trail, at least at first. Once the direhounds catch sight of it, well, that will be that."

Not far away, the Commandant was checking the tack on his tall, gray stallion Cloud. The horse wore a coat of iron rings interlaced with strips of *rhi-sar* leather, protecting his chest, sides, and flanks with skirts long enough, hopefully, to foil a rathorn's upward thrust. His rider wore corresponding light armor, designed for the hunt. Man and horse had the same sheen of misted steel, the same chill of purpose.

Two direhounds, impatient for the chase, turned on each other snapping and snarling. They moved almost too fast for the eye to follow, a blur of lean, white bodies, black legs, and square, black heads. Huntsmen grabbed them by their spiked collars and wrenched them apart, but not before one had caught the other's foreleg in its powerful jaws and snapped the bone with an audible crunch. The hunt-master knelt to assess the damage. The hound whined and was licking his face as he slipped a blade between its ribs.

"First blood of the hunt," said Erim uneasily as the randon cradled the dead hound, "and it's ours."

There would be more, thought Jame, eyeing the array of swords, boar-spears, and bows.

"I wish," she said to no one in particular, "that they would just leave him alone."

Vant gave her a sidelong glance. "Now, lady, we can't have a brute like that on the loose, can we? Or were you thinking you'd like to ride him?"

That caused a ripple of laughter; Jame's poor horsemanship was fast becoming the stuff of legend. The horse-master swore that she had found every way to fall off known to man or beast, and then invented a few more.

"Look," said someone.

They all leaned over the rail, craning to the left to watch as Gorbel entered the square. He was dressed in hunting leathers and carried a boar-spear as if he knew how to use it. The hunt-master stroked the hound's head one last time, lowered it to the ground, and rose to meet the Caineron Lordan.

What they said was inaudible to the onlookers, but Gorbel's growing anger spoke for itself. He turned, blustering, to the Commandant.

Sheth shot a sidelong smile at Harn Grip-hard, who stood stone-faced by the rail, watching, clad in his everyday, rumpled clothes. "Since the Highlord's commander does not deign to hunt down and kill the . . . er . . . emblem of his house," the Commandant announced in his clear, light voice to the college at large, "he stays here, in charge during my absence. Ask him."

Even as Gorbel turned, speechless and baffled, Harn was shaking his massive head. No.

Vant laughed as Caineron lordan stalked back to his barracks.

"Better luck next time, Gorbelly!"

"Be quiet," said Brier.

Vant turned to her from his haughty height although, indeed, he was slightly shorter than she. "*What* was that, five?"

Jame spoke without looking at either of them. "She meant, 'Shut up, ten.' It's tacky to gloat."

As Gorbel stalked past the Randir, they called out sympathetically to him. One named Simmel put his arm around the Caineron's shoulders and shook him playfully.

Mmm, thought Jame, remembering her uncle's ill-fated Randir crony, Roane. Whenever there was trouble, there seemed to be a Randir somewhere behind it, pushing.

In the crowd by the rail, she saw a thick coil of gold wrapped around a cadet's neck. The Randir seemed to feel Jame's eyes and glared back, one hand rising to caress the triangular head that rose from her collar to meet it. So. The Shanir had gotten her snake back, apparently uninjured. Good.

Was it really possible for an entire house to go rotten? Some Randir randon seemed all right. Others . . . she remembered the Tempter and the calculating, alien darkness that had seemed for a moment to peer out through her eyes. The Commandant had said that she was back, but Jame hadn't yet encountered her, nor did she wish to.

The Falconer's merlin swooped over the square with a scream, then wheeled toward the upper window of the mews where his master awaited him. Simultaneously came the belling of distant horns.

"They have the scent!" cried several voices. "Hurrah!"

Riders swung into the saddle and took the boar spears handed up to them. Archers strung their bows. Hounds yelped and pressed eagerly against the hall doors, black tails whipping in excitement. The doors opened. They surged through, down Old Tentir's hall, and out into the growing dawn. Swift feet and hooves followed.

Cadets leaned over the rail to watch them go, cheering, but then fell silent as the tumult of the hunt faded into the distance. Gorbel threw down his spear.

After that, it seemed quite prosaic to go in to breakfast with another round of lessons ahead.

 II

HOWEVER, it turned out to be a day of distractions.

Whatever the class, the cadets' attention kept turning to the hunt. For a long time, snatches of it could be heard in the distance—the bell of hounds, the sound of horns—borne on a shifting wind. The rathorn colt, it seemed, was keeping close to Tentir, playing hide-and-seek with its pursuers. In this, it was no doubt helped not only by the Riverland's odd topography but also by the disruptions caused by the recent weirdingstrom and quakes, which between them had displaced large chunks of the landscape, some as far south as the Cataracts.

Perhaps, some whispered, it could even use the folds of the land as the Merikit did.

Others laughed at this, but uneasily: no one knew for sure how the northern tribesmen could pop up wherever in the Riverland they chose. Some, like Lord Caineron, welcomed the odd native hunter as good sport, to be hunted in turn. Others remembered the fate of Kithorn and kept watch especially against the autumn cattle raids, but it did little good.

We are strangers here, Jame thought, not for the first time, *and the land doesn't welcome us.*

She and her ten were on their way, finally, to the day's last lesson.

The previous three had been exercises in confusion, with whole files of lancers tripping over each other's weapons, arrows loosed at random (except for Erim's, who couldn't seem to miss if he tried), and an irate strategy instructor dismissing half his class mildly concussed for inattention.

Harn had finally emerged and bellowed that the whole college had better settle down or, by Trinity, he would work off their fidgets with a punishment run the likes of which they had never seen and probably wouldn't survive.

Gorbel, bound for the same lesson as Jame, was still seething: "God's claws, I can track down that brute if anyone can. I'm the best hunter at Restormir except," he added hastily, "for Father."

While his cronies assured him that this was true and Jame's ten bit their tongues under Brier's stony gaze, Jame unhappily considered the rathorn. The Riverland wouldn't be safe for her, or at least as safe as it had ever been, until he was dead, but what a terrible waste!

Here was their classroom, a large chamber on the ground floor of Old Tentir, where they would practice with some of the more obscure weapons in the Kencyrath's armory. Jame stopped short on the threshold, her ten piling up behind her. Hanging on a rack were suits of protective leather armor, face-guards, and beside them, in pairs, heavy gauntlets tipped with steel claws.

Their instructor was a dark Brandan who looked as if he had had entirely too much experience with the wicked blades behind him. Indeed, one puckered eyelid drooped over an empty socket while three seamed scars ran parallel to it slantwise across his face.

"The Arrin-thar," he announced, gesturing to dangling weapons. "You see the intended connection with the lethal claws of the Arrin-ken, also with occasional rare Shanir. Find the pair that suits you best."

Alone among the excited chatter of her classmates, Jame fumbled through the swinging scythes, hoping desperately that none of them would fit.

"Here, lady," said the instructor, and thrust a pair at her. "These were made for a Kendar child—as playthings, no less—but you have hands almost as small." He pulled on his own and flexed their articulated fingers. Clink, clink, clink. "Well, Jameth?"

Jame stood holding the gauntlets in her own gloved hands, feeling numb, then nauseous.

"My name is Jame, ran, not Jameth." She gulped. "And I think that I'm going to be sick."

"Not good enough." He flipped down his face guard. "Defend yourself."

And he sprang at her.

She dropped the gauntlets.

The next moment passed in a blur of action, two figures at the heart of it leaping, striking, withdrawing.

The instructor looked down at his shirt—he hadn't bothered to don body armor against a novice—and watched it fall apart in five long gashes. The hairy chest beneath was similarly slashed, and the cuts just beginning to bleed.

Jame backed into a corner, hands gripped tightly behind her.

". . . sorry, sorry, sorry . . ."

The randon stalked after her, cadets scattering before him.

"Show me."

White faced and miserable, she held out her hands. He stripped off the gloves and examined her fingertips. Then he pressed her palms to make the ivory claws extend.

Gorbel's moon of a face appeared at the randon's elbow, wide eyed and goggling.

"Oh, how splendid!" he breathed, and then, as his friends pushed up behind him. "I mean, how grotesque. Father always said you were a freak."

For this, he got the randon's elbow casually jabbed into his eye and retreated, swearing.

"You'll need special training to use these properly," said the instructor in a matter-of-fact tone, releasing Jame's hands. "Gloves aren't a bad idea, though. Take note, all of you: always keep a weapon in reserve, the more unexpected, the better. D'you have clawed toes as well . . . er . . . Jame? Too bad. They can be useful. Now, on to practice."

The rest of the session passed in a daze for Jame. Wearing armor against the others' inexperience, encumbered by her own, she countered their flailing attacks automatically, initiating none of her own. Nor did it help that the instructor kept watching her, although he said nothing. At last the class was over and the cadets dismissed.

Outside the room, Jame almost ran head first into the Randir Tempter. All the more startling, the woman wore a heavy veil across the lower half of her face. She stepped aside without speaking, but the lines around her dark eyes shifted as if she smiled, unpleasantly: *Why should I interfere? You will destroy yourself soon enough.*

Jame had meant to slink back to her attic, but word of what had happened preceded her.

Timmon was waiting on the boardwalk. "From all the ruckus," he said, "I thought you must at least have sprouted fur and fangs." When he craned to see her hands, she presented them to him with a defiant glare, nails out. "Now these," he said, examining them, "are quite elegant. Just the same, you'll have to be careful how you use them in bed."

Jame realized that her ten had bunched up behind her, watching and listening, Vant with distaste, Brier without expression, the others obviously fascinated.

"Do you mind?" she snapped at them. As they reluctantly departed, she rounded on the Ardeth. "As for you . . ."

Timmon also retreated, throwing up his hands in mock surrender. "Keep 'em sheathed! I'm off too. And sleep well tonight, Lordan of Ivory," he called after her as she stalked away. "I'll see you in your dreams."

At the door of the Knorth barracks, Jame paused, hearing a babble of voices within: "Did you hear . . ."

"Did you see . . ."

"Oh no."

"Oh yes!"

Sudden silence fell as she stepped over the threshold. Nearly everyone was there, back from the last lesson, and all had turned to stare at her. Instinctively, she thrust her hands behind her back. Her movement broke the spell. At least half the room rushed at her, shouting questions:

"Oh, lady, can we see? Rue says they're five inches long" ("I did not!" Rue protested from the back of the crowd.) "and as sharp as knives!"

"Did you really make cat's meat of the instructor?"

"We knew you were a true Knorth!"

"Oh please, lady, show us!"

And, hesitantly, Jame did, flexing her long, black gloved fingers, the ivory nails, honed to lethal points, sliding out of their sheaths.

"Oooh!"

"So *that's* why the king post in the attic is all scratched up!" Rue exclaimed, suddenly enlightened.

Jame bolted up the stairs.

In her own quarters above, she leaned out the hole in the roof to gulp down cool mountain air, to wonder if, after all, she was going to be sick.

But here came Jorin, trotting across the floor, greeting her as if she had been gone a year. She sank down against the wall, gathered up as much of the ounce as would fit into her lap, and pressed her face into his rich fur. His purr shook them both, or perhaps not his purr alone.

"Shanir, god-spawn, unclean, unclean!"

Words shouted at a frightened child with bloody fingertips and nails. No: claws. Hide them. Chop them off. But too late: Father had seen. So much hate, such loathing for who and what she was.

Worse, Tori felt the same way, on a gut level perhaps inaccessible to reason. Father had trained him well, even as he had rebelled against that legacy of hate.

She, too, had rebelled, over and over again . . . but she had never quite lost the sense that it was all her fault. The claws. The rejection. Everything. That lesson, too, had sunk in deeper than reason.

Now Kendar who previously couldn't look her in the face had been avid to see what she had kept hidden in shame all her life. True, some had expressed horror. But not all. Not even most.

She remembered Marc's easy acceptance of her . . . deformity. Perhaps he was more typical of the Kendar attitude than she had thought. *"We are many,"* the Randir Tempter had said, speaking of the Kendar Shanir, *"and we are proud."*

Jorin stretched backward over her arm, bracing himself with a paw against her cheek. She took it, feeling the warm, thick pad, the hidden menace. Press here, and out they came, hooked and sharp. Jorin took back his paw and began to groom it, pausing to crunch on the tip of a nail.

The most natural thing in the world.

No. It wasn't the same . . . or was it?

She cupped his sleek, golden head with her ivory nails. He leaned back into them. *There. Scratch there.*

All her life, she had mistrusted her own judgment, depending instead on that of Kendar like Marc, like these cadets, like Brier.

But her brother's feelings still mattered. Dreadfully.

And there was far more to her Shanir nature than ten embellished fingers. As yet, Tentir had no exact knowledge what it had on its hands.

Below, the dinner horn sounded.

Had so much time passed? Apparently. Her stomach rebelled at the thought of food, but she couldn't hide here forever. Jame pushed Jorin off her lap and soberly went down to a meal for which she had no appetite.

III

I MUST BE DREAMING, thought Jame.

She had expected to fall asleep with difficulty that night—after all, one's life didn't turn upside down every day—but now she barely remembered falling into bed.

Not this bed, though. The attic offered nothing so soft nor such silken sheets, deliciously cool on bare, bruised skin. Eyes still closed, she stretched luxuriously, like a cat, and found that her hands were bound above her head.

. . . be careful how you use those claws in bed . . .

Her eyes snapped open. Surely, this was a dream. Curtains of red ribbons surrounded her, rippling, whispering together. More ribbons bound her wrists, but loosely as if to say, *Relax. Blame us if you must, but enjoy what you can't prevent. Truly, is it so bad to be a woman?*

There was a flaw in that logic—probably several—but Jame found it hard to think clearly over the seductive suspiration of silk on silk. Anyway, did it matter what happened in a dream? And this felt so very, very good . . .

The ribbons parted. Timmon stood over her, naked and smiling. "I promised you some fun," he said.

Abruptly his expression changed. "Oh, no. Not again."

He seemed to go flat, and then his image separated into long strips . . . no, into more ribbons, fluttering in futile protest.

Through them stumbled someone else. A spare body wired with muscle and laced with scars, black hair shot with white, silver-gray eyes . . .

Brother and sister stared at each other. "Oh *no!*" they said simultaneously, and Jame woke with a start in her attic loft on rough blankets, alone.

What a strange dream, she thought as her pounding heart slowed. *Even for me. Especially for me. Oh well.*

She curled up again in her scratchy nest, but this time sleep eluded her for a long, long time.

IV

DAWN CAME AT LAST, but no word from the hunt. The distant sounds had faded under a leaden, over-cast sky. Not even the keen eyes of the Falconer's merlin, circling above, could pierce the clouds that mantled the lower slopes of the Snowthorns.

After assembly, Gorbel again demanded that he be allowed to lead out his private pack of hounds, and again he was denied. Simmel led him off, whispering in his ear with a twisted smile that the Caineron did not see.

The Danior Tarn also begged for permission to join the hunt with his Molocar Torvo and also was denied, but more gently. The old hound gave a cavernous, nearly toothless yawn and fell asleep at his master's feet.

When Jame's ten set out to do their stint in rebuilding the quake-broken outer walls, she was told to stay behind. It occurred to her, watching them go, that she hadn't been outside Tentir since the rathorn attack at the river, that the class schedule had deliberately been changed to keep her in. The college was a large place. Nonetheless, she suddenly felt cramped and restless.

Having nothing else to do, she took Jorin and went in search of Harn Grip-hard.

On the way, she ran into Timmon, arm in arm with a Kendar girl of his house.

"Have any good dreams last night?" asked Timmon. "Because I didn't. At first. Then I remembered Narsa here, and the rest of the evening was quite jolly."

He toyed with a lock of the girl's dark hair as he spoke, glancing sidelong at Jame. It occurred to her that he was trying to make her jealous.

"Play your games, then," she said, lightly. "I wish you joy of him, cadet."

Timmon blinked at her and the girl glared, clutching his arm even more tightly.

Jame went her way, annoyed to find that she *was* vaguely, fleetingly jealous. But, after all, he hadn't been all that impressive naked, even in a dream.

. . . anyway, not compared to that other lean, neatly muscled body tempered by hardship and battle, those beautiful hands that wore their scars like elegant lacework gloves, those silver-shadowed eyes . . .

Stop it, Jame told herself crossly. *Things are complicated enough already.*

At length she found Harn in the subterranean stable.

A commotion drew her to the southernmost row of stalls, hard against Old Tentir's foundation. Over shouts of warning rose the eerie shriek of a terrified horse, followed by a series of crashes. Edging closer, Jame saw a large, piebald horse in its stall, on its back, with all four hooves in the air. She burst out laughing. Harn turned around and boxed her on the ear, hard.

"It isn't funny," he said.

The blow sent her reeling. Rage surged over shock and she came back at him, claws out; but his expression, impatient and preoccupied, stopped her like a dash of ice water in the face:

Not now.

The horse began to thrash again. A flying hoof smashed through wood, caught, was wrenched free. The animal kept rolling back against the wall and pausing to pant, its pale belly heaving. Then it lashed out again.

The bow-legged horse-master jerked a cadet out of the way. "D'you want your face flattened like mine, youngling? You and you. Pin him down."

A sargent and a third year cadet threw themselves on the horse's head and neck.

"Steady, steady . . ."

The master shook out a coil of rope and expertly snaked it around the far hind leg near the hock. "Now, let go!"

They sprang back.

The master pulled, aided a moment later by Harn, and the horse crashed over in a cloud of dust. It rested for moment, looking dazed, then lurched to its feet. Harn grunted approval when he saw that it was uninjured and turned to walk away. Jame followed him, rubbing her ear.

"Listen," he said, rounding on her. "When a horse gets cast in a stall like that, it can't get up by itself. It will struggle until it dies."

"Ran, I'm sorry I laughed. It wasn't funny at all. And yes, I did nearly flare at you."

"Huh." He gave her a brooding look. "But you didn't."

"Ran," she said as he turned again to leave, "tell me about the White Lady."

He swung back, so suddenly that she shrank from him. "Why?"

"Because I've seen her, first outside my quarters, calling to me, and then beside Perimal's Cauldron."

To her surprise, behind its garnish of grizzled stubble his broad face paled. "I said your being here was madness, and now this."

"Now what, ran?" she asked, bewildered by his agitation. Did he mean to hit her again, burst into tears, or faint? "Has it something to do with her being called 'The Shame of Tentir,' and why that, anyway?"

He loomed over her like a cliff face, as if poised to crush her questions with his sheer bulk, and perhaps her as well.

"Just leave!" he roared down at her, causing heads to turn across the stable and Jorin to bolt. "D'you hear me? Get out!"

She stared after him as he stumped off.

The horse-master came trotting up to see what all the shouting was about. "Now, now, remember what the Commandant said about not driving your instructors mad, lady," he said, adding, "not that it looks like with Harn Grip-hard you'd have far to go. What in Trinity's name d'you say to him?"

"Just that I'd seen the White Lady. Was that so awful?"

The master's shaggy eyebrows rose, as if attempting to scale the mottled heights of his bald head. "Well, it's a surprise, given that the poor thing's been dead these forty years. And no, I'll not tell you how or why if the senior randon of your own house won't. I've heard tell, though, that if a Knorth sees her, it means they're going to die."

"Oh," said Jame, digesting this. "Ran, did Harn just expel me from Tentir?"

"No, no." He clapped her bracingly on the shoulder as he might have to reassure an nervous filly. "You've still got a mort of tests to fail and horses to fall off. All things in good time."

THE HUNT RETURNED at dusk the next day in shocking disarray.

Everyone in it was muddy and bruised, with ripped clothes and shattered weapons. The dogs limped, heads down, and most of the horses had gone lame. The Commandant led his own mount with a sargent swaying on its back, his head wrapped in bloody rags. Other injured randon entered supported by friends or on makeshift litters.

"Trinity," said Harn, staring, as were most of the cadets who had gathered as the morning before at the practice ground rail, this time in stunned silence. "That damned colt did all of this?"

"Hardly any of it," answered Sheth, helping down the sargent. Members of the man's house rushed to help him. "I've sent for a healer," the Commandant told them.

"There are some broken limbs. Otherwise, this is the worst of it.

"No, not the rathorn," he repeated to Harn, preoccupied, as he turned to help the other wounded. "We ran into a tree, or rather a tree ran over us."

The rest of the story had to wait until dinner in the officers' mess. Nearly everyone attended, bandages, splints, and all. A healer, borrowed from the Scrollsmen's College at Mount Alban, was with the injured sargent. Otherwise, even the Commandant was present for once, although this was a mixed blessing: no one dared to speak of the hunt before he did and there he sat, calmly sipping the wine that he had ordered served instead of the customary cider, clad in a coat of rich, purple velvet with trimmed with royal blue. Unlike most of his fellow huntsmen, he had found time to bathe.

Harn too drank, more deeply than usual. He had been rattled by Jameth's sighting of the White Lady and, no doubt, had made a fool of himself, luckily during the Commandant's absence. Since then, he had had time to think. Whatever his feelings about Bel-tairi and the terrible events following her death, or disappearance, or whatever-it-had-been, he felt now that he had underestimated the Knorth Lordan. It was hard not to see her as a frighteningly vulnerable version of her brother or as a fragile child when compared to her fellow Kendar cadets, but Bran's news heartened him.

On the other hand, as usual, he found Sheth's reticence maddening. At last he slammed down his glass, ignoring it when it shattered. His neighbors flinched at the flying shards.

"Well?" he growled. "D'you mean to sit there all night smirking like a cat in cream? What *happened*, man?"

Sheth picked a splinter of glass out of his venison stew and laid it beside his plate. "Patience never was one of your virtues, was it, Ran Harn? All right."

He folded his hands and spoke as if to them, a thin smile wryly twisting his saturnine face. "As you may have guessed, we saw precious little of the rathorn. His trail kept ending up in a hopeless muddle, crossed, re-crossed, and crossed yet again. Clearly, he was playing with us and no doubt enjoying himself enormously. Then too, we kept stumbling on stray patches of weirding and the occasional case of arboreal drift."

Someone laughed, like Harn a bit drunk. "S'true. I got caught in a creeping grove of sumac and was nearly carried off, Trinity knows where."

"You were lucky," said another morosely, his hands such a welter of bandages that he could only glare at his untouched meal. "The cloud-of-thorns were on the move too. So were the wild roses. And the raspberry canes."

"Ah, the thorns of life," murmured Sheth. "So sweet. So sharp. Things didn't get really . . . er . . . interesting, though, until last night. We were bedding down when we first heard it. From the approaching lash of branches, I thought we were in for a storm, but there was no wind. Then it burst into our camp. I think," he added judiciously, "that we were simply in its way."

"In whose way?" demanded Harn, just short of an explosion.

"Why, didn't I say? It was a golden willow. Rampant."

"God's claws, Commandant! Don't y'know how to tell a story?" The bandaged randon leaned forward, elbows planted firmly in his dinner.

"Listen. First, as Sheth Sharp-tongue says, we hear this mighty thrashing in the forest. Myself, I wondered if the Dark Judge and judgment itself were about to fall on us. Then the earth begins to writhe. Roots are surging out of it and rocks are sinking in. See, the ground has turned as soft as quicksand and I'm fighting in its grip, all tangled up in runners like so many ropes of steel. Then comes the tree.

"God's truth, we all thought we were dead. Some were sinking, others picked up and flung aside. It had no more regard for us than . . . than for so much straw flung in its way. Less, if possible. Myself, I don't believe that the Riverland is alive and conscious, much less that it doesn't like us crawling over its wrinkled hide like . . . like . . . "

"Fleas?" suggested an Edirr, helpfully. "Lice? Wood ticks?"

"Argh. Brute nature. Brute Rathillien. That's all it is. Like a hundred other worlds before it."

"Ah, but we don't know about them, do we?" said the Commandant gently. "Only that none of them have put us to the test the way this world has."

"It needs to know its master," a Caineron muttered into his glass. "That's all."

"And if it refuses?" asked a Randir, with a sidelong smile at the others of her house.

"Then, I say, break it all to bits."

"Leaving us to stand on what?" Harn snorted. "This is ridiculous. Look at you, bandaged up to the eyebrows. Who broke whom? You Caineron and you Randir, who cut down all the trees around Wilden to stop them from drifting away. What has that gotten you? Mud-slides in season and a rain of frogs out of it. Is all the Chain of Creation to be bent to your will?"

"Yes!" shouted the Caineron, and banged their glasses on the table, more shattering in the process.

"If this keeps up," murmured one senior randon to another, "we'll have to start drinking from tin cups, or from cupped hands."

"So we are to rule the whole of creation," said Sheth, with a wry smile, regarding their battered ranks. "Never mind the Master or Perimal Darkling or a trail of lost, fallen worlds. Never mind betrayal, heartbreak, and thirty millennia of failure. And for whom, after all, do we accomplish this great feat—our hated god, our . . . er . . . beloved lords, ourselves?"

He had spoken this last softly so that most of his fellow Caineron hadn't heard. But Harn did.

"Which do you serve, randon?"

"Ah, my dear brother-in-arms. Grant me the space to decide."

Harn looked hard at him. "Choice, yes, so that it be done with honor."

The other inclined his head, acknowledging ruefully the Kencyrath's fundamental dilemma.

"I dunno about Rathillien," said one of the hunters with satisfaction, "but we spent all day chasing down and settling for that damn tree. It's chained to a boulder now, waiting for the axe. Prime bows, its wood will make, among other things."

"It's a prize all right," another agreed, "for whichever house reaches it first."

This sparked a widespread, increasingly loud argument: to whom did the willow belong? It turned out that the randon of the two nearest major houses—Caineron and Randir—had sent urgent messages to their lords requesting foresters. The Brandan claimed that they had put their mark on it first, the previous fall. Others pointed out, however, that they had subsequently lost it:

when the sap began to run that spring, not surprisingly so had the tree, right across the river south of the Danior's Shadow Rock. Other houses, smaller, farther away, or more altruistic, insisted that it belonged to Tentir, hard won with blood, bruises and sundry broken bones.

Before the randon could become too heated, Harn loudly broke in: "We stay-at-homes have some news too. Bran, show 'em."

The dark, scarred randon obligingly opened his shirt to reveal five scabbed-over gashes across his hairy torso. Then he explained how he had gotten them.

"So," said someone, after a blank moment. "Our kitten has claws."

"And why," murmured the Commandant, "am I not surprised?"

"We already know that she's a reasonably controlled berserker," Harn growled. "I'll swear to that."

"We won't," snapped a Randir. "When our tempter first chewed through her gag, she induced the Kendar in charge of her to jump down a well. Something at the bottom ate him."

"Trogs, probably," muttered someone. "And poor sanitation. Never trust a rock with teeth, or a midden that burps."

Hawthorn glanced around to make sure that the randon in question was absent. "Yet Lady Rawneth has since sent her pet tempter back to . . . er . . . grace our halls."

Since her return, she had, in fact, kept mostly to the Randir barracks, to no one's disappointment except (perhaps) the Randir.

"Odd," remarked a Danior. "We've been watching the Highlord for any of his father's destructive traits, and here they pop up in his sister. True, it's not as if she could read runes or reap souls . . ."

He paused, perhaps remembering when Knorth and Ardeth had danced and darkness had gaped. But nothing, after all, had come of that.

"Just the same," said another randon, maybe following the other's thought, maybe not, "d'you think Torisen knows?"

"He might," said Bran, securing his shirt. "We all know how the Highlord feels about the Shanir, and his attitude toward our Jameth has been . . . puzzling. Does he want her to succeed at Tentir or not? Does he really mean to keep her as his heir, perhaps to become the first highlady in our history? Does he even know his own mind in the matter?"

"Or perhaps," murmured a Randir, "he's lost said mind altogether. It's been known to happen in his family. Ask the Knorth: how secure do they feel in his power since the battle at the Cataracts, much less since he fled Kothifir for the Riverland as if the Shadows themselves were snapping at his heels?"

Harn started to rise, but Sheth's fingertips on his arm stopped him.

"Time will tell," the Commandant said gently. "Shouting won't."

"No offense, rans," said a Coman, his eyes flickering nervously from face to face, "but the rest aside, we all know there's only one person at Tentir qualified to train a natural Arrin-thari."

He jumped as Harn's fist crashed down on the table.

"No! We agreed that that was far too dangerous. Remember the mauled cadet. And look what he did to your face, Bran."

"Oh, I don't blame him for that. After all, at the time we were forcing him at spear-point into a cage."

"Just the same . . ."

"Enough," said the Commandant quietly, and the room lapsed momentarily into a strange, almost embarrassed silence.

Behind the wall, in the gloom of Old Tentir's secret ways, Graykin listened with interest.

"Speaking of the Highborn," said Hawthorn, "I'd watch out, if I were you, for the Ardeth Timmon."

"Why?" demanded a member of that house.

"Because you also produce strong Shanir, as we know to our grief from Pereden. Because his son may also be a dream-stalker, as well as a charmer. Because he's already snared a Kendar girl with his glamour and bedded her. We all know what damage that can cause, and how many Kendar Pereden ruined."

"Nonetheless, it's a house matter," said the Ardeth flatly. "Don't interfere."

"Still, he's bound to try for the Knorth Lordan."

"I pity him if he does," Harn said with a sudden bark of laughter. "God's teeth and toenails, didn't you hear? Our kitten has claws."

CHAPTER XIII

Blood and Ivory

Summer 45

I

JAME WOKE WITH A START, dew beading her eyelashes. She had taken to sleeping directly under the hole in the as yet unmended roof, to Jorin's dismay, but in the past few days it had made her feel less like a prisoner. During the night it had rained, hard, driving her back to shelter. As soon as the storm had passed, however, she had returned to watch the hazy stars emerge one by one.

Although she thought that she had dreamed again, after that, she remembered little except a voice calling:

. . . come, come, come . . .

Perhaps that was what had woken her.

She rose, taking care not to disturb the ounce, and looked out. The heavy cloud cover of the past few days had condensed into slow rivers of fog rolling silently down the mountain slopes to the river. Above, a crisp night sky sparkled with stars, the sliver of a waxing moon having long since set. It was either very late or very early, and deathly still.

In a corner, Graykin stirred, grumbled, and went back to sleep. He had told her the previous night of the conversation that he had overheard in the officers' mess. That had given her several things to think about.

. . . come, come . . .

This would be the third day of the hunt, and the seventh in the college's weekly rotation, meaning no classes. One might even sleep in and skip breakfast. If she could slip out unseen, no one would know she was gone until evening.

. . . come . . .

She dressed quietly, choosing her black, knife-fighter's *d'hen* over a cadet's jacket. It felt good to have the Talisman's old tools back in hand for a night's prowl, if through a different maze than that of Tai-tastigon. Solitary by nature, how she missed the freedom to come and go as she chose. As she extracted grapnel segments from the *d'hen*'s full sleeve and snapped them together, she wondered if she would ever become accustomed to acting with or through others. A long talk with the earnest Brandan master ten had given her a list of her responsibilities as head of her own barracks, which she had memorized and then passed on to Vant, to his ill-disguised disgust. Well, if she had to lump it, so could he.

Attach the line, anchor the hook, and swing out into the night. Hopefully, the Kendar with their dislike of heights would never think of such an escape route. On the ground, she freed the grapnel with a flick of her wrist and caught it as it fell.

The fading summons drew her northward across the foggy training fields, over the bridge under which the mud battle had been fought, to the outer wall. Despite ongoing repairs, parts of it were still down, tumbled by the quake, and the whole length unguarded. Of all the Riverland keeps, ironically, Tentir possessed the fewest fortifications. When Jame had asked Vant about this, he had snorted:

"The other houses defend themselves mostly against each other. Who would attack a school where all young randon train?"

The Merikit, Jame had said. The Seven Kings. The Shadow Guild. A rising of *rhi-sar*. Caldane, Lord Caineron, on a bad day.

Vant had only laughed, as if humoring a moron.

Beyond the wall was the orchard that each year supplied the college with its apple cider. The boughs were heavy with fruit ripening toward the autumn harvest, the ground beneath fragrant with windfalls that squelched and slipped underfoot. Beyond again were sloping pastures dappled with sleeping cows and sheep and other indistinct shapes that could have been anything. Although the eastern sky now showed the black silhouette of peaks, it was still very dark here in the valley below, and rather foggy.

Jame tripped over a stump hidden in deep grass, then over another. A hare, breaking cover almost under her feet, made her heart leap. Ahead loomed the forest, in this light a solid black mass poised like an avalanche to topple over the land stolen from it. Under its eaves, seedlings had already begun to reclaim what was theirs.

Jame stopped just short of those reaching shadows. For the first time, she wondered what she was doing here.

Two by two, in perfect silence, points of light sprang up in the trees, some low, some high, more and more and more.

The forest is watching me, she thought, and fished the *imu* medallion out of her pocket.

"I have the Earth Wife's favor," she said, holding it up, wondering even as she spoke if that was still true in all senses of the word.

She had promised to carry the little, clay face with its big ears into places where Mother Ragga otherwise was deaf, but she hadn't done anything yet about the duties foisted on her by the Merikit chief Chingetai. Damn the man anyway for making her his heir and, by implication, male, just to get out of a tight spot.

Still, wasn't that exactly what Tori had done too, following the Merikit's lead and Kirien's advice?

So here she stood at the boundary between two worlds, assigned much the same role in each, in danger of failing in both.

The forest's eyes blinked. Then out of its shadows burst a flight of luminous moths. They swirled around Jame with the flash and flutter of a thousand wings, dusting her with their glow. One landed on her wrist and flexed pale gray-green wings overlaid with a tracery of silver. Its furry antennae twiddled furiously.

"Have you a message for me?" Jame asked it, only half in jest.

If so, there was no time for it. The next moment the moths spiraled up into the sky as rushing bodies parted the thick grass. Jame found herself surrounded by a milling pack of hounds. They were muzzled lymers, she saw, scent trackers with fringed dewlaps and busy, intrusive noses.

One gave a muffled yelp and their black ranks parted to let through the direhounds. Jame stood very still among the glimmer of white backs. Teeth and eyes gleamed up at her. While not up to a Molocar's weight or strength, these hounds were killers. She had seen them practice on the weaker of their own kind: their mothers first taught them to eat meat by ripping apart the runt of each litter and feeding the bloody scraps to its stronger siblings.

Then horsemen rode among the roiling pack, whipping them off. But there were too few of them to be the college hunt—a bare dozen or less.

Someone laughed. "I don't believe it. First that Danior brat slinks out of Tentir with his mangy mutt and now here's the Knorth freak. Ho, my lord! Shall we loose the dogs again and see how fast a Knorth can run?"

Jame recognized the voice: it was one of Gorbel's Highborn cronies. The Caineron Lordan himself rode apart, leaning down from the saddle to let the lymers sniff a white cloth with dark stains—at a guess, rathorn blood wiped from thorns. The dogs milled excitedly around him, although some shrank away, whimpering. A Kendar cadet lashed them back into line. Then they were off, black on black under the trees, casting back and forth for the scent.

"My lord!" called the Highborn again.

Gorbel straightened. "What?" he said, preoccupied, intent on the dogs.

One gave a muffled yip and plunged into the forest, the rest a black tide flowing on his heels.

Gorbel shouted: "Ha!" and spurred after them.

Direhounds and horsemen followed. Jame dodged among them, sure they meant to ride her down. Instead, someone grabbed her by the collar and jerked her up across a horse's withers. A saddle horn punched her in the stomach with every stride. Branches whipped her buttocks and tore at her streaming hair. She started to slip. The horse shied violently as her nails bit into it and the rider cursed.

Trinity, anything to stop this nightmare ride.

Occasionally, prayers are answered.

Something hard clipped Jame on the back of the head and she tumbled into merciful darkness.

II

SOMEONE WAS GROANING.

Jame swallowed, dry-mouthed, and the sound stopped.

Incautiously, she opened her eyes and winced as sunlight stabbed into them. Time had passed. The day must be well advanced. Before her lay a dappled glen carpeted with ferns, lined with slender, gleaming birch trees. She frowned, trying to remember something, anything. Shouts, dogs yelping, pain.

That last was still with her. Her head throbbed with each heartbeat and her shoulders ached. She tried to straighten to ease the strain and discovered that her hands were bound tightly behind her, around a tree trunk.

Footsteps.

Someone sank onto his heels before her, bringing their eyes level.

"So. Awake at last."

She fumbled for a name to fit that narrow face with its mocking eyes. Simmel. A Randir.

"Where . . ."

"North of Tentir, lost in the folds of the hills. More than that, I can't tell you. The cursed land keeps shifting. Worse, that damn colt has crisscrossed it so often over the last few days that the lymers have run off in all directions and all but three of the Caineron after them." He laughed. "That house. So easily led."

"You mean . . . misled."

"That too. M'lord Gorbel insists, however, that we are on the true scent. Why? Because that Danior brat and his mangy mutt are still ahead of us. But it really isn't necessary to track the rathorn any farther." He brushed loose hair back from her face and let it slide through his fingers. "You see, now we have something he wants. You."

Jame tried to answer, but the words stuck in her dry throat.

"You'd like some water, I suppose," said the Randir, making no effort to get her any.

Behind her back, she extended her claws. Her hands were so numb that she didn't know if she was breaking the rope that bound them, strand by strand, or merely shredding her own wrists. She hawked and spat froth, wishing a moment later that she hadn't turned her head to do so. The Randir's hand had dropped to finger her *d'hen*.

"What a strange jacket," he murmured, spreading it open at the throat, regarding with detached interest the slight swell of breasts beneath her white shirt, the quick, secret pulse.

When he raised his eyes, his pupils had expanded until only a rim of white remained. From the abyss within, whatever lived in the Randir Tempter's eyes regarded Jame with amused, indolent contempt.

"So here you are, the last of Kinzi's female bloodline, the last Knorth lady."

As he spoke, his voice shifted timber to a drowsy half-purr that made Jame's skin crawl.

"And what do you think your great-grandmother, dear Kinzi, would make of you? Why, you're no lady at all, just a scrawny, mask-less hoyden playing soldier. Scarred, too. Damaged goods." His fingertips brushed her cheek, with a touch more of long, sharp nails than of his own short cut ones. He made a slight moue of disappointment. "I thought Kallystine had cut deeper, but never mind; even now she is paying for that mistake, and for many others."

"Who *are* you?"

"Even now you don't know. But then my name is legion, as are my forms and the eyes through which I see. Do you recognize these?"

He opened his jacket at the throat. Around his neck was a string of human teeth, the incisors chipped to sharp points. "The roots never stop bleeding," he said, more in his own voice than before, and bared his own sharpened teeth in a feral grin. "Ah, my family have been good servants to my lady, and my mother was one of the best. After you were done with her, my lady returned these to me, lest I forget. I will never forget, and neither should you."

Then Jame remembered, with a shiver. Rawneth had used the soul of one of her randon captains, a former instructor at Tentir and guard at Gothregor, a woman whose name Jame had never been able to learn, to create a demon to hunt Kindrie. There under the shadow of the Witch's tower at Wilden, Bane had literally ripped open its seams with the Ivory Knife and the demon essence had spilled out onto the pavement as a sort of black sludge with a set of teeth—these teeth—afloat in it before they too sank.

So that had been Simmel's mother and the Tempter's "cousin," caught in a situation not unlike Bane's own after the priest Ishtier had used his soul to create the Lower Town Monster—except that the Knife had presumably destroyed the randon's soul, but not necessarily her body. With Bane, the reverse might be true. Or not. Jame's head hurt enough as it was without trying to untangle such a riddle.

The Randir put a finger to his lips. "Shhhh. You mustn't frighten her away."

"Who?" Jame demanded, thoroughly confused as his voice changed again.

"Why, Kinzi's pretty little Whinno-hir, although not so pretty now. I thought she was dead. No matter. Today we finish what my sweet Greshan began."

A Caineron Highborn appeared behind him. "What, trifling with our bait? No fair, Simmel. We've earned that dubious pleasure, not you."

The Randir flinched. His face, sallow before, went white with shock as his pupils suddenly contracted back to normal. He lurched to his feet and stumbled behind a bush, where they could hear him violently retching.

"Odd people, the Randir," commented the Highborn.

Jame recognized him from her first class with the Caineron, the one who had wanted to play games. Now he watched her with bright-eyed intensity, and licked his lips.

"No," said Gorbel, behind him.

"But, my lord, think how proud your father will be of you! Besides, afterward who could tell?"

"I said, no." As the other withdrew, grumbling, Gorbel knelt and raised a leather water-bag to her lips.

Jame drank, feeling as if she could drain a lake.

"Enough," he said, and withdrew the bag.

"Why?"

"Once you helped the Ardeth Timmon save me from water," he said gruffly. "Now I save you with it. We're even."

That wasn't what she had meant. The Caineron was right: after what she had done to him and to his pet advisor, Caldane would love anyone who brought her to grief; and even as his current lordan, Gorbel's position in that snake-pit of a house was none too secure.

A shiver passed through the forest. Leaves rustled, trunks groaned, stirred by no breath of wind. Jame stiffened and tried to draw up her cramped legs.

"I think," she said, as casually as possible, "that I may be sitting on a snake."

"More likely a root. The rain last night loosened the soil. Arboreal drift, you know. Some trees prefer to spend the summer up-slope where it's cooler. Also, that damn willow is stirring things up."

"It's here?"

"Close enough, and on the move, dragging a chunk of mountain after it."

He had risen and spoke in a preoccupied voice, listening. The woods quivered again.

"Take cover. As for you," he looked down at Jame, expressionless, "wait."

Left alone, unable to do otherwise, she waited.

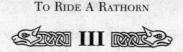

III

SOMETHING WAS COMING, something that glimmered between the white birch. The forest seemed to shift around it. Late spring flowers bloomed in the shadow of new leaves, stirred by a fresher breath than that of near midsummer. The Whinno-hir seemed to drift into the clearing like smoke, like mist. There at its edge she paused, shy as a doe with one delicate hoof poised in mid-air. Her coat was the color of fresh cream, her mane, tail, and stockings white, as were the dapples on her back and flanks. Large, dark eyes darted here and there, warily. Ears flicked. Then she snorted, tossed her head, and stomped.

Jame caught a trace of what she had scented: the infinitely personal reek that clung to the Heir's Coat. But she had long since laid that aside.

The hills fold space. Sometimes perhaps they also fold time. This wasn't the ragged creature that Jame had seen before, but what she had been. For a moment, it was forty-three years ago, and Greshan lurked behind her in ambush.

"Lady!" Her voice came out as hollow as an echo in an empty room, straining to cross decades. "It's a trap. Run!"

Twangggg . . .

The note of the bow seemed by itself to flick a crimson line across that cream colored shoulder, so fast did the arrow fly.

The Whinno-hir screamed, wheeled, and fled.

Simmel leaped from the bushes to follow, already fitting another arrow to his bow, but Gorbel caught him by the jacket and swung him around, hard.

"Never." Slap. "Hurt." Slap. "A Whinno-hir." Slap.

He let go and the Randir fell.

"I challenge you for this, lordling," he snarled through blood spilling from a split lip.

"Do. Then you can explain to the Commandant why. Oh, Perimal."

Half a dozen direhounds erupted from the undergrowth. They might not be scent trackers, but bloodshed almost under their noses whipped them to frenzy. Most charged after the wounded Whinno-hir. One made for the Randir. Gorbel caught the hound on his dagger as it leaped and flung it aside.

"Damn waste of a good dog. Horses!" he roared, turning. "After them, you fools, before they catch her!"

The three Caineron plunged away, two of them riding high in their stirrups, whooping, the third grim-faced with spurs clapped to his mount's sides.

Simmel lurched to his feet and smeared blood across his white face with a shaking hand. His trembling fingers caught the necklace of teeth and broke it. He looked beyond sick, like an apple half-devoured from within by worms. His skin grew taut over bone and his eyes sank.

"My lady honored me," he said, in a drying thread of a voice. "Then she left me. She left, with her will unfulfilled."

He was Randir. His lady was Rawneth, the Witch of Wilden. Of course. That was who had spoken to her through him.

"Your mistress has hag-ridden you," Jame said, to distract him, to gain time as she strained against her bonds.

"I've seen this before, with a . . . a creature named Bane. Where is your shadow, Randir? What's happened to your soul?"

His lips peeled back, teeth already falling from oozing gums, and went for Jame in a shamble. At last she wrenched her hands free. One came up with a rock in it. She smashed him on the side of the head and his skull crumpled like paper, empty. He fell, and in falling crumbled to dust and to a rain of bloody teeth within his cadet's uniform.

IV

JAME SCRABBLED OFF THE REMAINS OF ROPE, noting that her claws had indeed picked apart one length, but they had also badly lacerated the opposite wrists. Her own blood, still flowing freely, had loosened the knots.

A moment to tear strips of cloth from her shirt, another to bind up the bleeding wounds, and she was off, stumbling after the hunt. No tracker, she quickly went astray in the restless landscape. Somewhere hounds were baying and men shouting but, it seemed, in different directions. Perhaps Gorbel, that mighty hunter, had also gotten lost.

The ground rippled with roots to trip her. Aspens quivered, reaching for the cool heights. Valley oaks dug in their gnarled toes. A grove of sumac scattered wildly in all directions. The whole Riverland felt unstable, shifting—from the crack on her head or blood loss or arboreal drift, Jame couldn't tell. Dense undergrowth, swaying trees, a sky rapidly clouding over—which way was north, which south? Lost. And under it all was the nightmare sense of needing to get somewhere, fearing that it was already too late.

Shouts, crashes, a high, terrified whinny.

Jame floundered through bushes and stopped, staring. She had caught up with the wrong hunt. Again.

The Whinno-hir Bel-tairi plunged against the ropes that held her, jerking her captors back and forth. She was small and delicately made, but terror gave her strength. A violent lunge yanked a Kendar off his feet. She stood poised to trample him, but restrained herself, snorting, and he scrambled out of her way.

"Hold her, damn you!"

The man who spoke bent over a fire, stirring it with a metal rod. There was something of Torisen in his features, something of Ganth in his voice, but both on the turn. Though still young and handsome, he looked like a man with a secret taste for spoiled meat, his own flesh just beginning to ripen on the bone.

Jame stood rooted, staring at him. This, without doubt, was her long-dead uncle Greshan.

"Having been on your travels," he said to the Whinno-hir in a conversational tone, "you may not know this, but your mistress Kinzi, my dear grandmother, has seen fit to stand between me and my chosen consort. She has even talked Father into sending my brother to seek the contract that should be mine. Dear little Gangoid. Sweet little Gangrene. As if he were man enough for Rawneth, or for anything else. I will have her, you know. I always get what I want. But your lady must be taught not to meddle, and you will bear that message to her."

He drew out the iron, which by now was glowing red hot, and spat on it. Fixed to its end were the three curved lines of the rathorn sigil, incandescent with heat.

With an effort, the mare controlled herself, although her wide, dark eyes still rolled white. The men gasped and fell back a step. Their ropes now hung loosely around a slender woman with long, white hair and a triangular face.

Please, she said. *Please*.

"Well, well, well." Greshan thrust the iron back into the heart of the fire and rose. "I've heard that your kind can shape-change, but never believed it. Now, is this form true, or an illusion? Shall we find out?"

He sauntered around her, stepping over the slackened ropes. "You aren't bad looking . . . for an animal. I've had worse. Perhaps we can handle this another way, if you please me."

As he came up behind her, his hand dropped to loosen his belt. In a flash, she was again equine, lashing out with small, sharp hooves. He fell over backwards with a yelp and scuttled away. Once clear, he rose, his face going from white to blotchy red with anger.

"You mangy, flea-bitten nag, look what you did!"

She might have cracked open his skull. Instead, she had ripped his coat and knocked him into a mud puddle.

He grabbed the hot iron and stalked toward her.

"Bring her down!"

Ropes tightened around her legs. She crashed over on her side.

"You. Hold her head."

A wooden-faced Kendar forced it to the ground and knelt on her neck, one hand brutally twisted in her mane. Greshan stepped forward and thrust the glowing iron into the Whinno-hir's face.

Her scream and the stench of burning hair shocked Jame from her trance. She sprang at Greshan, the rathorn battle-shriek tearing from her throat and her claws out. He saw her. His eyes widened and his jaw dropped. So did the brand. But at the end of her lunge, he wasn't there. Face down in deep mould, she heard the fading echoes of shouts as the mare freed herself and then the receding beat of hooves. She was alone, the glen undisturbed by fire or struggle.

Did I dream it? She wondered, but then she felt a hard shape under her hand, under the loom of decades and drew it out. It was a rusted metal rod, its end bent into the sigil of a Knorth branding iron.

You can visit the past, Tirandys had once told her, speaking of the Master's House, but you can't change it.

"Damn, damn, *damn!*" said Jame.

However, this terrible story wasn't over yet.

Today, we finish what my sweet Greshan began.

The hounds were still on the trail of their prey and she was still lost. Jame pulled herself together and rose.

Water flows downhill. Find water.

SOME TIME LATER, how long she hardly knew, Jame found herself stumbling up a slope. Something beyond the ridge above her was moving, something big.

Overhead, golden leaves undulated against a leaden sky. Supple withies swayed back until the trunk invisible beneath them groaned, then surged forward with a great *swooshhhh*.

From the crest, she looked down on the errant golden willow. It had just passed by, a shimmering hillock of narrow leaves on long, wand-like stems, fighting its way up the bed of a mountain stream. Beneath, its roots writhed in a serpentine node, cracking out like whips to anchor and pull, digging into the stream bed to push. Its trunk swayed back, then surged forward. As it did so, the chain fettering it rose dripping from the stream and the huge boulder to which it was attached ground forward another inch. Back and forth, back and forth.

This was the tree that, not so long ago, had carried Jame and her cousin Kindrie across the Silver, away from the Randir's ravening pack, not that it had probably been aware of them clinging like a pair of aphids to its boughs. Now here it was, all but trapped, wood for the axe.

A moment's dizziness, and suddenly she was slithering down the steep slope, into the stream. Half obstructed as it was below by the boulder, it had risen far above its natural bed. Moreover, the willow's roots had churned it to the consistency of thick oatmeal lumpy with stones and apparently bottomless.

Flailing about, she managed to grab the overhanging branch of a tree that had survived the willow's passing. Whether she clawed her way out or the tree pulled her up, Jame had no idea. As she lay panting on the bank among its hunched roots (why did she have the impression that they had pulled themselves out of the willow's way?), a hoarse, hollow voice spoke above her, sounding not altogether pleased:

"You again, girl. I might have known."

Jame looked up.

The tree's trunk was a knobby, thick affair, easily twice as wide around as her arms could have reached. Shaggy bark clung to its bulges like an ill-fitting dress. Some eight feet up was a broad burl that suggested a contorted face, with a large hole where a major branch had long since broken off. The whole looked not unlike a natural *imu*.

"Earth Wife? Mother Ragga?"

"G'ah," said the voice, as if clearing its throat, and the hole spat out a shower of leave mold mixed with old bird bones, twigs, and one very angry squirrel. "Step-mother to you, if that. Get off my feet. Your blood is poison."

Jame let her head droop. The rag around her wrist was dripping red. ". . . could have told you that," she muttered, trying to tighten it with teeth and her free hand. ". . .'s hardly a secret anymore."

"Get up," said the hollow voice as the squirrel furiously scolded them both from a nearby branch. "G'aaah up! They have her."

Then Jame heard the Whinno-hir's despairing cry. Over it soared the rathorn's scream, mingling with the mad howl of the direhounds.

JAME CLAWED HER WAY TO HER FEET, bark shredding under her nails. The sounds were surprisingly close. Trinity, had they all been running in circles? She fought her way down stream through brambles, past the boulder, up the far slope. The ridge above was crowned with throttle-berries and under them ran the narrow paths of wild things. Clothed this time, but otherwise as wet and slippery with mud as she had been at the falls, Jame slithered between the roots until she could see into the hollow beyond.

On the far side, the Whinno-hir huddled, a pale blur, against the trunk of a giant fir. Bare, lower branches thrust out around her like so many brittle arms seeking to protect a ghost.

The rathorn colt also stood between her and the hounds. Three lay dead and mangled at his feet. A fourth dragged itself in circles, snapping furiously at its own useless hindquarters. The last two, one on each side, darted back and forth, trying to draw their quarry off balance.

The colt reared up, presenting his horned mask, greaves, and ivory sheathed belly. Head on, only his hind legs were vulnerable. Hackles rattled and rose, lifting the lower half of his mane, a spiky wave down his spine, and his tail. As the hounds lunged, he pivoted on his hocks and struck at them, fangs snapping, with the whip-crack speed of a snake. One came too close, and was impaled on the twin horns. As the colt flung him off, his mate lunged for the rathorn's throat, broke his teeth on the ivory armor, and went down with a shriek under sharp hooves.

The hound with the broken back had stopped circling. It snarled as the rathorn loomed over it. The hooves drove down again in a precise blow to the skull that shattered it.

Sudden silence.

There in the midst of carnage stood the rathorn like some fabulous cross between a dragon and a warhorse, all white except for his own blood and that of the hounds. The latter ran down the curved horns into grooves in the ivory mask, between the glittering red eyes, down to the mouth where it was caught by the flick of a pink tongue between white fangs.

Then he gave himself a very equine shake that set his mane flying and uttered a loud snort of satisfaction.

Jame could feel his eyes fix on her. He snorted again: "*Huuh!*"

She crawled out from under the bushes and stood, swaying slightly. "All right. You can see me and I can see you. What next?"

Below, undergrowth crackled and parted for Gorbel, closely followed by his two men. He gave a grunt of satisfaction, not unlike the rathorn's, and swung down from his mount, a wickedly sharp boar spear in hand. His companions kept to their saddles, but with difficulty: all three horses had caught the rathorn's disturbing scent. The colt lowered his bloody horns at them and snarled. They backed, wild-eyed, barely under control.

The Caineron took up a stance, perhaps by accident, between Jame and the ivory-clad beast. One of his own hounds lay disemboweled at his feet. Jame didn't like the odds for either man or beast. She slid down through the bracken to his Gorbel's side and touched his sleeve. "Please. Don't."

He shot her a look askance, taking in her filthy condition. "Been playing in the mud again, have you? Father would love to see you now."

"Well, I've seen him turning handle over spout in mid-air, filling his pants. Who d'you think is ahead so far?"

The sound he made might almost have been a laugh.

Then both horns and spear swung around to cover the opposite side of the hollow. Someone or thing was approaching. A snuffle, a sneeze, and the Molocar Torvo shambled panting into the clearing, followed by his master Tarn.

Both were utterly disheveled and matted with burrs. One of the Caineron snickered. Gorbel looked exasperated. When Tarn saw the rathorn, however, his face lit up with delight.

"See?" he demanded of them all. "*See?* I don't know what trail you lot followed to get here, but we came by the true one, every step of the way." He dropped to his knees and threw his arms the enormous, shaggy hound. "Good boy, Torvie, good boy!"

Torvo licked his master's face and slowly collapsed in the boy's embrace.

Tarn shook him. "Torvie, you idiot, this is no time for a nap. There's the rathorn. There! We still have to take it." The hound breathed in long, rasping sighs, with a rattle at the end of each, his half open eye-lids fluttered. "Torvie!"

Everyone was watching now, transfixed.

"Torvie, wake up! You're not going to die. No, no . . ."

The rathorn colt began to quiver. His hackles had fallen and he seemed somehow smaller than he had been, more vulnerable. His own grief had scabbed over, Jame realized, but never healed, like an abscess on the soul. What he saw now was not a boy and a dying hound but himself in the last moments of his dam's life, frantic that she not leave him, knowing that she must, but not yet, please, not yet.

The hound's breath rattled and stopped.

For a moment, no one breathed.

Then the rathorn screamed.

His grief and despair blasted the clearing, withering every leaf, killing every blade of grass. Jame fell to her knees, hands over her ears, but the sound was in her heart, in her soul, ripping open old scars.

She was with her first teacher and nurse, Winter, as Kin-Slayer in her father's hands sheared the Kendar woman nearly in two.

She was on the edge of the Escarpment, watching her mother plummet into the abyss.

She was crouching beside the body of the man who had taught her honor and given her love under the eaves of darkness.

Good-bye, Tirandys, Senethari. Good-bye.

A hand on her shoulder . . . Torisen? No. Gorbel.

"B-but I never cry," she told him, feeling tears track down her muddy face.

"Neither do I," he said, and perfunctorily wiped a streaming nose on his sleeve.

Somewhere beyond her own grief, she had glimpsed a fat man beating a woman over and over, despite her screams, until she lay still on the floor in a pool of blood that inched toward a child's bed.

Tarn bent over Torvo, sobbing. "It's my fault! It's all my fault!"

Otherwise, the clearing was empty.

Jame glanced toward where the Caineron had been.

"They ran away," said Gorbel flatly. "I might have too, if I'd been on horseback."

"The rathorn?"

Then they heard him shriek, not far away. He sounded terrified. Gorbel grabbed his spear and plunged off in the direction of the sound, with Jame hard on his heels.

❧ VII ❧

THEY CAME TO THE CHURNING STREAM, the boulder, and the willow. The latter two had progressed perhaps a foot since Jame had last seen it, but where was the rathorn?

The willow swung back and surged ahead, its leaves flowing molten gold. The chain rose dripping, and there was the colt, brought up with it. In his headlong flight, he had plunged into the quagmire and somehow gotten his lesser horn wedged into a link of the chain.

"Oh, shit," said Jame.

The colt snorted out mud, wheezed, and began feebly to struggle. The willow swung back and the chain sank again, dragging him down with it.

"Damn," said Gorbel. "There goes my trophy."

"Quit on me now and I'll hand you something you'll be even sorrier to lose. Come on."

Seen close up, the boulder really did look like a dislodged chunk of mountain. A very big chunk. With muddy water boiling around it. Jame took a running jump and for a moment hung from its slick rock-face by her nails. The roar of the water echoed in her head. Then she forced the world back into focus and clawed her way up. Luckily, the boulder was full of cracks and niches. When she reached the top, she looked back down to see Gorbel trying to follow her, still stubbornly clutching his boar spear. She grabbed its shaft below the head and braced herself. He climbed up hand over hand and collapsed gasping beside her.

"This . . . is . . . insane."

"But interesting. Look."

The willow was shedding wands. As they floated down, they grew thread-like roots and clustered around the rock's base, busily prying into its fractures. The cap of each rootlet excreted an acid that allowed both the saplings and their parent tree to anchor themselves with startling speed, years of erosion accomplished in minutes. Still, that might not be fast enough.

"Can you use that pig-sticker to pry this open?" she asked, shouting to make herself heard.

He examined the link that hooked the chain's ends together. "I might. Why?"

"Just do it, once I reach the colt."

He caught her arm. "Again, why?"

"Because I killed his dam."

Rathorn ivory is the second hardest substance on Rathillien, and it never stops growing. If they live long enough—and some scrollsmen argue that, like the Whinno-hir, they are potentially immortal—their armor eventually encases them in a living tomb.

The mare had been staggering under its weight, breathing in hissing gasps through bared fangs because the nasal pits of her mask had grown shut, as had one eye hole. He had walked beside her, crying, now a year-ling foal, now a slender, white-haired boy with red, red eyes: *No, you're not going to die! No, no . . .*

"You bagged a rathorn?" Gorbel's goggle eyes were suddenly those of a child, wide with wonder. "How?" he demanded eagerly. "With what weapon?"

"There isn't time . . ."

"Tell me, and I'll help."

"With a knife."

If you kill me, my child will kill you.

"Through the eye."

Kill me.

"At extremely close quarters."

The chain was rising again, and the rathorn with it. Gorbel still held Jame's arm, for a moment supporting her as she sagged. He peered at her face, white under its muddy mask, but if the cloth around her wrist was more red than brown, he didn't notice.

"Are you all right?"

I'm bleeding to death, Jame thought with odd detachment. *Well, either I have enough blood left in me to do this or I don't.*

"Besides," she said out loud, "I owe the tree too."

He was surprised into letting her go, and she stepped out onto the taut chain. The colt's weakening struggles barely caused a tremor, but at least he was still alive. The links were slick and knobby underfoot (Who brings a chain on a hunt? They must have sent to Restormir or Wilden for it.), but it was at least as thick as the rope that had stretched across the Great Hall.

When she reached the colt, she slid into the roiling water, onto his back. His red eyes snapped open and he began feebly to thrash, but already they were sinking again. Jame took a deep breath. Opaque water, almost liquid mud, closed over her head. Eyes squeezed shut, she slid her hands up the rathorn's neck and down his mask to the trapped horn. There. She began to work the link back and forth, inch by inch, up the length of ivory. The air in her lungs was turning to fire when the slack went out of the chain and they rose again.

Above water, she clung gasping to the colt's neck. He hung limp. She drove her nails into his crest.

"Wake up, dammit! You can't kill me if you die first!"

VIII

GORBEL WONDERED if the Knorth madness was indeed contagious and if so, whether he had caught it.

After all, here he was on top of a bloody big rock (*don't think how far off the ground you are; don't think*), trying to break a Trinity-be-damned chain with an ancestors-cursed boar spear, while trying to fend off a swarm of willow saplings. The boulder's face seethed with them as if with so many leafy snakes (*ugh*), all industriously rooting themselves in stone. Debris rattled down on all sides, along with occasional larger chunks.

Father had told him clearly enough what to do with the Knorth bitch: humiliate her; make her suffer; show the entire Kencyrath how insane both she and her brother were for thinking that a Highborn girl could ever become a randon.

But it wasn't so easy. She kept throwing him off-guard.

This . . . this was insane.

She had killed a rathorn mare. There, he envied her. She felt she owed a debt to the rathorn's foal. All right. He could see that, vaguely. But to a *tree*?

Madness.

And what about that sudden flash of . . . memory? . . . back in the clearing when the rathorn had let off that god-awful cry? Father beating Mother, smashing her skull, spattering blood and brains . . . no. His mother had died when he was still only a squalling brat. He didn't remember her at all, and he cried for no one. But his nose did run. It was running now.

Sudden pain lanced through his foot. A sapling had crawled onto it unnoticed and had sunken its roots through the boot into flesh. He yanked out the leafy wand as if it were a weed, but only the top part came. His foot continued to throb as if splinters had been driven deeply into it.

The willow swayed back and forward again with a rush. The chain around the boulder tightened. Its length rose, bringing with it a muddy mass that resolved itself into two figures, one clinging to the other. The rathorn hung by his horn like a slaughtered hog on a hook. Then he snorted mud out of his nostrils and again began struggling weakly to free himself. He had guts, that one. So (*face it*) did the Knorth.

But Trinity, what a way to ride a rathorn!

Stone shifted under foot. Gorbel wobbled, terror clutching his heart. One side of the rock sheared away, trailing saplings, and hit the water with a great, drenching splash. The rest of the boulder was breaking apart, the chain paying out link by link, faster and faster, as the willow pulled and its anchor gave way.

Jump. *Jump!*

Gorbel did, and nearly fainted on impact from the stabbing pain in his foot. He limped to high ground and clung to a tree, watching, as the boulder disintegrated. Set loose, the dammed stream crested in a muddy flash flood. Two figures tumbled with it, around a curve in the river bed, out of sight.

CHAPTER XIV

To Ride a Rathorn

Summer 45–53

I

. . . DROWNING, tumbling over and over, battered coughing on water, choking on air, arms and leg wrapped around the colt, her face pressed against his neck, white mane and black hair streaming together in her eyes . . .

. . . hang on hang on hang on . . .

Thick with debris, the river swept them on in the flash flood of its sudden release until, finally, the crest left them behind. The colt righted himself with a snort and struck out for the shore, but the water was still too deep and the current too swift.

Jame clung to him, her head spinning. No, she and the colt both were, around and around in a wide eddy. Here, sharp rocks like teeth rimmed the shore, gnashing the water to foam. The clear center of the vortex revealed stony terraces below, gaping like a vast, ribbed gullet. At the bottom, eyes as big as dinner plates reflected the moon, waiting.

It wasn't the River Snake, Jame thought, with intense if momentary relief. They hadn't yet reached that monster's abode beneath the Silver. However, Rathillien came in layers of reality. Either she had hit her head once too often or this was some new dimension of the Merikits' sacred space, from which the Four—water, air, earth, and fire: Eaten One, Falling Man, Earth Wife, and Burnt Man—ruled Rathillien in their singularly haphazard fashion.

"Great fish! Eaten One!" she cried to the maw beneath, sputtering through a face-full of spray. "What have we done to you? Spit us out!"

Bloop.

Monstrous bubbles set the water boiling around them and burst with the stink of fish breath.

Ah, why should I bother with you, who are no spawn of mine? Go your way. Go.

The whirlpool disgorged itself into a waterfall. They fell from what surely was an impossible height. Stranger still, an old man fell with them, his dingy-white beard whipping up over his shoulder. He was almost but not quite seated on a throne that fell just beneath him.

"Falling Man, South Wind, Tishooo!" Jame cried to him. "You helped me once at Gothregor. Will you again?"

"Pshaw." Needles clattered in gnarled hands. A knobby scarf laddered with dropped stitches flew upward and tried to wrap itself around his neck. He fended it off impatiently. "Knit one, purl two . . . I already did my part in blowing away the weirdingstrom. Leave me alone. I have a kingdom to rule."

"Tishooo, you're knitting your beard into your scarf."

"Well, how do *you* catch a dragon? Go away, girl. I'm busy."

They crashed into the pool at the base of the falls, into water throbbing with the pulse of its own descent, and were swept on. Jame could no longer feel her chilled hands or feet. *Much more of this*, she thought, not very clearly, *and I'm off*.

One last try.

"Earth Wife . . ."

WHAP.

They had tumbled into a tree's drooping limbs and one had slapped her smartly across the face. The colt snagged the bough with his curved horns. Half-dazed, still clinging to his back, she felt him swing around in the current, then clamber out of the water and up the bank. Wet, tangled roots that should have snared his hooves instead shifted, groaning, to provide footholds. At the top he stood for a moment with his head down, sides a heave and quivering legs astraddle. Then he gave himself a mighty shake.

Jame was lying on the ground before she realized that she had fallen off. Cracks of bright sky showed through a dark canopy of leaves overhead. She stared up at them, too tired to move or think. Between one blink and the next, or so it seemed, the light shifted and darkened toward a night fretted with stars. Time had passed. How much?

The air was very still, yet nearby leaves stirred.

"Talk, talk, talk." The words rustled and creaked as stiff leaves rubbed together. "Earth Wife this. Earth Wife that. Always wanting something. Always meddling. *Errr-eeek* . . . Wear down a mountain, you would, girl, or tear up a forest by the roots. And now this."

Jame rolled her head toward the voice. She lay not far from a large holly bush. Broad, glossy leaves edged with faintly luminous gold stirred fretfully. Some drew back, others bowed forward or curled into rolling lines. Light, shadow, and movement defined a crude, constantly changing face as large as the bush itself. It glowered down at Jame, spiked leaves rippling into a scowl.

"Said your blood was poison, girl, didn't I? What shall we do with you now, eh?"

Something has happened. Jame thought, fumbling through shards of memory. *What?*

She raised an unsteady hand to her head. The makeshift bandages had long since unraveled and been swept away by the current; the scratches, if one could call them that, oozed. She could see white tendons laid bare and veins narrowly missed. Trinity, had she cut that deep and never even felt it? A diagonal swathe of mingled fresh blood and dried was smeared across her forearm. Vaguely, she remembered hot breath on her wrist and a sense of bitter triumph not her own. A pause. Then had come the first, almost tentative rasp of a tongue against her bleeding flesh.

Sweet Trinity. He had tasted her blood.

Somewhere, someone was crying. It was a terrible sound, compounded of grief, rage, and a helpless, hopeless despair that shook her very soul.

"D'you want to see what you've done, you wretched, wicked girl?" hissed the leaves, rasping against each other in such agitation that spines snapped and flew in a stinging shower. "Then look."

Foliage peeled back layer by layer, opening not into the heart of the bush but into the dim, earth-floored lodge of Mother Ragga, the Earth Wife. Two figures huddled on the cold hearth, both white-haired but one a naked, shivering boy and the other a woman who held him in her arms. It was he who sobbed in deep wrenching gasps through pale lips stained with blood.

My blood, thought Jame.

The woman bent her head to draw the curtain of her hair over him and across the ruined half of her face. One dark, liquid eye regarded Jame askance.

Oh Kinzi-kin, child of darkness. How much worse than your uncle you have proved.

Then she froze, ears pricking through her tangled mane.

Jame heard it too.

Something was moving in the gathering dark. With it came a crackling and the stench of burnt fur.

"Now look what you've called up," hissed the Earth Wife, closing her branches like so many leafy arms. "As if we needed him!" Then she turned her face inward and disappeared.

Undergrowth and small trees snapped beneath a heavy tread, though the footfalls themselves were felt rather than heard as slow, deep shudders in the earth. Something huge prowled and growled through the darkening wood, circling, circling. Too weak to rise, Jame turned her head to catch glimpses as it passed, now a black shape defined by a hole in the star light, now by glowing cracks that opened and closed as it moved as if some terrible conflagration still smoldered deep within its flesh.

In the Ebonbane, by the chasm, it was muttering over and over. *On the hearth, in the Master's hall . . .*

Its words crackled and growled in Jame's mind, impatient, hungry. If fire had a voice, so it would have sounded. There was something else in it, though, something terrifyingly familiar, but her dazed brain refused to track down the memory.

An enormous head suddenly blotted out the sky above her, blunt, feline, and very, very close. The ears were charred stubs, the eyes caverns lit by deep, internal flames, the whole face a contorted mask of scar tissue.

Huh. It breathed waves of heat and greasy smoke in her face, then snuffled in her scent. *You.*

Jame had been expecting the Burnt Man who, Ancestors knew, was bad enough. But this was something else, or perhaps something more.

"Who . . . what *are* you?" she gasped, trying to cringe away.

The great head swung above her, scarred lips rippling back from white fangs bared half in grin, half in snarl. Flecks of bitter ash stung her face and clung to her lips, rank with the taste of ancient holocaust.

On the hearth, in the Master's hall, the changer Keral burned out my eyes. So many of my kin lay dead around me. So many. And all the while the Dream-weaver smiled and smiled as she danced out the souls of the fallen. But I did not fall. Dancer's daughter, in the Ebonbane, by the chasm, you escaped my judgment. But these mountains are mine.

Trinity, of course: it was the blind Arrin-ken whose presence she had sensed in her flight from Gothregor and up the Riverland, when the entire Snowthorn range had seemed like a crouching cat that held her under its paw.

Then, he had let her go. Now . . .

You have called on water, air, and earth. Now call on me. Do you seek judgment, Nemesis? Ask, and I will give it, blind justice for blind destruction. Ask!

The pressure to confess welled up like vomit. She had done so many bad things, or at least things for which she blamed herself. The great cat's will bore down on her, his hot breath scorching her face.

Confess. You know your guilt.

The Arrin-ken were the third of the three people who made up the Kencyrath. The Highborn ruled, the Kendar served, and the Arrin-ken kept the balance between them and their god—or had until millennia ago the great felines had withdrawn into the wilds of Rathillien for reasons still not entirely clear. However, they still sometimes used the so-called God-Voice to speak through unwilling Kencyr lips.

Oh. That was where she had last heard that terrible voice. In the subterranean Priests' College. Though the mouth of the renegade priest Ishtier.

Grief, pain, and rage had driven the great cat insane, but did that matter?

For us, the Arrin-ken Immalai had said, *good is no less terrible than evil*, nor were the two easily told apart. Who was to judge between them, if not those whom their ruthless god had chosen for that role? Least of all, who was she to question such a judgment?

In a moment, she would give this dark avenger what he wanted, and with it permission to burn her alive. Or would she become one of the Burnt Man's pack of the damned, the Burning Ones, with whom he hunted down those with the stench of guilt on them? An Arrin-ken's justice or the Burnt Man's? Kencyrath or Rathillien or both? It was all very confusing.

And yet again came the demand, singeing her eyelashes, rattling her to the depths of her being: *All things end, light, hope, and life. This you know full well, darkling-born, none better. Why delay? Come to judgment. Come!*

. . . get away get away get away . . .

She was still too weak to move, but her will to survive leaped out and seized that other mind now blood-bound to her own.

With a shriek, she/he/they burst out of the undergrowth. Before them, a monstrous darkness crouched, gloating, over its prey.

That puny thing is me? thought Jame.

Then the Arrin-ken raised its blind, smoldering face to them, and the stench of it rolled out in waves of heat that made the air quiver. The colt stopped short, appalled. Jame felt his hindquarters gather as if they were her own. The next moment, they had leaped over the great cat and were in wild flight down the riverbank.

. . . run run run . . .

THE COLT'S TERROR at this sudden invasion of his soul fed on Jame's of that which even now might pursue her. Their flight was madness and mindless, an eternity in growing darkness of crashing into, through, and between things that raked their sides and snatched at their feet.

After what felt like a millennium, Jame began to gather her wits. So did the colt. She could feel his revulsion at her presence in his mind and his attempts to throw her off. If she had indeed been on his back, he would have been rid of her long ago, and she of him. As it was, she felt his hatred and rage trying to pry her loose even as she struggled to free herself from him, but they were bound, body and soul. How could one throw off oneself?

To ride a rathorn . . .

Trinity, who would have thought it would be like this?

Hush, she found herself crooning to the colt. *Gently, gently. What good will it do to run yourself to death?*

Good enough to kill you, came the fierce answer.

And so he would, if he could. She felt the air burning in his lungs and his heart pounding. So did her own, back where her body lay.

So this is blood-binding, she thought, sickened to the bottom of her solitary soul. *No one should have such power over another being, and I don't even like being touched. Graykin was bad enough, but this . . . this is obscene. Am I too, for letting it happen?*

Gorbel's moon-like face hung over her, his lower lip pendulous with dismay.

"What's wrong?" he said, as if from a great distance.

She clutched his arm, and he flinched at the bite of her nails. "Gorbel, for Trinity's sake, kill me and set us both free!"

"What?"

"Just do it! Daddy will love you for it."

"Huh. I may not be clever like some, but I'm not stupid. Caldane, Lord Caineron, loves no one but himself. We don't play for love in my house, only for power. And survival. You've made a fine mess of your wrists. Hold still while I bind them. I said, hold still!"

She barely saw his hand before it caught her in the face with a jolting slap.

"Damn," she heard him mutter as the world dimmed.

III

IT FELT AS IF THEY HAD BEEN RUNNING FOR-EVER, on and on and on.

Sounds came and went.

Jame was vaguely aware of hounds baying and some-one (Gorbel?) shouting to attract the hunt's attention.

Time passed.

A thin, cool hand touched her brow, then held some-thing to her lips, forcing her to drink. "I don't know what's wrong," said a voice which, surely, she should know. "These injuries are bad, but nothing that *dwar* sleep won't heal . . . if she lets it. This constant agitation is killing her."

You try to calm down, she wanted to say, *with a bloody great cat breathing hot ash down your neck!*

Yes, there had been a cat. A blind Arrin-ken. Hunting them. Somehow mixed up with the Merikits' Burning Man.

And there had been a Whinno-hir mare—Bel-tairi, the Shame of Tentir, whatever that meant. She had tried to stop their mad flight crying, *Kinzi-kin! Nemesis! Do you want to kill him?*

Herself, perhaps; the rathorn colt, no.

Then the blind Arrin-ken had erupted from the under-growth, roaring, and the branches around him burst into flame. The colt jumped out of his skin, literally. One moment he was bucking like a lunatic, as if that could unseat an disembodied rider, the next he and Jame were looking down at his collapsed form. With its fierce anima-tion gone, it had looked almost as pathetic as Jame had under the Arrin-ken's paw. And then the blind brute had come at them again, not to be fooled by mere flesh and blood.

The rathorn bolted.

. . . run, run, run . . .

But where were the mountains, and what were these hills that rose and fell, swooping on wings of withered grass under the leaden eye of the moon? In a hollow, a patch of bloated flowers burst with a carrion stench under the colt's hooves. He slowed, snorting with alarm.

Oh no, thought Jame.

There probably were ways to step straight from the banks of the Silver into the Haunted Lands, several hundred leagues to the east on the other side of the Ebonbane.

With luck, though, this was only a nightmare, or the onset of terminal delirium.

However, given past experience, it was just as likely that she had somehow stumbled into her brother's soulscape. Again.

From the crest of the next rise, they looked down on the desolate ruins of a keep, just as Jame knew they would. Every line of it was familiar to her, from the squat tower to the broken walls, from the dry moat to the cracked, moon-like solar aglow over the lord's hall. She and Tori had grown up here, and here their father had died.

Memories: helping Cook dig poached eyes out of boiled potatoes, carefully, because if they burst they poisoned the food; the randon Tigon so hungry for meat that he cut off and roasted his own toes; Winter refusing to teach her how to fight because she was not a girl but—that awful thing—a lady. Ha. She had pounced on her brother after that, hoping to learn something from his reaction. Instead, she had only given him a bloody nose.

"Father says it's dangerous to teach you anything." Tori had said, snuffling into his sleeve. *"Will the things you learn always hurt people?"*

Jame had considered this, as she did again now, wondering if the answer had changed. *"Maybe. As long as I learn, does it matter?"*

"It does to me. I'm the one who usually gets hurt. Father says you're dangerous. He says you'll destroy me."

"That's silly. I love you."

"Father says destruction begins with love."

Love had destroyed their father, or rather the loss of it had with the gradual fading of their mother out of their lives and his increasingly desperate search for her.

Another memory, as sharp as a splinter of glass and as hard to forget: That day, she had played hide and seek with her brother (*"You be Father, I'll be Mother"*). There. Below. In the keep. And ended up dancing to entertain a warty faced death banner in the great hall.

At first, she had hadn't seen Father watching her. Then his husky voice had stopped her in mid-step.

"You've come back to me." He had looked half dazed with a relief so intense that it wiped twenty years off his face. *"Oh, I knew you would. I knew . . ."* But as he stepped hastily forward and saw her more clearly, the softness had run out of his expression like melting wax. *"You."*

I don't want to remember this, Jame thought, gripping the colt's tuft of a mane.

Simultaneously, she realized that she was not only in the rathorn's mind but on his back. Also, her hands had gone small and childish, without nails. The colt likewise had dwindled to a frightened foal, with mere bumps between his eyes and on his nose instead of those lethal horns.

Maybe this was a nightmare after all, and she was trapped in it. Perhaps this was a taste of the same terror that sometimes kept her brother awake for days on end rather than risk never being able to wake up again.

But fear only sharpened memory.

There in the hall, Father had stuck her hard across the face and slammed her back against the wall.

"*You changeling, you impostor, how dare you be so much like her? How dare you! And yet, and yet, you are . . . so like.*" His hands rose as if by themselves to cup her bruised face. "*So like . . .*" he breathed, and kissed her, hard, on the mouth.

"My lord!" Winter stood in the hall doorway.

He had drawn back with a gasp. "*No*. No! *I am* not *my brother!*" And he smashed his fist into the stone wall next to Jame's head, speckling her face with his blood. Then he had raged out, shouting for his horse, hell-bent on storming the Master's House itself to reclaim his lost love.

Winter had knelt beside her. "*All right, child?*"

Jame remembered nodding, and not being able to stop until the randon touched her shoulder. Then Winter had risen but paused, briefly, looking down at her. "*It isn't entirely his fault.*" she had said, and gone out to ready her lord's gaunt, gray stallion before someone got killed.

If not his fault, Jame had wondered as a child, *then whose?*

Now, the half-grown part of her mind caught the glimmer of an answer, and felt an unexpected stab of pity.

From the miseries of his own childhood, her father had risen to the pinnacle of power, only to fall with the loss of the one thing he had ever wanted. Love.

And for all his flaws, he was *not* like his brother, although Greshan had shaped him in ways that she was only beginning to understand.

So, who is the monster in the maze?

The question sprang into her mind as if asked by someone else. She recognized the test it posed, and the importance of the answer. Who was her true enemy?

Trinity. There were too many possibilities. Master Gerridon, the Witch of Wilden, Ishtier, Caldane, Torisen . . .

No, she told herself fiercely. Not him. Never.

Here and now, or rather down there in the keep that had become her brother's soul-image, the enemy was a mad, muttering voice behind a locked door.

"Tori!" she cried. Both she and the foal flinched as her shrill, child's voice cracked the leaden silence. Every nerve in her body cried, *Shut up, you fool! Run! Hide!* But she tried again, louder. "Daddy's boy! Come out, come out, wherever you are!"

The rathorn shook as the sky rumbled, or perhaps it was the earth. The sour wind shifted, this way and that, and the grass rustled like so many ribbons of dry snake skin.

Someone stood in the keep door, a thin, dark-haired boy her own age, give or take a minute either way. A white wolver pup crouched at his heels, just out of reach. The twins stared at each other. It was then. It was now. All they had had together lay between them, close enough to touch and yet years out of reach. The wind blew hard and the grass cringed, beginning to whine.

"Tori, get out!" she cried down at him, into the teeth of the rising gale, across the abyss of time. Could he hear her at all? "Go somewhere, anywhere, as far from here as you can!"

The wind veered again, now pushing at her back. It brought with it an all too familiar smell of must and dust and ancient sickness. She knew what was there before she turned to face it, but heart and stomach still lurched at the sight.

The Master's House loomed over them. Mist obscured its lower stories but the upper leaned as if poised to topple. Ashes of the dead blew in veils off its many roofs and gables, clouding the moon, thickening the air. Darkness stared out of a thousand broken windows and the reek of dull hunger exhaled—*HHAAAaaaa . . .* —through a hundred gaping doors. From the shadows within came the grinding of stone on stone as at a glacial pace the whole massive pile edged forward, for this was only the blind head of the House. The rest of it stretched back into Perimal Darkling and beyond, from fallen world to world, down the Chain of Creation. All those rooms of darkness drove it forward with a vast, inhuman momentum while its shadow rolled before it over the hills, and the grass wailed under it.

Jame gulped down nausea. If Tori's soul-image was bad, hers was worse. In the House was a hall with a green-shot floor. There, the woven eyes of the dead and the damned stared down from the walls at a sleeper huddled on the cold hearth, on a pile of Arrin-ken pelts.

And when the Master, finally, enters his hall, what then, Dancer's daughter? Will you rise and fight, or open your arms to him as you so nearly did once before? For what else, after all, were you bred?

Ah, but that time had not yet come.

"Hush," Jame breathed to the foal, her hand on his quivering neck. An ear flickered back to listen, then forward again, then back. "Hush. The Master is still in his house, the monster in its maze. In the end, either he will come out to meet us or we will go in after him. There. Aren't you glad now that you tried a taste of my blood?"

Perhaps she had spoken too soon.

A clot of darkness detached itself from the shadow of the House and rushed toward them over the swelling hills, glimpsed and gone and glimpsed again. Part of the rumble separated into pounding hooves.

"Oh no," said Jame.

The Master's gray stallion burst over the next rise and roared down on them. Its gaping jaws spewed foam and its steel-shod hooves threw up divots of turf that turned to dust in midair. The foal shrieked for his mother and bolted.

They dodged away among the rolling hills, the foal running in blind panic, Jame trying to keep him in the hollows, out of sight. This was hide and seek with a vengeance. It was also that buried childhood nightmare only recently unearthed by her abysmal attempts at horsemanship.

If you fail the Master, we'll just have to feed you to Iron-jaw, won't we?

She remembered the gray stallion charging her, ears back and teeth bared, when he had been only a horse and she only a child who had strayed into what might laughingly be called his pasture, given the noisome herbage of the Haunted Lands. Another time, Tori had dared her to ride him and, of course, she had been thrown, hard. There. That was the origin of the sick fear that cuddled her stomach to this day every time she put foot to stirrup and herself at the mercy of such a strong, unpredictable creature. Then her father had ridden the stallion to death and the changer Keral had claimed the haunt that it had become for his master.

The foal skidded around a mound, his hind legs nearly flying out from under him, and they swept down on a lone, white-haired figure on foot.

"Stop, or you'll kill yourselves!" he shouted, then jumped out of the way as they hurtled past.

"If we stop," Jame yelled back over her shoulder, "we'll die!"

Around another curve and there he was again, directly in their path with his thin hands up, terrified but determined. "I'm not joking!"

"Neither are we!"

The foal ran into him, stumbled, and fell head over heels. Thrown clear, Jame scrambled to her feet and spat out a mouthful of wriggling grass before it could take root.

The cause of their fall sat holding his head and groaning. Belatedly, Jame recognized her cousin Kindrie Soulwalker. Of course. That was the other voice she had heard in her sleep or delirium or whatever this was, and those were the thin, sensitive hands that had held a cup to her lips. Now he had entered the soulscape as a healer to help her, and been trampled for his pains.

"Sorry," she said to him, then "Run!"

The ground was thrumming like a vast drum. Over the crest came Iron-jaw and hurtled down on them, roaring. Kindrie stared, aghast, then abruptly vanished. The foal shied, squealing, directly into the stallion's path and went down under his hooves. The haunt wheeled and went for him, teeth bared. If he caught the young rathorn, he would shake him to death or snap his neck.

Jame leaped at the haunt's head. She meant to go for his eyes with her claws; however, her fingertips were still without nails. Instead, she found herself clinging to the stallion's neck, his hot breath reeking in her ear. One dead, white eye rolled toward her. He reared and tossed his head, trying to throw her off. If she fell, he would surely kill her.

So, she thought with an odd detachment, *do I die a helpless child or, finally, accept what I am and grow up?*

Her body seemed to decide for her. Skin split and bloody claws erupted from the tips of her fingers, just as they had when she had turned seven and faced her father over the dying Kendar Winter. She wrapped her legs around the haunt's neck. When he reared again, swinging her upward into his face, she drove her claws into that white marble of an eye. It burst, spraying an arc of black blood that clotted as it hit the air. Up he went and over, crashing down on his back. Jame sprang clear and ran. She heard him thrashing behind her, trying to roll away from such agony.

So some haunts can still feel pain, observed part of her mind. *Interesting*.

Another part, the one that wanted to live, thought only . . . *run run run* . . . and so she did, on and on and on, too scared to realize that she ran alone.

CHAPTER XV

Back to the Soulscape

Summer 53

I

SOMEONE WAS CALLING HER.

"Jame." And again, "Jame."

She knew that voice, although it seemed a lifetime since she had last heard it.

"Jame. Come on now, lass. Wake up."

Part of her was still running, lost among hills that rolled on forever, but the rest of her would rather die than not answer that call. Her eyes fluttered open. The moon glowed through tall windows, throwing tranquil bars of light on the floor, onto facing rows of cots empty except for the one in which she lay, but not alone. A strong arm held her. She knew that touch, that very smell, clean and honest as the man himself.

"Oh, Marc," she said. "I had such an awful dream."

But then, when she raised her hand to touch him, to be sure he was really there, she saw that her arm was heavily bandaged from wrist to elbow. No, it hadn't all been a dream. The worst part was true.

"Marc, I've done a terrible thing."

"Have you now." His big, rough hand gently stroked her hair. "You'd better tell me about it, then."

For a long while, however, neither of them spoke. They hadn't seen each other in nearly a year, not since the battle at the Cataracts. It seemed more like a lifetime ago, Jame thought, settling against the Kendar's broad chest, feeling him breathe and listening to his heart beat, steady and strong.

She remembered how they had first met. Dashing around a corner in Tai-tastigon with the stolen Peacock Gloves tucked into her wallet and the city guards on her heels, she had run head-on into what she at first had thought was a wall. Then it had put out big hands to catch her on the rebound.

He had walked all the way from East Kenshold—a big Kendar in late middle-age, turned out by the new lord of a minor house for defending the old lord's Whinno-hir mare from being ridden against her will. Before that, he had been a Caineron yondri with the Southern Host; before that, the last survivor of another minor house that had held Kithorn until the Merikit slaughtered everyone except Marc, who had been out hunting at the time and had come home to red ruin. By the time he had reached Tai-tastigon, seventy-odd years later, he had been tired unto death and ready to die, sure that at his age no Kencyr house would ever accept him again.

He had, however, woken in time to save her from a brigands' attack in the alley below—this, by climbing down two stories from the inn's loft "and then, to save time, falling the rest of the way," as he had put it later.

He was the most solidly decent person Jame had ever known, and she trusted his moral sense far more than she did her own.

However, he had assumed that she was Kendar with only enough Highborn blood to account for her various strange attributes. After all, Kencyr ladies were a breed apart, seldom seen outside their own halls and then only heavily masked. That one of them should be the infamous Talisman, apprentice to the greatest thief in Taitastigon, had never crossed his mind. At the time, Jame hadn't been sure herself what she was, and certainly hadn't guessed that the Highlord of the Kencyrath was her long-lost twin brother Tori.

Then she had found out, and so had Marc.

Would there ever be that easy friendship and equality between them again? Could there be between a Highborn and a Kendar? They hadn't yet crossed that bridge, yet here he was. Hang on to that.

Just then, Jorin trotted into the room and jumped up onto the cot. Jame yelped as his weight landed on her bandaged arm. Marc scooped up the ounce and rolled him over between them, upside-down.

"Hello, kitten," he said, rubbing the exposed, furry stomach. Jorin stretched, back arching, paws in the air, and began to purr.

"Where did you spring from?" Jame asked the Kendar over the cat's rumble.

"Oh, Gothregor. Everyone is back, except for those still attached to the Southern Host or elsewhere. Your lord brother will need every hand he can get for the haying, come midsummer."

Jame tried to imagine the seven foot tall Kendar wielding a scythe instead of his usual two-edged war axe. "He's got you out cutting the grass?"

"Nothing wrong with working the land, lass. I'll take that any day over a battlefield, where naught grows but bones from the earth after the first frost. Mind you, they say blood is a good fertilizer, but not one I'd use by choice."

Marc had never cared much for fighting, come to that. In battle, he usually feigned a berserker fit and scared the enemy into head-long flight. She had seen him once empty a hostile tavern the same way, with brigands flying through the doors, out the windows, and even up the chimney.

"Mostly, though," he said, "I've been seeing what can be done to put that big stained glass window back together. You know, the one facing east in the old keep, the map of Rathillien. A gorgeous thing. Somehow, though, it got smashed to pieces."

"Er . . . I'm afraid that was me. At the time, I had a pack of shadow assassins after me and used a rune to blow away their souls. Unfortunately, the window blew out too. So did a lot of death banners from the lower hall. Sorry."

There was a short pause, followed by a resigned sigh. "Ah well. I should have guessed as much. That's all right then, as long as it was in a good cause."

She started to turn to look at him, but stopped herself, in case he wasn't there after all. If this was a dream, she didn't want to wake.

"Are you teasing me?"

"Not at all. The window can be replaced. I hope. You can't. Besides, I enjoy the work."

He would, thought Jame, a bit envious given her own lack of talent. Marc had always had an artistic bent but precious little chance to develop it.

"Here."

He dropped something smooth and cool into her hand.

"We were melting down some salvaged shards of red glass—did you know the color comes in part from real gold?—when your lord brother nicked a finger and a drop of his blood fell into the mix. The result was . . . interesting."

Jame held the fragment up to the moon. Even such faint, silvery light woke a ruby glow in the heart of the glass. It seemed to her that she held something alive, but with a sort of life beyond her experience or comprehension.

"I'd like to experiment with other colors," said the big Kendar wistfully. "It's awkward, though, asking the Highlord of the Kencyrath to bleed on request."

Jame braced herself. She had to know. "I suppose," she said carefully, "that Tori has offered you a place in his—that is, in our house."

He shifted, to muffled protests both from cot and cat. "He did, yes. I declined the honor."

"But . . . why? Ancestors know, you've earned it."

"Oh," he said, trying to sound casual, "I thought I'd wait a bit, just to see what else might come along."

Jame nearly sat up, but the effort made her head spin.

"Marc," she said urgently, clutching his jacket, "you can't count on me ever having an establishment of my own, much less being allowed officially to bind Kendar to me. Think! Is Tori likely to give me that much power?"

"He made you his lordan, lass."

"Yes, but that was only to buy time. He can pitch me back into the Women's Halls whenever he wants, assuming the matriarchs don't toss me out again. Why, he hasn't even come to see if I've managed to get myself killed yet."

"Oh, he came." Marc chuckled. "You called him 'Daddy's boy' and told him to go away."

"Oh," said Jame blankly. "Oh dear. Wait a moment. How long have I been unconscious?"

"More than a week. Your cousin Kindrie went into the soulscape to see what was keeping you, and came back with two black eyes. He said something about being trampled by a rage of rathorns."

For the first time since waking, Jame remembered the rathorn colt. Trinity, where was he? It struck her now that she hadn't felt his presence since they had run in different directions to escape the haunt stallion. Surely she would know if he was dead . . . wouldn't she? What if she had left him trapped in the soulscape?

"I have to go back," she said, struggling to free herself from Marc's arms. "He won't know how to get out. He'll wander there, lost, until he dies."

"Gently, gently. Who will?"

"The colt. Marc, I said I'd done something awful, and I have. I've blood-bound a young rathorn."

He didn't push her away, but she felt his breath catch. "I didn't know you were a binder," he said, with a careful lack of emphasis. "Still, I suppose it's nothing you can help. Why bind a rathorn, though, of all creatures?"

"It wasn't intentional. He bit me."

"Ah. Well, there's no accounting for taste."

Jame felt a surge of relief. "Now you're laughing at me." If he could accept this, the worst thing she knew about herself, perhaps their friendship would survive after all.

But that didn't help the colt.

"I brought someone to meet you," said Marc, deliberately changing the subject.

She felt him move, then heard a flint rasp. The sudden flare of light momentarily blinded her. When her eyes cleared, she saw a child's wisp of a shadow cast on the far wall. Marc had set a lit candle down behind a lumpy saddle-bag on the table.

"This is my sister, Willow. Willow, meet my Lady Jamethiel. If you're good, she may let you call her Jame."

"I would be honored," said Jame, a little shaken, as the shadow sketched a wary salute.

She knew, of course, that her brother had found the child's bones at Kithorn the previous autumn and for some reason had carried them all the way south to the battle at the Cataracts. A little girl, trapped in death for decades under the ruins of her house . . . there she had hidden while her family was slaughtered above her, and there she had starved to death. But blood and bone trap the soul until fire sets it free, so here she still was.

Jorin's head popped up. He wriggled free, hopped down, and bounced at the shadow, which recoiled from him.

"He's frightening her," said Jame sharply.

"Give them a moment. Ah, that's my girl."

Cat and shadow had begun to chase each other back and forth, up and down the wall, while Marc moved the candle to give the game more scope.

"I keep meaning to give her to the pyre." He sighed. "After losing her once, though, it's hard to let go again."

In his tone, Jame heard the boy that he had been, who had lost everything he had ever loved. The old ache had never really healed, nor the loneliness gone away except, perhaps, for a time when two unlikely friends had shared a loft in Tai-tastigon.

"D'you suppose," he asked, "that it hurts her to stay like this?"

"I don't think so," said Jame, watching ounce and shadow child play, "but what do I know? You should ask Ashe."

He took a deep breath. "So I will. Until then, I'll hold on to her a bit longer, just to see what else might come along."

Neither spoke after that. Jame settled back against his shoulder and closed her eyes.

SOME TIME LATER she woke, or thought that she did.

The room had tarnished to a kind of thick, half light that belonged neither to day nor to night and cast no shadows but two. One was her own. The other sat cross-legged on a blanket, watching her, or so she assumed. It had a child's shape and some hint of shadowy features, but she could see through it to the wall beyond, to shelves thick with dust, lined with broken jars.

"This is a dream, isn't it?" she asked the silent watcher. "You're Willow, and this is where my brother found you, in the still room at Kithorn, under the charred hall."

No answer. Jame gathered herself to rise, but hesitated as the other drew back. "You're afraid of me. Why?"

Then she saw that her hands were tipped with six inch long ivory claws that rasped on the floor and would not retract. Her clothes had also changed to the close-fitting costume of a Senetha dancer with its oddly placed slashes. There were more of them than she remembered.

Reaper of souls. Who had called her that? *Dancer's daughter.* She felt her Shanir nature stir, dark, dangerous, and seductive.

"Is this what you see in me? Is this what you fear . . . for yourself? No. For your brother."

She settled carefully back against the wall.

"I'm sorry. I didn't mean to take your place in his life. When Marc and I first met, I'd lost my family too. I was . . . almost feral. You know," she added, reminding herself that, after all, this was only a child, "like a kitten that's grown up wild and never learned how to purr."

She frowned at her over-grown claws and clicked them together irritably. "Even for a dream, this is ridiculous. Maybe I should take up knitting. Knit one, purl two . . . but I'd only end up making cats' cradles and tying my hands together. I can't even pick my nose with these things without picking my brain, and there's little enough of that to begin with."

The shadow child uttered no sound, but something about her suggested a suppressed giggle.

Good, thought Jame, relaxing slightly, and continued, as much now to herself as to the child.

"It's hard to be Kencyr, much less a Highborn Shanir. Honor as we practice it is a cold, hard thing. It breaks some people. It turns others into monsters. I could easily be as bad as you fear I am . . . no, much worse . . . if I hadn't been shown kindness. First there were the Kendar at my home keep, then Tirandys, then Marc, and I love them all for it. I especially love your brother for reminding me what decency is, simply by being himself. I would rather die than hurt him. My word on it."

More tension left the small, shadowy figure, but a question lingered.

"Why can't I give him what he needs most, a home? Because I don't have one myself and perhaps never will." Jame thrust fingers into her loose hair in an exasperation which grew when her claws became entangled. She tugged, nearly poked herself in the eye, and swore in a language hopefully unknown to a child from remote Kithorn.

"So far, by accident, I've bound a half-bred Southron and a rathorn colt out for my blood (which he got, ancestors help him). Oh, and let's not forget my dear half-brother Bane, who flays little boys alive for sport, or used to. Maybe I don't deserve anyone better. The point is, though, not what they owe me but what I owe them, and so far as a bounden Highborn I've done a rotten job all around. I'm not going to promise Marc anything I can't give him. He deserves better than that."

Now, Jame thought, comes the hard part. She leaned forward, looking as serious as she could with both hands still tangled in her hair as if she was trying to tear it out by the roots.

"Willow, I need your help. This is a dream, part of the dreamscape. I need to go deeper, into the soulscape. I've gotten there before accidentally (and by now you probably think that 'Accident' is my middle name), but I don't know how to do it deliberately. You helped Kindrie to enter my brother's soul-image last winter on the march south, when he fell asleep and couldn't wake up. Will you help me now? Please. The colt is still trapped there. He's bound to me, however reluctantly, so I have to rescue him if I can, at the very least. Tirandys and the Kendar taught me that."

She didn't know how Willow would respond, or even if she understood. After all, this was a child, and one long dead at that.

Time stretched on and on in silence, until it lost all meaning. Dust drifted down. Flesh began to melt. The dancing costume now hung on wasted limbs and her hands had fallen to her lap, each still loosely gripping a mass of black hair with bits of dried scalp attached to it. Jame felt, dimly, that this should concern her, and there was a niggling sense of something else important, forgotten; but it was too much trouble to remember. All she wanted was to lie down and to sleep forever, but she was cold, so cold. Crawl across the floor through thick dust, lift the edge of the blanket . . . but someone was already under it, waiting, with eye sockets full of lonely shadow.

Those who receive kindness owe kindness in return.

Jame crept under the blanket and took the small bones in arms hardly less clothed in flesh. Dust fell. And silence. And the long night of the dead without a dawn.

III

THEN SOMEONE SPOKE HER NAME, or rather that hated corruption of it: "Jameth." And again, "Jameth."

The voice was muffled, but it was also clearly angry.

Jame stirred uneasily. She would rather sleep on and on, with no worries except perhaps that her teeth would eventually fall out, like her hair.

Wait a minute. That had been a dream, hadn't it? Trinity, she hoped so. Yes, she still had a full if rather tangled head of hair, and no clothes.

That last was changing, though. She felt her name draw her on, into a web of unseen thread. Coarse strands touched her, lightly at first, then with more persistence, snaring, entangling, thickening. And they stank. It was like being pressed face-first into dank, moldy cloth. Just as she was about to panic, she found herself on the other side, in a circular room. Like the death banner hall at Gothregor, it was dark and windowless, with an oppressively low ceiling. Torches flared at intervals around the stone walls. Between them hung dark tapestries full of lurking shadows that seemed furtively to shift as if aware of her presence. Opposite, however, fire light flickered on a familiar, gentle face.

Jame had never actually met her cousin Aerulan. After all, it was more than forty years since the massacre that had claimed all the Knorth ladies but one, the child Tieri, whom Aerulan had died protecting. However, over the past, dismal winter confined in the Women's Halls at Gothregor, wearing her dead cousin's clothes because Tori hadn't thought to provide her with anything more suitable, she had often visited Aerulan's banner where it had hung among the ranks of her family's dead—that is, until that last night when the Tishooo had blown them all out the window.

Now here they both were again, except . . . except it appeared to be Aerulan herself standing there, smiling back at her.

Blink. Look again.

While the other's face had the shape and fullness of life, it was marked by the fine weave of death, and its smile was a mere tug of stitches. Nonetheless, Aerulan's soul gazed out through warp and woof, clear-eyed and wryly amused.

So here we are again, cousin.

Was this another dream, or had she indeed reached the soulscape? If the latter, whose voice had drawn her and where was she now?

The answer came in the click of boot-heels and the jangle of heavy spurs, both muffled by the stone and thick cloth of the walls.

Brenwyr stalked past in a swirl of her divided riding skirt, arms folded tightly across her chest as if holding herself together. No longer smiling, Aerulan watched her pass. As the dead girl turned her head, Jame saw that it had no back except the concave reverse of her face, rough with tied off threads.

The Brandan Matriarch seemed oblivious to them both. What comfort could she take in that which she could not see, and who could see anything through an eyeless seeker's mask? In the Women's Halls, Jame had sometimes been forced to wear one herself as punishment for her restless wanderings. More commonly, though, the mask was used in a child's game. The girl wearing it lost not only her sight but her identity until she managed to catch another player. Then she passed on the mask and assumed the new seeker's name. In the end, everyone was someone else except for the girl left wearing the mask, who became no one, nameless and lost. Sometimes, she wore it for days until an older girl took pity on her and removed it.

But who could free a matriarch blinded by her own despair?

"What can I do? What can I do?" Brenwyr was muttering to herself in a rant as circular and obsessive as her pacing. "We had a contract, dammit! You were to have been mine forever. But then you died and the Gray Lord went into exile, and now his son tells my brother to forget the price. Adiraina says that he's only a man, that he doesn't understand, that he means to be kind. Ha! How can I keep you, and yet how can I bear to lose you again? This will destroy me. Worse, what if it drives me to destroy others?"

The shadows stirred in the tapestries as she passed, creeping forward, gaining definition. Her demons. Her memories.

Here stood a child grotesque in her brother's over-sized clothes, a knife in one hand, a hacked off hank of long, black hair dangling from the other. Every line of her unhappy face said, *It didn't work. I still hate myself.*

In the next tapestry, the same girl knelt beside the body of a woman who, arms full of boy's clothing, had tumbled down a flight of stairs and broken her neck.

Brenwyr beat her blind face with clenched fists. "Oh, mother, I didn't mean to curse you. I didn't. I didn't. But I am a Shanir maledight, a monster. What can I do but harm? Adiraina, grandmother-kin, you tell me to be strong and so I have been. The Iron Matriarch they call me, but they don't know. They don't know. Aerulan, sister-kin, you gave me strength, and love, and then you died. Oh, I cursed your murderer and doom fell on him, but you are still dead. And now must I lose your banner too? He tossed you to me, ancestors damn him, like a bone to a dog! The insult, the shame. I should curse him. No, no, I have already cursed his sister. 'Rootless and roofless' . . . damn you, Jameth!"

Jame flinched. That was the same harsh, heart-broken cry that had drawn her here.

Then she fought to keep her balance. Only now did she realize that she was again wearing Aerulan's clothes, including the tight underskirt that practically bound her legs together. To fall over at the Brandon's feet would be awkward, to say the least. She wondered in passing if "damn you" counted as a maledight curse.

Brenwyr said it again, with a breaking voice. "You stole her, seduced her with that accursed Knorth charm. Ah, how well I remember it. How I have felt it, even with you. On the road. In the cold. Did you sleep with her?"

That, thought Jame, still tottering precariously, was one way to put it. She had retrieved Aerulan's banner from the tree where the Tishooo had left it and taken it north with her. Yes, the nights had been cold. Yes, she had used the banner as a blanket for warmth and sometimes woke to feel her cousin's comforting arms around her. Willow wasn't the first of the dead with whom she had shared comfort. It probably wouldn't help, though, to say that she had slept not only with Brenwyr's beloved but under her.

As the matriarch paced on and on, the shadows kept pace with her from tapestry to tapestry, mirroring her thoughts, mocking them.

You are ugly, dangerous, a killer, they said. *Who could love you but one of the mad Knorth, and now she is dead. Maledight, monster. Curse yourself and die.*

Jame watched the roil of dark stitches and wondered. Doubtless, the Brandan Matriarch had a terrible opinion of herself, and the possible loss of Aerulan had stirred up all the destructive self-loathing at the bottom of her soul, but this seemed extreme. Moreover, she sensed another presence in the room, slyly lurking. If she, Jame, was here, why not someone else? As if in answer, the stitches of the nearest tapestry seethed like so many maggots into the semblance of a masked face that turned to look at Jame askance. It smiled.

I told you. My name is legion, as are my forms and the eyes through which I see. Miserable orphan of a ruined house, do you know me now?

"Oh, yes," breathed Jame, her fists clenching, nails biting palms. "We met in the eyes of your tempter and again when you spoke through that wretched boy whom you hag-rode to his death. Worm in the weave, I name you, and witch in the tower. Rawneth, the great bitch of Wilden."

The other began to laugh, and Jame went for her, claws first. The face distorted in a soundless scream as her nails hooked in it and tore downward. The fabric disintegrated into striped, twitching threads and slimy clots that slopped to the floor, stinking like the contents of an unplugged drain.

"Ugh," said Jame, regarding her befouled nails, wondering if she would ever get them clean again.

Brenwyr had spun around. "Who's there?" she demanded harshly. "Name yourself, so that I may know whom to curse."

Jame floundered to her feet, fighting not only the tight undergarment but the full outer skirt. Trinity, neither had been this bad in the real world. In them, she might hop or roll, but little else. The Brandan Matriarch was advancing on her, arms blindly groping. Her sleeves, her very hands, trailed threads as her entire soul-image began to unravel. Over her shoulder, Jame saw Aerulan.

Go, mouthed her cousin, so urgently that the stitches sealing her woven lips snapped and bled.

Jame ducked away, lost her balance again and, in a sharp ripping of undergarments, toppled through the hole left by the disintegrating tapestry. As she fell away into the outer darkness of the soulscape, she saw the receding image of Brenwyr. The matriarch had stopped, her shoulders slumped. Then she drew herself up and began slowly, grimly, to pull back together the frayed threads of her being.

IV

THE SOULSCAPE seemed to connect all individual soul-images, but it wasn't clear to Jame exactly how. One could get lost in here forever, or stumble into something really nasty, as she just had.

Trinity, could Rawneth wander here as she pleased, or did she only infest Brenwyr's soul-image? There, she had clearly found a chink in the Iron Matriarch's armor, and Brenwyr was too blinded by grief and rage to defend herself. Jame sensed that she had expelled the Witch at least temporarily. But there were other banners in Brenwyr's soul-image, other "eyes" through which that malignant creature might peer. Somehow, the matriarch must shed that accursed seeker's mask. Aerulan, or rather her banner, was the key, but one problem at a time.

It was hard, though, not to think what power it would give one to have free range of the soulscape. Trinity, what a way to find things out, if not to destroy one's enemies outright. She pictured herself armored and deadly, cutting a swathe through the rotten patches of the soulscape, up to the Master's very door. But why stop there? Why not pursue the monster into his maze and there destroy him once and for all? Why have such power if not to use it?

Nemesis.

The word emerged out of the darkness as a harsh cough, as if it were trying to dislodge clinkers in the throat. With it came the stench of burnt fur.

What have you done now?

The name drew her, but not as strongly as "Jameth" had done. After all, while she was clearly a nemesis, aligned with That-Which-Destroys, she wasn't yet *the* Nemesis, Third Face of God. Dammit, what had she done now except defend herself . . . and rip the guts out of a putrid banner in someone else's soul-image . . . and blood-bind a rathorn.

Where was the colt? What if she had really killed him . . . but wouldn't she know if she had? She reached deep into her own soul, to a part that ached like an over-taxed muscle. Weakness sent quivers through all her limbs. He hadn't the stamina for this. She felt his exhaustion threatening to undo them both.

No, she told herself. *Be strong. Be angry.*

That blasted cat, Arrin-ken be damned. If he must prowl the soulscape, why didn't he go after the Witch for tormenting Brenwyr? So much was rotten in the Kencyrath, both openly and in secret. Honor had been twisted until for some Highborn it was nothing but a Lawful Lie, and the breaking of it of little more importance. Where were the judges that should call such oathbreakers to justice? What worms ever now were undermining from within the fabric of the Three People so that all in the end might fall to ruin?

Her throat hurt. She had shouted her questions into the darkness. Now she waited for a reply.

Nothing.

Then, faintly, she heard someone calling her:

Kinzi-kin. Come. Please.

When she turned toward the voice, another tapestry hung before her. This one depicted a garden in full bloom, and all the blooms were white. Pushing it aside, she stepped into the Moon Garden.

FOR A MOMENT, Jame thought that she was in the real garden at Gothregor, which she had discovered the previous winter during her ceaseless wanderings through the empty eastern halls. It occupied a secret courtyard abutting the Ghost Walks, where the women of her house had lived before the massacre and, when she had last seen it, it had been a riot of snowy blossoms in the early spring.

So it still was, although the year had passed well into summer. Moreover, the lofty comfrey, lacy yarrow, heart's ease and self-heal all glowed softly in the dusk while pollen floated, glimmering, on the still air. At the north end grew a flowering apple tree where none had been before. Under it sat a pale lady, with the head of the rathorn cradled in her lap.

Lully lully lullaby, she sang in a low murmur, stroking his white neck and mane. *Dream of meadows, free of flies . . .*

"Isn't this Kindrie's soul-image?" Jame asked, perplexed. "How did you get here?"

The lady paused and raised her head, the right side turned away. *Who is Kindrie?*

Her lips didn't move. They never had, Jame realized, when she spoke, and that was only when she wore the aspect of a woman.

"Kinzi's great-grandson. He was born in this garden—the real one, I mean. His mother Tieri, Kinzi's grand-daughter, died here."

She glanced at the southern wall where Tieri's death banner should have hung. Moss and shadow suggested that gentle, sad face against the stones, but nothing more. For that matter, she supposed that while all soul-images were unique, people must model them after something familiar to them. She would have liked the garden for her own soul's haven, although for her it probably would sprout carnivorous daisies and flights of bright-winged carrion jewel-jaws.

The White Lady was shaking her head. *Names, names, names. Never born, never lived, never died.* Her hand stole up to her hidden cheek, touched it, jerked away. *Someone hurt me. Who? And my lady dead? No, no, no. This is all a bad dream, and so are you. Go away.*

She bent again over the colt, crooning,

Dream of friends who never lie,
And of love that never dies . . .

The whole garden had a strange texture, best seen out of the corner of the eye, a sort of cross-hatching.

At Perimal's Cauldron, the Whinno-hir had said that she had spoken to Kinzi, that the matriarch's blood had trapped her soul in the weave of her death.

Jame touched a nearby lily. Its white petals looked like cool, living velvet, but they felt like coarse, damp cloth. "I think," she said, "that we are in the background of Lady Kinzi's death banner."

If, however, this was the remnant of her great-grand-mother's soul-image, might some element of her still inhabit it?

But all life must end in sighs,
So lully lully lullaby.

A square of candle-light glimmered on the garden, silvering grass and flower, changing their shadows to pewter. It fell from an open window set high in the northern, outer wall, where the Ghost Walks began. During her visits here in the flesh, Jame had noticed the bricked up aperture, but had not known to whom that lovely view down into the garden had belonged, much less why it had been obstructed. Now a figure stood at the open window in dark silhouette against the flickering light. She had heard that Kinzi was a small, trim woman, and so was this silent watcher, although nothing could be seen of her face. What a long shadow that tiny figure had cast, until assassins cut it short.

Jame felt suddenly, acutely, self-conscious. She still wore the remnants of Aerulan's clothes, little better than tatters, and no mask. Moreover, the rags stank with the residual effluvium of the shredded tapestry. This time, not only had she arrived inappropriately clothed but reeking like an open sewer. She saluted the figure in the window with as much dignity as she could muster. Perhaps the other nodded slightly in reply, perhaps not. Life, death, and the abyss of time lay between them.

Lully lully lullaby . . .

The sad little song began again, lamenting all that had been lost. Lives, hope, honor, all gone, and only the victims were left to pay, and pay, and pay. A house in ruins. Her house. A family put to the knife, and that too hers. Vengeance be damned. Where was justice?

Be strong. Be angry.

Jame was pacing now, impatiently plucking off sodden
rags. She felt dangerous. She felt deadly. All that she
had shouted into the darkness echoed in her mind, the
challenge unanswered. Her god was no help—long ago,
those three faces had turned away—and his judges went
their own inscrutable way, far from the walks of those
whom they were to have served.

The garden fell gradually into shadow, the inner light
of its blooms flickering out one by one.

"You leave us in the dark, and damn us when we
stumble."

Her angry voice came back flat and muffled, off stone
walls that were in fact cloth, threadbare leavings of the
dead.

"You let honor perish and those who flaunt it prosper."

Remember that all men do lie,
If not in words, then deeds belie . . .

"You demand that we fight your battles, yet the weapons that you give us shatter in our hands."

To whom was she speaking? Did it matter? She flung
out the words like knives, not caring whom they hit.

"Yet through this all, we are bound to keep faith?"

"Watch where you tread."

The voice grumbled down, huge, like thunder in the
mountains. This time, there was an echo. Jame stopped
short. During her rant, space had changed around her.
She could still see the lit window, but it seemed lower
than before, the fire in it dying in a wrought iron grate.
Of Kinzi, if indeed it had been she, there was no sign.
Instead, Whinno-hir and rathorn colt huddled together
in the embers' ruddy glow. Walls still surrounded them
and the drum tower of the Ghost Walks still loomed over

head, but then the latter shifted on its foundations. Stone ground on stone. Grit rattled down. Was it going to fall? No. Slowly, ponderously, it began to rock. Back and forth. Back and forth. And it had gone all lumpy, more toward the bottom than the top, against which a faint, full moon seemed to be rising.

. . . click, click, click . . .

Needles, knitting—what, Jame couldn't see, but as for who . . . . She gulped.

"Mother Ragga, how did I . . . that is, how did we get into your lodge?"

A grunt of disgust made the air shake, as if something massive had fallen. What Jame had thought to be the moon leaned over her, glowering. Mother Ragga had a face not unlike a monstrous dumpling gone bad, soft here, bulging there, alight with mottled indignation.

"This is what the Merikit call sacred space— Rathillien's soulscape, as it were. You always did creep inside, girl, whenever you found a chink. Since those idiots invited you through the front door as my Favorite, though, there seems to be no keeping you out, short of killing you. I'm considering that."

"What? But why?"

"Look where you have trodden."

The upper reaches of the room might be the lodge, grown large enough to swallow an army whole, but the dirt floor where Ragga kept her earth map was still the Moon Garden, or what was left of it. Jame saw with dismay that in raging back and forth she had destroyed a wide swath of it. Comfrey, yarrow, and heart's-ease lay not just broken under her feet but rotting, with the threads of Kinzi's banner showing through like tendons laid bare. She flexed her hands, staring at the ivory gauntlets that gloved them. She wore armor from throat to loins but, like the rathorn, only on the front. The draft from behind was disconcerting.

She had dreamed of slashing through the soulscape, a warrior clad in gleaming ivory, destroying all that was rotten in it. What if, however, like the Ivory Knife, everything that she touched died, the fair with the foul? Was that what it meant to be the Third Face of God?

"You asked why," grumbled that enormous voice. "You ask much. But what will your answers cost? It isn't the Favorite's role to ask but to act, yet that might be worse. What about the summer solstice, eh?"

Jame had nearly forgotten, and it wasn't far off.

"Didn't we take care of my part in that on Summer's Eve?" she asked nervously. "After all, I've already fought last year's Favorite—sort of. It wasn't my idea to combine that rite with establishing the boundaries, nor to get dragged into either one of them, for that matter."

"Huh. Well I know it, and little it matters. There are rules. Remember, not only does the Favorite mate with the Earth Wife for the fertility of the land, but then she passes off her lover to her consort the Burnt Man as their son. It's called 'fooling death.'"

"Who makes up these games anyway?" Jame asked.

The rocking stopped for a moment. "Don't know. Doesn't matter. They just are. I might blink at some of 'em, but the Burnt Man won't. Not now, anyway. Since you became involved, he's somehow gotten mixed up with that blind judge of yours. Bad breath, a worse attitude, and he's out of his tiny little cinder of a mind. Then there's you, another disaster waiting to happen. Oh, you may regret it afterward and try to make amends, but some things once broken can never be mended."

And they will hunt you till you die, sang the Whinno-hir Bel-tairi on the Earth Wife's hearth, rocking the white-haired boy that was the rathorn colt.

And then your mouth will fill with flies,
So lully lully lullaby.

The Earth Wife's face filled half the sky, and her anger pressed down as one feels the weight of a mountain from within a cave or that of a boulder poised to fall. "Did you hear that, you wretched girl? What did you people do to this poor creature? She came to me wounded in body and soul. I sheltered her in my lodge—days, years, what does time matter? Then her lady called her forth. Is her torment to begin all over again? I tell you straight, I'd rather destroy the lot of you than go through that again. Don't think that I can't! And what's the matter with that colt?"

As Jame fumbled for the answer least likely to get her killed, the Whinno-hir spoke again:

My lady bade me find you.

They might have been back at Perimal's Cauldron, but the shock of that first meeting had passed into a dream-like acceptance.

My lady bids me warn you. Of the Knorth Highborn, only three of you are left.

Jame blinked. Three? "Lady, who . . . ?"

One is still too wounded to know himself, and the other's mind is poisoned against his own nature. You are the closest of the three to realizing who and what you are, but you also have the darkling glamour bred into your very bones. The haunt singer Ashe has warned my lady, and my lady has warned me.

"Wait a minute. How does Kinzi know—I mean, about the third? This side of the shadows, except for Tori and me, there's only our cousin Kindrie, and he was born long after the massacre."

The dead know what concerns the dead. My unfortunate granddaughter Tieri is dead, and so am I. While our blood traps us, we walk the Gray Land together, two of a silent host.

The Whinno-hir's voice changed. Her fire-cast shadow lengthened and thinned, as if cast by someone else, small and trim.

Jame gulped. The Gray Land? One by one, all the things she thought she knew about death were proving false, but she must keep to the point. "Lady, Kindrie is a bastard, or doesn't legitimacy count after all?"

It does. Blood of my blood, some things that matter very much are unfair, but true. It is also true that I told your father to draw strength from his anger, but he did not have the discipline to control what he called up. How could he, while he denied what he was?

Be strong, Jame had told herself. Be angry.

"Great-grandmother, I know who I am and what I may become."

Ah, but what if you are truly alone, with neither That-Which-Creates nor That-Which-Preserves to balance you? Have you the strength, alone, to balance yourself?

"Huh." The Earth Wife leaned back, her face a pocked moon rising, and the tower groaned as she resumed her slow rocking. "That's the kernel of the nut. Balance. We four have it—most of the time; you three don't. By stone and stock, you don't even seem to know who you are. As I understand it, you people have ruined world after world. Should Rathillien topple as well for your faults?"

"I think," said Jame carefully, "that without us this world is doomed. Mother Ragga, have you looked into the face of the shadows that loom over you? I have. As everyone keeps reminding me, I was raised among them. If I remembered more of those lost years, perhaps there would be less of me left to recover."

She paused, surprised by her own words. Of course, her lost childhood still bothered her. (*Confess.*) What had she done under shadows' eaves and what had been done to her? (*You know your faults.*) Perhaps, after all, she had deserved the latter, and much more beside.

Huh. *I know who I am*, she had just said, and of this much she was sure:

"Thanks to my Senethari Tirandys . . . and to Bender, his brother . . . my honor has survived."

"So far," grumbled the Earth Wife.

"Well, yes, but who can say more than that?"

Enough. I am sorry, child, but desperate times, desperate measures. Ashe is right: Tentir will test you as it has all Knorth lordan. Succeed or fail. Live or die. Now give back this poor boy's armor until you earn the right to wear it. Besides, he is cold.

So was Jame, all up her bare back. Half clothed was far worse than stark naked, but must she face the outer darkness in nothing but her skin? What if the blind Arrinken was waiting for her? On the other hand, did she really want to back out of the Earth Wife's presence or, worse, turn bare buttocks on her great-grandmother? Oh well.

At the thought, she felt suddenly lighter, with good reason: the armor was gone, or rather back where it belonged.

"I cared for the mare," grumbled that huge voice, thunder receding. "I will keep what watch I can over her fosterling until (if ever) you assume your responsibilities. Here."

Something scratchy dropped around her bare shoulders—a kind of blanket, knit of moss and lichen.

"Now sleep."

And, despite herself, she did.

CHAPTER XVI

Midsummer's Eve

Summer 53–60

I

JAME WOKE IN TENTIR'S INFIRMARY AND, to her great annoyance, was forced to spend another seven days there. She had never been flat on her back for so long before, nor was this usual for the fast-healing Kencyr.

"You should be glad you aren't dead," said Kindrie, who had been summoned to treat the wounded of the rathorn hunt and had stayed to keep an eye on her. "Soul-walking is dangerous, even when you aren't bled nearly dry."

Her slashed wrists had all but healed, settling into a random pattern of thin, white lines which, hopefully, would soon also disappear. She had to admit that Tori's scars were much more esthetically pleasing, but then his had been the work of Karnid fanatics, to whom everything formed a pattern.

More to the point, she was missing vital training. All too soon after midsummer would come the autumn cull both of unworthy cadets and of beasts unlikely to survive the coming winter. For herself, Jame would rather be salted for the larder than sent back to the Women's Halls at Gothregor. The sound of cadets at practice outside in the square made her fidget under the Earth Wife's thick, mossy blanket. So did the blanket itself, which tickled. Besides scratchy lichen, she suspected that it harbored a hidden population of woodlice, if not spiders and centipedes, but so far none had been fool enough to bite her. Then too, the moss was cool and comforting on this hot summer day.

"It would help if you ate something." Rue presented her latest offering. "Look, here's a nice bowl of gruel."

"Yum, yum," muttered Graykin from the far corner where he was pretending to be invisible.

"I wish," said Jame, exasperated, "that all of you would stop treating me like a moron."

"Then stop acting like one." Kindrie took the bowl and offered her a spoonful.

The Scrollsmen's College must agree with him, Jame thought, unconsciously drawing back from the dripping, gray gunk.

(*Toad eggs, dog vomit . . .*)

When she had first met her cousin that spring, he had seemed to have all the backbone of an angle-worm and a beaten air that had made her long to hit him. Of course, at the time, he had just escaped from what must have been a nightmare winter in the Priests' College at Wilden, in Lady Rawneth's shadow and under her thumb.

"You won't regain your strength if you don't eat," he said patiently.

"I'm not hungry."

(*Maggot larvae, cow drool . . .*)

Food had seldom been more than a necessary evil in her life, given her early acquaintance with the shrieking carrots and oozing onions of the Haunted Lands. Now the very thought of it nauseated her. Marc might have coaxed her into eating. However, after assuring himself that she was out of danger, or at least as much so as she ever was, he had gone back to tend an unpredictable glass furnace at Gothregor.

"If it decides to blow up," he had said, not too comfortingly, "I should be there."

Harn Grip-hard had gone with him, to prepare for the Minor Harvest. Tomorrow, Midsummer's Day, all cadets would go home to help with the haying.

Kindrie put down the bowl. "Very well. You can serve a rathorn rabbit, but you can't make him eat it. Before I forget, my lady Kirien sends her congratulations."

"For what?"

"Not being dead yet, I suppose. Also, Index says he's going up into the hills with you for the summer solstice."

"Damn that man. How often do I have to tell him that I'm not going at all?"

"Every day from now until then, I suppose. The solstice comes, what, six days after our Midsummer? You'd think our ancestors would have paid more attention to Rathillien's calendar, but we always have tried to impose our own systems on any threshold world where we happen to land. Anyway, you can hardly blame Index. Herbs are only his practical job. The Merikit were his field of study before your friend Marc wiped out a score of them, avenging Kithorn."

"For what it's worth, that winter killed Marc's taste for bloodshed for the rest of his life, which for a professional warrior is awkward."

"It also closed the hills to all Kencyr except, apparently, you."

"That wasn't my idea."

"No. A lot of things aren't, but they still happen."

"Oh, bugger this." Jame threw off the Earth Wife's gift, tripped over Jorin, and fell flat on her face. Rue returned her to bed while Graykin modestly averted his eyes.

"What *is* this thing?" asked the cadet, regarding the fibrous mat suspiciously.

"A reminder." Not that she was likely to forget, Index notwithstanding. What would the Merikit do on the solstice without the legitimate Favorite? Oh well. That was their problem.

"Even if you wanted to go up into the hills," said Kindrie, "I doubt if you would have the strength, especially if you carry on like this."

Jame growled at him, echoed by Jorin under the bed, nursing the paw on which she had trodden.

"You're enjoying this, aren't you?"

The ghost of a smile flickered across his thin face. "A bit," he admitted.

"Huh." She glowered at him for a moment. "Rue, Graykin, I want to talk to my cousin alone."

Rue sketched a salute and turned to leave. Graykin tried to sidle into the shadows behind the open door, but the cadet fished him out and pushed him before her, protesting, into the hall. The door closed behind them. Kindrie sat down on the opposite cot, looking nervous.

"Have you been mucking around with my soul-image again?" Jame asked him bluntly.

That, after all, was how a healer worked. Each person, consciously or not, visualized his or her soul in a particular way. The Knorth favored architectural models. A healer might spend what felt like a year inside an injured person's soulscape, rebuilding a fallen wall, and emerge an hour later to find his patient's broken ribs well on the mend. What repairs she might need now, Jame couldn't imagine.

But Kindrie was shaking his head, the window behind him making a halo of his white hair.

"No. The last time, remember, you threw me out so hard that I cracked my skull on an inconveniently placed anvil. This time, all you needed was a solid stint of *dwar* sleep. That, and food. Still, battered, half-drowned, and nearly exsanguinated—a busy day, even for you. But why did you ask about your soul-image?"

"I'm not sure." She frowned, trying to recapture impressions that had hardly registered at the time. "Something about it this time was . . . different. First, I was on the edge of Tori's soulscape—no, I didn't meddle with it, although I did shout a bit. Then there was the Master's House, but I was outside of it. In fact, it came after me. What in Perimal's name was that all about?"

"I'd forgotten," said Kindrie slowly. "We haven't had a chance to talk since Summer's Eve when I tried to heal your face."

Jame touched her scarred cheek. "And I never got a chance to thank you for your work on this. I know, I know: you could have done more if I hadn't thrown you out. That wasn't deliberate. Sorry about the anvil."

She still had to fight her revulsion at his priestling background. What the Shanir were to her brother, priests were to her, with better reason. Still, she kept reminding herself, Kindrie hadn't chosen to grow up at Wilden in the Priest's College. Born after the Knorth had nearly been wiped out by Shadow Assassins, Shanir, and (worse) illegitimate, he had been dropped into the priests' laps, so to speak, as an alternative to drowning him like an unwanted pup.

She wondered what those who had thrown him away so casually would think if they could see him now. Besides having become a powerful healer, he was beginning to show the fine-drawn Knorth features that one could trace on death banners back to the Fall. There was much of his mother Tieri's gentle melancholy in his eyes, but also much of his great-grandmother Kinzi's deceptive strength in the elegant bones of his face and hands. In fact, physically, he was starting to look like a cross between Tori and herself, except for the white hair and pale blue eyes. Were they a legacy from his unknown father? Who in Perimal's name could that have been, anyway?

Of the Knorth Highborn, only three of you are left.

And those three were the Kencyrath's last chance to produce the long-awaited Tyr-ridan, through whom their god was supposed to manifest himself and do battle with that ancient enemy, Perimal Darkling.

One is still too wounded to know himself, and the other's mind is poisoned against his own nature.

If she was becoming That-Which-Destroys, Tori presumably was destined to become That-Which-Creates, if he could overcome the poison instilled by his father, if he ever got the chance to make something new out of their increasingly compromised society.

As a potential third, That-Which-Preserves, who else was there and who better than the healer Kindrie, wounded by his past but slowly recovering from it?

Except that he was a bastard, and blood still mattered.

"About your soul-image," he was saying, "I know you believe that it's the Master's Hall. I thought so at first too. When I went into the soulscape to work on your injury, all of the hall's death banners had been slashed across the face, like you, then stitched up again with coarse thread to form raised welts. I wasted a lot of time unpicking stitches before I realized that they were only a diversion."

"I'm confused. Aren't disfigured faces what you would expect to find?"

"Yes, but there were too many of them, and they were laughing at me. Then I saw something white on the hearth. It was you, the real you, asleep, wearing partial rathorn armor, with a bleeding crack across the cheek. That's what I was trying to close when you woke up and threw me out."

"Oh."

Jame considered this, rather blankly. Perhaps she had worn the ivory armor in the soulscape before borrowing it this last time, as it were, off the colt's back. On that level, just as different versions of the Moon Garden might shelter more than one soul, so armor might shield whoever needed it, and she already had close links both personal and familial with those horned beasts of madness.

"I think," said Kindrie, "that it means you've begun to protect yourself against your past, like growing a callus, only in you it takes the form of an outbreak of ivory. Sleep could be another defense, if a passive one. There, they couldn't get at you. But now you're awake and out. Of the hall. Of the Master's House."

Jame snorted. "Into the Haunted Lands. Back among the dead. Not quite like my brother, though."

"No. For some reason he's still confined to that awful keep where you both grew up. You, though, seem to be free in the soulscape, though travel there is perilous and I'll thank you to remember that it just nearly killed you."

"At least Tori has the keep, and you have the Moon Garden. Will I ever have a true home or must I always wander, armored and perhaps armed, but roofless and rootless?"

The question burst from her with a force that surprised them both.

"That's what you really want? A home?"

"More than anything." Until she said it, she didn't realize how painfully true it was. What had her life been so far but a desperate search for a place where she belonged? Brenwyr hadn't needed to curse her, although it probably hadn't helped; she was the eternal outsider, the arch-iconoclast. Given her nature, what else could she be?

"I'm sorry," said Kindrie, seeing that she was upset. "Still, soul-images do change as we grow. You're only—what, nineteen years old? Twenty? More?"

There was no answer to this: thanks to the slower, erratic passage of time in Perimal Darkling, Jame didn't know. She felt ancient.

"I should tell you," said the Shanir, this time not meeting her eyes. "In the soulscape, your servant Graykin was guarding you in the shape of a half-starved mongrel dog, chained to the hearth. He's intensely jealous of anyone who gets close to you. That's his soul-image, and it's a pretty miserable one. It's not my business, but you should consider more carefully how you treat him."

Jame brushed this aside. Graykin was the least of her worries.

"Has Tori accepted you as a Knorth?" she asked abruptly.

"No." Again Kindrie looked away, biting his lip. "He tried, but . . . do you know how psychic bonding works? Most of the lords don't really understand, but when they bind a follower they give that person a small piece of their soul image, or maybe they give him or her a niche in their own soulscape, or maybe both. It's hard to explain, but there's definitely an element of give, whereas with blood binding it's all take, like . . . like . . . "

"Rape versus love?" Jame suggested, deliberately probing her own sense of guilt over the colt.

"In a way. When the Highlord offered me a place in his house, I was overjoyed." He looked at her askance through a fringe of white hair. "I'm looking for a place to belong too, you know, and I am Knorth, if only by bastard blood. That wouldn't matter to Torisen, but you know how he feels about the Shanir."

"He hates and fears us," said Jame flatly. "Father taught him that."

"Just the same, he tried. You know what his soulscape is like. Well, he gave me his hand, and there I was in that desolate keep. At the back of the hall was a door. Something was on the other side. Something that muttered and cursed and shook the handle."

Jame remembered being in her brother's soul-image and slamming that door against their father's madness, to save Tori's sanity, to give him peace.

The bolt is shot.

"Well," said Kindrie, taking a deep breath, "what he offered me was the lock on that door. I couldn't accept it. He isn't ready."

"Little man," said Jame, impressed, "you've grown."

His pale face flushed. It took Jame a moment to realize that he was angry. "I couldn't hurt him. You know that.

But since then I've wondered: is it good for him to have part of his soul-image locked off? That was your doing, wasn't it? I nearly caught you at it. Perhaps it seemed like a good idea at the time, but somehow it's weakened him. I've heard rumors. He's having trouble remembering his people's names."

This struck cold. "But if he can't remember . . ."

"The bond breaks. One Kendar has already killed himself because of it."

"Oh. Poor man. And poor Tori. Kindrie, this is awful. Can't we do something about it?"

He shook his head, frustrated. "I've thought and thought. He has to come to terms with what's behind that door, and he has to do it by himself. I think. At any rate, the way things stand right now, neither of us can get close enough to him to help."

Silence fell between them. The room was falling into shadow, the sounds outside of the day's last class fading as cadets dispersed for their free period before the Midsummer Eve's feast.

"So," said Jame at last, "that's why you're at Mount Alban instead of at Gothregor."

"Yes. The Scrollsmen's College has taken me in and the Jaran Lordan, Kirien, has been very kind. Of course," he added with a twist to his smile, "she's pleased to have a healer on hand. For a community mostly of aging scholars, the scrollsmen and the singers get into as many squabbles with each other as a bunch of children. Academia seems to have that effect on some people. I'm also helping Index put his herb shed back in order after the weirdingstrom."

Index knew where every bit of information could be found, be it in some ancient scroll or in a colleague's capacious memory. Besides supplying medicines, in its organization the herb shed was a mnemonic device —Index's index, as it were. Jame wondered if Kindrie had discovered that yet. She herself had only found out by accident.

"Well, he's not going to talk me into going up-river for some blasted fertility rite, and so you may tell him. I just want to go back to being a normal cadet."

"That," said a rough voice, "you'll never be."

Gorbel limped into the infirmary and dropped heavily into a chair. "Still here, are you?" he said to Kindrie. "Good. Do something about this damned foot of mine. Now."

"You'll have to excuse him," said Jame. "The Caineron consider good manners a weakness. Gorbel, this is Kindrie Soul-walker, my cousin and blood-kin to the Highlord."

"The Knorth Bastard, eh? Well, don't just stand there, man. This hurts!"

The Shanir gave Jame an unreadable look, then knelt to pull off the Caineron's boot. This took some effort: the foot within was badly swollen, with green lines radiating out from a central, raw puncture.

Kindrie sat back on his heels, staring. "I thought I'd dealt with this. All right. Let's see what's going on." He cupped Gorbel's broad, dirty foot in his long, delicate hands and bent over it.

"One of your blasted willow saplings sank a root into me," Gorbel explained to Jame, then flinched. "Trinity damn it, man, be careful! Anyway, the surgeon dug it out like a splinter, which hurt like Perimal. Now this."

"Gently, gently . . ." said the healer, and Gorbel's stubby toes slowly unclenched. He sagged in the chair, small eyes losing their focus and toad face relaxing.

"It's a forest in here," Kindrie murmured, deep in the other's soul-image. "Strange. He doesn't know what he is yet, hunter or prey. At the moment, he's trying to be a tree."

"Perhaps because trees don't feel pain, although I'm not so sure about that anymore. What about the willow?"

"That's the problem. I couldn't help while he had a physical object jammed through his foot—how would you like to be healed with an arrow still sticking out of you?—but the sapling's rootlets are loose now in his soulscape and, I suppose, in his blood. Damn. Have you ever tried to uproot a particularly persistent weed? Just when you think you've gotten it all, it springs up again on the other side of the garden. This is going to take awhile."

"Am I interrupting anything?" asked a voice at the door, and there stood Timmon with an armful of daises, beaming over them like a particularly self-satisfied sun. "You're awake at last. Good!"

"What are those for?" Jame asked as he appropriated a water jug for his bouquet.

"Why, hasn't anyone ever given you flowers before?"

"No. Once picked, they just die. What's the point?"

"You're suppose to admire them," murmured Kindrie, "and be grateful to the donor."

"So this is about you, Timmon, not about me or an armload of wilting greenery, however pretty. Does your girlfriend admire flowers too?"

"Everything is always about me," said the Ardeth cheerfully. "What girlfriend? Oh. The Kendar. Narsa. It's a nuisance how possessive some females get, especially when the fun is over. You'll be more sensible, of course. Actually, that Coman cadet Gari picked these flowers, but he asked me to bring them because he's come down with an infestation of termites."

"How uncomfortable for him."

"Oh, he's all right, as long as he keeps moving. Otherwise, the floor collapses under him. The master-ten of his house has him sleeping outside. Hello, what have we here?" He wandered over to regard Gorbel, who blinked slowly at him.

"A ssslight case," said the Caineron, slurring his words, "of ingrown tree." He made a sound like a small explosion that turned out to be a laugh. "That tickles," he informed Kindrie.

"My. I had no idea the infirmary was so entertaining."

"Nodd from where I'm sittin'. Want to change places?"

Jame propped herself up on an elbow, then surprised herself by modestly pulling up the moss. A spider scrambled down between her small breasts, diving for cover. "Timmon, you can't treat people that way, especially not Kendar. They're too vulnerable to the Highborn as it is."

Kindrie shot her a look: *remember Graykin.*

"Ah, you sound like Grandfather," said Timmon, pouting. "Now, my father Pereden amused himself however he pleased and he . . . "

". . . was a great man. So you've said. Repeatedly."

"There." Kindrie sat back on his heels with a sigh. "I hope I got it all. The swelling should go down soon. If it doesn't, or comes back, we'll try again."

"Come on," said Timmon, pulling Gorbel to his feet and scooping up the boot. "Let's get you back to your quarters. Good evening, my lady. Sweet dreams."

As they lurched out, one supporting the other, Kindrie turned to a rank of bottles on an infirmary shelf and took down a blue-tinted vial.

"Lord Ardeth's favorite," he said, uncorking it and pouring a small amount into a glass of water. "Tincture of hemlock. This will help you sleep."

Jame took the glass and sniffed it. "Ugh. Distillation of dead mouse, more likely."

"Now, now. If you're a good girl, maybe we'll let you go back to the Knorth barracks tomorrow."

She glowered at him, and drank. "You're enjoying all of this far, far too much."

Kindrie smiled, lit a thick candle with the hours of the night marked on it by bars, and left her alone.

II

BY NOW, it was early evening. The day's last light flooded through the infirmary windows and shadows crept after it up the walls. Below, cheerful, muted chatter spilled into the square from the barracks' dining halls.

Jame floated on the light, then sank into shadow. The hemlock began to take effect almost immediately on her empty stomach. It was a little like being drunk, as far as she could remember from her one experience, but with an unpleasant tingling of her limbs as if they were falling asleep. She drifted in and out of consciousness fitfully, not quite trusting herself to the drug. That was too much like losing control. The candle flame seemed to expand and contract as it flickered in the breeze through the open window. Light and dark, dark and light . . .

Fleetingly, someone touched her, leaving a slight, supple weight on her chest that had not been there before.

Jame blinked. The candle had burned down two rings. The college would be settling for the night and soon she would be only one sleeper out of hundreds, as was proper. She sighed and let go.

A low growl roused her, followed by a soft hiss.

"Can't you let the dead rest in peace?" she muttered, and with difficulty pried open her eyes.

Jorin had his forepaws on the edge of the cot and was leaning forward over it, every hair a bristle. Moonlight reflected in his wide, blind eyes. He growled again like distant thunder.

A hiss answered him, and the weight on her chest stirred. Whatever it was, it was so close that she had to stare cross-eyed at it to focus. A coil of molten gold had settled into the mossy blanket. Above it, weaving to and fro, rose a triangular head with glittering eyes. The gilded swamp adder hissed again, showing wicked white fangs and a flickering black tongue.

"For this you woke me up?" said Jame, hearing the hemlock slur in her voice, "Settle down, both of you. Jorin, here." The ounce slunk onto the bed and settled by her feet, still glaring. Bit by bit, his eyes closed.

Serpent and girl regarded each other.

Candle light gleamed off the zigzag pattern running down the adder's back, ochre at the top, shading to rich gold with a ridge of gilt at the bottom. Scales rustled softly as it breathed. Its throat and belly were the color of pale honey, its eyes a fiery orange.

"Oh, you beauty," Jame murmured and stroked its gleaming throat with a fingertip. It flowed over her hand and up her arm in a ripple of muscles to settle in a band of gold around her throat. Its tongue tickled her ear.

"Your mistress is going to be furious with you," she told it, "but never mind. Hushhhh."

And again the room was quiet.

 **III**

WHEN JAME WOKE AGAIN, someone tall stood over her. She blinked at the candle. It must still be an hour shy of midnight. What a long, confusing day.

"I thought," said the Commandant, "that I would check on you during last rounds. The healer makes a good report of you, except he says that you won't eat. Now why is that, I wonder?"

The answer was there, waiting, as if she had known it all along. "Ran, I've blood-bound a rathorn colt. He's very upset. I think he's trying to starve himself to death and take me with him."

"I . . . see. You Knorth do get yourselves into interesting scrapes. How will you handle this one?"

Jame frowned. "I'm not sure. Go up into the hills and find him, I suppose, when Kindrie lets me out of this bed. Between us, Bel and I should be able to do something."

"Ah." The Commandant drew up a chair and settled back in it, hawk-features receding into shadows over the glimmer of his white scarf of office. He folded his hands under his chin, stretched out his long legs, and crossed them at the ankles. "You refer to the Whinno-hir Beltairi. The White Lady. Recent sightings of her have been reported to me, but I dismissed them. To the best of my knowledge, she has been dead these forty years and more."

"My great-grandmother Kinzi sent her to find me."

"Ah. That explains everything, and nothing. I had believed that the last Knorth Matriarch was also dead. Have I perhaps been misinformed on that point as well?"

Jame didn't feel up to explaining, assuming that she could. Instead, she asked a question that had bothered her for a long time:

"Ran, why is Bel-tairi called 'The Shame of Tentir'? What could she have done, to deserve that?"

"It wasn't what she did but what was done to her."

"Do you mean my uncle Greshan branding her?"

A sigh answered her from the shadows. "That was only the start of it, or not quite the start."

Jame remembered her glimpse of the brutal past in that clearing on the hunt. "Greshan was courting Rawneth, but Kinzi forbade it. He took out his revenge on her Whinno-hir mare. Was that before or after my father stormed out of Tentir in the middle of the night?"

"After, by about a year. Now, where did you hear that? Have you spoken to your brother or to Harn Grip-hard?"

"Not to Tori. I don't think he knows anything about it. And when I asked Harn about the White Lady, he just roared that I should leave Tentir before it was too late. Then he stormed off."

"Did he now." The dry voice sounded amused. "My dear brother-in-arms. Always so excitable. But then we are speaking here of a very painful topic, both for your house and for Tentir. I will tell you this much: yes, your uncle the Knorth lordan put a branding iron to a Whinno-hir's face, and then he bragged about it to the whole college. That was bad. Worse followed. The Highlord, your grandfather, ordered that the entire affair be hushed up, as if that were possible. But his darling son mustn't be seen for the worthless bastard he was. Oh no. Even if it meant hunting down and killing an injured Whinno-hir. He hadn't finished the job, you see. He simply let her go, maimed as she was and weeping blood."

Silence fell for a moment. The Commandant seemed to taste again that bitter memory, holding it on his tongue like a drop of poison that must be swallowed. His voice, when he resumed, had flattened, all emotion suppressed.

"The entire Randon Council went on that grim hunt—nine in all, one from each major house and all former commandants of Tentir except for the Knorth, Hallik Hard-hand, whose turn it was to wear the white scarf. Greshan went too, all gay in his gilded leathers, but he came back slung across his saddle. A hunting accident, Hallik said. He also said that the mare must be dead. They had pursued her up a steep mountain trail and she must have fallen off into river below. The way ended in a sheer rock face, you see, with no sign of her."

He paused again, remembering. "I scaled that path as a cadet. Many of us did, afterward. It's a hard, rocky climb, even at a walk, and she was injured, running for her life. On one side, stone. On the other, far, far down, the black, roaring throat of the river. At the top . . . a curious thing. I thought at first that I saw the outline of a door in the rock wall, and the suggestion of carving around it. But the crack was barely fingernail deep and behind it, only more stone."

For the Whinno-hir, Jame thought, that door would have stood open into the Earth Wife's lodge, which could be found wherever it was needed. So that was how the White Lady had come to shelter, and yet left those behind sure of her death.

Her mind began to drift again. That damn hemlock. The next time Kindrie wanted her to sleep, he would have to do it another way, say, by hitting her over the head with a rock.

"I see that I am tiring you." The Commandant rose, his tall form seeming to stretch up to the ceiling. "Anyway, there is little more to tell. Hallik killed himself with the White Knife, your grandfather Gerraint died of grief, and your father Ganth Grayling, unprepared and unworthy, became highlord, to the near destruction of us all. If you want to know more, ask Harn when he returns. After all, Hallik was his father."

"Wait," she said, as the Commandant turned to leave. Hallik Hard-hand was Harn's father? And he had killed himself over a mere hunting accident? There had to be more to the story than that, but the questions she wanted to ask roiled in her drug-numbed mind like a handful of worms, impossible to sort head from tail. "Please," she heard herself say, "return this to the Randir. She must be worried about it."

Jame didn't realize how still the Commandant had become until he moved again, bending over her and carefully pinning the swamp adder behind its wicked little head. It gave a sleepy hiss as he lifted it from her neck and by reflex coiled itself around the warmth of his arm.

"You favor strange bed-fellows," he said, in an odd voice. "How did this come to be here?"

She could only shake her head, which set everything spinning. "Someone brought it. Dunno who."

"I . . . see. Be careful what you say about this, and to whom. The lords can collect no blood-price for anything that happens here, but the college has its own forms of justice. Good night."

"G'night, Senethari."

He paused in the doorway, gave her an enigmatic look, and went out, carefully holding his lethal charge.

 **IV**

SEVERAL MORE TIMES Jame half-woke during the night, thinking she had heard some disturbance. More likely, though, it was the echo of a dream.

Shouts, battle-cries, and then sargents bellowing, "Run, run, run!" to the thunder of feet on the boards of the arcade . . . obviously her drug-befuddled brain had drifted back to that first day at Tentir and the punishment run.

Oddly, each time she surfaced a different member of her ten-command was in the room, on guard. This puzzled her, but not enough to ask why they were there. When she at last fully woke in the early morning, Brier Iron-thorn sat on the window-ledge.

Jame regarded that hard, strong profile, that distant, proud expression. How little she truly knew about this woman. She remembered a bloody Brier on the Ardeth stair, blocking her way to the room above where Tori fought for his soul if not for his life:

"He saved me from the Caineron. Bound me. I am his, although I trust no Highborn fool enough to trust me. I don't trust you. You will only hurt him."

Such a bitter insight, and so tangled even in the Southron's own mind.

"You haven't yet taught me how they fight in the streets of Kothifir," she said.

Brier glanced at her. "There hasn't been time, lady. Do you still want to learn?" She turned back to contemplate the empty square, across which dawn was edging. She looked tired, and her clothes were dull with dust. "The randon would hardly thank me for corrupting your classic style."

"It's only classic because it's all I know—that, and some knife tricks."

When she pushed back the blanket of woven moss, it slid to the floor and crumbled to dust. Spiders scurried off in all directions. She stood up and swayed, suddenly light-headed. When her sight cleared, she found that Brier had moved swiftly to support her.

"Thank you. Now, where did Kindrie hide my clothes?"

Jame was nearly dressed when the healer arrived.

"I'm not sure about this," he said, watching her wobble on one foot as she tried to pull on a boot, then sit down abruptly on the bed. "I hear you didn't have a restful night, which is hardly surprising under the circumstances."

"Damn. Who else knows?"

"Everyone," said Brier briefly. "The Commandant sent me word late last night about your uninvited bed-mate, and Vant overheard. He's already tackled the Randir about it."

"Trinity. Have there been fights?"

"A few. Then the sargents stepped in and ran us all ragged. They're still keeping a thumb on the pot, hoping it won't come to a boil before the general exodus later this morning."

A sudden commotion erupted outside the infirmary door.

"No!" Rue was saying loudly. "Stay away from my lady, you . . . you . . ."

A scuffle, a yelp, and the door burst open. Rue tumbled into the room and rolled to her feet between Jame and the intruder. Brier instantly joined her. Peering between them, Jame saw a Randir cadet framed in the doorway.

"I did *not* put Addy in your bed," the Randir said.

By now, Jame had recognized her as the Shanir cadet from the Falconer's class, and had noted the rising bruise under one eye. Vant's work, probably.

"Who is Addy? Oh, I see."

Around the other's neck hung a thick, living, golden loop, which she half-steadied and half-caressed with one hand.

Slipping between the two Knorth, Jame offered her hand to the Randir's snake. Behind her, Rue yelped in alarm, but she had already welcomed the serpent as it slid, glittering, over her fingers.

"No," she said, having by now had time to think. "I don't believe you would risk Addy that way. It . . . that is, she . . . might have been killed, and you would certainly have been blamed. Besides, Highborn are almost impossible to poison, so as an assassination attempt it wasn't very bright." She didn't add that a shot of venom to the throat, in someone already weakened, might not have been all that easily shrugged off, but the Commandant wanted this incident played down, and so did she. "When did you miss her?"

"Around dinner time." The Randir regarded her with sharp mistrust. "You believe me?"

"I know what it means to be bound to a creature—human, animal, or reptile. Someone has tried to play a nasty trick on both our houses, and to take advantage of our differences. That offends me. If you find out who it is, will you let me know?"

"Agreed, if you will do the same for me."

Below in the square, the rally sounded and the barracks woke with a surly roar.

The Randir turned to leave, but Jame stopped her.

"If you'll wait a minute, I'll go down with you."

"Why?"

On her second attempt, with Rue's help, Jame managed to pull on her boot. She rose and stomped to settle the heel. "Brier tells me that there were clashes overnight. If we're seen together, that's one step toward calming things down, at least over this business. Another time, it may be different."

The Randir considered this, then gave a curt nod. "My name is Shade," she said, as if to seal this temporary truce.

"And mine is Jame."

When they entered the square, all nine houses had assembled. A ripple went through the waiting ranks and a murmur that the sargent on duty instantly quelled. Shade joined the Randir. Jame, walking on to the Knorth, felt eyes follow her and saw marks on a dozen faces of the previous night's unrest. The Commandant stood on his balcony watching. When Jame met his hooded gaze, he gave her a slight nod: Well done.

After breakfast, Jame ran down Vant.

"It wasn't the Randir," she told him bluntly, "or at least not the snake's owner."

"She told you that, I suppose," he said, baring his teeth. Two of them had been knocked out. "Did she also happen to mention that she's the Witch's grand-daughter?"

Whoa.

"Lord Randir is her father? I didn't know that he had any children."

"Only one, begat by way of experiment before his tastes settled. Anyway, did you think that the Caineron are the only house whose Highborn make sport with their Kendar?"

He spoke with such unusual, throttled rage that Jame blinked. She hadn't realized that he felt so strongly on the subject. It also occurred to her that she knew nothing of Vant's background, except that he was presumably descended from Those-Who-Returned, Knorth Kendar driven back by her father as he had stormed into exile and forced to serve as *yondri* in other houses until her brother had reclaimed both power and as many of his scattered people as he could hold, perhaps overreaching in the process.

But Vant's past was a puzzle for another day.

"Shade may be half darkling changer for all I know or care. On this, I believe her. So lay off."

As Vant departed, sour-faced, to organize the cadets' departure, Jame found Rue at her elbow.

"I assume that we're all under house rather than college discipline once we leave Tentir. True? Good. Saddle me a horse, a nice, quiet one, and wait for me with it outside the north gate. No, I'm not going with you. If my brother asks, tell him that I have unfinished business in the hills."

Brier had come up to hear this last. "Is it wise to go off on your own, lady? The land is treacherous. Besides, someone has just tried to kill you."

"I suspect that he . . . or she . . . will be marching out
with the others. I'll take my chances with Rathillien."
She paused and gave a snort of laughter. "Besides, I'll
probably have company soon enough."

# CHAPTER XVII

Into the Wilds

Summer 60–65

I

JAME STARED. "You have got to be joking."

Rue gave a self-conscious wriggle. "All the others are going home for the harvest, but Chumley here pulled up lame. Myself, I think he faked it for the inspection. He's perfectly sound now. Anyway, you asked for a quiet horse."

"I should hope so. If he gets frisky, the earth is going to shake."

They regarded the animal in question, a placid chestnut gelding with blonde mane and tail, built along the lines of an equine mountain range. He dropped his huge head to scratch a heavily feathered fetlock. Somewhere under all that hair must be a hoof the size of a buckler.

"Oh well," said Jame. "As long as you can find me a ladder."

Some time later, horse and rider ambled out of Tentir by a lesser gate—the fewer spectators the better, thought Jame, not to mention what people would make of her departure in the wrong direction.

Chumley might have grown bored pulling a cart, but he didn't object to a rider if, indeed, he even noticed her most of the time. He seemed quite happy to shamble along, head down, eyes half-closed under a heavy thatch of mane, finding the easiest way as if by accident.

Jame could have made faster time on foot.

However, then she would have had to carry the bulging saddle-bags that Rue had stuffed with as much food as she could lay her hands on in a hurry. Left to herself, Jame would have forgotten about provisions altogether. As Tirandys had once remarked, she never could remember to pack a lunch. Only by resolutely thinking about something else had she managed to choke down some breakfast.

On top of bags was strapped a bed-roll; and on top of that, Jame's knapsack, containing several things that would have made Rue stare if she had known about them.

They were following roughly the same route as the rathorn hunt, northward, across the toes of the Snowthorns. Sometimes the Silver glinted below as it wound down the valley floor. Sometimes voices floated up from the New Road as Jaran and Caineron cadets rode north to their home keeps of Valantir and Restormir, outpacing the slower travelers on the upper slopes. Mount Alban also lay in that direction, as did the ruins of Tagmeth and Kithorn, all three on the opposite bank. Beyond that were the hills claimed by the Merikit, then the Barrier that separated Rathillien from Perimal Darkling. However, Jame had no intention of going that far.

Actually, she didn't know where she was going or particularly care. The rathorn colt was out here somewhere, probably more aware of her than she was of him. She sensed that she could draw him to her by force if necessary, but that might break him and would surely defeat her purpose in seeking him out. They had to come to some understanding before he starved himself to death and either took her with him or left her unable to face a meal without nausea for the rest of her life. Besides, she felt responsible for him.

My stupid, stupid blood.

Meanwhile, it was a beautiful midsummer's day, warm in the sun, cool in the shade, with the tang of the evergreen ironwood in the breeze blowing off the heights. Clouds sailed southward down the valley against a sky as blue as a kitten's eye, their shadows drifting after them as if leisurely grazing on the upland meadows. Lavender true-love and pink shooting stars spangled grass that dipped and swayed in the wind. Among the trees, wood rose and blue bell lit the dappled shadows. Then the land plunged down into fern-laced ravines and up into stands of fluttering aspen which had at last achieved their summer arborage. Here a creek gurgled in its bed. There a jumble of boulders loomed as if tossed by some petulant giant at play. Above loomed the gray, misty heights of the Snowthorns, capped with white. Below, birds stilled at the clop of the travelers' approach, then burst into song when they had passed.

Jorin trotted ahead, occasionally dashing after butterflies when they caught Jame's eye. Mostly, however, she dozed, swaying on her mount's broad back, lulled by his placid, steady gait.

Take me where you will, she thought, just this side of sleep, hardly knowing whom she meant. *Dreamscape, soulscape, sacred space, over the hills or under them . . . wherever he waits for me.*

Once or twice she thought she glimpsed a keep sprawling below, but surely that was a waking dream. Valantir was some twenty-five miles north of Tentir and Restormir, the Caineron stronghold, that much farther again. At this pace, given the rough terrain, she would be surprised if they had made ten miles by the time the sun dipped below the peaks.

At dusk they halted beside a stream. Above, it coiled out of sight around pine and tamarack with a muted roar beyond that suggested a waterfall. Below, it slowed to meander down through a rich, sloping meadow fringed at the bottom with trees. This would do nicely.

Jame slid down from Chumley, and fell over. Her feet were numb. Also, it was a long, long way to the ground. Recovering, she unloaded the gelding and set him loose to graze in the meadow. Then she pitched camp under the boughs of a mountain ash with the chuckling stream nearby. As she gathered kindling, Jorin slipped off to hunt his dinner. Night fell.

A huge shape loomed out of the darkness, making her start, but it was only Chumley come looking for company. The gelding sank ponderously to his knees, then eased over onto his side with a groan of pleasure, his back to her small fire. Presently he began to snore. Leaning against him, Jame watched glow-bugs trundle about over the grass with their tiny lights like so many lost search parties while crickets sang derisively up at them.

At length she settled down under her blanket, devoutly hoping that the horse didn't roll over on her in the night. Only at the edge of sleep did she remember that she had forgotten to eat any supper. Jorin returned some time later and curled up beside her with a contented belch of raw muskrat.

In the morning, the rathorn came.

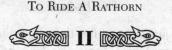

II

JAME WAS KNEELING on the pebbly margin of the stream, splashing cold water in her face, when a flash of white caught the corner of her eye. She rose, absently wiping her hands on her pants, and watched the rathorn colt canter toward her through the tall grass, the Whinno-hir Bel-tairi a pale shadow at his side.

Chumley was grazing by the river. His head jerked up as he caught their scents and he whickered uneasily. Bel swerved aside to reassure him, but the colt came straight on, gaining speed.

Hackles rose down his back, lifting his mane and the streaming flag of his tail. His head dropped to level the tips of his twin, curved horns. Jame watched his rapid approach, half terrified, half transfixed. He seemed to flow in a ripple of muscle and shifting ivory. If death were poetry, it would have scanned to the beat of those lethal hooves. And he wasn't slowing down.

I should climb a tree, thought Jame, just as Jorin did so behind her with a wild scrabble of claws and a shower of bark.

However, something told her to hold her ground and so she did, even as the rathorn hurtled down on her like an avalanche, filling the world with white thunder.

At the last moment he swerved aside in a stinging spray of gravel. Jame felt the wind of his passing and a sharp tug on her jacket where his nasal horn had plucked it open, drawing a bead of blood in the hollow of her throat. He skidded to a stop and wheeled on his hocks.

Here he came again.

This time just short of her the colt again slammed to a halt and reared, ivory hooves slashing the air on either side of her head. She noted almost with detachment that the light feathering concealed sharp dewclaw spurs, growing from the back of each fetlock joint. As his wild, musky smell filled her senses, she knew that he was trying to panic her into moving. Just a flinch either way and he would smash her skull, but he couldn't kill her outright.

Both realized this simultaneously. The rathorn dropped back to all fours and glared at her, nose to nose. Then he snorted, pivoted, and trotted away, tail arched, farting loudly.

"Hello to you too," said Jame, and abruptly sat down in the stream as her legs gave way under her.

The Whinno-hir had paused beside the gelding to snatch a few bites of grass. Against his looming bulk, she seemed no bigger than a foal, slender limbed, insubstantial. When Jame rose and wobbled toward her, she jerked up her head and froze in wide-eyed terror.

Suddenly the colt was between them. This time Jame couldn't help recoiling as his fangs snapped in her face, even though she was reasonably sure he didn't mean to bite it off. Before she could recover, both equines had galloped away.

Jame watched them out of sight, then went to coax Jorin down from his tree.

She spent the rest of the morning sorting out the supplies sent by Rue into what would keep, what wouldn't, and what was for her by definition inedible short of starvation, notably a wad of over-cooked sprouts mashed together in a bag like so many soggy, deformed little heads. Among the second group, snatched from ancestors knew what larder, was a whole roast chicken. After some thought, Jame shoved it and the other perishables back into a saddle bag, waded out into the stream, and wedged the lot in among stones so cold with mountain run-off that they numbed her hands.

Then she and Jorin went exploring.

To the west, hidden by trees, there was indeed a very respectable waterfall, tumbling into a deep pool, from there spilling into the swift stream that ran past her camp. Host trees overhung the water, their pale foliage fluttering upward in the misty draft. In the fall, the leaves would take flight for other hosts farther south. Some already seemed on the fret to go, as if sensing that the season was about to turn and the days to shorten.

This sheltered place would have been a much better campsite than the one she had chosen, Jame thought, and then saw that someone had had the same idea. Several yards from the waterfall, a shallow cave opened into the escarpment. Tucked under the cliff's over-hang was a stone-lined fire-pit, with embers still smoldering in a deep bed of white ash. More rocks formed a semi-circle outside. As Jame cautiously stepped between them toward the pit, her altered perspective suddenly changed them from random heaps to the crude semblance of human forms. One looked vaguely like a figure half-reclining, small boulders for the extended body, a pile of flat rocks for the torso, a round rock for a head, by nature even given the hint of a face. Imagination turned three more piles into seated men.

As Jame backed away from the cave, something made her look up. On top of the escarpment, on the lip of the falls, stood a man, looking down at her. She only saw him for a moment, long enough to note the hood that concealed most of his face and his hunting leathers, worn to a mottled green almost invisible against the undergrowth. She had barely drawn breath to hail him when he melted back into a clump of shrubs.

Jame scrambled up a spill of rocks to the top of the falls. By the time she got there, however, the stranger was gone, leaving not a foot-print, not a broken leaf, only a flight of azure-winged jewel-jaws spiraling up through the trees. If she hadn't stumbled across his campsite below, she would have thought that she had imagined him. Even so . . .

Turning, Jame looked back the way that she had come. From this height, she had a view over the host trees and pine spinney, down to the meadow where the chestnut gelding was rolling on his back, feathered hooves kicking the sky. For him, this must be paradise. Neither the rathorn nor the Whinno-hir were in sight, although a twinge in the bond that they now shared told her that the colt at least had not gone far. Beyond the trees at the meadow's foot there seemed to be a gap, and beyond that a high bluff crowned with more trees. She could hear the distant, hollow roar of water running between rocky walls. Could that be the Silver? Sunlight glinted on it farther upstream where it converged with another, smaller torrent. Between their fork rose the lower reaches of the northern Snowthorns, dismissed in the local parlance as "hills." Higher, more jagged mountains loomed beyond, including one at some distance whose heights were wreathed with smoke.

Wonderful, thought Jame. *Earthquakes, weirdingstroms, floods, and now maybe a volcano.*

She was about to descend when something across the river on top of the opposite cliff caught her attention. Although nearly masked with leaves, it looked like the remains of a curtain wall, enclosing a shattered tower. She had never seen it from this angle before, but it looked alarmingly like the ruins of Kithorn—which made no sense whatsoever. The nearest keep on the east bank to the north of Tentir was Mount Alban, home to the Scrollsmen's' College, but that would place her within spitting distance of the west bank Jaran fortress, Valantir, of which there was no sign.

Then she remembered that the Riverland fortifications had originally come in pairs, built by the ancient kingdoms of Bashti and Hathir to glare at each other across the Silver. Since then, a number had disappeared altogether, their stones dismantled to rebuild the nearest Kencyr keep. There must once have been at least a tower opposite Tentir. Perhaps this was its ruin, although that would place her much closer to the college than she had thought. Still, better that than opposite Kithorn, on Merikit land, only days from the summer solstice.

"Either way," she said to Jorin as they started back down toward their camp, "there's not much we can do about it short of running like hell, and I can't go anywhere until I've settled matters with that blasted rathorn."

Jorin ignored her in favor of a glittering, golden beetle that whirred past his nose. With a snap he ate it, and then was noisily sick. It had tasted awful. That night neither he nor Jame had any desire for food.

Perhaps it was the rumble of her empty stomach that roused Jame sometime later. *It can't be very late, though*, she thought, only half awake, looking up at a swollen gibbous moon that would soon be full. Just in time for the solstice. Odd. On Rathillien, was there some correlation between a full moon and the longest day? *Will have to ask Kirien or Index*, she thought drowsily.

Before she could sink back into sleep, however, some slight change in the stream's chuckle made her blink.

A man was bathing in it. Jame thought at first that it was Kindrie, but only because of the long white hair—too long, surely, unbound, waist-length, clinging to the stranger's shoulders and back. Moonlight turned his whole body into gleaming alabaster except where blue shadows traced wiry muscles and the threads of old scars. He scooped up water and dashed it in his face. It ran down, gleaming, over the hard lines of his chest, stomach, and loins.

Since when do I dream of naked men? Jame thought. *All right. Since Timmon. And Tori. But who is this? Trinity, I'm not dreaming . . . am I?*

The stranger waded ashore. He made hardly a sound on the pebbly bank, nor as he dried himself with wisps of grass, nor as he slipped back into his well-worn hunting leathers.

Glow-bugs traced his movements. He played with them, sculpting their flight with his white hands, expanding his gestures into wide, glowing sweeps. They danced with him, and he with them, wind-blowing kant-irs in a moon-silvered field. At times, in flight, his feet barely touched the bending grass. So her mother the Dream-weaver had danced, free of earth, free of pain or regret, free as the wind blows. Jame longed to join him, to shed all that weighed her down—her past, her responsibilities, herself—but dull flesh bound her, helpless. Instead, she watched until the moon set and sleep took her into dreams of aching grace.

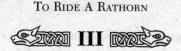

III

IN THE MORNING, a strange mare grazed beside Chumley in the field. Jame didn't see her at first, so perfectly did she blend with the play of sun and shadow on the grass. Even then, Jame didn't at first believe her eyes. Of the many strange things she had encountered in her life, a green horse ranked near the top. The mare greeted her with a friendly whicker, long, moss green tail swishing at flies. On closer inspection, Jame saw that although her eyes were the color of new leaves, her coat was actually pearl gray, subtly stained in all the shades of leaf and lichen, wood and stone. In fact, thought Jame, tracing the swoop of a line down her shoulder—tawny gold tinged with a rosy haze the color of ripening wheat—she was beautiful, a true work of art, and also excellently camouflaged.

Around her neck was a leather band. Curious, Jame slid a finger under it. Immediately, blood began to trickle down the mare's neck from a small, neat hole in her throat. It stopped as soon as Jame hastily released the band, which she now saw had a small plug on its inner surface. The mare had raised her head with a look of mild inquiry, but dropped it again to graze when she saw that nothing more was required of her.

How very odd. A campsite with stone figures for company, a naked man bathing, and now this. It seemed that she had encroached on someone's territory, but whose?

She was gnawing a wedge of rock-hard bread, hoping she wasn't about to break another tooth, when the rathorn returned, again accompanied by Bel. He swerved to inspect the newcomer, who squealed and kicked him in the face when he got too close. Jame winced, feeling his head ring inside its ivory mask. He retreated, then began to prance back and forth, slashing at weeds, deliberately ignoring both Jame and the strange mare.

Now that he wasn't trying to kill her, she had a chance to observe him more closely. For all his fluid stride and proudly cocked head, his white coat was dull and staring, his mane and tail tangled into elf-locks. As for his ribs, she could count them as easily as she could her own.

Despite that, he was no fool. She sensed that he understood as well as she did that they were now bound together, and had as little idea how to handle the situation. Of course, he was furious and resentful. If the situation had been reversed, she would have been tearing out her hair—or better yet, his. To be in the power of one's worst enemy . . . how did one live with that? How had she, during all those lost years in Perimal Darkling? But then at some fundamental level she had still been free, still been herself, thanks to Tirandys' subtle distortion of his master's orders. That would have ended in Gerridon's beribboned bed, where she would have taken her mother's place in more ways than one. Instead, someone (Bender?) had handed her a knife and she had reclaimed her life with its sharp edge.

This bond would be much harder to sever than the Master's wrist. If the old songs were right, it bound her and the rathorn together to death and perhaps beyond. Even more surely, she knew that if she pushed the colt too hard against his will, he would lash back as best he could, even to his own destruction. This had to be subtle. A courtship. Even a seduction.

Still, things weren't as bad as they had been. Their experiences together in the soulscape, while terrifying, had taken some of the edge off his anger at her. After all, they had arguably saved each other from the haunt stallion Iron-jaw and she had gone back for him, even if the Earth Wife's protection had turned out to make that unnecessary.

More important, he now had the company of the Whinno-hir Bel-tairi. As different as they were in many respects—not least in that she was prey and he a predator —both were herd animals. Much of his previous despair and incipient madness had been rooted in his isolation after his mother's death at Jame's hand. Captain Hawthorn had called the colt a rogue, a death's-head, adding that no rage would let him join it. Jame wondered if he had tried and been repulsed. That long, half-healed scar down his side above the protective armor suggested the work of another rathorn stallion's nasal tusk. For that matter, maybe he had been lurking around the Knorth horses not in search of meat but of companionship. After all, he hadn't attacked any of them. Poor boy.

Boy. When they had first met, she had judged him to be either a weanling or a yearling, but what did she know? Her only real experience with horses before that had been with her father's war-horse Iron Jaw and the monster that he had become.

How old was the rathorn colt now? Less than two years, at a guess, and, for all his inches, not yet full grown. She wondered at what age it would be safe to ride him, assuming they got that far without killing each other. Working in the stable, she had overheard the horse-master speak of a two-year-old filly whose knees had finally closed, whatever that meant beyond that she was now old enough to work. It made sense after all that a foal couldn't bear the weight of a rider before it was strong enough.

Then again, this was a rathorn, not a horse. As far as Jame knew, no one had ever ridden one before, at any age, or at least not lived to brag of it. "To ride a rathorn" was madness—wasn't it? Still, she couldn't help but wonder what it would be like in real life, not just in a dream of the soulscape.

She also wondered what the colt's name was. No doubt he had one, and it would be impertinent of her to try to saddle him with another.

"Snowfire?" she said experimentally, and he turned to glare at her down his long, gleaming nose. "Precious? All right, all right. You'll tell me when you're ready."

By now, it was afternoon.

Jame took a handful of oats from her knapsack and went to lay on her back in the long grass. Stems tickled her ears and insects crawled over her outflung arms. The sun beat on her face, turning her shut eyelids into red-veined curtains. Her skin began to glow. She remembered with unease that there were now only four days until the longest of the year, the summer solstice, but pushed the thought away.

She was almost asleep when she heard the cautious approach of hooves, then teeth tearing nearby grass. Through narrowed lids, she saw the Whinno-hir.

"I'm sorry I frightened you," she murmured, barely moving her lips. The sound of grazing stopped, but while the hooves shifted uneasily, they didn't move away. "What my uncle did to you was unforgivable, and I may turn out to be more like him than like my great-grand-mother Kinzi. Truly, though, I'm trying not to. Will you help me, for her sake? Can we at least start over?"

She let her fingers uncurl. After a long moment, velvet lips brushed her palm to scoop up the grain.

IV

THAT NIGHT, Jame woke to Jorin's low growl and lay still, holding him, her senses at full stretch. The crickets and night birds had fallen silent. She thought she had heard . . . no, smelled . . . something too, before she was fully awake, something that had darkened her last dreams with the shades of smoldering nightmare. Burnt fur. That was it.

She scanned the meadow and trees or what she could see of them, which was virtually nothing. The moon had long since set, and a haze shrouded the stars. No wind stirred the grass. Even the stream seemed oddly muted. She rose to add more wood to her campfire, moving slowly, deliberately.

Show no fear.

Why had that thought suddenly leaped into her mind?

Because he can smell fear, and guilt.

Out in the darkness, Chumley squealed and bolted, ponderous hooves thudding away.

Shouldn't have feigned lameness. Bet you're sorry now.

A swift rush through the grass and Bel-tairi appeared on the edge of the firelight. There she stood, poised for further flight with one fore-hoof raised, looking back over her shoulder into the darkness. Then, still looking back, she edged sideways in so close to the fire that she trod on its outer branches and jumped as they snapped.

A moment later, the rathorn colt joined her, taking the outer position of guard. Both ignored Jame, but through the colt's senses as well as through Jorin's she now heard the slow tread of great paws and smelled, much stronger than before, that peculiar, acrid stench of burnt hair. There, beyond the firelight, the Dark Judge paced. The equines turned with him, Jame now circling between them and the intruder with Jorin so close on her inner heel that he threatened to trip her.

. . . bloody, stupid Merikit . . .

The great cat's mutter rumbled through flesh and shuddered in the bone. Not just that: the earth itself shook. To the north, in the dark, rose a column of smoke, its dimensions defined by inner flickering tongues of lightning, its sullen mutter rolling down the valley. It seemed closer than it had by day unless (alarming thought) this was another mountain. What if the entire range erupted?

. . . think they can fool us, do they? Not again. Never again.

Us? thought Jame. *Who is "us"?*

By now she could make out the prowling hulk of the blind Arrin-ken, always so much larger than one expected. It seemed to flow around the margin of the camp, a net of fiery cracks cast over darkness, opening into it. The fire-bugs had left the field and swarmed about a dark, upright shape that walked silently at the great cat's side. When the insects touched the second figure, they flared briefly and fell so that its passage was marked by a thousand tiny deaths.

. . . burn, burn, burn them all, as we were burned.

The mutter deepened to a growl, under-laid with hunger and a terrible, gloating eagerness.

Eat away weakness. Consume sin. Devour guilt. You!

His massive head swung toward Jame as the earth shuddered again. His companion also turned. Dying fire-bugs flared in the latter's eye-sockets, giving a brief glimpse of a charred, ravaged face that had once been human.

Come to justice, little nemesis. Be purified in our flame for your holy purpose.

"No."

He was frightening Bel, and that angered her.

"I will judge myself, as I always have, and will accept no more mercy than I am prepared to give. Now go away, you pompous bully; you've upset m'lady."

Huh!

His contemptuous snort blew her campfire apart. To the north, a second dark, roiling cloud arose, defined by the hot cinders swirling in it and the forked lightning at its heart. A distant boom rolled down the valley like thunder, and the earth shook again.

Mare and colt both screamed. The next moment, the rathorn had charged the intruders, who dissolved into a shower of sparks before him. Jame caught the mare and made her stand, trembling, as she plucked burning embers out of her mane and tail.

"Death's-head!" she shouted after the colt. "Come back, you fool!"

Eventually he did, having made sure the others had really gone.

"Death's-head," Jame repeated, watching him solicitously lick a scorched patch on the mare's shoulder. "Are you sure you want that for a name?" He bared his fangs at her over Bel's back and hissed, reminding her of the Randir's adder. "All right, all right. After all, that's what you are. Death's-head and Nemesis it is, then, although for the element of surprise I would have preferred Snowball and Buttercup."

⟨≋⟩ **V** ⟨≋⟩

RECOVERING CHUMLEY took most of the next day, during which Jame came to the reluctant conclusion that she was nowhere near the randon college.

For one thing, the more she saw of those ruins on the opposite bank, the more like Kithorn they looked.

For another, she was fairly sure she would have noticed a smoking mountain in the immediate vicinity. Poor as she was at guessing distances on such a scale, she was fairly sure it couldn't be more than five miles away, although the previous day it had seemed more distant.

That morning the grass had been lightly dusted with ash, and the ground now trembled almost continually. What was more, behind a screen of smoke the mountain top seemed to be growing some sort of spine or protrusion like nothing she had ever seen before—a plug of half-cooled lava, perhaps, forced upward by titanic pressure from beneath. If the mountain should pop its cork, well, the thought did not encourage hope for a quiet life in the near future.

One disaster at a time, though. First, find Chumley.

In the beginning, the trail was clear: A near-ton of panicking horse-flesh tends to leave its mark. However, rough terrain intervened, and then Jorin ran into a patch of deadman's-breath that left him rolling on the ground, trying to escape his own nose.

Jame was about to give up when she heard Bel calling. She followed the sound to a deep ravine. The Whinnohir stood at the brink and there at the bottom was the gelding, up to his withers in brambles, looking unhurt but deeply embarrassed. He whickered plaintively up at her.

"All right," she said. "Hold your horses . . . er . . . that is, hold still."

She had brought her grapnel rope, which was hardly strong enough to haul up such a weight by brute force, even if she had had the strength to try. This would only work if Chumley stopped waiting to be rescued and started helping himself. Jame looped the rope twice around a smooth-barked tree and scrambled down. Luckily, the gelding still wore his halter. She secured the rope to it and encouraged him to climb, but kept sliding back herself.

Frustrated, she grabbed a handful of his flaxen mane, pulled herself up onto his broad back, and dug her heels into his sides. When he only shifted uneasily, she unsheathed her claws. Their use resulted in a surge upward. When he faltered, Jame flicked loose the slackened rope from around the tree and again pulled it taut, preventing him from sliding back down unless he wanted his neck to stretch like taffy. Thus by fits and starts they finally lurched up the slope and out of the ravine.

At the top, Jame slid down onto shaking legs and leaned against the gelding's sweat-stained side. Chumley was also trembling, but didn't draw away from her, which improved her opinion of his good sense, or at least of his good nature.

When they finally got back to the meadow, she cleaned the scratches on his neck and gave him a thorough grooming. Brushes, combs, and a hoof-pick had also been among her knapsack stash, on the advice of a bemused horse-master who couldn't imagine what a confirmed equinophobe like Jame wanted with them. However, she had had plenty of experience putting up her mounts after lessons, and even more when sharing her ten's various punishment duties.

The gelding leaned into the curry brush with a groan of pleasure. Remnants of his rough, winter coat came off in felt-like mats on the bristles and dried mud crumbled to dust. Then there were his hooves to pick, once one found them under all that heavy feathering, and his mane and tail to comb, tangled as they were with burrs and bracken.

As she worked, Jame wondered if in future she should hobble him. No, she decided. If he had to run again, better that he not trip and break his neck. Anyway, after the first shock of sharing pasture with a carnivorous rathorn, he had settled down remarkably fast. Rathorns used scent to communicate. Jame suspected that the colt could change the way he smelled to soothe potential prey just as he could to terrorize enemies. Bel enjoyed company as she grazed; therefore, Chumley had been made to feel welcome and seemed disinclined to stray, even after the previous night's visitors.

The Dark Judge and the Burnt Man, the worst (or least the most unstable and dangerous) of both worlds, Kencyrath and Rathillien. Now, there was trouble beyond the scope of her imagination, and only three days to go until the solstice.

The gelding took a long time, leaving Jame hot, sweaty, and plastered with loose horse hairs. Set free, he stretched like an over-grown cat, yawned hugely, and ambled off for a nice roll in the mud.

"Huh!" said Jame, dropping the brushes in disgust as she watched him undo all her hard work. Then she went to wash in the stream. She was considering a swim when the Whinno-hir's reflection appeared in the water behind her own and a soft nose nudged her shoulder.

Oh well, she thought. This too had been part of her plan.

As Kinzi's mount, Bel must have been groomed lovingly and often. Her body remembered it as the brushes slid over her coat even as she trembled, no doubt also remembering the last time she had been touched by human hands.

One usually began with the head. However, when the mare flinched away, Jame smoothed her mane to the right and started on the left side. At the withers, she paused to probe tense shoulder muscles with her finger tips, then knead them with her knuckles until Bel relaxed, sighing, shot-hipped. With brush and touch, Jame moved down the mare's body. Dull, dead hair lifted from creamy new growth; white dapples emerged on back and flanks. The white tail seemed to lengthen as she combed it until half of it trailed on the ground. The mane also proved surprisingly long, reaching below the mare's knees. However, not until Jame reached Bel's hooves did she realize what was happening.

As she held one in her hand, about to pick it clean, she noted how long it was in the toe. In fact, it grew as she watched, becoming wavy and turning up at the end like a dandy's slipper. Forty-odd years in the Earth Wife's lodge were catching up with the mare all at once. No wonder her hair was suddenly so long. If she had been a normal horse, not a potentially immortal Whinno-hir, she probably would have dropped dead of extreme old age on the spot, just when she had had been brought at last to accept life.

Bel shook free her foot and placed it gingerly on the ground. All four hooves now looked like curved skids and were obviously painful.

The rathorn's teeth closed on Jame's collar. He lifted her off her feet, gave her a hard shake, and let her drop, with a menacing snort down the back of her neck.

"Look," she said, on bruised knees, glowering up over her shoulder at him. "This isn't my fault. And no, I didn't think to bring farrier's tools, supposing I'd know what to do with them if I had them. D'you want me to float her back teeth too?"

It occurred to her even as she spoke that that too would probably be required, as it was with horses. Barbs grew on the outer edge of their teeth, designed to keep hay from falling out of their mouths as they chewed. However, unless these hooks were periodically filed down, they could rasp the inner cheek raw. If that was true, as with her hooves and hair, the Whinno-hir would now also have trouble eating. Of the four of them, that only left Jorin with a decent appetite, as long as he stayed away from pretty bugs.

A spill of white mane between the ears fell like a curtain over the mare's features. Jame parted it, slowly, carefully, unveiling a mystery.

A woman gazed steadily back at her out of one large, liquid eye set in half a flawless face. A savage scar seamed the other eye shut before curving off down her cheek to the rim of her nose. Jame traced it with a finger, overwhelmed with pity and rage. Nothing was bad enough for the man who had done this, never mind that he was long dead. She was Nemesis, dammit, or soon would be. Who said that vengeance stopped with the pyre?

A light touch brought her back to herself. As she examined Bel's scars, so Bel had been studying hers. The other's cool, slim hands slid up to cradle her face, lifting black hair as Jame's did white.

We are sisters of the brand, her voice murmured in Jame's mind. *We are stronger than what has been done to us. So my lady told me. So, thanks to you, I now understand. Be at rest in your strength, Kinzi-kin, as I now am in mine.*

She kissed Jame lightly on the lips, then let the black hair swing back over her face. By the time Jame had scooped it clear, the mare had moving gingerly away on her over-grown hooves, shaking each in turn before she stepped on it like a cat who has accidentally trod in something unpleasant. In her place, the rathorn stood glowering.

"What's the matter?" Jame twisted up her hair and clapped her cap back over it. "Haven't you ever seen two girls sharing secrets?" She retrieved a brush. "Your turn."

But the colt only gave a snort and trotted off.

VI

THAT NIGHT JAME sat by the fire combing her damp hair with her claws, trying to decide if she really needed any dinner. Jorin had already gone off to hunt his own.

Rescuing Chumley, not to mention grooming him and the mare, had been surprisingly hard work, and a swim in the chilly stream afterward had only restored her in part.

Face it, she thought glumly, teasing out a snarl. *You're starting to draw on reserves that you don't have. After all, there are reasons why people eat regular meals.*

The rathorn hadn't eaten yet either . . . in how many days? And he was a growing boy, if usually a blood-thirsty one. His anger at her had faded somewhat, unless he remembered to keep it fueled. Now, more than anything else, he was being stubborn.

I won't eat and you can't make me.

Idiot.

And so, of course, was she as well, for getting them all into this fix.

"I ought to have a sign nailed to my back," she muttered, getting her nails caught in her hair and impatiently yanking a dozen strands out by the roots. " 'Unsafe for man or beast.' "

"How about women and children?"

The gruff voice made Jame start.

On the other side of the fire, just beyond its light, sat a large, lumpy figure that might have been a hillock rising out of the grass. Jame could barely make out a shaggy head and hands with fingers like thick, knobby twigs. Click, click, click . . . it was knitting, and what it knitted was alive.

"Quip?" said the work, flexing on the long, thin needles that were its bones. Bright eyes in a fox-like face caught the firelight. "Quip!"

"Almost done, my sweetling. Patience."

"Some day," said Jame, "will you teach me how to knit? I'm hopeless with needle and thread, but that looks . . . well, restful. Most of the time."

The foxkin was flapping his one finished wing frantically, trying to escape. The Earth Wife wrestled him down. "Wait till I cast off, dumpling. D'you want to unravel in mid-air?" She examined the limb more closely and clucked in disapproval. "I've made a right mess of this. Too much on my mind. Hold still, pumpkin. This won't hurt . . . much."

"QUEEE!"

Jame winced as powerful fingers slid the work in question off the bone and ripped it out back to the shoulder.

The Earth Wife glared at her, eyes reflecting flames. Fire-bugs nestled in her wild hair, illuminating patches of its tangle and stray quadrants of her lumpy face. "Should I let it go a cripple? Here. You try." She tossed the living bundle to Jame, who nearly dropped it into the fire. "First, take off those stupid gloves. Then put the stitches back on the needle."

Jame hastily stripped off her gloves as the creature crawled about in her lap, making small, busy sounds to itself as if taking notes. Its body was quite solid, furry, and about twice the size of a bat's, but the wing stubs ended in a frill of loops. She picked up the latter one by one, sliding them onto a slender, white needle. The foxkin hooked his hind claws over the bone and hung upside down from it, regarding her inquisitively.

"Quip?"

"Now what?" Jame asked, holding the needle and its burden away from her face.

"Take the other needle in your left hand and slip its point through the first stitch from front to back. Now loop the yarn over the left needle, draw one stitch through the other, and lift the new stitch off to the left. Careful. Don't accidentally knit in his claws or he can't use 'em."

"Squeee!"

"And not so tight. Let it ride loose on the bone. I hear you had company last night, and the night before that—yes, through the big ears of that *imu* in your pocket. So the Burnt Man won't be fooled any longer, will he?"

"So the Dark Judge said." Jame focused on capturing the next stitch. How could someone so nimble-fingered at picking locks be so clumsy with any sort of needlework? "Is that bad?"

Mother Ragga snorted. The sound turned into a truly seismic belch that shook the ground and dislodged burning branches in the campfire in a shower of sparks. To the north, the volcano rumbled as if in sullen reply. Fire glowered at the base of the spine at its top, sending veins of incandescent scarlet upward. The clouds above reflected back a ruddy, smoldering glow. In the darkened meadow, Chumley neighed uneasily. Much more of this, and there would be another stampede.

" 'Is that bad?' " Mother Ragga repeated in what might have been a mincing imitation of Jame's voice. "By stock and stone, girl, I can't make out whether you're innocent or ignorant, not that one isn't as dangerous as t'other. I told you in the Moon Garden: there are rules. If the Burnt Man wasn't fooled before, at least he pretended to be, and so the seasons rolled on. Where are we now, if death won't yield to life? Somehow, that great, bloody burnt cat of yours is mucking things up. Got it in for you, has he? Why?"

Jame gave an uncomfortable shrug and dropped a stitch. "Damn. I'm apparently half way to becoming That-Which-Destroys, whether I like it or not. If I have a correspondence to any of the Four, it would probably be to fire. The burnt cat shares that link, but he has his own ideas about what should be destroyed."

"Huh. Namely everything. That's where you confuse me, girl. Granted, you can be lethal. What you did to the colt, now, that was nasty, but here you are, trying to help him, and the mare too. How does that fit with this three faced god-thingie of yours?"

"I've been asked that before." Jame probed for the lost stitch and accidentally poked the foxkin, who squealed in protest and nipped all the way around her fingertip with his sharp teeth, luckily without breaking the skin. "Sorry. It's a hard question. If the priests know . . . well, I'm not going to ask those bastards anything. There's honor, of course, but also responsibility and kindness. Good teachers taught me that. They also taught me to try to balance myself, not that I always succeed. Some things need to be broken. Others don't. I try to make distinctions and act accordingly. Then again, I'm not the Third Face of God yet and may never be, if the other two don't show up. But if I should become Regonereth, the Ivory Knife incarnate, destroying everything I touch, everything I love—well, I'll do what I was born to do, break what needs to be broken, and then break myself."

She hadn't quite thought it through before, but there it was, with a nice, solid thud. Such power without responsibility would pervert everything she had ever tried to accomplish and dishonor her Senethari, at least one of whom had died for her sake. The least she could do was back her word with her life.

The Earth Wife eyed her askance. "Huh. Give that back. I should have started you on something easy. Like a tube-worm."

Jame returned the incomplete foxkin, surprised at her own reluctance. Knitting might not always be restful, but she suspected that it was addictive, assuming the work in progress could be persuaded not to eat one's fingers.

She looked again at the glowering mountain. How close it now seemed, blotting out half the night sky, its fire-veined tip thrust, pulsing, up into the dark.

"Is it my imagination, or is that thing trying to creep up on us?"

"Schist, girl. You're in sacred space now. Sometimes it surprises even me."

"Oh." Jame considered this. On the whole, it was not reassuring. She glanced up again at the throbbing tip. "Impressive."

The shadowy figure gave a rumbling chuckle. "Aye, that he is. A hot lover to warm an old woman's bed. Too hot for those damn fool Merikit. Chingetai has gotten into the habit of underestimating us. Thinks he can trot in wearing the Burnt Man's soot and do what he likes."

"He wasn't there for most of the Summer's Eve rite," said Jame soberly. "He didn't see it from inside sacred space, the way I did, when the Four unmasked and turned a mummery into the real thing.

"That is Kithorn over there, isn't it? How in Perimal's name did I get here?"

"You asked, I answered: 'Take me where you will, wherever he waits.' The land folds at my bidding, doesn't it?"

"Yes, but I thought that if I brought Kencyr steel, even horse tack, over the Merikit border, some sort of alarm went off."

"So it should have, but now, thanks to that silly bugger Chingetai, all his borders are down, including those to the north, and there are tribes up there near the Barrier all too friendly with the shadows."

"I didn't know that," said Jame, startled.

"Har-*rumph*! Who d'you think guards the northern end of the Riverland, or should if he was paying attention? The Silver is a natural concourse to the heart of Rathillien. Last year, didn't you people stop a thrust up from the south? First bit of useful work you've done since you got here. Chingetai should have made his northern border secure at Summer's Eve, but instead he makes a grab for the entire Riverland and gets his fingers burned for his pains. Your doing, that, I hear tell."

"It wasn't deliberate. How was I to know that pocketing a Burnt Man's bone would spoil his plan? Er . . . does he know that I'm here?"

"The man's a fool, but not an idiot. On his doorstep, aren't you? Of course he knows. Thanks to him, you're my Favorite, and so I brought you here to play your part. But Chingetai doesn't want you showing what a mess he's made of things, so he means to use a substitute."

"But now the Burnt Man says he won't be fooled."

"Aye. Troubling, that, although he might just as well have meant getting a stick of a girl presented to him as his son instead of the strapping boy he expects." She burped again, hawked raucously like a mountain clearing its throat, and spat a gob of flame into the dying fire. "G'ah. Heartburn. Earth and fire don't mix well. I don't see how this is going to play out, and that's a fact. On top of it all, if there's a bloody big bang, we need the Tishooo to blow the ash northward over the Barrier, and he's home sulking. Thinks he should have a bigger part in the midsummer festival. Huh! Every year we get this nonsense. Mind you, I can protect the Merikit, little as they deserve it, and it might be a good thing in the long run to bury you lot up to your eyebrows in hot ash, but I don't half like this northern wind. It reeks of the shadows."

To Jame, it simply reeked, mostly of sulfur. She hadn't considered how a major eruption might affect the Riverland. When the mountain had been a mere smoking bump on the horizon, it hadn't seemed to matter much. Perhaps, in real space, that's where it still was, too far away to be a threat. On the other hand, what did she know about volcanoes, other than that they tended inconveniently to explode?

"Ah." The Earth Wife's mirror-fire eyes shifted to something behind Jame and her crooked mouth twitched into something like a smile, red light from within a jagged line between her lips. "Here's someone come to call. Hold still."

Even with the warning, Jame started as a pair of slim, white hands appeared over her shoulders. She thought they were going for her face but instead, as she held herself rigidly still, they gathered up her loose hair and smoothed it back.

"Soft," said a voice behind her, odd and husky as if it hadn't spoken in a long time, and it spoke in High Kens. Fingers took up combing out her tangled locks where she had left off. When she tried to turn, however, a firm hand on the top of her head prevented her.

"Who is it?" she hissed at the Earth Wife, even as the glimmer of an answer occurred to her. After all, how many people had she encountered since her arrival here, and how many Kencyr Highborn wandered the wilds, as free as the wind through the trees?

"You should know. He's one of you lot. The Merikit call him Mer-kanti."

Jame thought she could put a different name to the stranger, but not here, where the very sound of it might draw those enemies sworn to his destruction. Meanwhile, his deft fingers slide through her hair, smoothing, separating, gently tugging.

"That feels good," she murmured, surrendering to his touch.

The Earth wife laughed. "You folk are peculiar. D'you have to go into the wilderness to give and take pleasure freely? Mind you, Mer-kanti's passions are obscure. He finds company in stacked stones, a painted mare, and the flight of crown jewel-jaws. We feel him glide through our seasons. Earth, air, wind, and fire are all one to him, although daylight hurts his eyes. Look for him in shadow and darkness, or where the red blood flows."

"And those who hunt him?"

"The Merikit gave up long ago. Their quarrel with your kind was none of his making, and he spares where he might easily kill. Others come, sometimes, from the south, but they leave their bodies to richen my soil."

Although she held herself as still as still, Jame felt the pulse in her throat quickly under that light, caressing touch. "Their blood too?"

"Ah." She thought she heard the hint of smile in the other's voice. "That's his business, isn't it? But enough of that. I foresee fire and ash, a peculiar dawn and darkness at noon. What happens next depends in part on which way the wind blows, and I mistrust anything that comes from the north. Best you were gone, girl. After all, the solstice is tomorrow."

"What? It can't be . . . or did I somehow miss a day?"

"Yes, getting here. Sometimes folding the land takes time. By the way, I like your big horse. Not many are up to my weight. Fare you well. *Hic!*"

She tried to stifle it, but the belched flame erupted like a geyser from her mouth and set her straw thatch of hair on fire.

Jame leaped to her feet, meaning to push her into the stream to extinguish her, but Mother Ragga's blazing figure crumbled at her touch. Out of it sprang the terrified, singed foxkin, landing in Jame's arms and scuttling inside her jacket for shelter. Mer-kanti had disappeared. In the distance, the mountain grumbled and spat.

Jame sighed. *Life is strange*, she thought, and went to bed with a half-knit foxkin curled up under her chin.

CHAPTER XVIII

Solstice

Summer 66

I

JAME WOKE the next morning, disoriented.

Surely it had all been a dream, and not a very good one at that. The Burnt Man and the Dark Judge, the Earth Wife and the creeping mountain, a green mare and a half-knit foxkin . . .

". . . quip . . ." said something furry under her chin, and snuggled down again with a sleepy kneading of claws.

All right. She would grant the foxkin.

And the mountain. It was rather hard to miss in that it now loomed overhead, taking up most of the northern sky. If it had looked any closer, she would have been under it. Around that ridiculous spine at its top it was smoking like a chimney, assuming anyone would want to burn brimstone and rotten eggs. The ground under her head rumbled steadily—rock's equivalent of a warning growl: Just you wait.

Then she remembered. The wait was almost over. This was the summer solstice. That also rattled her, coming as it did a day before she had expected it, again like a bad dream.

But I'm not ready.

A sudden blare of horns made her jump and the foxkin dig in its claws. Distorted by hill and mountain, the ruckus presumably came from the Merikit village hidden by a turn farther up the Silver. A cloud of ash-laden vapor drifted eastward toward it from the volcano's peak, some settling to darken the summit snow, some lifting back into the air to distort the sunrise before the prevailing north wind caught and pushed it south. The solar rim had just appeared between two eastern peaks, a bow of improbable sharp blue spiked with turquoise rays in turn edged with shimmering green. So began the longest day of the year, in a haze of smoke, a discordant blat of horns, and a stench of sulfur.

For a moment, Jame wished that she had acceded to Index's demand and brought the old scrollsman with her. He might have had some idea what she should expect, at least from the Merikit. She felt like someone on the edge of a great pageant, knowing that she had an important role in it and fretting that she wasn't there. At the same time, no one would thank her for stepping forward to claim her part. The Earth Wife had as good as told her to leave. If she had any sense, she would have saddled Chumley last night and ridden away as fast as his great, galumphing hooves would take her.

She rose and began in a distracted way to break up camp as the foxkin rummaged, chittering, in a saddle-bag, looking for breakfast. Over the past few days, Jame had forced herself to eat a bit of this or that—hard bread, a crust of cheese, some withered apples, even the squishy little sprout heads, although those had come back up faster than they had gone down. Not much remained. However, the foxkin's busy quest reminded her of the other bag of provisions, still sunk in the icy water. She waded out to retrieve it.

The contents were, of course, wet and cold, but also well-preserved. Jame extracted the roast chicken and sniffed at it suspiciously. To her surprise, it smelled good. Since when had anything done that? She tore off a leg and was about to take a gingerly nibble when the rathorn's head snaked over her shoulder and snatched it out of her hand.

Jame sprang to her feet, aghast. She tried to grab it back before he swallowed any bone splinters, but the colt backed away, raising his head out of reach like a horse refusing the bit. Then he spat out a mouthful of intact bones, gulped down the meat, and made another dive at the carcass. Both suddenly ravenous, they wrestled over it briefly before it tore apart. Jame tumbled over backward, clutching a pair of wings. The colt retreated, snorting, with the rest.

Gnawing on her prize, she watched him pin his to the ground with a dew-spur and frantically rasp flesh from bone with his tongue. The latter must be barbed, as with some large hunting cats. All this time, she had only needed the proper treat to break his stubborn resistance, but how could she have guessed that he had a passion for cooked meat? For that matter, it seemed to have surprised him as much as it had her; after all, there weren't many roast chickens running about loose in the wild.

The last scrap gone, he shoved his nose into the wet saddlebag looking for more, then jerked it back with the foxkin clinging to his nasal horn. As he backed in a circle, trying to shake the creature loose, Jame gathered the chicken bones before Jorin could get at them and threw the lot into the stream. It too was beginning to steam and stink; ground water as well as run-off must contribute to it. She had retrieved the saddle-bag none too soon. Meanwhile, Chumley, the painted mare (where had she come from?), Bel, and Jorin were lined up, accidentally according to height, watching the rathorn's wild gyrations with wary fascination.

As the foxkin scuttled over his ivory mask, the colt's red eyes crossed, trying to follow it.

"Quip!" it said, popping up between his ears and sticking its sharp, inquisitive nose into one of them.

The colt squealed, reared, and went over backward, scattering his audience but not shaking his tormenter. He lurched back to his feet and careened off, bucking, across the meadow.

Meanwhile, Jame had dumped the contents of the bag onto the ground. Was there anything left to tempt the colt or, for that matter, herself? Ah. Some beef jerky and a few slabs of smoked ham, perfect for a picnic under an active volcano.

Before she could decide what to eat and what to offer, the sun lifted clear of the mountains and drums in the Merikit village greeted its ascent.

"BOOM-Wah-wah . . . BOOM-Wah-wah . . . "

The sound was approaching, gaining definition as the procession cleared intervening hills, but she couldn't see it from the meadow. Nor was there any reason why she had to, Jame told herself. She couldn't do any good although, given her nature, she might inadvertently do harm. Still, the drums called.

"BOOM-Wah-wah-BOOM!"

She stuffed a greasy slab of meat into a pocket and set off at a trot down the meadow. By the time she reached the bottom and dived among the ferns under the shadow of overhanging boughs, she was running. Before her, the stream leaping over a cliff into the torrent below. On the other side of the Silver's chasm rose sandstone bluffs, still deep in shadow, with the ruins of Kithorn on their summit. Could she snag her grapnel on the opposite heights and swing over? No. Too far. Then climb.

Of the trees offered to her, a black walnut some two hundred feet downstream loomed the tallest. She stripped off her gloves and tucked them into her belt, wishing for the first time that she had clawed toes as well as fingers. The corrugated bark gave good hand-holds, though, as did sturdy boughs. Her hands soon stank of the bruised leaves' distinctive, astringent scent. The trunk bifurcated, once, twice, and again into a limb stretching over the Silver. Jame crawled out on it.

A good thing I'm not afraid of heights, she thought, then froze as the branch dipped, groaning, under her weight. From below rose the thunder of water and mist that wrapped the tree in wet, slippery moss. She was a long, long way up.

At least from here she could see over the broken wall and tower, which her brother had accidentally burned down the previous fall. How strange, as it were, to be looking into Marc's past. After all, he had grown up in the shattered keep now spread out below her. Like a score of minor keeps dotting the edges of Rathillien, all but forgotten, Kithorn had kept watch on the Barrier with Perimal Darkling according to the Kencyrath's ancient trust. Yes, she had been here before, but too close really to see how small a place it was, how desperate its defiance against the dark must have been.

In the center of its inner court was a wide well-mouth, rimmed with serpentine marble, the relic of a time long before Hathir and Bashti had laid their arrogant claims to this ancient land. All the Riverland keeps were built on the sites of Bashtiri or Hathiri fortresses, but these in turn had been raised over the ruins of still older hill forts. However, none of the latter were more potent than this one.

From her perch, Jame couldn't quite see over the well's lip down to the ring of teeth within or the muscular red throat below that, but she knew they were there. After all, on Summer Eve she had been dropped down it and had had to climb back up, fast, for this was the mouth of the River Snake whose vast length ran beneath the Silver from one end to the other, whose restless stirrings could throw the land into convulsions.

Although Marc's lord had allowed the Merikit private access for their rituals, he had not known what they were doing until he had accidentally learned, in a year of violent quakes, that they meant to throw a hero down the well to fight the snake. This he had forbidden. Afraid that their world was about to be shaken apart, the Merikit had tried to take the garrison hostage to prevent its interference, but someone had panicked, ending with the slaughter of every Kencyr there except for Marc, who had been off by himself, hunting. And so the hills had been closed.

If the Earth Wife had spoken true, the terrible irony was that the Kencyr and the Merikit shared a charge to maintain the Barrier against Perimal Darkling here at the Riverland's northern end. Instead, the Merikit cut Kencyr throats and the Kencyr—at least in Lord Cainer-on's case—spread flayed Merikit skins on their floors as trophies of the hunt. What a waste on both sides, thought Jame, and what a potentially fatal error.

The drums stopped. A number of Merikit were already in the courtyard, hanging back around the edges, but all attention focused on the four bizarre, gnarled figures who now entered. Ash-smeared, with goat-udders swaying under their long, unbound hair, the shamans trotted around a square drawn in charcoal on the flagstones, at whose center was the well-mouth. Jame couldn't hear them over the water, but she knew that the bells strapped to their ankles were going chink-chink-chink in unison with each step. Interspersed between them were three other Merikit made up to represent Earth Wife, Falling Man, and the Eaten One—earth, air, and water. Last of all came fire, the Burnt Man, muffled in a cloak. That, undoubtedly, was the chief, Chingetai, pretending to be invisible until his time came to take center stage.

He entered the square with the rest of the Four, each at his own corner, and the shamans prepared to close it. That left two, the Favorite and the Challenger, the first in red britches, the second in green.

It seemed that Chingetai meant to enact the entire solstice fertility rite, just as if he hadn't already done so, prematurely, on Summer Eve, and gotten saddled with her, Jame, as the Earth Wife's current Favorite and his presumed heir. Jame recognized the substitute Favorite as the former Challenger—the one who had jammed the victor's ivy crown on her head and shoved her into the square in his place. He didn't look any happier in red than he had in green. His opponent also seemed reluctant to enter the square, only doing so when poked from behind with a spear.

Bloody, stupid Merikit, the Dark Judge had said. *Think they can fool us, do they? Not again. Never again.*

The hillmen had good reason to be nervous. In trying to change the rules, Chingetai was literally playing with fire, and with their lives.

Tied to the smithy door was a goat, who would hardly have looked so bored if it had known what role it was about to play. At least the loser wasn't going to share Sonny's fate, which had almost been Jame's own.

Now should come the closing of the square and the opening of sacred space, but nothing happened.

Of course, thought Jame. *They were already in sacred space, or what passed for it this time around.*

The shaman in Chingetai's corner—probably Tungit, Index's old friend—tried to build a bone-fire, but it kept falling apart. He spoke urgently over his shoulder to the chief, but a sharp gesture silenced him. Jame suddenly wondered if, like his dead son, Chingetai couldn't see the changed landscape around him. Some people were like that, psychically blind. Perhaps, to him, the smoking mountain was still a bump in the distance. Perhaps that would even save him if it exploded. She guessed, though, that both Tungit and the substitute Favorite could see all too clearly what loomed above, and that it made them very, very nervous.

When the Challenger glanced away for a moment, the Favorite snatched off his ivy crown, popped it onto the other's head, and threw himself on the ground. He had deliberately forfeited without a fight. Again.

A moment's stunned pause, and then Chingetai surged out of his corner, roaring with rage. The Burnt Man's bone-fire scattered before him.

WHOOP.

The earth leaped, throwing everyone off their feet.

Jame's tree shook as if hit solidly in the trunk by something massive. She scrabbled to maintain her grip in a hail of falling leaves and unripe nuts, slipped, and found herself hanging upside down by her knees, cap gone, hair tumbling free. Through the quivering canopy overhead, she saw snatches of the mountain top as it exploded. The spine disintegrated into a black, billowing cloud, out of which shot chunks of red-hot rock, trailing fire.

A trick of the wind brought a crash and a horrified shout from Kithorn. Twisting around, still upside-down, Jame saw that a boulder half the size of the smithy had smashed into the square beside the well. There was Red Britches, still curled up like a hedgehog, and Chingetai, and Tungit, but where was Green Britches, the new Favorite? Silly question. Smashed to bloody pulp under the boulder, of course. What very bad luck, or what very good aim.

A whistling sound made her look up.

"Oh schist," she said, as another flaming rock punched through the upper branches.

It struck the limb from which she dangled and smashed it. She fell, snatching at leaf and stem, twig and branch, until a sturdy bough seemed to leap up at her. It hit her in the side, or rather she hit it, and there she hung for a moment, stunned and breathless. A huge splash and a jet of steam up through the leaves marked the fireball's plunge into the river. Would she follow it? River or ground, broken neck or back?

Neither.

She slid off the bough and fell again, into someone's arms. For a moment, dazed, she looked up into the pale, hooded face of the man whom the Merikit called Merkanti.

"Run," he said, in a voice rusty with disuse, and dropped her.

More fiery stones fell, incandescent against a lime-green rain of leaves and unripe walnuts. Jame lurched to her feet, trying to gather her wits; even for her, that had been a jarring fall—three of them, in fact, in rapid succession. She limped toward the meadow, met by Jorin as he bounded toward her through the ferns, chirping in alarm.

They emerged down-meadow from the stream, to a sight that stopped her in her tracks. A huge, black cloud towered above the shattered mountain top. Vivid pink lightning snapped within it, its crack almost swallowed by the volcano's roar. As the cloud rose, flattened, and spread, the morning light dimmed to a murky yellow. Underfoot, the ground shuddered continuously.

Jorin pressed against her leg, his terror as clear as speech. Time to leave. Now.

"Not yet," she told him.

She set off slant-wise across the field, going as fast as she could with a hand pressed against a savage stitch in her side. Please Trinity she hadn't broken a rib. Or two. Or three. Something white drew her. There stood the Whinno-hir Bel-tairi, trembling, with one foot barely touching the ground. She must have tried to run with her over-grown hooves and pulled up lame. Yes, dammit. Drawing closer, Jame saw the bulge between knee and pastern of a bowed tendon.

A white-haired boy, stood at her head, trying to coax her forward. As Jame approached, he turned a stricken, desperate face toward her and mouthed a plea for help that came out as a half-strangled bleat.

Jame knelt and ran her hand down the mare's leg. It was already hot and swollen, unusable without the risk of permanent damage. Now what?

She shot a glance over her shoulder at the mountain. Perhaps the worst was over. However, black clouds still billowed from the ragged heights and sections of the upper slope were giving way in massive landslides of melted snow and mud. Trinity, Jame thought, watching two hundred foot tall ironwoods topple like pins. How clear and close it all seemed. If the Merikit village was anywhere near the foot of that monster, it would be swallowed whole, yet the Earth Wife had said that she could protect it. How?

The answer came from high up on the south-west flank of the volcano. There, a broad area bulged outward, then split open in an even greater explosion than the first. For a moment, molded in shifting chaos, Jame saw the Earth Wife's face, mouth hugely agape, vomiting fire. Ten seconds, fifteen . . .

BOOM!

The concussion made her stagger and Jorin skitter sideways, while mare and colt cried out as if with one terrified voice.

Gray and white debris boiled out of the cleft mountain and rolled down the face opposite the Merikit village with a rumble that shook the earth. Unlike the first eruption's storm cloud, this was a dirty, spreading avalanche. Both, however, seemed to move slowly—a trick, perhaps, of distance. After all, despite how close the mountain appeared, it had taken that massive concussion some time to reach her. Mother Ragga had turned the major eruption away from the Merikit. Perhaps those in the meadow were also safe, but somehow Jame doubted it. The Burnt Man had been thwarted once. He would not be again, if he could help it, especially not with the Dark Judge muttering vengeance in his charred stub of an ear.

"Bel can't run," she said to the boy, "but perhaps she can ride."

Understanding lit his face. In a moment, he had reverted to the equine—if, in fact, his quasi-human appearance had been real at all—and Bel sank down on the grass with a cry of pain. Jame caught her cold, white hands.

"Lady, please. You must."

She helped her rise, and was very relieved to find that she was as light for a woman as she had been for a horse. It still took an effort to lift her onto the rathorn's back against the savage throb in her side.

The colt lunged away as soon as he felt his rider's weight, but then he swerved to circle Jame. She felt his confusion as he cantered past, just out of reach. His instincts were screaming at him to run, to escape, to save what he valued most. Under that like bile lay long cherished hatred. If he couldn't kill his dam's slayer outright, he could leave her to her fate, except that the bond between them held as strongly as the chain that had trapped him in the riverbed. Under that in turn was something else, something new, furiously denied but still there.

No time to explore that now.

"Go," she told him. "Get m'lady away from here, as far as you can." When he hesitated, she told him again, unwilling to force her command on him but ready to do so if she must. "I'll find another way. Go!"

He tossed his head—*Huh. If you insist*—and was gone, a swift, pale shadow across the darkening grass.

Jame turned back to the stream. It surprised her how much she wished she had gone with Bel—not just to escape, either, but to race the wind on that splendid creature. To ride a rathorn might be madness, but what divine folly, worth any cost. Well, not quite. She feared that the colt's legs weren't strong enough to carry two, at least as far and fast as necessary. Besides, there by the water stood Chumley, whose great hooves could still surely take her to safety.

More rocks fell, trailing smoke and fire. Most were no bigger than a clenched fist, but some roaring past overhead were huge, and shattered on impact, leaving great craters in the soft ground. At least their fall now seemed random and they were easy to dodge if one kept an eye on their flight.

As she neared the river bank, Jame saw that Chumley wasn't half screened by grass as she had thought but by the painted mare. Mer-kanti stood between the two horses with a hand on each, steadying them. Several paces in front of him was a large, smoldering boulder, half-buried in the stream's gravel margin. Jame slowed, staring, then approached cautiously. The rock's crust was laced with fiery cracks, and some pieces had fallen away like unusually thick bits of shell from a gigantic, boiled egg. Out of one crack protruded a scrap of burnt material. In its filigree of ash, clearly preserved, were the loops and whorls of knit-work.

Jame fell to her knees beside the boulder, close enough to feel the waves of heat rolling off of it.

"Mother Ragga? Earth Wife? Are you in there?"

Another bit of lava-shell fell, hissing, onto the wet river pebbles. The thing was hollow. Inside, something moved, and coughed.

"Well, what are you waiting for?" said a thin, peevish voice. "Get me out of here."

Jame incautiously grabbed a patch of shell to pull it loose, and her gloves burst into fire. She plunged them into the steaming stream, then sat down abruptly on the stony bank with her scorched hands jammed into her arm-pits, and swore while Jorin slunk around her, chirping urgently. Dammit, that had been her last pair of gloves.

"What are you staring at?" she demanded over her shoulder. "Can't you help?"

The hooded man lifted a hand from Chumley's shoulder, then quickly dropped it again to stop the enormous horse from bolting. The message was clear: if he lost physical contact with either beast, instinct would throw it into blind flight. Presumably they needed both if he, Jame, and the Earth Wife all must flee.

". . . water . . . waaater . . . "

The odd, gargling voice came from the stream. There, dead trout floated past, silver bellies up, but one particularly large fish had caught on the rocks broadside to the swift current. Its back was steel blue speckled with black, its eyes already glazed and turning white as the water boiled it alive. From its gaping mouth came again that desperate plea:

". . . waaaater . . . !"

All right. A talking fish. This was, after all, still sacred space, home also to the Eaten One.

"I can't make the stream run clean again, or cool it down," Jame said, exasperated. "I can't save you. Sweet Trinity, who do you think I am?"

"Water." This time the croaked word came from Merkanti, and he nodded toward the lava-shell.

"Oh," said Jame.

She grabbed the empty saddle bag, dipped it into the stream, and dumped its contents on the hot shell, which exploded, knocking her over backward. She heard

Chumley scream and through the steam saw him rear above her, looming higher than the mountain, it seemed, all flared nostrils, bared yellow teeth, and eyes rolling white with terror. Mer-kanti's thin, strong hand slid up the chestnut neck as far as it could reach and the gelding came down again with a snort, enormous hooves crashing to earth on either side of Jame's head. Belatedly, she yelped and scrambled clear.

The top had blown off the hollow rock, leaving a rough bowl full of something at first impossible to identify. Then a bony hand rose from a pale welter of flesh, clutched the edge of the bowl, and raised a thin arm drooping with loose skin. A face turned upward, and what a face. Sagging flesh hung off the skull except where eyes, nose, and mouth pinned it in place. Only by those ancient, gummy eyes did Jame recognize the Earth Wife's formerly plump features. The lava's heat had made her fat run like melting wax within her skin, settling to swell the lowest points. She stared at her wasted arm, festooned in rolls of hanging skin, and her toothless mouth gaped in a wail.

"Just look at me! Damn you, Burnie, was this fair? Was this right? Oh, bury me quick! I want to die!"

She dropped her face back into the folds of her flesh. Steeling herself, Jame reached in, rummaged about, and pulled the Earth Wife's head up again by its thin, gray braid.

"You can't die," she said. "You're Rathillien, or one quarter of it, anyway. Pull yourself together!"

"I'm blind!" Mother Ragga howled, and indeed at the moment she was: the tension on her hair had caused her skull to sink within its sack of skin and her eyes with it to the bottom of deep, indrawn dimples.

Jame could have shaken her, but was afraid that she would slosh.

Hot ash stung her face. It had started to descend unnoticed, as a fine dust growing rapidly thicker. This would be fall-out from the first eruption. The roiling clouds of the second still churned down the mountain side—closer, it seemed, and picking up speed.

"Listen," she said desperately. "You like my horse, don't you? I'll give him to you."

"Present?" said the sunken mouth, suddenly hopeful. Nothing, it seemed, could quell the Earth Wife's greed for gifts.

"Yes, but you've got to accept him *now*. Come on. D'you want . . . er . . . Burnie to win?"

She left go of the braid and Mother Ragga's skull rose to meet its features. She stared avidly at Chumley who stared back at her, ears pricked, fascinated by this strange creature with the peep-a-boo face.

"Nice horse," she crooned. "Big horse. *My* horse."

Mer-kanti slid his hand up to the gelding's withers and pressed down. Chumley sank ponderously to his knees.

When the Earth Wife rose and leaned, reaching eagerly for him, she looked like a skeleton wearing a half-collapsed tent of skin, and a small skeleton at that, coming barely to Jame's chin. It might have belonged to a child, weighed down by an old woman's mortality, anchored by it, too: liquefied fat had settled in her legs and feet, swelling them to grotesque proportions. Jame struggled to lift one leg from the lava shell. It squished in her grasp like a thin boot full of mud. Raising the White Lady had been hard. This was like trying to shift the foundations of the earth.

She heaved, the shell tipped, and Mother Ragga spilled out on top of her. Jame found herself buried under folds of hot, sweaty skin, inside of which anonymous organs oozed, gurgling. G'ah, what a smell, like all the old women in the world baked in a pie. She struggled to her knees. Sharp bones dug into her back. After an agonized, fumbling moment, the mass lifted and she could breathe again.

"Next time . . ." she gasped, staggering to her feet, "bring your own . . . damn mounting block."

Mother Ragga had indeed gotten one leg over Chumley's broad back. Now she was slowly toppling off the other side. Up came her near foot, a bloated bag of skin with thick, yellow nails half-sunken at one end. Jame grabbed it and pulled down to center the ungainly rider. As she did so, the sudden stab of sore ribs caught her in the side like a dagger thrust.

She found herself back on aching knees, trying to catch her breath. The world had gone gray for a moment, more likely for several. She thought she remembered Chumley lurching to his feet with a squeal and the Earth Wife's shriek trailing off into the distance. Yes, they were gone. Her claws were out and bloodied. Without meaning to, she had raked the gelding's side, trying to stop her fall. No wonder he had bolted.

So had the painted mare.

Jame looked up just in time to see her plunge away across the meadow with Mer-kanti on foot beside her, gripping her mane. How beautifully he moved, barely touching the grass, wind-blowing Senethari at its finest. Just before both vanished into the deepening twilight, he swung up onto the mare's back.

Jame shook off her dazed wonder. "Wait!" she cried, struggling to her feet. "Come back!"

But he too was gone.

The world was still gray, and growing darker by the second. Ash fell thickly now, like a hot, dirty snowstorm stinking of sulfur. Jame shrugged off her jacket and draped it over her head. The improvised hood protected her eyes as did the curtain of her loose hair, but it was now impossible to see more than a few feet ahead. Then for a dazzling moment lightning shattered the sky, followed by a crack of thunder. In the stunned blindness that followed, panic reached her through senses not her own.

"Jorin!" she cried, and without thinking took a deep breath of the ash-laden air to call again. When her convulsive coughing stopped, she reached out to the ounce with her senses, but there was no answer.

Lost. Gone.

That meant nothing, she told herself. The link between them often broke at the most inconvenient times. But what would he do in this thickening nightmare? Curl up in an ash bank and wait for her to find him or for the storm to pass? Small chance of the former, unless she tripped over him. If the latter, he would die. Worse was coming. She knew it.

It's all your fault.

Insidious whisper, borne on an uneasy, shifting wind. Who or what spoke, if not her own guilt?

You destroy everyone who trusts you, everyone whom you love.

"No," she said, denial ash-bitter in her mouth, parching her throat.

But what if it were true?

As if called, the dead came to her on the swirling breath of distant fire: Dally, dragging his flayed skin behind him; Prince Odallian, melting into a puddle of flesh corrupt through no sin of his own; Tirandys, smiling on his pyre. Ash they had all become, because of her. As ash they returned.

"If I become Regonereth, the Ivory Knife incarnate," she had told the Earth Wife, "I'll do what I was born to do, break what needs to be broken, and then break myself."

Then break and die.

"No," she said again. Blink hard, and they were gone. A trick of the mind. Besides, as much as she regretted their deaths, none of them had been her fault.

Or were they? Think.

Between the stab and crack of lightning, the gray world was unnervingly quiet, the ash a blanket that muffled the senses. In that dead silence there was far too much time for thought.

True. However good her intentions, around her things happened. Even her most innocent action could become a pebble cast into the pool of events, with ripples far beyond her control. Then too, not all her actions had been inconsequential in themselves, as witnessed by the string of ruins that she had left in her wake.

Still, buildings didn't necessarily fall down or burn up whenever she walked into them, as she had told Timmon.

No, just most of the time. And how much worse it would surely become as her god-cursed nature worked its way to the surface like a festering wound.

Then lance it and die. You know you are poison.

Why else had everyone abandoned her, not once but over and over again? Why should they stay, sensing what she was?

G'ah, she thought, giving herself a shake that was half a shudder. *Horses bolt and death sweeps people away, whether they wish it to or not. Am I to blame for that?*

For everything, breathed the gray wind. *Someone must be.*

That brought her up short. "Now wait just a minute."

No. Behold those who would judge you.

Lightning flickered across the sky, illuminating it in quick jabs that made the intervals of darkness between all the more intense. A shape formed within the dance of ash, gaining definition with each flash and drawing closer without seeming to move. It was slim and elegant with a pale face under an unruly shock of black hair threaded with white. Silver-gray eyes caught each lightning flare and held it in the dark that followed. Jame couldn't clearly see his hands, but she knew them to be as fine-boned as his face and gloved in a lacework of scars. Her sudden longing for their touch was so sharp that it hurt. Here at last was someone who, surely, would not abandon her.

Then he saw her, and turned away.

It's only a trick, part of her mind insisted, but it hurt too much to ignore.

"Torisen!" she cried after him. "Brother, don't leave me!"

"Why not?" He paused to answer her but askance, not meeting her eyes. "What can you be to me but my destruction?"

"But I love you!"

"Destruction begins with love. So our father taught us. So our mother taught him. So he was doomed to dust and bitter death, all honor spent. Would you likewise doom me?"

"No! Never! How can you say so?"

"Because I know what you are."

His features shifted, his voice as well, growing harsh with anger and bewildered pain.

"Filthy Shanir." Her father turned to glare at her, as gray with ash as his name. Death had hollowed his face to dry patches of skin clinging to the skull, but his silver eyes blazed. "How dare you look so much like your mother and not be her? Tricked. Betrayed. Poison fruit of a tainted tree, where is my sword, my ring, my life?"

Before that cry of pain Jame recoiled a step, but only one. Once his rage had thrown her into panic-stricken flight. It could still made her flinch. But she remembered what she had heard at Tentir about a cadet humiliated by his lord father, tormented by his lordan brother, driven out prey to passions at which she could only guess.

There was the crux. She didn't yet know what had happened to her father that night in the lordan's quarters. Perhaps neither did who or whatever now challenged her.

"Father," she said, "if that's who you are, tell me: that night, in that hot, stinking room, what broke you? I want to understand. Please tell me."

He stared at her. What flickered through those dead eyes—surprise, chagrin, anger? Then he threw back his head and howled. He didn't want to be understood, much less pitied. What was he, after all, without his mantle of rage? Already he was changing. Gone, the patched, gray coat worn thin by years of bitter exile and the prematurely gray hair; gone, that thin, haunted face.

Sleek and smug, Greshan smiled at her, and twitched straight his exquisitely embroidered jacket with a coarse hand.

Jame's fists clenched, nails biting palms. Was this how her father had learned to live with himself, by becoming the thing that had marred him?

"No," she said to that smirking face. "He made mistakes. He hurt a lot of people, including me. But he never put hot iron to the face of an innocent, nor tormented little boys for fun. He didn't become you."

The other's smile twisted and slipped. She wanted to rip it off his face altogether, and that foul coat off his back.

"What happened in your apartment, uncle?" she demanded, both pleased and annoyed that he seemed to drift away as she advanced on him. Lightning and darkness flickered back and forth to a muffled shout of thunder. "What did you do, or try to do, that left your Randir friend nailed to the floor with a knife through his guts, your servant in flames, and you fouling yourself in a corner? Brave man. Great warrior. Daddy's boy. How did you die, and why did your death cause a man like Hallik Hard-hand to turn the White Knife on himself? Answer, dammit!"

She tried to pin him with her rage, but he slipped away, dissolving into darkness.

Again came that flicker of doubt. What was all this anyway—guilt, hallucination, or something else altogether? Who was it that must have someone to blame, who kept trying to push her in directions she didn't want to go? That had happened before, at least twice recently.

Then she knew.

"All right," she told the chaos that seethed around her. "Enough fun and games. Show yourself."

Ahhhhhhh . . . breathed the storm, and the air grew ominously still. Murky yellow light filtered down from above, gray motes afloat in it. Ash no longer fell on Jame but circled in a dark storm wall of which she was the eye. Although it was still sweltering hot, she resumed her jacket and defiantly shook out her hair, the better to face whatever was coming to face her.

A huge shape moved in the shifting darkness, ill-defined by clots and flowing streamers of ash. Here was the bulge of a great shoulder; there, the cavernous socket of an eye; and all the time gigantic paws soundless in themselves kept pace with the shuddering earth.

Jame turned with it. This was the third time in recent days that she and the blind Arrin-ken had danced around each other, if one counted the first when she had been flat on her back, half dead from blood loss and scared half out of her wits. On some level, she was still afraid—how not, faced with such a creature?—but she was also angry.

Be angry, whispered her Shanir blood. *Be strong. Be like your father.*

"Now that I have your attention," she said, hardly knowing if fear or rage shook her voice, "I have a question. You are a judge. Trinity knows, the Kencyrath need justice. So why don't you go after bastards like Lord Caineron, who would corrupt all that we are, or that lying priest Ishtier? Where were you when the Witch of Wilden made her pact with the Shadow Guild to slaughter my family or when my dear uncle Greshan played his filthy game with Bel?"

A flame-savaged face turned toward her, baring its fangs.

The innocent are not my concern. She flinched involuntarily as his voice snarled in her head, like teeth scraping the inside of her skull. *I judge only those of the Old Blood with destruction ripening in their veins, if their own kind are too cowardly to judge them first. Such as you. Dare you call yourself innocent? Dancer's daughter, you were born guilty.*

"That I deny, nor am I yet damned."

Liar!

His terrible face snapped at her out of shifting shadows, itself a shadow but ravaged with such hunger that it seemed ready to devour itself for want of other food.

A surge of near-berserker rage made Jame stumble. *Careful,* she thought, fighting to regain both control and balance. *Fall now and you fall forever . . . like your father. But you know who you are and what you may become.*

"Liar?" she repeated as levelly as she could, hearing her voice quiver, catching it. Without thinking, she began to move in the kantirs of the Senethar, wind-blowing with a touch of water-flowing, gliding around the savage eddies of his anger. "That too I deny."

The dance imposed its own discipline. Move the hand just so to cup the wind. Dip and sway around an errant coil of ash as hot as thwarted vengeance, as cold as lost hope. Such self-devouring anger! Such despair! Here were fires that might consume the world, yet hunger for more. Ah, gently, gently. Feel the cool flow of water over scorched skin. Spill the wind through spread fingers and comb it with the heavy silk of black hair until all flowed smooth. There. Let it go.

"I am not like you, burnt cat, blind judge. I came from the darkness, but I do not embrace it. What is there in the Master's House but dust and ashes? You were burned there, so you make yourself a fire to burn others. Does their pain ease your own?"

Yes!

Such deadly vehemence, causing even ash to flare in fiery motes, but the dance threaded through it, catching him unawares. God's claws, this was dangerous. Don't think. Dance.

The great head, half-seen, swung . . . in assent, denial, confusion?

No. If I hurt, if I burn, it is to make me what I am, to do what I must. What other reason can there be?

"Must everything have a reason?"

YES! How else are we to endure such misery if in the end there is no one to punish for it?

What did one say to that? If you can't live with a run of bad luck, stop whining and die? Or was he right? Cause and effect. One understood that. But effect without cause? What if, after all, the world was nothing but random chance, without justice or sense? Better madness than to believe that.

Never mind. He was answering questions despite himself. Ask more.

"You say you judge those Shanir allied with the Third Face of God, That-Which-Destroys. Whom *have* you judged?"

Arrrr . . . not Greshan. He would have been my meat, ripe and rich, but his own kind judged him first.

Jame blinked. What?

The Brandan matriarch, Brenwyr, a maledight and matricide. Despite that, however, she is still innocent. Soon, soon may she fall. You have pushed her hard, little nemesis. Already she totters on the edge of her doom. The Witch, ah, the Witch. I will have her in the end, when she uncloaks and her defenses at last fall. But they are nothing, nothing, while the Master lives and so does his servant Keral, who burned out my eyes.

"There you name true evil," said Jame, and heard her voice begin to purr with the seductive power of the dance.

Ah. That was better. Her ribs no longer hurt, nor did she feel the weight of her own body. Doubts, too, began to fall away. Why have such power if not to use it?

"You name your failures, Lord Cat. What have you accomplished in this great crusade of yours? What are you but a stinking shadow to frighten children if you cannot strike at evil's root, there, under shadow's eaves?"

He howled and raked at his own flesh as if to punish it. The air thickened with flakes of charred skin.

Do you think I have not tried? Year after bitter year, I have prowled the Barrier, seeking a way through, but no Arrin-ken may enter Perimal Darkling until the coming of the Tyr-ridan, and that is never, because our god has forsaken us.

If he and the Kencyrath managed to kill off every destructive Shanir, they guaranteed that failure. Jame suspected she wasn't the first potential Nemesis, only quite possibly the last. She was about to say as much, but the great cat still spoke as if under bitter compulsion, and his words stunned her.

Once, only once, he came within reach. I felt him cross into this world, into a garden of white flowers, but by the time I arrived he was gone, leaving yet another marred innocent. I would have judged her, punished her, but she had license for what she did. She showed me. The one I should have judged, the one who had doomed her, was then long dead, and he her own father! All things end, light, hope, and life. All come to judgment—except the guilty.

Trinity.

The dance flew out of Jame's mind, and its power spiraled away. Up to that moment, she hadn't realized that she was air-borne on its wings.

Dammit, she thought, spitting out grass and trying to catch the breath that surprise and the ground had slammed out of her. *I've got to stop falling from great heights. It's unhealthy. But* what *did he say?*

Fire and ash roared up in a shape that towered above her, an awakened holocaust with flame raging in its jaws and the deep pits of its eyes.

Child of darkness, Dancer's daughter, you dare play your filthy games with ME?

Clearly, the dance had released him too. What had she been trying to do, anyway? Not reap his soul. Not quite. But the dark thrill remained of searching an Arrinken for weakness as for cracks of bitter honey in his soul, like Rawneth in Brenwyr's soul-image.

I could have shattered him, she thought, amazed, appalled. *He almost came apart in my hands.*

Did that, finally, make her guilty and thus subject to his judgment? But he hadn't broken, and neither had she.

The ash storm ignited into a hurricane of fire that ringed her, roaring with his voice. Green grass withered and kindled; strands of her hair, lifting, sizzled and stank. Her face stung. He would burn her alive through sheer mindless fury, justice be damned, and in doing so he would damn himself.

"Lord!" she cried. Heat had almost closed her throat. Was that feeble croak her voice? "A judgment! Am I fallen? If not, are the innocent now your meat?"

The great cat sprang at her, and the flames rose with him.

This is my pyre, she thought, staring up as the fiery wave crested above her. Incandescent orange and glowing red, laced with gold and a deep, luminous blue . . . *How beautiful.*

At the top of his leap, a blast of scorching wind caught him. He fought it, howling, but it shredded him. Jame fell flat on the ground, claws out to anchor her against the gale. What in Perimal's name . . . ? In a lull of sorts, she raised her head and saw that the Arrin-ken had vanished, but what was coming in his place?

The wind had whipped away most of the low-level ash, leaving the newly-risen sun a pallid smudge in the sky. Movement to the north caught Jame's eye. Very, very close, boiling clouds from the second irruption rose from the valley that converged just below Kithorn with the Silver. The head of the avalanche had momentarily disappeared behind a high bluff, but now it rolled back into sight at the northern end of the meadow. Its vanguard appeared to be not clouds but huge, tumbling figures, gray, black and white, veined with fire. A raised, baleful head, the stump of a foot, a hand with charred stubs for fingers, reaching, then over it would go as another took its place and another after that in a seething, eager muddle.

"*Wha, wha, wha?*" came their questing cry.

Then they saw her.

"*HA!*"

Jame had leaped up. Their booming, triumphant shout and a second tempest blast struck her almost simultaneously, bowling her over. She rolled to her feet and fled, all but flying before the wind with the Burning Ones hot on her heels.

There was no way that she could outrun them. Belatedly, she remembered the cliff over the waterfall, high enough perhaps to take her above their reach, but that lay behind her now. When she turned her head to gauge how far, the wind smacked her hard in the face. Through a blur of stinging tears, she saw the Burnt Man's host roar across the stream, which exploded into steam at their touch.

Run, run, run . . .

Immediately in front of her stood a door, surrounded by the seared meadow, half sunk into it. Serpentine forms and gap-mouthed *imus* rioted over its wooden posts and lintel. It hadn't been there before.

Jame couldn't have stopped if she had wanted to. She crashed into it and it gave way, spilling her down a step onto the dirt floor of the Earth Wife's lodge. A large shape took up one entire end of the room—Chumley, whickering in alarm and hitting his head against the low ceiling. The room was full of animals, sleepily growling, squawking, and squeaking in protest at her sudden arrival. Jorin pounced her in delight before she had stopped rolling. On the other side of a smoky fire sat Mother Ragga herself, lumpen in her chair with the half-knit foxkin bright-eyed in her lap.

"Well?" she said, sounding petulant. "If you're staying, shut the door."

Jame did.

CHAPTER XIX

Darkness at Noon

Summer 66

I

BELOW GOTHREGOR, the Silver bent to the east before resuming its southward course. Long ago, the low-lying ground within this angle had been cleared and enclosed along the edge by an earthen dike. Every spring part of the snow-swollen river was diverted into the resulting three hundred acre meadow and then drained out its lower end, leaving a new, rich layer of silt through which the early grass soon shot vivid green blades. On the far side, where the land rose to meet the Snowthorn's foothills, long terraces supported bright ribbons of flax, barley, rye, oats, and wheat, all ripening toward the Great Harvest at the end of summer. At midsummer, though, attention fixed on the lower meadow and the haying, which took every hand that the Knorth could muster to bring in the harvest before the weather turned.

First came a line of reapers with a hiss and flash of scythes, the hay falling in swathes at their feet. The next line of workers turned over these sheaves with rakes to loosen them for proper drying. Twenty great wains, drawn by horse or oxen, lumbered behind them between the rows. Onto these the hay was pitched under the expert eye of the load-masters. When a wain was full, it pulled aside to one of the growing stacks. The hayricks themselves were meticulously constructed and, in their way, things of beauty. Each sat on a stone foundation which in turn was covered with a deep layer of green bracken, both to raise the hay off the damp ground and to protect it from rats, who could no more chew through the tough branches than through horse hair. Set on top of that was a wooden structure in the shape of an open-sided pyramid, against which the hay was stacked, again under careful supervision.

All in all, the Lesser Harvest progressed smoothly, well oiled by centuries of practice.

Torisen worked with the reapers, hot, sweaty, and not as smoothly as he would have liked. In past years, he had either been with the Southern Host or saddled with other duties, making this his first season in the field. He knew his Kendar would prefer that he stayed aloof, pretending to oversee—after all, what would their enemies say if they saw the Knorth lord slaving away beside the least of his house? However, Torisen didn't care. At least he had mastered the long-armed scythe well enough not to cut off anyone's foot; and if his row was less orderly than those of more experienced mowers, well, he could learn. After all, there were his hands, both of them, moving at his will. The bandages and splints had come off weeks ago, but his relief remained, as sharp and clear as the moment he had first flexed his mended fingers and known that he wouldn't be a cripple after all.

Besides, it was pleasant to be under orders again, even those of someone as ill-tempered as the harvest-master.

The man was behind him now, shouting at a raker in a voice as raspy and irritating as the chaff that worked itself into everything.

"Here now, you cow-handed cadet! Turn those swathes and loosen 'em properly. What, you've never heard of tight-packed hay heating 'til it bursts into flames?"

The cadet Vant stifled a derisive snort. *Who are you*, it said, *to be telling me anything?* As a ten-commander, he had already made it clear that he resented playing such a menial role in the harvest, never mind that everyone from senior randon to the highlord himself labored beside him.

"You think that's funny?" The harvest-master must be almost in the cadet's face, up on his toes to bring their eyes level. "Well, I've seen it happen, boy, a whole field of burning ricks, pale tongues of fire in the summer sun, and that winter the cattle lowing with hunger so loud that no one could sleep. So shut up and do your work properly!"

Torisen felt those hard, impatient eyes turn to fix on his back. *I dare you*, he thought.

"Huh!" said the master, and stomped off to shout at someone else.

Marc and Brier Iron-thorn worked side by side down the line, two tall, strong figures swinging their blades in identical, effortless arcs. The girl's hair glowed sullen red, swaying back and forth as she moved. The man's beard was a thick, white bush with some lingering touches of fox, his head sunburned and peeling under its crown of thinning, reddish hair. Someone was always hiding his hat for a joke; this time he apparently hadn't found it yet. He said something to his companion and she laughed, white teeth ablaze in that dark face which seemed bred into some Southron Kendar. Torisen had never heard Brier Iron-thorn laugh before, or even seen her smile.

He wondered again why Marc—ever so gently, as if not wanting to cause pain—had turned down his offer of a permanent place with the Knorth. Anyone else in the Kendar's position would surely have jumped at the chance. For that matter, any decent lord should have been glad to have him. True, in his mid-nineties he was past his fighting prime, but he had so much else to offer for those who valued kindness and inherent decency, not to mention his growing skill as an artisan. The man was waiting, but for what? In the meantime, ironically, in part because of his refusal to accept Knorth service, his was one of the few names that Torisen was absolutely sure he would never forget.

Not that he had misplaced anyone since the unfortunate Mullen. His people wouldn't let him. In his presence, everyone had pointedly called each other by name until he had demanded that they stop as it gave him a headache. Dammit, didn't they trust him?

Don't answer that.

Kindrie had also declined a place in his service. At the time Torisen had been both surprised and relieved, if puzzled. According to the Matriarchs, an illegitimate Highborn was kin to no one, but that didn't change the fact that Kindrie was the son of Torisen's unfortunate aunt Tieri—a first cousin. And the Shanir was desperate for a home. Why, then, had he turned away at the last minute?

For that matter, Torisen hadn't formally bound his sister Jamethiel. It had never occurred to him to try, nor had she seemed either to expect or want it.

There was another sore spot, dimming his pleasure in the day: Jame's ten-command had come to help with the harvest, but without her. The Min-drear cadet Rue had said that his sister had unfinished business in the hills. What, for Ancestors' sake? Surely she couldn't be mad enough to try to pick up with the Merikit where she had left off at Kithorn on Summer's Eve. He remembered now, uneasily, that she hadn't agreed with him that such a thing was out of the question. Her quiet independence alarmed him, as if she only submitted to authority when she wanted to.

Am I losing control? he wondered, not for the first time. *Of my sister, of my people, of myself? Was I wrong to assume my father's title with his curse hanging over me? Can the disowned inherit power any more than the illegitimate?*

But he had seen how close the Kencyrath was to falling apart. As he had sensed Ganth's death, so had others, if less clearly. Some Highborn, soon, would have claimed the Highlord's seat. Caineron, probably. Or Ardeth. Or Randir. Then there would have been civil war and slaughter enough to make the White Hills pale by comparison. Those seeds of destruction were also part of his father's legacy.

No matter what I do, Torisen thought, swinging his scythe with untoward force, making the Kendar next to him hastily step aside, *I stand in his shadow.*

"Rest!" bellowed the harvest-master.

Reapers grounded their tools and reached for the water bottles hanging from their belts. Some sat down, drew out cheese and onion wrapped in black bread, and began to munch on it. A ripple of talk and laughter passed down the line, some of it directed at the workers behind them whose failure to keep up had caused this welcome halt. As it was, they had almost reached the bottom of the meadow. Tubs of oil and sand were brought forward along with the hones to whet the blades for the final assault.

Harn trudged up, an eight-foot pitchfork cocked like an ungainly spear over his shoulder.

"Hot work," he said, offering Torisen a swig from his bottle, which turned out to contain hard cider. He squinted up at the hazy sky and at the sun, which was ringed by a halo. "Odd light, odd weather. D'you suppose it's going to storm?"

Rain was coming, thought Torisen. He could feel it in his new-knit bones. And something else, somehow connected to his delinquent sister . . . but to think that was ridiculous. All natural disasters weren't Jame's fault—maybe just the unnatural ones.

There had been several jolts around dawn, enough to crumble some already damaged walls and to stir fears of another earthquake like the one that spring, whose marks could still be seen up and down the Riverland. Torisen looked northward. Early that morning, from window of his turret quarters, he had seen a plume of smoke on the horizon. Now clouds were coming—strange, lobed ones white against a darkening sky. The air stirred, laced with a hint of . . . what? Rotten eggs? Birds flew overhead, all going south.

Someone shouted a warning as a herd of deer bounded across the field between and sometimes over harvesters, who threw themselves flat to avoid the flying hooves. At a stag's heels, snapping, ran a white streak. The wolver pup Yce had grown over the summer, although not as much as a wolf cub would have, and she chased anything that fled her. Deer, cows, sheep, people . . .

"Just wait until she gets big enough to make her first kill," Harn said grimly, watching. "One taste of fresh blood, and there'll be no stopping her."

Yce gave up pursuit and loped back to Torisen, as usual stopping just out of reach.

"What am I going to do with you?" he asked her, "and what in Perimal's name do you want of me?"

No answer but that unnerving, ice-blue stare.

More than ever, she reminded him of his sister. Both seemed to be challenging him in ways he couldn't understand, or perhaps didn't want to.

Again came that sick sense of lost control, like tumbling down an abyss by stages with no bottom in sight.

. . . *Daddy's boy, run, hide* . . .

Words spoken in delirium. Ridiculous that they should have struck so deep, that they continued to hurt. She hadn't known what she was saying, of course.

He still didn't know how his sister had come to be injured. Apparently no one did, although Torisen sensed that the Caineron Gorbel knew more than he would admit. Something odd was going on between the two lordans, if by "odd" one meant anything besides the inevitable house rivalries, which in the past had bordered on the lethal. And then there was the Ardeth Timmon as well. Pereden's son. Adric's favorite. What had he to do with Jame, and why did both of them keep edging into his most intimate dreams?

G'ah, think of something else. But he couldn't.

After half a lifetime his twin sister had returned, but she kept slipping away again into one outlandish situation after another. She was younger than he now, but sometimes she seemed older, with eyes that hinted at experiences beyond his comprehension and at a certain rising irritation: *You might at least* try *to understand.*

On top of all that, she was now a cadet at Tentir, where he had longed with all his heart to go.

She is gaining strength, boy, murmured the voice in his head, behind the locked door. *Even your war-leader Harn speaks well of her. The randon like a fighter, and she is becoming one of them. What if, eventually, they prefer her to you?*

Madness. Don't listen.

Besides, not everyone at Tentir wanted her there. The cadet Vant, although an ass in other respects, had said as much. To many, she was a freak, her mere presence at the college an insult to all randon past and present. Vant had also hinted that no one expected her actually to stay the course. M'lord shouldn't worry. His people at Tentir knew his mind.

Ha, thought Torisen. He wished that he knew it himself.

Harn nudged him. "Company."

Two riders were coming down the New Road, one a randon guard, the other . . . damn. A lady. Torisen mopped his sweaty face, silently cursing.

He had thought that, here in the middle of a hay field, he would be safe from the Matriarchs. As Rowan had predicted, their schemes had grown subtler since the farce of the first few days, but they were far from giving up. Over the past few weeks he had been presented with everything from an unhappy bald girl, her head newly shaven (someone must have noticed his strong reaction to long, black hair, but taken it the wrong way), to the wide-eyed seven-year-old who had first asked him to marry her outside Adiraina's quarters.

Occasionally, on the sly, he visited the Jaran Matriarch Trishien to reassure himself that all Highborn women weren't mad; and if she should have news of Jame by way of Kirien, all the better, although he took care never to ask directly.

Rowan's suggestion floated in the back of his mind. If nothing else, it would be sweet to confound them all by taking his sister as his consort—only for show, of course.

Torisen slipped back on the black jacket that he had discarded in the heat. One should show one's enemies respect, and wear whatever protection was available.

"Hello!"

He straightened, surprised at the hail. Decorum kept most of his would-be consorts silent, except for the seven-year-old whose naive, highly improper stream of questions no one had been able either to stop or to divert.

Then he recognized the newcomer as Lyra, Caineron's young daughter, and relaxed. It was hard to feel threatened by a girl nicknamed "Lack-wit." Besides, at Kithorn she had stopped her sister Kallystine from slapping him with the same razor ring that his former consort had used to slash Jame's face. Even if the girl's interference had been an accident, as she claimed, he owed her for it.

Not waiting for help, Lyra tumbled off her pony in a swirl of flame red velvet and plunged across the rough meadow toward him. Bemused Kendar drew aside to let her pass. From the freedom with which she moved, Torisen guessed that she had left her tight under-skirt back in the Women's Halls. Then she saw Marc and threw herself into his arms with a squeal of delight.

"I saw you in the courtyard, working with all those pretty bits of glass, but they wouldn't let me go out to say hello. Hello!"

Marc laughed, gently returning her enthusiastic hug. The top of her head only came up to the lower edge of his rib cage. "I saw you too, lady, at an upper window waving and, I think, shouting. Then someone pulled you away."

"That was the sewing mistress. It's so funny when she gets hysterical. Just ask, 'Why?' and off she goes. Young ladies aren't supposed to ask questions, you see, which I think is stupid, so I ask them all the time."

"You must be very popular with your teachers," said Torisen, amused. "I didn't realize that you knew Marcarn."

"Oh yes!" She turned to beam at him—quite a pretty girl, actually, from what one could see behind her deceptively demure half-mask; and no fool either, despite her nickname and manner. "Marc rescued us from the palace at Karkinaroth. That was after it caught fire and before it fell down, of course. In between, poor Prince Odalian died." Her pert face dimmed at the memory, a cloud crossing the sun, but immediately brightened again. "Then we three rode a barge down the Tardy to Hurlen, along with that darling ounce Jorin. That was fun. Such exciting things happen when your sister is around!"

"I've noticed," he said, with a smile that was half grimace. "But she's not here now. To what do we owe the honor of your presence, lady? Surely the Matriarchs didn't send you."

"Oh no," she said blithely. "They threw a bucket of water over the sewing mistress, just when she was getting interesting, and sent me to my room to practice knot stitches, but that's so boring! Nearly everything is, in the Women's Halls. I'd ask to go home, but Kallystine would probably kill me. Anyway, I just had to get out of the Halls for a while. I would have come alone, except Marrow here spotted me and besides I needed help with the basket. I thought I'd bring you a picnic lunch. It *is* almost noon, you know."

Torisen had noticed the wicker hamper that the cadet guard Marrow carried self-consciously slung over her arm. He also noted that harried look on her face of someone rushed into something without time to think it through. No doubt her captain would give her seven kinds of hell over this later.

Lyra spread a white garment over the hummocky stubble—so she hadn't left her under-skirt behind after all—and dumped the contents of the basket onto it.

"There!" she said. "I brought some of everything that I like to eat."

Torisen accepted a purple sugarplum scrolled with cream frosting. Marzipan, chocolate rolled in crumbled walnut, snails encased in ginger shells . . . the Caineron larder was obviously much better stocked with luxuries than the Knorth, and probably with everything else as well.

"So you know our kitten as well as our Marcarn." Harn popped something bright green into his mouth, made a face, and swallowed it whole. "I think that one was still alive."

"Well, you wouldn't want to eat a *dead* candied cockroach, would you? Oh yes, Jame and I are like sisters. After Hurlen, though, we didn't see each other again until she showed up at Restormir just before the weirdingstrom. *You* know," she added, turning to Brier. "You were there too."

"I've heard something about that," said Harn. He eyed the rest of Lyra's offerings, but didn't take any. Around them Kendar were settling down to their more mundane repasts, pretending not to listen. "What *did* happen, cadet?"

The rest of Brier's ten in the second row stared at her with ill-concealed horror. Vant, down the line, went white under his peeling sunburn. The story was by now well known in the barracks at Tentir, with many unintended embellishments gained by repetition. So far, though, no senior randon had gotten around to asking for a formal account of it, probably afraid of what they would hear.

Brier gave her report in a voice so flat that one could have rolled a marble across it. They had encountered the lordan while on patrol. She had stated that her servant Graykin was Lord Caineron's prisoner and that she was honor-bound to rescue him. They had helped her accomplish this.

Everyone waited for the Southron to go on, but she had come to a full stop. Vant sighed with relief.

"Oh, you don't know how to tell a story at all!" said Lyra impatiently. "Listen. Everyone was up in the Crown—that's Restormir's tower—getting beastly drunk and making a row. I was with Gran in her rooftop garden, but she sent me down to fetch some food from the kitchen, and who do you think I ran into there? Jame and a bunch of cadets, chasing a chicken. No, that's not quite right. My uncles and cousins and brothers were chasing it to make soup—Father's drinking had made all our servants sick, you see, so we had to fend for ourselves—and it (the chicken) ran into the pantry where we were hiding. That's when Jame told me why she was there. Gricki—that is, Graykin—used to be my servant at Karkinaroth. He's also my half-brother by some Southron kitchen maid. Anyway, Father was mad at him for changing houses and so he jabbed all these red-hot hooks through his skin."

Lyra paused, remembering, suddenly sober. "He screamed," she said. "A lot. No one should have to scream like that.

"Anyway, then Father attached wires and swung him out into the Crown's central shaft. For a while he made him dance like a puppet. Then he got bored and left, thinking that the hooks would eventually tear through Gricki's skin and that he would fall all the way down to the Pit."

"That's a good two hundred feet," one Kendar muttered to another. Both had turned pale at the thought of dangling from such a height. Others also looked sick.

"But he didn't fall," Lyra continued. "We reeled him in . . . well, I helped a bit . . . and unhooked him. By then, though, Father was coming. I ran. Then Father caught you."

She looked up at Brier, a bit uncertainly.

"He said something about binding you by the seed, whatever that means, and ordered you to kneel. It scares me when he uses that voice. Somehow, there's no disobeying it. I was back on top in Gran's garden by then, kneeling on the edge, so I couldn't see anything, but I could hear. Jame said, 'BOO!' and Father said, 'HIC!' and the next thing I know, he bobs out over the rail, into the shaft, floating upside down with his pants undone and flapping in his face."

"Sweet Trinity," breathed Harn. "Sheth said something at the Cataracts about Caineron 'not quite feeling in touch with things.' What in Perimal's name did our kitten do to him?"

"I don't know," said Lyra, "but he's terrified of her. Then she said, 'Make sport of decent Kendar, will you? Play God almighty in your high tower, huh? Well, the next time the urge takes you, remember me. And this. And keep looking down.'

"Then he started to scream.

"Brier, you said, 'You don't know what you've done.'

"And she said, 'I seldom do, but I do it anyway. This is what I am, Brier Iron-thorn. Remember that.'

"And neither of us ever will forget, will we? Because she said it in a voice just like Father's."

II

FOR A MOMENT, no one spoke.

The wind shifted to and fro between them, swirling eddies of chaff like ghosts trying to rise from the shorn field, then slumping back among the rows. Vanguards of the north wind and of the tardy Tishooo from the south skirmished in the upper air.

Harn shot Torisen a look under his heavy brows. "Remind me later to tell you about something else that's happened. At Tentir. Concerning Caineron's councilor Corrudin."

Torisen didn't want to hear it. He had heard too much already.

Lyra's recitation had left her looking frightened, as if she hadn't realized what she was going to say until she had said it. Now she jumped and squealed as a dead bird plummeted to earth beside her. They were falling all over the field. So was a light fall of what at first appeared to be dirty snow. The clouds were almost upon them, growling with muffled thunder, pulling a shroud over the sun.

Marc tasted a flake that had fallen on his hand and spat it out. "Ash," he said. "I was afraid of this. Some mountain to the north has blown its top."

The harvest-master bustled up, scowling. "That hasn't happened in my lifetime," he said, as if to assert that it wasn't possible now. "Say you're right, though, we're way to the south. How much of the damn stuff could we possibly get?"

"Anywhere from a dusting to several feet." Marc looked apologetic. "Usually Old Man Tishooo blows the worst of it northward over the Barrier, but this time he seems to have been slow off the mark. It may also rain."

The master stared at him, then cast a wild glance at the upper terraces where cat's-paws of wind tossed the ripening grain in its gleaming bands. Golden brown barley bowed to shine silver gold. Wheat bent more stiffly, its beards of grain barely open.

"We might gather some," he muttered. "A few bushels of early wheat, at least, or rye, or oats, just in case . . ."

Torisen glanced at Marc, who shook his head. There wasn't time. "We must save what we can here in the water meadow," he said, "and hope for the best."

The master looked stricken. Just as hay was vital to the beasts' winter survival, so the Greater Harvest at summer's end was to anything on two legs.

Famine didn't scare him, Torisen realized. He was afraid that if supplies ran short, his lord would send most of his people south while he himself stayed to hold the keep with a token garrison. As weak as the Highlord had recently shown himself to be, to leave Gothregor unguarded was to risk having it seized by a stronger house. On the other hand, of those he sent away, how many would he forget? Mullen had flayed himself alive to escape such a fate.

All the weight of his position fell back on his shoulders, no longer to be escaped, harder than ever to bear. *They depend on me. I gave them that right when I assumed my father's place.*

He touched the Kendar's shoulder.

"It will be all right, Stav." *Somehow.* "Carry on."

The harvest-master blinked at the sound of his own name, and that sudden flare of panic faded from his eyes. He gave his lord a brusque, awkward nod and turned to the assembled troops. "Forget the last standing grass. Get those hayricks covered. Move!"

As Kendar sprang into action all over the field, Marc picked up a frightened Lyra, set her on her pony's back, and handed the reins to the already mounted cadet guard. "Ride for Gothregor," he said. "Fast. Tell them to bring in the livestock, hood the wells, close all chimney dampers, secure the shutters, and stuff as many cracks as possible with rags. At the very least, this is going to be messy." Lyra yelped as lightning split the sky and her pony shied. "Go. We'll follow as quickly as we can. And don't lock us out!" he bellowed after them.

At the bottom of their loads, all wains carried mats woven of wiry rye stalks. Kendar now hauled these out and started to pitch them over the hayricks. It took four to cover each stack. Frantic hands laced together the edges with wisps of straw and bound them to iron rings set in the stone foundations. Before some mats could be secured, they tore free to flap and flail while swearing Kendar fought to control them.

The winds were picking up, and they came from both directions. The Tishooo and the northern wind clashed overhead, warm and cold, clear and ash-laden, roiling together, with sudden cracks of blue sky between them and sharper cracks of lightning. Wrestling funnels dipped and swayed above the field, lashing it with their tails. Chaff flew. Horses screamed. Then the stack which Torisen was trying to cover exploded in his face.

Nearby, a Kendar cried out as the wind drove sharp straws like needles into her eyes.

Torisen found himself flat on his back, staring up at an ascending maelstrom of hay. It seemed to take shape as it rose, assuming the nebulous form of something huge with wings that spanned the entire valley. There might or might not have been the figure riding it, an old man whose beard streamed behind him. Against him came the clouds of ash, and they too had gained both form and voice.

"*Wha, wha, wha?*" howled the roiling, black figures of the Burning Ones. "*Tha!*"

They dived at Torisen.

My father's curse, he thought, watching them come. *My own weakness. I deserve this.*

The wolver pup Yce was suddenly crouching over him with her over-sized paws heavy on his chest and her white teeth bared at the falling sky. The thing of hay and wind swooped, every straw pricked to the attack, but what good is chaff against fire? Torisen threw his arms around the pup and rolled to protect her as flaming debris rained down on them. He found himself holding a small body shaken by its own pounding heart. Small hands, short fingered, long nailed, clutched his shirt. A child looked up at him with terrified blue eyes set in a mask of creamy fur, then buried her face against his chest. He tightened his grip.

Me, you can have; her, never.

The field burned around them, but the flames cast curiously little light. Falling ash had clamped a tight, black bowl over the earth. In the outer darkness, things fought with muffled bellows of thunder, but not even the lightning stroke of their blows penetrated the gloom. Then the sky split open and the deluge descended like a cataract.

The fires hissed out.

The world filled with noise and hard driven water.

Torisen stumbled to his feet, still clutching the child who was also a wolf, and nearly fell again. Mixed ash and mud slithered under foot, in a blinding rain. It had also turned surprisingly cold. Would the other ricks stand, or had they already lost the Lesser Harvest? Where was everyone? Please Trinity someone had pulled the injured Kendar to safety and tended her wounds. It was a terrible thing to be maimed. Kindrie could help her, but he wasn't here. Because of Torisen. Because of something the healer had seen or felt in that moment when their hands had touched, his cringing at the mere thought of accepting a Shanir, the other's thin and cool and suddenly withdrawn.

"My lord, I can't do it."

Why? What corruption in him could repel one already tainted by the Old Blood? What, but a father's curse?

I am doomed and damned, he thought. *That too perhaps I deserve, but not my people as well!*

A vertical crack of light opened in the chaos and widened slightly. As it did so, faint horizontal lines joined it above and below. Trinity. It was a door, in the middle of a field. As he stood gaping at it, a familiar voice spoke from inside:

"Well? Don't you know enough to come in out of the rain?"

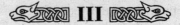

III

TORISEN DECIDED that he was dreaming, or had finally gone barking mad. Either seemed more likely that that the destroyed haystack had been built around such a large, stone hut, or rather a full-sized lodge. Down several steps was an earthen floor covered with lumpy forms. Opposite, a small fire smoked and flared on a sunken hearth, its light picking out low rafters from which hung an odd assortment of shapes. Most appeared to be drowsy bats and foxkin but one, larger, rustled leathery wings and glared sleepily at him with obsidian eyes set in a wizened, almost human face.

"Watch out for that one," said Jame behind him, closing the door. "It blew north with the weirdingstrom, and I don't think it's had a decent meal since."

As his eyes adjusted to the gloom, Torisen saw that the room was full of sleeping creatures. Hawks and sparrows, side by side, perched one-legged on the mantle, chair backs, and the enormous antlers of a snoring moose. Badgers and otters rolled up together for warmth under a table. That huge mound by the door was a cave bear, covered by a living coat of ermine which rose and fell with his stentorian breathing. As for the cauldron of water beside him, surreptitiously seething . . .

Stiff whiskers broke the surface, then a wide, gaping mouth and a pair of round, knowing eyes.

"Bloop," said the catfish solemnly, and sank back out of sight.

"What *is* all this?" Torisen asked, more convinced than ever that he had fallen into some insane dream.

"They're refugees, of course."

Jame picked her way across the room to a chair next to the fire.

"Not everyone could get to shelter when the ash-flow came . . ."

She removed a hedgehog from the seat and settling it in a basket of knit-work on the floor.

"Quip!" said the knitting in drowsy protest.

". . . but a lot did. It must have been a madhouse in here before Mother Ragga told them all to shut up and go to sleep."

She stepped up onto the chair, balancing carefully on its arms as it creaked under her, and began to do something to the upper end of an unusually large bundle suspended from the rafters.

The wolver pup wriggled out of Torisen's arms and bounded toward the hearth, where a cat rose, hissing, to meet him. It was a surprisingly big cat, Torisen noted, as its arched back rose higher and higher. Flames surrounded it in a nimbus of red-gold, bristling fur and its eyes reflected only fire.

"You'd better call off your friend," said Jame. "Jorin is in no mood for games, and I haven't the time. Who is she, anyway?"

"Yce, an orphan from the Deep Weald, or so Grimly tells me."

"Ice?"

"Close enough. It's a wolver term for a frozen crust over deep snow. The name seemed appropriate."

Pup and ounce met on the hearth. After a moment's hostile posing for honor's sake, they settled down side by side, not touching and studiously ignoring each other, to watch the fire.

"This is a very strange place," said Torisen, wiping rain out of his eyes the better to see it. "Where are we?"

"Inside the Earth Wife's lodge, which in turn could be anywhere. It moves around a lot. I found it in a meadow near Kithorn, just before a volcano caught up with me. Now I'm guessing we're closer to Gothregor, or were when you came through the door. But I'm forgetting my manners. Mother Ragga, this is my brother Torisen, Highlord of the Kencyrath. Tori, this is Mother Ragga, also known as the Earth Wife."

The lower edge of the bundle stirred. Knobby hands lifted what turned out to be the hem of an inverted outer skirt and a florid, upside-down face peered out, like a pudding hanging in a sack.

"Highlord, eh? About time we met. Welcome to my house, if not necessarily to my world."

The features started to rotate sickeningly, as if for a better look, but Jame gave her a warning slap.

"Stop that. D'you want to get stuck with your head on the wrong way?"

Torisen saw that the upper end of the bundle was a much patched underskirt held up, as was the whole body, by a rope around the ankles. Above that, close to the supporting beam, were a pair of enormously swollen feet. Jame resumed squeezing the sausage-like toes as if trying to milk an upside-down cow.

"That tickles!" protested Mother Ragga.

"I told you, this isn't my sort of job."

"What," asked Torisen, bemused, "hanging old women up by their heels?"

"That either. But Kindrie is the healer, not me—not that he could probably do any better. Y'see, the volcano melted all the fat in her body and it settled to what was then the lowest point. I'm trying to work it back into place before it cools and hardens where it is. This was her idea, by the way, and it seems to be working, if slowly."

The bundle twitched irritably. "Well, hurry up! I'm getting dizzy." Then she yelped as she was suddenly jerked up, her feet jamming hard against the underside of the rafter. Dislodged dust drifted down.

"Chumley!" Jame called into the darkness at the end of the room. "Stand still, you great lummox!"

Torisen traced the taut line of rope over the beam and down into the gloom. Beyond the mounds of sleeping animals, he could just make out an enormous pair of hindquarters with a flaxen tail swishing complacently between them. The rope appeared to be secured to the beast's other end.

"There's a horse in the corner," he said. "Also, I think, a meadow."

He could see now that the room had no far wall. Where it should have been, there was a sea of grass lit only by the dance of fireflies and a few reluctant stars low on the horizon. Night, and no mountains. They were no longer in the Riverland, or at least that side of the lodge wasn't. Unconcerned, the big horse continued to graze.

"This is madness," he said.

"Oh, for Ancestors' sake." Jame stopped squeezing the Earth Wife's toes and began vigorously to knead her calves through the patched underskirt, ignoring muffled squawks of pain and a certain amount of thrashing below. "You must have seen as many strange things as I have—well, almost as many. Neither of us has lead an exactly normal life. Things happen to us. Powers seek us out. You know that, although you seem Perimal-bent on denying it. How can either of us be sure what's sane and what isn't?"

Torisen started to protest then stopped, considering his words. "We are a house noted for our madness, or so everyone says. Are they wrong? What about our father?"

His sister paused, frowning. "There's more to his story than we were ever told—if not enough to forgive him, perhaps enough to understand and take warning. Tori, since Summer Eve, have you had any strange dreams?"

He stiffened, remembering a flurry of them, some of which he had no intention of repeating to his sister. "All dreams are strange. What about it?"

She also looked acutely ill at ease, but determined. "I had one that first night at Tentir and another, later. Do you remember dreaming that you were a cadet at the college, and being summoned up to the lordan's quarters late one night?"

He did. Twice. Trinity, that second time . . .

"Do you remember who you were, and who waited for you on the hearth, wearing a particular coat?"

His mouth felt dry. "It was beautiful, all the colors of creation, but the man wearing it . . ."

". . . was Greshan, our uncle. A monster. It was also me, somewhere inside him, only able to watch through his foul eyes. And you were there too, inside a young Ganth, our father."

He remembered, as hard as he had tried to forget. "So? It was only a dream." After all, he had been cured, mysteriously, miraculously, of those nightmares that had driven him to the edge of madness—or had he only been relieved of the foresight that had led him to try so hard to fight them off?

She sighed. "Perhaps they are only nightmares, frightening but harmless. I hope you're right. If not, though,

I have to warn you: there will be at least one more, maybe several, in that room, before that hearth, and the last will be worse than all the others rolled up together. Something terrible happened to our father there. No one alive today knows what it was, but something at Tentir seems to be trying to show me, to show us.

"Tori, listen: There have been schemes within schemes, enemies behind enemies, treachery, murder, bloody betrayal. What happened to our house was no accident. I'm sure of that, although I don't yet understand it all. But what started then isn't over yet, however strange its course has been. Some of the answers lie at Tentir."

She gave him a quick, almost feral smile, all white teeth and a flash of inhuman, silver eyes.

"Trust me in this at least: I'm good at hunting down hidden enemies."

He believed her, and it frightened him.

She had turned back to contemplate the Earth Wife's swaying feet. "Y'know, I think that bump did more to shift things than all my prodding has. Chumley, again."

Obligingly, the massive horse shifted back and forth where he stood, with each forward surge reaching farther for fresh tufts of grass. Thud, thud, thud went the soles of the swollen feet against the rafter, to accompanying yelps from below.

"Oh, stop complaining, you big baby. You did ask me to hurry up. This is my revenge," she murmured aside to Torisen, "for a good many frights and indignities. No doubt she'll get her own back later, by the bucket full, and I'll be lucky to survive it."

The prospect, however, didn't seem to alarm her. What kind of a life had she lead, to take such things so casually?

Don't ask.

Instead, he regarded her intently, seeking reassurance. They were, after all, twins. How different could they be?

Both had always been slight and fine-boned, even for Highborn, but quick and agile. If he was stronger, she made up for it by constantly surprising him. She did so now, stepping up onto the chair's back and balancing there as it teetered, apparently for a closer look at the thumping progress. She moved like a dancer or a fighter, with easy balance and a chilling disregard for personal safety. Like her, he took far too many unnecessary risks, or so Harn kept telling him.

Torisen also didn't think much about his own appearance. If his servant Burr caught him at a weak moment, he might consent to wear the Highlord's finery, but otherwise why bother? Plain, simple, and black suited him best. Maybe that was why in part he hadn't thought to supply his sister with garments befitting her rank. For that matter, she hadn't asked for them. She didn't seem to care much about what she wore either, given some of the clothes he had seen her in—that outlandish dress at the Cataracts, for example, formerly the property of an overweight Hurlen street-walker. Given a preference, though, she also seemed to favor plain and black, like that oddly cut jacket slung aside on the floor.

Was she handsome?

People kept telling him that they both had the classic Knorth features. For that matter, several times she had been mistaken for him on the battlefield—something which he found profoundly disturbing.

Was she beautiful?

Not by the standards of Kallystine's voluptuous charms that had drawn him despite his better judgment. His former consort had been adept at intoxicating the senses, but with an after-taste that had made him both loathe and mistrust his own passion. One of the Highborn subsequently thrown at him, a ridiculously young Ardeth girl, had seen enough to suggest that Kallystine had used potions to entrap him.

Women.

He would trust his life and honor to most Kendar, but too few Highborn. Kirien and the Matriarch Trishien, maybe, but Jame?

Did he trust his own sister?

No! said the voice in the back of his mind. *Never*!

Yet he felt drawn to that lithe body with its clean, spare lines and to that wry smile as to a cool breath in an overheated room. If Kallystine had been poison, perhaps here was the antidote.

Then, for the first time, he realized that Jame wasn't wearing gloves. Even with their nails sheathed, those long, slim fingers made him shiver, threat and promise in one touch.

Her face also looked oddly bare, and not for the lack of a mask.

"What happened to your eyebrows?"

She touched her forehead, annoyed. "I got too close to a fire. So did you, apparently. Your jacket may be soaked, but it's also scorched and still smoldering."

Torisen shrugged it off and dropped it on a pile of snow-footed ferrets, who woke briefly to quarrel among themselves before settling back to sleep under the reeking cloth.

Now that he looked, he saw that her clothes were also charred in patches and hanging in long strips, as if fiery claws had tried but failed to catch her. The heavy fall of her long black hair covered her better than the tattered remains of her shirt, although both slid away from delicate curves as she moved. Had the Burning Ones been after her too? If so, why? She had her own secrets, he reminded himself, years' worth of them between the time when their father had driven her out and when he had taken her back in.

As he studied her, so she did him.

"There were strands of white in your hair the last time I saw you," she said. "Now they're gone. So are your scars."

Torisen stared at his unmarked hands. He had grown so used to the phantom pain of the Karnids' red-hot gloves that only now, when it was gone, did he miss it.

"For the first time since we were children," she said slowly, giving voice to his sudden dread, "I think that we're the same age."

They regarded each other, she (infuriatingly) amused, he on the verge of panic.

"For how long?"

"Probably only while we're in the Earth Wife's lodge. Mother Ragga, is this your idea of a joke?"

Between grunts as her horny soles hit the rafter, something like a stifled chuckle emerged from the inverted skirt. ". . . seemed only fair. Taking advantage . . ."

"I was not!" Torisen burst out, and then, to his horror, found himself blushing as he hadn't since his youth. Trinity, was he about to be thrown back to those long-gone, miserable days? On the whole he would rather drop dead, here and now, than live through them again. Maybe Jame would too.

Had he taken unfair advantage of the years he had gained on her? After all, they were twins and always would be, however strangely their lives had diverged. He wasn't even sure which one of them had been born first. But that didn't matter. As the male, he would always come first and she be his inferior—but that wasn't how it felt. Did he need to be older, to feel that he had control over her, and why was that so important anyway?

Because destruction begins with love, and you love her.

"No," he said out loud. When in doubt, attack. "Lyra tells me that you ordered her father to step off a balcony two hundred feet up, and he did."

"You disapprove?"

"No. I mean, yes! Who are you to order the lord of any house to do something like that, and what did you do to Caldane at the Cataracts anyway?"

"Finally, you ask! He held me prisoner in his tent, and I had to escape to bring you Father's ring and sword. I slipped him a powder I had picked up on my travels, not knowing what it would do to him, at that point not really caring." She suddenly grinned. "If you ever want to get an . . . er . . . rise out of m'lord Caldane, just startle him into an attack of the hiccups."

"Harn said something about Caineron's advisor, Corrudin." He didn't want to know, but could no more prevent himself from asking than he had from fretting endlessly about his bandaged hand. "What did you do to him?"

"That filthy man." Her abrupt, deep anger made the room's temperature drop. Rumbling, sleepy complaints rose from all sides. "He tried to make me order Brier Iron-thorn to lick the mud off my boots. I told him to back off and he did, right out a third story window. I wish he had broken his neck."

" 'This is what I am,' " Torisen quoted, teeth chattering, breath hanging on the air. " 'Remember that.' "

"Yes. Sorry. Corrudin and I both abused our power, which probably makes me no better than he is, at least in Brier's eyes. I do care what she thinks, you know, and Marc too. If they disapprove, then I've still gotten it wrong somehow. It's so hard to find a balance. Sweet Trinity, haven't you ever made someone do something he or she didn't want to?"

"Not like that!"

Even as he spoke, however, he remembered forcing the Ardeth Matriarch Adiraina to tell him what had happened to his sister in the Women's Halls that winter. Afterward, Grimly had called it "a good trick," and he had nearly snapped the Wolver's head off for suggesting that he had done anything unusual. It wasn't the same, though. It couldn't be. He certainly didn't feel that power in himself now. On the other hand, this young body didn't know that the man who had sired it was dead. In this strange house, in this displaced moment, that authority hadn't yet passed to him.

Then again, perhaps it never had, and never would.

"Damn you, boy, for deserting me. Faithless, honorless . . . I curse you and cast you out. Blood and bone, you are no son of mine . . ."

Words spoken in searing bitterness by a dying man. By his father. How could any curse be more terrible?

To his horror, he felt himself growing younger, smaller, while the edges of the Earth Wife's lodge dimmed around him into the dusty corners of the Haunted Lands keep where he had grown up, which he never seemed able entirely to escape.

"Tori, stop it!"

She had jumped down from the chair and crossed the room to seize him. As her nails bit into his shoulders, the keep faded.

Something crunched, and the wolver pup backed off, shaking her head. Seeing him apparently under attack, she had bitten his sister's leg, or tried to. Something white and hard showed through Jame's torn pants at shin level.

"Oh no, child," she said to Yce. "You don't want to taste my blood, or my brother's either." And Torisen knew, somehow, that the pup would never try to again.

"What's happening to you?" he demanded. While he could clearly see the fine lines of her face, simultaneously it wore a sketchy half-mask of ivory, more like a rudimentary helm than any frivolous product of the Women's World. Then the ivory faded as had the shadows of the keep, although he sensed that neither had gone far.

"This lodge exists in Rathillien's sacred space. From there, it seems to be a short step to the Kencyr soulscape. I don't entirely understand that. It may be as the Earth Wife wills, or as our needs demand. My soul-image is changing. They can, you know. You should try it. Get away from that foul keep, from that voice of madness, before it's too late!"

" 'Daddy's boy. Run. Hide.' "

"Er . . . sorry. I didn't mean it quite like that, and I don't think I told you to hide. Oh, Perimal. You can't leave, can you? Not while that door stays locked with half of what you are on the other side."

This time he grabbed her, hard. "What are you talking about? Filthy Shanir, what have you done to me?"

She didn't flinch, but her gaze was stricken. "Now you sound like Father. I've gotten it wrong again, haven't I? Kindrie told me as much. But I was only trying to help, to buy you some time. You weren't ready then to open that door. Are you now?"

Involuntarily, he glanced over his shoulder at what was somehow the door both to the Earth Wife's lodge and to the ramparts of the Haunted Lands' keep.

Someone knocked on it.

Without thinking, the twins found themselves in each other's arms. Torisen held his sister tight, his face buried in the glorious richness of her hair as if to hide in it. Her breasts pressed against him in odd, soft contrast to the firm, boyish lines of her body beneath his hands. Gray eyes met gray, mirroring each other. Her lips tasted like wild honey, sweet and bitter at once.

"Stay," she murmured. "I will stay with you."

Thump, thump, thump, fists on the door, feet on the rafters, his heart against his ribs . . .

On the keep stairs, heavy footsteps descended. Two children huddled together in bed, terrified. They had heard him in the room above, smashing Mother's things, raving. *"Betrayed, betrayed, whore, slut, love . . . oh, return to me, return!"* Now he was coming for them, the last vestige of her that he possessed, the last bit that he could still hurt, and if he found them together . . .

Torisen thrust his sister away in sudden panic. "I can't stay. I won't."

He had to get out. Better anywhere than here.

The door flew open as he threw himself at it and he fell out, face first. The wolver pup landed on his back and bounded off again, driving him yet deeper into the mud.

"Well," said Harn's voice over him, hoarse with exasperation and relief. "There you are at last."

IV

Jame stared at the door. It had swung shut in her face, but not before she had glimpsed the gray, sodden hay field beyond and recognized Gothregor's outline against a leaden northern sky. At least Tori was safely home. Just the same . . .

"Damn, damn, damn," she muttered, touching her lips where his lips had touched them. Her whole body tingled from that unexpected contact, which had been almost as much an assault as a kiss. But if so, who had attacked whom, and why did she long for a rematch?

She turned, and the bat-thing from the south lunged at her, all gaping mouth and teeth, hissing. She punched it in the face. Its nose flattened with a faint crunch of cartilage, and its red eyes crossed.

"Oh, go suck an egg," she told it as it slunk, whimpering, into a corner.

Then she went to let Mother Ragga down before all the fat went to her head.

CHAPTER XX

The Bear Pit

Summer 68–90

I

EVERYONE AGREED afterward that it had been the most eventful Minor Harvest in living memory.

All the northern keeps received at least a dusting of ash and a day of darkness, reeking of sulfur, not unlike the end of the world. Beasts ran mad in the fields, the Silver seethed white with debris, and scrollsmen gleefully collected samples from the ramparts of Mount Alban. Later, one swore that he had recreated a miniature volcano, but as the glass globe containing it immediately exploded, his claim went unrecorded—and no, colleagues said, the chaos to which his room had been reduced proved nothing, unless he wanted to credit the college kitchen with similar feats of spontaneous creation on a daily basis.

Gothregor suffered the worst of ash, wind, and rain, due to the clash of the north wind and the Tishooo directly overhead. Half a dozen hay ricks were torn apart or burnt down, but the rest stood firm under their hoods of woven rye while their stone foundations raised them above the subsequent torrent of ash-laden mud.

The stepped fields above, however, were utterly destroyed, and their precious crops with them.

The only good thing was that a day later the Highlord had suddenly reappeared, face down and dazed but otherwise unhurt, in the middle of the ruined field.

The day after that, his sister the lordan Jameth limped back into Tentir by a side door, apparently hoping that her return would escape immediate notice. It didn't.

Vant stopped short in the doorway of the Knorth barracks, staring at this dirty, singed apparition with its clothes hanging off it in rags and its eyebrows gone.

"Lady, what in Perimal's name happened to you?"

"Don't ask," she snarled, echoed by the ounce at her heels. "Just tell Rue to get me hot water, fresh clothes, and food. Lots of it. I'm starved."

II

THE RANDOM COLLEGE quickly settled back into its routine, with a growing sense of urgency. All too soon would come the autumn cull and the end of many hopes.

Jame in particular had cause to worry. After a slow start, she had lost more training time than any other cadet due to various mishaps, and now she was hindered by severely bruised if not broken ribs. Her ten-command began to look worried and Vant increasingly smug.

It disturbed her to learn, by accident, that the cull would not be like the summer testing, as she had assumed.

She and Timmon were on their way down from sword practice on the second floor of Old Tentir. Jame, as usual, had been disarmed with unnerving speed. This time the blade had spun straight out the window, to be caught below by the Commandant and returned with a polite request that in future the Knorth Lordan was, please, not to substitute disemboweling her instructors for driving them insane.

Huh, thought Jame sourly. Sheth hadn't even had to ask whose escaped weapon it was.

"That's another black stone for you, for sure," said Timmon cheerfully. "Maybe you'll break the college record and get all eleven of them. You know," he added, seeing her puzzled expression. "Black stone, white stone, leave or stay."

"I *don't* know. What are you talking about?"

"I keep forgetting. You weren't raised in the randon tradition, were you? See, each member of the Randon Council has one black stone and one white. That's . . ."

"Eighteen in all. I can count, you know."

"Actually, it's twenty-two, because the Highlord's war leader—Ran Harn, in this case—and the Commandant each get an extra black and white to play with. You look confused. Now, attend, child, while I teach you the facts of life."

He sat down on the steps, obliging her to do the same and other cadets to swerve, cursing, around them.

Jame gritted her teeth. She hated it when Timmon went all superior on her or forced her to follow his lead. Even more, though, she feared these sudden gulfs of ignorance that kept opening up under her feet, threatening to swallow her whole.

"Did you notice that rather severe Ardeth randon watching us at play just now, when you threw your sword out the window? Remember his gray silk scarf? That's the mark of a randon council member, one of nine, each a former commandant of Tentir except for the one currently wearing the white scarf."

"Sheth Sharp-tongue."

"Indeed. You may also have noticed other gray scarves wandering around the college recently. Even Harn Griphard had dug up some ratty bit of gray cloth to mark his rank—honestly, your house and its clothes! Anyway, they're taking note of the best and the worst of us. Sometime before Autumn Eve, they meet in the college Map Room to cast the stones.

"Imagine the scene: It's nightfall. The room is lit with a thousand candles, illuminating the murals of all our greatest battles. The Council sits in a circle on the floor. Behind each stands a sargent of his or her house. Also there's a scrollsman tucked away in a corner somewhere to keep score.

"So. Starting with the Highlord's house, the attendant randon calls out the name of each cadet in turn. As lordan, you'll come either first or last, as I will for the Ardeth. If no one casts a stone, you're in. The same goes for one or more unchallenged whites. Get only black, though, and you're out."

His blithe tone began to make Jame feel queasy. Of his own success, he apparently had no doubt. It was that stress on the second-person pronoun "you" that twisted her guts.

"Yes," she said, "but what if there's a mix of black and white stones?"

"Ah, then it gets interesting. In the second round, get at least six white stones and you're in, or at least six black and you're out. If it's four or five either way, though, they consider it too close to call, so on to round three, where Harn's and Sheth's extra stones come into play. There, simple majority rules."

"Enough," she said, standing up. "You're making my head hurt."

"Ah, don't fret." He also rose, with a laugh. "If you do get thrown out, you can always try a contract with me. Trust me, it would be fun. We could practice tonight, to see if we suit each other."

Just then, an Ardeth girl brushed past them on the way down the stairs, ramming her elbow into Jame's sore ribs as if by accident. Timmon caught her as she lurched sideways and nearly fell.

"Narsa!" he shouted after the descending Kendar. "Stop that!"

Jame caught her breath and drew herself upright, out of his embrace. She had recognized Timmon's one night conquest from so many weeks ago before he had given up trying to make her jealous.

"Still after you, is she?"

Timmon looked exasperated. "I keep telling her that it's over. Why won't she believe me?"

"You, my boy, have been a bit too free with your glamour, and don't look at me like that: You know what I mean."

"There was never a problem with it until you came along," he muttered, no longer meeting her eyes.

"None that you deigned to notice, anyway; and from now on stay out of my dreams. One of these nights, you're going to get hurt."

They had reached the great hall and stopped to watch the Danior cadet Tarn wrestling with a Molocar pup. Young as it was, all bumbling paws and flopping dewlaps, it easily bowled him over and sat on his chest, licking his face.

"The Caineron Lordan gave him to me," he explained, trying to escape its great, sloppy tongue. "We haven't bonded yet, and of course nothing can replace Torvo—Turvie, stop that!—but still . . ."

He laughed as the pup rolled onto its back, grinning idiotically, and presented its belly to be rubbed.

Jame pressed her hand to her forehead in sudden pain. "Ouch."

"Now what?" Timmon demanded, half solicitous, half exasperated.

"Nothing. Someone I've been expecting has just arrived." She flinched again. "Quit it! I hear you. I'm coming. Excuse me," she said to Timmon. "I've got to find the horse-master."

On the ramp down to the underground stable, she met Gorbel and the other four Highborn of his ten-command, on their way up from their last lesson of the day. The Caineron Lordan grunted when he saw her and would have limped past without speaking.

"It was kind of you to give Tarn that puppy," she said, stopping him.

"Huh." His eyes, bloodshot and sullen, refused to meet her own. Obviously his willow-infected foot still hurt despite Kindrie's best efforts. "Runt of the litter, wasn't it? Either that or throw it to the direhounds."

One of the Caineron made a low comment to another, and both snickered. Gorbel had come back from Restormir with a new set of Highborn "friends" or, more likely, spies for his father. Jame wondered how they could rank as cadets, arriving this late in the season, long past the tests. The Commandant hadn't said anything, but then neither had he about Gorbel.

At a guess, the Caineron Lordan had also gotten an earful from Caldane about fraternizing with the hated Knorth, however accidentally. Jame sighed. It looked as if they were going to be enemies again, not that they had ever had much of a chance at friendship. A shame, that: Gorbel was better than most of his house, when his father left him alone. She stepped aside and let him go.

The horse-master stood at the door of the tack-room, watching with disapproval as the five Kendar Caineron cleaned up after the Highborn whom they served.

"You ride it, you care for it," he muttered aside to Jame. "M'lord Gorbel knows that. What cause has he suddenly to go all high and mighty?"

"I think his father is riding him. Hard. And his foot hurts, which is partly my fault. Master, I need your help."

He raised bushy eyebrows at her. "*Now* what have you done, stampeded the herd off to Hurlen?"

"No, they're quite close," she said, somewhat distract-edly, adding as if to the air, "*Stop* that, or d'you want me to start shouting back?"

"Here now, lady, are you all right?"

"Oh, I'm not the one hurt . . . much. Please, master, come with me, and bring your tools."

"Which? What for?"

"Over-grown hooves, back teeth that need floating, a bowed tendon, and a roast chicken. No, sorry, I'm sup-posed to bring that last one. Meet you at the north gate."

Some fifteen minutes later Jame emerged from Tentir with a soggy bundle hidden under her jacket, leaking grease onto her shirt. The horse-master waited, a bulging leather work-bag slung over his shoulder.

"I think," he said, "that you three lordan have run mad. That fool Timmon just tried to charm his way into coming too."

Of course his curiosity would have been piqued, thought Jame, looking anxiously about for the Ardeth's grinning face.

"No, no. I set him to cleaning tack—a proper punishment for all the times he's left his own mount in a muck sweat. The last I saw, the Caineron were jamming the tack-room door, pretending to be deaf and pointedly polishing spurs, with him boxed inside. Ha. Let him practice his guiles on that lot. Now, which way?"

Jame paused to check her mental compass. "West, above the college."

He grunted and set off. Like most of his charges, the horse-master had four gaits: walk, trot, canter, and bolt. Their brisk pace soon had Jame clutching a stitch in her side. They passed between the trees, climbing toward where the lower slopes of the Snowthorns were strewn with enormous, fallen boulders, like so many snaggle-teeth set in a giant's lower jaw. Most of them still had drifts of volcanic ash piled against their western sides where the pounding rain had failed to wash them completely away.

Rounding a huge rock, they came on a pale lady with long, white hair, sitting on a stone. She leaped up with a frightened cry, swayed, and became a Whinno-hir standing on three feet with the fourth raised, delicate hoof trembling.

The horse-master had stopped dead, staring. "M'lady? Bel-tairi? I thought you were dead!" He dropped his bag with a muffled, complicated crash and threw his arms around her neck. The mare suppressed a start, then bent her head gently to return the embrace.

A sharp clatter of hooves, and there was the rathorn colt, ears flat, crest rising all down his spine.

"It's all right!" Jame hastily stepped between them. "I told you: what do I know about these things? But he can help. Here." She tossed the soggy bag at the colt's feet. He ripped it open and began to tear at the roast fowl, all the time keeping a wary eye on the two Kencyr.

"Seems you've been busy, lady," said the horse-master to Jame. He blew his nose on his sleeve and reached for his tools. "Ancestors know, you're the last person on Rathillien I would expect to be keeping such company, nor yet a Whinno-hir with a rathorn, for that matter. How did it happen, and where's m'lady Bel been these forty years past, while we all mourned her as dead?"

While he bound the bowed tendon back into place and trimmed the mare's hooves, Jame tried to explain, if not the whole story, at least as much as applied to the two equines. It was, perforce, a narrative full of holes.

"Let's see if I've got this straight," said the horse-master at last, as he lifted one of Bel's rear hoofs and began to rasp it flat. "M'lady here gets branded by that bastard Greshan, then chased to the top of a mountain path where she finds a stone door opening into . . . what? Oh, right: the lodge of the Earth Wife, whoever that might be. There she falls asleep for the next forty-odd years until she hears Lady Kinzi's death banner calling to her. Once she's found that, she comes looking for you. At that point, four decades' worth of teeth and toenails all catch up with her at once."

"Er, yes, more or less." She noted that he had skipped over the mystery of Greshan's death, if indeed it was a mystery and not simply a hunting accident as Hallik Hard-hand had reported, before killing himself. On the other hand, how many would know the truth, besides those who had been there? "You believe me?"

"I'm not about to call the Highlord's sister a liar. Besides, here Bel-tairi is." He started gently to brush her mane away from the ruined side of her face, but let it alone when she flinched. Instead, he turned his attention to the over-grown sweep of her tail, tangled with briers but still magnificent. "A pity to cut that. Braid it, maybe, but later." He drew a long file out of his sack. "Open wide, m'lady."

When the Whinno-hir did, looking nervous, he unceremoniously slid his hand into her mouth, seized her tongue, and drew it out to one side.

"Here, make yourself useful. Hang on to this, firm but gentle. Don't pull it."

Jame found herself gripping that surprisingly thick, muscular organ. It twitched. The mare's eye rolled with alarm as the master slid the file between her back teeth and her raw, inner cheek, but Jame's hold immobilized her as he began to rasp away the barbs. The sound was awful.

A hot, menacingly snort blasted down the back of Jame's neck.

"Don't give me that look," she told the rathorn over her shoulder. "This is apparently how it's done, and it doesn't seem to hurt her."

"Not if done right," said the master briskly. "Change sides. Hold. And that's that. A few weeks for the mouth to heal, a bit longer for the tendon, decent forage with plenty of oats, and all will be right again."

"Except for her poor face," said Jame, watching the mare wander off, gingerly working her jaw.

"Well, yes. No helping that, worse luck, but one can live with scars, as well you know." He bent to clean and stow his tools. "About the rathorn, now. You say he's gotten himself blood-bound to you—a damn fool thing to do, but there it is. How d'you mean to handle that?"

Jame sat down on a rock and considered. The colt crouched some distance away like a great cat, pinning his prey with a dew-spur, occasionally raising his head to spit a bone at her.

How indeed?

So far, he had communicated with her mostly in blasts of raw emotion, usually rage or fear. He was intelligent, though, with a complex language of his own comprised, as far as she could tell, largely of scents and images. No doubt he already understood her better than she did him, although she suspected that he would pretend to misunderstand whenever it suited him. They hadn't come yet to a true test of wills.

Just you try, said those red, red eyes, with a glint of unholy anticipation.

Jame sighed. Sooner or later, she would have to. In the meantime, ancestors help them, they were stuck with each other.

The master stood and shouldered his bag. "You're going to need help," he said flatly.

Jame had been hoping for just such an offer, but now she hesitated. This was clearly a job as much for a dragon-tamer as for a horse-trainer; and while the bond between them prevented the colt from deliberately killing her, she sensed that he would cheerfully slaughter anyone else who annoyed him.

"I think," she said, "that he and I should get better acquainted first. I'm right, aren't I, that he's still too young to put under saddle?"

"By half a year at least, if he were a horse. With a rathorn, who knows?" He shook his head—in exasperation or amusement, it was hard to tell. "Mad, the pair of you. No, I won't speak of this to anyone, nor of m'lady Bel's return. Yet. Small blame to her, poor thing, but Trinity only knows what ancient stink her reappearance may stir up."

On the point of leaving, he paused and looked back at them with a sudden lop-sided smile under his flattened nose.

"Ah, but what a thing that will be, someday, to ride a rathorn—assuming he doesn't have you for breakfast first."

THREE WEEKS PASSED.

By now Jame's ribs had healed, although the bruise on her side remained a wonder to behold, if anyone had been there to see it. On her return that first night, Graykin had announced that he had found lodgings more to his taste and had departed, meager possessions in hand. Jame wondered where he had gone and what he found, day after day, to occupy himself, but was too pleased at her sudden privacy to ask questions on the increasingly rare occasions when he reported to her. She hadn't realized until then how much she had grown to dislike his nightly, disapproving presence. God's claws, if she didn't care how she looked, why should he?

On the other hand, Harn had finally exerted his authority during her absence to repair the barracks roof. She supposed the work had to be done sometime. Still, it irked her not to see the stars at night slowly wheeling overhead or to wake in the morning with dew on her face.

. . . *rootless and roofless* . . .

Huh. Maybe she just didn't like roofs.

Worse, though, with the attic enclosed, for the first time she became aware of the stale reek of the lordan's quarters below, seeping up through the floor-boards. The smell gave her bad dreams, or rather the same dream over and over, in which she sat drunk beside a roaring hearth, listening with a terrible, gloating anticipation to hesitant steps as they approached on the outer stair. Then the door would open and she would see her brother's bewildered eyes set in their father's incongruously young, terrified face.

One night, the door opened and Timmon stood on the threshold, his smirk melting into dismay.

"Eek!" he said.

"You have the most uncomfortable dreams," he informed her the next day. "Just once, why can't I find you frolicking naked in a meadow or something?"

"I frolic poorly, and I did warn you. That dream is particularly dangerous. Stay out of it."

She certainly wished that she could, but some sly, malignant force seemed to be behind it, pushing. Sooner or later, as she had warned Tori, they would both have to see it through, but not just yet.

In the meantime, partly to escape it, partly to keep Bel and the rathorn company, she took to sleeping up among the boulders, sometimes waking in the early dawn to find herself bracketed by their warm bodies. Whenever that happened, the colt always lurched to his feet with a snort of disgust as if to say, *How dare you sneak up on me?*

Often, though, she woke to the arrival of the horse-master, come to apply fresh poultices and to re-bandage the mare's leg. A bowed tendon, obviously, was not to be taken lightly. As night turned to pallid dawn, he often stood with her by the hour in a mountain stream, up to their respective knees in icy water and his flat nose running with the cold. Meanwhile, a diet of oats and lush summer grass began to fill in the flesh between her ribs and to restore the gloss to her coat.

The colt foraged for himself, although he still complained bitterly whenever Jame forgot to bring him treats or anything other than his beloved roast fowl.

"So learn how to catch and cook them yourself," she told his retreating back as he stalked away from an offering of (admittedly) rather tough stewed kidneys.

She emptied the sack on the ground in case he changed his mind and tucked her hands under her armpits to warm them. It might be summer, but mornings on the mountain were cold. She missed her gloves, the last pair having gone up in flames while rescuing the Earth Wife. Rue could knit her mittens by the dozen, but was struggling with bits of soft leather to make acceptable alternatives with fingers.

The horse-master came back with the Whinno-hir limping after him. "Fifteen minutes' walk twice a day," he said. "Slow and sure. Not to fret, lass: she's getting there, although things would go much faster with a few leaves of comfrey and yarrow from your grandmother's moon garden. That in a mash of linseed oil and mangle-wart would do wonders."

He paused. "A word of warning: sleeping up here is all well and good, and I daresay that colt won't let anything happen to you, however foul his temper, but be careful.

The hill-tribes have started raiding southward earlier than usual, and coming in larger numbers. There's already been trouble at Restormir and Valantir with their outlying herds. I dunno what's gotten into old Chingetai. He must realize that if his folk start killing ours, there'll be Perimal to pay."

Jame wondered too. The Merikit had made a proper mess of their midsummer rites and were lucky as a result not to have been buried up to their necks in volcanic ash or mud slides, if not molten lava. Could the chief's power be so undermined that he had to prove himself with these dangerous raids or—here was a thought—what about the tribes living farther north, near the Barrier, whom the Earth Wife had mentioned? Thanks to Chingetai's earlier scheme, the Merikits' territory now lay open and unguarded in all directions.

Below in New Tentir, the morning horn sounded.

Late again, Jame thought, dashing breathless into the square with Jorin on her heels. Rue slipped a chunk of bread into her hand as she passed. At least she had managed to enforce her order that the rest of the Knorth eat breakfast whether she was there or not, despite Vant's protests. No doubt he had taken his complaint to higher authorities. Having heard nothing back, Jame only hoped that no one was keeping a secret ledger against her, full of black stones.

As she took her place before her house, twitching grass-stained clothes straight, the master sargent on duty stepped forward to announce the day's assignments. For Jame's ten, this amounted to field maneuvers and archery before lunch, the Sene and composition afterward, partnered respectively with ten-commands from the Coman, Danior, Edirr, and Jaran. Only the last caused a murmur of dismay among the Knorth: according to rumor, the scholarly Jaran were taught their letters before they learned how to walk. Now, how unnatural and unfair was that?

Nonetheless, Jame enjoyed her classes. Maneuvers involved not just formation work but directed attacks, each member of the ten responding to her gestures like the fingers of a hand. They were learning to work well together, knowing each other's strengths and weaknesses, trusting that however unorthodox her orders, they usually got results. There were, Jame supposed, some advantages in coming to such work with no preconceived ideas, assuming that one didn't confuse one's own command more than one did the enemy. In the meantime, it was rather fun to see how often she could make Brier blink with well-concealed surprise.

During archery practice, as an experiment, they blindfolded Erim and spun him around until he wobbled like a drunkard. His subsequent shots hit a half-inch sapling, a rabbit hole, and the sargent's hat. He could hit anything, he admitted afterward, somewhat shame-faced, as long as it wasn't alive.

After lunch, they practiced the Sene with the Edirr, who could be trusted to bring imagination and enthusiasm to any endeavor. It took skill to shift from Senetha to Senethar in time to the flute, which played for one but not for the other, stopping and starting at the player's whim. Dance to fight, fight to dance, the forms flowed together and apart. At one point, Jame found herself part of a line of Knorth dancers all moving as one, met by an Edirr row that mirrored their actions. At such a moment, it felt as if the world itself was finally coming into balance, the same thrill running down every nerve.

Then the instructor clapped to end the lesson.

Jame and her Edirr opposite relaxed and saluted each other with a mutual sigh of appreciation:

Ah, that was nice.

On the way to the last class, an unfamiliar sargent pulled Jame aside and directed her to follow him into a section of Old Tentir where she had never been before. There, he showed her into an interior room some thirty feet square, its wooden walls deeply gouged and prickly with splinters. Even more unusual, a wide circle had been cut in the ceiling so that it opened into the room above. A waist-high wall surrounded the hole and several dark figures lined it, back-lit by torches. The glimmers of a white scarf and of a pale gray one marked the presence of two randon council members.

The sargent handed Jame a padded jacket and a leather hood with a metal grill over the face, then withdrew. So, she thought, shrugging on the heavy coat and buckling it. This was the infamous fight pit, where the Arrin-thar was taught and cadets were thrown to the monster. After the last lesson, it felt like a sudden plunge into the dark heart of the Kencyrath, where secrets were sealed with spilt blood and tied up with entrails.

She wasn't surprised when the door opposite opened and Bear shambled in.

He was every bit as large as she remembered, barefoot, and as shabbily dressed. Tangled gray hair tumbled into the horrible cleft in his skull. He yawned, rubbed his eyes, then saw her and uttered a grunt of mingled surprise and interest.

She made herself stand still as he lumbered over to her, his personal miasma rolling forward with him. Trinity, didn't anyone ever provide the poor man with bath water? Then again, he might simply drink it. He touched her hair—since she had lost her last cap, she had taken to braiding it—and sniffed its scent on his fingertips. His claws were huge, more overgrown than the last time she had seen him and beginning to curve in on themselves, as did his toenails to the extent that walking must surely be painful. He took her hands, turned them over, and pressed the palms to make her own much smaller claws extend.

"Huh," he said, satisfied, letting them go.

She pulled on the hood and mask. He had none. Did the watchers think she would never break through his guard, or didn't they care?

"*We gave him a White Knife,*" Harn had said. "*He picked his toenails with it. Some would poison his food or rush him with spears like a cornered boar, but God curse anyone who takes the life of such a man without a fair fight.*"

They saluted each other, formal on her part, sketchy on his as if he only half remembered how. For that matter, she recalled precious little of her one lesson with the clawed gloves. At the time, she had been too shocked by the instructor's matter-of-fact acceptance that she had the real things. He had said then that she would need special training. Well, here it was.

She imitated Bear's pose, hands up, claws out, weight balanced between one foot advanced and the other withdrawn. He began a series of movements, slowly, so that she could mirror them. These must be the practice kantirs of the Arrin-thar, similar to those of the Senethar or the Sene but darker and deeper.

Here we reach the hidden nature, she thought. *Here is the secret compact with our god, who has made us his champions and his monsters. Remember, you have five razors on each hand—you, who don't even like knives. But you are no one's prey, and no one can disarm you without destroying what you are.*

After a lifetime of concealment, the change in focus felt very strange, and almost exhilarating.

Bear's actions became faster and surer as his body remembered what his mind had forgotten. His claws raked the air in slashes that could tear out a throat or rip off a face. Strike lower to disembowel.

He clapped.

Jame stopped, startled, then surrendered her hands to his so that he might shape them properly. Of course: her nails, like his, curved, although not as much. A straight, fire-leaping spear-strike wouldn't work. She must angle the blow, so, to penetrate the muscle wall and scoop out the vitals within. Huh. Just what she needed: something to make her more dangerous. Never mind. One used what one was given.

Faster now.

They no longer mirrored each other but struck and countered, advancing, retreating. He was nearly three times her size and weight, his enormous hands surprisingly fast, but his half-crippled feet less so. Use that. She must play agile ounce to his massive Arrin-ken. Slip under his swing, slash at his side in passing . . . damn, why hadn't they given him armor? He turned, nearly catching her. A huge grin split his bearded face. She wouldn't trick him that way again.

For some time, there had been a growing disturbance on the balcony, erupting suddenly into a scuffle.

". . . told you this was too dangerous!" someone was shouting. It sounded like Harn. "Stop them!"

Despite herself, Jame glanced up. At that moment, Bear's open palm strike caught her in the face guard and smashed her back against the wall. He had, of course, expected her to block or dodge. All she could see, and that not very clearly because they were so close, were his claws driven through and entangled in the metal mesh.

A roar. A thud that shook the floor. Harn must have jumped down into the pit and be coming at them. Bear swung around to face him, perforce swinging her with him, nearly off her feet. He shook his hand to free it, only managing to shake her as she gripped his wrist until she thought her neck would snap. If she was lucky, only the hood would rip off.

"Er . . ." she said, aware that probably no one could hear her. "Help?"

Then she remembered, and clapped her hands.

Bear stopped immediately. Harn did too, if only because several randon had grabbed him by the arms and were holding him.

"Child?" Sheth spoke mildly, somewhere behind her, also from the pit floor. For a moment there, it must have rained randon. "Are you all right?"

"In a minute." To herself, she sounded muffled and half-strangled, which was close to the case. "Can someone please get this hood off of me?"

She felt strong fingers unlace the cords behind her head and at last was able to wriggle free, wincing as caught strands of hair pulled out at the root. Her head at least still seemed to be attached, as she discovered by gingerly rotating it.

Bear had stepped back, one huge hand still tangled in the mask, the other absently scratching himself. That filthy lair of his must breed fleas by the dynasty. He also needed new clothes even worse than she did, especially pants.

"You know," Sheth was saying gently to Harn, "you nearly got your lordan killed. Bear was under control. You weren't."

The burly randon stared at him, then shook off his captors and blundered away. As Timmon had noted, he was indeed wearing what looked like a gray rag around his neck, probably the closest thing to a council scarf that he could find. Jame started after him, but Sheth stopped her. "Let him go. He needs to think about this."

"Ran, does it help or hurt him that I'm here?"

The Commandant considered this. "A good question, but then I don't know the answer, for any of us. We will just have to see, won't we?"

He had turned to go when she spoke again, on impulse: "Commandant, Bear is your older brother, isn't he? You were the one who pulled him out of the pyre, there, in the White Hills, when he had been left for dead."

He paused, a dark elegant shape in the door way, head bowed, face averted. "Ah, yes. And did that help or hurt? I don't know the answer to that question either."

Then he was gone.

◁▷ **CHAPTER XXI** ◁▷
Loyalty or Honor

Summer 90–110

I

JAME TRACKED Bear back to his den by his bloody footprints. After the guards had locked him in, the Commandant stood for some time, motionless, brooding outside the door. Then he turned in a swirl of his black coat and left. When all footsteps had faded away, Jame slithered inside through the food-flap.

The apartment was much as she remembered it, dark, hot, and airless, but she had time now to see that otherwise it was fairly comfortable with solid furniture, lively (if hard to make out) tapestries, and toys such as the little wooden warriors strewn enticingly about the floor. The Commandant had done the best he could for his brother. Unfortunately, Bear was in no shape to keep it clean, and any walls will close in when one can't escape them.

The big randon had subsided into his tattered chair before the fireplace and was slowly dismantling the guard mask still entangled in his claws. He must have kept it, Jame thought, to play with like a puzzle, as good a distraction as any for so damaged a brain. He grunted when he

1049

saw her but didn't rise. Considering the state of his bare feet, she wasn't surprised. The toenails were much worse than she had realized: several of them curled all the way under until the sharp points pierced the heavily calloused soles of his feet. That he could walk at all, much less fight, amazed her.

To one side was a table with fresh food and drink set out on it. Besides that, she found a small shaft set into the wall that allowed one to haul water up from the springs beneath Old Tentir. This she heated in a basin over the fire and finally got Bear to put his feet in it. The water immediately turned black with dirt. Several basins later, with his toes clean and beginning to wrinkle, she drew out a huge, hairy foot, braced it on her thigh, and began to pry an embedded claw out of the calloused sole. Bear nearly kicked her into the fireplace. It hadn't occurred to her that the big man might be ticklish.

"What I really need," she said to him, picking herself up, "is a nail clipper from the kennel. And maybe a file."

For the moment, however, she must make do with her knife. Finally, she worked out the first claw, rather like digging a nail out of a board, and trimmed off its needle point. Another came out red at the tip, with a sluggish ooze of blood and a faint whiff of corruption. Kendar don't infect easily. Nonetheless, Bear was very lucky not to have suffered worse damage than this. It occurred to her, as she whittled down lethal, overgrown tips, that perhaps this was what Bear had been trying to do when they handed him the White Knife. Life was too strong in him to cut it short, but no one should have to suffer perennially sore feet. Such a simple thing— perhaps too simple for anyone but another Arrin-thari to have noticed.

"There," she said, sitting back on her heels. "The next time, I'll bring the proper tools and do a proper job, on your hands too. These nails are still going to need a lot of filing."

"G-g-g-g-g . . ."

"Good?"

"G-g-g-g-g . . ."

"Girl?"

He leaned forward and patted her clumsily on the head. Unfortunately, the hand he used was still spiky with wire so it took awhile, again, to disentangle her hair without tearing out patches of it.

Maybe I should ask Rue to make me a new cap as well as gloves, Jame thought as she wriggled out into the hallway. Long, lovely locks were all very well, but not if people kept nearly scalping her . . . and be damned if she was going to crop it short, however much Harn grumbled.

OTHER LESSONS with Bear followed, none as dramatic as the first but all invaluable.

Harn stayed away, for which Jame was sorry. Although their situations were very different, she wished Harn could see that Bear wasn't a monstrosity so that, by extension, he might feel less like one himself. She certainly felt more at ease at least with that aspect of her Shanir nature than she had since childhood—not that she appreciated being born one of her god's pet monsters. Surely, though, it was better to have such weapons than to face life without them. After all, whatever her heritage, what mattered was what she did with it—or did it? Whenever her thoughts reached that point, she still felt confused. Had she free will in these matters, or did her blood damn her, whatever she did? But to accept the latter was to surrender responsibility for her own fate as Bane had done, and look where that had led him.

At any rate, it was impossible for her to deal with Bear without seeing him as Marc so easily could have been, under similar circumstances.

And Bear had taken that terrible injury fighting a useless battle led by her father. There, if you please, lay the true madness, sprung from her own blood, nurtured in the broken world it had created.

She was sure that exercise helped both Bear's temper and health and would gladly have taken him on midnight rambles or down to one of the hot water pits in the fire timber hall for a proper bath. However, his was a door fitted with a lock that for once she couldn't pick, perhaps because it was Kendar work, and Bear certainly couldn't squeeze through the flap. At least she was able to get his clothes washed and repaired, once she induced him to shed them—an operation that left him huddled naked as far under his cot as he could get, scarlet with embarrassment, probably wishing somewhere in his befuddled brain that this mad Knorth female with her fetish for clean clothes had never come into his life.

Jorin usually stayed in the outer hallway. Occasionally through him, Jame caught the hint of an amused presence outside, but when she flipped up the panel to look, no one was there but the ounce, sometimes batting around an exotic fruit or a new toy soldier for Bear.

III

THE DAYS OF HIGH SUMMER PASSED, divided for Jame between lessons and barracks duty, rathorn colt and Whinno-hir mare, Bear and a changing assortment of gray scarved senior randon, who always seemed to be there, watching, at the worst possible moments.

On the good side, Bel-tairi was healing rapidly.

"Soon she'll be fit to ride," the horse-master said, with a side-long glance at Jame.

However, Jame had no idea if the mare would permit such a liberty. Bel was still bound to her great-grand-mother, as far as she could tell, or at least to the blood that bound Kinzi's soul to her death banner. Death was proving to be at least as complicated as life.

The colt continued to run wild. With Bel for company, however, he didn't plague the remount herd so, except for random sightings, only Jame and the horse-master knew that he still haunted the area. Sometimes the master brought out harnesses and lunge lines, but on the rare occasions when the colt allowed them to be strapped on, it was only for the pleasure of tearing them apart. Normal training for him, obviously, was out of the question.

"Never mind," said the master with a sigh, watching the colt prance off flinging aside snapped leather straps and broken rope. "I'll think of something."

Jame hoped so. She had an odd feeling that they would never be complete without each other, but how was she to ride such a creature when she still could barely stay on the quietest lesson horse? Forget the bridle bit. As with the Whinno-hir, she sensed that the colt would never submit to one. A halter, maybe, for appearance's sake. At the very least, though, she was going to need a tightly girthed saddle and stirrups.

Still, he was young, and so was she. There was time.

More worrying were reports that hill tribes had begun to raid farther south, and more aggressively. A Caineron flock had been slaughtered in the high fields, the carcasses left to rot, and the Kendar herders flayed alive. Worse, not only were their skins taken but their raw flesh was smeared with sheep fat so that, when found, they were still alive, in agony, begging for the White Knife. Perhaps one shouldn't wonder at such barbarity, given Caldane's practices, but it still didn't sound right to Jame. From what little she knew of the Merikit, they weren't given to wasteful, wanton cruelty. Nonetheless, Caldane now regularly hunted them, pushing farther and farther into northern lands once closed to him, thwarted only by the mysterious folds in the land from striking at the heart of Merikit territory.

She could only guess what the scrollsman Index felt after his years of study and friendship with the Merikit. He had given up demanding that she take him with her up into the hills, which was ominous in itself. She hoped he wasn't going to do something stupid, while simultaneously feeling guilty that she hadn't come up with a plan of her own. She was, after all, still the Earth Wife's Favorite and, technically, Chingetai's heir.

And the Burnt Man's son, she reminded herself.

Trinity knew, she had no desire to face that nightmare again, Burnt Man and Dark Judge combined, ready to pass judgment on such an errant darkling as herself. To them, she must represent the worst of both worlds, much as they did to her.

Then there was Torisen. She heard nothing more about her brother's problem in remembering the names of those Kendar bound to him. Sometimes, though, she felt a shiver ripple through the fabric of her house and for days after that, everyone would call each other by name in her presence. She wasn't sure what good it would do, but she began to learn every Knorth name she could, alive or dead, until her head hurt.

IV

ONE NIGHT late in the barracks dining room, Jame dawdled over a cup of cider, listening to Vant set the next day's duty roster with the other ten-commanders of their house. As this was one of his chores, she didn't have to be there, but it amused her how his eyes kept sliding toward her and how at such times he lost focus on the matter at hand.

Just then, a sort of muffled rumpus broke out overhead, punctuated by Graykin's sharp voice raised in protest.

Jame rose. "Carry on," she said to the ten-commanders. "The roster sounds fine, Vant, except that you have cadet Cherry cooking dinner and cleaning the latrine simultaneously. What goes in does come out, but usually not that fast, unless Cherry is a much worse cook than I realized."

With that, she went quickly up the stair with Jorin on her heels. The second story dorm was quiet. Above,

however, feet tramped back and forth between the front
common room and the lordan's quarters to the back.

From the landing, Jame saw that the latter's anteroom
door stood wide open, as did that of the larger, inner
chamber. Flames leaped in the over-sized fireplace. She
fell back a step before the heat, feeling for a moment as
if she had suddenly walked into her as yet unresolved,
recurrent nightmare. The floor was even strewn with
clothes.

Inside, Rue was directing the dismantlement of the
northern wall of chests, while Graykin stood before the
southern ramparts as if ready to defend them with his
life.

"What's going on?" Jame asked the assembly at large.

Rue set a pugnacious jaw.

"Well, lady, you keep coming back clad in naught but
rags, if that. It isn't proper."

What she meant was *Consider our pride, if not your
own*, and Jame knew it. Clothes weren't that important
to her, but the other houses were beginning to laugh at
the increasingly shabby Knorth lordan.

She glanced at her servant, who glared back at her
defiantly.

"There's plenty dumped out on the floor already," he
said. "Tell them to leave this side alone."

Besides his normal, dusty gear, he wore an elegant if
filthy scarf woven of silvery silk, embroidered along the
borders in peacock blue with animals engaged in enthusiastic if highly improbable frolics. No doubt he had pil-
fered it from one of the chests. Well, she had told him
to take whatever he wanted. She also suspected that he
had wormed through the southern barrier to set up his
new lodgings in the deserted rooms beyond. It was easy

to forget that the lordan's suite extended in both directions down the length of the western wall.

"Leave the south side of the room intact for the time being," she told Rue. "Trinity knows, there's enough here already for me to wear a different set of clothes every day for a year."

Rue wrinkled her pug nose at the armful she had scooped up. "But not all of it is salvageable." She tossed the lot into the flames, which snatched it and roared up the chimney. "Ugh, that stink!"

Jame regarded the room's north wall. "Let's have it all down," she said abruptly. "I want to see what's behind it."

Cadets stared at her for a moment, then Rue gave a whoop of delight and practically threw herself at the barrier. Jame backed out of the way as the others leaped to help. It hadn't occurred to her that they had been itching to reclaim the lost rooms—more like to exorcise them. It had to happen sooner or later.

But am I ready? she asked herself, and didn't know the answer.

Not all the chests contained clothes. Some held ornate weapons more for show than use, pretty baubles, broken musical instruments, scrolls with many interesting illustrations along the lines of the scarf, and enough ointments, unguents, and cosmetics to have kept the courtesans of Tai-tastigon in business for a year.

There were also cracked kegs leaking a gooey, amber substance and crates of corked bottles of every size, shape, and color.

Beyond that was a door.

When Rue stepped forward to open it, however, Jame stopped her.

"After all," she said, bracing herself, "he was my uncle."

It was unlocked, but its rusty hinges ground like iron teeth and all was dark within. Dar ran to fetch lights. As she waited, Jame tested the stale air both with her own senses and with Jorin's. Here and now, though, the attic smelled worse than the darkness before her. When Rue handed her a lit candle, she entered cautiously, to find dust, small empty rooms, smaller windows in the outer wall, and at the end of the hall, a kitchen. These were the servants' quarters.

Looking back down the long, dusty hall, she saw Graykin still in the central room, glowering back at her, guarding the unseen master chambers behind him that he had claimed as his own.

He was welcome to them.

Jame sighed for the lost, airy freedom of her attic.

"If those rooms were cleaned up," she said as they left the dreary wing, "I suppose I could live there. It will certainly be warmer than the attic, come winter. Rue, ask Ran Harn if we can knock out some walls to make larger spaces, and maybe enlarge some windows. Cold be damned. I hate feeling shut in."

Rue agreed with such enthusiasm that Jame realized her odd choice of living quarters had been as much a source of embarrassment to her house as her sparse wardrobe. Speaking of which . . .

"As a council member, Ran Harn needs a proper scarf. Graykin, give me that, please. Consider it rent," she added as he hesitated to surrender his prize. "Rue, wash it and do something about that border. We can't have the Knorth war leader sporting hounds in heat, or hopping hares, or whatever these beasties are supposed to be."

In the common room across the landing, cadets both female and male were busily sorting, cutting, and sewing. Dusk had fallen. Candles cast pools of light through which needle and knife flashed like silvery fish. The cadets might be serving their own pride as much as her need, but the cheerful babble of their voices and the sacrifice of their scant free time touched Jame.

"Use most of this to make new clothes for the cadets," she told Rue. "Truly, I only need a serviceable wardrobe, not an enormous or fancy one, and some of us are even shabbier than I am. Remember, we're a poor house. I'll wear whatever you can salvage for me—within reason —but not that damned jacket."

The Lordan's Coat sprawled on a chair in the corner, as if sent there in punishment like a naughty child. Even untenanted, it had an air of indolent, stupid malice to it as faint but persistent as its reek, and just as personal.

Rue made a face. "Beautiful needlework it may be, but a foul thing nonetheless. You wouldn't think that one man could leave such a taint."

"Master Gerridon did," said Jame grimly, not adding that he, too, had been her uncle.

The smell reminded her that she had only reclaimed a few, dusty rooms. Greshan's personal quarters and the nightmare he had left behind had not yet been exorcized. In that, the coat seemed to mock her, the past overshadowing the present and threatening the future. For that matter, if she failed the autumn cull, all here would sink back into obscurity; and she knew, perhaps better than anyone, what malignant strength that darkness held.

Given that, it was a comfort to pass through the candle-glow of the common room, greeting those cadets whom she knew by name, learning the names of others.

As master ten of the entire barracks she should have done this long ago, except for distractions and a lingering fear that many (like Vant) wished that she would just go away. Their cheerful welcome on this particular evening warmed her. Had she really, somehow, come to be accepted?

But at the door, watching, stood Brier Iron-thorn, as wooden faced as ever, judgment reserved.

No, thought Jame sadly, slipping past the big Southron and down the stair with Jorin on her heels. She wasn't home yet.

THE REMAINS of an incredible sunset hung over the black bulk of the western mountains, smears and whorls of red, orange, and yellow, lurid and smoldering, as if the entire sky were a great fire dying down to ash. Such spectacles had become common since the eruption, and the light on cloudy days was often an odd, murky yellow tinged with olive green shadows. The wind picked up. Dust rattled in the practice square and the tin roof of the surrounding arcade flexed with a hollow boom like imitation thunder. Warm light spilled from barracks' doors and windows. Supper over, cadets and randon alike were settling down to their favorite evening pursuits before bed.

Jame walked south, then east around the square, bound for Old Tentir—not the most direct route, but she preferred to stay clear of the Caineron and Randir quarters when by herself. After all, why ask for trouble?

She wondered, looking across at them: where did one draw the line between house and college loyalties? Just before their oath-taking, the Commandant had said, "While you attend this college, it is your home and all within it are your family, wherever you were born, whomever you call 'enemy' outside these walls. Here we are all blood-kin."

So far, it hadn't quite worked out that way . . . or had it? There were rivalries between barracks, of course, that turned many lessons into fierce competitions; but that was nothing, and good in its way. Here, everyone competed all the time, enthusiastically.

However, you didn't tie blood-kin to a tree as bait for a rathorn, or try to feed them to a poor, mad monster in his lair, or drop poisonous snakes on them as they slept.

As for the first, though, Gorbel probably hadn't meant to harm her, intending to get the rathorn before it got her.

The Randir had indeed tossed her into Bear's den, but that was before she had formally become a cadet.

True, she still had no idea who had introduced her to Addy the gilded swamp adder so informally.

Then there was the Randir Tempter . . . but presumably, whether the Witch watched through the randon's eyes or not, she was only doing her job. She and the Commandant both tested weaknesses and exposed flaws—valuable work, as far as that went. Jame had certainly learned more about self-control here in a half a season than in years outside the college walls.

Yes, but if so why had no one tested Greshan . . . unless that role had fallen to the unfortunate Roane?

Was Roane the Randir also a tempter? If so, how far had he intended to go before he passed judgment on the Knorth lordan? Too far, it seemed, as Roane had ended up dead, warping her father's life forever in the process. How far were the current tempter and commandant prepared to go?

Could one be at Tentir, but not of it?

Clearly, her uncle Greshan hadn't belonged here, only attending because that was what the Knorth lordan was supposed to do. From what she had heard, he had made no attempt to fulfill a cadet's duties. Did Gorbel belong? Did Timmon? Did she? The Commandant had said that the college had its own rules, its own justice, and that by the end she would know for sure whether or not she had succeeded. Getting out alive would be a good start. Ah, but winning one's randon collar would be even better.

Jorin's ears flicked as something stirred on the other side of the square. The lower story of the Randir barracks was dark, the main door almost invisible in the arcade's shadow, but figures were slipping out of it and moving quickly, silently, toward Old Tentir. Some seemed to be carrying bows.

What in Perimal's name . . . ?

Keeping to the shadows herself, Jame entered the great hall by its southern-most door. On the other side was the ramp leading down to the stables. That was where they were going. She had been bound there herself, to ask the horse-master some minor question about Bel. If those were bows, who or what were the Randir hunting with such stealth in such an unlikely place at this time of night? Should she tell someone or find out first, if she could, what was going on? The latter appealed more. She crossed the hall and descended, moving briskly and openly, as if nothing were wrong.

Most of the subterranean stable was dark, its inmates fed and settled for the night. Here and there for light, candles floated in pans of water, open flame being a serious danger when surrounded by so much dry wood and hay. As she passed, Jame glimpsed pale, hooded faces drawing back into the dark and heard the restless movements of horses. Jorin growled, until a soft word from her quieted him. But he had caught a familiar scent, and they followed it, down again into the fire-timber hall, where giant upright trunks of iron-wood smoldered in their pits, fifty feet from brick floor to ceiling. Here among other facilities was the farrier's forge, glowing red.

A gray mare stood patiently in cross-ties, waiting to be fitted with new shoes. The horse-master himself manned bellows, tongs, and hammer, his bald head shining with sweat that ran freely down his face, unimpeded by his flattened nose. When he saw Jame, his eyebrows rose but he continued as if a visit by the Knorth Lordan at such an hour was nothing unusual.

"What a beautiful animal," said Jame, running a hand down the mare's neck.

Encircling it was a thin leather band. All traces of paint had been washed away, but between the band and those mild, leaf-green eyes, the creature was unmistakable. Jame was greatly relieved that Mer-kanti had outrun the volcano; she had been worried about him. But what was either he or his mare doing here?

"Her name is Mirah." He lifted a fore-hoof to check it against the shoe. Jame bent as if to examine his work. "Her master is in danger," he breathed, lips barely moving. "The bastards have set an ambush. You've got to warn him."

"Where is he?"

"Probably in Ran Harn's apartment."

Jame straightened with a casual "Good night, then," hoping that her sudden departure would take the lurkers off guard. She hadn't spotted any in the fire timber hall, but three surrounded her at the top of the ramp, bows drawn.

"Now what?" she asked them.

Coming up behind, farrier's hammer in hand, the horse-master dropped one with an arm-shattering blow. An arrow flew wild, and in the stable's darkness a horse screamed. Confused, the second archer wavered between two targets, and Jame took him down with a fire-leaping kick. Turning, she found that the third had melted back into the shadows.

"Run," said the horse-master.

Jame did, with Jorin bounding ahead. From behind came the master's defiant war-cry, a hawk's jeering shriek, cut short. She hadn't known that he was Edirr.

The stable was awake now, nervous horses bugling, hooves ringing on wood, great flanks crashing into slat walls and boards cracking. Dark figures flitted through the chaos, on the hunt. The hunted fled, dodging down aisles, around corners, through stalls, under hooves. The ramp up to the great hall would surely be guarded.

Jorin's nose twitched at a sharp, well-remembered smell. Bales of hay hid the back wall, but behind them was the hole that the wyrm had eaten through solid stone that first night at Tentir, which now seemed so long ago. Jame scrambled through it and up the steep, slippery stairs on all fours, toward a faint line of light. Yes, here was the secret door, still ajar, and beyond it the charred ruins of the Knorth guest quarters. The weakened floor groaned under her feet and clouds of stale dust made Jorin sneeze.

Had anyone heard? Were they being followed?

Out into the hall. Now, which way?

The maze of Old Tentir had proved harder to master even than the labyrinth that was Tai-tastigon. Someone either expert at misdirection or mentally unhinged had designed it so that one never quite knew where one was, at least within the public halls. Jame guessed that east lay to the left and set off in that direction, only to find herself in a room with many doors, one of which opened on a blank wall, another on a sheer drop, and a third on a flight of stairs going up. She climbed. At the top, fading light met her through the arched windows of the eastern third story. Down the corridor to the left was the base of Harn's tower.

At the foot of the tight, spiral stair, the ounce paused and Jame with him, panting, catching through his senses the smell of fresh blood. She sprinted up the steps two at a time, only to trip over Jorin at the top and fall flat on her face at Harn's feet.

"Well," he said, looking down at her. "Look what the cat dragged in."

By dusk, the small room was pleasant and homey. Its windows stood open to the north and south so that the evening breeze blew in one and out the other. A fire played in the grate, its light dancing on the two large chairs drawn up on either side of it. A platter on the table held the remains of . . . what? In shape it looked vaguely like a roast bustard, but it was covered with brown and white fluttering wings. These suddenly took flight, circled the room, and settled upon the occupant of the chair turned toward the stair-head. Those who landed on his face, hair, and hands turned white, the others a mossy green veined with gold to match his hunting leathers. Mer-kanti smiled at Jame through the restless mask of their wings.

"Soft," he said, greeting her in his rusty voice.

Jame rose, thoroughly rattled. "I thought jewel-jaws were blue," she said, no doubt sounding as stupid as she felt.

"The common ones are." Harn poured a glass of wine and handed it to her. "Drink this. It's said to be good for out-of-breath idiots. These 'jaws could be blue too, if they wanted, but they're a species called crown jewels that can match almost any background. They still do like blood, though."

Mer-kanti put a hand over his goblet to ward off questing feelers. The glass's content, a dark, opaque red, clearly wasn't wine. Jame noted that Harn wore a bandage around his wrist.

"When we were both cadets here," Harn said, "he could still eat raw meat. Now only blood and milk will stay down. Honey too, but it hurts his teeth. Mine too, for that matter. Still, this"—he nodded at his wrist—"at least makes a difference from horse blood."

Jame remembered the band and plug on Mirah's neck, the permanently open wound. The thought made her a little queasy, but it didn't seem to bother the mare.

"And the . . . er . . . crown jewel-jaws?"

"He migrates south with 'em. The Riverland is no place for man or insect, come winter."

"Harn, you're forgetting your manners," said the Commandant from the other chair, whose back was turned to Jame. "I believe these two know each other, but not formally."

"Huh. Lady Jameth, Lordan of the Knorth, meet Lord Randiroc, Lordan of the Randir—yes, yes, Wilden's so-called missing heir, although not as lost as some would like."

Jame felt as if someone had jabbed her in the ribs. "Mer-kanti—that is, Lord Randiroc, they've set an ambush for you in the stable. A trap. I think Mirah is the bait."

The Randir rose so quickly that he left a shell of himself in glimmering wings.

"Surely they wouldn't hurt her," said Harn, distressed, "and who d'you mean by 'they' anyhow?"

"They hurt the horse-master," said Jame grimly. "I heard him cry out. And 'they' came from the Randir barracks, or at least seemed to."

Harn caught the Randir's arm as the latter started for the door. "Wait a minute. No need to charge in by the front door. We can slip down the private stair in the Knorth guest quarters."

"That's how I came up," said Jame. "They'll be watching it."

"Well, there are other hidden ways. Your gray sneak isn't the only one who knows Tentir's secret passages."

"As many at least as you can fit through, and there are fewer of those each year."

The Commandant's words were light but not his expression. He rose, seeming to fill the small room with his dark presence. "We are not 'sneaking' anywhere. This is Tentir, and they mean to pollute its honor by spilling innocent blood."

"These are also probably cadets, however misguided. Let me at least sound the alarm. That may bring them to their senses."

Jame had never heard Harn use that tone before, much less beg for anything.

"You always were too soft on others, and too hard on yourself," said the Commandant in a quiet voice that yet rasped like drawn steel. "We may live in a world of shifting values, but some lines cannot be crossed." When Harn still blocked his way, he put him gently aside. "My old friend, you should understand. Tonight, I am Tentir."

Some slight noise below caught Jame's attention. She ran down the stairs and at their foot collided with someone. They fought briefly, soundlessly, until Jame drove her opponent back against the wall hard enough to knock the wind out of her. It was the Randir cadet Shade.

The Commandant and Harn descended the stairs, the latter still arguing, the former as still as death. Jame pushed her adversary back into the shadows and held her there, a hand over her mouth, as they passed.

Trinity, she thought. *Don't bite me. Please.*

Then came the Randir Lordan, in a mantle of fluttering jewel-jaws. He paused and looked at them. A surprisingly sweet smile crossed his pale face.

"Nightshade, my cousin," he said.

Jame dropped her hand. Shade looked stunned.

"Randiroc," she said, hoarsely. "My lord."

The two cadets stumbled after the randon, Jame supporting the Randir. "Cousin" could mean almost any relation within the bonds of blood-kinship. "My lord" was less ambiguous, especially the way that Shade had said it. She had probably never met this man before, her natural lord, whom she had been taught from childhood to hate.

The Commandant meant to approach the stables without stealth, by public ways. Jame knew another, faster route, and hustled Shade along it. As they went, both felt the Commandant's silent call go out to all the college's Shanir. No wonder he was taking his time, allowing them to respond. Whatever happened, there would be witnesses.

Below in the hay-sweet darkness, she depended on Jorin's nose and ears to slip past the hidden assassins, whoever they were. Would the Randir really be this blatant, here of all places? Despite all that she had seen, like Harn she didn't want to believe it. Tentir should mean so much more than that.

They hid behind one of the massive pillars that surrounded the underground arena. The stable had quieted somewhat, although hooves still shifted uneasily on straw. Mirah stood alone in the center of the torch-lit space, head drooping, hip-shot. She might have been asleep on her feet, shoeing done, awaiting her master's return.

However, the leather band around her neck hung low, unbuckled. In its place was something thicker, something golden, something that bent sinuously to lap at the thin stream of blood that trickled down the mare's neck.

Shade's breath caught. "That's Addy," she said. "I left her in the barracks. I never thought . . ."

Jame grabbed her arm. "Wait. Has she bitten Mirah?"

"No, or the mare would be dead. Addy likes warm blood. When she only nips her prey, her saliva paralyzes it. She can live off a stunned rat for days before she eats it, but she will strike if alarmed."

She started forward again, and again Jame held her back.

"If either one flinches, both, eventually, will die. D'you think they will spare a horse-slayer? But I know both of them. Who else at Tentir can say the same? Let me try."

The Randir shivered under her hands, wide eyes on the golden band. Unconsciously, the tip of her tongue slid over teeth which, for the first time, Jame realized, were not filed.

"Go then," she said hoarsely. "Now."

Jame had also heard feet on the ramp, Harn's voice still raised in protest. From farther away, through Jorin's senses, came puzzled calls and questions as the Shanir responded to the Commandant's summons. She stepped out into the open and walked toward the mare. The faint groan of drawn bows almost made her stop. How many? Twenty, at least. She might not be their target of choice, but she was there, in the way, and if these were indeed Randir, they bore her no love.

Glancing behind her, she saw Shade on her knees, arms clasped tight around Jorin to restrain him. Knorth and Randir they might be, but here at least they understood each other perfectly.

"Hush," she said softly to Mirah, running a hand down the mare's sleek back. "Are you half-asleep, dreaming? Dream on, a moment longer."

The adder had raised her head and flicked a black, forked tongue, tasting the air.

"Yes, you too know my scent. Your lady awaits. Be still while I return you to her."

She slid her hand under the serpent's head and lifted her away from the trickle of blood. The adder loosed her grip on the mare's neck and curled her thick body trustingly around Jame's arm.

"There. Good girl."

The Commandant stood at the arena's side, watching. He waited until Jame had retreated—not too fast, not too slow—then strolled forward with Harn and Randiroc

on his heels. The former stumped, scowling, daring anything to happen. The latter moved with his usual seemingly weightless stride. When he stopped beside the
mare, apparitions of him drifted on in the uncertain light,
defined by a flutter of wings. He slid the leather band
into place and fastened it. The dribble of blood stopped.
Mirah leaned against him with a sigh and closed her
green eyes.

Meanwhile, the Commandant paced slowly around
them, his long, black coat swishing with each stride.
Again, Jame was reminded of an Arrin-ken, but not of
that charred, stalking menace that was the Dark Judge,
warped by pain and hate. Here too was judgment incarnate, but cool and precise, wearing the mantle of power
as he did his white scarf of office—with negligent grace,
but not to be taken lightly.

"So," he said to the shadows. "Here we are. You will
perhaps recall that I once spoke to you of the special
contract that you enter when you take the cadet's-oath.
As I said then, whatever your house, whomever your
enemies there, within these walls we are all blood-kin."

As he spoke, the Shanir arrived: the Falconer; the
horse-master, looking rather dazed, with a lump rising
on his bald head; Tarn with his Molocar pup; Gari with
a humming halo of bees; Timmon, faintly luminous; Gorbel, his hair in cowlicks, clad in a glorious, untied dressing robe with nothing on underneath—cadets,
sargents, officers.

"*We are many,*" the Randir Tempter had said, "*and
we are proud.*"

There, even, was Bear, his claws ragged and bloody
with splinters from ripping apart the door of his prison
in answer to his brother's call. He joined the others in

watchful silence at the foot of the ramp and waited, shifting his great weight from foot to foot. Among them too was the senior Randir officer, a raw-boned, gray-scarved woman named Awl. Sheth acknowledged her with a nod. Other members of the Randon Council stood in the background. As most, like Harn, were pure Kendar, not all could be Shanir; some other instinct or message must have brought them. All nine were present, Jame realized, for the first time all summer. The autumn cull must be near, even tonight, but at the moment that hardly seemed to matter.

"You may also recall," said the Commandant to those other hidden watchers, "that I spoke of honor, and nothing about honor has ever been easy. So, ask yourselves and answer truthfully: here and now, which is more important to you, loyalty to your house or to your oath of fellowship to Tentir? Those who choose their house, come forth."

A blank moment followed. Then a score of Randir cadets stumbled out into the open, bows at the slack. Shade started forward too, but stopped when Jame touched her shoulder and spun around, glaring.

"Think," said Jame.

She didn't know how far the Randir had been in this plot, but she hadn't been carrying a bow.

"Stay. Please."

Shade gave her a brooding look, then a curt, reluctant nod.

Sheth regarded the other cadets, not without compassion. They looked very young and stricken, as if suddenly awakened from a nightmare only to find that it was real. "I release you from the college," he said, "without prejudice. You were tempted and you fell. The politics of your house are . . . complex, if not torturous, but they have no place here. Apply again a year hence, when you have had time to think, if you still wish to become randon."

The senior Randir gave a slight, stiff nod, accepting his judgment. Whether her lord or lady would be as understanding was another matter.

Sheth's hawk eyes swept back to the shadows. "You have also made your choice. Do you hold to it?"

An arrow flashed out of the shadows. Randiroc caught it in mid-flight, snapped it in two, and dropped the pieces. He was, after all, in addition to everything else, a weapons-master.

"I see," said the Commandant.

The rest will slip away, thought Jame. *What have we done here but unmask a few weak souls?*

But then she felt another presence in the shadows and remembered the oath ceremony in the great hall under the house banners, when she had suddenly known that someone was swearing falsely. Over that lay a second memory, like one stink on top of another, of a much different hall and a far stranger banner, where black stitches crawled like maggots into the semblance of a smile.

My name is legion, as are my forms and the eyes through which I see.

The worm was back in the weave.

Jame found herself walking out into the arena, her Shanir senses questing. Everyone was staring at her, but that didn't matter. She would find the wrong thing and she would break it. Again. And again. And again. Until it stayed broken forever.

This is what I am. This is what I do.

As she drew parallel to the Commandant, another arrow hissed out of the darkness. He thrust her aside, then made a faint sound and rocked back on his heels.

"Now that," he said mildly, "was uncalled for."

The shaft had gone through high on his right shoulder, taking his scarf of office with it. White silk began to turn red.

Jame was vaguely aware of a struggle as many hands gripped Bear to restrain him. She stepped forward on the Commandant's right, and Gorbel on his left. Their voices caught each other's pitch perfectly and launched it with all the strength of their outrage into the shadows:

"COME OUT."

The Randir Tempter stumbled into the open, her bow falling from palsied hands. She clawed away her half-mask. The lower half of her face was a shredded ruin, and she spat red through a full set of sharpened, bleeding teeth. Gorbel fell back, staring. No one else moved.

"Damned Knorth." That voice, however mangled, was not her own, nor was the soul that glared out of her eyes. "Again and again and again, you thwart me, even when such is not your intent. Worthless chit. Damaged goods."

"Not half as damaged as the woman whom you now ride."

The Witch laughed through her servant's mask of pain, a wet, ragged sound. "My people obey me willingly. Child of a fallen house, what do you know of such devotion, such sacrifice, such worship?"

"Only what I have seen of their results. They aren't pretty."

They were circling each other now, so close that Jame could see her own reflection in those wide, black eyes, in pupils with barely a rim. She felt her anger grow, a cold, balanced thing, a weapon poised to strike. Their breath hung between them on the suddenly chill air and the floor under their feet rimed with ice.

"The cadet Simmel gave his life for you, lady, but you left him to die alone."

"Not quite alone. You were there. In fact, I believe that you killed him. Did you enjoy it, Kinzi-kin? Was his death sweet?"

"Dust and bloody teeth scattered in the dirt. I took no pleasure in it, snake-heart, nor in what you are doing to your servant now, enemy of my house that she is."

The Tempter bared her sharp teeth, or perhaps the Witch did, twitching the other's raw sinews like some ghastly puppeteer. "You Knorth, hypocrites from first to last. The Old Blood runs strong in you. You savor it, girl, don't you? Did your father, the night that he slew my dear cousin Roane? Well, did he?"

Jame stared at her. "You don't know what really happened, do you? Your lover Greshan wouldn't tell you, for all your wiles, and that still galls you, after all these years."

"Just as it does you, dear child." She raised a hand as if to caress Jame's hair, but Jame slid away from it. "Something changed your father. Several things. And this was one of the first. His blood is yours, and your brother's as well. Is his final madness also your joint inheritance? How much easier it is to hate than to understand, but can either of you truly know yourself until you understand him? Little girl, dare you try?"

The Witch knew something about the haunted room, about the lordan's coat, about nightmares faced or fled. Such things weren't spoken of outside the Knorth barracks, but they were hardly secrets either.

Her black eyes turned to sweep contemptuously over the silent, watching randon.

"And you, Tentir, such noble talk of honor when my darling Greshan's blood is still wet upon your hands. What are decades to such guilt as that? Be assured: he will yet have his revenge, and soon."

She swung back to smile almost playfully at Jame. "But first, dear child, I think I will finish Kallystine's work and rip off your face."

Her hands curled into claws and her ruined mouth gaped, wide, then wider, all sharp teeth bared to bite, to tear.

"Steady," murmured someone. It sounded like the Commandant, but his voice was strangely blurred, as if with the hum of wings. "Wait, wait . . ."

Jame smiled into that terrible face, without humor, without mercy.

"I told you once, as the Randir Tempter, never to touch me again and now, in her form, you can't. But I can touch you."

She extended a claw and drew it delicately in a swooping curve down the woman's face from the forehead, across the bridge of the nose, down to circle that ghastly mouth. Her finger tip left a thin, red line.

"There. The first stroke of the rathorn brand. Of course, when your dear Greshan did this to the Whinnohir Bel-tairi, he used searing iron. What is it about innocence that drives you to destroy it?"

She traced a second red curve from one nostril up around a sharp cheekbone. "The lesser horn. Slayer of innocents, you ordered the assassination of all my female blood-kin, didn't you? Why? What did you and Kinzi quarrel about that it should lead to such slaughter?

"The line of the greater horn, you know," she added, conversationally, "will cut across your eye, as it did across Bel's."

Then Jame heard it under the other's voice, the deep temptation that had been there all along:

Give up. Give in. Become the monster that you know you are.

The Randir began to laugh, half-choking on the ruins of her tongue. "Oh, child of darkness. Tempt me to speak, would you? But I am older than you, and stronger. How you betray yourself! Tricked. Trapped. Here, before all those whose opinions you value most. Cut deeper, then, and prove me right."

Silver eyes reflected back from the gloating, obsidian stare. Behind them both, the angry, frustrated thrum of wings swelled.

Jame's smile grew. "So be it."

She cupped the woman's face in her hands, claws extending, and kissed her on the lips. "Tempter, victim of a greater temptation, randon, sister, farewell. I'm sorry." Then she drove her thumbs into the other's mouth, back to the hinges, forcing her jaws open.

"Gari, now!"

The bee swarm roared over Jame's shoulders, around her head, and down the Randir's throat. Eyes widened in shock as they began to sting and to die, inside her, yet more came, and more. They crawled down Jame's arms in a furry, furious pelt, down her hands, down into that seething mouth. The Randir began to gag and thrash, but she couldn't touch the one who held her. When she fell, Jame went down with her, straddling her body as it bucked and convulsed under her.

"This is your servant!" she shouted into those bulging eyes, at the alien presence within. "Keep faith with her and stay to honor her death!" But the black pupils were already contracting as the Witch fled.

Jame let go and sat back heavily on the floor.

"Damn you," she muttered, close to tears. "Witch, bitch, worm, damn you to the Gray Lands and there let the dead have their way with you forever."

She had no wish to witness those final, terrible death throes, but it seemed as if someone should. At last the body lay still, except where dying bees crawled beneath its clothes, their entrails torn out with their stingers. Then came a bright flutter of carrion jewel-jaws that settled, eagerly, on whatever exposed flesh they could find.

Timmon leaned against a pillar, throwing up his dinner.

"I just told them to go," Gari was saying, again and again. "I didn't tell them to do that. I didn't . . . I didn't . . ."

Sheth put his uninjured arm around the boy, and the cadet clung to him, sobbing. "Of course you didn't," the Commandant said gently.

"Huh." Gorbel nudged the body with his foot, only just not kicking it in case some of the bees were still alive and armed. "You do come up with interesting ways to kill people, Knorth."

"Oh, shut up," said Jame.

She considered vomiting too, but decided it wouldn't make her feel any better. Nothing she could think of would. But here was Jorin, anxiously nuzzling her ear, trying to crawl into her lap where he hadn't fit since he was a kitten. She held him, surprised to find that she was both chilled and shivering.

The Commandant stood over her. "All right, child?"

She gave a laugh that was half a sob. "You keep asking me that, ran."

"With you, the question continually arises."

"Er . . . you do know that you still have an arrow stuck through your shoulder, don't you?"

"I had noticed," he said dryly.

Harn snapped off the head and pulled out the shaft, which had punched Sheth's silk scarf of office through the wound from entry to exit. "No splinters there," he said. "Finally, the damned thing has served a purpose."

Jame climbed to her feet, trying to pull herself together. She thought distractedly that she must give Harn the silver silk scarf as soon as possible, cavorting beasties be damned. It seemed a lifetime since she had first seen it wrapped around Graykin's dirty neck.

"I'm curious," said the Commandant to her. "What did the Tempter mean about you killing Simmel? That young man's fate has always puzzled me. All we ever found were his clothes and a pile of teeth."

"Well, ran, I did hit him in the head with a rock, but that's not why he crumbled to dust."

"I see. Or rather, I don't. Perhaps, at some future date, you will enlighten me."

By now, the others who had lain in ambush had slipped away. Making no fuss about it, the hunt-master gave a lymer the scent from the feathers of the arrow that Randiroc had snapped in two. When the tracker had found the scent and sped up the ramp in pursuit, he loosed a direhound after it.

"This has not been one of Tentir's better days," remarked the Commandant. "It might, however, have been worse."

He turned aside to speak with the Randir Lordan. Mirah had sunk to the ground asleep, legs folded neatly under her, head cradled in her master's arms. Clearly, she would not be fit to travel at least until morning.

Harn stared down at the Randir's body. "Trinity, girl, Blackie would never . . ."

"No, ran, I don't suppose he would; but I am not my brother."

The big Kendar regarded her soberly for a moment, chewing on the inside of his cheek. "It will be Autumn's Eve in ten days," he said. "Blackie hasn't asked for you, but tomorrow you should leave for Gothregor to stand by him on the night. I think he's going to need you."

His eyes were still on her, hesitant but heavy with judgment.

"Tonight we cast the stones for the autumn cull. I'm sorry, but I don't think you will be coming back."

VI

JAME LEFT THE STABLE, feeling numb.

The college was still in the process of rousing; the departure of its Shanir, without a general alarm, had been too sudden to create more than an initial stir, but now word was filtering back to the barracks that something startling if not terrible had happened. Lights flared in rooms among groggy sleepers. Those who hadn't yet gone to bed stood in their barracks doorways, bootless, calling questions to which there were few if any answers. Jame slipped by them as if invisible.

Outside her own barracks, she stopped to lean on the rail. Across the practice square, on the second floor of

Old Tentir, candle light glowed through the peach-colored screens of the Map Room and spilled out onto the Commandant's balcony. There, tonight, the casting of the stones, the autumn cull, would take place, but probably not for awhile yet: the Commandant would need to have his shoulder properly patched up, and then there was that mess below to sort out. She wondered what they would do with the Tempter's body. On her way out, she had heard Sheth say something about putting it outside the walls, to be claimed by whomever cared to take the trouble. If not, he had said, let Randiroc's jewel-jaws have it.

Was that fair? Was it right? She didn't know.

Almost at her feet, on the other side of the low wall and in its moon-cast shadow, the direhound raised its black head and snarled up at her over its prey. Front paws on the rail, Jorin growled back. The white lymer crouched to one side, its tracking done, patiently waiting for its reward of fresh entrails.

"I know the hunt-master doesn't starve you," she told them both. "Return to him." The hound bared bloody fangs and crouched to spring. "Go."

As one, they flattened and went, slinking.

Huddled as the body was, she could only guess that the Randir cadet was male. Given the great pool of blood in which he lay, he was most certainly dead. So. Those were the fingers that had smoothed the arrow's feathers, set its notch to the string, and loosed it at a man whom this cadet had been told was a mortal enemy of his house.

"I'm afraid," she said to him, "that you've been both gulled and culled. Perhaps I have been and will be too, soon."

Maybe Harn was right. Maybe she didn't belong at Tentir and should be cast out. On the simple level of skill, except in a few areas she still trailed far behind the rest of her class. There was still a huge gap between their experience and hers. And she was dangerous—but would she be any less so elsewhere? Sending her back to Gothregor for anything longer than a visit was chancy, to say the least. What did one do with a nemesis, anyway, between catastrophes?

"I have *got* to learn how to knit," Jame muttered to herself. "What's the worst I can do with a ball of yarn and a pair of needles? No, don't answer that."

"I've been looking for you," said a grim voice, and there was Shade, with Addy draped around her neck like a thick, golden collar. She glanced over the railing. "Quirl. He always was a fool. Then again, I wasn't so bloody smart this evening either. Why did you do it?"

"Do what, or rather, which? It's been a busy night."

The other snorted. "You might well say so. I mean, why did you stop me? I could be packing now too, or more likely looking for a White Knife. My lady grand-dam does not like failure."

Jame had forgotten that Shade was Rawneth's half-Kendar grand-daughter and that Lord Kenan was her father, not that either seemed to count for much among the Randir.

"Would you have done it? Shot a fellow randon from ambush in the heart of Tentir?"

Shade scowled. "I don't know what I was going to do. Listening to the Tempter, it sounded right: kill the enemy of our house; accomplish what even the dread Shadow Assassins have failed to do, these forty years past; protect our blood. Then I followed you, and spoke to him, and suddenly nothing was simple anymore." She shook her head. "It was always so clear before. Us against you. That's the way I was raised. No questions. No hesitation. Tentir is changing that, and so are you. I don't like it. It makes my head hurt." She shot Jame a look askance. "I was there, you know, in the stable. That devil hound went for me first because I was closest, but he veered off."

"Why not? You hands were clean."

"Is that why you stopped me from stepping forward?"

"I suppose. Also, I like your snake." Jame looked up at the Map Room where shadows were beginning to move against the peach-colored screens. "Tonight, for me too, there were moments of such blinding clarity, when I knew exactly what I had to do and how to do it."

She rubbed her mouth, as if to wipe away the cold touch of the Tempter's lips: *Victim of a greater temptation, randon, sister, farewell.* Somehow, she had known that the swarm was coming, and why, and how to open the way for it. No doubt. No hesitation. No question, even now. Only guilt.

Jame sighed. "Now so much is murky again. Right and wrong, good and evil, honor and loyalty . . ."

"You sound more familiar with confusion than with certainty. I don't envy you." Shade nodded toward the body almost at their feet. "That's certain, at least."

"Death? I'm beginning to think that it's the most complicated thing of all, next to honor."

She straightened and stretched, feeling the strain of the day in all the muscles down her back, hearing her spine creak.

"The cull is about to begin, the stones to be cast. I wish you luck, Randir. For my part, this is probably my last night at the college, and I have one last thing to do while I still have the chance."

The other looked at her suspiciously. "What?"

Jame had started to turn toward the barracks door but hesitated, looking back. A wry smile twisted her face. "Why, sleep, of course. And dream."

꧁ **CHAPTER XXII** ꧂

Casting the Stones

Summer 110

I

RUE MET HER AT THE BARRACKS DOOR, with a startled glance after the retreating Randir, then another at the general stir along arcade.

"Lady, what's going on?"

Jame didn't feel like explaining, assuming she could, so she chose the simplest answer: "The autumn cull has begun."

The cadet shot an aghast look across the square at the lit windows of the Map Room. "What, tonight?"

Other Knorth cadets crowded behind her in a rising babble of voices: "What did she say?"

"They're casting the stones!"

"But what's this about a pile of corpses in the stable?"

"Never mind that. It's the cull!"

Jame recaptured Rue's attention with difficulty.

"Take the gray silk scarf to Ran Harn. Hurry."

"B-but I haven't even had time to wash it, and as for the embroidery . . ."

"Never mind that. He's about to cast the stones with what looks like a dirty sock tied around his neck. Go."

She climbed the stairs against a swift tide of descending cadets. They had all known this was coming, of course, but to have it suddenly upon them was another thing altogether. It didn't look as if anyone else would either want or get much sleep that night.

The Lordan's Coat still sprawled, ignobly abandoned, in the corner of the third floor common room. Dragging it by the collar as if by the scruff of the neck, she entered the lordan's apartment and closed both doors behind her. Jorin slipped through on her heels.

The inner room had been left a desolation of discarded clothes, empty chests, and tarnished trinkets, the tawdry remains of a worthless life and of a death largely unmourned. Even the smell seemed old, a dusty, faint reek of mortality. The door to the north wing servants' quarters stood ajar, and a thin, cold breath of air moved through it like a long sigh. Jame closed it. Then, feeling a bit foolish, she balanced a chair against it so that it would topple if the door moved.

Somewhere behind all those other boxes against the south wall, there was another door, but she didn't care to dig it out. Either Graykin was asleep in whatever nest he had made there or, more likely, he was out earning his keep by spying on the Map Room. Whichever, what she had to do now was none of his business. With a certain grim amusement, she booby-trapped that side of the room too with an assortment of knickknacks and bottles sure to crunch or roll under the unwary foot.

There. I warned you never to spy on me again.

A few embers glowed on the hearth among heaps of smoldering rags. Jame tossed in the wreckage of a cedar chest to rouse the flames and held her hands up to them as they flared. She still felt very cold, and shaken, and not at all prepared for what came next.

For that matter, was it really necessary, or even wise? One couldn't be physically hurt in dreams as one could in the soulscape, or so she supposed, but if she had actually begun to dream true, nightmares of the past might tell her things that hurt far worse than any punch in the nose. Did she really want to know what had happened in this room to her father so long ago? The old days held so many dark things, some perhaps best left undisturbed.

Ah, but the past wasn't dead, only asleep, waiting to rise again and to strike. She had the Witch's promise of that.

"*Something changed your father,*" Rawneth had said through the Tempter's bleeding lips. "*His blood is yours, and your brother's as well. Is his final madness also your joint inheritance? Can either of you truly know yourself until you understand him?*"

Huh. So much for any choice in the matter. This concerned Tori as much as it did her. Besides, in her experience if you turned your back on a problem, it tended to bite you in the ass.

Here was a pile of not too musty clothing, perhaps dropped by Rue in her rush downstairs. Jame heaped them on the raised hearth in a rough bed, lay down, still fully clothed, and tried to make herself comfortable. The fire warmed her back and Jorin crept into her arms, but she continued to shiver.

From the shadows by the door where she had let it fall, the Lordan's Coat smirked at her. There was no other word for the expression conveyed by those peaked folds of stitch-thickened cloth, too heavy to crumple even when unceremoniously dropped. With a sigh, over Jorin's protest at being disturbed, she rose to fetch it. After all, why else had she brought the damn thing in here with her? Rue had cleaned it as best she could and darned the ripped lining, but at the least movement the old stench seeped out of it, as strong, personal, and offensive as ever. As Jame returned to the hearth with it, she considered throwing it on the fire. Heirloom or not, Greshan had surely tainted it past repair. But if it had become the flayed skin of old nightmares, she still needed to learn its secrets.

With a smug reek, the coat settled over her in an unwelcome embrace. Wrinkles in the garments upon which she lay creased her flesh and Jorin grumbled as she shifted restlessly. The fire snarled over its wooden prey. From outside came the muted stir of the barracks.

Never in her life had she felt less like falling asleep.

 **II**

"WHAT ARE YOU GRINNING AT?"

Harn Grip-hard glared at the senior Edirr randon, sitting cross-legged third to his right around the circle, beyond the haughty Ardeth and a Danior who seemed far too young to be here, in such august company. As in the hall below, the Randon Council kept to the order of their house banners, but in a circle without head or foot.

"Oh, nothing, nothing," said the Edirr hastily, and turned to speak to the grave Brandan on his right.

Harn tugged at the silk scarf. Pretty it might be, but slippery; he had had to knot it around his thick neck to keep it from slithering off. Now, however, he felt as if it

was trying to strangle him. Either that, or guilt: The cadet
Rue had intercepted him just outside the Map Room
with a quick, hissed message that the Knorth Lordan had
said he should wear it—this, when Jameth must know
that he was about to betray her.

He squinted surreptitiously at the embroidered border
that seemed to amuse the Edirr so much. Seen upside
down, it looked like an abstract pattern, peacock blue
thread on shimmering gray. Nothing to laugh at there,
or anywhere else tonight that he could see.

The Tempter's grisly fate didn't bother him—much:
clearly, the woman had crossed any number of lines,
putting an arrow through Sheth Sharp-tongue being the
least of them.

But that boy in the square with his throat torn out . . .
such a pitiful, little heap he had made, his eyes and
mouth agape with frozen horror. Harn remembered him
alive, small for his age with a thin, intent face, struggling
to keep up. A child. The Tempter would have used that:
*Here is your chance to prove yourself, to be blooded in
your lady's service.*

Blood. The ground had been soaked with it. His own
hands felt wet and greasy—only with sweat, he told himself; but when he closed his eyes, all he saw was red.

*What's happening to us, Blackie? How can such a
thing occur, here of all places? Have we failed in honor,
or has honor failed us?*

He rolled two stones in his palm—one white quartz,
the other black limestone, both polished smooth by a
mountain stream and warming to his touch. Two more
of each lay before him. Like the rest of the Council, he
had spent the last few weeks making up his mind which
stone each cadet had earned, white or black, in or out.

Some of the choices hadn't been easy. One was getting harder by the minute. Perhaps he should ask for a delay. After such a night, were any of them fit to judge wisely?

The senior Randir Awl sat across from him, her back roughly to the east wall as his was to the balcony and the west. Murals flickered by candle-light all around them, each the bloody chaos of battle resolved into clean lines and glowing color. There on the north wall was the newest: the Cataracts. Awl had done fine service at the Lower Huddles and on many other so-called fields of honor, often by his side. A good woman. A good randon. Tonight, though, she looked like the unburnt dead. At her left hand was a knobby bone, the vertebra of a large snake; at her right, a black . . . thing, compact but convoluted, as if tightly wound, with an oily sheen—both no doubt the choice of her lady the Witch. Harn was angry for his colleague's sake. What had happened tonight wasn't her fault. Why did clean hands such as hers have to touch such things?

But she hadn't asked to delay the cull.

The Commandant sat to his left, beyond the Jaran. Candle-glow picked out the hawk-sharp lines of his face and a fresh, white scarf serving as a sling. His shoulder must throb with every heartbeat, but he showed no sign of it except perhaps for the gathering shadows under his eyes.

He hadn't asked for a delay either.

Harn sighed. If Sheth could do this with a bloody hole punched through him, so could he. Oh, but it was hard.

"We know why we are here." The Commandant's voice was flat. *This is our sworn duty*, its inflection said, *and we may not turn from it.* "The college cannot support its current population over the coming winter. More important, only the best belong here, and we have now had time to determine who they are. A score have already departed this night."

Awl's thin lips tightened, but she didn't speak nor did anyone look at her.

"We need to cull at least a hundred more. Are we agreed? Then let the stones fall—for the good of our randon fellowship, for our houses, for the Kencyrath as a whole, and for our personal honor, tonight so grievously wounded. May duty heal us all."

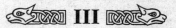 III

THIS IS RIDICULOUS, thought Jame, still fidgeting on the hearth.

Never patient where his comfort was concerned, Jorin had long since retreated to a quiet corner. She herself had slept sound in stranger places than this. So, why not tonight?

Earlier, she had wished she had some of Kindrie's foul tincture of hemlock. That in turn had reminded her of the bottles Rue had unearthed and, rising, she had found one still marginally drinkable, in a square green bottle sealed with wax and soft lead. Tubain had kept a similar jar behind the counter at the Res aB'tyrr in Tai-tastigon, until Cleppetty had made him empty it into the gutter. Jame remembered the curb-stones smoking. But Highborn, she reminded herself, were very hard to poison. Anise, tansy, wormwood, and a kick like a cart horse.

One swallow had numbed her mouth and made her eyes sting; but that, apparently, was all.

Oh, why couldn't she sleep?

"Because you will always fail," said the Tempter's voice, filtered through a hum of insects.

She hawked to clear her throat. An ejected bee tumbled out onto the floor, its guts ripped out with its stinger. It righted itself, unsteadily, and bumbled into the fire where flames kindled its wings. The Randir herself stood in shadow, her form still yet strangely a-seethe.

"You haven't the focus," she said. "Lover of confusion, of chaos, of destruction."

"I am not! I just don't see things as simply as you Randir do. Poor Shade. I made her head hurt. Mine is throbbing now too."

"Serves yuh right." Simmel balanced on the wobbly chair set against the side door, gumming his words without teeth. Grains of dust trickled out of his ears and empty eye sockets, *tick, tick, tick*, onto the floor. "Look at m' poor head, all s-smashed an' hollow."

"Thank your lady for that," Jame snapped. "She's the one who emptied your skull, not me, and you let her. The world is *not* black and white."

"It is tonight," said the Tempter, with a ghastly, toothy smile full of mangled, wriggling bees. "White stone, in; black stone, out."

Jame felt warmth against her back. She thought it was the fire, until it stirred restlessly.

"I'm going to fail," murmured her brother. "So many faces, so many names . . . how can I remember them all?"

They might have been children again in the keep in the Haunted Lands, huddled together in bed for comfort, for protection.

"Mullen. Marc. I will never forget them, but one is dead and the other refused my bond. Father said I was weak, and I am. I am. I am."

All right, Jame thought. *I'm asleep after all, but is this my dream or his?*

"I'm going to fail . . ."

She tried to turn, but the lordan's jacket fought her. How many arms did the thing have anyway, and why couldn't it keep them to itself?

"Tori, let me help you. Dammit"—this in a sputter to the coat, as it wrapped a boneless sleeve around her face and tried to stuff itself down her throat—"Ummph . . . let me go! Tori!"

Could he hear her? Was he even there anymore?

With a great effort she flung off the coat and scrambled to her feet, to find by the draft that she had shed all her other clothing as well. Simmel snickered from the shadows.

"Oh, shut up," she snarled at him. "You're not so pretty yourself."

"Remember me!" dry voices cried from the ashes of the past, from the crack and greedy hiss of the pyre. "Remember me! I brought your grandfather word of his son's death, and for that he cursed me."

"I honored seven contracts, at last dying in childbirth far from home."

"I fought beside your father in the White Hills, and died at the hands of my own mate for the sake of our unborn child."

"I saved Tentir's honor at the point of the White Knife or thought that I did, but all in vain . . ."

She could almost see them now in the arc of the fireplace, a vast, gray host crowding around her brother, reaching out to him with unraveling hands. How many there were, all the past Highborn and Kendar of their house whose blood, like Kinzi's and Aerulan's, trapped their souls in the weave of their death.

Torisen held out his beautiful, scarred hands—to embrace or to ward them off?

"Yes, yes, I know my duty and am honor bound to it, but so many names, so many faces—how can I remember you all?"

That last gray shape who had spoken of honor, Tentir, and the White Knife . . . he had been a big Kendar with large hands and a broad, almost familiar face.

I know him, thought Jame. *I* know *him!*

"Tori!" she called over the wasteland of ashen heads, of gray faces turning slowly toward her even as they crumbled to ruin. "That's Hallik Hard-hand, Harn's father! And that other must be Sere, Winter's mate. Don't you remember his face painted on the walls of our parents' bedroom? I know others as well, dead and alive. Let me help!"

But could he hear her? The cries had grown shrill, demanding: "Me!"

"Me!"

"Take me!"

Banners unraveled and rewove to clothe the living. Highborn ladies swarmed around Torisen in a swirl of stolen funereal finery, clawing strips off each other to reach him. What are the claims of the dead compared to the ravenous hunger of the living?

"Take me!"

"Me!"

"Me!"

What was this, a feeding frenzy?

Jame plunged in among them, naked and thoroughly exasperated. They scattered before her with faint, horrified shrieks at her unmasked face. No doubt about it: This was Tori's nightmare, asleep and awake. If even a fraction of it was true, the Women's World had lost its mind, or at least its head. No wonder Tori was running scared. But where was he, or rather where were they?

She had followed him to a cold, dark place which, surely, she should know by that thin, sour smell, but it was so very, very dark, and it felt safer somehow not to know, or to be noticed. Voices muttered, rising and falling, woven together with the dense texture of an argument that never ends but only repeats with endless variations.

". . . hands, hands, hands," Torisen was saying. He sounded much younger than he had a moment ago, and his voice cracked with helpless exhaustion. "How they clutch and cling! They will drag me down, but I swore never to fail another as I did Mullen. I s-swore!"

A hoarse, muffled voice answered him, an insidious murmur from within. "We all swear. Many swore to me, and all swore false. I have lost thousands. I lost you, my only son. What is one man compared to that?"

"He was just that, a man, and he trusted me. They all do."

"All who trust are fools. I trusted you. Trust no one."

"But she's my s-sister, my twin, my other half. Why can't I trust her and accept her help?"

It was the voice of a child, pleading against the dark. Jame wanted to shout at it, "Oh, grow up! Don't ask. Tell him!" But her own voice caught in her throat.

"Because, boy, she is Shanir."

"Is—is that really so bad?"

Now she was truly struck dumb. When had Tori begun to question that, the bedrock of their early training?

"Anar taught us the old stories. Mother sang them to us in the dark, before she went away. Once, those of the Old Blood did great things . . ."

"Terrible things."

"That too. Yet everything else in life is gray. Why is only this black and white?"

. . . white stone, black stone, in or out . . .

"You ask me that, again and again and again. Do you think, if you whine long enough, I can change night to day? Weak, foolish, faithless boy. Shall I tell you, again, what that filthy Shanir, my brother Greshan, did to me as a child, no older than you are now? Shall I show you?"

No! Jame wanted to shout. *Leave him alone, you bully!* But fear swallowed her voice.

"See. Hear. Learn," said that loathsome voice, gloating over each word. "Just a drop of his blood on the knife's tip, not strong enough to bind for more than an hour or two, just long enough to make the game more interesting. Dear little Gangrene. You went crying to Father the last time, but he didn't believe you, and he never will. Not against me. You're a worthless, sniveling liar, and everyone knows it. Now open wide like a good little boy or I'll break your teeth—again—with the blade. There. Now, come to me."

And Jame woke on the cold hearth, with the iron taste of blood in her mouth from her own bitten tongue and her brother's cry of horror echoing in her mind.

 **IV**

THE FIRST ROUND of the cull went much as expected, although with a few surprises. Naturally, the Highlord's house began, and the first name called by the sargent standing behind Harn Grip-hard was that of the Knorth Lordan.

For a long moment, no one moved except for Harn, tugging again at his gray silk scarf. No stone cast, black or white, meant that Jameth was in. Then the senior Jaran leaned forward and rolled an ivory ball carved with lesser runes into the circle. Harn felt the room swim. Must he be the one after all to cast the black? But the Randir spared him. Whether on her own judgment or by order of her lady, she let drop her black ball. It neither bounced nor rolled, but fell with a plop and lay there, twitching slightly.

Again, everyone waited, but no one moved. Then Jaran and Randir scooped up their markers and the next name was called.

Harn let his breath out in a loud *whoosh*, causing the Commandant to shoot him an amused glance. Jameth's fate would not be decided until the second round, or possibly the third and last.

Judgment was also suspended on the Caineron and Ardeth lordans. Politics aside, some felt that the former was too clumsy and the latter too casual to make good randon. Brier Iron-thorn also received one white and one black stone. No one doubted her ability, but several were still wary of her sudden change of houses. Such things rarely happened, and caused great suspicion when they did. At the end of the first round, the fates of some two hundred cadets remained undecided.

By now, it was well into the night, the thick candles banded with the hours half burnt.

"At this rate," murmured the young Danior to the Brandan in the pause between rounds, "we won't be done until dawn. D'you think the Commandant will last that long?"

The Brandan gave a short, mirthless laugh. "I've seen Sheth Sharp-tongue direct a battle, aye, and fight in it for three days running, with a thigh slashed two inches deep. We only found out about it at the end, when he dismounted and collapsed from loss of blood. Awl worries me more. Every time she touches that damn black ball, something goes out of her."

"And Harn?"

"You sit closer to him than I do. Keep watch. I don't like his color, or the way he keeps tightening that blasted scarf; and I don't trust the Ardeth to help, although he sits closer still."

They both glanced at the senior Ardeth who stood aside, sipping amber wine from a crystal glass. He and the Jaran were the only pure Highborn currently on the Randon Council, although otherwise they were as different from each other as fine leather and rough silk.

"So Lord Ardeth still isn't speaking to Blackie."

"Not directly." The Brandan took a swig of watered cider. Only Harn was drinking his neat, and hard. "We hear rumors that he's trying to get at the Highlord through his matriarch, Adiraina. Our own matriarch hasn't been near Gothregor since she returned the Knorth death banner."

Tactfully, the Danior didn't comment on this. Everyone knew that Brenwyr was unwell and that her lord brother worried about her, but whatever ailed her belonged to the impenetrable, no doubt trivial mysteries of the Women's World.

The Commandant returned to the circle and sank into his place on the floor, followed soon after with some cracking of stiff joints by the rest of the Council. The second round of the cull was about to begin.

GETTING BACK TO SLEEP required several more pulls on the green bottle, taken reluctantly: Jame remembered all too clearly how helpless she had felt when Kindrie had dosed her with hemlock. Dreams were tricky enough as it was, she thought as she dropped back into her noisome nest on the hearth, head and stomach roiling.

As it was, she no longer knew who was dreaming what. Had that last been a dream at all, or had she descended far enough to eavesdrop on Tori at the bolted door in his soul-image? Even then, it had been strange, that slip from her father's voice to her uncle's. Greshan, a bloodbinder? It didn't surprise her much, nor that his Shanir powers should have proved so much weaker than her father's, considering that the older boy had only been able to bind the younger for short periods of time. It certainly helped to explain Ganth's hatred of the Old Blood, without forcing him to realize that he possessed it himself.

What a miserable childhood he must have had, almost as bad as her own. What had it been like, to live under the shadow of such alternating cruelty and neglect? Her mind drifted toward sleep, trying to imagine the boy her father had been.

It was Autumn's Eve.

The boy wandered in his grandmother's Moon Garden, between banks of tall, pale comfrey and lacy yarrow, between primrose and arching fern. He had the slight build of his house and the fine, strong bones just emerging from childhood, but undercut by an anxious air like that of a beaten puppy. All around were healing herbs, but none to cure the emptiness within, the echoing sense of worthlessness so carefully nurtured by his older brother, the Knorth Lordan.

Another walked beside him in his moon-cast shadow: daughter-to-be, child of his ruined future. *If he thinks so little of you*, it asked, *why does he bother to torment you at all?*

The boy didn't know. All he asked was to be left alone. Somehow, though, he was like a secret itch that his brother felt compelled to scratch until it bled.

He glanced unhappily up at a dark window set high in the garden's northern wall. Only with his grandmother Kinzi did he feel safe, but the Knorth Matriarch was visiting her friend Adiraina in the Women's Halls. He would wait here until she came home. Then he would go up to say good night and hear a kind word in return.

He turned, and found that he was no longer alone. The door to the outer halls had silently opened. Just inside it stood a slim, masked girl clad in black, white, and silver, her eyes fixed, greedily, on that dark, upper window.

Jame half-woke with a sick start.

That's Rawneth, she thought, gulping down green nausea. *Young, beautiful, and oh, so hungry. But for what?*

Now they were in Kinzi's apartment, and Rawneth was looking through the Matriarch's possessions.

This is wrong. Why did you bring her here?

She had been so kind to him in the garden, so sympathetic. Why hadn't he gone with his father on this Autumn's Eve to remember the Knorth dead? The Highlord hadn't asked him? Oh. Well, perhaps Lord Gerraint thought that he would be bored and it was, really, such a long, dull ceremony. Anyway, it was the Lordan's duty to attend his father tonight. What, Greshan hadn't gone either? He was out hunting? How curious.

He reminded himself that she was only sixteen, a bare three years his senior, but so poised that they might have belonged to different generations. The lower third of her full skirt, her arms, and her mask were black, her bodice white, tight laced with silver—the markings of an elegant direhound.

She had always wanted to see the Knorth quarters, especially those of the Knorth Matriarch. Would he show her? How her dark eyes glittered behind her mask, how red those thin lips against that white skin. Her fingertips, long nailed, caressed his cheek and he shuddered, torn between desire and repulsion, hardly knowing which stirred him more. Show me. Please?

Now he stood back watching, increasingly uncomfortable, as her pretense of delicate curiosity fell away and she began to paw through Kinzi's things like a dog on the scent, digging avidly for dirt. What she found was a square of fine linen, covered with tiny knot-stitches.

"Well, well, well."

Greshan lounged in the doorway. He reeked of the hunt, of sweat, blood, and offal, a filthy, gorgeously embroidered coat draped over one shoulder. Tunic laces hung loose, half undone, at his throat.

"What have you brought me, Gander? Will I enjoy it?"

They circled each other beside Kinzi's bed. Her long, black hair stirred and rose about her as if in an updraft, although the room was close and still. Her fingertips brushed against his bare chest, leaving faint red lines. He slid his hand through her shining hair, then suddenly gripped it and jerked her face up to his. She stifled a cry, but tears of pain glittered in her pale cheeks. He bent his head, licked them off, and shuddered.

"Bitter," he said thickly. "And potent. Is the magic in your blood as strong?"

"Taste it and see."

The tendrils of black hair that had wound about his hand slowly relaxed into a caress. She gave a husky laugh.

"You should meet my cousin Roane. He likes to play games too."

"Later. Gangray, get out."

She eyed Ganth askance over Greshan's shoulder, black eyes glittering half in mockery, half in challenge. "Oh, let the little boy watch . . . unless he wishes to join us and become a man."

Then everything stopped.

Kinzi stood in the doorway. The Knorth Matriarch was a tiny, neat, old woman with a crown of tightly plaited white hair which, unbound, would have brushed the floor; but all one really saw, in that frozen moment, were her eyes, as hard, bright, and cold as burnished silver.

"Leave," she said to her older grandson. "Now."

Greshan goggled at her, made a choking sound, and reeled past, out of the room.

Knorth and Randir faced each other.

"So. You would bind the Highlord's heir if you could."

"Do you think it beyond me, Matriarch?"

"I think you believe that very little is."

They were circling each other now, gliding, the tall, elegant girl and the tiny, old woman. The boy, forgotten, backed into the corner, as far away as he could get. It seemed to him as if the room was tilting this way and that, twisted by the clash of their wills; but there was no question who was the stronger.

Kinzi held out her small hand. "Give me that."

All this time, Rawneth had been clutching the embroidery with its fine pattern of knot work. Now she tried instinctively to hide it behind her back, but Kinzi's hand was still out. Step by grudging step, she drew the younger woman to her and took the cloth from her.

"If I were to tell the Highlord what those knots say . . ." Rawneth began defiantly.

"Would you indeed, and betray the very heart of the Women's World? What Adiraina writes in the love-knots of this old letter is meant for me alone."

"If I told. . . ."

"You would be excluded forever from the solace of sisterkin-ship—if, indeed, anyone should ever want you. As it is, I cast you out from the Women's Halls. Never come back. And leave my grandson alone. He may be a fool, but he is not for the likes of you, nor do you want him for anything but his bloodlines. I smell your ambition, girl, rank as a whore's lust."

The Randir drew herself up, trembling with rage.

"Do you think you Knorth will rule the Kencyrath forever," she spat, "you, who are already so few? And who will come next, when your oh-so-pure blood is finally spent? Do you think about that, old woman, in the long nights? You should. Change is coming. I have foreseen it. I am part of it."

"Not today. Not while I live. Go, snake-heart. Now."

And Rawneth went, out of the room, out of the Knorth quarters, out of Gothregor.

Kinzi sank onto her bed and dropped her head into her trembling hands. She looked suddenly smaller and more vulnerable than the boy had ever seen her. It frightened him.

She looked up. "Ah, child. You shouldn't have seen that. Forget."

His eyes went blank and he stood swaying like one asleep on his feet. Clearly, he had indeed forgotten.

Her gaze shifted to the watcher who stood in his shadow. "Perhaps that was wrong of me. I never made him face what he was, or knew what his brother had done to him as a child until it was too late, the harm already done, and he grown out of reach. I made so many mistakes. We all did. And now you live with the consequences."

Lady . . .

It was hard to speak as a dream within a dream, to a past in which she did not exist. Her voice sounded to her like the thin whine of the winter wind under a door.

Rawneth. The Witch. I see how your quarrel started, but why did it end like that, in such slaughter?

Kinzi seemed about to answer, but then her look sharpened, and her voice as well. "Child, you have company. Wake up."

"W-w-wha . . . ?"

Jame lurched out of sleep, thoroughly disoriented. Where was she . . . and why was someone scrabbling at the jacket, trying to get at her throat? She freed a hand with difficulty from the coat's embrace, caught the other by the wrist, and stopped the knife's descent. Along its fire-lit edge, she met a young Kendar's furious glare.

"Narsa, what in Perimal's name . . ."

"I told you: Timmon is mine."

The Ardeth cadet bore down on the steel until the point touched the hollow of her throat, but then Jame gathered her wits and kicked her off. Both rolled off the raised hearth and onto their feet, one surprised to find that, as in her dream, she was naked. And unarmed. And furious.

"Dammit, I was finally about to get some answers, and you come busting in with your stupid jealousy! Oh." The floor seemed to lurch; no, that had been her own unsteady legs. The square bottle was striking back.

Wonderful, she thought. *I'm about to fight for my life while half-drunk.*

"I told you . . ."

"And I'm telling you: he's not mine." Jame sat down on the hearth, to make a virtue of necessity. "Take him if you can get him, with my blessings, or find someone better."

"Y-you've bewitched him!" The knife wove before the Ardeth, but her eyes spilled over with such tears that it seemed unlikely she could strike true with it. Her thin face was already blotched and swollen with weeping. "He can't talk about anyone but you, especially tonight. Jameth this, Jameth that, on and on and on . . ."

"You're the one who put Addy in my bed," said Jame, suddenly enlightened. "You did me a good turn there, but you've got to stop sneaking up on me while I'm asleep. Someone could get hurt."

"Witch!" Narsa threw the knife at her, missed, and fled, wailing.

As Jame fished in the ashes of the dying fire for the blade, Jorin ambled out of the shadows, yawning.

"Some guardian you are," she told him.

How was she supposed to dream true with all these interruptions? For that matter, how did one tell the true from the false in such matters? That last dream had felt painfully real. How like Greshan, and Rawneth, and—here came a pause—that poor boy, who would one day become her father. But nowhere had she caught so much as a glimpse of her brother, Tori.

Jame sighed. Painful or not, it hadn't been the dream she was after. She would have to try again.

Whatever was in the green bottle seemed to help, even if it made waking more a nightmare than sleep. She picked it up, feeling by its heft that it was still half full, with a solid residue at the bottom.

A warning sounded in the back of her mind: *The more you drink, the less control you will have.* Under that came a more urgent whisper: *Think. The Witch's taunt has set you on this path: Little girl, dare you try?*

She wasn't thinking clearly and she knew it; but the taunt galled, as it was meant to. Caution be damned.

Yes, I dare.

She up-ended the bottle and, half choking, drained it.

THE SECOND ROUND of the cull slowly drew to its close. This time, the Council had reversed the order so that the Knorth came last. Before that, the stones were cast again and again, settling the fate of cadet after cadet. Three black and six white, in. Six black and three white, out.

The Danior sniffed. "Do you smell something burning?"

A sargent went to investigate. On his return, he bent to whisper in the Commandant's ear, then resumed his station.

"Well?" demanded the Ardeth.

Sheth dismissed the matter with an incautious shrug, followed by a suppressed wince. "There has been a small fire in the stable, but it is under control. Proceed."

Finally, only one cadet remained in doubt: the Knorth Lordan, Jameth.

The Randir and Jaran cast as they had at first, the former against, the latter for. The Ardeth also tossed an obsidian sphere into the circle: even if it hadn't suited M'lord Adric that the Knorth girl should escape his schemes, the senior randon of his house didn't approve of her being at Tentir on general principles. The Danior, defiantly, cast white, as did the Edirr, with a mischievous grin. Coman, black. Brandan, white.

"That's four white and three black," murmured the Commandant. He fingered a stone, then sighed and cast it.

Black.

"Why?" burst out the Danior. "I thought you liked her."

"So I do."

"What, then? Did M'lord Caldane order you to vote against her?"

"Of course."

"And you agreed?"

The Danior's voice cracked slightly. He wasn't asking as much for one cadet, even a lordan, as for Tentir. The others stirred uneasily. All knew that politics played a role at this level, but none cared to admit it, especially when it ran counter to their own instincts. If the best among them surrendered his judgment to his lord's will, what case could the rest make for following their conscience rather than orders?

"I take my lord's wishes into consideration," said Sheth levelly, "but only that. As for the Knorth Jameth, as we all know by now, she has great power and is learning—for the most part—how to control it. As for skills, her Senethar is excellent. Although she might still learn something from Randiroc about wind-blowing, I doubt if anyone in generations has seen a purer style."

"Yes." The Coman leaned forward, as pugnacious as his young lord. "But where did she learn it, eh? Who was her Senethari?"

This, indeed, still caused debate in the officers' messhall. In Jameth, they seemed to have an effect without a cause, a pupil without a teacher. If she had belonged to any other house, they could have shrugged it off as chance, however unlikely. With the Knorth, however, one had to wonder.

"Well, whoever it was," the Brandan said, "we are her teachers now. Her weapons' mastery is less than satisfactory . . ."

"Flying swords," murmured the Ardeth. "A new form of combat, perhaps? I seem to remember that her brother once favored throwing knives."

". . . however, it isn't hopeless. She can learn. The same goes for leadership."

"But don't forget," interposed the Randir, startling the others because she had spoken so little that evening, "we aren't talking about an ordinary cadet here. She is the Highlord's heir and his possible successor."

Several members of the Council snorted.

"Blackie will never carry through with that," said the Coman. "We all know that he's just buying time. I've even heard that he's considering taking her as his consort when she fails here."

"If she fails."

"When, you mean."

"No, if!"

"No, dammit, when! Remember, none of us thought she would get even this far."

"D'you really think Blackie might contract for her?" the Danior asked Harn undercover of the general uproar, leaning past a disdainful Ardeth who pretended not to hear him. "After all, that was the Knorth way with powerful Shanir before the Fall, and it's not as if he has to ask anyone's permission now."

Harn grunted. "How should I know? Nobody tells me anything."

"Gently, gently." Sheth eased his arm in its sling with a faint grimace. As the candles had waned, the shadows under his eyes had grown. "You begin to sound like a conclave of scrollsmen. No offense, Jurien."

The Jaran Highborn shrugged. He sat on that council as well and might one day, when he retired as a randon, become its director. "Why should I take offense at the truth? Academia has made squabbling a fine art. You, my dear friends, are mere novices by comparison. For that matter, Mount Alban would be pleased to offer the Knorth Lordan a place, if Tentir is fool enough to toss her out. With her brother's permission, of course. She has a mind, that girl. I suggest that we dismiss it at our peril. Anyway, she needn't graduate from Tentir to become Highlord. Ganth didn't. Torisen didn't."

"And here she is vulnerable."

Everyone turned to the Commandant. After all, so far he had only listed reasons why the Knorth Lordan should stay.

"There are the usual risks, of course, but so far she has proved equal to them. If anything, we have been in more danger from her than she from us."

Somebody laughed. Others glared.

"However, this is the Highlord's heir, subject to special judgment. If she passes this cull, the next may prove far more deadly. Come summer, do you really think that she will pass unchallenged, or must she suffer the fate of her uncle? Yes, I both like and value her, too well to want her blood on my hands."

"Nor on mine." Harn let fall his black stone to lie beside Sheth's. He tugged at his already tight scarf, turning an alarming shade of purple in the process. "My house brought death and bitter shame on Tentir once. Never again."

That seemed to take his last breath. As he strained, gaping, to draw another, the Danior made a dive for him across the Ardeth. However, the sargent standing behind Harn reached him first, slipping a knife under the scarf, as if to cut his throat, but instead slicing free the silk.

"I think," said the Commandant, as Harn sat gasping, his face slowly changing from purple to mottled red, "that a short recess is in order."

Four white, five black.

It was nearly dawn. Soon would come the third and last round of the cull when Commandant and Knorth war-leader must cast their extra votes, with only one cadet in question.

❧ IV ❧

JAME SAT SHIVERING on the ledge of the raised hearth, the Lordan's Coat draped over her shoulders, staring at Narsa's knife which had been driven deep into the floor at the center of the old blood stain. New blood spread out around it and welled up through cracks as if the very wood bled.

Trinity, what a terrible dream.

She had suddenly found herself straddling the hips of a prone Timmon, both of them naked. He had looked as surprised as she had felt, but then he had smiled.

"At last!"

The smile twitched and faded from unease to dawning alarm.

"I think," he had said uncertainly, "that I'm going to throw up again."

"Not on me, you aren't. I told you this dream was dangerous."

Then she had looked down and realized that she was gripping not what she had thought but the hilt of the knife as it jutted obscenely out of Timmon's stomach. Her fingers were still cramped with the effort that it had taken to drive the steel through him, and his blood spilled out over her hands.

With that, she had started awake on the hearth and hastily leaned over its edge to vomit green slime onto the floor, where it was now eating a hole in the wood. Oh, for a drink of cold, clean water. A river. An ocean. But those were passing thoughts.

She also hoped that Timmon was all right. Huh. If nothing else, maybe this would teach him to stay out of her dreams, even when summoned.

What appalled her most, however, was that that had only been the end of the nightmare. In the shock of waking, she had forgotten the rest.

At least she had stopped shivering. The fire roared at her back, fed with more shattered crates, warming her through the heavy, embroidered coat. She had the odd sensation of expanding to fill it. A warmth also filled her stomach, replacing the previous clammy nausea. There was a cup of wine in her hand. She sipped it, and felt the glow within increase.

That's funny, she thought, and heard someone chuckle thickly—herself, but not in her voice.

A soft laugh echoed her from the other side of the hearth, from a dark Randir face. Who . . . oh.

"M'dear friend, Roane."

That slurred voice again. Not hers. His. Greshan's.

"Well, of course," it said. "After all, I *am* the Knorth Lordan."

"Of course you are," murmured the Randir, and touched his glass to his lips without drinking.

The Knorth knew vaguely that he had had far more wine tonight than his companion.

Can't hold his liquor and knows it. Not like me.

He took another gulp and started to say something so clever that he burst out laughing at the mere thought of it. Wine spurted out his nose like blood onto his white shirt. That, too, struck him as exquisitely funny.

Behind Roane, in the shadows, stood two figures, watching. He squinted at them. One had a strangely shaped head, as if it had been smashed flat on one side; the other seemed to be chewing on something that squirmed and faintly buzzed. More Randir. Roane had strange servants. Well, damn them all with their superior, knowing airs. He would show them something that they wouldn't soon forget. The best joke yet.

"No, truly," he heard himself cry, "such games we used to play, my brother and I. The things I made him do!"

"Did he enjoy them?"

"Now, if he had, where would have been the fun? Once the poor little fool even tried to tell Father, who called him a liar to his face for his pains."

He was leaning forward now, supporting himself with a hand heavy with glittering golden rings, the gifts of a doting parent.

Wrap the old fool 'round m'little finger. Be done with him soon. Then we'll see how a true highlord can rule.

In the meantime, there was this damned Randir with his knowing smirk, as if he knew how much Greshan's younger brother vexed him, and how much it irked him that he *was* vexed.

"Killed our mother, didn't he? Giving birth. Father hates him for that. So do I."

Saying too much. Stop it.

He dropped his voice conspiratorially. "Listen. This very minute, he sleeps below in his virtuous cot. Dear little Gangrene, all grown up and come to play soldier. Shall we summon him, eh? See if he remembers our old midnight game?"

"Why not? It might be . . . amusing. Permit me."

Roane's misshapen servant stepped forward in response to a languid gesture and silently left the room.

Greshan licked his lips, feeling a sudden flush of anticipation. It had been a long time. Not that the real pleasure came from the act, but from the control, the sense of superiority. No one stood up for Ganth Grayling but their grandmother Kinzi, and he was sure that the little bastard hadn't told her anything. He had that much pride at least. Too much pride. To think that dear little Gander had actually come here, as if to make something of himself. What arrogance. Clearly, he hadn't yet learned his place, which was to be, always and forever, infinitely his brother's inferior.

The door opened. On the threshold stood a slim figure, backed by the odd clot that was Roane's servant. The latter shoved the former inside and closed the door after them. The lock snicked. At a push, the boy stumbled forward through a welter of discarded clothes and came into the light.

Jame looked into Torisen's wary eyes.

We have been here before, haven't we? they seemed to ask.

Yes. Now we are here again.

The others' voices became a distant mutter. Greshan was telling his brother Ganth to take off his clothes. Fingers fumbling numbly, the thin boy with the strangely familiar face removed his tunic. Knorth and Randir laughed at his slight build.

"Now the pants," said Greshan.

Tori, remember in the Earth Wife's lodge? I warned you this was coming. Fight him! Resist!

When the boy didn't move, the ruin that was Simmel grabbed one of his arms and the Tempter, coming out of the shadows, seized the other. Her ruined lips moved, dribbling insectile fragments, as she whispered honeyed poison in his ear. Roane sauntered toward him, turning a familiar knife in his hands. Now he was behind the young cadet who was, simultaneously, Ganth Grayling in the past and Torisen Black Lord in the present.

Jame shivered. She had wanted to learn what had happened to her father, not to force Tori to relive it; but she had also wanted him to see, to understand. Was this all her fault?

She felt her ears clear, as if water had drained out of them.

"Little boys should do as they are told," Roane was saying softly.

He teased the knife point under the captive's waist band and, with a flick of the wrist, cut it.

"In your grandfather Gerraint's day, your house was soft, rotting from within. There sits the sodden proof on the hearth."

The blade slid neatly down first one leg, then the other. *Snick, snick*. Clothes fell away.

"Such a one I could have molded to my purpose, or so I believed."

He was speaking directly to Torisen now, a dead voice out of the dead past, yet with a familiar under-note. Simmel snickered. The Tempter broke into her ghastly grin. Both pressed in on their prisoner who stood rigid between them. This was the boy whom Jame had met in the Earth Wife's lodge, her twin brother as he should always have been, her age, her peer, but now so terribly vulnerable. Granted, being stripped naked didn't help.

Simmel leaned in, mumbling through a mouthful of dust. "You're weak, and y'know it."

From the other side came the Tempter's insidious, buzzing whisper: "Your people trust you and you fail them. How many more will slip through your fingers?"

Torisen's hands clenched into fists. They had been unmarked in the Earth Wife's lodge, but now the hint of white scars rose on them. The Randirs' words had hurt. Sinews flexed up his arms as he tested the grip in which he was held. For someone so slight, he had wiry muscles and balance, but not yet the experience he would gain with age.

I'm sorry, Jame tried to tell him.

The corner of his mouth almost twitched in response: *You would be.*

Roane followed his gaze. "You see her in his eyes, don't you? Your sister. The Shanir freak from nowhere. She will fail you too, or worse. See how alike they are, uncle and niece, monsters both."

We are not!

"Monsters, or alike?"

Snarling, Jame struggled to free herself. *Just you wait.*

Although she could see and hear clearly, Greshan's essence still enfolded her like the rank folds of his coat. This might be her dream, but she no longer felt in control of it.

A trap. A trick. But whose, and how?

"Witch." Her voice was his, thick, hard to manage. "You planned this."

Roane smiled, mockingly, askance, teeth white and sharp, eyes obsidian. "I hoped, and the liquor helped. Dear, dead Greshan. How else was I to learn what you would never tell me?"

"Don't . . ."

Jame felt his dull alarm, like the noxious gas of corruption rising through mud.

"Ah, but why not? We might have savored this together. Lover, how we would have laughed! But the past has weight. Set in motion, it must follow its course." Long-nailed fingers caressed the captive's cheek. Torisen stiffened. "Now be a good little boy," purred that two-toned voice, Roane and Rawneth together. "Submit."

As the Randir moved behind him, his gaze becoming remote and stony. So he must have looked when the Karnid torturers had presented him with their gloves of white-hot wire. Now as then, he would endure and survive; but oh, the pain and the scars, the branded memory . . .

Jame felt something inside her snap.

Be angry. Be strong.

"You will not hurt my brother," she said, and she spoke from the clutch of cold hands, over her shoulder to a man dead these forty years.

Her hands twisted in their clammy grasp and gripped them in turn. She sent Simmel floundering, suddenly boneless, into the figure on the hearth and the Tempter headfirst into the fire. The knife's point skittered across her hip, drawing its own hot line of pain. As Roane's wrist shot past, she grabbed it, pulled, and bent. They were on the floor now, she on top, Narsa's blade between them. Firelight shifted across their faces as the Tempter staggered about the room, wrapped in flames. Flakes of charred cloth and skin whirled away. Then a swarm of blazing bees erupted from her and she fell.

Jame looked down into the Randir's wide, obsidian eyes, and smiled. "The past does have weight," she said. "Let's see how you like it." And she drove the knife into his belly. Down it went with all her cold fury behind it through muscle walls, scraping against the spine, into the floor. Blood welled up over her hands. Then, slowly, she screwed the blade home.

Something shadowy blundered away from the hearth with a faint cry of horror and the fading stink of voided bowels. Her brother stood in its place, a black silhouette against the flames.

"This is what happened," she told him, breathing hard, trying to collect herself. "Our father's berserker nature saved him, but he couldn't face what he was or what he had done, so he left Tentir that night. Tori? Do you hear me?"

But he was gone.

Jame looked down at a knife stuck in the floor, in the middle of the old stain, and at her own bloody hands, the palms cut on the blade's edge.

"Oh, schist," she said, then bent over to retch painfully from the bottom of her soul.

 **CHAPTER XXIII**

Touchstone

Summer 111

I

AN HOUR OR SO BEFORE DAWN, the horse-master emerged from Old Tentir into the training square. There he paused, rubbing his hands together for warmth against the early morning chill, noting the unusual but subdued stir in the barracks. Some cadets still kept vigil, perhaps playing gen to stay awake. Others probably dozed on benches or the floor, waiting for word of the cull's outcome. Only the most phlegmatic or exhausted would be in bed.

Where had he been, some fifty years ago, on this night? For a moment he couldn't remember and felt mildly alarmed. Had that Randir bash to the skull scrambled his few remaining wits? After all, it wasn't as if he had any hair left to cushion the odd blow. Then to his relief it came back to him: He had been in the stable. With the dun mare. Waiting for her to foal. Of course, she had waited until he turned his back. They always did. A fine colt that had been—three white socks twinkling in the dusk as if they ran by themselves. Odd to think that the mare and all her babies were long dead, although their blood still ran strong in the herd. Wild Ginger and steady Brownie, foolish Knicker who spooked at everything and naughty Marne with that sly, side-long look before she kicked . . . .

Come Autumn's Eve, he would walk between the stalls naming all their occupants, past and present, perhaps pausing by an empty box to listen to a mare suckle a newborn foal, fifty years ago.

Above, the Map Room windows glowed softly. The Council was still hard at it. The horse-master had guessed that they would have a long session, if only because of one particular cadet. Being who and what he was, he worried more about the fate of two unlikely equines. Still, it was a pity that such a fog of distractions surrounded the Knorth Lordan. With any other cadet . . . ah, well, there it was: she wasn't just a cadet but a lordan, and Knorth, and female. Too many complications, too much to make the Council nervous, especially these days. Things were much simpler in the stable—usually.

He applied his flattened nose to his sleeve, sniffed, and made a face at the stench that clung to it. *You've lived to see strange times, old man.*

Shouldering his leather work bag, he left the college by its lesser northern gate and headed west along its outer wall, toward the hills above.

It was still dark with a freckling of stars overhead and a waning gibbous moon perched atop the western peaks, about to roll down the far side. The air was crisp and still, his breath a haze through which he walked. He thought about winter fodder, and bedding, and the stable fit to burst with horses on the coldest days when all must be brought in or risk lung infection. The Commandant would probably allow him to use the Great Hall for the over-flow or for quarantine if the winter cough broke out again. Some Highborn might complain—what, a manure pile under our precious house banners?—but Sheth Sharp-tongue was too sensible to listen to such nonsense. If he weren't also so moody, he would have made a good horse. That, from the master, was the highest form of praise.

At last here was the jumble of massive, pale boulders, glimmering in the dark. Among them, he came suddenly on the White Lady seated on a rock by the stream. With a flash of white limbs, she leaped to her feet, all four of them, a human cry turning half way through into a mare's frightened whinny.

"Now, now . . ." he said, to soothe her, but from behind came a hasty step.

The master turned, swinging his heavy bag, clouting the rathorn on the nose.

"Behave, you," he told the colt as it retreated with an outraged snort, shaking its head. "Sorry, lady. I didn't mean to frighten you."

Then it was his turn to start. With a splash and a gasp, the Knorth Jameth sat up in the stream and clawed wet hair out of her eyes.

"If you're trying to drown yourself," he told her, "the water is too shallow."

"I have a headache. Or maybe a hangover."

"You aren't sure?"

"I've only been drunk once before."

She rose, wobbling in the swift current as smooth river stones shifted underfoot. Long, black hair clung to her like a sleek pelt, leaving slim, white arms and legs incongruously bare except for rising goose-bumps.

"Cold water helped, the last time. At least now I don't feel like turning my stomach inside out."

He handed her a cloth as she waded ashore. "Here. Rub yourself down."

While she wrung out her hair and then hastily dressed to a chill clatter of teeth, he unwrapped the mare's leg and felt it. No heat. The tendon had settled firmly back into place and the swelling had at last subsided.

"Good as new," he said, pleased. "Still, we'll keep it bandaged for a few days more to be sure."

"Master, what's that smell? You reek like a pyre."

He paused, remembering. "Well, now, that was a strange thing. We'd put the Tempter's body in an empty stall, hoping that the Commandant would change his mind about exposing it outside the walls. After all, the woman was a randon. Then I heard horses cry out and smelt that greasy smoke. No mistaking it. Her body had burst into flames as if someone had spoken the pyric rune over her, but nobody was there. It burned down to ash, all but the hands, feet, and skull, which split open in the heat. The straw beneath was scorched, but nothing else. Very strange indeed."

"Yes," said the Knorth. "Very strange."

From her tone, he might almost have thought that she knew more about it than he did, but that was silly.

"Randi . . . ."

He stopped himself. Best not to say that name in the open. Such were the days in which they lived, where the innocent suffered rather than the guilty and the past threatened to overshadow the present. Without thinking, he slid his hand up the Whinno-hir's leg to pat her shoulder. Greshan had paid for what he had done to her but, in the master's opinion, not enough.

"That's to say, Mer-kanti is saddling Mirah. H'uh. Actually, he was in the stable with her all night, keeping watch and playing artist. If you're traveling with him and that cadet as far as Gothregor, you should go."

"I take it that Gari passed the cull."

"Yes." He had heard that much, at least, before the fire. "On the first round, without a challenge."

"Good."

She was standing over him now, absently braiding the mare's silky white forelock and mane to cover the marred half of her face. The Whinno-hir leaned into her with a sigh, cheek to cheek, scar to scar. Sisters of the brand.

"Master, you've been at the college a long time, haven't you?"

So long that he had almost forgotten his own name, his own house. So long that all the family he cared to claim ran on four legs.

"Were you here when my father was a cadet?"

"Yes." What next?

"He never really had a chance, did he?"

"No."

"I didn't think so. Still, in the end, he found his strength and fought back. For that, if nothing else, I accept the consequences." She gave a strange little laugh, with a catch in it. "I once called Tori 'daddy's boy,' but in this I am truly my father's daughter, and my uncle's niece. Who would have thought that I had so much in common with either of them? Nonetheless, Tentir gave me my chance. Thank you, master."

For what? he wondered, hearing her turn to depart, wishing there was something he could do or say. He knew where he was with horses. With people, though, especially Highborn fillies . . . .

When in doubt, groom.

He picked up a brush, but the mare stepped away from him. She was following the Knorth.

Jameth turned, frowning. Behind her, the eastern sky blushed with dawn.

"Bel, are you sure?" Her eyes sought his. "Master, are *you* sure that she's sound?"

He scooped up his tools and thrust them back into the sack. An idea had sparked in his mind. "She can bear your weight, if that's what you mean, assuming you take it easy. Nine days to reach Gothregor at eight or nine miles per day. Yes. The exercise would do her good."

Still she hesitated. "Well, if you think so . . ."

"I do."

"All right. Thank you, Bel-tairi. I would be honored."

The colt followed them anxiously. At the gate, as clear as speech, the mare told him to wait. Then they entered the training square.

The master dropped his sack. "Finish grooming her here," he said briskly. "I'll find suitable tack and bring it up."

She cast an uneasy glance around the surrounding barracks, then up at the Map Room's balcony. "This is awfully public. You said once that Bel's return might raise all sorts of ancient stink."

"None worse than what we've already smelt tonight. Carry on."

With that, he left at a trot for Old Tentir and the stable. *We'll see*, he thought, grinning as he went. *Oh yes, we'll just see!*

II

THE COMMANDANT stood by the balcony, watching the western peaks above the college slowly emerge as the eastern sky lightened. It had been a long night. His shoulder throbbed in time to the beat of his heart, but he thought little of that. A randon's life was full of such minor pains. Worse was his sense of failure. He had hoped that fulfilling their duty would restore the Council's sense of confidence and honor, but how could it when even he felt compelled to compromise?

Oh, I knew you were trouble, he thought wryly of the last cadet whose fate remained undecided. *From the moment you rode into Tentir and tumbled off your horse practically at my feet. You test us, more than we test you. Your house always has. Against you words ring hollow, the form but not the substance of honor. Black stone, white stone, touchstone.*

Behind him, except for the Knorth, the Council was drifting toward the circle. Even those such as the Ardeth who had shown no hesitation before now seemed strangely reluctant. No doubt they told themselves that this was a small matter, easily decided—foolish, even. Trivial. However, it wasn't.

What were you thinking, Torisen Black Lord, when you handed us this dilemma? Did you even know yourself? You are not one of us, but this girl will be—if she survives Tentir's judgment.

Meanwhile, Harn had literally backed himself into a corner and stood there twisting the slashed scarf in his thick hands as if trying to figure out how to hang himself with it. The Commandant almost smiled. It had been an interesting challenge, over the years, keeping his old classmate alive and more or less sane. He knew how deeply flawed Harn believed himself to be, but he also understood the man's value. In his own rough way, Harn was also a touchstone, and a test. One reason the Commandant had suspended judgment on Torisen as highlord was that he had seen, from the start, how the boy had helped Harn keep his mental balance.

So too, unexpectedly, had the girl Jameth.

The Ardeth seemed to think that her very presence at the college would ultimately destroy it.

The Commandant considered this. She might, if sufficiently annoyed. Then too, as she had once said to him with that odd, almost embarrassed air of defiance, "Some things need to be broken."

Indeed.

We have been playing with fire, he thought. *Fire destroys, but it also purifies, and we are in desperate need of that too. Over the years, too many secrets have festered here. Yet now Harn and I are about to compromise our judgment, because we have seen too many Knorth die. Because we are sick of death. The others won't let her survive Tentir. They dare not. The last Knorth lady, her brother the last Knorth Highlord. Change is coming, one way or another. Will it strengthen or destroy us? Where does one stand in such a time, if not on honor, but what if honor means the death of another innocent?*

Hoofbeats sounded below. The horse-master had entered the square from the north gate, followed by the Knorth Lordan and a small, cream-colored mare with white mane, tail, and stockings, dappled with more white across the rump. No, not just a mare. A Whinno-hir. And not just any one at that.

The master dropped his bag of tools and darted away. The Knorth looked around again, nervous, not seeing the watcher above. Then, puzzled but obedient, she drew a brush from the bag and began to ply it against the mare's already shining coat.

Sheth slowly straightened.

"Well?" said the Ardeth behind him, impatient. "Let's be done."

"I think," said the Commandant, "that you should see this first."

Cadets began to emerge from the barracks in a trickle, then in a tide as word spread. Some stumbled, half-asleep; others didn't understand the excitement.

"So?" grumbled one of Gorbel's Highborn ten-command, kneading his eyes and yawning. "It's the Knorth freak and a white pony."

"Shut up," said Gorbel, his frog-face scrunched into a hard stare.

The horse-master returned with the tack. He placed a pad on the mare's back, then tossed a saddle over it. Meanwhile, Jame slid the bridle over Bel's head, noting as she did so that the bit had been removed. Rue ran out of the Knorth barracks with a packed saddle bag, Jorin trotting on her heels. Jame spotted Timmon at the rail. Seeing that she had seen him, he advanced with a sulky air to meet her.

"Are you all right?" she asked, voice pitched low in the presence of so many interested witnesses.

He rubbed his stomach and grimaced. "I've got a dirty, big bruise, if that's what you mean."

"Sorry. Somehow, I ended up on top of three different people last night, and none of it was any fun."

The corner of his mouth twitched despite him. "Then you weren't doing it right."

There was a stir on the balcony and a groan from its wooden supports as Council members crowded forward, staring down: "Is that . . . ?"

"It can't be. She's dead."

"I tell you, it *is*."

"Bel-tairi!"

The mare regarded them askance, ears flickering nervously, one hoof pawing the ground. She seemed on the verge of flight. Laying a hand on her shoulder, Jame glared up at the swarm of gaping faces. Her uncle might have committed the original sin against Bel, but damn them all for trying to consummate his evil against a true innocent.

Cowards, she thought. *Lack-faiths, toadies. Cursed be* . . . no, not that. Harn's father, Hallik Hard-hand, had paid the price . . . but for what, exactly?

Quivering muscles stilled under her touch. With ears pinned and teeth bared, the Whinno-hir gave a defiant cry that rang off the stones of Old Tentir like a bugle blast fit to wake the dead from their ashes.

Yes. Me, it seemed to say. *I'm back*.

From inside the Map Room came what seemed to be an answering shout of alarm. Like a released spring, the Randir's black "stone" had uncoiled into a host of frantic, fleeing snakelets. Awl pinned one under her boot by the head as its whip-thin body frantically lashed her. She considered for a moment, then, deliberately, brought her weight down on it with a muffled crunch.

A band of tension seemed to snap in the room.

Sargents pursued the rest as they slithered for cover. The senior Edirr and Danior gleefully joined in the hunt, the Brandan and Coman more sedately, while the Jaran tried without success to capture one alive for study. Meanwhile, with an air of supreme distain, the Ardeth stepped up onto the table, as if the better to look down his nose at such unseemly proceedings.

In the confusion, by chance or design, a white stone rolled into the circle, then another and another.

The Commandant sighed. To no one in particular, he said, "I give up. Come what may, who dares to vote against the cadet who has redeemed the Shame of Tentir?"

And he cast his two white markers into the circle, to join nine others. Only Harn hadn't remembered to vote: he was too busy jumping up and down on a bloody smear that had been a Randir snake, in imminent danger of smashing both it and himself through the floor.

The Commandant began to clap softly in time to his colleague's stomping feet. He stepped out onto the balcony and looked down, still striking sound hand against injured, ignoring the jarring pain to his shoulder. The Knorth cadets took it up, led by Rue, then the Jaran, the Brandan, the Danior, and the Edirr. Reluctantly, the Ardeth joined in, then the Caineron, following their lordan's slow, heavy lead. A few Randir cadets clapped, but then self-consciously fell as silent as their officers. Standing to the front with Addy a golden loop around her neck, Shade tapped the rail with a fingertip.

All of this commotion reminded the mare where she was, surrounded by those who had once been her enemies. Jame swung up into the saddle, half to reassure Bel, half because she didn't trust her ability to mount if the Whinno-hir spooked again. Trinity, how little control one had without a bit. Moreover, there had been no time to tighten the girth or adjust the stirrup leathers. The whole world seemed to reel. Above, shadows lurched across the Map Room curtains as if the Council has spontaneously broken into a wild, noisy dance.

"What's going on?" she asked Timmon, clutching Bel's mane.

He grinned up at her, his bruise forgotten. "Congratulations. You've survived the cull. Travel safe and return soon."

With that, he slapped Bel on the rump and she sprang forward with Jame nearly out of the saddle. They careened through the great hall of Old Tentir, joined at the stable ramp by Gari on a raw-boned bay and a golden-green mare with rider. Luckily, the outer doors were open. Out they burst into the morning sun, down to the New Road, then south toward Gothregor. An ounce streaked at their heels, and above among the trees a pale, horned shadow kept pace.

Jame managed to hang on to the bolting mare until Tentir was out of sight around the road's curve. Then she fell off.

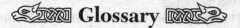

Glossary

ADIRAINA: *blind Matriarch of the Ardeth, beloved of Kinzi; a Shanir who can determine bloodlines by touch*

ADRIC: *Lord Ardeth of Omiroth, Torisen's former mentor*

AERULAN: *female cousin to Torisen, beloved of Brenwyr, slain in the Massacre of the Knorth women*

ANAR: *a scrollsman who taught Torisen and Jame in the Haunted Lands keep when they were children*

ANARCHIES: *a forest on the western slopes of the Ebonbane mountain range, where the Builders disturbed Rathillien's native powers and were destroyed by them*

ARGENTIEL: *That-Which-Preserves, the Second Face of the Three-Faced-God*

ARON: *an Ardeth sargent at Tentir*

ARRIN-KEN: *huge, immortal, cat-like creatures; third of the three people who make up the Kencyrath along with the Highborn and the Kendar judges*

ARRIN-THAR: *a rare form of armed combat using clawed gantlets*

ASHE: *a haunt singer*

AWL: *a senior Randir officer*

BANE: *guards The Book Bound in Pale Leather and the Ivory Knife; half-brother to Jame; may be alive or dead*

BARRIER, THE: *a wall of mist between Rathillien and Perimal Darkling*

BASHTI: *an ancient kingdom paired with Hathir on either side of the River Silver*

BASHTIRI SHADOW GUILD: *a guild of assassins, noted for their determination and invisibility*

BEAR: *a randon who was brain-damaged by an axe during the battle of the White Hills; Commandant Sheth's older brother*

BEL-TAIRI: *Kinzi's Whinno-hir mare, sister to Brithany, also called the White Lady and the Shame of Tentir*

BENDER: *brother of Tirandys*

BLOOD-BINDER: *a Shanir able to control anyone who tastes his or her blood*

BONE-KIN: *distant kin, as opposed to blood-kin*

BOOK BOUND IN PALE LEATHER, THE: *a compendium of runes; one of the three objects of power lost during the Fall*

BRANT: *Lord Brandan of Falkirr, Brenwyr's brother*

BREAKNECK ROCK: *a rock jutting out over Tentir's favorite swimming hole*

BRENWYR: *sister of Brant; the Brandon Matriarch, also known as the Iron Matriarch; a maledight: beloved of Aerulan*

BRIER IRON-THORN: *a Kendar cadet, formerly Caineron, now Knorth; second in command (or Five) of Jame's ten-command*

BRITHANY: *a Whinno-hir and matriarch of the herd; Adric's mount, grand-dam of Torisen's warhorse Storm*

BUILDERS, THE: *a mysterious, now probably extinct race of architects who built temples for the Three-faced God on threshold worlds*

BURNT MAN, THE: *one of the Four who present Rathillien; an avenger linked to fire*

BURR: *Kendar servant and friend of Torisen*

CALDANE: *Lord Caineron of Restormir*

CATARACTS, THE: *site of a great battle between the Kencyr Host and the Waster Horde*

CATTILA: *the Caineron Matriarch, Caldane's great-grandmother*

CHAIN OF CREATION: *a series of over-lapping worlds, each the threshold to a different dimension*

CHAOS SERPENTS: *vast serpents under the earth whose writhing creates earthquakes*

CHANGERS: *Kencyr who fell with the Master and, through mating with the shadows of Perimal Darkling, have gained the ability to shape-shift*

CHERRY: *an Edirr cadet*

CHINGETAI: *the Merikit chief*

CLEPPETTY: *a friend of Jame's in Tai-tastigon; housekeeper at an inn called the Res aB'tyrr*

CLOUD: *Commandant Sheth's warhorse*

CORRUDIN: *Lord Caldane's uncle and chief advisor*

DALLY: *a young male friend of Jame in Tai-tastigon*

DAR: *a Knorth cadet, one of Jame's ten-command*

DARK JUDGE: *an Arrin-ken allied to the Third Face of God, That-Which-Destroys, also to the Burnt Man*

DARKLING CRAWLER: *a wyrm, or very large creepy-crawly with a poisonous bite*

DARKWYR SIGN: *a gesture made to avert evil*

DEATH BANNERS: *tapestry portraits of the dead woven of threads taken from the clothes in which they died.*

DEATH'S-HEAD: *a rogue rathorn, also the name adopted by the rathorn colt whose mother Jame killed*

D'HEN: *a knife-fighter's jacket, with one tight sleeve and one full, reinforced with steel mesh, to turn attacker's blade*

DIANTHE: *the Danior Matriarch*

DIREHOUNDS: *savage hunting dogs with black legs and head, white body*

DREAMSCAPE: *as with the soulscape, Kencyr dreams can touch, even overlap. However, on this superficial level one can only observe and sometimes communicate, not act.*

DWAR: *a forced sleep that promotes healing*

EARTH WIFE, THE: *also known as Mother Ragga; fertility goddess representing the earth*

EARTH WIFE'S FAVORITE: *a role in a Merikit rite, usually undertaken by a young man who acts as the Earth Wife's lover while pretending to be her son by the Burnt Man*

EAST KENSHOLD: *a Kencyr border keep on the Eastern Sea*

EBONBANE, THE: *the mountain range that separates the Eastern Lands from the Central Lands*

ELDER GODS: *those who came before the Old Pantheon.*

ERIM: *a Knorth cadet; one of Jame's ten-command*

ESCARPMENT, THE: *three hundred foot tall cliffs on the northern edge of the Southern Wastes*

FAITH-BREAKERS, THE: *Knorth Kendar who refused to follow Ganth into exile and subsequently found places in other houses.*

FALCONER, THE: *the blind master of hawks at Tentir, who also teaches all Shanir with the ability to bond to other creatures*

FALL, THE: *some 3000 years ago, the current Highlord, Gerridon, betrayed his people when promised* *immortality by Perimal Darkling. This caused the Kencyrath's flight to Rathillien*

FOUR, THE: *Rathillien's elemental powers, represented by the Eaten One (water), the Falling Man (air), the Earth Wife (earth), and the Burnt Man (fire); real people who suddenly at the point of death found themselves gods due to the activation of the Kencyr temples*

GANTH GRAY LORD: *the former Highlord; Jame and Torisen's father*

GARI: *a Coman cadet, bonded to insects*

GEN: *a game*

GERRAINT: *father of Ganth*

GERRIDON: *twin of Jamethiel Dream-weaver, also known as the Master, who as Highlord betrayed the Kencyrath to Perimal Darkling in return for immortality; see the Fall*

GORBEL: *present Caineron lordan*

GORGO: *a Tastigon rain god of the Old Pantheon*

GRAY LANDS: *where the unburnt Kencyr dead walk*

GRAYKIN: *Jame's servant; Caldane's Southron, bastard half-caste son*

GRESHAN GREED-HEART: *Knorth Lordan before Jame, uncle to Jame, brother to Ganth*

GRIMLY: *a wolver poet*

GRIMLY HOLT, THE: *wood on the edge of the Great Weald where Grimly's pack lives*

GRONDIN: *Caldane's first established son*

HALLICK HARD-HAND: *Knorth commander during time of Greshan; father of Harn*

HARN GRIP-HARD: *Torisen's randon friend and war-leader, a former commandant of Tentir, also a berserker who fears that he is losing control*

HATHIR: *an ancient kingdom paired with Bashti on either side of River Silver*

HAUNTED LANDS, THE: *land north of Tai-tastigon, under the influence of Perimal Darkling, where Jame and Torisen were born during their father's exile*

HAUNTS: *anything that has been tainted by the Haunted Lands and is therefore neither quite dead nor quite alive; usually mindless*

HAWTHORN: *a Brandan captain at Tentir*

HEART OF THE WOODS: *a place of ancient power, near where the battle of the Cataracts took place*

HIGH KEEP: *the Min-drear border keep far to the north, home of Rue*

HIGH KENS: *a highly formal and archaic version of the Kencyr language*

HIGHLORD: *leader of the Kencyrath, always (at least until now) a Knorth*

HIGRON: *Caldane's sixth established son*

HOLLENS: *Lord Danior of Shadow Rock, also known as Holly*

HONOR'S PARADOX: *Where does honor lie, in obedience to one's lord or to oneself?*

HURLEN: *a town of wooden towers on islets at the convergence of the Silver and Tardy Rivers*

IMMALAI: *an Arrin-ken of the Ebonbane*

IMU: *a sign of the Elder Gods*

INDEX: *a scrollsman herbalist who studied the Merikit*

IRON-JAW: *Ganth's warhorse, now a haunt*

ISHTIER: *a renegade priest of the Priests' College*

IVORY KNIFE, THE: *one of the three lost objects of power whose least scratch is fatal, now guarded by Bane*

JAME: *also called Jamethiel Priest's-bane and (incorrectly) Jameth; Torisen's twin sister, but ten years his junior*

JAMETHIEL DREAM-WEAVER: *caused the Fall, twin sister of Gerridon and mother of the twins Jame and Tori*

JEWEL-JAWS: *a type of carnivorous insect*

KIRIEN: *a scrollswoman and the Jaran lordan*

JORIN: *a blind, Royal Gold hunting ounce, bound to Jame*

JURIEN: *Jaran Highborn and Randon Council member*

KALLYSTINE: *Caineron's daughter, Torisen's consort for a time, who slashed Jame's face*

KARIDIA: *the Coman Matriarch*

KARNID: *religious fanatics who live in the Southern Wastes. Their torture permanently scarred Torisen's hands.*

KENAN: *Lord Randir of Wilden, father of Shade, son of Rawneth*

KENCYR HOUSES: [see chart]

KENCYRATH: *The Three People, chosen by the Three-faced God to fight Perimal Darkling*

KENDAR: *one of the Three People, usually servant class*

KERAL: *a darkling changer*

KEST: *a Knorth cadet; one of Jame's ten-command*

KILLY: *a Knorth cadet; one of Jame's ten-command*

KINDRIE SOUL-WALKER: *a Shanir healer, first cousin to Jame and Torisen*

KIN-SLAYER: *sword belonging to Torisen*

KINZI: *great-grandmother to Torisen, sister-kin to Adiraina, the last Knorth Matriarch*

KITHORN: *northernmost of the Riverland keeps, now on Merikit land. Marc's former home*

KIRIEN: *the Jaran Lordan or Heir, a scrollswoman*

KOREY: *Lord Coman of Kraggen*

KOTHIFIR: *a city on the edge of the Southern Wastes, called the Cruel*

LAWFUL LIE: *Kencyr singers (and some diplomats) are allowed a certain poetic license with the truth*

LOOGAN: *Gorgo's priest*

LORDAN: *a lord's designed heir, male or female*

LOWER HUDDLES: *a field near Hurlen where battle of Cataracts took place*

LOWER TOWN MONSTER: *the demon created by Ishtier around Bane's soul*

LYMERS: *hounds, scent trackers*

LYRA LACK-WIT: *Caldane's young daughter, formerly consort to Prince Odalian of Karkinaroth, nicknamed "Lack-wit"*

MALEDIGHT: *a Shanir who can kill with a curse*

MARC, MARCARN: *Kendar friend of Jameth, seven foot tall, ninety-five years old, a former warrior*

MARROW: *cadet guard, Knorth*

MASSACRE, THE: *nearly thirty years ago, Shadow Assassins killed all the Knorth ladies except for Tieri; no one knows why, but Jame has her suspicions*

MASTER, THE: *Gerridon*

MASTER'S HOUSE, THE: *where Jame went when her father drove her out; the House extends back down the Chain of Creation from fallen world to world, stopping just short of Rathillien*

MERIKIT: *a native hill tribe, living north of Kithorn*

MER-KANTI: *the Merkits' name for Randiroc*

MIN-DREAR: *a minor Kencyr house*

MINT: *a Knorth cadet, one of Jame's ten-command*

MIRAH: *a gray mare painted green and ridden by Mer-kant*

MOLOCAR: *an enormous war hound*

MOON GARDEN, THE: *Kinzi's secret courtyard at Gothregor, where Kindrie was born and which still serves as his soul-image*

MOTHER RAGGA: *also known as the Earth Wife; one of the Merikit's four elemental gods*

MOUNT ALBAN: *home of the Scrollsmen's College*

NARSA: *a female Ardeth cadet, in love with Timmon*

NEW ROAD: *flanks the Silver River on the western side*

NEW TENTIR: *the hollow square of barracks behind Old Tentir where the cadets live*

NIALL: *a Knorth cadet, replacement for Kest; survivor/ veteran of the Cataracts*

OLD BLOOD, THE: *see Shanir*

OLD TENTIR: *the original stone keep*

PEACOCK GLOVES: *stolen by Jame in Tai-tastigon*

PENTILLA: *a young Ardeth highborn woman*

PEREDEN: *son of Ardeth, who supposedly died fighting the Waster Horde in the Southern Wastes; Timmon's father*

PERIMAL DARKLING: *a kind of shadow that is eating its way up the Chain of Creation from threshold world to world. Under it, the living and the dead, the past and the present become confused.*

PRIEST'S COLLEGE, THE: *located at Wilden*

QUILL: *a Knorth cadet, one of Jame's ten-command*

QUIRL: *a Randir cadet who died trying to assassinate Randiroc*

RAGGA: *Mother Ragga, the Earth Wife of Peshtar*

RANDIROC: *the so-called lost Randir Heir or Lordan, a randon and Shanir, hiding in the wilds from the Witch of Wilden who has set Shadow Assassins to kill him*

RANDON: *a military officer and graduate of Tentir*

RANDON COLLEGE: *where randon cadets are trained*

RAN: *a term of address to a randon, male or female*

RATHILLLIEN: *the planet's name*

RATHORN: *an ivory armored, carnivorous equine, usually with a bad temper*

RAWNETH: *the Randir Matriarch, also called the Witch of Wilden*

REGONERETH: *the third face of god, That-Which-Destroys*

RES A'BTYRR: *an inn in Tai-tastigon*

RESTORMIR: *the Caineron keep*

RIVER ROAD: *an ancient road on east side of Silver River*

RIVER SILVER: *runs down the Riverland, then between Hathir and Bashti to the Cataracts*

RIVER SNAKE: *the huge chaos serpent that stretches underground from one end of the Silver to the other, causing earthquakes if not fed*

RIVERLAND, THE: *a long, narrow strip of land ceded to the Kencyrath at the northern end of the Silver*

ROANE: *Randir, cousin of the Witch of Wilden, killed by Ganth*

ROSE IRON-THORN: *Brier's mother*

ROWAN: *female friend of Torisen, randon and steward of Gothregor*

RUE: *randon cadet from Min-drear, one of Jame's ten-command*

SARGENT: *a sort of non-commissioned randon officer, almost always Kendar, addressed as "sar"*

SCROLLSMEN'S COLLEGE: *at Mount Alban across from Valantir; also home to the singers*

SENETHA: *dance form of the Senethar*

SENETHAR: *unarmed combat divided into four disciplines: water-flowing, earth-moving, fire-leaping, and wind-blowing*

SENETHARI: *a master and teacher of the Senethar*

SEVEN KINGS OF THE CENTRAL LANDS: *Bashti and Hathir have devolved into seven minor kingdoms who are always at war with each other, often using Kencyr mercenaries*

SHADE: *also known as Nightshade; a Randir cadet, bound to a golden swamp adder; half-Kendar bastard daughter of Lord Kenan of Randir, grand-daughter of the Randir Matriarch Rawneth*

SHADOW ASSASSINS: *a mysterious cult of assassins who make themselves invisible (and ultimately insane) with tattoos that cover every inch of their bodies*

SHADOW ROCK: *the Danior keep*

SHANIR: *sometimes referred to as the Old Blood; some Kencyr have odd powers such as the ability to blood-bind or to bond with animals, aligned to one of the Three Faces of God; to be Shanir, one must have at least some Highborn blood.*

SHETH SHARP-TONGUE: *Commandant of Tentir, Caineron, Caldane's war-leader*

SIMMEL: *a Randir cadet and crony of Gorbel*

SISTER-KINSHIP: *sometimes Highborn women of different houses form lasting bonds with each other, about which their lords know nothing.*

SNOWTHORNS: *the mountain range through which the Riverland runs*

"SONNY": *Chingetai's son, the Merikit Favorite*

"SONNY BOY": *Sonny's younger brother.*

SOUL-IMAGES: *each Kencyr sees his or her soul in terms of an image such as a house or a puzzle or a garden. A healer works with this image to promote physical and mental health.*

SOULSCAPE: *all soul images overlap at some point, forming an interwoven psychic landscape; the Kencyrath's collective subconscious*

STAV: *harvest-master at Gothregor*

TAI-TASTIGON: *a city in the Eastern Lands where Jame and Marc met*

TARDY: *a river that converges with the Silver at Hurlen*

TARN: *a Danior cadet, bound to an old Molocar named Torvo, then to a Molocan pup named Torvi*

TELARIEN: *Jame's grandmother, killed in the Massacre*

TEN-COMMAND: *the basic squad unit of cadets; its leader is referred to as Ten and the second-in-command as Five*

THOSE-WHO-RETURNED: *Knorth Kendar who were driven back by Ganth when they attempted to go into exile with him; most became yondri-gon*

THREE PEOPLE, THE: *Highborn, Kendar, and Arrin-ken, who together are the Kencyrath*

TIERI: *a highborn Knorth, Ganth's sister, mother of Kindrie and first cousin of Torisen, whose life was saved during the massacre by Aerulan*

TIGGERI: *Caldane's seventh established son*

TIGON: *a randon from Jame's youth*

TIMMON: *a cadet, also, the Ardeth Lordan; son of Peredon (Peri), grandson of Adric*

TIRANDYS: *male darkling changer, Jame's former Senethari or teacher, deceased*

TISHOOO: *the southern wind, also called the Falling Man*

TORISEN BLACK LORD: *High Lord of the Kencyrath, son of Ganth Gray Lord, who stopped the Waster horde at the Cataracts*

TRISHIEN: *the Jaran Matriarch, a scrollswoman*

TROGS: *rocks with teeth, given to infesting wells, dungeons, and latrines*

TUBAIN: *owner of the Res aB'yrr*

TUNGIT: *a Merikit shaman and old friend of Index*

TYR-RIDAN: *human vessels for the Three-faced God to manifest itself through in the final battle with Perimal Darkling.*

UPPER MEADOWS: *a field near Hurlen where the battle of Cataracts took place*

URAKARN OF THE SOUTHERN WASTES: *citadel of the Karnids*

VALANTIR: *Jaran fortress north of Tentir*

VANT: *an officious Knorth cadet*

WASTER HORDE, THE: *a vast, nomadic, cannibalistic collection of tribes who endlessly circle the Southern Wastes, preying on each other*

WEALD, THE GREAT: *a large forest in the Central Lands, home to the wolvers*

WEIRDINGSTROM: *a magical storm capable of transporting people and things instantaneously anywhere*

WEIRD-WALKING: *using the weirding mist to travel deliberately*

WHITE HILLS, THE: *south of the Riverland, where Ganth Gray Lord fought a great battle following the Massacre, lost, and was driven into exile.*

WHITE KNIFE: *suicide knife, an honorable death*

WHITE LADY, THE: *the Whinno-hir Bel-tairi*

WILDEN: *the Randir fortress*

WILLOW: *little sister of Marcarn, killed when Kithorn fell*

WINTER: *a Kendar randon, first nurse to Jame, killed by Ganth*

WOLVER GRIMLY: *shape-shifter, friend of Torison*

WOLVERS: *creatures who shift easily between human and lupine forms, expert singers, usually peaceful unless they come from the deep Weald*

WOMEN'S WORLD: *the Council of Matriarchs in Gothregor trains young highborn women and initiates them into sister-kinship*

WYRM: *also called a darkling crawler*

YCE: *an orphan wolver cub from the deep Weald, rescued by Torisen*

YOLINDRA: *Matriarch of the Edirr*

YONDRI, YONDRI-GON: *a Kendar who has lost his or her house and has been offered temporary shelter by another; sometimes called "threshold dwellers"*

MAJOR KENCYR HOUSES

House	Lord	Matriarch	Lordan	Keeps	Emblem
Knorth	Torisen		Jame	Gothregor	Rathorn
Caineron	Caldane	Cattila	Gorbel	Restormir	Serpent devouring its young
Ardeth	Adric	Adiraina	Timmon	Omiroth	Full moon
Jaran	Jedrak	Trishien	Kirien	Valanhir	Stricken tree
Danior	Hollens	Dianthe	?	Shadow Rock	Wolf's mask, snarling
Brandan	Brant	Brenwyr	?	Falkirr	Leaping flames
Coman	Korey	Karidia	?	Kraggen	Double-edged sword
Randir	Kenan	Rawneth	?	Wilden	Fist grasping the sun
Edirr	Essien and Essiar	Yolindra	?	Kestrie	Stooping hawk

1145

The Randon College

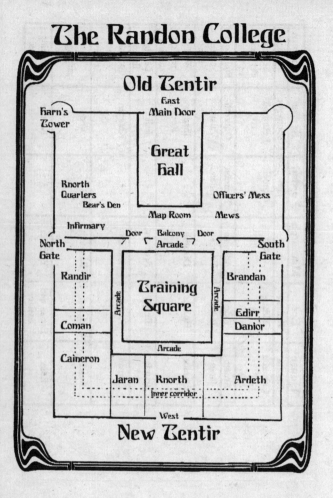

Old Tentir

Harn's Tower

East Main Door

Great Hall

Knorth Quarters

Bear's Den

Officers' Mess

Map Room

Mews

Infirmary

North Gate

Door

Balcony Arcade

Door

South Gate

Randir

Arcade

Training Square

Arcade

Brandan

Coman

Edirr

Danior

Caineron

Arcade

Jaran

Knorth

Ardeth

inner corridor

West

New Tentir

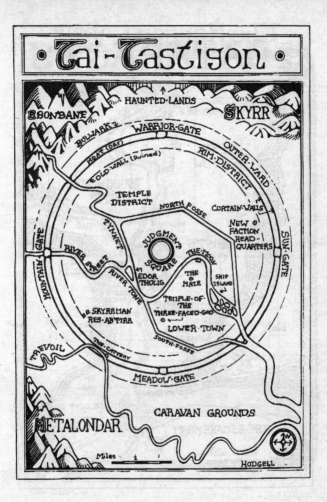

· Tai-Tastigon ·

HAUNTED·LANDS

EBONBANE

SKYRR

BULWARK

WARRIOR·GATE

OUTER·WARD

MOAT (DRY)

RIM·DISTRICT

OLD·WALL (Ruined)

TEMPLE
DISTRICT

NORTH FOSSE

CURTAIN·WALLS

TYNNET

NEW
FACTION
HEAD-
QUARTERS

SUN·GATE

MOUNTAIN·GATE

RIVER·STREET

JUDGMENT
SQUARE

THE·MOON

RIVER TONE

EDOR·
THULIG

THE
MAZE

SHIP
ISLAND

TEMPLE·OF·
THE·
THREE·FACED·GOD

SKYRRMAN
RES·AB·TYRR

LOWER·TOWN

SOUTH·FOSSE

TREVOIL

THE·CATTERY

MEADOW·GATE

METALONDAR

CARAVAN GROUNDS

Miles

HODGELL

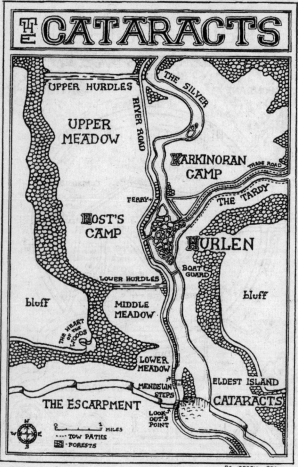

THE CATARACTS

UPPER HURDLES

THE SILVER

UPPER MEADOW

RIVER ROAD

KARKINORAN CAMP

TRADE ROAD

FERRY

THE TARDY

HOST'S CAMP

HURLEN

LOWER HURDLES

BOAT GUARD

bluff

MIDDLE MEADOW

bluff

THE HEART OF THE WOODS

LOWER MEADOW

MENDELIN STEPS

ELDEST ISLAND

THE ESCARPMENT

LOOK-OUT'S POINT

CATARACTS

N W E S

2 · · · · 1 MILES
- - - · TOW PATHS
▦ · FORESTS

P.C. HODGELL - .1984

Maps

Epic Urban Adventure by a New Star of Fantasy

DRAW ONE IN THE DARK

by Sarah A. Hoyt

Every one of us has a beast inside. But for Kyrie Smith, the beast is no metaphor. Thrust into an ever-changing world of shifters, where shape-shifting dragons, giant cats and other beasts wage a secret war behind humanity's back, Kyrie tries to control her inner animal and remain human as best she can....

"Analytically, it's a tour de force: logical, built from assumptions, with no contradictions, which is astonishing given the subject matter. It's also gripping enough that I finished it in one day."
—Jerry Pournelle

1-4165-2092-9 • $25.00

16th Century Europe...intrigue, knights, courtesans, magic, demons...

Historical Fantasy From Masters of the Genre

The Shadow of the Lion
Mercedes Lackey, Eric Flint & Dave Freer

Venice, 1537. A failed magician, a fugitive orphan, a reluctant prince, a devious courtesan, and a man of faith must make uneasy alliance or the city will be consumed by evil beyond human comprehension.   0-7434-7147-4 • $7.99

This Rough Magic
Mercedes Lackey, Eric Flint & Dave Freer

The demon Chernobog, defeated by the Lion of Venice, besieges the isle of Corfu in order to control the Adriatic. Far from the Lion's help, two knights organize guerrillas, and a young woman uncovers the island's ancient mystic powers. If she can ally with them, she may be able to repel the invaders—but only at a bitter personal price.

0-7434-9909-3 • $7.99

Much Fall of Blood
Mercedes Lackey, Eric Flint & Dave Freer

Prince Manfred and Erik were supposed to be on a diplomatic mission—until a civil war broke out, forcing them into an alliance with the Mongol's Golden Horde and the magical forces of Valahia. Not to mention a captive prince named Vlad and wolflike nonhumans disguised as gypsies.

HC 978-1-4391-3351-4 $27.00

IF YOU LIKE...
YOU SHOULD TRY...

DAVID DRAKE
David Weber

DAVID WEBER
John Ringo

JOHN RINGO
Michael Z. Williamson
Tom Kratman

ANNE MCCAFFREY
Mercedes Lackey

MERCEDES LACKEY
Wen Spencer, Andre Norton
Andre Norton
James H. Schmitz

LARRY NIVEN
James P. Hogan
Travis S. Taylor

ROBERT A. HEINLEIN
Jerry Pournelle
Lois McMaster Bujold
Michael Z. Williamson

HEINLEIN'S "JUVENILES"
Rats, Bats & Vats series by Eric Flint & Dave Freer

HORATIO HORNBLOWER OR
PATRICK O'BRIAN
David Weber's Honor Harrington series
David Drake's RCN series

HARRY POTTER
Mercedes Lackey's Urban Fantasy series

THE LORD OF THE RINGS
Elizabeth Moon's The Deed of Paksenarrion

H.P. LOVECRAFT
Princess of Wands by John Ringo

GEORGETTE HEYER
Lois McMaster Bujold
Catherine Asaro

GREEK MYTHOLOGY
Pyramid Scheme by Eric Flint & Dave Freer
Forge of the Titans by Steve White
Blood of the Heroes by Steve White

NORSE MYTHOLOGY
Northworld Trilogy by David Drake
A Mankind Witch by Dave Freer